For Honor and Love

A Story of WWII on the Home Front and in the Pacific

James H. Maynard
Capt. USNR Ret.

Edited by Joseph Hertzburg

Cover design by David Maynard

Printed in the United States of America
Published by Braughler Books LLC., Springboro, Ohio

First printing, 2019

ISBN: 978-1-970063-28-8 (softcover)
ISBN: 978-1-970063-29-5 (ebook)

Library of Congress Control Number: 2019912022

Ordering information: Special discounts are available on quantity purchases by bookstores, corporations, associations, and others. For details, contact the publisher at:

sales@braughlerbooks.com

or at 937-58-BOOKS

For questions or comments about this book, please write to:

info@braughlerbooks.com

Braughler™
Books
braughlerbooks.com

Dedication

To the 'greatest generation' of men and women from Oxford and Miami University who served in World War II with honor and love. And to the valiant men of the United States Navy submarine service, the first in combat and the last to leave.

They that go down to the sea in ships, that do business in great waters;
They see the works of the Lord, and his wonders in the deep.
For he commands and raises the stormy wind,
Which lift the waves
They mount up to the heaven,
They go down again to the depths…

Psalm 107:23-26

Contents

Foreword

For Honor and Love is a novel of World War II on the home front and in the Pacific aboard a U.S. submarine. The silent service's boats were the first combatants to respond to the Japanese surprise attack on the U.S. Pacific Fleet based at Pearl Harbor, Hawaii. Many of the events portrayed in this work of fiction are based on actual actions taken by the Navy to destroy the lines of supply to the Japanese island nation. The historic happenings at home are set in the village of Oxford, Ohio, the home of Miami University. December 7, 1941 became a day of infamy when Japanese Navy carrier-based aircraft attacked Army, and Navy bases and ships on a beautiful Sunday morning as reveille sounded. Over two thousand sailors and civilians were killed in just a few hours. One of the first casualties was a new ensign pilot assigned to the U.S.S. Arizona, William Lawrence of Oxford Ohio, a graduate of Miami University. He died along with 1238 shipmates, when a Japanese dive bomber scored a direct hit on the ship's magazines.

The lives of the citizens of Oxford and the students of Miami University were changed overnight. Miami opened its doors to the Navy and Miami faculty began the training of enlisted and officers. Oxford experienced rationing of food, sugar, meat and gasoline. Draft boards and rationing boards were established, brown outs of the lights in the village were practiced, there were war bond drives and USO gatherings with occasional dances on the weekends, by the Campus Owls and even some of the popular big bands. Then came the tragic stories of the personal loss of loved ones as the nation's enemy conquered Wake island, the Philippines, Guam and most of Southeast Asia. Young students put aside their caps and gowns and put on the uniforms of the Army, Navy and Marines. They took the oath to "…protect and defend the Constitution of the United States against all enemies …So help me God." Many never lived to return to the beautiful campus of Miami University. By the end of the war 180 Miami men gave their lives and many were wounded in defense of the nation.

For Honor and Love is a story of men and women's devotion to causes greater than themselves, who cherished duty, honor, love of others and country, and became known as the 'greatest generation.'

Acknowledgements

I am indebted to so many who helped me in the preparation of this narrative. I realize it is taking a risk to list them all, because someone may be inadvertently omitted. First of all, I want to thank my family, especially Billie Ann, my wife of over 65 years, and my steady date while we were students at Miami, for her help in editing the manuscript's drafts, her encouragement, along with many friends and classmates, that kept me going.

My special thanks to Valerie Elliott and staff of the Smith Library of Regional History, a division of Lane Public Libraries, for their help in my research of Oxford during the war years and for providing copies of photos of navy trainees; to Jane Baer for my interviews with her about campus life as a coed at Miami during the war; for interviews with Captain Ken Glass USNR Ret., Miami Associate Dean of Education and a WWII TBM torpedo plane pilot who flew combat missions from the carrier the USS *Hornet*; to retired Captain Gary Gibbons USN, my NROTC classmate, fraternity brother and submarine captain who helped answer my questions on technical operations of fleet type submarines. To Bill Modrow and Jackie Johnson, of the Miami University King Library Special Collections and Archives Department, for assistance with issues of *The Miami Student* and photographs. To Ethel Hock, who printed my first draft and answered my many computer questions. To Rima Walker and Cathy Arra, Florida neighbors and teachers of English, for offering helpful suggestions. To Jennifer Post, author and noted New York Interior Designer for her support and encouragement. To Janet Ziegler, retired from the English Department of Miami University, for her suggestions with sentence structure and to my friend, Police Chief Mike Dickey, for his astute critique of my drafts. A special word of thanks goes to Dave Bouslog, author of *Maru Killer, the war patrols of the submarine Seahorse*, for reading my drafts and his advice. His non-fiction work of the *Seahorse* is one of the finest books about the Silent Service during the war.

A word of thanks to the noted author of historical fiction and my former Ohio neighbor, John Jakes, for answering my question on writing historical novels. I am indebted to my son David, Miami Fine Arts '81, and my grandson Daniel, both professional artists, for their inspirational cover for this work of fiction. It's been said, *'A picture is worth ten thousand words,'* and they have captured the theme of the story, Honor and Love. David Braughler and staff of Braughler Books have done a masterful job of layout, design and production of this neophyte's first book of fiction. David's advice, patience and understanding, deserve the highest praise.

And much special appreciation is due to my friend Joseph Hertzberg in New York City for his many questions and countless hours of careful proof reading and editing of the many drafts of this manuscript. *His words of encouragement and support made this work possible.* Any mistakes are mine and mine alone.

Lastly, a very special debt of gratitude to the Lord, who graciously gave me some bonus years in the sunset time of my life to bring this to you.

James Maynard
Hamilton, Ohio

PERMISSIONS WITH GRATITUDE FOR:

Photographs of Naval personnel in Oxford from Gilson Wright's collections World War II courtesy of Ms. Valerie Elliott and the staff of the Smith Library of Regional History, a division of the Lane Public Libraries, Oxford, Ohio.

Photographs of the war years and the copy of the December 8, 1941, front page of The Miami Student, courtesy of William Modrow and Jacqueline Johnson of the Miami University Archives.

The poem The Spires of Oxford by Winifred M. Letts. E.P. Dutton and Company 1918, Penguin Books, New York.

The poem *The Oxford Press* courtesy of Randy Listerman from his book Poems of Oxford, Ohio, and Braughler Books, Springboro, Ohio.

For the cover courtesy of David Maynard, Miami University Fine Arts '81, and a photo of Navy officer from Alamy Stock Photos.

To Daniel Maynard for his drawings of the Beta Bells and the Dedication spire.

For the license to use the words in the title For Honor and Love, derivatives of Miami's theme Love and Honor, with grateful appreciation to Laura Driscoll, Manager of University Trademarks and Licensing, Miami University, Oxford, Ohio.

World War II US Submarine, Gato Class

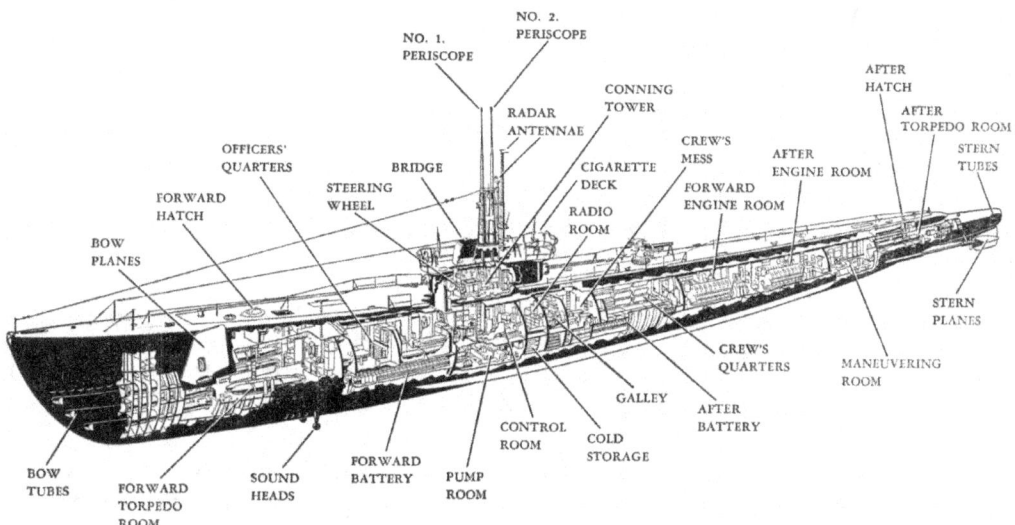

Diagram of compartments of fleet type submarine
United States Submarine Operations in World War II, US Naval Institute

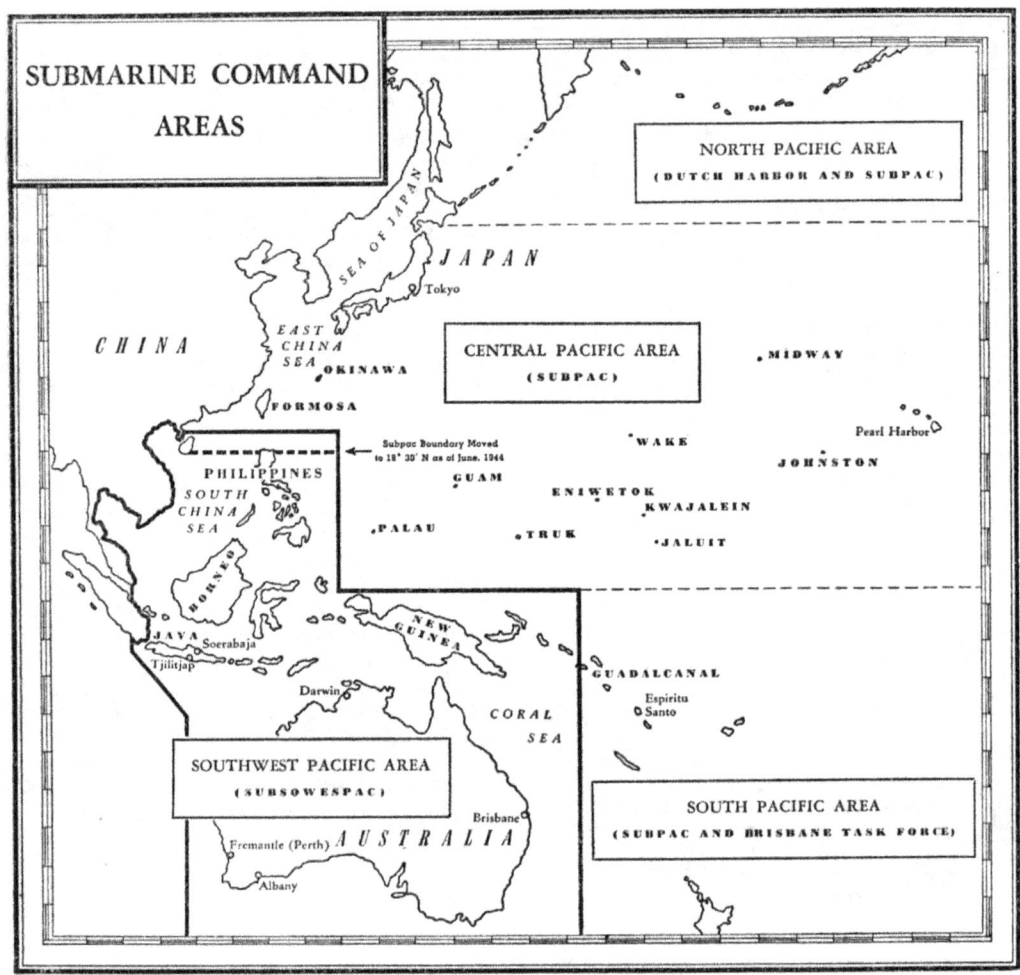

United States Submarine Operations in World War II, US Naval Institute

Part One

The Attack

CHAPTER 1

September 1942,
Two Hundred Miles South of Japan

The United States submarine, *Thornfish,* surfaced on patrol in the Pacific south of the Japanese mainland, its bow knifing through the East China Sea. Spokes of orange and gold from the setting sun glanced over the gentle waves, its peaceful appearance masking the threat of the enemy. A young naval reservist, Ensign Robert A. Walker Jr., USNR, was standing his first watch as the officer of the deck. A graduate of Miami University, class of 1941, and out of Officers' Training School only six months, he was determined to be the best OOD aboard this new submarine. A fierce competitor in sports in college as a star end on the Redskins football team, the rugged athlete excelled in sports and academics, graduating cum laude with Phi Beta Kappa honors. His Beta fraternity brothers affectionately called him 'dummy' for being so darn smart.

Rob grew up in an academic world. His father, Dr. Robert A. Walker, recognized as one of the most prominent geologists in the country, had become a full professor of geology at Miami. In college, Rob was considered a "townie," meaning his folks lived in Oxford, the home of Miami University. Rather than living at home, however, he chose to live in a dormitory on campus so that he could feel more like a fulltime student. The tall, handsome blond with steel blue eyes never lacked for a date among the many coeds now seeking a college education. Following in his father's footsteps, he majored in geology and was seriously considering getting a master's degree and then a job with a mining company. The attack on Pearl Harbor changed his life forever. He joined the Navy after the outbreak of the war, choosing submarine service because he wanted combat, and in the silent service he would get plenty.

The turbulent waters caused by a recent typhoon had subsided. It was hard to believe that in these placid waters immediate destruction could await the sub, not only from enemy aircraft patrolling from bases less than 200 miles away, but from enemy submarines lurking in the depths off their home waters. The crew welcomed the tranquil sea especially since they had their first good hot meal in days.

Below the bridge in the conning tower, the helmsman steering the sub followed a prescribed course change every few minutes while surfaced. The zigzag maneuver, along the base course, provided some degree of protection from an attack by an enemy submarine. Rob held his binoculars, sweeping the open waters before him, looking for anything that would be an indication of enemy ships on the horizon.

The Chief of the Boat, Chief Electrician Lawrence O'Neil, came up the conning tower hatch to the bridge and shouted, "Permission to come up sir?" Officers and men, when required to be topside, are required to ask permission of the OOD. "Come up chief," Rob replied. He climbed the ladder to the bridge and in an instant stood by Rob, taking in the fresh air and the beautiful sunset over the western Pacific. The senior chief had become a mentor to the new ensign. Both came from Ohio. The top enlisted man on the *Thornfish* took an immediate liking to his ensign. His willingness to learn, his respect for men in his division, and his desire to succeed in every aspect of his training impressed the old man. The son of an Irish immigrant, O'Neil joined the Navy during the Great Depression after finding no work in his hometown, Mansfield, Ohio. The Navy became his salvation. Since Rob had not attended submarine officers' school, the chief had become a personal trainer for the new officer. The Navy seldom assigned anyone to a submarine without having graduated from sub school in New London, Connecticut. Rob was confident that he would more than make up for his by-passing the traditional six months training. The chief was puzzled that the Bureau of Navigation, that made officer assignments, had ordered Ensign Walker directly to the submarine without the benefit of the submarine school. He was unaware that the Secretary of the Navy had ordered the detailer in the BuNav, to immediately assign him to a submarine upon graduation. To avoid any favoritism, BuNav chose two from his class to report directly to submarines. The other newly commissioned officer went directly to a submarine operating in Alaskan waters.

Rob was impressed by the *Thornfish* the moment he saw it for the first time tied alongside pier two at the submarine base at Pearl Harbor. One of the newest fleet boats in the Pacific fleet, it's sleek gray hull three hundred and fifty feet long, with a raked bow, long low deck with a five-inch gun and powerful diesel engines that murmured through mufflers at the stern, thrilled him when he stepped aboard. He knew he was joining a fighting vessel. But he couldn't understand why the submariners called their magnificent vessels, *boats*. He asked his mentor one day and the chief explained, "Because the first subs *were s*mall boats and it stuck with the Navy forever."

Chief O'Neil said, "How's it going sir?" Turning to acknowledge his presence, Rob mentally added him to the number of people topside in case it became necessary to dive in an emergency. Rob replied, "Ok, chief. I'm glad to be standing watch as the officer of the deck, but it is sure a lot of responsibility!" Rob was fully aware of the duties of the officer of the deck in Navy Regulations: "*He must be able to handle the ship underway without supervision. The captain should be able to have a peaceful conscience while the ship is running darkened at night knowing that officer has the officer of the deck watch.*

Such an officer must possess intelligence, judgment and a keen sense of observation and he must know his boat." As the officer of the deck, the OOD is in complete charge of the submarine reporting only to the Commanding Officer while on watch. The lives of 70 others depend on him and his watch team. Rob qualified as OOD after some four and a half months on board, a new record for qualification on the *Thornfish*.

Rob and his mentor stood looking at the sunset without saying more. Above them in the periscope shears were four lookouts, each with binoculars covering their assigned areas of one-fourth of the entire 360 degrees around the boat searching not only for enemy aircraft but ships, mines and even the periscopes of an enemy submarine.

"Ensign, could I give you a bit of advice sir?" asked the senior chief. His raspy voice sounded like thunder at times, probably due to drinking too much Irish whiskey over many years of hard work.

"Sure, go ahead chief."

Everyone on the *Thornfish* respected the chief. A center on his high school football team, college eluded him for lack of money. Hard as nails, he had been on the submarine, *Squalus,* when it sank off Portsmouth, New Hampshire in 1939. The *Squalus* was in its initial sea trials after being in the shipyard for overhaul and sank in 230 feet of water when the main induction valve failed to close. Tons of water flowed into the engineering spaces. Within several hours, deadly hydrogen gas began to accumulate in the battery well. Chief Electrician O'Neil saved the ship by descending into the after-battery compartment at the risk of his own life and disconnecting the batteries with deadly electrical arcs sparking all around him. Had he not been successful, the hydrogen gas in the battery well would have exploded killing everyone. Only 33 survived. Despite his valiant effort, the Navy never awarded him a medal for his heroism.

"Be careful sir. Captain Custer is getting very agitated. This is his second patrol. The first was zero, no ships sunk. His boss gave him a second chance. He can make mistakes; so, don't you add to his anxiety." Rob was stunned to hear this from the chief. He continued, "The captain doesn't think much of reserve officers anyway, and even though you catch on better than any of the officers, he'll be watching your every move." With that, he took another deep breath of fresh air and disappeared down the hatch.

When Rob enlisted, he intentionally avoided telling his recruiter that he had lived in Japan for two years during the time his father served as an Adjunct Professor of Volcanology at the University of Tokyo. While there he attended the American School and learned enough Japanese to get along with some of his teenage Japanese friends. He knew that if the Navy were aware that he had some language skills, especially Japanese, they would have stuck him in naval intelligence somewhere. Rob felt a real sense of betrayal when the Japanese made their sneak attack at Pearl Harbor. Those two hours over Oahu changed his life and the entire nation's forever.

Down below, the *Thornfish's* captain, Lieutenant Commander J.J. Custer, U.S. Naval Academy class of 1927, was feeling subtle pressure from the crew for not having sunk any ships after three weeks on patrol off the Chinese coast. Other submarine captains had lost their commands after returning from patrols with most of their torpedoes, so he was determined to sink ships on this combat patrol. Small in stature, with piercing green eyes, some of his academy classmates said he suffered from short man's disease. His nickname, in the yearbook was---'The Judge.'

Despite his dour personality, Custer managed to carve out a successful career path by being an overly aggressive staff officer. He made life miserable for submariners in the training command when he was deputy chief of staff for training for the submarine division based in New London, Connecticut. He knew Navy Regulations inside and out. His subordinates knew they'd better cross every T and dot every I for Custer but his selection for command surprised many of his contemporaries. In the days leading up to Pearl Harbor, however, submarine commands were assigned by seniority and only to Naval Academy graduates. Due to his ship's excellent performance in under-way trials off Hawaii, *Thornfish* was assigned a choice hunting ground for their second patrol. The area between Formosa and the southern islands of the Japanese mainland was teaming with convoys on their way north to Japan, carrying raw materials, rubber, oil, and rice from Borneo and Sumatra.

Submarine pre-war tactics stipulated that merchant ships were not to be sunk unless they were positively carrying war materials. Attacks on warships were to be carried out while submerged, and submarines were to remain underwater during daylight hours using sound bearings to position for attacks rather than visual bearings through the periscope. Safer that way, so they thought.

All that changed on December 8. The Commander of Submarines, Pacific Fleet, issued an order to all submarines: "Initiate immediate unrestricted submarine warfare." That included both warships and merchant vessels. Successful submarine captains took risks by staying on the surface as long as possible during attacks. However, Lieutenant Commander Custer, the 35-year-old captain of the *Thornfish,* found it difficult to set aside his prewar mindset and training.

Rob scanned the western sky as the sun slowly began to set when suddenly the radar operator in the conning tower shouted, "Enemy plane five miles out directly ahead!" Rob turned and immediately yelled, "Clear the bridge!" The forward lookouts saw the plane, a Mitsubishi twin-engine bomber with its bomb bay doors open; they jumped from their perches above the bridge, scrambling down the hatch, as Rob sounded the diving alarm…Aoogah… Aoogah. Rob, the last man down, quickly slid down the ladder into the conning tower. The quartermaster slammed the hatch behind him locking it while Rob descended into the control room and assumed the dive as diving officer.

When the diving alarm sounded the *Thornfish's* captain was in his stateroom reading a paperback western novel. He sprang from his bed wearing only his skivvies and sandals, and as he passed through the control room and up the ladder to the conning tower, he immediately ordered, "Right full rudder, all ahead flank. Walker get me down now!"

Upon hearing the diving alarm, the machinist mate in the control room opened the vents on the main ballast tanks allowing seawater to flood the tanks submerging the submarine. Back aft in the galley, Willy McKinney, the first-class negro cook, reached up and grasped the lever in his hand that would trigger the closing of the main induction just in case that the hydraulic system in the control room failed. He thought of the *Squalus* on every dive. The electricians in the maneuvering room had already changed propulsion from diesel engines to batteries and increased speed from standard to flank speed.

"Green board sir," Rob shouted to the captain who was now by the periscope in the conning tower. The board showed the condition of all the hatches and openings to the sea. Green board meant that they were shut, and the air pressure in the submarine was positive and holding. The captain ordered Rob to flood the negative tank and to take her down to 350 feet near the boat's test depth.

Suddenly, WHAM! A bomb exploded close by on the port side near where they would have been if the captain had not ordered right full rudder. The explosion shook the boat, cork insulation flew off some of the overhead and light bulbs shattered in the control room.

Rob, standing behind the men on the diving planes, ordered full dive on both bow and stern planes. He watched the bubble indicator displaying the degree of inclination, up or down, and began to ease the dive as it approached 350 feet. He ordered, "Blow negative to the mark!" Immediately the second-class machinist mate, at the air manifold, let high-pressure air into the negative tank and blew enough water from the tank to achieve neutral buoyancy. The boat leveled off at 350 feet as ordered.

The executive officer, standing behind Rob in the control room, monitored the entire situation. All this took only a few minutes but too long to suit the captain. No more bombs fell. After a half an hour, they surfaced in the gathering twilight.

At breakfast the next morning Lieutenant Dick Morrison, the executive officer, announced that all officers not on watch and the chief of the boat O'Neil were to be in the wardroom for a meeting at 1100. John Young, a new ensign fresh out of sub school, spoke without thinking, "What's the meeting about sir?" The XO ignored his question saying, "Well just be here on time. That's all, gentlemen."

Rob stared at the scrambled eggs on his plate wondering if he would be the subject of the meeting.

CHAPTER 2

The Meeting

At 1100, the officers not on watch gathered in the wardroom, sitting on the bench seats on either side of the single wardroom table covered with green cloth. In emergencies, the table could serve as first-aid and an operating table for any severely wounded men. There were only two chairs reserved at each end of the table. One at the far end for the captain and the exec at the other end. Behind the exec's chair, several coffee pots, enclosed in stainless steel straps, sat on the shelf leading to the officers' pantry.

Rob sat at the far end of the bench sipping coffee when the XO slipped into his chair next to him. He leaned over and whispered in Rob's ear, "Relax, you did fine yesterday." The executive officer, a Midwesterner from Nebraska and a Naval Academy graduate, had a reputation as a warrior. He was on the wrestling team at the academy and built like a tank. His sandy crew cut hair, his square jaw, and strong physique seemed intimidating to those that first met him. The crew respected him as a strong, calm leader who looked after his men. Lieutenant Morrison knew every man's name and his background. He had made two combat patrols on the *Argonaut* before coming to the *Thornfish* as exec. He originally enlisted in the Navy and, while a seaman recruit, applied for and was granted acceptance at Bainbridge, Maryland, the Navy's prep school for the academy. After one year at Bainbridge, he became a plebe in the summer of 1933.

Just then, the captain entered and took his seat at the head of the table. He looked tired. Every line in his face was taunt. Bags under his eyes revealed a lack of sleep. Normally on large ships, the officers would stand when the captain entered, but the protocol was not possible in small submarine wardrooms. The Filipino steward set a fresh cup of coffee in front of the captain. Custer stared at the cup looking at its Naval Academy logo before speaking. Without any pleasantries, the CO began by saying "Gentlemen, we nearly bought the farm yesterday." His eyes scanned every officer making sure the meaning was clear to all. Had the bomb been any closer, the beneficiaries of their $10,000 government insurance policies would have had enough money to pay off the mortgage on the family farm. He added, "Fortunately, I turned off our track. Otherwise, that Jap bomb would have landed right on top of us. Changing course slowed our decent, but the movement away from our track saved us." He glared at Rob and said, "Mister Walker, why didn't your lookouts see the damned plane?" Without waiting for a reply and his voice getting stronger, he said, "Why did the radar fail to pick up the plane so close? How long would it take for a plane going, let's say 180 knots, to go five miles?" Custer asked, "If *Thornfish* is going 15 knots toward him, Ensign Walker what is the relative speed difference and how many minutes would we have to dive?" Rob replied, "Sir, I would estimate that the travel time for that plane at that speed would be on top of us in no more than three minutes if we stopped, and less time since we headed in his direction at 15 knots." The captain frowned, and with an analyzing gaze said, "Correct, less than three minutes." Then he repeated, "Less than three minutes gentlemen, and we are dead." Custer Looked directly at Rob and said, "Ensign Walker, I expect you to have a taunt bridge watch. One of the forward lookouts should have seen the plane." Rob said, "Sir, it's no excuse but the only reason that we didn't see it was that he was coming at us from a low altitude right out of the sun."

Turning his attention to LT Morrison, the exec, the captain asked, "Dick how often do we tune the radar, and when was it last tuned? I am damned sure that it should have picked up that Jap more than five miles out. I want a report on this today, and from now on we will tune the radar each watch while surfaced." As he said that, the chief of the boat came in and not having a place to sit down, stood by the exec at the other end of the table. Captain Custer, his voice level getting louder with each word, said, "Chief O'Neil, I was not pleased with the performance of our lookouts yesterday. I want you to retrain all of them. We've got to do a better job up there." The chief replied," Yes sir, I 'm sorry to be late, but we have a problem developing with number four main engine. But I understand your concern, and I will start the retraining today captain." LT Jerry Abrams, the *Thornfish's* engineering officer, and the third senior officer asked, "What's wrong with number four chief? Why wasn't I informed?" Everyone could see that the chief was uncomfortable as he turned to the lieutenant and said, "Well sir, it just happened. I was going to tell you as soon as I could. It's not a huge problem yet, but we have a knock in one of the pistons, and we may have to shut number 4 down and replace a shim." Captain Custer interrupted, "Ok chief, get on it right away, you're excused from the meeting, but I want a full report on the status of number four and get on with the retraining of lookouts. I want to see a schedule and what is being done." The chief replied smartly, "Aye, Sir" and left, followed by the engineering officer. As they exited the wardroom, the IMC, general announcing system, blared "Captain to the bridge! Smoke on the horizon!" The OOD on the bridge had changed course immediately upon sighting the column of black smoke and was heading at flank speed toward the enemy column now showing on the SJ radar screen. Most likely, it was delayed by the recent typhoon and was making better than 12 knots. Multiple contacts meant a large convoy was likely heading for home.

The captain shouted to his exec, "Dick, station the tracking party, I'll be on the bridge." Rob breathed a sigh of relief, as he headed to his station in the conning tower. When the captain reached the bridge, he found the boat headed directly toward the sight of the smoke of the enemy ships.

With the tracking team below working on the best solution for the attack, the XO headed to the bridge. "Captain it looks like a big one on the radar," Dick shouted over the roar of the three Fairbanks Morris diesel engines moving *Thornfish* at 17 knots. "Radar shows at least five large ships with a couple of destroyers in the front. We can scoot around the convoy and be in a firing position in about three hours on three engines, and less if we can get the fourth one online." Custer ignored his comments and said, "Dick, go below and check on the engine problem right away. I'm really worried about the land-based aircraft spotting us."

Rob's position assignment as an assistant on the Target Data Computer (TDC) was an important job, especially for a young ensign. The target data computer, an analog computer, solves the firing solution taking data from the bearing and range of the target, and entering speed and course and distance to the track needed to attack enemy ships. Rob was good at it. He liked math and became comfortable using the device. Rob started generating the course and speed of the convoy from radar ranges and bearings given by the radar operator in the tiny conning tower. Directly below in the control room, the plotting team soon determined its data on the convoy's track. Their figures indicated the convoy was on a base course of north, speed 11 knots. Their estimates nearly matched Rob's computer solution. They determined that the enemy could be intercepted in two and a half hours if *Thornfish* took a course of 350 degrees at a speed of 18 knots on the surface. The XO returned from the engine room just as the plotting team reached their conclusion. He looked at the plot, agreed with their assessment, and started to climb up to the bridge to confer with the captain about the plan of attack. As he started up the ladder to the conning tower, the OOD shouted, "Clear the bridge, Dive, Dive," and the klaxon blared as Dick swung aside to avoid being nearly knocked off the ladder by the lookouts scrambling down from the bridge to the control room. Jerry Abrams came in the control room breathless taking his position as diving officer, standing behind the two lookouts now operating the bow and stern planes. Captain Custer ordered the diving officer to level off at periscope depth about 60 feet.

The exec charged up the ladder to the conning tower to see what was going on. He asked the captain, now standing by the periscope, what happened. "Enemy plane sir?" asked Dick expecting a plane had been spotted visually. Captain Custer replied, "No, but we can't afford to take a chance with these guys. They must know we are in the neighborhood, and they will be looking for us in the daylight; there may be a plane over the horizon that our radar would not pick up, and we'd be toast." Dick's face flushed, "But with all due respect sir, we have no chance of attacking if we remain submerged. We're going to let them get away!" Custer turned and looked daggers at his exec shouting, "Dick are you trying to get us killed?" The exec bit his lip and descended to the control room and ordered, "Secure the tracking team." Rob was shocked. The captain had let the enemy escape, and he knew the crew was more than disappointed at their captain's lack of aggressiveness. *Thornfish* cruised submerged for the rest of the day.

Rob was exhausted, so he decided to skip the evening meal and grab some shut-eye before taking the mid-watch. Despite his need for sleep, he found slumber difficult. He worried about his failure to see the enemy plane boring in on them during his watch that previous evening. He went over and over what led up to the attack and how he responded to the emergency. What more could he have done? Why didn't the lookouts see the plane sooner? Why didn't the radar pick up the plane further out than five miles? He tossed and turned reflecting on his first combat experience. As he began to doze, thoughts of his Irish sweetheart Molly filled his reverie. Her picture was taped to the bulkhead by his pillow. She was the most beautiful girl he had ever met, and he was smitten right from the first time he saw her in Alumni Library. How all this all began filled his mind before finally nodding off.

CHAPTER 3

The Christmas Dance

December 6, 1941 was a very cold day in Oxford, Ohio. City employees were installing wreaths and lights on all the lamp posts uptown. The Lions Club was selling Christmas trees under the water tower in the town square. Merchants had their display windows decorated with gifts wrapped with red ribbons and bows. Snow began falling through Saturday morning. The university campus, with its Georgian style buildings, was covered with about two inches by noon. Preparations for the big band dance in Withrow Court were about completed. The theme for the annual Christmas blast was *"In the Mood,"* from the popular song by Glen Miller's band. Don Bester's Big Band would play for the campus hop. Students expected a great college weekend. Campus dormitories were decorated with Christmas trees, tinsel, and garlands woven with colored lights. Fraternity row, with the alpha chapters of Sigma Chi, Phi Delta Theta, and Beta Theta Pi, was decked out with all the trimmings. Another fraternity house was dark. A week earlier, some of its brothers made a very big mistake. They wanted to decorate their fraternity house with a very large tree. Late one night they stole into the university's formal gardens and cut down a beautiful Colorado Blue Spruce. The decades old thirty-foot blue spruce was gone forever. When the perpetrators were found, the University Student Disciplinary Board, led by the Dean of Men, closed the fraternity for the rest of the school year. Rob Walker was very glad he had chosen to be a Beta. During the second semester of his freshman year, all the fraternities on campus held rush week. He was invited to pledge the party boys in Kappa Iota Delta, known as the KIDs on campus, but decided the Betas, known as the brainy guys, were a better fit for him.

Rob graduated at the top of his senior class at McGuffey High School in Oxford, where he lived all his life except for two exciting years during high school when he attended the American School in Tokyo. Rob's father, an internationally renowned expert on volcanoes, spent many of his summers researching volcanoes in Mexico, Hawaii, and the Pacific Rim. Rob grew up collecting rocks and fossils, and every family vacation seemed more like a field trip than a real vacation. In 1935, during the Great Depression, his father was granted a two-year leave of absence from Miami to be a visiting professor of volcanology in Tokyo. Dr. Walker and his wife and son Rob lived near the University of Tokyo and young Robert became friends with some of his Japanese classmates. He learned to converse in Japanese, but never mastered the writing skills. The two years in Japan were a great adventure for the entire family. While there, Rob's father became acquainted with the American ambassador to Japan and became a friend of his naval attaché, Captain Howard Morris USN. He was a Buckeye from Dayton, thirty miles from Oxford, and had attended Miami for one year before enrolling at the U.S. Naval Academy.

Miami University, a land grant college, was founded in 1809 the year that Abraham Lincoln was born. Named for the Miami Indian Tribe living for centuries in the area, the student population had grown to one hundred in 1824. It had only one academic building, Old Main, later renamed for a Miami graduate, Benjamin Harrison, the twenty-third President of the United States. One member of the class of 1825 was a young man named Stephen C. Rowan, who later became a Vice Admiral in the United States Navy and had four Navy warships named after him. In the decades following Admiral Rowan, Miami would develop a rich tradition with the United States Navy.

Rob, the popular tall six-foot-four athlete with blond crew cut hair, had an unassuming air about him that caused some cute coeds to compare him with the shy movie actor, Jimmy Stewart. But during his senior year, he had a steady girlfriend, Molly Gaynor, a junior in the School of Education, and he soon made her the love of his life.

Rob met Molly quite by accident in the reading room wing of Alumni Library. Its high ceilings, with arched windows, a reference desk and walls lined with books, made a sterile impression for students trying to study. The central portion, with its stacks, reading rooms, and a 70-foot-high rotunda was built with funds from Andrew Carnegie who put up half of the $90,000 cost. The rotunda in the entrance featured a black bronze statue of George Washington, dressed in his splendid uniform. The right toe of the tall statue was worn from decades of students passing by patting it for good luck. The main reading room had rectangular tables seating up to 12 on hardback uncomfortable chairs.

One afternoon, Rob was studying the Federalist Papers in preparation for his American Government class. While engrossed in his studies, the guy across from him whispered, "Rob you've got to check this one out!" Rob looked up and saw Molly for the first time. With books under her arms, she glided gracefully down the aisle between the tables. Every male's eyes locked on her. Standing about five- feet seven, with her blonde hair swept back in a ponytail, high cheekbones, a beautiful smile and a figure that would be the winner in the Miss America contest, she approached Rob's table. Some wag nearby was staring so intently he dropped his book with a bang that resounded through the room. Startled and a little embarrassed, Molly suddenly sat down in the chair next to Rob. "Hi, is this seat taken?" She whispered as she smoothed her hair. "Yes, it is, it's reserved for you." She glanced his way. "Thanks, are you sure? I was a little startled by the noise when that guy dropped his book!" Rob whispered, "He does this every time he sees a pretty girl in the library." She replied, "Well he must drop a lot of books then because there's a lot of pretty coeds at Miami."

After two hours of fitful studying, Rob finally got up enough courage to ask Molly to join him for a toasted roll at Tuffy's. The little shop was a favorite of the students specializing in sandwiches, snacks, and famous for its toasted rolls smothered in vanilla ice cream. The shop, tucked in the basement of a three-floor apartment building, had an ice cream bar with chrome stools decorated in red and white, the colors of Miami University, and small booths along the windows overlooking Tallawanda Street. It was the beginning of a beautiful relationship.

· · · · ·

The Christmas dance began at about eight o'clock and would be over about midnight. Female students at Miami had to be in their dorms by ten on weeknights, and midnight on the weekends. Molly was a resident assistant and had to be on hand to check the girls in. Doris Henry, the House Mother, would invariably be at the door making sure no one was inebriated. Drinking alcohol was not permitted on campus or in the city of Oxford with the exception being 3.2 beer.

Against his father's better judgment, Rob talked him into letting him use his car to pick up Molly for the dance. Students were forbidden to have cars or ride in them on campus. But tonight, with the snow, Rob was excited to have her ride in his dad's new 1941 Ford coupe. It was jet black with wide white wall tires.

Don Bester's orchestra, with its trombones, saxophones and clarinets, sounded much like Glen Miller's famous band. Couples crowded on the dance floor jitterbugging to, *"I've, got a gal in Kalamazoo, zoo.... zoo."* Molly and Rob stole the show with their jitterbugging to the music of Bester's band.

Toward midnight, with the lights low, Molly and Rob held each other close as they slow danced to *Moonlight Sonata.* She wanted the night not to end. Little did she know that it would be their last dance for a long, long time.

Rob drove Molly to her dormitory, parking in the small driveway leading to the service entrance. The little windup clock on the dash was approaching midnight, and the windows of the car were steaming from their rapid embraces. Rob reached into his tux pocket and took out his Beta fraternity pin. He drew Molly close and said he wanted her to be his sweetheart forever and placed the pin on her ample bosom. He said, "Molly, I love you!"

She whispered, "Not as much as I love you, Rob Walker." They kissed long and hard, and she suddenly shouted, "I'm going to be late! I've got to check on the girls coming in, and added, "I'm going to put your pin on my pajamas tonight." With that, she bounced out of the car and ran through the snow to the door turning briefly to blow a kiss to Rob as he climbed back into his dad's Ford.

Light snow was falling when Moly awoke the next morning. As she looked out her window, the campus was like a fairyland. She was so excited about last night and what the future might bring with Rob. She showered and quickly dressed for Sunday Mass at St. Mary's Catholic Church. She walked through the soft snow thinking of being with Rob in the afternoon. Exams were just a few weeks away, and they would be on a study date later in the day at Alumni Library.

As she entered the little church, Father Tom Fitzgerald met her at in the narthex. He had a wonderful way with young people and had a close relationship with all the students in his parish. As time permitted, he would greet them personally each Sunday. If Hollywood were to cast an Irish Catholic Priest for a movie, they would pick Father Tom. Small of stature, but with a broad smile and a chiseled countenance that showed his age and rough younger years, he was a favorite of the college kids. Uptown he always wore his Miami Redskin jacket rather than his priestly attire. He was a great storyteller and his sermons, spiked with Irish humor, packed out the church every Sunday morning.

But this Sunday was different. The title of his short sermon was "Consider the Lilies" from a passage in Mathew's Gospel. Father Tom spoke in somber tones about the war in Europe that was about to engulf the United States. The terrible loss of life, especially civilians, in the battle of Britain, and the German blitzkrieg that overran the Low Countries and France. Times were bad and getting worse. But the good news is Jesus is still in control. He told his disciples not to worry because the Heavenly Father considers them more than anything else in all creation. Look at the lilies, they neither toil nor spin yet Solomon in all his glory was not arrayed like the lilies. And he threw in a little Irish saying, "If you worry you die. If you don't worry you die, so why worry?"

As a boy, Rob's parents took him to church every Sunday. They were members of the Oxford Methodist Church where he had been baptized and confirmed. The church had two stately high spires that were the highest in Oxford and had a mellow bell that Rob often got a chance to toll calling the town to church on Sundays and usually interrupting the sermon of the pastor of the nearby Presbyterian Church. But after confirmation and during college Rob seldom attended. And this Sunday, Rob slept in.

· · · · ·

Rob awoke about eleven on Sunday, December 7, in his room in Elliott Hall. His roommates had gone. He looked through frosted windows with sleepy eyes at the snow falling outside. As a senior and an honors student, he rated his first choice of rooms and chose 210, a huge corner room, for its view over the campus from its many windows. Constructed in 1829, it was the first dormitory on campus and was originally called North Hall. Built for $7,000 it was called by the architect, "plain, but strong." Initially, each room had its wood-burning stove that students used to heat their rooms and cook their meals. It was patterned after Yale University's Connecticut Hall and had been renovated just three years earlier and renamed after Dr. Charles Elliott, Miami's professor of Greek and Logic from 1849-1863.

Rob's back hurt when he awoke. He thought he needed to get a new mattress, but after showering and dressing, he felt much better. Rob pulled his heavy mackinaw jacket over his Miami Redskin letter sweater and headed for the Beta House for a late breakfast. He passed the Beta Bells Tower given to the University in 1940 by his fraternity's alpha chapter. They rang loud and clear in the cold crisp December air. From seven in the morning to ten at night the bells tolled the hour and quarter hour. Residents in the nearby dormitories seldom noticed them after being there a few weeks. The brisk north wind made him pick up his steps as he passed Lewis Place, the home of the university's presidents. Built in 1838 by Romeo Lewis of Connecticut, a successful mining engineer, the beautiful white brick sixteen-room home had a fireplace in each room. His heirs sold the house to the university in 1929 for $25,000 for Miami presidents' residence.

Rob turned the collar of his coat up to cover his face as he trudged along High Street towards the Beta House at the corner of Campus and High Street. He decided he would only stay for a meal and then head back to his room to pick up some books before going to see Molly. Rob had enough credit hours to graduate in the winter commencement, but he wanted to finish his next semester and receive his diploma with the rest of his class. The spring semester of 1942 would be easy he thought and would give him some time to decide if he wanted to get his master's degree. Getting his M.S. at Miami would allow him some more time to be with Molly during her senior year. Then maybe a June wedding.

Rob took off his heavy coat and hung it by the front door and passed through the dining room with its ancient maple table and chairs pausing only for a few seconds to warm his hands by the fireplace and head into the kitchen. Mrs. Bonham, the cook and housemother of the club, stood cleaning the large black stove.

He called out "Mrs. Bonham; you look lovely today."

"Flattery will get you nowhere Robert Walker. You know the kitchen is closed."

Undismayed Rob replied, "What if I were to give you a million dollars for some scrambled eggs and bacon, would you do it for me?"

"No but sit down, and I'll get you some for being so nice."

He sat down on a stool next to the preparation table and noticed that she looked worried. Daniele Bonham had been the chief cook and bottle washer for years at the house. Now in her fifties, she was still a good-looking woman, although she had put on a little weight lately. Rob asked, "Anything wrong Mrs. Bonham? Are you OK?"

"Rob, I'm concerned about the war. The boys were talking about it at lunch today, it looks bad. We're going to be drawn into it for sure."

Rob replied, "Well FDR doesn't want to get any of our troops in it, but the Navy is surely helping the Brits now, we gave them 50 of our destroyers last year you know."

As she started cracking the eggs over the frying pan, she said," Well then tell me why he started the draft a year ago? You boys all had to sign up."

"Well if I'm drafted, I'm going in the Navy! I've always liked the sea ever since our family went to Japan on the liner."

"Well, maybe you'll be safer there. I lost my favorite uncle in the Great War to end all wars; he was gassed on the Western Front."

"I'm sorry. War is a terrible way to settle things. I like submarines. I was able to go aboard one when I was in Japan. They're fascinating."

As she placed the scrambled eggs on a plate, she said, "Well, don't be foolish Rob, it is very dangerous. Do you remember the submarine *Squalus* when it sank off Maine a couple of years ago?"

"Yeah, but they rescued them. Mrs. Bonham do you have any coffee left?"

As she poured black coffee in the large white cup, she continued in a stern motherly tone, "They rescued some of the crew. Where did you ever get the idea of going into the submarine service? And how did you ever get to go on a Japanese submarine?"

"Well, it's funny you asked. My father spent two years in Japan as an adjunct visiting professor of volcanoes at the University of Tokyo. They have lots of them in Japan. Our family went with him, and I attended the American School in Tokyo. I became a good friend with one of the Japanese students in my class whose father was a captain in the Japanese Navy. He commanded a squadron of submarines, and we were given a tour of one of their subs, an I-15, at their Navy base at Yokosuka. It was a huge submarine. They wouldn't let me in some of the compartments, but I did get a very interesting tour nevertheless."

As she sat down across from him at the table, she said, "Well just remember the *Squalus*, those that survived were lucky."

Rob looked at his watch and said, "Gosh, its one-thirty, I've got to go, time to hit the books. My finals are in two weeks. Thanks for saving my life!"

She laughed and said, "Get out of here… you're going to see your beautiful girl-friend, I know you."

"Mrs. Bonham, I gave Molly my pin last night! We're in love!

Daniele smiled and hugged Rob. "Wonderful, she is such a sweetheart. Hang on to her Rob."

As he pulled on his coat, Rob thought of going to see Molly, but he'd have to get his books first. As he passed down the hall one of the brothers yelled, "Hey Dummy, we need a fourth for bridge, take off that coat and join us." Rob was one of the best bridge players at the Beta House. He loved the strategy of the game. He glanced at the card table and replied, "Can't do it now guys, got to hit the books."

He pressed on as the snow was now coming down again. He quickly strode down Slant Walk passing Harrison Hall, its stately towers and beautiful brick facades were decorated with garlands and white snow.

As he entered Elliott dormitory, Rob shed his overcoat and checked his mailbox before climbing the stairs to his room. There was just one envelope addressed to him; it was from his draft board in Oxford. He tore it open and found a notice about the draft. He was relieved a bit. They only wanted him to fill out a form regarding his status in school and expected graduation date.

His roommates had returned. Both were zoology majors intending to pursue medical degrees next year. Bill Harmon met him at the door. "Rob, I want to apologize right here and now." Bill, a tall and lanky southerner from North Carolina, came to school in Oxford because his mother had graduated from Miami. He explained that he and their other roommate had been playing a little game last night in Rob's absence. They were trying to see who could jump completely around the room without stepping on the floor. Hopping from chairs to desks to beds and back they had broken the springs in Rob's bed.

"Rob I'm sorry, Dick and I promise that we'll go to the lumber yard tomorrow and get a piece of plywood cut to size and put it under your bedsprings."

Rob looked at his bed and said sarcastically, "Thanks a lot… no wonder my back hurt so much this morning. My bed looks like a hammock! Maybe it's an omen Bill. I might be going in the Navy, who knows."

Bill's radio was tuned to some music on WLW, Cincinnati's Crosley Broadcasting Company's premier 50,000-watt clear channel station known as the nation's station. Suddenly Peter Grant, the announcer, said in a very excited tone, "We interrupt this program to bring you a news bulletin. The Japanese have attacked Pearl Harbor!"

CHAPTER 4

Pearl Harbor, Hawaii
This Is Not a Drill!

Hours earlier, about 7:35 am, Pearl Harbor time, a Japanese floatplane from the Cruiser Chikuma approached north of Pearl Harbor and radioed, "Enemy formation at anchor. Nine battleships, one heavy cruiser, six light cruisers in the harbor." His excited broadcast was received by Captain Mitsuo Fuchida, the commander of the entire 250 carrier aircraft echelons whose planes flying from four Japanese aircraft carriers, were now only twenty-five miles from the naval base. He immediately told his radio operator, "Notify all planes to attack."

The signal TO, TO, TO, an abbreviation for the *totsugeki* meaning charge, was broadcast as Fuchida's bomber rounded Barbers Point. Then another blast was issued "TO RA, TO RA, TO RA."

A few minutes before eight o'clock the carnage began. The Japanese planes attacked the Army's Schofield Barracks, high in the hills before descending to Wheeler airfield where Army Air Corps planes were parked wing tip to wing tip. On Ford Island, bombs blasted the Navy's floatplane slips and amphibious PBY aircraft. Torpedo aircraft attacked the battleships moored adjacent to Ford Island just as the ships' colors were about to be raised at 0800. The commander of the U.S. Navy 2nd Patrol Wing radioed the alarm at 07:58, "Air Raid Pearl Harbor. This is not a drill."

Within minutes the Naval Radio Station sent a message to Washington informing the Navy Department of the attack. As the first wave of Japanese aircraft was ending, the Secretary of the Navy, Frank Knox, received a dispatch and immediately telephoned the White House. Everyone there believed it was a mistake; it must be an attack on the Philippines. But as confirmation began to arrive shortly after two p.m. Washington time, the news was broadcast to a shocked nation a few hours later.

For security reasons, the extent of the terrific damage done to our forces was withheld. The death toll after the two raids was 2,403 including 68 civilians. 1,178 were wounded. Over half of the Navy casualties were from the USS *Arizona* that completely blew apart when a bomb penetrated the forward ammunition magazine. One of those lost was a naval aviator, Ensign William Lawrence, a graduate of Miami University, who had been recently assigned to the battleship. He was an architectural student at Miami and one of 16 in his aviation class at Pensacola Naval Air Station. Upon receiving his wings, he visited his mother in Oxford before leaving for his new duty station as an aviator flying the observation plane on the USS *Arizona*.

The Japanese carrier task force launched two attacks that morning. Over 18 ships had been sunk or destroyed beyond use. Four battleships plus *Utah* were sunk, four heavily damaged, three light cruisers, and three destroyers were destroyed. By a stroke of luck or divine providence, the Navy's carriers were at sea and escaped damage. So also, all the submarines at Pearl Harbor, and most importantly, all oil tanks were completely left intact. Had Admiral Nagaimo, the task force commander, decided to make a third attack the devastation would have been even more enormous.

Rob was stunned. How could the Japanese do such a dastardly thing? A sneak attack with no warning whatsoever seemed so out of character with the young men he had known in Japan only a few years earlier.

Rob's roommate said, "This won't last long. The U.S Navy will clobber those slant-eyed, bucktoothed, yellow-bellies. They'll learn not to mess with our military soon enough. I'll give them six months, and it'll be all over." Rob said, "Don't be so sure. No, it won't. The Japanese are industrious and have a huge military now."

The three of them sat by their little portable radio listening for any more information. Finally, Rob said he was going to Hepburn Hall to find Molly.

Bounding up the steps of Hepburn, he entered the front door and saw a crowd of coeds surrounding the upright Philco radio in the living room. Rob immediately checked with the student Resident Assistant behind the desk and inquired about Molly.

She said, "Molly left the dorm a little while ago and said she was going to the newspaper office across campus." Molly, in her second year as a student reporter, was in line to be one of the editors next semester. *The Miami Student* newspaper was the oldest college newspaper founded in 1826. Rob knew she would be there a long time, so he decided to go back to the fraternity house.

As he walked toward the Beta House a few blocks away, he began to think about his future. The draft board would have his latest information next week, and they would know his expected graduation date. He did not want to join the Army, and the Navy appealed the most to him. He loved the sea, and the appealing adventure promised in the recruiting posters, *"Join the Navy and see the world."* He decided to talk it over with his parents.

When he arrived at the Beta Theta Pi house, Rob was met with loud conversations in every room. The brothers were mad as hell. He heard someone yell, "Those dirty Japs will pay the price for this." Some of the brothers were already talking about going to Cincinnati to visit the military recruiters to check out the various services.

Arnold Jessen, the Beta president, jumped up on a chair and hollered, "OK guys, pipe down and listen. Let's do this; I want three volunteers to go with me to Cincy tomorrow morning and get information on the services and how to sign up. No need for all of us to go. I can get a car, and four of us will come back with all the details. Whatever we do, we need to finish out the semester in two weeks. Any objections?"

Mrs. Bonham stood observing the chaos in the doorway to the kitchen, clutching her apron trying to wipe away her tears. Rob, seeing her crying, went over and hugged her and said. "Don't worry; we'll be ok."

Rob headed for his folks' home. Their house located at the corner of Spring Street and Campus Avenue was one of Oxford's old historic homes. It appealed to them for its frame construction with a large front porch that just looked plain but comfortable. Professor Walker had finished shoveling the front walk and was putting the snow shovel aside next to the front door when he saw Rob coming up the sidewalk.

Rob broke the news to his father of the attack. His dad said, "This is bad Rob; I knew they would eventually do something like this. Tojo is the instigator I'm sure. He's a real warmonger."

He continued, "I've met Admiral Yamamoto. He's a smart guy and would be very reluctant to attack us. He attended Harvard and was assigned to the Japanese embassy in Washington years ago. He knows America like no other Japanese, but I'm sure he knows he has awakened a sleeping giant."

Rob's father had met many high officials in the Japanese government while teaching at Tokyo University. He once met General Hideki Tojo at the Fourth of July celebration party at the American Embassy and didn't like him. His first impressions were usually right. He sized up Tojo right away as a cunning, calculating and very aggressive man. He was now Premier of Japan having assumed power in 1937 from a weak government. The rise of militarism in Japan had its roots in the West. A significant German military strategist named Major Mercel impressed the minds of the upper echelons of the Japanese military. They reorganized their command structure along the lines of the Prussian general staff. By the 1930s the military had gained control of the political bureaucracy and became a "state within a state." Empowered by a strange law that stipulated failure to have any two cabinet posts filled in the government would cause the Premier to resign. Hence the posts filled by one Army and one Navy cabinet posts could cause the government to fall, which it eventually did. Tojo emerged the victor in 1937.

His dad noticed Rob was shivering, "Come on in son and let me get you some hot coffee. Where's Molly?" Before Rob could answer his mother appeared at the door and admonished them, "Don't stand there, get in here right now, you both will catch a cold!"

Mary Catherine Walker was a very attractive woman in her middle years. Tall and very elegant, she and her professor husband made a handsome couple and always made the invitation list for major campus social events. She was born and raised in Cincinnati and educated at Wellesley college, the most prestigious school for women. A direct descendant of William Howard Taft, the twenty-seventh President of the United States and later Chief Justice of the Supreme Court, she inherited his intellect but also some of his disdain for politics. She was not a diplomat. People always knew where she stood on any issue regardless of the consequences and to some, she was very intimidating.

"Let me get you men some hot coffee," she said as she led the way to the kitchen. The room furnished in white had white walls, a white ceiling, and white linoleum floors. Rob often thought he was raised in an igloo. White cabinets with glass fronts showed every cup in its place; every plate stacked one on top of the other with saucers standing by as in military formation. She hated germs, and Rob grew up with the assignment as a family dishwasher. Polio was a constant fear of every mother. As a boy, Rob couldn't go to the swimming pool in the summer or the circus when it came to Dayton or Cincinnati because his mother feared crowds might have infected persons in them.

Rob broke the news of the attack to his mother. She had not heard any radio broadcasts. His mother sat in her favorite kitchen chair and put her hands over her face, stifling some tears that rarely flowed from her eyes. She finally said, "Well, Rob tell me more about what you have heard about the attack. Before he could reply Dr. Walker immediately turned the little radio on in the kitchen and they sat still listening to the latest news. Then he volunteered, "General Tojo is responsible."

Mrs. Walker interrupted, "No, I think it's Emperor Hirohito. Those damn Japs don't do anything without his highness' OK."

Father corrected, "They're Japanese my dear, not Japs." She continued, "Well they are Japanese to you and Japs to me, especially after what they did today." She looked directly at them and added, "FDR is going to have to declare war on the bastards."

Rob's father corrected her, "He can't, only Congress can make a declaration of war."

Rob could see this wasn't going anywhere, so he interjected, "Let's talk about us. Dad you know a lot about Japan, and you may be called to go to Washington. And the draft board just sent me a notice asking when I'm to graduate." He added, "I'd like to go into the Navy. Some of the guys from the fraternity are going to Cincy tomorrow morning to scope out the services for all of us, and I might go too. I have enough credits to graduate this month, and I may enlist in the Navy."

Mary Catherine stiffened as she took the coffee pot off the stove. She interrupted, "No you're not young man! Forget that! You need to graduate in June, and the draft board will give you that at least. Besides, I know most of the men on the Oxford Board, and they can be persuaded. And that's final." Then she stammered, "But…but if you must go in the service, I can get you assigned to the Navy intelligence in Washington. You know some Japanese language, and they could use you there. And my uncle Robert has a lot of influence with the Navy." One thing Mary Catherine learned as a young girl: women do not have a lot of power. The best way to get what you want is to manipulate men. Subterfuge and manipulation were a woman's best friend. Robert A. Taft, the senator from Ohio and a Republican, was Mary Catherine's favorite uncle and, as a member of the Senate Military Affairs Committee, he had a lot of clout.

Rob didn't say anything. He didn't feel like arguing with his mother, so he went to the little white GE refrigerator and found a bottle of milk and poured a bit of the cream off the top into his coffee. "Dad, do you suppose you could get your ham operator friend in Honolulu to get on the air with you?"

"Great idea Rob! I'll try." Rob's father had been a ham operator for years, and he jumped up and left the room to go to the attic and tune his wireless radio. Rob took his cup and went to the hallway to try to telephone Molly at the *Student's* office. But the Walkers had a party line, and it was already full of chatter about the attack, so he realized it would be nearly impossible to get through. He returned to the kitchen and saw his mother crying. She was listening to the Crosley Radio on the shelf above the kitchen sink. The reporter was telling his broadcast audience that the president would be meeting with his cabinet tonight at 8:30 p.m.

"Why are they doing this? We're going to be dragged into a war in the Pacific and most likely in Europe. We're safe here in America. Think of all the men that were killed in the war in Europe twenty years ago."

Rob's eyes were focused far off; he finally said, "Mother we do not have a choice now." Suddenly Rob's father yelled, "Rob, come up; I've got my contact, hurry!"

Rob bounded up the stairs to the second floor past his bedroom and then up the narrow staircase to the cold attic where he used to play as a child. It was familiar territory. After Rob entered college, his father built a desk in the attic and placed all his ham radio equipment on it with a large antenna run out the rafters to the roof. His dad had earphones on sitting by a small electric heater and was jotting down notes as his radio friend in Hawaii described the scene of the carnage going on below his house high in the hills overlooking Pearl Harbor.

"There are fires everywhere. It's been chaos for hours… one battleship capsized, *Arizona* sunk, *Maryland* hit badly, but *Nevada* got underway but heavily attacked…now beached off Hospital Point. The water in the harbor is on fire…Ford Island hangars are destroyed…a few of our planes got up…. I saw one Jap plane so close I could see the pilot's face…there's smoke everywhere…we may be attacked again. …Sirens going on and on…. Oh, oh… God, got to go now" …. Sign off."

As he took his headphones off, Rob's father shook his head and said, "This is terrible Rob, we're in for a long, long war I'm afraid."

The Japanese air attack lasted two hours, but those two hours would change the world.

CHAPTER 5

The Mobilization

Molly Gaynor, dressed in a black sweater and a plaid skirt, her soft blond hair tied in a ponytail, was busy typing an article about the attack on the office Underwood manual typewriter when her boyfriend Rob entered the front door of *The Miami Student* newspaper office. The tiny rooms set aside to produce the four-or-five-page weekly paper were far from glamorous. Secluded in the basement of Irvin Hall, it had a linoleum floor that badly needed replacing. Wooden desks, cast off from academic offices long after they were usable, were stacked end to end. A long conference table took up most of the space at one end of the largest room. Coffee cups, most of them with lipstick on the rim, were hung on hooks near the small table containing the large coffee pot.

Rob moved a chair next to Molly's desk and said, "Hi Sweetie," and gave her a quick kiss. The office was a beehive of activity. Each staff member had a specific assignment to cover the events as the news came in over the wire services. Molly's was to cover the news of the initial attack as the meager information developed. They agreed that the headline for Monday's edition would be '**WAR DECLARED, President Pledges Nation to Fight to Final Victory**.' The front page would contain the text of the President's address to Congress and the nation, transcribed by one of the students in shorthand from the radio broadcast. A cartoon by a *Miami Student* artist would show a male student standing in front of a mirror that reflected him in uniform.

Molly said, "I'm worried Rob. You're likely to be drafted. How can the Japanese do this to us? Why do they hate us?"

Rob replied, "I don't know, it may be because we cut them off from oil after they invaded China. Japan has little natural resources themselves, so that may be one reason. Then the government is completely controlled by the military now. And General Tojo, the Premier, reports directly to the Emperor. Dad met Tojo once when we were in Japan, and he didn't like him one bit."

The editor called the staff to a meeting in his office, so Molly pulled the paper from her typewriter and said. "When can I see you? Come to my dorm tonight, before 10, OK?"

"Sure, I'll try to be there around 9."

"I Ask For A State Of War"--- Roosevelt

EXTRA The Miami Student EXTRA

Oldest College Newspaper In The United States

Vol. 67, No. 24   Monday, December 8, 1941   PRICE FIVE CENTS

WAR DECLARED

President Pledges Nation To Fight Till Final Victory

Congress Majority; One Negative Vote Recorded For War

"Infamous Attacks" By Japanese Cause Final Declaration

Joe College

Speaking before the joint session of the Senate and the House of Representatives assembled in the House chamber room in Washington, D. C., Pres. F. D. Roosevelt at 12:30 p.m. today (EST) delivered the following message:

Mr. Vice-President, Mr. Speaker, Members of the Senate and of the House of Representatives:

Yesterday, December 7, 1941, a date which will live in infamy, the United States of America was suddenly and deliberately attacked by naval and air forces of the Empire of Japan. The United States was at peace with that nation and at the solicitation of Japan was still in conversation with its government and its members looking toward the maintenance of peace in the Pacific. Indeed, one hour after Japanese Air squadrons had commenced bombing at the American island of Oahu, the Japanese Ambassador to the United States and his colleague delivered to our Secretary of State a formal reply to a recent American message, and while this reply stated that it seemed useless to continue the existing diplomatic negotiations, it contained no threat or hint of war or of armed attack. It will be recorded that the distance of Hawaii from Japan makes it obvious that the attack was deliberately planned many days or even weeks ago. During the intervening time the Japanese Government had deliberately sought to deceive the United States by false statement and expressions of hope for continued peace. The attack yesterday on the Hawaiian Islands has caused severe damage to American naval and military forces. I regret to tell you that very many American lives have been lost. In addition, American ships have been reported torpedoed on the High Seas between San Francisco and Honolulu. Yesterday the Japanese Government also launched an attack against Malaya. Last night Japanese forces attacked Hongkong. Last night Japanese forces attacked Guam. Last night Japanese forces attacked the Philippine Islands. Last night the Japanese forces attacked Wake Island and this morning the Japanese attacked Midway Island. Japan has therefore undertaken a surprise offensive extending throughout the Pacific area. The facts of yesterday and today speak for themselves. The people of the United States have already formed their opinions and will understand the implications to the very life and safety of our nation. As Commander-in-Chief of the Army and Navy, I have directed that all measures be taken for our defense, but always will our whole nation remember the character of the onslaught against us. No matter how long it may take us to overcome this premeditated invasion the American people in their righteous might will win through to absolute victory. I believe that I interpret the will of the Congress and of the people when I assert that we will not only defend ourselves to the uttermost but will make it very certain that this form of treachery shall never again endanger us.

Hostilities exist. There is no blinking at the fact that our people and territory and our interests are in grave danger. With confidence in our armed forces, with the unbounding determination of our people, we will gain the inevitable triumph SO HELP US GOD!

I ask that the Congress declare that since the unprovoked and dastardly attack by Japan on December 7, 1941, a state of war has existed between the United States and the Japanese Empire.

The address of the President, but a little longer than Lincoln's Gettysburg address, made historic occasions; the Call to Arms of the American Colonies after the Battle of Lexington and Concord, James Madison's call for war against this nation in 1812, James K. Polk's battle America to war against Mexico, Lincoln's fateful call for 75,000 volunteers after the firing on Fort Sumter.

But perhaps the best comparison, even more to the times that forged war on April 2, 1917, the ever-to-be-remembered speech of Winston Churchill, as he took the prime ministry of Great Britain in the darkest days of the war. Roosevelt's clarion call that "we shall win the inevitable victory, so help us God" may well rank with Mr. Churchill's bulldoggish plea for "Blood and tears and toil and sweat!"

Former Congressman French Gives Views

Student Poll Taken On War

A sizeable majority of 85.55 per cent of the 83 represents five Miami men contacted in a hurried poll taken late last night by The Miami Student were in full accord with the government in the belief that the United States should declare war on Japan immediately.

Last night men in all the fraternity houses, and representatives of various men's dorms were contacted and asked two questions in an attempt to fathom general campus opinion on the sudden attack on Honolulu and the subsequent declaration of war by Japan. Men of all frat classes were questioned.

Dr. Salvadori To Be Speaker In Assembly

This, Our Task

By a vote of 82-0 in the Senate and 388-1 in the House of Representatives, the Congress of the United States declared the recognition of a state of war between the United States of America and the Japanese Empire.

The actual declaration of war read:

"Whereas the Imperial Government of Japan has committed unprovoked repeated acts of war against the United States and the people of the United States of America, therefore be it resolved by the Senate and the House of Representatives of the United States and the Congress assembled, a state of war between the United States and the Imperial Japanese Government which has thus been thrust upon the United States is hereby formally declared and the President is authorized and directed to employ the entire military and naval forces of the United States to carry on war against the Japanese Government and to bring the conflict to a successful termination. All of the resources of the country are hereby pledged by the Congress of the United States.

The single vote against the war resolution was that of Miss Jeanette Rankin of Montana, who also voted against the first World War.

The final declaration came at approximately 1:30 p.m. Monday, December 8, 1941.

Front page of Miami Student December 8, 1941
Courtesy Miami University Archives

As he walked back to Elliott Hall, hitting the books was far from his mind. Rob began mulling over the tragic events. He didn't want to discuss the information his father had received from his ham radio buddy in Pearl Harbor with Molly for her article in *The Miami Student*. The Navy would do that in its own good time. He wondered where his best Japanese friend was now. Jimmu had studied very hard to gain admittance to the Japanese Imperial Naval Academy, and if he did, he might have graduated and volunteered for the submarine service as his father had done. Maybe he would too. He decided he would go to Cincinnati tomorrow to see the recruiters and check out his chances of getting into the Navy and the submarine service. He turned to head back across Slant Walk towards his fraternity house. Darkness had settled on the campus. The winter solstice was only a couple of weeks away, and it seemed colder than ever.

* * * * *

His fraternity brothers' anger had subsided a bit, and plans were being made for a "scouting party" to go to the recruiting offices in Cincinnati in the morning. The president of the Betas asked Rob and two others to accompany him to Cincy and they decided to meet at the fraternity house at 8 am. He was able to borrow a car from the faculty advisor to the Betas. Knowing it was against the rules, he nevertheless agreed under the circumstances.

Rob left the Beta House a little before nine and walked back along Slant Walk towards Molly's dorm when he saw her coming toward him all bundled up with snow swirling around her.

"Hi, honey!" Rob said as he grabbed her hand. I was coming over to the office to find you."

"Well we put the paper on hold until after the President addresses Congress in the morning, and we plan to include most of his speech in our edition. One of our girls can do shorthand and will transcribe his words. All the wire services sound pretty grim Rob; it looks like we took a beating from them."

"Yea, I know a little bit more than they do I'm afraid."

"How did you find out more information?"

"From dad's friend, a ham operator in Pearl Harbor." Molly stopped. "What?"

"My father spoke with him on his radio during the air raid!"

"Tell me about it; I need to know more for our paper's edition."

"No, can't do it as it could tell the enemy more than they should know."

"But the public has a right to know, that's what we journalists do, we report the news!"

"I shouldn't have mentioned it. But it will all come out soon enough. Let's get a toasted roll at Tuffy's and warm up. We need to talk about us." Molly agreed but kept her anger inside.

They crossed High Street and ducked into Tuffy's shop for one of his famous rolls. It was about closing time. The place was almost vacant, so they had their selection of booths and found one furthest from the door and the cold. Rob ordered two coffees and rolls with ice cream, and as they sat facing each other in the tiny booth, their knees touched. They didn't move. She looked great even after having worked all afternoon on the story of the attack. When the coffee arrived, he told her of his plans to go to the Navy recruiting office in the morning.

"Rob please don't do anything rash. You'll have time to graduate in the spring. Can't we have that time together at least?"

"We'll see. I have enough credits now to graduate this month. I'd like to join the Navy if possible. I'd like submarine duty."

"Oh my God, no. You can't be serious! It's too dangerous."

"You sound just like my mother."

"She doesn't like me."

"How do you know that? She has never said one bad thing about you."

"Well, it is my intuition, I guess. Maybe it's because she knows I'm from across the tracks. Or because I'm Irish Catholic."

He stared at his cup and said, "No, it's just my mother. She is hard to please, even for me. But let's not talk about her."

Tears were welling up in Molly's eyes. Rob grabbed a handkerchief for her. "Honey don't worry."

"That's what Father Tom preached about this morning at church. He talked about the chaos that the world is in and spoke of Jesus Sermon on the Mount from Matthew's Gospel. The title of his sermon was *Consider the Lilies*, and I'll never forget it. Despite all the trouble in the world, he said "Jesus tells us not to be anxious about your life, what you eat or drink or clothes; he said look at the birds of the air, they neither sow nor reap yet our Heavenly Father feeds them, aren't we more valuable than the birds? And look at the lilies how they grow, they neither toil nor spin yet not even Solomon and all his glory was not arrayed like one of these."

Rob dug into his toasted roll and replied, "I've heard Father Tom is a great guy. Maybe I should go to church with you next Sunday."

Rob was getting a little uncomfortable and stared out the window at the light from the streetlight reflecting on the falling snow. Molly noticed his discomfort, but she took a deep breath and said, "Rob, have you ever committed yourself to follow Jesus?"

Caught off guard, Rob was at a loss for words. He looked at Molly and saw a side of her that he had never seen before. He paused for what Molly seemed to be minutes. "Well, I guess I did at my confirmation, but that was a long time ago; I was raised Methodist and haven't been to church for a while. I'm not very religious... anyhow it's getting late; I think we'd better be going. You have to be in soon, and I have a full day ahead of me."

As they walked back to her dorm, he put his arm around her, and they walked in silence until they stood on the front porch of Hepburn. Despite the cold, he pulled her close and kissed her and then said, "You're right, let's not be anxious. Everything will work out for us and the USA."

She replied, "Rob, please don't do anything stupid tomorrow. Promise?"

The next morning Rob met Arnie Jessen at the fraternity house and piled in his borrowed Plymouth sedan with two other fraternity brothers. They stopped at the Marathon gas station on the town square and chipped in to fill up the tank with regular leaded gas for 15 cents a gallon and headed toward Cincinnati south on U.S.27. The snow had stopped, and the roads had been cleared. As they drove down U.S.27, the car was filled with jabbering about the war, but Rob's thoughts turned to Molly's concerns and her question about his belief. He felt like a hypocrite. She is searching for answers, and he is looking to sign up to kill an enemy. He decided to put the matter off for now. Maybe later.

An hour later they arrived at the U.S. Post Office on Fountain Square in downtown Cincinnati. They saw a long line of men shivering in the cold waiting to get into the building to sign up for service. Arnie was from Cincy and had worked there during Christmas break last year. He said, "I know an entrance behind the Post Office; we might sneak in there."

They pulled the black sedan into the alley; they found a door and hoped it would be open. Arnie parked in an official parking spot, and the four of them bounded out and entered the large service door. Once inside they climbed the stairs that opened on the main floor.

The Armed Forces Recruiting offices were on the second floor. Arnie had made assignments for the four of them. One was to go to the Army desk, one to the Army Air Corps, one to the Marines and one to the Navy. Rob was assigned the Navy desk.

They all went to the men's room and got rid of the morning coffee. Just as they emerged onto the main floor the loudspeaker called everyone to pause, the President of the United States was about to address Congress. Taking advantage of the crowd's attention, the men slipped upstairs and into their respective recruiting lines.

Franklin Delano Roosevelt, the 32nd President of the United States, gave a brief but stirring speech to the Congress. He began by saying "Yesterday, December 7, 1941, a day which will live in infamy, the United States of America was suddenly and deliberately attacked by naval and air forces of the Empire of Japan." No one spoke or moved until he concluded his address by saying "I, therefore, ask that The Congress declare that since the unprovoked and dastardly attack by Japan, a state of war has existed between the United States and the Japanese Empire." The place erupted in cheers that echoed through every corridor in the old U. S. Post Office on Fountain Square.

Rob stood in the line for information of the Navy for over two hours. He finally entered the small office with a desk and two chairs set before it. Behind the desk sat a chief petty officer dressed in blues with gold diagonal stripes on his sleeve. Three rows of ribbons indicated he had been successful in his career. "Well young man, what can the Navy do for you?" Rob studied the senior chief's weatherworn face, his receding crew cut gray hair made him look like a person used to leadership and a person that would have little room for incompetence. "Well sir, I'd like some information about joining the Navy, for me and my buddies at Miami." The chief looked at Rob's letter sweater, "What did you letter in son?" Rob, a little embarrassed, had forgotten he had worn his red and white turtleneck sweater with the big M on the front. "Football sir." The chief seemed very pleased, "Well we can always use some good football players. Ever heard of Slade Cutter at the Naval Academy? I knew him when I was stationed at Annapolis. Slade was a champion prizefighter, a heavyweight. And the football player that won the Army-Navy game with a field goal in the final few minutes. He is in submarines now. Rob's eyes lit up. "I'm interested in subs sir; I want subs too! "The chief pointed to his silver dolphin submarine insignia above the ribbons on his chest and said, "I'm a submariner so let me give you all the interesting brochures on the submarine service and a bunch of other bits of information for your buddies."

On the way home, the brothers constantly chattered about the information they had obtained from the military recruiters during the return trip to Oxford, but Rob was lost in thoughts of what he should do. His parents and Molly wanted him to stay in school, but he felt betrayed by the Japanese. It would be only a matter of time before they would run out of the raw materials needed to support their aggression. Submarines would be on the leading edge of the efforts to defeat Japan by cutting off their supply lines, and he wanted to be a part of that action. As he watched the winter sky dim, he made up his mind. Submarine service would be his first and only choice. He hoped the Navy would agree.

President Roosevelt yielded to his advisors by not declaring war on Germany. Instead, he waited to see what Hitler would do since the Axis Powers, Germany, Japan, and Italy had a mutual aid pact to go to the other's aid. Sure enough, December 8, 1941, Germany declared war on the United States. The Navy was somewhat relieved as they were already at war with the German U boats in the North Atlantic. Now it was official.

The following days slipped by quickly. The whole campus was full of activity. Rumors were flying about what the next semester would bring. Courses were to be offered next semester in navigation, map reading, basic aviation and even Morse code. The president of the university called an all-campus convocation to encourage students to study harder and look for ways to aid the war effort. In Oxford, public school children were joining the war effort by going from door to door gathering scrap metal and rubber to help the war effort.

Rob found it difficult to study. It was his final semester, and he had a 3.9 average going into his exams. His father taught a course in geophysical prospecting for oil. Rob took it in the fall and loved it. Combining the physical sciences, geology, physics, and math with stratigraphy, it was the fascinating culmination of his four years as a geology major. He aced the course without any help from his dad.

In the last few days, Dr. Walker and his wife had many conversations about Rob's interest in the submarine service. Mary Catherine was opposed to it. She was determined to intercede with her uncle, a powerful senator in Washington, to get him a billet in naval intelligence service. She knew he could arrange it easily. Rob would most likely be stationed in Washington, and with his father's connections with the state department from his years in Japan, he would be on a fast track for promotions. She was completely unaware that Rob had already had an appointment with the Navy recruiter in Hamilton, the county seat of Butler County Ohio, for an interview for an appointment to Navy Officer Candidate School.

Dr. Walker was aware of it because he had agreed to give Rob a ride to the appointment on the afternoon of December 17 right after his final exam. He decided the better part of valor would be to tell his wife after the appointment.

Rob appreciated his father taking the time to drive him to Hamilton. He knew he was anxious to get his final papers graded, but Dr. Walker wanted to know as much as he could about what the service had to offer his son. He hoped that submarine service would not be available to him.

As they parked the car, they noted the beauty of the old Courthouse made from Bedford limestone and marble; it looked like it would last for an eternity. Once in the building, they were directed to the lower level to the Navy recruiting office. Rob was a little early for his appointment. They both sat down in hard well-worn wooden chairs that lined the hallway. Rob thought that they might have been in prior service in some railroad waiting room. Dr. Walker found a Hamilton newspaper and began to read. The headline was about the imminent fall of the British colony of Hong Kong and below it the capture of Wake Island by the Japanese.

"My God he exclaimed! How could they hit all these islands so quickly? MacArthur is being bombed daily in the Philippines. He is pleading for reinforcements!"

A young sailor in his dress blues appeared at the door to the office and called out "Robert Walker?" Rob stood and was ushered into the temporary recruiting office where a petty officer sat behind a gray steel desk. Rob's dad followed, and they were offered chairs that were more comfortable than the ones in the hall. The first-class machinist mate was a seasoned old hand with four rows of ribbons on the left breast of his uniform. He asked, "What can I do for you young man?"

Rob replied, "I want to join the Navy."

"Good choice, but why?"

"Well, sir I'm interested in submarine service and the Army doesn't have one." The old sailor laughed and said "Well sit down, you've come to the right place. Let's get started" He opened the desk drawer and with his fingers more familiar with the mechanics of diesel engines, opened a folder full of application papers. "You know a physical exam is required. But I'd say you look very physically equipped. He picked up the phone and made an appointment for his physical at the Federal Building on Fountain Square in Cincinnati. As his father looked on, Rob filled out his application and signed on the dotted line. The first step to join the United States Navy was done.

Rob drove his dad's car on the way back to Oxford. The sun was low on the horizon as they sped up Route 27. Lights in the farmhouses were coming on. Fence rows still had snow piled against them. The crops were in. It had been a good bountiful crop this year. The war effort would be greatly blessed. Rob's father sat quietly in the passenger seat holding a tightly rolled up newspaper in his hands. No words were exchanged for a long while. Finally, his father said, "You're set on the submarine service, aren't you?"

Rob replied, "Yes, if they'll have me."

"The recruiter said that you would not know for sure until you graduate from Midshipmen's School. Maybe I can put a good word in for you with one of my friends that I knew when we were in Japan. He was a Navy submariner, stationed at the American Embassy. I think he was there to keep an eye on the Japanese. He was a captain then and is now a rear admiral stationed in the Bureau of Navigation in Washington. They make personnel assignments. If he's no longer in Washington, with the war now, he may have been transferred. I have another option."

Rob asked, "What would that be?"

"Well, your mother's uncle, the senator. He is on the Armed Services Committee and has a lot of influence with the Navy."

"WOW! That would be swell dad." Rob's fingers tightened on the steering wheel.

"But Rob, we need to keep this just between us, no one else, especially your mother. She is completely opposed to you going into submarines. Where do you think they will send you for OCS?"

"Well he said one of three places. Either to the USS *Connecticut,* an old battleship in New York Harbor or Notre Dame, or more likely, Northwestern's campus in Chicago. They are training hundreds of midshipmen right now in a high rise right off Michigan Avenue next to Lake Michigan."

"God, it's cold there son, in the winter the wind blows down from Canada unabated. You'll freeze your butt off."

"I hear Chicago is a great town, lots of fun too."

"We'll see."

· · · · ·

Three weeks later Rob was on his way to Chicago for Midshipmen's School at the Northwestern University Chicago Campus. Rob's dad was right. It was ten above zero when Rob's train from Dayton arrived at the Chicago terminal. As he left the passenger car, Rob carried his suitcase in his right hand and pulled the collar on his Harris Tweed overcoat with the left. A small Navy bus met him and several other enlistees who had boarded the train as it made its way through the snow-covered country in Indiana.

Rob had boarded the Penn Central Railroad passenger train in Dayton the night before. Dr. Walker loaded Rob's one small suitcase in the trunk and Rob and Molly piled in the front seat next to his dad and they set off in the Ford for the thirty-mile trip to Dayton. Rob's mother declined to go with them as she knew she would not be able to hold her emotions in check. Deep down she harbored some resentment toward her son because he refused to remain in school and graduate with his class in the spring. They arrived at the station in downtown Dayton and hurried to the elevated platforms as the bells of the Clock Tower above them struck ten. Molly, Rob and his father, stood on the platform stamping their feet trying to keep circulation in their legs in the cold January air. The eighteen-wheeler locomotive belching black smoke, bell ringing, towing ten passenger cars entered the station on track A only fifteen minutes late.

Professor Walker said goodbye to his son trying to conceal his emotions. He discreetly withdrew to his car leaving Molly and Rob to say farewell. Molly and Rob stood and embraced for a final kiss. Rob drew her close as she whispered, "Rob I love you so much. I will wait for you no matter what happens. Please stay safe. I will pray for you every day. I'll write… please send me your new address when you get there." Tears welled up in her eyes, Rob kissed them away saying, "I love you honey and always will. Keep the faith and I'll be safe. We will win this war, and I promise to keep you in my heart forever." The engine bell started to ring and ring, the shrill whistle blew, and the conductor yelled "All Aboard!" Seeing Rob and Molly still holding each other, he came over to Rob and said, "Sir, we're boarding now." Rob turned and hugged her the last time. It would be a long time before they would embrace again. Rob climbed the stairs to the coach and hurried to the window seat to wave a farewell to Molly. She started running alongside the coach as it gathered speed among clouds of steam. Molly stood alone at the end of the empty platform waiting until the last car disappeared in the night.

· · · · ·

Rob heard reveille sounding through the corridors of the newly built Abbott Hall on the Chicago campus of Northwestern University. It was six a.m. He rose and looked out the window. Snow had fallen throughout the night, now blowing over the streets of Michigan Avenue. The lake was almost frozen over. He shared a four-man room, one of many housing over 500 midshipmen officer candidates. It was Rob's first day transitioning from civilian life. Northwestern would train over 25,000 Navy officers during the war, among them a young ensign by the name of John F. Kennedy.

After assembly and roll call, breakfast was served in the cafeteria, uniforms were issued, haircuts taken, and physicals were given while standing naked in line for hours. At the end of the day, they were introduced to close order drill led by screaming Marine sergeants. At taps, he fell exhausted into his bunk. Lights out at ten p.m.

The next weeks were filled with studies: naval orientation, naval ordnance, navigation, engineering, communications, and naval justice. He learned about seamanship on a yard patrol craft moored alongside the pier at the Chicago Yacht Club. He wrote home how much he enjoyed conning the vessel, doing bumper drills, and learning how to handle the small patrol boat mooring to the dock. His favorite subject was the introduction to navigation. He loved the precision of the stars, the math and how much the science depends on precise time. He disliked the latrine duties, KP, peeling potatoes, and standing in line for everything, but it was part of the indoctrination of midshipmen. The term midshipman dated back as far as the sixteenth century when midshipmen were ratings that worked on board naval vessels in amidships and were generally berthed there. Rob likened midshipmen to the ham in the middle of the sandwich, you're neither an officer nor an enlisted man.

There was little time for recreation. Rob hit the books more than his roommates. But Sammy his best friend at the school loved movies so he and Rob took them in when liberty sounded. Some of the year's favorites played at the Fox Movie-Tone Theater in the Loop. His favorites, *Casablanca*, and *Yankee Doodle Dandy*. Rob sat dumbstruck at the newsreels, narrated by Lowell Thomas, showing the fall of Wake Island, Guam, Singapore and telling of the struggles of General MacArthur's forces in the Philippines holding out on beleaguered Corregidor. The anger building inside him made him want to get into the fray as soon as possible. He knew submarines were going to be the first line of offense, and he wanted to get aboard one as soon as he graduated.

The days flew by for the ninety-day wonders. Rob stood at the top of his class. Orders from BUNAV were received and distributed a week before graduation. Rob received his first choice of duty: report to Submarine Squadron 6 in Pearl Harbor for further assignment to a submarine. His superiors were surprised that he was ordered straight to submarines without the benefit of the submarine school. There were only two in his class directly assigned to submarines. Two of Rob's roommates were assigned to surface ships, and Sammy to aviation training at Pensacola.

Molly wrote two or sometimes three letters every week. Rob found time to answer them on weekends. Graduation would be held in the auditorium of Abbott Hall on March 25, 1942 and Rob invited Molly and his parents. They planned to drive to Chicago on the 24th staying at the Palmer House the most elegant hotel in town. Molly was so happy to get the invitation to join the Walkers for Rob's graduation.

Arriving at five p.m. they checked in the hotel, climbing the travertine marble-clad double staircase leading from the Monroe Street entrance to the grand reception room. Molly was awestruck at the beauty of the place. Dr. Walker had to use some influence to get two reservations as the hotel was booked constantly due to the war. Molly's room was on the fifth floor and the Walkers' suite on the seventh. After changing they met in the main lobby on Monroe Street awaiting Rob's arrival. Molly wore a sleeveless black dress, cut low in front, with a white scarf around her shoulders. Rob's fraternity pin was displayed prominently on her breast. Molly was very nervously awaiting Rob's arrival. And Rob was apprehensive and eager at the same time, eager to see Molly and apprehensive about having to tell his mother he had received orders to submarines. Molly couldn't stand it any longer, so she went out to the porter station near the entrance looking for Rob. She had just made it when a tall Navy man wearing a black bridge coat with brass buttons came through the revolving door. It was Rob! She rushed to him and fell into his arms. Rob said, "Where have you been all my life? Molly I love you! You are beautiful!" She kissed him while newly arrivals crowded past them. Molly exclaimed, "Rob you look great, the Navy is taking good care of you, you are more handsome than ever, my gosh you look so marvelous in your uniform!" Arm in arm they found his parents in the bar having a drink. Mary Catherine Walker stood and gave her son a long hug and kissed his cheek. "You've lost weight, the Navy isn't feeding you enough!" Rob replied, "No mother," looking at his dad, he winked, "I'm getting a lot to eat, just doing a lot of physical training, it's part of the curriculum."

They dined in the classical-style Empire Room up a short flight of stairs off the lobby. It was the main dining room which later in the evening, became a nightclub. The lavish decorations reflected the Palmer House architect Steven Root who once wrote that the room was ornamented with "flat ebony pilasters against dark green walls and softly tapestried panels, the whole lightened by gold leaf decorations." Dinner with the Walkers in the beautiful dining room began with Dr. Walker ordering a cheese fondue appetizer made with Gruyere and Emmantled Cheese reheated in a silver bowl on their table; for their main course Rob chose lake trout and Molly a filet mignon with creamed horseradish sauce on the side. The elegant dinner was wonderful and served by attentive waiters. She was so grateful and thanked the Walkers. Rob explained the schedules for the graduation ceremonies the next day and their seating arrangements. Everything went smoothly until Rob's mother asked, "Rob have you received your orders yet?" Rob glanced at his father, took a drink of water and said, "Yes Mother, I just received them. I'm going to Pearl Harbor." She looked startled, "But are you going into intelligence work?" Rob replied, "No mother, I'm going to be assigned to a submarine based in Hawaii. I think the Navy gave me my first choice of duty because of my class standing." Rob looked around the table, Molly had a slight smile, Rob's father looked pained, and Mrs. Walker lips were pursed, her arms crossed her chest. She started to say something, and Dr. Walker interrupted, "Let's have some dessert, shall we?" He beckoned to the waiter and breathed a sigh of relief. His wife was not relieved, she was worried.

After dessert the Walkers decided to go to their room. Dr. Walker was tired after the long drive from Oxford, and he knew he'd get an earful before he went to bed. They would meet Molly in the dining room for breakfast in the morning and then go to the graduation ceremonies. Rob had to be back in his dorm room at Northwestern soon, but he and Molly went to the ballroom to dance. There were two large ballrooms upstairs on the fourth floor planned by the famous architect's Root and Burnham, architects of the Palmer House and many buildings in Chicago. They were the inventors of the first skyscrapers. The ballrooms were designed around the Louis XVI period with red lacquer panels set off with gold trim and mirrors. Molly thought it a bit overdone, but she didn't care as she was with Rob the love of her life. Popular orchestras appeared there frequently featuring swing bands, such as Jimmy Dorsey, Benny Goodman, Vaughn Monroe, Freddie Martin and others. As Rob and Molly entered the room the lights were low, and the band was playing a Glen Miller tune, *Moonlight Serenade*. Rob held Molly tight, as they danced to the familiar music, Rob whispered, "It's like old times darling, I miss you so." Molly said softly, "I've been so lonely without you, these three months seem like three years." They danced to the small band's songs made popular by Tex Beneke's version of *Hey! BaBaReBop*, Glen Miller's *In the Mood*, and Tommy Dorsey's *Chicago*.

Nearly out of breath, they slow danced cheek to cheek to a song by the Gershwins', *Love is Here to Stay*, the words sung by the band's young vocalist melted their hearts. Molly said, "Oh Rob, I wish this night would never end. This song will be our song forever. Always remember, *Love is Here to Stay*." Rob held her close and said, "I will, Molly." They sat at a small table by the dance floor holding hands, talking about their life together and what the future might hold for them and suddenly it was the last dance. They danced to *Goodnight Sweetheart* twirling to the music holding each other as close as possible. It was time to go.

Rob got his bridge coat from the hatcheck girl and walked Molly to her room. They exited the walnut panel elevator on the fifth-floor bidding goodnight to the young elevator operator, and they moved down the hall hand in hand, not even noticing the beautifully inlaid paneling and an expensive carpet of this famous hotel. At her door he paused, he wanted to go in her room, but he decided the honorable thing to do would be to leave as quickly as possible before things got out of hand. He drew her close once again and kissed her goodnight. Rob said, "Honey, what a wonderful evening! I'll see you in the morning in the auditorium at Abbott Hall, here are the tickets." Rob turned and started to walk down the hall; Molly called after him "Honey, come here." She opened the door and said, "Come in and see my room, it's beautiful." Rob was stunned. She led him over to the wide window overlooking Monroe Street. The city lights were dazzling. Office buildings were lighted despite the brownout, the elevated train was speeding by, gold and red neon signs blinking, taxicabs racing down the street with their light signaling they had a paying fare. "Sit down honey, I've got to use the bathroom. Rob wasn't sure what to do but he sat in the lounge chair and admired his new watch, a Rolex his father had given him that evening for a graduation present from college and the Navy. It was 2 a.m. He turned the radio on and found a music station still broadcasting after midnight. It was playing one of the top twenty-five songs on the Hit Parade, *I'll be seeing you.*

Molly came out of the bathroom, clad in her bathrobe. She turned the lights out and said, "Darling, let's dance." The only light was from neon signs blinking in the street below. Molly put her arms around him and kissed him deeply. As they danced, she whispered, "Rob, I have a confession, would it be bad if we slept here tonight? It may be our only chance for a long time or forever." Rob's hands found her warm breasts, their lips met in an endless embrace. As his hands raced over her, she gasped, "Oh Rob!" He suddenly broke away from their torrid embrace and staggered over to the door. His heart was racing, "Molly I want you more than anything in the world, but think about it, I guess I'm old fashioned, but could we save ourselves for a wonderful honeymoon when I return someday? But if I don't make it through the war, you'll be a virgin for your husband." Everything in her upbringing and her Catholic faith ruled against premarital sex, but her heart was overruling her beliefs. She wanted Rob so much: *What's wrong with me? What's wrong with Rob?* She was crushed but, in her heart, she knew that he was right. Rob closed the door softly. It was 3 a.m. He took a cab to his dorm. He needed a cold shower.

Molly's tiny bedside radio was playing *I Remember You* as she sobbed before finally drifting off to sleep. She was still a virgin.

· · · · ·

The auditorium of Abbott Hall was packed with guests and graduating officer candidates when Molly and the Walkers entered the huge room, tickets in hand looking for their assigned seats. Once seated Molly looked in vain for Rob, all she could see were the rows of officer caps. The Navy band from the Great Lakes Boot Camp began playing a stirring march of John Philip Sousa, *Stars and Stripes Forever, The Thunderer, and Sabers and Spurs.* While the music was playing, Mrs. Walker told her husband, "These men all look alike." Dr. Walker smiled, "That promotes unity, that's why they call what they are wearing *uniforms.*" Molly chuckled softly not wanting to embarrass her hostess. Attention to colors was sounded and all stood as the band played the National Anthem. Shivers ran through Molly as the Navy men saluted and all guests stood at attention with their hands over their breasts. The chaplain gave a warm invocation imploring God, "To give these men courage and divine guidance in the fight against tyranny. Each one has given the United States of America a blank check for giving their very lives if necessary, in defense of our nation."

Molly didn't hear much of the address by the Commandant of the Naval District as the words of giving a blank check for their lives reverberated in her mind. Suddenly it was time for the administering of the Oath of Office. All the officers stood as the Admiral led them in reciting the oath:

"I, and state your full name, do solemnly swear that I will support and defend the Constitution of the United States against all enemies, foreign and domestic; that I will bear true faith and allegiance to the same; that I take this obligation freely, without any mental reservation or purpose of evasion; and that I will well and faithfully discharge the duties of the office on which I am about to enter. So, help me God."

The Commandant said, "Gentlemen, welcome as Commissioned Officers in the United States Navy!"

CHAPTER 6

Oxford, Fall 1942

Molly Gaynor was beginning her senior year and had landed a part-time job in the Dean's office doing secretarial work, filing and typing occasional letters for her new boss. It was a great job. Her hours were scheduled around her class time permitting her some occasional free minutes during lunch to type letters to Rob. And she continued reporting campus news for the *Student* newspaper. She liked keeping busy, it helped pass the time away. Molly longed to see her Navy man. She carried a photo of Rob in his new uniform in her billfold. He had written in the corner *Molly, with all my love, Rob.*

The last time she had been with Rob was after his graduation from Northwestern. His orders permitted him to take a plane from Glenview Naval Air Station, north of Chicago, direct to Alameda Naval Air Station, California, and then on to Pearl Harbor.

She remembered him saying that the star above the single gold stripe on his sleeve indicated that he was a line officer, and a line officer could do anything. She knew he could, but she was very worried about Rob being in submarines. She knew he wanted combat and he was successful in getting assigned to the *Thornfish*. But being in a submarine was extremely dangerous even in peacetime, let alone in war.

Newspaper reports were full of stinging defeats of the U.S. Military. Wake Island had fallen around Christmas, 1941, and the Japs had invaded Guam in April. The British lost Singapore in February, and General Wainwright surrendered the entire U.S. Army in the Philippines in early April. Most were defending the Bataan peninsula when ordered to surrender. Reports were leaking out that some 60,000 Filipino and American soldiers were taken prisoner and forced to march some 70 miles without food and water to Camp O'Donnell. Thousands died from torture, no food or water, and bayoneting along the way.

Despite all the bad news for America, there were several bright spots. One was the bombing of Tokyo by LT Colonel Jimmy Doolittle's B-25 bombers on April 18, 1942. Sixteen B-25 medium bombers launched from USS *Hornet*, four hundred miles off the coast of Japan flew without fighter escort to bomb Tokyo. The raid did little damage, but those 30 seconds over Tokyo electrified the nation. The other bright spot for The United States was the Navy's victory at Midway in June. It was at the little American island base, situated halfway across the Pacific, where the tide of war would turn. A large Japanese invasion force was turned back and nearly destroyed by American dive bombers and torpedo planes flying off the carrier the USS *Yorktown*. Thanks to early warnings of Japanese communications decoded by Navy intelligence at Pearl Harbor, the U.S. Navy sank all four of the Jap carriers in the invasion fleet, the same ones that attacked Pearl Harbor six months earlier. It would mark the turning point of the Pacific war.

The Miami campus was beginning to feel the effects of the war. The male student population was declining every month as men volunteered or were drafted. Some Miami professors and instructors were volunteering to serve in the armed forces. And many of the professors were changing their normal courses of instruction to teach radio, navigation, and aeronautics.

Molly's letters to Rob always included the latest campus news including some occasional gossip. She was selected to become one of the editors of the *Student* next semester. Her responsibility included writing about the Navy training on campus. The college's newspaper was now staffed almost entirely with females as the male population of the university declined. She was able to get a lot of information from eager sailors wanting to get better acquainted with the pretty reporter. Some clippings of her reporting of campus news were usually tucked into the envelopes along with her love letters to Rob.

Molly was the first of the Gaynors to go to college. Her father immigrated to America from Ireland in the early twenties. After months of trying to find work in New York and seeing occasional signs in store windows, IRISH NEED NOT APPLY, he hopped a freight train and a few days later, found himself in the yard of the Erie Rail Road in Marion, Ohio. He often told the family how he outran some railroad workers that were chasing "hobos" and made it to the City Mission in town. He could only stay three nights and then would be on his own. The third day the kindly Reverend Bob, head of the mission, found him a job as an apprentice laying brick and ceramic tile.

Frank Gaynor was glad to get out of the mission. He heard some fiery preachers each night. Local pastors took turns speaking to the men in the evenings before dinner. Being an Irish Catholic, he was unaccustomed to evangelistic preaching. One evening, during the sermon that they all had to attend before getting their evening meal, the scrubby guy in the pew next to him was eating popcorn out of a box. The preacher was earnestly speaking about Jesus raising Lazarus from the dead, and his coming out of the tomb bound in linen grave clothes. As the preacher got louder and louder, the man, completely engrossed in the fiery sermon, finished his popcorn and then began to eat the box! Frank could hardly contain himself from laughing. He loved to tell the story over and over.

Molly was the third child born to a family of seven. Her mother, Irene Catherine

Kennedy, met Frank at a Catholic dance in Columbus, and they were married four months later. Frank became a very good bricklayer and started his own company in October 1929, just as the stock market crashed. Her mother took in laundry to supplement their meager income and worked cleaning homes for some of the wealthy in Marion. Molly loved school even as a child and her mother taught her to read before she entered first grade. Always a step ahead of her classmates, she graduated from Marion Harding High second in her class of 52.

During dinner one evening, she announced to her parents that she wanted to go to college. Molly had been chosen salutatorian of her class and was convinced she could gain entrance to college especially as an Ohio high school graduate and near the top of her class. Her father didn't say anything for a few moments. All her siblings were staring intently at their father. No Gaynor had ever gone to college. Her two older brothers began work with the tile business as soon as they hung up their high school graduation robes. Molly broke the silence, "Father did you hear me? I want to go on to college and maybe become a scientist or maybe even an aviator."

Molly's mother turned her head in disbelief; no one ever dared to interrupt father.

After a few more bites of his fried chicken, Frank finally said in his stilted Irish brogue, "Molly Gaynor, you'll do no such thing. Aviation is dangerous and not a job for women, and scientists are men's jobs, so don't even think about it. Besides, we don't have the money to send any of you kids to college, so you'll need to start looking for work as soon as you graduate." After a few more bites of chicken he added, "Even if we did, you'd have to become a teacher because that's what women do and it's always a good job to fall back on when things get tough like they are right now."

Molly got up from the table without saying a word, picked up her plate and turned her head to hide her tears as she made her way to the kitchen; then she took her plate and smashed it in the sink. This Irish girl's stubborn streak was aroused. She was determined she would not work in a tile plant or be the wife of a bricklayer. No, she would go to school and be somebody! She chose Miami University in Oxford, Ohio, as her first choice.

CHAPTER 7

The Surprise

Thornfish cruised submerged during the daylight hours the following day, with brief periods of observations coming to periscope depth at very slow speed so as not to leave a wake in the calm sea. In the late afternoon, Captain Custer ordered the diving officer to make his depth 58 feet to give a maximum height of the exposed scope for a good look around. He squatted on the deck by the periscope well and folded the handles down as the quartermaster raised the search periscope. It broke the surface, and the captain yelled, "Dick come up here! Am I seeing things? Is that a Jap floatplane on the horizon?" Dick climbed the ladder from the control room to the conning tower two steps at a time. He took the handles noting the relative bearing on the circular ring surrounding the base of the periscope. He confirmed what the captain had seen and ordered, "down scope." Ahead on the horizon was a Japanese single engine Mitsubishi floatplane drifting along with two aviators in the cockpit.

Custer said, "Dick they were probably scouting for a convoy, and had mechanical problems, don't you think?" Dick replied, "Sir, probably so, but we might be able to take them prisoner if we surface quickly; they might have some charts and other info on convoys that would be helpful. I'd like to get some target practice in for our gunners too. We'll surprise them by surfacing quickly and ram the plane enough to prevent them from getting off a radio distress call." Looking directly at Custer he said, "Let's do it sir."

Captain Custer looked perplexed, "Dick, I don't know...there could be another plane or a destroyer on its way, and we'd be caught red-handed. No, it's not a good idea." Dick wasn't going to give up easily. "Sir, I think headquarters would be very pleased to get some good intelligence on convoys and perhaps charts of minefields." That sparked some interest in Custer's mind. That would make a great entry in his patrol report. He stared at the compass repeater for a few moments and then said, "Ok Dick, this is your deal, I hope you're right. I don't want too many men on deck in case we have to dive, so select your best men on the twenty mm and machine guns. We may have a shootout ahead of us."

The *Thornfish* had several men assigned to do boarding of enemy vessels if the opportunity presented itself. Before they left Pearl, five enlisted and one officer had been given two weeks training by the Marines qualifying them with small arms weapons, capture and interrogation. Because of his size and athleticism, Ensign Walker had been selected to lead the team.

While the boarding party was assembling in the control room, the exec and the captain conferred about how to approach the plane. The captain's idea was a direct one. He was worried that Jap headquarters had already been radioed by the downed aircraft and would certainly have a plane on the way to find it and direct a surface ship to the scene. He didn't want to stay surfaced any longer than he had to.

Dick added a caution saying, "Captain, this guy might have a depth charge hanging under his wing, I recommend that we circle it and make sure it's OK before we go in.

Custer then said, "All right Dick, good idea, let's go," and ordered all engines ahead one third, and *Thornfish* began circling the enemy aircraft. LT Morrison was right; no depth charges were hanging under the floatplane.

The exec went on the intercom and informed the crew of the situation and the need for speed in boarding the plane. Gun crews would man the two 20 mm guns and keep them trained on the plane while the captain conned the bow of *Thornfish* behind the wing of the Mitsubishi. Ensign Walker's team would then board the floatplane and take the two airmen prisoners if they did not resist. If the Japs indicated that they were going to use any weapons, they could fire at will.

The captain ordered surface, and *Thornfish* rose in smooth seas only a hundred yards from the plane's startled crew. The battle surface was done like clockwork, just as they had done in weeks of training. The gun crews loaded their weapons and trained the 20 mm guns directly on the cockpit. Ensign Walker and his team rushed to the bow as Custer conned the *Thornfish's* bow closer to the enemy plane.

In their haste, the captain failed to have the standard Navy booklet English to Japanese dictionary brought to the bridge. He was about to order it brought up when he heard Ensign Walker yelling at them in Japanese. He couldn't believe it!

Rob said in Japanese, "Hands up! Surrender. You will not be harmed. Put your weapons on the wing NOW."

He recognized that one was the pilot and the other the radioman. They stood up, and suddenly the pilot pulled out his pistol and started shooting. Fortunately, he was a bad shot. The boarding party's marksman shot him with a Thompson submachine gun. The radioman immediately jumped into the water and started swimming towards the *Thornfish*. Rob ordered his best swimmer to go after him. And in a few minutes, he had the shaky Jap laid on the bow. Captain then eased the bow of the sub so close that Rob could climb aboard the Mitsubishi. He quickly determined that the pilot was dead and then pulled the charts and any papers he could find from the cockpit.

Tucking them into his backpack, he took the pilot's pistol as a souvenir. As Rob was descending from the wing, Custer ordered all hands below as radar had a high-speed surface contact coming over the horizon.

Once Rob was back on board, the *Thornfish* slowly backed away from the plane and Captain Custer ordered, "Clear the bridge," and as soon as everyone was below, he sounded the diving alarm and *Thornfish* submerged before the Japanese destroyer arrived on the scene. Once at periscope depth, the captain saw the destroyer heading for the downed aircraft. The exec had an idea. "Sir, he's going to stop to investigate the damaged plane. He'll be a perfect target for us, dead in the water. We can't miss."

"Dick, if we miss, we will be in for a shellacking."

The XO passed the word throughout the boat of the plan. The crew was excited. Finally, they would see some action against a surface vessel. Submariners were only permitted to wear the Submarine Combat Patrol Pin on their uniforms after successfully sinking an enemy ship while on patrol.

The order was passed to man battle stations torpedo. Captain Custer was on the attack periscope; the executive officer in the conning tower, supervising the attack team. Jerry Abrams, the Engineering Officer, was in the control room as diving officer, and Rob Walker was at the Target Data Computer in the conning tower. Custer ordered the forward torpedo doors opened. They would fire three torpedoes, set at depth 10 feet, spread to hit in the destroyer's bow, amidships, and one in the after part of the ship. He conned the sub to a position 800 yards from the plane and exposed the attack periscope for far too many seconds each time he observed to get range and bearing to the target as it raced toward the damaged plane.

The captain called out target information "Angle on the bow port twenty, range 2000 yards, speed estimated ten knots and slowing." Perspiration caused him to wipe his eyes and forehead. His hands were clammy as he moved the handles on the scope.

"We've got a Chidori Class coming our way! They are the best the Japs have."

Custer made a final periscope observation before firing. The range and bearing checked with Rob's TDC solution. As the destroyer slowed to check the damaged plane, the captain gave the order to fire when ready. The exec standing by Rob, pushed the firing button for torpedo number 1, then 2, and 3. *Thornfish's* sonar man reported, "All cleared the boat, hot straight and normal." The range had now closed to 900 yards. The XO manned the scope to check the wakes and found them dead on. They couldn't miss. The three Mark-14 steam torpedoes, 21 inches in diameter, and 18 feet long sped out of the torpedo tubes at 45 knots. Each carried 450 pounds of TNT in the warhead, but steam torpedoes always leave a wake in the water as soon as they're fired. In daylight, they offered the enemy a perfect trail to the submarine firing the torpedoes. Rob, with a stopwatch in his hand, counted the seconds awaiting the explosions. Five, four, three, two, and mark…. but no thunderous hits were heard. The exec raised the periscope and took a quick look and exclaimed, "They went under the tin can! He's seen us and is coming after us! Captain, we need to get deep, now!"

Captain Custer seemed dazed. He mumbled yes but gave no orders to conn the ship. Dick saw that he was not responding, yelled to the diving officer, "All ahead flank, flood negative, twenty degrees down angle, make your depth 300 feet. Rig for depth charge!" The pings from the sonar of the enemy ship echoed throughout the boat as they descended. He then ordered left full rudder to bring *Thornfish* almost under the damaged plane, where last seen. The sound of the screws of the destroyer above them grew louder as it crossed over the submarine. But no depth charges were dropped. Dick thought this is too good to be true.

During training, the crew had only been exposed to two depth charges dropped by a friendly DD to acquaint them with depth charging. But it was nothing compared to what they were about to endure. The enemy destroyer had slowed to allow their sonar echoes to be more effective. Dropping depth charges would interfere with their trying to locate the submerged submarine. Their sonar pulses sounded loudly in the boat even though *Thornfish* had quieted all but essential machinery and slowed the speed to three knots to creep away from the hunter above.

Captain Custer was visibly shaken even though no depth charges had fallen around the submarine. The exec, sensing he needed help, stayed close to him in the conning tower. Suddenly WHAM! WHAM! WHAM! Three depth charges exploded near the sub as it was slinking away from their tormentor above. All hell broke loose in the sub. The thunder below was so close that the cylindrical hull of the sub seemed to compress. Seawater poured in through packing glands in some of the valves. Insulation popped off the bulkheads, lights went out, and the emergency battle lanterns came on giving an eerie light in the control room.

Dick grabbed the captain's shoulder and said, "Captain, we've got to go deeper. The diving officer says that there is a temperature gradient now and we can try to get under it. Maybe their sonar won't detect us." The captain was about to reply when another blast of four depth charges exploded close but not as close as before. Captain Custer froze.

Dick told the diving officer "I have the conn." And then ordered, "Make your depth 400 feet. Come right to new course 010. All compartments report damage."

Thornfish silently crept away with course changes always trying to maintain a slim profile as the enemy sonar continued to track the sub. During the first hour of evasive action, a total of 36 depth charges rained down on *Thornfish*. Men not on duty lay in their bunks, some praying quietly, and a few not so quietly. The temperature inside rose to 100 degrees with the ship's air conditioning secured. The diving officer had to pump bilges several times during the ordeal to maintain depth control with so little speed on the boat.

Captain Custer remained in the conning tower even though it was drenched from the water coming in through the periscope's shears. Rob, standing in his battle station at the TDC, thought to himself is this going to be "Custer's Last Stand?" He stared in disbelief of the captain's lack of command and was very thankful that the XO dared to take charge of the emergencies.

During a lull in the action the exec said, "Captain, I'm going down below and see how the men are holding up."

"Very well, Dick," he replied weakly. He added, "Give me a damage report as soon as possible." It was the first words the captain had spoken since Dick acted after firing the torpedoes.

As Dick made his way through the boat, he found the crew glad to see him. One lad, who was experiencing his first depth charge attack, asked, "What are the chances we make it, Sir?"

Dick replied, "Well we are going to make it. That Jap is good, but we are better." Then he added loudly, "We're going to get out of here soon before he gets help from some of his buddies. Don't worry guys. I've got a plan."

As he made his way aft, he regretted saying the words "I've got a plan." He thought "I should have said the captain has a plan or we have a plan."

When he reached the maneuvering room, he talked with the engineering officer. "Jerry, how's the damage repair going?" The exec had a lot of confidence in his engineer. Jerry Abrams, a Reserve Officer and an electrical engineering graduate of Purdue University. He was granted a commission after graduation in 1939. A slim, agile former high school basketball player in his hometown of Fort Wayne, Indiana, he was always fascinated with submarines. It began when his dad gave him a beautifully bound book about submarines for Christmas. He was surprised that the Navy assigned him his first choice for active duty, submarine school at New London, Connecticut.

He replied, "Our main problem sir, is damage to the main induction pipe. We've got sea water coming in somewhere. After this is over, I'd like permission to have one of our skinniest men go in and find it."

"OK, Jerry, we'll do it as soon as we can surface. We'll need a full charge on the batteries. How are they holding up now?"

"We have about a 45% life left sir. But we're going to have to start a charge as soon as we get up."

"Roger that," replied the executive officer as he turned and quickly started toward the forward torpedo room. He also wanted to see how the Japanese radioman was doing. Immediately after being hauled aboard *Thornfish*, the Japanese prisoner had been handcuffed to a bunk in between two torpedoes in the forward torpedo room. He was a young man, radioman third class. He watched nervously as the torpedo men checked and rechecked their weapons.

The exec didn't make it to the forward room. As he entered the control room, Dick saw the ashen faces of the men and knew he had better take charge once again. Sonar then reported multiple screws approaching from 270 degrees. Two or three destroyers were now on their way to sink *Thornfish*. He was about to order a course change when another volley of depth charges exploded above them. The Japs were setting the depth charges too shallow. Good news for *Thornfish*. Dick checked the bathometer watching the temperature chart and said, "We've got a chance; we're going deeper."

The diving officer quickly said, "Sir with all due respect, we are almost at test depth now. If we go deeper, we may crush the hull."

"If we don't, they will crush us with those ash cans." Then he began to enact his plan. "There's a cold dense mass of water just below us. If we get in under it, the Jap sonar will be deflected as we creep away." Then he ordered the diving officer, "Make your depth 450 feet!"

As *Thornfish* quietly descended, the hull began to groan, and creek as the water pressure claimed every square inch of the hull. Soon water sprayed through packing glands of piping exposed to the sea. Damage control parties made their way through the vessel making the most vital repairs first.

Dick joined the captain once again in the conning tower and related all that was being done to save the ship. When the exec told the captain of his plan to escape, he became very agitated. "Dick, you're going to kill us all!" Dick thought to himself "*I've heard that before!*"

To his credit, and everyone on board, the plan worked. After reaching the ordered depth, *Thornfish* silently went ahead on both screws and made an abrupt change of course to the north. Thirty minutes later, with the sound of ash cans in the distance, Dick Morrison breathed easier as the sub came to periscope depth. Captain Custer ordered "Up Scope," and the search periscope broke the darkening surface. Once satisfied that the Jap destroyers, still dropping depth charges, were looking for them in vain, he ordered, "All engines ahead standard, prepare to surface."

Aoogah, Aoogah, Aoogah! Three blasts on the ship's announcing system to surface sent a signal of relief throughout the ship…they had survived their baptism of fire. *Thornfish* welcomed the night.

Once on the surface, the engineering officer chose machinist mate Stephen "Skinny" Krause to enter the main induction pipe to try to find the leak. Krause was selected because he had a very slender build. The main induction is a pipe running on the outside of the submarine's hull, 36 inches in diameter at it's opening in the superstructure behind the bridge but narrowing to 22 inches before entering the pressure hull to the forward and after engine rooms. It is vital for the operation of the engines. Air for the diesel engines, as well as for ventilation of all compartments, must come through the induction piping while on the surface. If sea water filled the pipes, it would weigh about 8,000 pounds and would have to be drained to the negative tank and accounted for in the weights and measures needed to provide stability in a submarine. Every change in weight must be compensated for to provide stability surfaced and especially when submerged.

Armed with a battle lantern and a sound powered phone "Skinny Krause" began his arduous task of determining the source of the leak. Within minutes he found a crack in the piping going to the after-engine room. The depth charging had cracked a joint, and it would have to be repaired by welding from above. Skinny reported this to LT Abrams, who went to ask permission of the captain to send welders to make repairs.

The captain had finally regained some composure. Jerry found him conferring with the exec in the control room. A top-secret message addressed to *Thornfish* had just been received in the radio room. An enemy cruiser, Chikuma class, had been damaged by torpedoes from the *Garfish* sixty nautical miles south of where they were. The cruiser, accompanied by a destroyer, was heading north toward Japan undoubtedly for repairs. It would take *Thornfish* hours at top speed to intercept, but with welders working in the superstructure it would require them to reduce speed in the sea state now roughing up the ship.

Jerry said, "Captain, we found the leak in the main induction. It's going to take my engineers some time to make repairs by welding from the outside superstructure. I'm not…." The captain interrupted, "Just tell me how long it will take Jerry!"

"Yes sir, our best estimate is about an hour."

Custer turned to the XO, "What do you think Dick? Can we make it in time if we delay an hour?"

"Sir let me get with my tracking team, and we'll get the answers."

"OK, do it NOW."

Thornfish had gotten a shellacking, just as Captain Custer had predicted. After getting damage reports from all compartments, he once again turned to his executive officer for advice.

"Dick, what is the tracking team's estimate?"

"Ensign Walker already laid out a track that considered the delay for one hour for the main induction repair, and another option for the possibility of a more direct approach. Our idea is to have us stay in a course with the waves to lessen the danger to the men working under the superstructure. By blowing all ballast tanks dry, including safety and negative, and riding as high as we can, we can make turns toward the cruiser while the welding is going on."

Captain Custer replied, "But can we get a charge in for the batteries and intercept with the induction shut?"

"I know his idea is a little risky sir, but we would have to open the conning tower hatch and maybe the after-torpedo room hatch to let air in for the diesels."

"You're right there. A pooping sea coming up from the stern could flood the after room. I don't know. It's damn risky, so don't open the after-engine room hatch. When is sunrise? We need to be in a position to attack before then."

"Sunrise is 0543. We believe that by using three engines at ten knots while we are welding, and then 18 knots after repairs and with number 4 engine on a charge of the batteries, we can make it before then."

"Ok, make it so if you agree. But we need to change course to intercept now."

Dick said, "I've already done that sir."

Custer looked away; he didn't like that. *He's trying to take command.* Then he added, "Those guys back aft on deck are going to get soaked for sure."

Dick agreed but worried about having a man overboard in the rough waters' topside. He decided to go aft to check on the men. Welding on a submarine is difficult even in dry dock, but with increasing wind and waves at two a.m. in cramped spaces under the deck aft of the conning tower, it was a Herculean task. Two machinist mates volunteered to do the job, knowing full well that if an emergency dive had to be made to avoid being hit by an enemy submarine's torpedo, they would be lost.

Chief O'Neil was supervising the operation when the XO climbed down from the bridge and worked his way aft holding on to the lifelines. Dick Morrison shouted over the roar of the engines, the howling wind and seas breaking over the fantail, "Chief how are they doing down there?"

"Not good sir, with the waves breaking over us, we can't do it. Can we get a better course to ride for a while? The wind seems to have hauled around off our starboard beam since we started."

"Ok chief, we'll head into the wind and hope the new course will help your men."

By changing course, the sub rode better making the welding job a little easier. Satisfied that the work was going well enough, the exec returned to the control room. The dispatch from Pearl was an Ultra message that was the result of the great job our code breakers had done in breaking the Japanese Navy message traffic. Standing over the DRT, the dead reckoning tracer, he looked at the plot the attack team had laid out. The one thing that bothered him was the increasing sea state and the workers in the superstructure. The change in course to accommodate the welders would increase the time required for the attack, but right now their plan was the best they could do.

He left the attack team and moved to the forward torpedo room to check on the men there and to look at the enemy radioman. The exec called Rob to go with him.

His unexpected knowledge of the Japanese language interested him. As they moved through the forward battery and officers' quarters, he asked Rob, "How in the hell did you ever get to know Japanese?" As they entered the hatch to the torpedo room, he replied, "Well Sir, I spent a couple of years in Japan when my father taught there at the University of Tokyo." He found the little radioman still handcuffed to a bunk, shaken and very frightened.

The XO ordered him freed while he talked with the men. Rob helped the lad up; he judged that he must be no more than 17 or 18 years old. He talked with him trying to calm him down after having been through some terrifying depth charging at the hands of his fellow countrymen. Rob thought he might have some valuable information for them regarding ship movements off the coast of Formosa. The young man told him that his plane was from the air base on Formosa and was on a search plan looking for submarines when they ran out of gas. He said their maintenance was lousy and the fuel gauge showed they had several hours more fuel left when the engine quit. His pilot skillfully landed the plane in the water, and they radioed for assistance. They were shocked by *Thornfish's* sudden appearance. After assuring the prisoner as much as possible that he would not be hurt, Rob turned him over to Grabowski, the senior torpedo man, to show him how to use the head; Rob translated as he was shown the complicated steps to flush the toilet. Several valves had to be used in sequence to dispose of the waste properly. Otherwise, a wrong turn could make things very messy as air pressure would blow the contents over the entire tiny water closet.

Before he could say more, the word was passed over the 1 MC announcing system for the executive officer to report to the bridge. Dick turned to Rob and said, "Better get back to the plotting board, the captain will want an update on our progress."

Rob made his way past the officers' quarters stopping in the wardroom for a quick cup of coffee. The Filipino steward on duty had just made a fresh pot. He poured it into a china mug and didn't bother to add his usual canned milk. He was learning to drink it black and hot. Balancing his cup, he entered the control room glancing at the clock and the course and speed indicators before joining the attack team at the DRT.

CHAPTER 8

Battle Stations

The noise in the control room made it difficult to hear because air for the diesel engines was being taken in through the opened conning tower hatch, creating a wind tunnel effect throughout the boat. Quartermaster third class Ryan informed Rob that the bridge had just reported that repairs to the main induction piping would be completed in less than 20 minutes. According to the plot, the latest and best estimate was that *Thornfish* would arrive in an attack position at dawn. The exec joined them and approved the track that had been laid out just as Captain Custer descended the ladder from the conning tower.

The captain glanced at the track and turned to the exec and said, "Dick make sure we get to the attack position before dawn. I'm going to try to get a couple of hours sleep. When the welding is done make flank speed on three engines and charge batteries on number four. Put it in my night order book and wake me when radar contact is made."

"Aye Sir." Traditionally, every commanding officer is required by Navy Regulations to provide his night orders for the night watches as to what they are to do, what navigation aids might be observed and when to awaken the CO when certain conditions are met. But not included was the traditional ration of liquor for all hands after having been depth charged. Even though it was 2300, the exec allowed all hands not on watch to get their ration of whiskey and then turn in to get some sleep before the general alarm's bell like tones, nicknamed the Bells of St. Mary's, announced, 'Battle Stations, Torpedo.'

The machinist mates who finished the welding job got a double ration for their heroic efforts. Rob took his one small bottle to the forward torpedo room and gave it to the Japanese radioman. The torpedomen had already nicknamed him "Tojo." He bowed gratefully and said thanks, then drank it all and collapsed on the deck in a deep sleep.

At 0215 radar picked up the two enemy ships at 30,000 yards. The radarman was proud of the fine tuning he had done to his SJ radar two hours after surfacing. The attack team in the control room soon determined the enemy's course and speed and began to assess its zigzag pattern. If they could continue at flank speed till dawn and get in position several miles ahead of the track, it would make the *Thornfish's* approach better. The destroyer guarding the crippled cruiser was making fan-shaped course changes every fifteen minutes immediately ahead of the cruiser while listening for subs. The damaged enemy cruiser could only make a speed of advance of ten knots. As noted in the captain's night order book, the OOD sent a messenger to notify the captain. He mumbled an acknowledgment of the messenger's contact information of the range, course, and speed of the enemy, but remained in his bunk.

On the bridge, Jerry standing his watch as OOD, asked the executive officer to come up for a consultation. He was concerned that they were burning too much fuel. They had to conserve enough for the return to Midway for a refueling stop before going on to Pearl Harbor. His calculations indicated that they would have to reduce speed on the homeward leg and use two engines. The XO thanked Jerry and told him that they would relook at it after the torpedo action in the morning.

After he returned to the control room, Rob asked permission from the XO to catch a few z's himself. LT Morrison replied, "Sure, go ahead, I'm going to secure the tracking team except for Ryan." The control room had become strangely quiet now that the main induction was repaired and the air for the engines was being fed through the boat in a normal fashion. It was a good thing because the seas were getting stronger and *Thornfish* was getting a rough ride in the increasing sea state. Rob made his way past the wardroom to his junior officer's stateroom and removed his shoes before climbing in his bed. He was asleep as soon as he stretched out in his bunk.

"It's 0315 sir!" The quartermaster of the watch had to shake Rob's shoulder to wake him gently. "Time to go on watch, sir. The weather topside is rain, and 50 degrees now. The officer of the deck told me to tell you that the wind has shifted astern, and we have a pooping sea. You should have your lifebelt on. Bridge watch is tied in now." Rob shared his stateroom with John Young, the newest ensign on board. Both were on the same watch schedule, Rob as OOD and John as junior officer of the deck. Rob awakened John as they both were scheduled to be on watch from 0400 to 0800. Rob washed his face with cold water in the stainless-steel lavatory, dried off and pulled his black crewneck wool sweater over his khaki shirt, followed by his foul weather jacket. John was stirring preparing himself to go on watch.

As Rob exited his room, he blew a kiss to the picture of Molly he had taped to the bulkhead to keep it from getting broken. On the way to the bridge he noticed the curtain to the captain's room was drawn and the room still darkened. He thought the old man would need sleep as the morning would bring a lot of action when they contacted the enemy cruiser. He stopped by the wardroom for a cup of very strong black coffee. In the conning tower, Rob checked the charts and the course, speed and distance to the target on the radar before climbing the ladder to the bridge. The PPI scope was a great advance for submarine radar. It presented a circular picture from the ship's center out to the extent of the radar's range. He could see the pips of the enemy ships displayed on the scope.

Jerry, the officer of the deck, and his entire bridge team were strapped with strong ropes tightly around their waists. The following sea posed a grave danger to submariners. Submariners called it a pooping sea. A huge wave could roll up the after part of the deck without them seeing it and fill the voids under the bridge instantly flooding it like a huge bathtub floating the men on the bridge overboard. It was raining very hard, and the visibility was very poor. They would depend on the radar to get them into position ahead of the enemy ships. Rob received the status of the engines, battery charge and the number of personnel topside from Jerry and after a few questions, he saluted and said the time-honored words, "I relieve you, sir." John inspected the compartments before appearing on the darkened bridge.

Later, the hatch to the conning tower opened and the exec climbed up holding on as the ship took a deep dip in the mounting seas. After asking permission to come up, Dick said, "Well I'm not going to get any stars this morning Rob, that's for sure. I was hoping that we'd get a break in the weather... I need a fix to get our position right. I've been dead reckoning too long. Our target is now on our port bow about 16000 yards, so with our speed, we should be ahead of their track just before dawn. But we just noticed that the cruiser has slowed to eight knots. That's going to help our approach. They must be having difficulty with the weather or taking on too much water from the torpedo they took from *Garfish*."

"Aye Sir. What's your plan of attack sir?"

"Well if they maintain the same speed, we should be able to make a night surface attack before dawn and then dive. Maybe we can get both the cruiser and the escort. Wouldn't that be something?"

Rob replied, "It sure would be sir. The crew is getting anxious to get their combat patrol pins."

I'm going below to wake the captain; make sure you get us a thousand yards ahead of the destroyer."

"Aye, Aye Sir."

John Young, junior officer of the deck, was doing well in his first assignment out of submarine school. Rob sent him below to check on the progress of tracking with surface search radar. He reported that the enemy cruiser had changed course to the northwest on an apparent zigzag leg. Rob hoped that the next leg would bring him close to the attack position. It should be a sure shot he thought.

Fifteen minutes later the JOOD reported that the two ships had changed course and were heading their way. Rob wondered, where's the captain? They should be going to battle stations torpedo. Below decks, the executive officer had awakened the captain and while he was dressing briefed him on the situation. The ship was rigged for red meaning all white lights were extinguished in the below deck spaces to allow for quicker adjustment to night time vision when surfaced. In the control room, Captain Custer leaned over the DRT and looked at the plot. "Dick, we'll need time to get in position and submerge for the attack… can we still make it?"

Dick was taken back because he believed a night surface attack would be the best strategy. It would enable them to get in quickly, fire and retire before the destroyer could even know where they were.

"Captain, may I recommend we make a surface attack while it's still dark? With this weather, we can sneak in between the two ships without being seen, fire on the cruiser and if we're lucky to shoot some fish at the escort and then submerge. I can stay on the bridge and using the TBT (Target Bearing Transmitter) get in position within 800 yards. We can fire a spread of four torpedoes and dive immediately."

In the red glow of the night vision lighting, the captain's face tensed as he considered the exec's idea. He thought, *what if these guys have radar? The destroyer might even ram them while surfaced. What if they pick Thornfish up in a searchlight? Their five-inch guns would blow us right out of the water. It's too risky. Standard operating procedures call for me to use a submerged attack. But the crew will think I'm a coward. They already think the XO is the real captain. No, if I let him try it'll be curtains for us unless we are lucky.*

Dick noticed the captain's hands tighten on the side of the plotting table. Sweat dripped from his brow. Dick realized the captain was almost paralyzed in the face of danger. He could make some bad decisions in a night surface attack. He whispered, "Sir, what if I man the bridge myself along with Ensign Walker? He has great night vision and could observe the enemy vessels while I concentrate on the TBT. You can remain in the conning tower supervising the attack team." No response. Against his better judgment, the XO gave the captain another option. "Sir, we could stay surfaced ahead of the two ships, submerge at dawn and make the attack. But if the enemy ships zigzag away from us, our chances are reduced, and we would have to surface and do another end around, taking time and making it riskier in the daylight from air attacks." Captain Custer turned and gave a direct order, "We'll do plan B, a submerged attack at dawn." He abruptly left the control room and returned to his stateroom.

One hour before dawn the general quarters bells rang throughout *Thornfish*, calling all hands to battle stations torpedo. In the control room, the exec took the microphone and announced the battle plan. "We're going to finish off the cruiser and maybe get the DD if we're lucky. Stay calm, do your job just as you've been trained to do. Even though it's early, we'll break out the rum when we're done."

Cheers erupted throughout the boat.

The *Thornfish* was now about four thousand yards ahead of the enemy destroyer. Shortly after arriving on the bridge the XO received reports that all battle stations were manned and ready. "Very well," he acknowledged in traditional Navy style. He turned to John and told him to go below and inform the captain that the boat was manned for torpedo action and that he had ordered a change of course.

John jumped down the ladders and, in a few seconds, was in the control room. He expected to find the captain hunched over the DRT plot, but he was not there. He found him sitting at his desk in his stateroom; a small white light illuminated the entire room. "Sir, the XO reports the boat manned and ready for torpedo action. "Very Well," he replied and told the young JOOD he would be on the bridge shortly. Then John added, "Sir the enemy has changed course, and we changed course to stay ahead of him now." Custer shouted "Ensign, I know that! I saw it on my compass repeater here on this bulkhead!"

Five minutes later, the captain climbed through the conning tower hatch to the bridge. The darkness enveloped him, as his night vision had been impaired by the white light in his stateroom. The exec shouted over the furious wind telling the captain the current situation and the need to have the maximum speed possible to maintain contact with the enemy. "It's no use" the CO shouted, "Dawn will be breaking in a few minutes, and we'll be exposed. Prepare to dive!"

Dick was stunned. "But sir, we are letting a major warship escape."

"I am the captain, and you are to carry out my orders! Dive the boat!"

"Aye, Aye Sir."

As *Thornfish* slid beneath the turbulent waves, the exec was biting his lip for fear of verbalizing his frustration with the Commanding Officer in front of the men in the conning tower. He could only give him the benefit of knowing his pre-war conservative training for submarine tactics in combat. And his age. Thirty-six is too old to command in wartime. Younger men do best. The German U-Boat captains averaged under twenty-eight.

The sub resumed the course along the original track of the enemy ships. Good fortune was about to smile on the crew. Harrington, the third-class sonar man, was one of the best in their squadron. He picked up the sound of the Jap screws coming closer. Dick took the periscope and in the early morning twilight, saw the destroyer and the cruiser had changed course and were heading back toward *Thornfish*. "Will miracles never cease," Dick shouted! "Boys make ready for action. Get me some target data on my next bearing mark. This guy is going to be coming close." The destroyer's sonar was pinging searching for any lurking submarine. Captain Custer returned to the conning tower. He had an uneasy and overly fearful respect for the Japanese sonar equipment. The exec did not share his CO's concern. Earlier, with the *Thornfish* on the surface five thousand yards ahead of the tin can, they had not been picked up by either their sonar or radar.

Dick said, "Captain my recommendation is to go beneath the DD and come to periscope depth 800 yards from the cruiser now limping along at six knots. We'll get off four Mark-14's from the bow tubes and then maybe fire four from the stern tube at the escort." Reluctantly Custer agreed.

The exec ordered Jerry, the battle station diving officer, "make your depth 60 feet."

"Up scope!" He could see the two enemy vessels outlined against the horizon in dawn's early light.

"Angle on the bow of the DD is starboard fifty, and the cruiser is starboard 10." He was able to get a range of 3000 yards to the cruiser. The Jap destroyer was ahead of the cruiser by about 2000 yards making a sweep in an arc ahead of the enemy ship it was protecting. Rob on the TDC was cranking in the readings as the exec called them out.

Turning to the general announcing system, the exec told the crew their plan. He could feel the excitement building in the boat. The captain broke his silence by ordering the diving officer in the control room below him to level the boat at 100 feet. The sound of the destroyer's screws reverberated through the ship as they passed under it. An occasional ping from the enemy's sonar indicated that they had not been picked up yet. "Set your torpedo depth at 15 feet and high speed." The Mark-14 steam torpedoes would leave the sub at a maximum speed of 45 knots but leave a trail of bubbles on their way. Then Jerry was ordered to bring the *Thornfish* back to periscope depth. At 65 feet the captain said, "Up scope." As soon as the periscope broke through the surface, Custer made a 360-degree sweep of the surface. Dick shouted, "Captain we need a bearing and range to the target Sir!" Instead of moving the scope to the bearing of the cruiser he locked on the destroyer that had changed course and was heading for *Thornfish*. "Sir the cruiser is going to go by us! For God's sake give me a bearing and range to the target!" Dick then ordered the word: "down scope!" They had exposed the periscope too long. Captain Custer seemed paralyzed. Dick, visibly shaken, turned to Rob and said, "give me the range and bearing now." Looking at his target computer, Rob replied, "Target course 350, speed 6 knots, bearing the range should be 1000 yards and closing." The XO ordered the helmsman, "Come right to new course 270, all ahead slow… standby to fire. Up Scope."

As the periscope broke water, he gave the range at 900 yards. The crosshairs of the periscope were put right in the center of the damaged cruiser. The exec said, "Fire one!" Rob pushed the firing button on the control panel in the conning tower. Marvin Grabowski, the first-class torpedo man in the forward torpedo room, checked the firing lever as number one left the boat followed by the command, "Fire two, fire three, fire four! Down Scope. Take her deep Jerry, NOW!" The exec's commands echoed down the control room hatch, and the planes men put full dive on the bow planes and stern planes. Harrington shouted, "Torpedoes hot straight and normal sir!"

Dick ordered, "Rig for depth charge." As *Thornfish* descended in the deep, the negative tank was flooded completely, and the crew was ordered to rush forward in the boat to the forward torpedo room to give extra weight to get *Thornfish* down. As they passed 100 feet the destroyer charged right over them. To everyone's surprise, no depth charges were dropped.

WHAM…WHAM! Two torpedoes found their mark, but two sped astern of the cruiser. Dick ordered the depth at 300 feet. And instead of turning, which would slow them down, he elected to go directly under the sinking cruiser.

For the next two hours, the destroyer worked havoc on *Thornfish*, dropping thirty-one depth charges. Fortunately for *Thornfish*, they were set too shallow, and with the help of a friendly thermocline that deflected sound waves above them, they were able to creep away to safety. It was tempting to return to the area of the sinking, but with a destroyer captain that knew what he was doing, Dick decided to leave the scene. He was sure the DD was trying to save survivors. *Thornfish* remained submerged for the rest of the day the crew was exhausted and needed rest. But before lunch, the XO gave the order to break out the "Kickapoo Joy Juice" for all hands. So, before lunch, the pharmacist mate and the supply officer, John Young, went to the storage locker beneath the deck plates in the crew's mess and retrieved small bottles of bourbon whiskey and distributed to all hands not on watch. It was a celebration as the crew would now qualify for the combat action pin having given the coup de grace to the crippled cruiser. Captain Custer frowned at the idea of alcohol on the ship. Josephus Daniels, Secretary of the Navy, prohibited the use of alcoholic beverages in Navy vessels in 1921.

The crew rested even though the air in the boat was stale and full of foul orders. Finally, just before sunset, *Thornfish* rose to periscope depth and the captain made a careful search all around the horizon before surfacing. The exec and his quartermaster stood in the control room at the plotting table working on the stars they would use to develop their position. It had been several days since they had been able to get a good fix. Machinist mates armed with battle lanterns were ready to make a quick survey of any damage to the sub from the depth charge attack. During the depth charging, something outside the hull later began banging, and it had to be repaired.

The klaxon sounded when the captain ordered "Surface."

As *Thornfish* broke the surface, the main induction valve opened, and the big nine-cylinder diesel engines roared to life. Two on propulsion, one on the charging of the batteries, and the fourth shut down while the engineers worked on the noisy cylinder making temporary repairs with shims on the connecting rods. The quartermaster opened the hatch from the conning tower to the bridge, and the captain followed by the exec sprinted up the ladder. The noisy low-pressure blower came on to drive more water out of the main ballast tanks, to increase buoyancy. Four lookouts mounted their positions high above the bridge in the periscope shears. Lieutenant junior grade Robinson was the officer of the deck.

Dick sensed that his boss was more relaxed than he had seen him during the entire war patrol. In fact, Captain Custer stooped below the windscreen and pulled out a cigar from his foul weather jacket and after several attempts finally got it lit. "These things stink enough out here Dick, so I never have one inside our boat. But I enjoy one now and then, would you like one?" Dick politely declined the offer, and the captain said, "Dick, I appreciate your assistance during the attack. I'll tell you confidentially, I don't think I'm cut out for this anymore." Dick was stunned. He thought, *"The captain had hardly done anything in the attack. He froze, and now he tells me that I assisted him."* Custer took a few more puffs on his cigar and continued, "I just received several messages from Pearl; we are to proceed to Midway for repairs and rest, but on the way, we are to go to Guam and do some reconnaissance of Apra Harbor. Then I received a second report of a convoy that is scheduled to leave the port of Apra heading towards Saipan. We may be in the area in time to intercept it."

Dick replied, "Yes Sir, the only thing is we'll have to be careful on our fuel consumption; it could get a little dicey with all the diesel fuel we used in the running around lately. It's going to be tricky too, lots of air cover from the Japs at Guam." The former U.S. Possession in the Marianas had fallen to the Japanese invasion force only six months ago. "Anyway, I'd like for you to start drafting our patrol report, I'll need it at least two days before entering port at Midway."

"Aye, Aye Sir," Dick replied. The CO turned and started toward the hatch and put his cigar out. Then he said "Dick I'm concerned about these reserve officers. They lack some of the stuff we got at the academy. Please keep a sharp eye on them." Before Dick could reply the captain disappeared down the hatch. Dick was certain that he especially meant Ensign Walker, who came to the boat directly out of OCS without the benefit of going to going to sub school. The captain often wondered how he got orders to *Thornfish*. Besides, reserve officers were getting good billets that he believed should go to Naval Academy graduates. Born and raised in Virginia, the captain was a WASP, White, Anglo Saxon, Protestant; he disliked Negroes and Jews and did not want them in responsible jobs in the Navy. One night he had the colored steward's mate relieved from lookout duty over the XO's strenuous objection. The exec argued that the black man had the best night vision on *Thornfish*, but his objection went unheeded. His engineer was a Jew. But because he was his best and only engineer, he put aside his prejudice.

En route to Guam the *Thornfish* crew began temporary repairs to the many leaks due to the depth charge attacks. Down below Rob began interrogating the captured Japanese radioman. The crew began to have some affection for him. They had him work cleaning the decks, the head, shower and in the galley helping with scrubbing pots and pans, mess tables and decks. He was a willing worker. Rob learned he was only 18 years old, and a native of Yokohama. He volunteered for the air service to escape being conscripted into the Army. He loved flying but disliked the poor maintenance of the Jap Navy. He told Rob for them not to worry about the enemy planes bombing their sub as they couldn't hit the side of a barn.

Slowly Tojo learned some words of English. Some wag in the galley taught him a few words to use and had him take some fresh breakfast rolls to the captain in the wardroom at breakfast several days later. Dressed in clean whites, with a broad apron, he proudly walked along the passageway to the wardroom and put the hot rolls on the table before the captain. He bowed, smiled politely, and said in his newly learned language, "Good morning captain, you son of a bitch. Here are your shitty rolls!" Captain Custer's face suddenly turned red and glared at the smiling steward. Everyone at the table looked at the CO expecting some real fireworks. In what seemed an eternity, the captain started laughing soon joined by all the wardroom officers. Tojo's shitty rolls became a legend on *Thornfish*!

CHAPTER 9

The Stress of Command

That afternoon, Rob sat down with Tojo in the crew's mess along with the note-books and charts he had recovered from his floatplane. He corrected the young sailor's language used at breakfast and then learned from the Japanese radioman where he was based, the range of his aircraft, the call signs he used, and most importantly, he learned of the enemy's radars on the China Coast, their frequencies and range of effective return. The intelligence would be very valuable to COMSUBPAC in assigning patrols in the future. Of utmost importance was the chart showing mines recently placed in defense of local ports.

Rob gathered up his notes, the charts, and Japanese radio code books and headed to the wardroom. The exec stopped him while he was passing through the control room, and said, "Rob, the captain wants to see you in the wardroom. I'll join you in a few minutes." Rob replied, "Yes Sir." *Now what?* He thought.

Captain Custer was seated at the head of the table drinking coffee. "You wanted to see me, sir?"

"Sit down Walker! I want to know if you put that Jap prisoner up to the prank you pulled this morning."

Rob gulped and quickly replied, "No sir."

"But you know his language. How did you learn Japanese anyhow?" Rob told the captain about his two years spent in Tokyo with his parents and attending the American School.

"Well with your knowledge of some Japanese, you could be an asset to the Navy in intelligence. Why didn't you apply for Intel? "

"Well Sir, I wanted combat and figured the submarine service would be on the front lines. I like it here and want to stay on the *Thornfish*."

"We'll see." Rob felt the accusatory threat of his commanding officer once again. The captain turned to the charts and books taken from the Jap floatplane. The exec came in and poured himself a mug of coffee and sat down with them. Rob explained what he had learned from the Japanese prisoner and that he was very willing to share information. He added that the crew liked him and that some of the stewards in the crew's mess had instigated the prank. Custer disliked practical jokes and especially ones from a prisoner of war. He made it clear that there would be no more such shenanigans on the *Thornfish.*

Rob was about to ask if he could be excused when the captain turned to Dick and asked him about the qualification check-offs of the new junior officers.

"Rob is about done with his, captain. Ensign Young is about the same. We should have them ready for their underway exams before the next patrol."

"Very well, keep their noses to the grindstone. I want only qualified officers on this boat! I'll never know how in the hell they sent me an officer right out of OCS. A ninety-day wonder! It took me four years to graduate from the Academy and get commissioned and then a year on *Idaho,* and then six months at sub school before I set foot aboard a sub."

All unqualified officers had a rigorous list of some 156 tasks that had to be accomplished by them and signed off on their qualification book. Then they would be given their underway test firing torpedoes at a target and answering questions from a board of three submarine commanders. Rob was setting a record for qualification checkoffs, and if everything went well in Pearl Harbor, he could get qualified in less than a year on board.

After Rob left the wardroom, Custer told his exec that he had decided to write the patrol report himself. Dick was surprised as the executive officer normally prepared the report from the ship's logs and plots of contacts with the enemy ships, a very time-consuming job. Dick realized that the captain wanted to frame the report in his favor and eliminate any references to his lack of engagement and his inability to function in the stress of combat. It could be a serious misrepresentation of the facts and any mistakes probably would be blamed on the executive officer.

Rob skipped the evening meal and turned in early as he had the mid-watch from midnight to 4 am. Fully clothed, as he lay on his bunk, he glanced at Molly's picture posted to the bulkhead and wondered if she was still waiting for him. Dog-tired, he had no problem in getting to sleep.

· · · · ·

The executive officer on fleet submarines, in addition to having responsibility for the military efficiency and administration of the boat, has the duties of the navigator. Since *Thornfish* only had seven officers, it sometimes became necessary for the XO to stand watches. This morning Dick took the four to eight o'clock watch to let Jerry Abrams, the engineering officer, who was scheduled to take the watch, get some needed rest. While on watch Dick could take his star sights and work them out later. His quartermaster was getting very proficient in celestial navigation and could do most of the work himself. *Thornfish* was on the course the exec had laid out to intercept the enemy convoy.

They were using three engines on propulsion moving the boat along at 15 knots; the fourth engine was now charging the batteries. Some of the damage from the depth charges had been repaired. At 0345 he relieved Rob, the OOD, and sent him below to get some shut-eye. Alone on the bridge except for the four lookouts above him in the sail, his thoughts turned to the patrol report. There would be some good news and some bad. The good was the capture of the downed Jap plane's charts and other information that would be of value to the intel boys, and the sinking of the crippled cruiser. But the bad news was the failures to take on the enemy when the clear opportunity presented itself. Captain Custer was aware that boats were usually lost on their first patrol or their fifth. The first, due to inexperience, and the fifth contempt for the Japanese capabilities. This was Custer's second war patrol, but he was still far too cautious and too old to command a new fleet boat. But most of all, Dick was concerned about the captain's fear in the face of the enemy. He had too high a regard for the enemy's sonar capabilities. And more importantly, he froze in the face of danger. Only the actions by the XO himself allowed the *Thornfish* to escape from the destroyers. He was the de facto captain of *Thornfish* on this patrol. And Captain Custer knew it, and his patrol report would most likely be a whitewash of anything detrimental to his career.

As he stood on the bridge with the stars forming a beautiful canopy of light overhead, Dick thought *how could this universe happen? Surely there is a creator that put everything in its place.* Without the glare of city lights, the stars at night at sea are bright enough one could almost feel like touching them. Dick had grown to love the sea. The beauty of the ocean and even its challenges in heavy weather fascinated him. As he looked at the water moving in the wake of the *Thornfish's* bow, he could see the plankton glowing in the displaced water; the tiny plankton provides food for the largest whales. WOW, he said to himself, wonder of wonders! How peaceful everything seemed now, but he knew that danger could lurk beyond the next wave.

The XO didn't see salt water until he arrived at Annapolis in the summer of his plebe year. Dick was raised in Hastings, Nebraska. The entire region is flat as a pancake. Acres and acres of wheat and corn are produced every year in this the heart of the nation's bread basket. Hastings is so flat that the city had to have the annual soap box derby on the railroad overpass, the highest place in town. When he arrived at Annapolis in the summer of 1933, he joined the Naval Academy Sailing Squadron and later made an ocean race to Bermuda in his senior year. Sailing is an essential part of training at the Academy. Midshipmen learn the effects of wind, tide, and current on the sailboats that have no engines. He became an excellent ship handler because of his midshipman training. He received high marks during sub school for handling the sub alongside piers in the narrow ship channel at the sub base New London, Connecticut.

After this patrol, he hoped that the captain would recommend him for command.

He had proved himself under dire circumstances in combat. He was organized, aggressive, and capable of command. But he worried that Custer would not sign off on him. A low mark on his fitness report, even though it would be satisfactory, could permanently harm his career.

Another worry crossed his mind. The message that *Thornfish* received indicated that this was an important convoy. All eyes in headquarters would be on the performance of *Thornfish*, the only sub in the area positioned to be able to intercept the enemy ships. Perhaps a capital ship, cruiser or battleship might be involved. *Thornfish* must get inside the convoy and wreak havoc. But knowing Custer, he was afraid that the Captain would find another excuse to evade attacking the enemy ships. *What if the captain froze again? Should I relieve him?* He decided that he would recheck Navy Regulations for relieving a commanding officer. But that would have to wait. Dawn was breaking in the east as the quartermaster requested permission to come up on the bridge bringing with him his sextant and the stopwatch. Time for star sights. With the assistance of his quartermaster, he got a great fix, five stars with azimuths about every 75 degrees. He needed a good fix since the ship had gone too long on dead reckoning. The captain would be very pleased. Custer always wanted the ship's 0800 position report handed to him promptly at 0800. He was relieved at 0745 by the oncoming OOD and went below and stopped by the wardroom expecting to find the captain at breakfast but he was not there. He went to his small stateroom and gently knocked, with no answer. He drew the curtain back and saw the captain asleep with a 45-caliber pistol by his hand. Dick shouted, "Captain!" Custer awoke from a deep sleep. He growled, "What do you want?" Dick said. "Captain you scared the shit out of me! Why the pistol?" His eyes were bloodshot. There were four or five empty small mini bottles of Jack Daniels on the deck by his bed. Rubbing his eyes, he replied, "Dick I'm losing my mind. I know I'm going to screw up!"

Dick interjected, "Well shooting yourself is not the answer sir. I'm going to have the pharmacist come up and give you some medicine. You've been under a lot of strain, sir. Command is not easy in peacetime and harder in war," and he reached down and took the 45. Hearing the commotion, Ensign Walker came out of his room just in time to see the exec standing by the captain with the 45 in his right hand. Dick turned and saw him standing in the passageway. He yelled, "Ensign, not a word of this to anyone, do you understand me?" "Aye, Sir," Rob replied, still confused about the gun in the exec's hand and what might have just happened in the captain's stateroom.

"Get the pharmacist here on the double with some sedative!" While Rob was gone, Dick took the gun and locked it in his safe, then put the empty bottles in his room on his desk. He returned to the captain and tried to provide him the information that a commanding officer would need to know before approaching the enemy's track. But it was no use; he was too groggy. The pharmacist came quickly and checked the captain's blood pressure, temperature, and his pulse. He smelled the alcohol on the captain's breath and told the exec, "He has high blood pressure, and his heart rate is too fast, I think he needs rest more than anything right now." With the XO's permission, he prepared a shot of sedative. "I think he'll be alright sir, but if you agree, I'll give him a little sedative to relax him and check on him every hour."

"How long will he be out?"

"I'd say about eight hours at the most sir." Dick thought about it. He would still be able to function before we encountered the convoy.

"Very well. Keep me informed of his condition."

"Aye, sir." The captain slept well, but the exec had not slept for 24 hours. He was running on adrenalin and mug after mug of black coffee. While his captain slept, Dick and the chief of the boat went throughout every compartment encouraging the men to do their best and to know the importance of the enemy convoy. Then he went to his stateroom and broke out Navy Regulations. No one had ever relieved a commanding officer in the United States Submarine Service during combat. It could end his naval career, but he vowed he wouldn't do it unless it were imperative for the safety of the vessel or if the captain froze again in fear and was unable to function.

Thornfish's captain didn't come out of his room as the *Thornfish* sped along the surface to rendezvous with the enemy convoy. Dick told the quartermaster to enter in the log that the captain needed sedation due to stress and to log in the time of his return to the conning tower should he appear.

Rob had the afternoon watch on the bridge. The weather was turning ugly. Before going on watch, he read the Fox report, radio messages sent to all Navy vessels in the western Pacific, that said to expect a low-pressure area that could become a typhoon. About midway through the watch, the exec came up on the bridge. He shouted over the thunder of the engines and the howling wind, "I just went over our attack plan with our team in the control room, and we'll make radar contact with the Japs about 1600. If we've planned right, we will be able to submerge and make our attack from a point well ahead of the convoy at sunset."

Rob said, "Roger sir. How is the captain doing?" Dick stared at the waves now crashing over the sub's bow, and finally said, "The captain is not well. I'm afraid that the strain of combat is getting to him, and we can't have that in a leader, especially the captain of a submarine in wartime." Rob was a little taken back by the exec's forthrightness. But Dick continued "I am apprehensive about the combat we're going to be in soon. If worse comes to worse, I may have to assume command temporarily at least. I took the captain's 45 and locked it in my safe. And the empty Jack Daniels bottles are in my room."

"Yes sir, I understand sir. I agree. I think he needs medical attention."

"Well, I had known Captain Custer mainly by reputation before he took command of the *Thornfish*. He is a perfectionist. A real stickler for following the rules and regulations, and probably an obsessive-compulsive personality. Just a reminder ensign, you must not say anything about what happened earlier today to anyone."

After the warning, Dick made his way to the hatch, now closed in case a rogue wave came crashing over the bridge. He told Rob to get some sleep as soon as he got off watch because he wouldn't get any for a while. As the *Thornfish* plowed thorough increasingly rough seas, the crew, not on watch, caught up on their sleep. But before he crashed in his bunk, Rob made notes in his officer's workbook about the incident he had observed earlier in the day. As he slept, he had a bad dream. Molly had found someone else.

· · · · ·

At 1600 the radar picked up the first pips of the target on the PPI scope. Gradually the entire enemy force, some 20,000 yards away, came into view on the radar scope. There were four ships, including two escorts, zigzagging in unison thirty degrees off their base course of 030 degrees true. Dick posted his tracking team and began developing the courses needed to get *Thornfish* positioned for the best shot at the big one. Sunset was two and a half hours away, and Dick needed to go over his plan with the captain, if he was able, before calling the ship to battle stations.

Dick's plan was simple: lay in wait ahead of the enemy's track. If he zigzagged right, he would increase speed and follow when he turned back to the base course, he would fire four torpedoes from the bow tubes. Then turn and fire at the other ships in the van with his stern tubes. If he zigged left of his track, then they would wait till the range was about 800 to 1000 yards and then fire as before and dive deep for evasion from the escorts. He wanted the captain to act as approach officer while he manned the periscope feeding range and bearings to the TDC. He sent for the pharmacist mate to come to the control room. "Jenkins, what is the condition of the captain now?" Jenkins had just come from the captain's stateroom. "He's awake now sir, he's groggy but is getting dressed and wants a cup of coffee. His blood pressure is still way too high, his heart rate is high, but his temperature is normal."

Dick went over the attack plans with the team once more and then went into officer's country and found the captain in the wardroom. Unbeknownst to Dick, the captain had just stopped in his exec's stateroom. While looking for his gun, Custer saw Navy Regulations open on the exec's desk, to the *Paragraph 1088, Relieving Command at Sea*. He read it and then opened Dick's desk and found the empty mini bottles and put them in the garbage bag in the officers' galley. He knew what Dick was up to. And he couldn't find his gun.

Dick found the captain pouring himself another cup of black coffee; his hands were shaking so much that the coffee spilled onto the green tablecloth. Dick grabbed his mug and successfully got a cup full and sat down. "Sir, are you feeling better? You scared me this morning." But he was appalled at his appearance. He was haggard, unshaven, bad breath, eyes red and hands that wouldn't hold still.

Custer said, "Well that's over with. I'm OK. Forget it. Now, what's the situation topside?"

"Rough weather sir it looks like we're heading into a tropical low that could be bad. I've gone over the entire battle plan with the tracking team several times." And Dick began to sketch it out on a napkin before them. Dick reminded him that he would man the attack periscope and the captain would act as the approach officer. Custer replied, his raspy voice trailing off, "Ok with me."

"With your permission sir, I'm going to the bridge and prepare to dive as soon as we have to."

"Very Well, keep me posted." As Dick got up to leave the captain added, "And Dick don't do anything you'll regret later." He continued to slurp his coffee.

Dick left without acknowledging the captain's warning but mulled it over as he climbed onto the submarine's small bridge. *Did he know?* An hour later with the enemy force about three miles ahead in the rain-shrouded storm, he ordered the OOD to get his lookouts down and sound the diving alarm when he was ready. Two blasts on the alarm sent *Thornfish* plunging back into the depths of the Marianna waters, the deepest in the Pacific Ocean. Leveling off at 65 feet, Jerry had a hard time controlling depth with the rough waters about his boat. Broaching could happen even with his best men on the bow and stern planes. Responding to the diving alarm, Captain Custer passed through the control room and climbed the ladder to the conning tower. His scarecrow appearance shocked even the hardiest of the attack team members. He looked more like a ghost than a submarine captain.

Leveling off at 65 feet, periscope depth, he slowed to three knots and raised the periscope to look around. When the periscope broke the surface, the captain could only see the waves breaking over the lens of the scope. He then announced to the conning tower personnel, "I will man the attack scope and LT Morrison will make the approach."

The exec was dumbfounded.

The eyes of the officers and men in the conning tower were trained on Dick. It was decision time for the second in command. No one in the submarine service had ever exercised Article 1088 of Navy Regs relieving a commanding officer, in peace or war. But Captain Custer was not well. He had been drinking while in command. That would disqualify him should Dick have to relieve him. He froze during depth charging; he let targets get away due to his timidity. But he had not purposely endangered the boat or the crew so far at least. Dick quickly considered that now was not the time. Perhaps the captain was trying to gain some self-respect and act with valor for a change.

Dick said, "Aye, Aye Sir." Then he turned to the chief of the watch ordered him to sound the alarm, battle stations torpedo. The Bells of St. Mary's rang throughout the boat.

"Down scope," the captain barked to the quartermaster now trying to read the relative bearings on the ring around the periscope. "Harrington get me sound bearings now!" The sonar man reported, "contact bearing, zero six five, sir."

Dick spoke, "Captain we must increase speed, or he's going to pass us," Dick interjected. The captain replied, "Very well, all ahead full." In twenty minutes, the sound bearings gradually changed keeping the sub ahead of the enemy fleet.

Dick said, "Captain, we're going to need visual bearings to get these guys. We've got to raise the periscope five feet at least in these seas." That would mean the diving officer would have to level off at 55 feet. But the danger is, at just about any speed in rough seas, one miscue by the men on the bow and stern planes could make *Thornfish* broach in full view of the enemy. Dick argued with the captain saying that as they slowed down and raised the periscope five feet above the waves, it would be difficult for the enemy to spot them in these rough seas. Reluctantly, the captain agreed. In a few minutes, after several sound bearings, the plotting team got an estimated course 035 degrees and a speed of 15 knots of the enemy ships. If the *Thornfish's* luck held out, they would have a target angle of about 80 to 90 degrees, perfect for a torpedo attack. All they had to do was sit and wait unless the enemy changed course.

The captain then raised the attack periscope. Smaller than the normal search scope, the attack periscope was harder to detect.

Custer ordered, "Open the outer doors on tubes one, two, three, and four. Up scope!"

"We've got a troopship and a tanker." The troopship was a converted passenger-cargo ship with an angle on the bow port 45 degrees. Range estimate 1100 yards.

Dick had Rob set gyro angles on the Target Data Computer for the torpedos to split the bow, midship and stern part of the target. They couldn't miss. Suddenly the sonar man reported pinging and screws of the escorts coming toward them. Captain Custer had the attack scope raised, turned and began searching for the new threat. Dick yelled, "Captain for God's sake give us the final bearing and shoot on the troopship." There was no response. The CO seemed almost paralyzed. Seeing the deteriorating situation enfolding, Dick seized the initiative, took the captain's trembling hands off the periscope, and said, "I'll get the final bearing for you captain."

Then Captain Custer shouted, "Flood negative, make your depth 300 feet!" It was too much for the executive officer.

Dick turned toward the hatch and told the diving officer below in the control room, "Belay that order! I am assuming command of *Thornfish* under Navy Regulations. The Captain is not well. Get Chief O'Neil to the conning tower immediately!" Then Dick grabbed the periscope. The attack periscope was raised some five feet above the swells, and Dick ordered, "Open the outer doors on tubes one, two, three, and four. Set torpedo depth 15 feet. Final bearing and shoot on target!"

Rob replied, "Tubes doors already opened sir!"

"Very well, Standby by... Mark! Bearing one five seven. Target angle on the bow port eight zero.

"Fire one! Fire two! Fire three! Fire four!"

The *Thornfish* shuddered as the torpedoes left the tubes. The high-pressure impulse air used to expel the torpedoes was vented back into the boat, causing the air pressure to increase noticeably inside the sub. The sonar man reported all torpedoes were running hot, straight, and normal, to the team in the conning tower. The quartermaster with his stopwatch in hand began to count off the seconds for the steam torpedoes, speeding towards the enemy ship at 45 knots.

Wham ... Wham! Two hit the target. One amidships and one at the stern. Custer was shaking so violently that Dick ordered the chief of the watch to get the pharmacist mate to come to the conning tower on the double! Suddenly, Custer's eyes widened and in a fit of rage he started to raise his arm to strike his exec while his back was turned to him. Rob standing by the TDC reached out and grabbed Custer's arm in midair and held him until he could be restrained by the pharmacist. Rob joined the Navy and wanted combat, but not in the confines of his ship.

CHAPTER 10

The Attack

While Custer was being attended to, Dick ordered the sub to swing 180 degrees to fire at the tanker with his stern tubes. Raising the attack scope, he ordered bearing, mark! Range 1100 yards open the outer doors on stern tubes, ready set, final bearing range, Rob said, "The TDC checks Ok…" Fire! Two Mark-14 torpedoes exited the stern tubes at 45 knots, set for 15 feet. They had a perfect set up for the tanker. Sonar again reported a hot, straight, and normal run for both torpedoes. Target angle 90, dead on for a shot at the side of the tanker, but when the fish hit the tanker, there was no explosion. They were duds. What the hell happened? It was too late. Dick had to take evasive action. The exec ordered a 20 degree down angle and the flooding of the negative tank to evade the destroyer now overhead about to drop depth charges. All the while the chief of the boat was having a hard time with their former commanding officer. Custer struggled to get free as the burly chief and the pharmacist mate slid along the sloping deck past the wardroom carrying Custer to his cabin. He kept screaming, "You're going to get us all killed. Don't listen to him! I am your captain. Don't do this!" Custer screamed again, "No, you're stupid. Get me down! Flood negative, 300 feet!" They held him down until a sedative was injected, he began to relax. But the chief of the boat posted a guard at his stateroom.

Dick ordered Jerry to make his depth 350 feet, rig for depth charge, and silent running. All pumps and air-conditioning, along with moving motors were silenced. The diving planes were put in manual. Just as *Thornfish* reached 300 feet, WHAM, WHAM, WHAM. The ashcans erupted overhead. They were too close. Cork insulation flew from the overhead in the control room, the lights dimmed and went out. Men in the control room fell. Emergency lamps came on, and leaks sprang up in nearly every compartment. *Thornfish* was in deep trouble.

Rob stood at the TDC watching the new commanding officer order evasive moves, trying to get under the thermal layer that might save them. He was in awe of his calm assertiveness. As the *Thornfish* ran silent and deep, Rob wondered what Captain Custer would have done in this situation. In the next 30 minutes, over 25 depth charges from the two escorts overhead were recorded in the control room; damage to the boat was horrendous. Dick ordered depth 400 feet well below test depth for their sub. No one spoke a word as the depth gage crept below 375 feet and then on down. Explosions were still too close for comfort. Dick ordered 450 feet. The boat began to creak and groan as the pressure against the steel hull increased.

Dick called for Rob and the chief of the boat to go through the boat to check for damage and encourage the crew. They first went forward to the torpedo room, and Rob found Tojo sitting on the deck rolled up in a ball trembling. Rob laid his hand on the lad's shoulder and said a few words to him in Japanese. The young radioman looked up and broke into a grin and said, "thank you" in English. Suddenly a column of water erupted from the fathometer housing on the port side of the torpedo room! The entire forward torpedo room started to fill with water. Rob ordered everyone to evacuate the compartment and close the watertight door. Rob and Chief O'Neil remained in the flooding compartment. As the last man left, including Tojo, the chief grabbed the leading petty officer and said, "Not you, Grabowski!" Grabowski, the senior man, had to find the stop valve that would shut off the flow of seawater. A huge man, he quickly found the valve but even with his strength could not shut it due to the intense sea pressure. Rob knew they had to surface to stop the flow, now nearly knee deep. Rob got on the 1 MC announcing system and told his new commanding officer that they could not stop the flooding, as the water pressure was too great. They had to get up and get up now.

In the control room, the depth gage read 500 feet. Jerry, the diving officer, yelled, "Sir, I can't control the depth we're sinking." *Thornfish* was in extremis. Dick knew what they had to do…he ordered Jerry to increase speed and blow the bow buoyancy tank. The danger was that they might broach right in the midst of the enemy ships, but he ordered Jerry to bring the ship to periscope depth. If all else failed, they would have to blow the safety tank and negative tank.

The bow buoyancy tank provides buoyancy in surfacing in heavy weather or an emergency. The negative tank holds 14,000 pounds of seawater and enables the sub to dive when filled. The safety tank is a special ballast tank with the strength of the pressure hull that can be blown to compensate for flooding in the boat. All three would have to be used to save the boat. Dick had the word passed over the 1 MC to prepare for battle surface. If *Thornfish* were to be sunk, they'd go down fighting with their five-inch deck gun. By carefully blowing the tanks, and increasing the speed of *Thornfish*, Jerry brought the boat to periscope depth. As *Thornfish* ascended, the pressure on the fathometer valve in the torpedo room decreased, and Grabowski finally shut off the flooding water. Pumping started immediately to dewater the compartment. Dick called the stern torpedo room to prepare to fire tubes seven and eight. The sound of destroyer screws grew louder and louder throughout the boat. The crew was ready for action.

"Boys we're going to get us a destroyer," Dick shouted. "Up Scope."

The embattled sub leveled out at periscope depth, and Dick manned the attack scope. The screws of the destroyer were growing closer as the scope broke the surface. Rob had returned to the conning tower and manned the TDC. He awaited the bearing and range and target course from Dick. "Standby, mark. Range 900 yards and closing… angle on the bow zero!" The DD was going to ram *Thornfish*!

Dick calmly turned to Rob and told him "Standby, make your torpedo depth 10 feet. Fire seven…fire eight! Impulse air rushed into the boat as the fish left the stern tubes. "Down scope. Right full rudder, all ahead flank! The new captain yelled at Jerry, the diving officer, "make your depth 100 feet. We're going right under the DD!" Sonar reported both fish were hot, straight, and normal. But the torpedoes had to run 400 yards before their warheads would be activated. The onrushing escort was probably just a little more than that when WHAM…. WHAM …. both torpedoes hit the destroyer. The sound of the destruction echoed throughout the sub. Cheers erupted. Dick ordered the *Thornfish* back to periscope depth.

When he raised the search periscope, it was almost dark. He ordered the radar mast raised and the PPI scope showed no sign of the enemy destroyer. Three blasts of the announcing alarm sent *Thornfish* up.

The former executive officer led the way to the bridge as soon as *Thornfish* surfaced. Lookouts climbed up into the shears and held on for dear life as the angry seas tossed the submarine back and forth. The radar operator raised the search scope and trained it on the bearing of the contact. "Bridge, Radar, there's only one pip now, the other DD I'm sure." Dick's immediate thought was to go after the remaining destroyer. Then there was a break in the deluge of rain, and he could see searchlights were being trained on the waters where the troop transport went down. The lingering DD was trying to rescue survivors. It would make a perfect target, but with his damaged sub he decided not to chance having to endure any more harm to the boat and the tanker was out of radar range. Dick would radio the estimated position of the tanker hoping that another submarine would intercept it before reaching Saipan.

The new captain announced over the 1 MC, "Well done sailors! You have cleaned their clock. I'm proud of all of you. We'll break out the brandy as soon as we clear the area. We are not going to take on the other DD now; we don't have enough juice left. So, we'll be heading to Midway, well-done men." More cheers could be heard even on the bridge with the howling wind screaming through the periscope shears. But then he added "Men, I regret to inform you that I had to relieve the captain. He is suffering from a medical condition I believe, and by regulations, I have formally relieved Captain Custer and put him on the sick list. I'm now in command of *Thornfish*. That's all."

Dick then ordered Rob to come up and take the deck as OOD. The quartermaster held out a foul weather jacket for Rob as he ascended the ladder to the bridge. It was raining buckets. The *Thornfish's* new captain spoke over the fury around them, "Rob, as soon as the engineer gives you the word that the main induction valve is ok, start two engines and put a third on a battery charge. We have very little juice left in our batteries, so we've got to conserve them. I want you to weave the boat from one rain squall to another. The radar can tell you where they are. I'll give you a course to clear the area, let's use one-third speed, for now. I'm going below to check on the damage."

"Aye sir." A few minutes later the new captain, still soaking wet, gave Rob a new course to clear the area and head towards Midway. As he passed through the compartment to the after-engine room, Dick began to mull over the action report, he had to send to Commander Submarines Pacific Fleet. What should he say about Captain Custer? The truth. But it would have to wait. Right now, he needed sleep.

CHAPTER 11

The Message

Thornfish's patrol lasted 60 days. The crew performed exceptionally well under fire. The crew knew what to do in emergencies. There was little time, however, for personal qualification for the Dolphins, the coveted submarine badge, identifying them as qualified submariners. Dick estimated about five days were needed to arrive at Midway Island for refueling and minor repairs. Major repairs would have to wait until they arrived at Pearl, or the West Coast if they were lucky. The crew enjoyed their ration of whiskey after the successful attack on the Jap convoy. Thornfish's crew morale improved greatly after Dick took command. Sailors know that a ship reflects the character and personality of the captain. Dick knew his men and was genuinely concerned about their welfare. Captain Custer was different. His goal was to advance himself.

After *Thornfish* exited the patrol area, Dick sent a message:

To: Commander Submarines Pacific Fleet.

Thornfish SS 499 attacked an enemy convoy of four ships consisting of a troop transport a tanker and two escorts apparently en route to Saipan 25 October 1942, Lat.15deg. 30min north long. 144deg. 35 min E X Sank troop transport also a DD. Fired two MK 14 torpedoes at the tanker and made hits with both but did not explode. X While undergoing repeated depth charge attacks the tanker proceeded independently on base course 030. Estimated speed 12 knots. X Thornfish heavily damaged and before surfacing fired two Mk14 and sank an oncoming destroyer. X While commencing torpedo action on the convoy it became necessary to relieve the captain LCDR J.J. Custer USN due to medical reasons by Navy Regulations Article 1088. X LT Richard Morrison USN executive office relieved the Captain at 0617 Zulu time over the protests of the Captain. X Proceeding to Midway for repairs anticipate ETA dawn 31 October. X Request immediate medical assistance upon arrival for LCDR Custer and assistance with a Japanese prisoner. V/R Richard Morrison LT USN Commanding.

Later in the evening, the new commanding officer called a meeting of all officers and chiefs not on watch for a meeting in the wardroom. The wardroom was full of excitement as the officers recounted the successful attack on the enemy convoy. Captain Morrison appeared after a few minutes and sat down at the head of the table, and the levity ceased. His somber countenance was seldom seen on *Thornfish*.

"Gentlemen what happened this morning is unprecedented in the submarine service." He slowly opened a copy of the message sent earlier to Pearl.

"I sent the following message to Commander Submarines Pacific Fleet." As he read the message his voiced cracked several times. When he came to the sentence relieving the commanding officer, his voice grew stronger. He picked up the copy of the Navy Regulations from the small bookcase on the serving shelf. He opened to page 95 and read:

Article 1088 Relief of a Commanding Officer by a Subordinate.

1. It is conceivable that most unusual and extraordinary circumstances may arise in which the relief from duty of a commanding officer by a subordinate becomes necessary, either by placing the commanding officer under arrest or on the sick list. Such action shall never be taken without the approval of the Commandant of the Marine Corps or the Chief of Naval Personnel, as appropriate or the senior officer present, except when a reference to such higher authority is undoubtedly impracticable because of the delay involved or for clearly obvious reasons.

Dick closed the book and said, "Gentlemen, I believe that Commander Custer has a serious medical condition most likely brought on by the stress of combat. I have placed him on the sick list and have so noted in the ship's log. I acted without reservation or prompting by anyone on board *Thornfish*. It was and is my responsibility alone. I undoubtedly will have to answer for my action to higher authority. If there is an inquiry, some of you may be asked to testify. If you are asked, just tell the truth. Until then I expect each one of you to do his best to maintain order and discipline on this vessel. We have serious damage to control. In a separate message, Jerry and I will list all repairs needed at Midway and beyond at Pearl."

At this point are there any questions?"

The chief of the boat said, "Yes sir. How is the captain, I mean Commander Custer doing now?"

"The pharmacist mate is looking after him. He is well sedated. He will be taking his meals in his stateroom for now. A messenger will be stationed outside his cabin until we reach Midway. I have asked for immediate medical assistance for him when we arrive."

Dick looked at each of the men and said, "Any others?" There were no more questions.

"OK, now I am going to go over your assignments. Mr. Abrams will assume duties as exec including navigator, assisted by Rob."

Although one of the newer officers on board, Rob was very respected by the crew. They recognized him as a natural leader, seeing in him one who was working hard to qualify. They were impressed too with his handling of the prisoner Tojo, and his action with the seaplane incident. His bravery in the forward torpedo room when the fathometer casualty occurred endeared him to all the crew. It took a lot of courage to order the torpedo men out of the compartment and shut the watertight door and staying in the flooding compartment to save the sub.

Ensign Rob Walker had a lot of responsibility for a junior officer. He was qualified as officer of the deck, the communications officer, and a member of the attack team under the direct supervision of his executive officer. Rob was continuing his progress on his checkoffs for qualification for his Dolphins, the emblem sought by every submariner signifying qualified in submarines. He must know every compartment, every system, every valve, the main propulsion system, how to load and fire torpedoes, how to start the diesel engines, apply charges to the forward and after batteries, the engine capabilities. Chief O'Neil, continued to mentor Rob, coaching him on the systems, air, hydraulics, and engineering.

En route to Midway Rob finally found some time to dash off a letter each day to Molly. All letters leaving the ship had to be read by officers to avoid having any information included in them that might be of value to the enemy. Rob didn't like the censorship job, but since he was a censor for the crew's letters, he knew his would be read so Rob didn't feel comfortable with a lot of mush in his letters.

The new captain of *Thornfish*, however, had lots of problems. Immediate repairs had to be made on the main induction valve. Number four engine was still giving them fits. Now in command, he had all the command responsibilities, plus most of the administration that the exec normally handled. And he had to write the patrol report. He knew it had to reflect the actions and inactions of the *Thornfish* accurately. Good news and bad news. The report would be read not only by those in higher authority but by many submarine commanders. Lots of lessons could be learned from reading other patrol reports. There was no reason to reinvent the wheel.

Dick felt somewhat sorry for the former captain. He was trained in prewar tactics; never stay on the surface during the daylight hours; make attacks submerged using sound bearings rather than visual bearings wherever possible. The result was that early in the war when submarine captains were selected mainly on their seniority, few had ever had any combat experience. Their executive officers were younger, and some had more combat experience than their captains. The German submarine service experienced the same problem. They found that age produced more cautious commanders and fewer sinkings. The German submarine commanders' ages were less than 28 years.

Admiral Lockwood, Commander U.S. Submarines, began relieving any captain that lacked aggressiveness.

· · · · ·

The storm abated soon after their latest combat was over. The bad weather had been a blessing. It allowed them to stay surfaced and evade the remaining escort. To get experience in navigation, Rob was now assigned to the four to eight watch to assist in the early morning star sights. He loved it because while surfaced, he could enjoy the beauty of the celestial skies while learning the basics of celestial navigation. Alone on the bridge, except for the lookouts above him in the shears, his thoughts raced from what he would do in an emergency to that of Molly and what their future might be after the war. Sometimes he wished that they would have eloped before he entered the Navy. But the risk of him not coming back was too great. He wondered what might have happened to his former Japanese student friend, his classmate at the American School in Tokyo some seven years ago. He knew he wanted to be in submarines following in his father's footsteps. Jimmysan, as Rob called him, was full of fun. He invited Rob to take a vacation with him when school let out in August. He planned to climb Mt. Fujiyama. There is a saying in Japan that "He who comes to Japan and does not climb Mt. Fujiyama is a fool. He who climbs it twice is a bigger fool." After much discussion with his parents, especially his mother, they gave him permission for a three-day trip to the famous mountain some 12,000 feet above sea level.

The train of five passenger cars and one freight car pulled by a black locomotive pulled out of the station exactly on time. The boys found an empty seat and spread out their backpacks on the empty bench opposite their seats. The passenger cars had seats facing one another, with windows open, and soot covering the curtains flying in the wind. Each car was painted green with windows trimmed in bright red. A conductor with a very official look, dressed in black uniform, came by soon after they left the station and punched their tickets. "Fujiyama, yes? The snow is gone. Have a good climb!"

They passed through the green foothills with rice paddies carved into the hill embankments. Women with pointed straw hats were bent over working their crops. Young children played on the banks of the waterfilled paddies while their older siblings joined the women working in the fields. *But where were the men?* Rob wondered.

They arrived at the base of the mountain at about five in the evening. The boys started climbing in the cool of the evening and planned to stay overnight in one of the nine stations along the steep zigzag trail that led up the mountain. Rob's mother had packed both boys some sandwiches, rice cookies, and many candy bars. They strode swiftly after leaving the train and stopped only to fill their canteens and eat a sandwich before starting their arduous climb. Rob took a picture of Jimmysan with his small 35 mm camera that he had purchased used in Oxford from John Minnis' drug store. Although it was secondhand, he took some great photos with it. After their hurried meal, the boys set out on the first leg of their climb. They climbed steadily until darkness overcame them. At the first station, they purchased a climbing pole that would be etched at each station along the climb. At station number four they rested for the night. The small shelter was nearly full of Japanese climbers. After purchasing some green tea and rice cookies, they laid down on the floor on bamboo mats with their backpacks as pillows. It became quite chilly during the night. The quilts that the hostess gave them were very fitting for the Japanese but only covered about half of Rob's tall body. After a restless night, Rob and Jimmysan woke at dawn and after a quick candy bar, they went out on the trail. The sun was rising in the east, and they viewed a spectacular sunrise over Tokyo Bay. The colors on the water were gold and orange tinted with hues of violet and purple. Rob took his camera from its leather case and began to take photos as the sun rose above the distant horizon.

Rob said, "What a beautiful sunrise and what a beautiful country."

Jimmysan replied, "Yes but I don't know how much longer it will be beautiful."

"What do you mean?" As they resumed their climb, Jimmy continued by saying,

"Well, my father says war is inevitable now with America and Great Britain." Rob was surprised. It was the first time his friend had ever mentioned the militarization that was taking over Japan's economy and politics. He went on, "The government has been taken over by the military. General Tojo is going to be Prime Minister soon, and when he does, he will be intent on war. Especially, father says, if the Western Nations ever place an embargo on our sources of oil, rubber, tin and iron ore, Japan would make a surprise attack. We are an island nation with little natural resources. We must use these vital products to survive."

Rob stopped suddenly. He had forgotten his camera! He had left it on a ledge by the station they had stayed in, and now he was faced with the dilemma, to go back and retrieve it or just leave it? After all, it only cost 10 dollars. But he reluctantly retraced his steps while pondering what he had just heard from the son of a prominent Japanese submarine commander.

CHAPTER 12

The Orders

Rob was shaken from his reverie by the lookouts above him. "Mine ahead!" They had spotted a floating mine dead ahead of *Thornfish* in the early dawn light. The mine started to pass close aboard on the port bow. He alertly ordered, "Left full rudder!" as the stern cleared the mine. "Sound the collision alarm!" A close call for all hands. Captain Morrison bounded up the ladder to the bridge. "Where is it, Rob?"

"Astern of us now captain."

"All stop! Let's get some target practice, Rob. Call up the twenty-millimeter crew." In a few minutes, they had dispatched the mine, perhaps saving another submarine's certain death. Dick complimented the lookouts for their finding the mine in very difficult waters. They saved their ship and their shipmates' lives. And he praised Rob for his seamanship in avoiding disaster.

Thornfish arrived off the entrance to Midway's narrow channel at dawn as forecast in their ETA. Getting into the inner harbor was not easy. Ancient coral reefs guarded the narrow entrance on either side of the passage. Dick maneuvered *Thornfish* expertly and made a two-bell landing alongside the pier. There were no hula girls, bands or even spectators awaiting their arrival. Sailors in dungarees slipped the mooring line over the bollards and made the sub secure alongside the pier. A Jeep approached with a Marine lieutenant and two guards to take the prisoner from the sub. The crew had given Tojo a large package of sugar, cigarettes, and candy bars, in a pillowcase. Pinned to it was a note to the Marines: "Take good care of this prisoner. He's a good guy and helped us a lot." The Marines tied a blindfold on their prisoner. Rob tried to prevent it, but the guards said regulations required it.

Rob went with the young Jap radioman down the gangway to the awaiting Jeep. He told the lieutenant the story of his capture and the vital intelligence he had provided.

In Japanese, he said warmly to Tojo, "After the war, perhaps we will meet again!"

"Thanks, you sir," Tojo replied in broken English.

Soon the pier became a beehive of activity as the repair crews started to arrive. The Navy yard commander appeared shortly after in a Jeep, along with his aide. He wanted to go over the repair list he had received earlier by a message from Jerry. A few minutes later an olive drab Marine ambulance arrived and parked ahead of the gangway. A medical doctor got out of the passenger side and asked permission to come aboard. Dick met him and escorted him down the ladders to the wardroom. LCDR J.J. Custer was seated at the head of the wardroom table drinking coffee. He appeared in freshly starched khakis that hung loosely on his small frame, clean shaven and clear-eyed. Outwardly at least, he was his old self, confident and calm.

After an awkward silence, Dick introduced Custer to the medical doctor and left the wardroom. As he turned to go into the control room a messenger from the base operations office met him by the ladder. "Sir, I have a message from the Commander of Submarines Pacific Fleet for you and one for Lieutenant Commander Custer."

"Very well, give me mine." He opened it.

From: Commander Submarines Pacific Fleet

Via: Commander Submarine Squadron 6

To LT Richard P Morrison USN USS Thornfish SS499

1. You are hereby appointed as Commanding Officer USS Thornfish SS 499.

2. A Board of Inquiry (BOI) will be convened at Commander Submarines' Headquarters once Thornfish returns to Pearl Harbor to review the circumstances for the relieving of the commanding officer LCDR J.J. Custer USN in accordance with Article 1088 Navy Regulations. You will be named as a respondent in the inquiry.

Dick read the message and dismissed the Marine corporal, folded the message and gave it to the officer of the deck for entry in the ship's log. As he entered the control room, he was elated that he had achieved his goal of command at sea. But it was not the way he wanted. In one sense it was good news, but it could be bad news. Only time would tell.

The messenger knocked on the wardroom entrance and saluted LCDR Custer and handed him his message. He opened it with trembling hands. He knew what was in it. He slowly read:

From: Commander Submarines Pacific Fleet

Via: Commander Submarine Squadron 6

To: LCDR J.J. Custer USN

This is to inform you that you are officially relieved as commanding officer USS Thornfish. Upon receipt of this message you are directed to proceed to medical facilities Midway

for a physical examination. Upon completion of the physical examination proceed using first available transportation to Headquarters Commander Submarines Pacific Fleet for temporary duty with the staff submarine squadron. A Board of Inquiry will be convened to inquire as to the circumstances of your relief at sea in accordance with Article 1088 U.S. Navy Regulations as soon as practicable after Thornfish returns to the Naval Base Pearl Harbor.

Custer bit his lip as he folded the message and put it in his shirt pocket. He finished his coffee and took his cup across the passageway to his stateroom, placing it on his desk. His personal effects would be sent to the officers' quarters on the base. He took one last look at his stateroom and took a small photograph of his wife and two children stuffing it in his pocket with the message relieving him from command. Then he walked swiftly to the main deck. There would be no change of command ceremony as is customary. As the former commanding officer, accompanied by the doctor, appeared on the deck the new captain, along with the officer of the deck and Jerry stood at attention. Dick ordered "Attention on Deck, Hand Salute." Custer returned his salute as he departed *Thornfish* for the last time. Dick was depressed. He knew Custer was crushed. But then he recalled Custer's words said in candor during the patrol, *"Dick, I'm not cut out for this."*

He was right. *It was Custer's last stand.*

· · · · ·

Midway is a small barren island, aptly named for being midway across the Pacific, and inhabited by funny seabirds called Gooney Birds by the occupants of the small isle. The gangly creatures could hardly fly. They waddle sometimes down the single runway, often interfering with plane traffic. Before the war Midway was a refueling stop for the famous China Clipper seaplanes that featured first-class accommodations for passengers during the long flight over the Pacific Ocean. The former Pan American Hotel had been taken over by the Navy for officers' quarters when they made Midway a submarine base. It cut travel time by five days for subs that were normally based in Hawaii en route to their patrol areas. The entire crew was housed on the base. Sixty days in a cramped foul-smelling submarine was long enough. The crew needed rest, showers, fresh water and beer. There was plenty of the latter. For recreation, there were movies and softball games, and on a few occasions, rough and tumble football games. One memorable game was played with the *Sea Horse* Captain, Slade Cutter. Slade, class of 1935 at the Naval Academy, was a heavyweight boxing champion and the football player who won the Army-Navy game with a last-minute field goal in the muddy classic of 1934. Having no football on Midway, they played a pickup football game using a billiard ball for the football. Ned Beach, an officer from another boat, made the mistake of trying to tackle Slade and got flattened.

The Japanese Navy planned an invasion of Midway only a few months earlier. June 2, 3, and 4, 1942, would become the turning point in the war. The Japanese lost four carriers, the *Akagi, Kaga, Sorry,* and *Hiryu,* the ones that attacked Pearl Harbor only six months earlier. The Americans lost the carrier *Yorktown* and all the planes of torpedo squadron eight flying off the *Yorktown.* Flying at 180 knots, 200 feet above the water, the Jap gunners cut down all the slow-moving TBM bombers. But they distracted the enemy's gunners long enough to allow the American dive bombers high above time to scream down on the carriers. The Japanese invasion fleet was defeated. The tide had turned.

The six officers from *Thornfish* enjoyed private rooms for now. Captain Morrison enjoyed a suite complete with a refrigerator stocked with cold beer. When another sub returned from patrol, some of the junior officers would have to double up. The beautiful beach was inviting. The sand was pristine. The crew, housed in temporary barracks some distance from the officers took to the water right away, and some got badly sunburned. Their commanding officer was one of them. LT Morrison stopped in the medical office to get some zinc oxide and as he waited for the pharmacist to bring him a small jar, LCDR Custer came out of the doctor's office. Seeing Dick, he said curtly, "See you in Court!" Dick didn't respond. He just looked away and held his breath.

Later in the day, he joined some of his officers in the bar of the small officers' club. Seated in the far corner was J.J. Custer holding forth to a small group of officers from the naval station. He had been drinking for a while as he loudly proclaimed how the crew of *Thornfish* was timid in the face of danger. Then he started lashing out at his former executive officer, "He was always doing stupid things, dumb enough to get us all killed. It was all I could do to stop him from his rash decisions." Dick was about to explode. He started to get up and Jerry, seated next to him, grabbed his wrist so forcefully it hurt his CO. "Captain it's not worth it sir. Let him be. His words will do him in. Let's get out of here." They rose, and all went out on the veranda and sat on white lawn chairs quietly watching the sun setting over the western Pacific.

That evening Rob dashed off a letter to Molly.

Honey, we're back from patrol. Lots of excitement. I'm striving for my Dolphins every day, standing watches, learning how to trim the tanks for the first dive of the morning. I have been checked out on just about every system, and each compartment on the boat. Chief O'Neil has been a great help. I think he likes me. We get along great. He is a natural leader. He was one of the heroes a couple of years ago when the Squalus went down off Portsmouth, New Hampshire. He saved the ship by going down in the after battery and disconnecting the batteries that were going to explode from the buildup of hydrogen. I am enjoying some refreshments now, getting showers, swimming, playing softball and reading and rereading your sweet letters. I had a stack of them when we returned to base. I'm reading every line, every word, and every thought of you. I miss you so much. I love you.

Rob, xxxx, ooo

The next morning Captain Morrison called a meeting of the officers in the conference room of the barracks. He read the message from Commander Submarines Pacific Fleet authorizing him to assume command of the *Thornfish*. He continued, "Gentlemen, we need to focus on getting the Midway repairs done, and I'm going to turn the meeting over to Jerry for his status report." The *Thornfish's* engineer reported on the progress of the repairs. The main induction valve had been fixed, and the temporary repairs on number four main engine piston would be completed in a day or so. He said we can safely dive the boat, but further major repairs will be needed at the yard at Pearl.

"When do you think we can get underway?" the captain asked.

Jerry replied, "Well sir, if everything goes ok, we should be ready for sea in 48 hours." The roar of airplane engines drowned out any further comments. A lone Liberator bomber landed on the single airstrip and began taxiing to the hangar. When the noise abated, Jerry concluded his brief report. Jerry was one of the boat's finest officers, bright, alert and thoughtful and with a good sense of humor, his men loved him. His former captain, however, did not share their feelings. Custer did not like LT Abrams, not only because he was a Jew, but because he was a reserve officer. And he told LT Abrams that one day in the wardroom. LCDR Custer told him that he had been a shipmate of a Jew named Hyman Rickover on a sub based in Panama in the thirties. He disliked him immensely. Rickover was smart and always right. The story goes that Custer's sentiments were shared by many of his classmates at the Academy. Rumor had it that Rickover's photo in the class yearbook was printed on perforated pages so that it could be torn out easily. Despite his excellent performance of his duties on *Thornfish*, Jerry's fitness reports were average to satisfactory.

After the meeting, Dick walked back to the *Thornfish*, and as he neared the gangway, a Navy Jeep drove up with a senior officer as a passenger.

"Dick it's great to see you!" He turned to see his old shipmate from the *Argonaut*, Commander Ben Miller. Dick saluted and extended his hand to his old friend.

"What are you doing here Ben?

"Well, I'm doing a little reconnaissance mission for the boss." The boss was the Commander of Submarine Squadron 6, Pearl Harbor. They quickly disappeared down the ladder to the wardroom for some Navy coffee. After the exchange of pleasantries,

Commander Miller said, "Well, I have come to get an advanced look at your patrol report for our commander. He is concerned about the problems brewing in Pearl for the Article 1088 issue."

Dick replied, "Well Sir, the report is not quite finished yet, but you can read what I have written so far."

"Great. Let me at it."

Dick went to the captain's stateroom that he now occupied himself. He opened the safe and removed the report and unfolded the tracks of the torpedo attacks that they had made, and the ones broken off by Captain Custer. The narrative was some six pages, beginning with the low morale after weeks of evading combat in the East China Sea that had abundant enemy shipping and concluding with the attack on the convoy from Guam that led to the relief of Captain Custer.

While the commander sat drinking his coffee and reading the report, Dick excused himself and made a quick trip aft to the engine compartment to see the progress on the repairs of number four diesel engine. As he entered the engineering space, an old looking lieutenant was talking with Jerry about the problem with the connecting rods on several cylinders. He was a *Mustang*, one who had risen through the ranks and was commissioned later in his career. He greeted Dick and said, "Sir I'm afraid the crankshaft is out of round and will have to be replaced. We can't do that here at Midway, so it will have to wait until you get to the yard at Pearl." Dick replied, "Ok but will the shims you put on hold together until we reach Pearl Harbor?"

"Yes Sir, I'm pretty sure the shims will work long enough to get you there. You are lucky captain."

"How so?"

"Well, you don't have HOR engines. A few weeks ago, we had to send a tug out in case the *Pompano* couldn't make it in. They finally had to surface and come into Midway on batteries.

"I know about those engines. Everyone in the sub service does. They stink!"

Most of the new submarines had Fairbanks-Morse diesel engines or General Motors engines. But a few were equipped with a newer engine manufactured along the lines of German diesels that were more powerful but caused a lot of trouble for their submarines. Their higher operating temperatures sometimes caused the piston rods to fail. Teeth on gear trains chipped and set up vibrations in the crankshaft that caused twisting and eventually breakage. The engines were called "whores" by the engineers as a result of their frequent breakdowns. Manufactured in Hamilton, Ohio, near Cincinnati, by the Hooven-Owens-Rentschler Company, the Navy assigned Commander Lew Parks to be a resident inspector at their Hamilton facilities. Lew Parks later commanded a new construction submarine, the *Pompano,* that was equipped with HOR engines.

The engines gave off a lot of heavy smoke and were never reliable. All were changed to other manufacturers later in the war.

When Dick returned to the wardroom, Ben had just finished reading most of the draft of the patrol report. Dick poured him another cup of coffee and one for himself. In the privacy of the wardroom, Ben Miller said, "Dick you have an outstanding report. It shows aggressiveness and tactical excellence under very difficult conditions."

Dick replied, "Thanks Ben, but I want you to know I have an outstanding crew. I'm particularly impressed with the caliber of reserve officers we have. Jerry Abrams is a terrific engineer, a Purdue graduate in electrical engineering, and Ensigns Walker and Young have both made some significant contributions. Ben agreed, "Yes, I see Ensign Walker has some Japanese language ability too; that will be valuable to the Navy."

"It has already," Dick said. "He was instrumental in our capture of the Jap radioman and got a lot of good intelligence for the Intel folks back in Pearl. He has performed exceptionally well and helped save the boat when the forward room began to flood."

"Dick, I think you should recommend him for a commendation medal, or maybe a bronze star."

"I intend to do that Ben."

Then Ben turned to the page describing the relieving of LCDR Custer. He reread the paragraphs describing the episode.

"Before the attack on the convoy, the captain made several bad decisions. Just before the attack Captain Custer changed our battle plan. We had previously agreed that the exec would man the periscope giving angle on the bow, bearings, and ranges to the attack team, and the captain would serve as the approach officer. The reason for this was that in prior attempts at attacking enemy ships the captain often froze and would leave the periscope up too long. This endangered *Thornfish* and happened again in this situation. The urgent message we received from headquarters said that this convoy was very important. During this time, the captain seemed to me to have something like a seizure. His hands were trembling, his countenance distraught, and commands almost inaudible. I immediately took his hands from the periscope handles and said that I would make the observations, but when he ordered deep submergence, I relieved him and countermanded his diving orders. We then resumed the attack without the captain's assistance. I ordered the chief of the boat to lead him below and ordered the pharmacist mate to attend to him. Later, when time allowed, I placed the captain on the sick list and had the time and date along with an entry made in the ship's log of my relieving the captain in accordance with Article 1088 of Navy Regulations, and that he had been placed on the ship's sick list. I ordered a guard placed at his stateroom in the event he needed assistance.

"Note: A few hours before our first radar contact with the enemy I went below to check on the captain as he was not present with our tactical team. I found him in bed with a 45 semi-automatic pistol beside him and four empty small bottles of bourbon whiskey we would distribute to the crew after being depth charged. I was afraid that he was considering suicide, and I immediately took the gun from him and unloaded it and placed it in my safe and took the empty bottles to my room. I told Captain Custer that he should have medical attention, and I called the pharmacist mate to check on him. He administered a mild sedative, and the captain fell asleep for the remainder of the day. While all this was going on, Ensign Robert Walker, USNR, was in the passageway just outside the wardroom, and hearing the commotion, came in time to observe the situation unfolding. I ordered him to get the pharmacist mate and to tell no one of the incident."

At this point, Ben interrupted the reading and said, "Dick I think you should rewrite this and omit the narrative about the circumstances leading up to Custer being relieved. As you know these patrol reports are given wide dissemination for other submarine commanders to benefit from the lessons learned by other submarines on patrol. All that I think needs to be said is that the captain was not well, and you were forced to exercise Article 1088. The details you mentioned will become known during the Board of Inquiry."

Dick took a long sip of his coffee and put his cup down carefully. Looking directly at his chief of staff he reluctantly replied, "Perhaps you are right, sir. I'll make the change."

"Good." I don't think you have anything to worry about in Pearl. Do you want someone to represent you at the inquiry?"

Dick said, "No I think I can handle it ok."

"Very well. I've got to be going. Thanks for the coffee and I'll see you in Pearl. Do you need anything from the staff now?"

"Yes, I'm going to need some help with our repairs as soon as we return. And I am going to need a good exec, do you know of someone? Would you help me get a good one?" Ben said, "Sure you'll get the best one I can find." As they made their way to the main deck, Ben said, "By the way, I'm going to have a passenger with me on my return trip this evening, a Lieutenant Commander J.J. Custer."

Dick said," You'll get an earful, Ben."

CHAPTER 13

Return to Pearl

Thornfish's return to the Navy yard at Pearl Harbor took nearly seven days, but they were days full of qualification checkoffs for the crew including the younger officers. But Rob found some time to learn the wardrooms favorite game, cribbage. Rob learned from an expert, Captain Morrison. He learned well enough to beat the captain two out of three games the last day out from the base. To mark the occasion, the ship's cooks baked Rob a cake decorated with red cards of three aces and two queens over white icing.

At 0700 21 November, the *Thornfish* rendezvoused with the USS *Latimore,* DE 346, twenty miles from the entrance to Pearl Harbor. The destroyer escort provided cover for the surfaced sub protecting it from friendly fire from any overzealous airmen on patrol off the Hawaiian Island of Oahu.

As they entered port, Captain Morrison had all the crew not on watch, standing at attention on deck as they passed the hulk of the capsized *Oklahoma* still containing the bodies of 400 sailors trapped when the ship overturned, and the mangled superstructure of the USS *Arizona* where over 1200 men died shortly after 0800 December 7. The boatswain mate's whistle ordered all hands to render salutes. The *Thornfish* swiftly navigated the channel to the sub-base and moored port side to the pier with a one bell landing under the superb ship handling of its captain. There were no hula girls, or bands or admirals to greet them. A lone Jeep driven by Commander Ben Miller met the boat as the lines were passed over to the waiting white hats on the pier to secure the sub to the dock. Ben Miller, chief of staff of the *Thornfish's* squadron, saluted smartly as he jogged up the gangway and asked the officer of the deck for permission to come aboard as custom and tradition dictated since the birth of the United States Navy in 1775. Captain Morrison met him at the head of the gangway and led him to the wardroom for the traditional cup of coffee.

"You were right Dick" exclaimed the chief of staff as they sat down at the wardroom table covered neatly with its green tablecloth. "I sure got an earful from Custer during our flight home last week. He is very bitter. He thinks you engineered the take over from the very beginning of the patrol. He said he even saw the ship's copy of Navy Regs open to Article 1088 on your desk one day. He says that the crew regarded you as the captain. And you were always trying to get the ship killed by your overzealous behavior when encountering the enemy."

Dick didn't say a word. "And to top it all off, he thinks he should get the Navy Cross for sinking the cruiser!"

"Well, maybe he should," Dick finally said. After a long pause, he added, "But he choked up during the attack Ben."

"By the way Dick, Custer wants his 45 back. He said he had it since his days as *George* on the old S-boat he was on in the Canal Zone." As the ship's supply officer, he had to go ashore and get cash to pay the crew and used the sidearm during his trips to and from the base. *George* was the name that all junior officers got when they came aboard their first sub. *George's* first assignment was usually a commissary and supply officer.

"He'll get it back after the Board of Inquiry. When's it going to be Ben?"

"Next week sometime. I think it will be the Monday after Thanksgiving."

"Well, that will give me a little time to prepare."

"I would like to help you get ready OK. You've got a lot to do. Can we get started in the morning? We have a couple of buses coming in a few minutes to take your crew to the Royal Hawaiian. I've got a Jeep, and I'll drive you there myself."

Admiral Lockwood, Commander of Submarines, Pacific Fleet, did a marvelous thing for his submariners when he took command. He provided relief crews for all returning boats immediately upon their arrival from patrols. The regular crews including their captains, officers and enlisted men were relieved and sent on two weeks rest and recreation (R&R) while repairs of damage and equipment were accomplished. Included in R&R was housing in The Royal Hawaiian Hotel, the finest hotel on Oahu. The Navy leased the entire facility situated on the Waikiki Beach after December 7. Only submariners could use its rooms. Commanding officers were allowed suites overlooking famous Waikiki Beach. Its pink façade, nicknamed the Pink Palace, was surrounded by palm trees and white sand encircled by fierce barbed wire and constantly guarded by armed Marine guards.

Rob, his fellow officers, and crew boarded a drab gray bus for the long drive from the submarine base to the hotel. On the way, they passed the Aloha Tower, at the harbor where Japanese embassy personnel spied on the anchored fleet in the harbor before the attack. A long line of sailors dressed in their white uniforms lined the side street, and Rob asked the driver what was going on there. He laughed and said they are waiting for biological physical therapy. "You mean these sailors are all suffering wounds?" asked Rob. That brought laughter from the civilian driver, a small Hawaiian man in a sweaty blue driver's uniform. He was laughing so hard he almost crashed into a parked Navy shore patrol van.

"Well sir, the kind of therapy they want is only for their dicks. They get a maximum of four minutes with the girls on the second floor!" Rob couldn't believe it. The line extended for a whole block. And all those in the front of the bus had a lot of fun telling others about the "biological physical therapy" that cost only $2.00 per session.

The driver asked, "Do you want me to stop now sir, and wait for all of you?"

Rob replied, "No, not now at least!" But the crew shouted in unison, "Stop the bus!"

* * * * *

Rob shared a room with John Young that overlooked the courtyard and Tiki Bar. After a long hot shower, he put on a clean khaki work uniform and began to read the mail he had received since Midway. There were five letters from Molly and two from his parents. Molly's were written on thin airmail stationery addressed simply to Ensign Robert A. Walker, USNR USS *Thornfish* C/O Fleet Post Office San Francisco, California. Airmail postage was six cents. In one letter she enclosed a recent picture of her at her desk in *The Student* newspaper. She looked great, but Rob was hoping that she would have one in her bathing suit. She would even look better than Betty Grable, every service man's pinup girl.

Her letters were full of news about what was happening on campus. The Navy was there in force. Contracts were being awarded to train cooks and bakers, and radio operators both men and women in uniform. Female Marines were being sent to Miami University as well as WAVES (Women Accepted for Voluntary Emergency Services). Molly loved working for *The Student*. Some of its reporters, editors, and even the business workers wanted to be journalists. Most majored in English, but a few like Molly were in the School of Education. She tried to please her father who insisted that she learn to be a teacher, but Molly had her sights on other things; the fast pace of the newspaper office, the excitement to meet deadlines, and the chance to meet interesting people appealed to her. She began to think more about what she would do after graduation in the spring. Her family wanted her to return to Marion and become a teacher. But she still harbored a secret desire to learn to fly, and Miami's new airfield might enable her to learn while she was still in school. Another option would be to get a job with a newspaper. Perhaps the *Cincinnati Enquirer* might need female reporters. One thing for sure, she didn't want to return to Marion, Ohio. It's a wonderful town but too close to home. She had even given some thought about joining the WAVES. All were first sent to Hunter College in New York for basic training. Then depending on their aptitude, some were sent directly to Miami for radio school. One day a train carrying some 50 WAVES all with red hair arrived in Oxford to begin training as radio operators. The Navy ordered them by mistake. It seems the Personnel Department, using punch cards, pulled cards for red hair instead of radio aptitude. They all began their training with enthusiasm, nevertheless.

But it was the two letters from his parents that bothered him. The one from his father mentioned that he had been asked to come to Washington to work with the Office of Strategic Services. He was strongly considering it, but a few lines later his father said that he was concerned about his mother's health. She had some medical issues and was not well. And his mother's letter gave him concern as well. She made no mention of her medical problems, but she was still trying to get him transferred to Washington to work in Navy intelligence. Her letter said that she was planning to ask her uncle Bob, senator from Ohio, to intercede directly with the Secretary of the Navy to get him transferred. The other thing that bothered Rob was that she made no mention of seeing Molly. Rob thought he could get his father to try to keep her from interfering with his choice of service, but he knew he couldn't change her attitude about Molly. She was a very opinionated woman, especially about the Irish Catholic girl from across the tracks. Only time would heal whatever was causing her to dislike his girlfriend.

He put the letters in his duffle bag and decided to get something to eat. He'd answer the letters to his folks and Molly tomorrow. Right now, he was hungry. He was looking forward to some mahi-mahi and a cold beer. He bounced down the stairs to the dining room only to find most of the *Thornfish's* officers seated around a round table in the bar with a terrific view of Diamond Head. Jerry Abrams yelled, "Hey Rocky, come over here and join us." Rocky was the new nickname Jerry had given Rob after learning that he was a geology major, a rock hound, as they were called on his college campus. The Royal Hawaiian bar was completely open on all sides, covered with a decorative metal roof and bordered with coconut leaves and long sea grass. Situated right on Waikiki Beach, it was the prime place for cocktails and only a few steps to the beautiful dining room. Happy hour prices were in effect, ten cents for a beer and fifteen cents for a cocktail. He took the empty seat beside Jerry, and a gorgeous Hawaiian waitress came over to ask him what he would like to drink. Rob said, "I'll have a draft beer please." Jerry interrupted, "Wait, have you ever had a gimlet?"

"No, what's that?"

"Well, that's what we're all having. I learned it from the limeys; it's got either gin or vodka with a little Roses' sweetened lime juice and some ice. Try it, it's great." Rob asked the young waitress her name. She replied, "Lily."

"Ok Lily, what do you think? Let's do both, a beer and a gimlet." She smiled and walked away with the eyes of the entire group locked on her.

"Eyes in the boat sailors," ordered Jerry. Lily was gorgeous. Her long dark hair ranged down her back. Her high cheekbones, beautiful dark eyes highlighted by her light tan complexion revealed her Asian-American heritage. Her perfect figure was amply displayed by a short skirt and an even shorter Hawaiian shirt.

John broke their glances by saying, "WOW, Rob, a gin gimlet, and a beer! You must have had some bad news in that pile of letters you just got, was it a Dear John?" Just as he said that he knew he had misspoken and said sheepishly, "I'm sorry Rob."

Rob replied, "No, it's ok John, I'm a little uptight and need to relax for a couple of days."

John said, "We all do. But hey, we're having a volleyball game on the beach tomorrow with the guys from the *Haddock* that just pulled in. Want to join us?"

"Sure. We have all five of us here now; maybe the captain will join in too."

"I doubt it, he's preparing for the Board of Inquiry," replied Jerry as he took a long sip of his gin gimlet. "I think it's scheduled for the first of next week." Turning to Rob, he said, "Are you going to have to testify Rocky?"

"I'm not sure; nobody has said anything to me about it." The beautiful waitress brought him his drinks and, in an effort, to deflect any more questions about the Board of Inquiry, Rob changed the subject to the most recent war news. Tom, the new first lieutenant on board, spoke up. "From what I have heard, the news is not very good. We're getting our ass kicked in the Pacific and the Atlantic. U-boats are patrolling up and down our east coast and wreaking havoc. The problem is complicated because we are not convoying these ships, especially tankers. East coast beaches are black with oil now. Cities are still lit up all night silhouetting our ships as they hug the coastline, making perfect targets for German U-boats."

Tom, a recent graduate of sub school, was fitting in nicely with the crew. A tall, lanky guy with a broad southern drawl, he came from a long line of the military going back to the Civil War. His alma mater, VMI, Virginia Military Institute, had produced many fine officers for the U.S. Military. A reserve officer, he made it clear to all that he was intent on making the Navy a career. He majored in military history at VMI. He rattled off some of the losses in the Pacific: Guam fell December 10, 1941, Wake Island at Christmas. In January 1942, the Japs invaded and captured Manila in the Philippines and invaded the Solomon Islands. Singapore fell in February and in April the U. S. Army surrendered all their forces on Bataan. And Corregidor, the island fortress in Manila Bay, surrendered a month later.

Rob broke in by saying, "Look, our job is more important than ever. While I was in Japan, I once talked with one of my schoolmates. His father, a Japanese submarine squadron commander, said that the Japanese Empire was completely dependent on maintaining the sea-lanes as all their raw materials, except coal and some copper, were imported. So, gentlemen, we have to sink every merchant ship we find." John said, "Well, we have to do a lot better than we did on the last patrol."

Jerry glanced at Rob and intentionally interrupted, "I'm buying another round," signaling the lovely waitress. To break the ice after John's last remark, he told another of his Jewish jokes. Irving went up to Mount Saini to talk with God. He asked God,

"How long are a million years in your eyes?" God replied, "Like a minute for you." Then Irving asked God, "How much is a million dollars to you?" God said," like a penny for you." Irving quickly replied, "How about a penny for me?" God said, "Ok, in a minute!"

No one got up early the next morning. All the officers were worn out after their 60-day war patrol. But by 1100, after a huge breakfast, the *Thornfish* volleyball team was assembled on the beach. The white sand beach was inviting even with the barbed wire strung along the entire shoreline and interspersed with machine gun emplacements. Further down the beach Fort DeRussy, manned with eight-inch guns, was protected with two feet of reinforced concrete.

The *Haddock* team arrived more than a few minutes late and hung over from last night. Both teams wore t-shirts, as their bodies were just as white as the sands of Waikiki. It didn't take long to determine the better volleyball team. *Thornfish* creamed the *Haddock*, three games in a row. Rob was the star player in every position of the six on his team. Afterward, he was dripping with sweat and crashed in a beach chair. He sat for some minutes just watching the foaming waves roll on the beach and turned his thoughts to home. Molly was probably going home for Thanksgiving if she could hitch a ride with someone going near Marion. His folks were most likely eating their Thanksgiving dinner with his mom's relatives in Cincinnati. It would be his first Thanksgiving without family and his best girl. He slumped in the chair and was soon fast asleep.

He felt a hand on his shoulder, "Sailor, you better not stay out here very long, or you'll have a terrific sunburn." It was the beautiful waitress. She extended her hand and pulled him up.

"What's your name sailor?" she asked.

"Rob "

"Do you have a last name?"

"Sure, I'm Rob Walker, but what's yours?"

"I'm Lily. Lily Edmonds."

Rob admired her features. They were Asian, but her stature was American. Tall, with a beautiful face, permanent golden tan and a warm smile, Lily was the most popular waitress at the Pink Palace as the submariners called the Royal Hawaiian. Built in 1927 and painted pink, it was owned by the Matson Shipping Line and leased to the Navy for the duration of the war. Set back only a few hundred yards from the famous Waikiki Beach, it was the favorite vacation spot for the rich and famous before the war.

"Come on in. Get out of the sun, and I'll have the bartender fix you a gin gimlet. You like them, don't you?"

Rob sat at the Tiki Bar and ordered a sandwich and sipped his gimlet. The place was beginning to fill up with late rising Navy customers. Lily came over and asked, "What are you doing for Thanksgiving? Are you going to the Hickam Officers Club with the rest of the crew?"

"Maybe."

"I've got the day off. Would you like to take a little tour of the island?"

"Well, that's nice of you to ask, I've never seen anything of Oahu." Rob thought it really wouldn't be wrong, would it? I think it would be interesting and get my mind off things. He was still concerned about being called to testify at the Board of Inquiry.

"But Lily, gas is rationed now. Can you get gas for your car?"

"I don't have a car."

"Well, that's going to be a long walk if we tour the island!"

"Oh silly, it's my mom's. She is working, and after I take her to her job, we'll have the car for a while. She's a maid for one of the wealthy Japanese-Hawaiians who lives in the hills overlooking Honolulu. My mom was born in Japan, so she is an Issie and is not welcomed in a lot of homes in Honolulu."

"I hope things will change with time. I spent a couple of years in Japan when my father worked there, and I grew to respect the people I met, but it is a much different culture than ours. Time heals all wounds they say."

"I hope you're right ensign."

Rob asked, "What time shall we meet?"

"Let's make it about nine forty-five. Can you get up that early?"

Rob laughed, "You're funny. No, let's make it a quarter of ten." Lily's giggle's caused patrons to look up. "You joker!"

Rob went up the stairs to his room. He was tired. Sitting at the desk by the window overlooking the beach, Rob reread his letters from Molly. What a sweetheart. He was so lucky to have her. Her letters were always full of news. She was a reporter at heart he thought. She's even one of the editors now of *The Miami Student* newspaper. She should have majored in English, but her father insisted on her becoming a school teacher. Always something to fall back on he said. Molly's letters brought him up to date with the happenings in Miami. The Navy was taking over things. They occupied Fisher Hall, one of the oldest dorms on campus and rumored to have been an insane asylum in the early days of Oxford. Rob longed for her. He thought of their last embrace in Chicago before he left for duty overseas and how she wanted him, but he refused. Submarine service was his choice, but it was a dangerous choice. Rob told her that he loved her so much that if he didn't survive the war, he wanted her to have the first time with her future husband.

But both females in his life wanted him in the intelligence service. His mother was, at this late date, still trying to get the Navy to order him to Washington. As he sat in his easy chair by the window of his small room, his eyelids closed and he daydreamed about his time in Japan with his Japanese teenage friend, Jimmu Kamatsu, while climbing Mount Fujiyama. The boys took photos of themselves with Rob's 35 mm camera when they finally reached the top of the volcano. It was noon, and at the 12,000-foot elevation, cold August winds were blowing over the top of the mountain. They could see Tokyo Bay with merchant ships weaving their way in the shipping channels near the harbor at Yokohama. The sea and the blue sky melted together on the eastern horizon.

The tranquility was interrupted by Jimmysan, "Robbie, we've got to get down now. We have a room reservation at the inn below, and a hot bath awaits us. Let's go down the fast way."

Rob replied, "What's the fast way?"

"Well, we're going to slide down on the cinders all the way." One side of the mountain was covered in fine loose volcanic cinders. If they could keep their balance, they would be down in a few hours.

"Let's go," Rob yelled over the howling wind. They were off. Their white tennis shoes soon turned black as they skied down the mountain. It was great fun. Near the bottom, the cinders gave way to lush green sawgrass. The path to the hotel led through a small grove of apple trees. Fuji apples were almost ripe. Rob thought about grabbing one but why take a farmer's fruit.

The hotel was beautiful; the road behind a meadow led to the front of the building. It had two stories made of volcanic brick trimmed in teak wood. Broad windows were covered with shutters that let the cool air in at night and shut the light out in the daytime. They checked in at the front desk. Jimmysan's father, Captain Kamatsu, Imperial Japanese Navy, had made reservations for two rooms. The porter took their backpacks, and he led them to their rooms. He stopped at Rob's room, slid the small paper-thin sliding door aside revealing a small but pleasant room. The bed was not much larger than a matt and only a few inches thick. A quilt covered the bed but would not cover Rob's tall frame. A small wash basin and a toilet were tucked in a small closet but with no shower. The porter bowed and left just as Jimmysan came to the door and smiled, "How do you like your accommodations Robbie?"

"OK, thanks for getting them," replied Rob. "Where can we shower?"

"Follow me." The stairway at the end of the hall led down to the showers and hot tubs. The room was tiled in small square inlaid pieces depicting the surrounding countryside and the picture of Mount Fujiyama. The boys stripped and jumped in the showers. The showers were open and the water warm. After their showers, Rob followed his friend to the hot tub. The tub measured about eight by ten feet. It was beautifully inlayed with small square blue- green tiles. The heat emanating from the hot tub made them cautious about jumping in. As they descended the stairs at the end of the pool, they found the water perfect. "How did you find this place Jimmysan," asked Rob. "Well, my father has been here before and suggested we stay here overnight. I think it's a great idea, don't you? Especially since he is paying for both of us." Rob replied, "No, I will pay for my room." Jimmu insisted, "No, he has already paid. It's my 16th birthday present. Enjoy it, Rob." Then the boys heard people talking. Rob looked up and saw a man and a woman, completely naked with their two children, a boy and a girl, come to the edge of the hot tub and asked if they could join them. "Of course," Jimmy said. They watched as the family descended the stairs into the tub. "This is common in our country Rob." Rob gasped, "Golleee!"

Back in their rooms, the young men changed into clean clothes, and placed their dirty ones into a bag and left them outside of their room. They would be cleaned overnight and returned in the early hours the next morning. They wandered down to the dining room. A waiter ushered them to their table in the pergola. Behind Mt Fuji, the evening sky was gloriously tinted with clouds of deep purple and hints of orange. They were seated in front of a hibachi glowing with hot coals. Two young very attractive waitresses came over and sat down beside them. "We will cook for you," they exclaimed. Small chunks of meat were sizzling hot when the vegetables were added, and a huge bowl of rice arrived from the kitchen. Jimmy showed Rob how to use the chopsticks and after a few clumsy moments, he managed to use them. The beverage of choice was rice beer, high in alcohol content. After they finished their meal, Rob said to one of the girls, "That meat was delicious. What is it?" She laughed, "It's dog!" He wasn't certain if she was kidding him.

Speaking in English, Rob asked Jimmy what he wanted to do with his life after school.

"It's already been planned for me."

"What do you mean?"

"My father is set on me attending the Japanese Imperial Naval Academy. But I would like to attend an American University, perhaps Harvard. My father studied for a year at Harvard when he was a commander."

"What about my school, Miami of Ohio? It's a great academic university and one of the most beautiful campuses in the country."

"Well, maybe it could happen if my dad gets the duty he has requested, as Naval Attaché in Washington, DC. My father is fluent in English as you know."

"That would be great! I hope it will work out for both of you."

After dinner, the girls serving them led them upstairs to a private party room. They left their sandals outside the door. The room was decked out with red velvet drapes embroidered with small images of Mt Fujiyama. In the center of the room was a small table and they motioned them to be seated on the floor. One of the girls brought out a deck of Japanese playing cards. We will teach you a game. They giggled and said it is like poker.

"You know poker?" they asked Rob.

"We can't play. We didn't bring any money."

"No need. It is called strip poker." These girls were good. In three quick hands, both boys were completely naked. Embarrassed they said," OK you win." But before they could move the girls stood and said," No you win!" And they opened their kimonos and stood naked before them. "What the…?" Rob said.

"We give you boys a lesson. This your first time, yes? Come." The girls led them into a small bedroom adjacent to the playroom and motioned for them to lie down.

"You can swim, yes? It's just like swimming. Come and see." It was Rob's first "swim."

CHAPTER 14

The Admiral's Decision

A loud knock on the door jarred Rob awake. He opened it to find a Marine corporal dressed in working khakis standing with a message in his hand, "Ensign Walker?"

"Yes"

"Sir, here's a message for you from Commander Submarines Pacific Fleet." Rob dismissed the messenger and returned to his chair and opened the envelope.

From: Commander Submarines Pacific Fleet

To: Ensign Robert A. Walker USNR.

You are directed to report to the office of Commander Submarines Pacific Fleet at 1000 Monday next for possible testimony at a Board of Inquiry. Call base transportation tele: 02369 to arrange for your transportation from The Royal Hawaiian.

Signed, Angus McDougal, Captain USN, Chief of Staff.

Rob sat motionless formulating what he would say. Then he remembered the admonition of LT Morrison, his new CO, "Just tell the truth."

Rob tried to push the thoughts of the Board of Inquiry aside. Tomorrow was Thanksgiving. He would take a tour of Oahu with Lily and then have some turkey at the Club at Hickam with his friends from the Horny Thorny as some of the crew affectionally called the *Thornfish*. Perhaps he could get a phone call through to the states. He would have to stand in the line of course to make his phone call, but maybe he could catch Molly in Oxford if she didn't get a ride to Marion.

To clear his mind, he decided to go for a swim. First, he had to buy a swimsuit. He found the ship's store open in the lobby and purchased a blue bathing suit with the hotel logo; it would be a good souvenir too. He found a pair of white shorts, and an outlandish Hawaiian aloha shirt. To complete his outfit, he chose a good pair of sandals and suntan lotion. Rob enjoyed an hour's swim off the Waikiki Beach with his T-shirt on to ward off sunburn. There were no lifeguards, of course, just Marine sentries perched high up in an observation tower down at the end of the narrow white sands. Protective rows of barbed wire lined the beach as far as the eye could see.

The exercise was just what he needed. After two months of no physical exercise, he needed the energetic use of all his muscles. After a long shower, he dressed in his working uniform and wrote some letters. First to Molly and then to his parents.

The admiral's quarters, a beautiful white bungalow, built on a hill overlooking the entire sub base was surrounded by bougainvillea and palm trees. Below were buildings housing torpedo shops, repairs facilities for radar, sonar, motor shops and a hundred-foot-high water tower used for training submariners to escape a sunken sub. During the air attack on Pearl Harbor, the Japanese didn't attack the submarine facilities and the fuel oil storage tanks. If they had, it would have set the Pacific campaign back months. American submarines were the first to respond after the air raid on Pearl Harbor.

The admiral's wife loved their quarters. They had moved over 15 times in his career and Hawaii was her favorite. But due to the possible invasion by the Japs, all dependents had been ordered to return to the continental U.S. The admiral was alone for the duration. It was five o'clock and Captain Angus McDougal, his chief of staff, joined him for a drink on the admiral's screened in lanai. Angus could tell his boss was disturbed by something; the tall, lanky admiral unbuttoned his white dress shirt and started pacing the floor.

"What's wrong admiral?" He stopped before replying, "I think I may have made a mistake, Angus."

"How so sir?" The admiral went to his wet bar and took out a bottle of Johnny Walker Black Label Scotch, poured two drinks over ice and handed one to his chief of staff.

"Well about this Inquiry. First, I should have just let his Division Commander handle it. We've never had a case like this. Although we came close on one occasion."

Angus was puzzled, "You mean the Midway incident?"

"Yes, a couple of *Pompano* officers threw their commanding officer out of their BOQ window while on R and R at Midway. Fortunately, it was a first-floor window, and no one got hurt.'

Angus chuckled, "Yes sir that was a strange one. He was relieved by his squadron CO for lack of confidence in him for letting subordinates treat him like that. But sir, if I might speak freely, you did the right thing. The submarine force needs to know that we take relieving a captain during combat as very serious. The other thing sir, captain, I mean Commander Custer, is making a lot of noise about his being relieved. We have to put a stop to that right away."

"Angus you may have something there. Is Custer going to be represented by counsel?"

"I believe so sir."

"Hmmm." He took another long sip, "Boy that's good scotch. There's another problem too Angus. What do we do about keeping Morrison as captain of the *Thornfish*?

I don't want a divided crew on that boat. One that favored Custer and the other Morrison. The best solution would be for me to transfer Morrison to another boat. The *Tiger Fish* is in Panama now. Her Captain has had a heart attack we think. I could transfer him to the *Tiger*."

"But admiral, I've talked with Ben Miller, the Division Chief of Staff; he went aboard the *Thornfish* after its arrival at Midway, and the crew loves LT Morrison. They'd do anything for him."

"Ben's a good guy. If Ben likes him, I'll agree. What year was Morrison at the academy?"

"Class of '36 and a very aggressive officer. He's up for promotion to Lieutenant Commander. He'll do fine and will sink a lot of ships I 'm sure."

"Ok, get everyone involved to be in our conference room at 1000 Monday. Let's get this over with. We've got to get *Thornfish* back to sea as soon as possible."

"Yes, Sir. But before I leave, I have a copy of the *Thornfish's* patrol report for you to read and approve the endorsement I have prepared, if you concur. I think you'll want to sign it after the board meets Monday. Some of these men deserve medals for their actions, sir."

"Ok, Angus, now are you up to a few hands of gin rummy?"

CHAPTER 15

The Swim

"Alright Ensign Walker, I'll see you at zero niner forty-five tomorrow morning," Lily said rather softly, poking fun at Rob about his time joke. Rob was seated at the bar with his shipmate John Young and a noisy, happy hour crowd. John nudged Rob, "Hey is she interested in you or what? She's gorgeous. But she sure has some Asian blood in her."

"That's enough of that John, we're just friends. Platonic friends. She's got a car, and she's going to take me on a brief tour over to Bellows Army Air Base in the morning. You want to come along?" John replied, "Naw, I think I'll sleep in, I'm still trying to get caught up. Thanks anyway." Rob liked John. He had gotten to know him better as they stood watches together on the bridge of the sub. Despite his impetuous and sometimes ill-timed comments, he possessed a quality that Rob did not have, one of inner peace.

After dinner that evening Rob returned to his room and reread all of Molly's letters. Every one of them ended with "*I am praying for you and your shipmates every day. Love and kisses, Molly. And remember, Our Love is Here to Stay!*"

The next morning promptly at 0945 Rob, dressed in his new outlandish civvies and sandals, met Lily outside the hotel. He couldn't believe her auto. It was a brand-new red Chevy convertible. He jumped in the passenger side amid whistles and catcalls from sailors walking by.

"Let's go," he shouted, and off they went along the avenue toward the east end of Oahu.

Lily said, "Hang on, we're in for a great day!"

"Where did you get this car?"

"It was my dad's. He bought it in November before the attack. It was to be his retirement gift to mom. He had it on order for almost a year." They drove along the beach road through a residential section composed of small one-story homes.

Where is your dad stationed now?" Rob asked

"I hope in heaven. He was killed in the attack. He was a chief aviation boatswain on Ford Island and was about ready to retire in Hawaii. But with the world situation deteriorating, he decided in November that he would re-enlist for four more years. The

Navy had just transferred him to the USS *Arizona*. That Sunday he went aboard about 7 a.m. to get ready for an admiral's inspection. An hour later he was dead.

"Lily, I'm sorry. One of my college's graduates died on the *Arizona*. He was an ensign named William Lawrence. He had just reported aboard a week or so earlier. He was a naval aviator assigned to the observation detachment on the battleship. Wonder if he ever met your father?"

"We'll never know of course. Let's hope they are flying around heaven together now."

Lily was crying. She pulled over, and Rob put his arm around her and held her until her sobs disappeared.

Rob said, "Let's take a walk." Ahead was a small park with picnic tables along the beach. They sat down on one of them close to the water's edge, and silently looked at the swells in the ocean breaking on the reef offshore. Finally, Rob said, "You know it's hard to believe that there is a war raging all around the Pacific now, and in Europe. It's so peaceful here."

"My father loved this island. He wanted to spend the rest of his life here. He met my mother when he was stationed here years ago. She is Japanese. So, I guess I'm a half-nisei. It's hard for us now. We are under a cloud of suspicion all the time. The Japanese government had a lot of intelligence agents stationed here. They say there were a lot of them on the West Coast too. You probably heard that President Roosevelt has ordered all Japanese-Americans on the West Coast to be put into internment camps."

"No, I can't believe that. He wouldn't do such a thing."

"Well the US Supreme Court has agreed that it's ok. Thousands are being taken from their homes and put in camps out in the desert."

Rob remained silent watching a seagull darting close by coming in for a landing.

"Are you okay? Can we go on now?"

"Yes," she whispered.

"Mind if I drive?"

"Sure, if you have a driver's license," she giggled.

"Well, if an Ohio license is valid on Hawaii, yes."

Lily responded, "It's a good idea especially if we get stopped by shore patrol! You do have your Navy ID, right?"

As they passed Diamond Head, she mentioned that she used to climb to the top through the tunnels now occupied by sentries and fortifications. The road wound along the shoreline. Waves were breaking along the volcanic rocks guarding the coast of southeast Oahu. She relaxed in the warmth of the sun high in the sky. Lily had her eyes closed. Her hair was blowing in the wind falling on her soft shoulders. She was clad in a brief Hawaiian dress not much longer than a man's shirt. Rob broke her reverie by saying, "We're coming up on Hanauma Bay Lily."

"Let's stop Rob!"

Rob slowed, made a right turn and carefully drove down the narrow, winding gravel road to the beach. The palm trees were swaying in the wind. The Bay, nestled in an old volcanic cone open on one end to the sea, seemed idyllic to Rob. Its horseshoe bay made it a great place to swim and observe the variety of tropical fish numbering over 450 different kinds. Rob parked the convertible under the shade of a palm tree. There was not a soul around.

"Let's go for a swim Rob."

"No, I didn't bring my swimsuit."

"I didn't either. No problem, you wear skivvies, don't you? We'll use them."

With that, she jumped out of the car and pulled her dress over her head revealing her beautiful body clad only in her bra and briefs and colorful sandals. She threw her dress in the back seat and darted for the blue, green clear water. "Follow me!"

Rob took off his shorts and shirt and wearing only his boxer underwear and t-shirt, he followed his hostess into the warm water. The warm sand felt good on his feet. He waded out to Lily now standing in waist deep water.

"Rob, come here and look at this black Sea Urchin." He looked down and saw a baseball size black ball, with spines all over it.

"Don't touch them," Lily yelled. "They sting, and the poison is awful!" Rob looked in the water and saw a variety of tropical fish. Lily said, "The naturalists say that there over 400 different kinds of fish here." Rainbow colored Parrotfish were eating at the base of some coral, dark blue Tangs in schools darted around them. Yellow Grunts darted to and fro. He spied a Flounder lying flat in the white sands almost completely invisible. Rob swam out to the far reef at the entrance of the horseshoe- shaped bay; he loved the exercise. He returned to the shore and found Lily at the car lifting a picnic basket out of the trunk. *Wow, this is living* he thought. She had thought of everything including small grass mats that she rolled out in the shade of the nearby palm tree.

As they enjoyed small tuna sandwiches, Lily said, "Tell me about your family." She handed him a cold Pabst Blue Ribbon beer from her cooler. "Mr. Rob, you know a lot about my family, but you haven't said anything about yours."

Rob took the steel can and opened it. "Golly that's a good beer. Well, there isn't much to tell. I'm an only child. My father is a professor at Miami University in a little college town in Ohio named after Oxford University in England. I grew up there, went to college at Miami, majored in geology, and after graduation, I got my commission at Northwestern University's Officers School in Chicago. My dad and mother and I lived in Japan for two years while I was a sophomore and junior in high school. I learned enough to speak some Japanese but not to write."

She glanced at his hands, "You're not married, are you? I don't see a ring. But my father mentioned that sometimes those wedding bands come off when the ship leaves homeport."

"No, I'm not married. I have a girlfriend at home."

"What's her name?"

"Molly," Rob said almost reverently.

Lily asked, "Does she have a middle name? Mine is Kaga. It's Japanese meaning Increasing Joy. My mom insisted on that name and my dad the other, Lily."

"That's a beautiful name. But it's also the name of an aircraft carrier that attacked Pearl Harbor." Lily clarified by saying, "I know. I have not told many people my middle name; is she pretty?"

"She sure is. She's Irish."

"Are you in love?"

"Yes."

Lily smiled, "She is a very lucky young lady, and then she began talking to Rob in Japanese. She was speaking so fast that he finally had to say, "STOP! You're going too fast for me."

"OK" how is this?" and she began speaking at a much slower pace.

"That's better."

"While you were in Japan, did you climb Fuji?"

"Of course, there's a saying that, 'He who goes to Japan and doesn't climb Mt Fuji is a fool. He who climbs it twice is a bigger fool.'"

She laughed, "Yes, I've heard that saying many times. But I have never been to Japan. I'd like to do that sometime after the war; perhaps you'd join me." Before he could say a word, she leaned over, and her eyes met his and suddenly she kissed him deeply. Then she rose and grabbed his hand, "Let's get a shower, Rob." He looked around; there wasn't anything like a shower on the beach.

"Oh yes there is. I know a secret waterfall a few hundred yards inland. We'll wash off this sand and salt. But you have to have your sandals on." Still in her scanty under-wear, she led him through the lush growth of tropical vegetation to a small waterfall with delightful fresh water cascading over the thirty-foot cliff. "Oahu has over 400 waterfalls that have been identified. Most are inaccessible."

Lily blended into the water, hands held high and disappeared underneath the thin veil of water tumbling down the cliff. Rob, still in his underwear, stood watching the silvery streams of water falling on the volcanic rock before him. He could only guess that she had found an alcove underneath the falls created by eons of erosion. Suddenly Lily reappeared, wearing only the sandals on her feet. Startled, Rob started to turn away, but before he could move, Lily reached out to him and drew him under the falls. Rob felt as though he was being lured into the alcove by one of the nymphs in

Homer's Odyssey. She embraced him tightly, and in a moment any resistance he felt was eroded like the water against rocks. His mind flashed back to the time he and Jimmysan stayed at the Fuji Hotel years ago, where he was invited for his first "swim." And now he was going for another.

· · · · ·

The sun was arcing lower over the hills surrounding Hanuman Bay when they emerged from the falls. Rob led the way out to the car. They picked up their mats and picnic baskets and placed them in the trunk. Lily said she would drive. She shifted the gears smoothly as the Chevy climbed the steep road from the beach; Rob sat in the passenger seat, wondering what he'd gotten into. Lily was exciting and vibrant, with no pretense or façade. Rob thought she is what you see. She seemed infatuated with him; why he didn't know, or perhaps didn't want to know. What he had just experienced was something that any red-blooded American sailor could ever hope for. But his thoughts returned to what she had said before their first kiss, "*Perhaps after the war, you could join me in climbing Mt Fuji.*" But then another thought crossed his mind; "*He who climbs it twice is a bigger fool.*" *That would be me*, thought Rob.

Back on the hard road, Lily turned right heading north on the coastal highway.

"Where are we headed now? "asked Rob.

"Our next attraction is the famous Halona Blowhole," Lily laughed. "We'll see a geyser. You should know about them since you're a geologist, Rob."

"Well, the only ones I know much about are the geysers in Yellowstone National Park in Wyoming. They're heated by molten lava near the surface of the earth's crust. This must be something different."

"You'll see in just a few minutes."

They pulled into the roadside park overlooking the Halona Blowhole. The ocean waves were crashing against black volcanic rock. Nestled along the beach was a former lava tube that created the phenomenon. Gases formed a hollow tube that once spread hot molten lava, but now allowed ocean wave action to force the water up through the tube exiting as a fine spray resembling steam. It blew with each significant wave. Lily parked the car in a remote area but where they could observe the sight. Rob watched and thought how some of his geology classmates would love to see this geologist delight.

"Rob, those clouds coming in look like rain to me. Help me put the top up on the convertible." Rob hopped out still dressed in his now dry white skivvies and said, "It's a good thing no one is around. I could be arrested for public indecency."

"Not on Oahu, we are very casual."

They got the top up just in time before the downpour started. They sat in the car just staring at the rain flooding the windshield. It was as though someone had dumped buckets full of water on them. Lily finally turned toward him and broke the silence,

"Rob, I'm getting horny again." With that Lily slipped out from behind the steering wheel and pounced on him whispering, "Push the seat back Rob." It was an order from the enchantress that he tried to resist but couldn't.

Some fifteen minutes later the rain stopped, and a beautiful rainbow appeared in the mist offshore. Satisfied, she said, "What a blessing Rob," as she put on her dress. "We see a lot of rainbows in the Islands. The timing of this one is perfect! You know the rainbow was a sign in the Old Testament to Noah of God's eternal covenant. You are a marvelous lover Rob. But we'd better go now. Mother may need a ride back from her work."

Rob drove, and Lily snuggled up to him and soon fell asleep. As he navigated the Kalanianaole Highway curving shore road, he thought about the day's events. His tour of Oahu was completely unexpected. Lily fascinated him. She was wonderful, but he felt guilty. He argued with himself. *I'm not married.* He thought, *this could be my last sexual experience. Five subs have been lost in the past nine months, maybe more that are kept secret. I don't know what awaits Thornfish on our next patrol. What's wrong with a fling with a gorgeous and warm-hearted girl? It could be my last. But I can't get romantically involved with her and still be faithful to Molly. No, it's not fair to her. But then she needn't know; she's five thousand miles away, and I'm meeting some needs of Lily right here and now. She is still suffering from the loss of her father on the Arizona. Gosh, she sure makes me feel good. And is she religious? She mentioned the sign of the rainbow to Noah. Where did she learn that?*

He slowed as they approached the Royal Hawaiian and Lily awoke.

"Where are we?"

"Near the hotel Lily."

"Let's not stop now. Mom may need a ride from her maid service job up in Ariea. Let's go home and see if she left me a note. It's just fifteen minutes from here."

"OK but remember we are going to the O club at Hickam Army Air Base for dinner."

Lily acted as the navigator as they wound up through the residential area of Honolulu high above the city. Mother's home was a one-story ranch with a beautiful lanai overlooking the city below. They got out, and Lily fumbled trying to open the door with her key. Rob followed and entered the living room appointed with oriental furniture. The large room opened onto a lanai that ran the length of the house. Lily commented as they walked on the deck, "Ordinarily the lights of the city would be coming on soon. But now with the possibility of an invasion, the city is dark at night." She showed him the kitchen and found a note from her mom on the table. Lily opened it and read aloud, "Lily, honey, I've been asked to stay over the weekend by the folks I'm working for, so I won't be home till Sunday. Hope you don't mind. Please pick me up Sunday afternoon at 1 pm. Happy Thanksgiving and don't forget to go to church if you're not working. I love you Lily, Mom."

"Rob let me show you the rest of the house." She went down the hall, "Mom's room on the right and mine straight ahead." Her room was bright and cheery, with white wicker furniture and a small desk and chair at the window overlooking the city. She looked at the bed, and slowly walked to the door and shut it. "We're alone Rob, and I'm still horny."

Once again, the enchantress worked her magic on Rob. They never made it to the Officers' Club.

Afterward, they sat on a small swing couch on the lanai and watched the sun dip below the horizon over Ewa Beach. Lily said, "Is Molly good in bed?" Rob was taken back with her forthrightness and slowly replied, "I don't know, never tried. She is a virgin. And a strong Catholic. But she wanted me before we parted the last time at school, but we decided with the uncertainty of war to wait."

"Well, maybe I'm supposed to do for you what Molly wanted. Just a thought."

"Well it's a wonderful thought, Lily, you are so much like Molly."

"How so?"

"Well, you are both strong-willed, beautiful in facial features and body, coy, demure and ready for adventure and very exciting."

"Rob I'm afraid…I could fall in love with you. Would there ever be room in your big heart for the two of us?" Before Rob could reply, she kissed him long and hard. Rob said, "We'd better be going. It'll be dark soon, and I don't want you out on the road with those dimmed headlights." Island blackout rules required that all autos have their headlights taped to allow only 10 per cent of light to show.

"What's your schedule tomorrow?"

"I've got to work at the bar at 1100."

Rob replied, "I've got to catch up on my correspondence and then check in at the sub base. But the most important thing I've got to do is get ready for my underway qualification for my Dolphins." To qualify in submarines, every submariner must pass an underway test, making an actual approach at a surface ship target, fire a torpedo successfully and hit the evading target. Then, if they pass their underway, they must go before a board composed of three submarine captains and answer their questions on emergency procedures, rules of the road, administration, and operation of all major equipment on the complicated submarine. "I'm scheduled week after next. So, I've got a lot to do before then."

"How may I help you, Rob?" She asked coyly. "I can give you a massage." Rob laughed, "Ok you win, that will help I'm sure." He didn't say anything about the Board of Inquiry.

Lily drove back to the hotel. They said little, both were lost in their thoughts. When she pulled in front of the Pink Palace, she kissed him and said, "Rob this has been the best day of my life. Let's do it again, soon."

Rob replied, "Can you get off Saturday night? We may have a ship's party."

"I'll sure try. See you tomorrow."

Rob watched her convertible leave with only a sliver of light to illuminate her way. He lingered at the curb watching her dim tail lights until they faded away into the distance. He was beginning to miss her already.

CHAPTER 16

Rocks and Shoals

Custer was a bitter man. And those he associated with, after being relieved of command, were getting weary of his constant derision of his former crew and stories about the 'mutinous atmosphere in the ship.' His antagonist was his executive officer, Lieutenant Dick Morrison. Bitterness is infectious. It's like an incurable disease for some. His started in his childhood. J.J.'s father was an alcoholic contractor always moving with a variety of jobs; an overly protective mother smothered him. He was never allowed to go to the movies or the circus in the summertime as a boy for fear, as his mother thought, of catching dreaded polio. He grew up with few friends, making studies his avenue of escape. His brother, four years younger, got the dreaded disease that left him crippled for life. Despite his small stature. J.J. could run like a deer and won state championships in the 100-yard dash and the 440. Hard work in studies and his track record helped him gain a Congressional appointment to the U.S. Naval Academy.

At the Academy, his work ethic and determination helped him to graduate in the top ten percent of his class. He got his first choice of duty for naval air training and was accepted. But J.J. washed out of flight training at Pensacola because he became very airsick during aerobatics. He vomited during his first barrel roll. Fear of failure gripped him constantly. He knew he would throw up again on his next try. And he did. Repeatedly. The medics could do nothing for him. After he washed out, J.J. asked for assignment to submarine service. The Navy complied with orders to sub school at New London, Connecticut, for six months, and he graduated near the top of his class.

As an obsessive-compulsive, he followed the "Rocks and Shoals," the familiar name for the Articles for the Government of the Navy, to the letter. During his four years as a midshipman, parts of the articles were read a least once a month to the entire battalion. The first three dealt with moral and religious values including the worship of Almighty God. But it was **Article 4.10** that made him apprehensive. *"The punishment of death, or such other punishment as a court-martial may adjudge, may be inflicted on any person in the naval service who intentionally or willfully suffers any vessel of the Navy to be stranded, or run upon rocks or shoals, or improperly hazarded or maliciously or willfully injures any* *vessel of the Navy or any part of her tackle, armament, or equipment, whereby the safety of the vessel is hazarded or the lives of the crew exposed to danger."*

His first submarine assignment was aboard an old S-boat based in Panama. He narrowly escaped death when his submarine was rammed at night by a Navy patrol boat. The tragic accident spared him and a dozen survivors before the sub sank in 100 fathoms. Ensign Custer vowed he'd never let that happen to him when he achieved command. Caution was his master. Even while driving an automobile his wife would say, "J.J., you're not going to a funeral. Speed up!" Her promptings seldom helped.

Before the attack on Pearl Harbor, the United States Submarine Service had never experienced combat. The old S-boats, with their short range of operation, were mainly used for defense in coastal waters off the shores of America and the Canal Zone. The newer long-range fleet subs coming off the shipyard ways in large numbers were larger, more comfortable, and even air-conditioned. They could patrol some 13,000 nautical miles without refueling.

In 1940 the President ordered the Pacific Fleet, based along the west coast of the United States, to permanently change their homeports to Pearl Harbor to show Japan that we were reinforcing our forces in the Western Pacific. Despite the warnings of naval intelligence, the Navy high command in Hawaii and Washington were asleep when the Japanese planes attacked Pearl Harbor on December 7. The Army and Navy chiefs in Hawaii were relieved of their commands. But none of those in command in Washington were punished.

J.J. Custer was an early riser and on Sunday, December 7, he stood at the beach in front of his home at the officers' quarters on Ewa Beach and saw the entire devastation of the Navy air base at Ford Island, and the battleships moored to piers. His duty station was at the submarine base, and he commandeered a Navy motor whaleboat and rescued many sailors in the oil covered waters. The carnage he experienced that day, a day of infamy as President Roosevelt so eloquently said in his speech to Congress the day after the attack, only exacerbated his bitter hatred for the Japanese.

* * * * *

The *Thornfish's* crew two-week Rest and Recreation was about half over. Rob's final week would be filled with the possible appearance at the Board of Inquiry and preparations for his underway examination for qualification in submarines. But this Saturday night was going to be special. He had invited Lily to the dance at the O club where some of the ship's officers would be having a blast with some of the local Navy nurses. Lily had the night off and met him in front of the hotel in her mother's red convertible. He invited his roommate, John Young and his date, Kate, a young attractive Navy nurse, to join them for the evening dance.

The Officers' Club at Hickam Army Airbase sustained little damage from the attack on December 7 and was open for business. Set in among willowy palm trees alongside the broad sandy beach, it was a perfect place for an enjoyable evening apart from the war.

Rob's date for the occasion was stunning. Lily, dressed in a tight sliver low cut dress that accentuated every curve on her body, was a show stopper. Her Asian-American features highlighted by her long black hair made her the most attractive woman there. Rob saw his ship's officers table across the crowded room, and as he and John and their dates threaded their way across the dance floor, the five-piece band was playing *"I Don't Want to Set the World on Fire, I just want to set a flame in your heart."* One of the Army junior officers, who had too much to drink, jumped up to the microphone and began singing the words, *"I don't want to set the world on fire, I want to set a flame in Tokyo!"* It brought thunderous applause despite his bad vocals. Rob and Lily joined his friends, and they all stood as Lily and Kate approached the table. Officers and gentlemen always arise when ladies joined them. Rob seated Lily alongside his chair and ordered two shrimp cocktails and two gin gimlets from the waiter. The conversation was difficult while the band played. Finally, they took a break, and talk flowed. Jerry Abrams was the only married officer present. Captain Morrison had not yet arrived. Jerry said, "We're going to get a new exec next week. I don't know yet who it will be." John said, "Why not you, sir?" Jerry replied, "Well I could do it but I'm a reserve officer, and so far, the personnel department favors academy grads, and never for command."

"Well, that's not fair."

"I know, but life isn't fair John. I'm sure that whoever is slated will be an experienced combat officer. Captain Morrison is going to go after the enemy, and there's no room for the fainthearted."

Lily interrupted, "Let's not talk about the war; let's just enjoy the moment."

Jerry bowed his head and said, "OK you win. You're right; we need to have fun tonight."

The band struck up another of the top ten songs, *Don't Sit Under the Apple Tree With Anyone Else But Me.* The female vocalist sang it beautifully, but the words *anyone else but me* echoed through Rob's mind. Lily sensed his thoughts and said, "Rob let's dance." She rose and took his hand and led him to the dance floor. The band was playing *Moonlight Becomes You.* She danced close with her head on his shoulder, lost in her dreams of a love affair that for her wouldn't cool down. Rob's thoughts were of what Molly might be doing tonight. She's sitting at her dorm window, her apple tree, not wanting to go to a dance without Rob. He felt miserable. When the music ended, they returned to their table and picked at their appetizers. As they were about to order dinner, a gaunt man dressed in white pants and a bizarre Hawaiian shirt, came staggering over to their table. At first glance no one noticed him. It was J.J. Custer, who had already had one too many to drink.

"Well if it isn't my old shipmates! What nefarious things are you all plotting now?" He stepped closer and said, "Aren't you going to ask me to sit down?"

Jerry Abrams, the senior man present at the table, replied, "Sir, to answer your question, we are not up to any nefarious activities, we are just trying to have an enjoyable evening. And I don't think it wise to seat you now with the Board of Inquiry meeting Monday; after that perhaps we could, sir."

Custer then turned his attention to the ladies present and went over to where Lily was sitting and said loudly, "Well lookie here; we have a Jap sitting here. You know she may be a spy." At that Lily became enraged. She stood up and slapped Custer in the mouth. "You bitch!" He cried, obviously embarrassed, holding his hand over his face, "I know where you work, and I'm going to get you fired." Rob stood up knocking his chair over as he lunged for Custer. Jerry jumped in the nick of time and blocked Rob's advance. A crowd started to gather around. "Mr. Custer," Jerry yelled," she is an American citizen… her father died on the *Arizona*. Please leave now before this gets out of hand." At this Custer retreated, staggering across the dance floor.

Lily was sobbing as Rob led her out onto the veranda, where it was quiet, and they could be alone. They sat on a couch, overlooking the calm ocean. A full moon lighted the crest of each wave breaking on the beach in front of them. The serenity helped calm her, and she finally said, "We have a war out there and one going on in here." Then she added, "Thanks for sticking up for me Rob."

"Well, you didn't deserve that. He is out of control. He was our Commanding Officer on the *Thornfish* and was relieved of command while we were underway by the executive officer, that's why I may have to testify at a Board of Inquiry Monday. They're looking into the circumstances leading up to his being relieved. He is bitter, and he's not used to drinking. He was a teetotaler before all this happened."

"I didn't know he was a submarine commander. Do you think he can get me fired?"

"No, don't worry about him." The band started playing the most popular song of the 1942 hit parade, "*I'm Dreaming of a White Christmas*." Rob stood and pulled Lily to him "Let's dance." They slow danced alone on the veranda, while the crowd on the dance floor seemed unusually quiet. Military families would be separated this Christmas, and thoughts of home filled their hearts.

CHAPTER 17

Oxford, Christmas 1942

Six thousand miles east of Hawaii, the lights in the little town of Oxford, Ohio, were dimmed this Christmas season. Outside decorations were missing from the fraternity houses and dormitories, and campus buildings that were brightly trimmed last year were dark. A few of the fraternity houses had closed for the duration since most of their occupants had gone off to war. The local Lions Club was still selling cut Christmas trees in a lot underneath the water tower. Molly Gaynor purchased some candies and a fruitcake at the grocery store uptown and hurried along High Street in the cold December air heading for Rob's parents' home on Campus Avenue. As she passed the Christmas tree lot, she said hello to the lone old timer shivering in the cold waiting for a customer to buy a tree. It was almost dark when she arrived at the Walker's home and climbed the steps to the front porch. She looked at the swing that she and Rob once sat in and thought how long it would be before we could do that again. She rang the bell, and no one answered. The lights in the hallway were on. She tried the doorknob, and it opened, and she entered saying, "Mrs. Walker, it's me, Molly. May I come in?" Mary Catherine Walker said faintly, "Yes, come in the kitchen, Molly." Molly entered the hallway leading to the kitchen; it was filled with family pictures of vacations past and those of their stay in Japan. Many pictures of Rob when he was a little boy adorned the family photo section. Two beautiful woodblock prints of colorful geisha girls were placed on an opposite wall and hanging next to them was the hiking stick Rob used when he climbed Mount Fujiyama. Markers of all nine stations were burned into the wood with the last one marking the top of the mountain.

Mrs. Walker looked tired. Her recent illness had taken a lot out of her. Molly entered the kitchen "the white room," as Rob called it. He used to joke about it was like living inside a ping pong ball. Everything was in its place. No dirty dishes. She still had a maid come once a week, working four hours for five dollars, including tip. But a loaf of bread cost ten cents and coffee forty-five cents for a tin of Maxwell House, *good to the last drop* as advertised. Gasoline was now rationed but only cost fifteen cents a gallon at the Marathon gas station on the north side of the town square.

"Mrs. Walker, I brought you something. I know you like fruitcake, and I found a good one uptown. And here's some hard licorice candy you like." Mary Catherine's continence brightened as she opened the sack of goodies. She was very partial to both items. "Molly that's so thoughtful of you. Thank you so much." She had mellowed a lot over the past few months of her illness, Molly thought. Molly was her only real companion now that her husband had taken a leave of absence from the university to go to work for the War Department in Washington. The ladies at the nearby Methodist Church had been a big help too. But her standoff nature made barriers to real friendship. She had learned to knit sox for the boys in uniform, however, at the church on Wednesday mornings. She constantly worried about her only son now in dangerous duty in the Pacific on a submarine. She had written two letters to her uncle, the senator in Washington, to implore him to get Rob duty in Washington without success. She was determined to go to Washington to see her husband as soon as she could travel, but her real purpose was to confront her uncle face to face about Rob.

Molly sat down at the kitchen table as Mary Catherine opened her presents.

"I didn't have time to wrap them, Mrs. Walker."

"That's ok, you know I love these. Let's have a piece of cake now." The fruitcake, enclosed in a tin painted with reindeers and a Santa around the circumference of the tin, had a lid with a wreath of holly and berries. She took the cake out and unwrapped the cellophane. Molly took a knife from the countertop and cut two pieces for them and placed them on two white plates.

Molly said, "Mrs. Walker, could we pray before eating these treats?" Taken a little back, she replied, "Of course." Molly grasped her hand. It felt cold. She prayed, "Lord, we thank you for your goodness to us. Please bless the food and we pray especially for Rob and his father where ever they are in serving our country. Please protect them and may your angels have charge over them. We ask this in Jesus name. Amen." Mary Catherine gently squeezed her hand. Molly looked up, and there were tears in her eyes. She dabbed her eyes with her napkin and said, "I'm OK, thanks for the prayer, I needed that right now." Mrs. Walker made coffee for two, and as they sat at the table, she began to ask what was happening on Miami's campus; *she loves gossip*, Molly thought. As a reporter and one of the editors of *The Miami Student* newspaper, she got some of the inside information about student activities and occasional faculty gossip, so Molly filled her in with some of the choice tidbits. The conversation turned once again to the war and Rob. "Have you heard from him lately?" she asked offhandedly, "I've only had one letter since he returned to Hawaii. He's worried about my health. I didn't tell him; it must have come from his father in Washington. I sent his Christmas presents six weeks ago; I sure hope he gets them before Christmas."

"I sent mine about the same time. I got him an ID bracelet, engraved with his name, Ens. Robert A. Walker, Jr USNR, on the outside and in the little secret compartment under the name, I included a small Bible verse. It said, "The Lord bless you and keep you; and give you peace."

"What a wonderful verse for him Molly. I know he'll appreciate it very much."

Molly didn't tell her what else was inscribed on the underside of the bracelet. It said… "*All my love forever Molly.*"

CHAPTER 18

The Royal Hawaiian

The dance at the O club was over, and Rob and his friends left in Lily's convertible, winding through streets on Hickam Airbase still being repaired due to the attack nearly a year ago. The top was down, and the cool night air was delightful. Kate threw her hands high in the air as an Army Jeep with young officers passed them by giving them the high sign. John said, "How do these junior Army guys get their own Jeep when we Navy guys have to walk?" Later that evening, officers from the *Pompano*, a sub in Rob's squadron, commandeered an Army Jeep parked in front of the Pink Palace with the keys left in it. The sub's captain, Lou Parks, his exec, Slade Cutter, found a rifle in the back seat of the Jeep and went on a drunken spree shooting at street lights, the water tower, and buoys in the harbor before being hauled over by MP's. Their two-hour joy ride almost got them thrown in the "slammer" when the MP's finally caught up with them. They appealed to a high government official, a relative of Parks, who interceded on their behalf, otherwise the *Pompano* would have left on patrol without the culprits, its captain and his executive officer. The incident enhanced the *Pompano's* reputation as the *Hooligans' Navy*.

Lily parked her car a few spaces from the main entrance to the hotel, and as they got out Captain Morrison arrived in a Navy sedan. He thanked the driver, and as he turned to enter the hotel, he saw his two junior officers and their dates about to enter the front door. He hollered at Ensign Walker and Rob, rather startled, came to attention. He didn't salute his captain as naval officers don't salute when they aren't covered with a hat. "Hello Sir," Rob exclaimed. "I'd like you to meet our friends."

After the introductions, Rob said "Would you like to join us for a nightcap Sir?"

"No, I'll take a raincheck. I've had a long evening and didn't even get to the O club to be with you all. Our division commander's staff wanted me to attend a briefing."

"It's just as well sir, Lieutenant Commander Custer showed up rather inebriated and caused a bad scene. So, it was best that you weren't there." Captain Morrison didn't say anything, just shook his head and walked on into the lobby. They followed him, and the Marine guard saluted as they entered the grand lobby. John had a sudden idea. Why not take the girls upstairs and show them their room? Rob was surprised at John's idea. It wasn't quite like him. The only problem: The Marine guard on duty near the stairs was posted to prevent females from getting into the hotel guest rooms. John said he would distract the guard and the others could quietly slip by. Ladies were allowed in the lobby and the bar and restaurant, so John asked the guard to show him where the head was located. Rob and the dates slipped up the stairs without being seen. Their room was on the third floor overlooking the waterfront. It was spartanly furnished but did have a bathroom which the ladies used right away. On the top of the desk were letters from Molly that Rob discreetly managed to put in a drawer while Lily was in the bathroom. Lily came into the room, opened the windows and let the cool night air blowing in from the ocean fill the room. The sound of music from the dance floor could be heard. The band's vocalist was singing, "*Saturday Night is the loneliest night of the week, that's when my baby and I used to dance cheek to cheek.*" John turned the lights off in the room. The moonlight filtered in through the palm trees casting fingers of moving light on the new dance floor. Lily took off her high heels and the couples danced to the lingering sound of the music. Lily drew Rob close, she whispered, "Rob will you stay with me tonight? I need you so." Her dark brown eyes were filled with tears falling on Rob's cheek. He found her request hard to refuse… "Sure" he said softly.

· · · · ·

Hours earlier, Molly Gaynor's Saturday night found her studying for her finals as the semester ended. She had a hard time concentrating. Her spirit was restless. Rob was on her mind all evening. She was worried. She decided to write to Rob. She began:

Dearest Rob,

I miss you so much. It's Saturday night and the night I seem to miss you the most. I tried studying for my finals this evening and just couldn't keep you off my mind. I hope you're ok. I'm doing as well as can be expected without you. I just saw your mother and she is doing better now. She is planning to travel to Washington over the Christmas holidays to see your dad. I think she plans to stay with him for a couple of weeks. Her health is still not what it should be. I try to check in on her every few days. She still has a housekeeper coming once a week. We have a few Christmas decorations this year. Even in the dorms. The war has changed this campus so much. They're talking about closing the Beta house for the duration, or maybe renting it to females, who need rooms now. Old Fisher Hall has been taken over by the Navy for enlisted training. They are teaching men to be cooks and bakers and radiomen. Rumors are floating around, no pun intended, that female Navy enlisted will be coming here to train too. They call them WAVES. Cute name. My brother is in the South Pacific we think. He is in the Marines. One more to worry about. Well, I must close now. I love you so much. Keep safe.

All my love forever, Molly

Remember, Our love is here to stay...

Xxxooooxxxooo

P.S. Ted Lewis and his band canceled Saturday night. Some mix up on dates they said. The Coca-Cola Company sponsors them. They said they would probably have another name band come soon, but you never know these days. Anyway, you'll be pleased to know that the Campus Owls still play every Saturday night at the Huddle! Wouldn't it be wonderful if we could be there this Saturday night? It's my loneliest night of the week.

Here are some clippings from The Oxford Press and the Student. I'm still one of the editors. I 'm trying to find a ride home for Christmas. The B & O has a train scheduled that goes to Lima; dad can pick me up there.

Molly didn't tell him that his mother was still determined to speak with her uncle, the senior senator from Ohio, during Christmas about getting him transferred out of submarines. Nor did she say anything about the handsome sports editor of *The Student* who was 4-F. He tried to enlist in the Marines, but they disqualified him due to a hernia. He was making a play for her.

CHAPTER 19

The Base Chapel
Pearl Harbor

Since the attack on December 7, the Base Chapel services were well attended. The white framed church had a bell displayed outside from one of the early sailing vessels that had explored Hawaii. A young protestant chaplain conducted the Sunday morning service. His sermon based on a text from the Gospel of John, was about the band of brothers, a theme taken from Shakespeare, how dependent we are on each other in a time of crisis. After the benediction, two senior staff officers, both Navy captains, dressed in their summer dress whites, edged closer to the door leading out onto the sidewalk overlooking the harbor. Both officers thanked the minister, a reserve lieutenant commander from Asbury Seminary in Kentucky, and then went outside to chat.

Captain Angus McDougal, the admiral's chief of staff, stood under the shade of the nearby palm trees talking with the senior member of the Board of Inquiry, Captain James Harris. "I shouldn't be saying this Jim since you are the senior member of the Board of Inquiry tomorrow, but I think you should know the admiral's thoughts about this board. The admiral has two things in mind for it to accomplish: one, be fair, and two, be fast. He wants the *Thornfish* back on patrol *with Dick Morrison* in command as soon as the boat is ready for sea. Ben Miller has already interviewed Dick Morrison after his boat arrived at Midway, so he could be challenged for prejudicial judgment if he were called to testify. But the admiral wanted to take that chance. He knows Ben has good judgment." He paused to catch Jim's reaction, and continued, "You know our boss would have relieved Custer anyway for lack of aggressiveness. It's too bad that the incident had to happen." Both captains knew the numbers: as 1942 was ending, some 40 skippers out of 135 were relieved for illness, stress and, as some called it, failures of aggression, another term for poor performance.

Captain Harris said, "You're right Angus, I concur completely. By the way, did you hear about the incident last night at the Hickam O club?"

"No," replied Angus. "Well, there was an altercation with some of the *Thornfish's* officers. Custer was there and had too much to drink and made a scene with the men and their dates. Anyway, cooler heads prevailed, and it didn't get too bad. Shore patrol was not called."

"O.K., well we need to get him assigned elsewhere. You know Custer has some good attributes. He is a good trainer, but he was educated in the old school; he is like some of the academy CO's in his year group. They were trained to be too damned cautious."

"I know only too well; the Germans have the same problem. Admiral Donitz fired their senior commanders. Now our intelligence services say the oldest German submarine captain is 28."

· · · · ·

At 0845 Monday morning Rob, dressed in his service dress whites, stood outside the hotel waiting for the Jeep to take him to the submarine base. As he waited, he thought about his latest encounter with the lovely Lily. Saturday night had been something else. He awoke Sunday morning in Lily's small bed, staring at the ceiling. At first, he didn't realize where he was. Lily was gone, but the smell of bacon cooking drifted into the room from the kitchen where she was busy preparing breakfast. Rob arose and stopped at the kitchen door and admired her. She was standing at the range, dressed only in her pajama tops. He softly crept up behind her and enfolded her in his arms. She turned and kissed him, "Hi, sleepy head." She said. "I was about ready to hold reveille for you. Come and sit down and have some coffee. After breakfast, we can make love again."

"Lily you're wearing me out." She seemed insatiable. The night left little sleep for Rob. "I'm going to have to spend the rest of my R & R just resting up!"

"You're funny. Sit down. How do you like your eggs?" They ate on the lanai. She had set Noritake China plates on the white-glass-topped wicker dining table. The view was marvelous, but the view of Lily was even better. In the distance, they could see Navy vessels moving in the channel accompanying a Navy carrier. Rob noticed a large telescope on a tripod on the end of the veranda. "Is that your telescope?" he asked. "No, it was my father's. He loved to sit here and watch the planes taking off from Ford Island where he once worked." Rob glanced at his watch. It was almost ten o'clock. He needed to get back to the hotel, but Lily started asking questions about the embarrassing encounter last night. She wanted to know more about *Thornfish's* former Commanding Officer. What was he like? Why was he so mean? Rob explained that the captain had become ill during the patrol and had to be relieved by the executive officer. It was done in accordance with Navy Regulations. But the captain is fighting it, and the Board of Inquiry is to determine if the proper action was taken.

"And you're going to have to testify tomorrow, correct?"

"Possibly, I'm not sure yet. I must be ready and be at the sub base by ten."

"Are you going to pick up your mother soon?" Rob asked. He reminded Lily that her mother had left a note for her to pick her up at one o'clock. She nodded. Rob chuckled, "You'd better take me back to the Royal before you pick her up."

"Rob, I'd like you to meet my mom. She is a great lady. You'd like her."

"I'm sure I would. I bet she is a beautiful woman too. Maybe we can meet before we deploy. Could we have dinner with her some evening?"

"I suppose," Lily replied with little enthusiasm in her voice. Rob asked, "Don't you have to work this evening?"

"Yes, I'm afraid so. I'd rather be with you. We have so little time left."

Rob showered and dressed while Lily cleaned the dishes. He made the bed while Lily showered and put on a short white dress. As they were about to leave, a car pulled up in the driveway. Lily went into the living room and looked out the front window. "Oh No! Rob, it's mom!" she cried.

Valerie Edmonds got out of the black Lincoln sedan and thanked the driver for bringing her home. She had worked for a Japanese-Hawaiian family for the past six months doing light housework and cooking Japanese meals. Even though her clients were born in Hawaii, being of Japanese descent made them suspect of being either spies or at least Japanese sympathizers. Heiro, her employer, a wealthy executive manufacturing shoes for the Islanders, had tried to obtain orders for military shoes but was turned down for no apparent reason.

Lily was frozen with fear. Her first impulse was to have Rob hide in her bedroom. But Rob had to get back to the hotel. What to do? Her composure returned as she made up her mind. "I'm going to introduce you, Rob. We are going to have a second breakfast here, that's all. Ok? Please go to the kitchen and get a cup of coffee. I'll handle Mother."

Valerie Edmonds put her key in the lock and opened the door. She was surprised to see Lily standing in the hallway. "Hi Honey. I got off a little early, and my employer had his driver take me home, saving you a trip."

"Thanks, mom." Lily blushed, "Come in I want you to meet someone."

"What? Don't tell me that you've got a man here now?"

"Yes, he's a friend from the hotel. I invited him for a late breakfast. He is an ensign in submarines whom I met recently."

"He's here for breakfast? I hope that's all he wants," she said emphatically. Rob was in the kitchen pouring himself a cup of coffee. He was about to sit down when Lily and her mother entered the room. Lily said, "Mom, this is Ensign Robert Walker from the USS *Thornfish*." He stood and extended his hand, "Mrs. Edmonds, I'm pleased to meet you, ma'am." Somehow her apprehension melted a bit when she took his hand. She said, "Please sit down. May I call you Robert?"

"Sure. Or Rob, everybody does. My fraternity brothers called me dummy." She laughed, "You're no dummy, why?" she asked. "Well because I was an honors student, I guess. Anyway, it was in fun."

Valerie Edmonds was born in Nagoya, Japan, and orphaned when she was eight years old. Catholic nuns eventually raised her in Nagoya, where every student had to take English as a second language. After graduating from high school, she found work with the Noritake China Company. Her first job was painting the gold edges on plates as they spun around on turntables. During tours of the factory, customers would often see the girls placing decals on the plates before firing. Tourists would ask, "I thought your Noritake China was hand painted." The guide would reply, "Yes, they are, see?" The guide pointed to the girls painting the gold strip on the edges of the plate as they spun around.

Valerie's striking beauty, intelligence and language ability eventually landed her a job in sales. After several years she was sent to Honolulu, Hawaii, to represent their interests in Japanese dinnerware. She met Frank Edmonds, her future husband, when he was a petty officer assigned to the aviation department on Ford Island. It was love at first sight. After they married, she quit her job when Kaga, Lily's middle name, was born. Her upbringing in the orphanage made her both a tough competitor and a strong Catholic. But as tough as she was, she wasn't prepared to lose her husband on December 7. He was about to retire, but the winds of war interrupted their plans to settle in Honolulu in their new home overlooking the harbor. Frank, against her better judgment, decided to reenlist in November for four more years and was assigned to the USS *Arizona*. After the attack, Val was unable to find work; she finally turned to maid service for some of the Japanese-Americans she knew. Lily became a waitress at the Royal Hawaiian Hotel. Between the two of them, they could make ends meet. Fortunately, both the house and the car that Frank dearly loved would be paid off when the government check arrived. Congress authorized ten thousand dollars to be paid to the next of kin of those in the military killed in combat.

"Well Rob, you look hungry. I'm going to fix your breakfast. How do you like your eggs? Rob and Lily joined by her mom, had breakfast on the lanai, his second breakfast of the morning. Mrs. Edmonds wanted to know all about his service in subs. Were you ever depth charged? Rob looked uncomfortable, and Lily interjected, "Mom he can't discuss operations, its secret you know."

"I'm sorry, I should know better. My husband had secrets too that he would never share."

Rob said, "He must have been a fine man."

"He was, and he was so handsome. He loved the Navy. I desperately wanted him to retire, but he knew that war with Japan was coming soon and wanted to help." She paused and held back a sob and then spoke to Lily in Japanese. "I like him. He's so good-looking, and he seems like a real gentleman. Where did you meet him?" Rob smiled at Lily. He understood.

After his late second breakfast, Lily drove Rob back to the hotel. On the way, she said, "Rob, mom likes you. You were so nice to her. I know you'll be busy this next week. Do you think you could squeeze in a bit of time for dinner with us some evening? We could do it at the hotel."

"Sure, I'll try, how about Wednesday night?" She kissed him saying sayonara, goodbye in Japanese, put the Chevy in gear and pulled away from the curb. Rob entered the lobby and checked his mail. There was a letter in the room key box. He took it and his key and went up the stairs two at a time. Once in his room, he took off his clothes and flopped on the bed. He started to open the envelope but fell asleep before he could read the first line of his father's letter. Rob was exhausted. Lily was wearing him out. He needed rest.

Across town, Sunday afternoon, Lieutenant Commander J.J. Custer USN was meeting with his counsel in his home at Ewa Beach officers' housing. They needed to go over last-minute details about the meeting the next morning. The home assigned to him when he first reported for duty as commanding officer of the *Thornfish,* was a three-bedroom bungalow right on the waterside of the complex. LT Marvin Cohen, a young reserve lieutenant, appointed to represent him during the Board of Inquiry's inquiry, was right out of Stanford University Law School. Custer disliked reservists, especially Jewish ones, but was resigned to the fact that there was no alternative for him. His counsel had been allowed to read the report of the *Thornfish's* two-month patrol but could not take notes due to its secret classification. The paragraphs about his client's relief were disturbing to the young legal officer. After reading it, he knew that there wasn't much of a chance for him to be believed. But after hours of discussion, it became clear to him that all Custer, a very virulent man, wanted was vengeance. Custer confided to him that he gave LT Morrison a barely satisfactory fitness report on his last annual appraisal. It would be a career killer for any future advancement. His counsel thought that should be enough retribution. He wondered, *why fight for more?* After three cups of coffee, he finally said "Commander, I think the crux of the matter is the state of your physical and mental condition at the time of and leading up to your relief. Much will depend on the medical department's testimony but especially that of the pharmacist mate on board the *Thornfish*."

"Well, they had me doped up."

"They?" Custer's eyes narrowed, "Yes, the XO and the pharmacist mate. Well, I mean Morrison... he had the pharmacist dope me up, over my strenuous objections. They kept me from preparing for the attack and during the attack."

"Are you prepared to testify that Morrison deliberately conspired to take over command of the *Thornfish*?"

"Absolutely!"

CHAPTER 20

The Board of Inquiry

Monday morning Rob rose early and descended the stairs to the dining room for some eggs and bacon. He was hungry. On the way to the dining room, he met Captain Morrison on the stairway. He said, "Rob, are you ready for the big day? "

"Yes, sir, I don't know if I'll be needed, but I'll be there."

"Good, you can ride with me. The Navy Jeep will be here at 0900 to take us to the conference room at the sub base. Uniform will be summer whites."

"Yes sir, thanks for the ride. We're all pulling for you."

"Thanks, it will work out for the best I'm sure."

Rob returned to his room after breakfast, showered and sat on the edge of his bed and opened the latest letter from Molly. Toward the end of her letter, she said,

"You know something tells me that you need prayer. I pray for you daily, and your shipmates, but something is prompting me to pray for you more earnestly. In fact, I have been fasting too. (And I could lose a little weight too!) I hope you're ok. Please let me know as soon as possible. Father Tom has had some great sermons lately. The little church is still packed out every Sunday. One year ago, we were at peace. What a difference a year makes. The Navy has invaded Oxford. We have more sailors arriving every day for training as radio operators. Some are cute too. They have a sentry station near the entrance to Fisher Hall with Navy guards 24 hours a day. (They need to keep the girls away!!) A new display board is being constructed on the town square uptown with the names of all the locals in the military. Your name is on it too! I mailed your little Christmas present four weeks ago. I hope you receive it before Christmas. Please help make this war end soon. I love you so very much.

Your sweetheart who's still sitting under the apple tree waiting for you to come home.

Love and kisses. Molly. I pray for you every day XO XO XO

PS Don't forget... Our love is here to stay!"

Rob laid down on the bed and thought how do I deserve such a sweetheart? I am so rotten.

The Jeep arrived at the hotel promptly at 0900. The Marine driver saluted smartly, and Rob got in the rear seat and Captain Morrison sat in the front passenger seat. The Jeep wound through downtown Honolulu and then onto Highway 1 to the Naval Base. Twenty minutes later they were ushered into the Flag Officers' Wardroom where a mess attendant filled cups of fresh hot black coffee and offered them sweet rolls. Rob looked over the admiral's wardroom and admired its nice furnishings, not luxurious, but not spartan like the *Thornfish's* that could be turned into an operating room at a moment's notice. This is the way the brass lives, what a way to fight a war. About 0945 Commander Ben Miller came in and greeted the officers and asked them to accompany him to the conference room where the inquiry would be held. In the hallway outside, Chief O'Neil was waiting patiently along with Pharmacists Mate Jenkins, and the Quartermaster Mitchell. They looked sharp in their starched white uniforms. They rose to attention as the new *Thornfish's* captain approached. He greeted them warmly, and they sat down in hardback chairs outside the conference room waiting to testify if called. As witnesses, they were excluded from the Board of Inquiry's room and had to wait until called.

Rob joined them taking a seat alongside Chief O'Neil. "How's your R&R going sir?" asked the chief.

"OK chief, but I have to tell you I need to get back to sea. I need a rest!"

"Sounds like you've had a great time. But you'll be taking your qualification test at sea next week, won't you?"

"I'm going to try if they think I'm ready." Chief O'Neil said, "You are ready sir, I have seen a lot of officers going through their qualifications, and you are going to do fine."

Lieutenant Morrison, accompanied by Division Chief of Staff Ben Miller, entered the conference room. A long table covered with green cloth typical of those in every wardroom of every Navy ship occupied the end of the room. Three chairs were placed on the table. In front were nameplates of the three board members. On the right side of the room was a small table where LCDR Custer had already been seated. He gave a slight Mona Lisa smile and nodded at Dick Morrison. Beside him was his legal counsel, LT Marvin C. Cohen USNR. On the left side of the room was a table reserved for LT Morrison. In between, in the middle of the room, a small table and chair were already occupied by the Recorder, a Navy lieutenant commander, who would serve as the government's representative. Beside him sat a Navy yeoman stenographer. A Navy steward was placing a small podium facing the three members of the board. Ben took a chair at the rear of the room. Just then someone shouted, 'attention on deck', as the three officers comprising the members of the Board of Inquiry, entered the room. They immediately stood behind the large green covered table, and the senior member said, "Please take your seats gentleman." The senior member, Captain James Harris, introduced himself and the two other members of the board, Captain Eli Zimmer, and Commander Stephen Lunsford. All three officers had Dolphins above their ribbons and had commanded submarines.

Captain Harris introduced the board's Recorder, LCDR Arnold Lytle USN, from the legal office, Naval Base Pearl Harbor. He then read the instructions from Commander Submarines Pacific Fleet authorizing the board and its purpose.

He put the paper down and said, "Gentlemen this is a Board of Inquiry. No judicial punishment will be rendered. This board is simply to inquire into the facts about the relief of command during a combat situation wherein LCDR John J. Custer, USN, commanding the USS *Thornfish*, was relieved by the executive officer of the USS *Thornfish*, LT Richard M. Morrison USN. Lieutenant Commander Custer has made some very serious charges about his being relieved that need to be heard and evaluated. LT Morrison is named as the Respondent in this investigation. *We will determine whether his actions were justified.* The results and any recommendations resulting from the inquiry will be forwarded to the convening authority for his action.

Dick Morrison, sitting alone, felt a pang in his stomach, something he had not experienced even when he had been depth charged.

Captain Harris consulted with his board and then continued, "For the record, please note that the two parties to this investigation are present this morning. It also should be noted that Commander Custer has counsel to represent him." He glanced down at his notes and read, "LT Marvin C. Cohen, USNR, legal officer staff COMSUBPAC. It is also noted that LT Morrison, the Respondent, does not have counsel. "

He looked directly at Dick Morrison, "Lieutenant, these proceeding may be adversarial; are you aware you are entitled to counsel?"

Dick replied, "Yes sir, I am aware of that, and I choose not to."

"Very well." Then addressing the entire assembly, he said, "This inquiry will undoubtedly have information of a sensitive security nature. Therefore, I am ordering the information contained in today's session of this board be classified as Secret. Is everyone *in this room* cleared for at least Secret Security Classification? If so, please stand state your name and your current security clearance," He turned to the Recorder and said, "Commander Lytle proceed to log each one in the record." After logging each officer in the minutes of the meeting, the Senior Member administered the oath to both parties to this investigation by saying, "Do you swear, or affirm, that the testimony you are about to give is the truth and the whole truth so help you, God?"

LT Morrison, with his right hand raised, replied, "I do." Commander Custer said, "I do."

Captain Harris directed the Recorder to proceed. The Recorder in Boards of Inquiry is a senior legal officer and represents the Navy in the proceedings. He began by reading the message from the *Thornfish* received by headquarters on October 25, 1942. It read,

> *Thornfish*, SS 499, attacked an enemy convoy of four ships, consisting of a troop transport, a tanker, and two escorts apparently en route Saipan, 24 October 1942, at 1900 local time, Lat.15 deg. 30'N, long. 142 deg. 40' E. *Thornfish* sank 8000-ton troop transport. Fired two MK 14 torpedoes at the tanker with a track angle of 60 degrees from 900 yards and made hits with both but did not explode. While *Thornfish* was undergoing repeated depth charge attacks, the tanker proceeded independently on course estimate 030. Speed 15 knots. *Thornfish* heavily damaged and before surfacing fired two Mk-14 torpedoes and sank an oncoming destroyer. While commencing torpedo action on the convoy, it became necessary to relieve Captain LCDR J. J. Custer USN, due to medical reasons in accordance with Navy Regulations, Article 1088. LT Richard Morrison, USN, relieved the captain at approximately 1845 local time and placed him on the sick list for medical reasons. Proceeding to Midway for repairs anticipate ETA dawn 31 October. Request immediate medical assistance upon arrival for LCDR Custer and assistance with a Japanese prisoner. Richard Morrison LT USN Commanding.

The Recorder asked that the message be entered in the minutes of the inquiry. "Affirmative without objection." Captain Harris ordered. There was one: Custer's counsel objected to the words: for medical reasons and being put on the sick list.

"So noted," added the senior member. Commander Lytle then asked permission to read and enter into the record Article 1088 Navy Regulations relief of a Commanding Officer by a Subordinate. Again, "So ordered without objection." Commander Lytle read in a deliberate and steady voice:

> **Art. 1088. 1. It is conceivable that most unusual and extraordinary circumstances may arise in which the relief from duty of a commanding officer by a subordinate becomes necessary, either by placing the commanding officer under arrest or on the sick list. Such action shall never be taken without the approval of the Commandant of the Marine Corps or the Chief of Naval Personnel, as appropriate or the senior officer present, except when a reference to such higher authority is undoubtedly impracticable because of the delay involved or for clearly obvious reasons."**

He then called the first witness, LT Morrison.

"Sir, would you please state your name for the record and give your account of the events leading up to the relief of the Captain of the *Thornfish*? Remember you are under oath."

LT Morrison then began an account of the principal events culminating in the relief of the Captain. "The situation developed over a period during this our second patrol under the command of Lieutenant Commander Custer. In several attack situations, the captain became very agitated. His demeanor worsened during some approaches to enemy ships, especially where destroyer escorts were present. He would show great personal stress often leaving the periscope exposed longer than he should have, endangering the ship. It seemed to me that he had panic attacks; his face would be contorted, heavy sweat, hands locked on the handles of the periscope. His commands would be inaudible. His voice was interrupted by Custer's counsel, "I object sir," directing his remarks to the members of the board, "LT Morrison is giving personal suppositions, without facts of the tactical situation."

Captain Harris replied, "Well that's what we asked for, his personal recollections of events leading up to the incident. The tactical considerations will be covered later I'm sure. Proceed, Mr. Morrison." Dick Morrison's composure was calm as he told the board the story leading up to the incident in combat on 24 October. He related, "Before the attack on the convoy, the captain made several bad decisions. Just before the attack Captain Custer changed the battle plan. We had previously agreed that the exec would man the attack periscope giving target angle, bearings and ranges to the attack team and Captain Custer would serve as approach officer. The reason for this was that in prior attempts at attacking enemy ships the captain often froze and would leave the periscope up too long." Across the room, Commander Custer's eyes widened and were staring daggers at his former XO. His fists were clenched as if he were in a prize fight. At the word *froze* he started to get up, and only the strong arm of his counsel held him in check. Unaware of this, LT Morrison continued his testimony. "This endangered *Thornfish* and happened again in this situation. The urgent message we received from Headquarters designated this convoy as very important, and we planned to attack aggressively.

"During this time the captain seemed to me to have something like a seizure. His hands were trembling, his countenance distraught, and commands almost inaudible. I immediately removed his hands from the periscope handles and said that I would make the observations for him, but when he suddenly ordered deep submergence, I relieved him and countermanded his diving orders. He protested vehemently. I had to order the chief of the boat to lead him below, and I ordered the pharmacist mate to attend him. We then resumed the attack without the captain's assistance. Later, when time permitted, I placed the captain on the sick list and had the quartermaster record an entry in the ship's log that I relieved Captain Custer in accordance with Article 1088, Navy Regulations, and that he was placed on the ship's sick list. I ordered a guard placed at his stateroom in the event he needed assistance. The pharmacist mate administered a shot of sedative to the captain to calm him. During this time, the crew of *Thornfish* performed with extraordinary courage and professionalism, sinking the enemy troop ship and putting two torpedoes amidships of the tanker that failed to explode. After enduring one of the most severe depth charge attacks during our patrol, *Thornfish* was forced to surface, but first, we sank one of the destroyers with a shot of two Mark-14's right down his bow."

The board and the other party to the investigation were held in rapt attention to every word of the story being related by LT Morrison. Dick paused and took a drink of water. Captain Harris said. "Lieutenant Morrison do you have anything further to relate regarding this incident?"

Dick glanced at Commander Custer and said, "Yes sir." And then he continued. "What I am about to tell you I do so reluctantly. But it is important to know what went on before my relieving him. A few hours after receiving the dispatch from COMSUBPAC, I went below to check on the captain, as he was not present with our tactical team planning our strategy. I found him in bed in his stateroom with a 45 semi-automatic pistol beside him in his bed and some small empty bottles of bourbon whiskey scattered on the deck, the kind we sometimes distributed to the crew after being depth charged. I was afraid that he was considering suicide, and I immediately took the gun from him and unloaded it. I said, "Captain, what the hell is going on? You scared the shit out of me." Captain Custer said, "Dick I don't know if I can handle this much longer." I said, "Captain, suicide is no way to handle this." At this, Mr. Cohen stood up and was about to object, and the Recorder prevented him and said for him to let LT Morrison finish his testimony. Dick said, "Thank you, sir, I'm about finished." He continued, "About this time, Ensign Walker, our assistant TDC operator, was in the passageway and hearing the commotion, came by and observed the captain and me. I ordered him to get the pharmacist on the double and cautioned him not to say a word to anyone about this. I took the gun and placed it in my safe and put the empty bottles in my room. The pharmacist examined the captain, took his blood pressure and temperature and gave him a shot of sedative. The captain remained asleep for the rest of the day. He awoke upon hearing the call for general quarters, battle stations torpedo. When he came into the conning tower, the crew was shocked at his appearance. He was not himself. He looked terrible. His hands were shaking. Everyone knew something was wrong. I again had the medic come and check on him. The captain refused, however, insisting he was all right. In my judgment, he was not well, but I did not act until the situation was in extremis. That's about it, sir." LT Morrison returned to his table and sat down.

During a Board of Inquiry, the Recorder acts somewhat as a prosecutor but not as an adversary as in courts-martial. Lieutenant Commander Lytle 's job was to be more of a facilitator, to probe to gain as much information as possible for the board. He turned to Custer's counsel and said, "do you have any questions of the witness?" Cohen stood erect, "Yes, sir but first I'd like to make a statement, if I may, on behalf of my client."

"Proceed."

Custer's counsel moved to the podium. "As a preface to my questions, I'd like to read from a guidebook to the naval service compiled by our ally, the Royal Navy. These words apply *to any Navy* and anyone in command. I quote, "The captain carries the ultimate responsibility for every word spoken by and for every action of an individual on board his ship. He also has the most immediate responsibility for her safety and war efficiency. For conduct in war, he is guided by the Articles of War, which enjoins that he shall 'use his utmost exertion to bring his ship into action and during such action, in his own person, encourages his inferior officers and men to fight courageously.'" Then he paused, for emphasis and continued the quotation, "Here you will see that two of his responsibilities the safety of his ship and the taking of her into action, must be balanced one against the other."

Custer's lawyer moved across the room with his notes in hand and stood directly in front of Lieutenant Morrison. In a loud stentorian tone, he said, "Mr. Morrison do you believe that the captain of a naval vessel must be held responsible for the safety of the ship?"

"Yes, certainly."

"Did Commander Custer ever say to you that you were going to get us killed?"

"Yes,"

"How many times would you say he said that?"

Dick gripped the edges of his table and looked directly at the board and said, "On several occasions."

"Do you believe that Captain Custer had the safety of *Thornfish* as his primary responsibility?"

"Yes. But as you just read the captain is to put his vessel in action with the enemy and to fight courageously." Counsel consulted his notes and continued saying, "LT Morrison, you have made several remarks in your testimony that Captain Custer needed medical attention. Have you been trained as a Doctor of Medicine? Have you any expertise to make an intelligent decision about the medical condition of the captain of the *Thornfish*?"

"No."

"In your testimony, you read from Article 1088 of Navy Regulations. During the patrol had you read these words *before* the 24th of October?"

"Yes, but only for information if it ever became necessary."

"But isn't it true that you had planned all along to take advantage of the relief of a Commanding Officer by a subordinate to take command from LCDR Custer? Did the crew look upon you as the real commanding officer of the *Thornfish*? Did you ever comment during a depth charge attack that *you* had a plan of escape?"

"Yes, I did one time during a severe depth charge attack, but I never had any plans to take command from the captain. You'll have to ask the crew about their regard for me. I did all I could to always support the captain. It was only during the heat of combat when he failed to command that I had to take the action I did. I am solely responsible. My medical training is limited to that of first aid that all of us are trained for. But I have common sense, and if you look sick, act sick, and the medic says you're sick, you are sick, and if bad enough then you need medical help. That was the case in this instance."

Custer's counsel stared at his notes for a long time and finally said, "That's all for now."

The next witness called was Ensign Robert A. Walker, USNR.

As he entered the room, he made an impressive appearance. His lanky frame was dressed in a crisp white uniform; blond hair clipped in a burr and cool blue eyes with facial features that hinted strongly of intelligence. He paused, waiting for instructions, as the Recorder directed him to the podium and whispered where he should stand. He then said so everyone could hear, "Raise your right hand, Ensign Walker, do you swear or affirm, to tell the truth, and the whole truth, so help you, God?" Rob replied in an equally loud voice, "I do." The Recorder took his seat and asked, "First of all, are you cleared for Secret?"

"No sir, I haven't received my formal clearance yet, I think they must be a running a little behind schedule." That brought a few chuckles from the board. He looked at LT Morrison and added, "But I have a temporary one from my commanding officer."

"Ok, we'll work around that for now. Please tell the board what you saw on the day the captain of the *Thornfish* was indisposed in his stateroom."

"Well, I was getting ready to go on watch and had stopped in my room to get some foul weather gear when I heard some shouting coming from the captain's stateroom. I ran over and found the executive officer standing in the captain's doorway with a pistol in his hand."

"Please describe what happened."

"Well, I saw the captain lying in his bunk, with some empty little whiskey bottles on the deck by his bed. Our exec was standing there holding a handgun, I think it was a 45.

"What did you do?"

"LT Morrison told me to get the pharmacist mate on the double, and that the captain was ill. And he told me not to say anything about it to anyone"

"What happened then?"

"Well, I got the medic and returned to the captain's cabin where the XO was still trying to talk to the captain."

"Was the captain coherent?" Rob replied that he wasn't sure, and that the medic was attending him. "What did the medic do then?"

"Well, he checked his pulse, took his blood pressure with the cuff thing and his temperature. I think he then gave him a shot of something. That seemed to calm him down."

"You mean the captain was agitated? "

"Well I believe so sir."

"All right let's move on. After the combat with the Jap convoy the next day, what was the situation in the wardroom? I mean about the captain being relieved."

"Well the exec, no I mean the new captain, called a meeting of all officers, chiefs and leading petty officers, not on watch, in the wardroom. It was crowded, some stood in the passageway. The wardroom was full of excitement over the results of the very successful attack on the enemy convoy. Captain Morrison appeared and took a seat at the head of the table. We could see that he was troubled. It was unusual for him."

"What did he say?"

"Well as I recall, he said something about what had happened was unprecedented in the U.S. Navy Submarine Service. He read from his message to Pearl Harbor that he had sent regarding the results of the attack on the Jap convoy and relief of Captain Custer, and then he read from an article in Navy Regs regarding the relief of a Commanding Officer by a subordinate. The thing I remember most was that he sincerely believed that LCDR Custer had a serious medical condition most likely brought on by the stress of combat. He said he had to relieve him and put him on the sick list. He said he acted without reservation or prompting by anyone on board. He said it was his responsibility alone and that he would have to answer for it later most likely by a Board of Inquiry. He added that some of us might be asked to testify and if we were asked, we were just to tell the truth. That's about it, sir."

"Thank you, ensign." Turning to Custer's counsel, he said, "Do you have questions of the witness?" "Yes," replied the counsel. "Proceed." Lieutenant Cohen got up slowly and walked over to the center of the room near where Rob was standing. He held a yellow legal tablet in his right hand and waved it as if he had a knife in his hand. He appeared to have a list of questions for the young ensign.

He began by asking Rob some rapid-fire questions about how long he had been in the Navy, how long aboard the *Thornfish*, had he ever had medical training, and what his station was in general quarters. And finally, as assistant TDC operator, counsel asked: "Were you present in the conning tower during the time Captain Custer was relieved?" Rob said, "Affirmative sir," thinking all this line of questioning was leading up to some crucial question for him to answer. "How would you describe the captain?" Rob turned and looked directly at his former CO, "Well, sir, when I first saw him come up the ladder, Captain Custer I mean, he looked terrible. He didn't say anything to any of us, just went over and stood by the periscope and ordered periscope depth. I remember his hands were really shaking." LT. Cohen moved closer to Rob and said, "What happened next?" Rob thought *he is trying to make me uncomfortable*. "Well, I was pretty busy cranking in some estimated target data in the Target Data Computer from sonar and waiting for direct bearings and ranges when the captain raised the periscope. There was some confusion in who was making the approach and who was doing the periscope observations. We all thought the XO was going to do the periscope. That was the plan." The Recorder interjected with a question of his own. "Why, the XO? Shouldn't the captain be doing that?" Rob paused in thought and looked at LT Morrison, and then said, "Yes, but in the past attacks on the enemy, Captain Custer tended to freeze and leave the scope up too long and failed to give us the information we needed to generate target data." Suddenly Custer jumped up and yelled, "That's a lie! I keep hearing that I froze. I never froze, I was just cautious in getting proper data. Don't listen to this 90-day wonder. He doesn't know a god-damned thing. Never even went to sub school, he's not qualified, and this fraternity boy is telling you what I did wrong... a commander who was standing OOD watches when he was in diapers. For Pete's sake."

At that, the senior member slammed his coffee cup down, coffee spilling on the papers in front of him. A little embarrassed he said, "Well I don't have a gavel, but I'll have no more outbursts of this kind. You will get time to present your side of this, in the meantime, sit down Mr. Custer!" His counsel arose and said, "Sir, may we have a recess please?"

"Granted. Fifteen minutes."

. . . . .

Everyone stood at attention as the board members filed out of the conference room. Ensign Walker was shaken. Custer stomped out of the room glaring at Rob. Rob took a chair in the back of the room where Commander Ben Miller was seated. They didn't talk for a minute or so, and finally Ben said, "Let me get you a glass of water." Rob wiped his brow with his handkerchief, and said, "Thanks I could use some sir." Ben Miller, Chief of Staff of his division, was very impressed with this young reserve officer. His record, even in the short time he had been aboard the *Thornfish*, was impressive. He had approved a nomination from LT Morrison to have him awarded the Bronze

Star with Combat V for his action with the downed Jap scout plane and another award of the Navy Commendation Medal for his efforts in controlling the flooding of the forward torpedo room on *Thornfish*. He would want Rob on any submarine in the Pacific Fleet. He handed Rob a glass of ice water and said, "Rob you're doing fine, remember what your CO said, "Just tell the truth."

When the board re-entered the room, the assembled officers stood until the senior member, Captain Harris, said, "Take your seats. I want to remind everyone that this is a Board of Inquiry and not a tavern; we'll have no more outbursts. Counsel resume your questioning of the witness."

Custer's counsel then asked Rob, "You're still under oath, ensign, I want to go back to your statement that the captain froze. In your vast experience, how long should a commander take in periscope observations? Rob caught his implication of *vast experience*, "Well sir, my experience is limited to my training on *Thornfish*. Captain Custer was a good instructor. And our boat, I was told, was one of the best trained submarines the evaluators had observed. During our training under Captain Custer, before going on our patrol, he would insist on the briefest observations when closing in and tracking a target. He required ten seconds for the initial check and then just up and dip on subsequent ones." Counsel didn't like his answer but continued "Now tell the board how long it took when Captain Custer, to use your term, froze?"

"Sir, Captain Morrison would be the best person to answer that question." Cohen frowned and said, "But you made the statement, so you should have some recollections of the events you referred to, now please tell the board." Rob gripped his hands firmly on the podium, "Well sir, after the first few incidents, I started watching the clock on the TDC. One time he had it exposed over 60 seconds, and finally, the exec had to take his hands off the scope and lower it. The captain's hands were trembling and sweaty, and he mumbled his commands. He was shaken especially when escorts were pinging their sonar. In more than one attempted attack, the XO had to take charge of the attack itself. A good example of what I am saying was the attack we made on the crippled cruiser and its escorts. I'm sure our patrol report will verify some of what I just said." Counsel was very upset by Rob's last remarks. He looked at his notes and said, "I have no further questions of this witness."

Custer's face was ashen; his hands started trembling. He took a drink of water and whispered something to his counsel. He started to rise from his chair, and his counsel held onto his arm; he sat down. LT Morrison sat at his table, poker-faced, staring at the ceiling fan overhead. As Rob left the room, Commander Miller, the Chief of Staff, gave him a hidden thumbs up.

During the next hour, the Recorder called as a witness, Chief O'Neil, the chief of the boat, and the pharmacist mate who attended Custer on board the *Thornfish*. Chief

O'Neil related his duties aboard the submarine and the morale of the crew while on patrol. When asked how the crew responded to LT Morrison as executive officer, he gave a very favorable report. The crew he said, loved him and would do anything for him. By contrast, LCDR Custer seemed distant and unsure of himself especially during combat situations, but he was a good trainer and ran a taut ship. He was a slave driver doing exercise after exercise until we had it right. He insisted on perfection and made everyman on board know his stuff before going on patrol. O'Neil said he had served on several submarines, including the *Squalus*, and the *Thornfish* was the best-trained sub he had ever been on. But the crew was dismayed by the lack of aggressiveness in pursuing the enemy ships they had encountered.

The pharmacist mate Jenkins recently promoted to second-class petty officer, gave a riveting testimony of the captain's mental and physical problems. He noted that the captain seemed depressed and he treated him for periods of insomnia. He supplied him with sleeping pills and occasionally medicinal whiskey. He noted that the captain had lost a lot of weight while on patrol. He had high blood pressure, and he cautioned the captain to limit his salt intake. The Recorder stood and asked several questions of the witness. "Please describe the scene when you were ordered by Ensign Walker to report to the captain's stateroom on the double."

"Well sir, I found Captain Custer lying in his bunk with the exec standing by him, and there were some small bottles of medicinal whiskey on the deck beside his bunk.

"Were they empty?"

"Yes, sir."

"How many would you say?"

"I'm not sure, probably three or four."

"How did you treat him?" The petty officer methodically described how he took his temperature, blood pressure, listened to his heart with a stethoscope and then stepped out into the passageway and discussed his findings with the exec. "Who decided to administer a sedative?" Asked Commander Lytle. "We both did. We were hesitant but the captain was in dire need of a sedative to relax him. He was extremely agitated."

The Recorder asked one final question of the Petty Officer Jenkins. "How long after you administered the sedative did the captain return to duty?" The petty officer did not reply right away. He thought about it and finally replied, "I'd say about eight hours. The ship's log should provide the time he came into the conning tower though." The recorder made some notes and then asked. "In your opinion, how long would the effects of the sedative you administered last?"

"I'm not sure sir, it would depend on the amount given, the individual's weight, food consumed, etc. But I think probably about 12 hours max."

"Did you examine him then to see if he was recovered from his meds?

"The XO had me check him in the conning tower after he had arrived, and we were at torpedo battle stations. He looked bad. His eyes were sunken; he was tired. He was perspiring and seemed confused to me. I did not get a chance to check his vitals as we were ready for battle.

The Recorder consulted his notes and said, "I have no further questions."

The senior member looked at the clock and said, "It's almost noon, we'll adjourn for lunch and resume at 1400 with the testimony of Lieutenant Commander Custer. After his testimony, I have asked the Recorder to read a summary statement from the medical department on Midway and at submarine base Pearl Harbor as to their evaluation of LCDR Custer. I'd like to wrap this up by 1600. I remind everyone not to discuss the proceedings of this inquiry with anyone outside of those in this room." All stood as the members cleared the room.

Rob decided not to talk with anyone during lunch. He wandered over to the O club and took lunch cafeteria style. He ordered a cheeseburger with mustard and a Coke and sat alone at a table by the window overlooking the sub base. He could see the *Thornfish* with a crane hovered over it installing a new surface radar. He would go down and check on the progress tomorrow if possible. His new captain was giving him a new assignment. He was to be the electronics officer as a collateral part of his duties as ships communicator. He hoped that this trial would be over, and he would not have to testify any further. But regardless, he would have to wait in the hallway in case he was called to answer more questions. He decided not to waste his time. He found some stationery at the O Club with their letterhead and decided he'd write Molly and his parents while waiting.

In the senior officers' dining room, Dick Morrison and his boss Ben Miller sat at a table covered with a white tablecloth; each plate set with napkins and silverware. They each ordered from a menu and recorded their selection on a small tablet with the Commander Pacific Fleet Submarines' logo printed at the top. They didn't discuss the hearing. Their conversation centered on the *Thornfish's* repairs and the preparations for getting the boat ready for combat. There would be 17 new personnel on board replacing crew members who had been ordered to new constructions or repair crews. Training was key to the success and safety of everyone on board. Each man depended on the other for their very lives on a submarine, especially so in combat. One mistake could sink the ship. LT Morrison was extremely anxious to get back into the fray. Ben Miller said that they had lost five submarines in the past few months. He confided to Dick that most of the failure of boats in the Pacific fleet was due to the poor performance of skippers and bad torpedoes. He said that some 40 commanding officers had been relieved so far due to poor health, battle fatigue or mostly for nonproductivity. The Navy was still relying on filling commands by seniority, not aggressiveness.

Dick said, "Ben, I need to get a couple of my junior officers qualified as soon as possible. Could you arrange for a torpedo exercise for me week after next? That way we'll have one week of work up and the second week for the test." Ben replied, "I'll do my best. It will all depend on the availability of the destroyer. By the way, we have a new XO for you. His name is Rogers, and he's a go-getter. You'll like him. He was an engineer on the *Haddock*; he did two patrols on it and he will fit in well. Good sense of humor. Practical joker at times. Good record." Dick said, "How soon will he be available?" Next week, Ben assured him.

Dick Morrison was quick to respond, "You know Jerry Abrams would make a fine exec, and I'd like to recommend him after this next patrol. I'm pretty sure that his fitness reports from Custer will not be good. Jerry is a Jew, and Custer hates Jews for some reason. This guy is terrific and will make a good exec and sub captain one of these days." Ben took a long drink of water and said, "Well don't be too sure about that. There's an old boys club to overcome that wants only Academy types to command." Dick finished his iced tea and asked, "Ben, can you get me a productive patrol area for *Thornfish*? We're going to sink ships!" Ben replied, "Yes, I'll see what I can do. I will try to get you assigned to where the hunting is best now, the East China Sea, the Emperor's backyard pool."

· · · · ·

The board reconvened exactly at 1400. Captain Harris reminded the parties they were still under oath. Glancing at his watch, the senior member repeated his earlier statement that this inquiry was to be fair to all parties and directed counsel to proceed.

LT Cohen began by relating his client's service record. His long service in submarines and that he excelled at all assignments prior to the command of the *Thornfish*, and he extolled his reputation as a strict disciplinarian who drove others and himself to do their best following the Articles of Government of the Navy and Navy Regulations to a T. Regarding the former, he cited the longstanding tradition at the Naval Academy of the battalion having to read the Articles especially the one of Rocks and Shoals every month. He paused and read from a portion beginning with **Article 4.10.**

The punishment of death, or such other punishment as a court-martial may adjudge, may be inflicted on any person in the naval service who intentionally or willfully suffers any vessel of the Navy to be stranded, or run upon rocks or shoals, or improperly hazarded or maliciously or willfully injures any vessel of, or any part of her tackle, armament whereby the safety of the vessel is hazarded, or the lives of the crew exposed to danger.

He then paused and said, "Sirs, I want you to give special attention to **Article 4.15. The punishment of death or other such punishment as a court-martial may adjudge** may be inflicted on any person in the naval service who does not properly observe the orders of his Commanding Officer and use his utmost exertions to carry them into execution when ordered to prepare for or join in, or when actually engaged in, battle, or while in the sight of the enemy."

Commander Custer would now like to tell his side of the story which LT Morrison correctly said is without precedent in the U.S. Navy submarine service. Custer arose, and walked over to the podium; his starched white uniform hung loosely on him. He had lost a lot of weight, and his pale face revealed a troubled man.

He began, "First of all, I want to apologize to this board for my impertinent and ill-timed remarks. Frankly I got carried away with some of the testimony which I feel is both unjust and untrue. The incident of 24 October 1942 will be remembered long after we leave the service. There was no reason for the takeover of the *Thornfish*, crewed by one of the best in the Navy except for a few officers who were determined to undermine my authority. My counsel just read Article 4, and I held the safety of my command top priority. Not one person on *Thornfish* would challenge that statement. I alone was responsible for the well-being and safety of all hands. I realize I'm a hard taskmaster, but that's what it takes to make a successful patrol. We did sink a Japanese heavy cruiser. But in several instances during our patrol, when I was searching for targets and escorts were about to attack us, I needed time to assess the tactical situation. Ensign Walker's testimony this morning was a distortion of what happened. I did have problems seeing the target with the high waves that required us to ride higher than normal. So, it took a little longer than normal to get my bearings. In heavy seas the danger of broaching and discovery was extreme. I might also add that I was recovering from an overdose of sedatives given by the pharmacist by direct order of my exec." Custer's counsel interrupted his client. "Sir, are you implying that Mr. Morrison was deliberately trying to conspire to relieve you and that he intentionally had you doped up so that you were prevented from functioning properly in the attack? Did he use this incident as an excuse to relieve you?" The Recorder cut him off. "Counselor, you are leading your witness, let him tell his account. This is a warning, no more of this." Undeterred Cohen continued, "Commander Custer, would you tell the board what led you to believe Mr. Morrison was insubordinate?"

"Yes, on one occasion, I was on my way to the bridge and stopped by the exec's stateroom and found our copy of Navy Regulations on his desk opened to the page containing Article 1088; someone had made a note in the margin by the article. I knew then what he was contemplating."

"When was this?" Custer answered, "About four weeks into our patrol." His counsel continued, "Did you confront him about this?"

"No, I did not, but looking back I should have."

"Were there other times he showed insubordination?" Custer said, "Well just before the mutiny…" LT Morrison jumped to his feet, addressing the board he said, "Sir, I'm challenging that last statement. There was no mutiny or mutinous thoughts preceding his relief. The facts are that Captain Custer was relieved for cause. The cause being unfit for command due to medical conditions. I ask that that last statement be stricken from the record." Captain Harris, replied, "So ordered." Custer continued, "Just before I was relieved, on my way to the conning tower, I stopped by the XO 's stateroom and once again found Navy Regs opened to Article 1088. But even before that there were a lot of times when he would challenge my decisions to avoid escorts, and I could tell he was really upset." He turned and looked directly at Morrison and said, "And frankly I did have to admonish him by telling him he was trying to get us all killed."

Commander Lytle, the Recorder, stood and slowly walked over to Commander Custer and looked intently at him, "Sir, did you observe anything that your executive officer said to any officer or member of the crew that undermined your authority as Commanding Officer? Custer's face flushed, and he looked down at the floor and said softly, "No." Captain Harris said, "Please repeat so we could hear you." He looked up and said loudly, "No."

Commander Stephen Lunsford, the junior member of the board, asked a direct question of Custer. "Lieutenant Commander Custer, LT Morrison said that before you were relieved, he found you in your bed with a 45-caliber government-issued pistol by your pillow. And he found some empty bottles of whiskey, is that correct?"

Custer bit his lip, "Well, I suppose I had one or two before dinner."

"You are aware that consumption of alcohol is forbidden in naval vessels."

"Yes but, as you know, the captain can relax it for medicinal purposes after the stress of battle."

"So, you were under great stress, correct?" Custer's countenance changed. He was perplexed about how to answer this line of questioning. If he said he was stressed out it would add to his nemesis' contention that he was unable to command. If he said no, he was just drinking, he would be guilty of abuse of alcohol while on duty. Before he could reply, Commander Lunsford said, "Each bottle contains about one and a half ounces of liquor, even if you had only two that would be a lot of whiskeys. LT Morrison testified that he feared you were considering suicide. Were you considering suicide?" Custer was visibly upset. He wiped his face with his handkerchief, his hands were trembling. He stared at the table in front of him. "No." His words slurred, "Actually… I was thinking of cleaning my gun. I had that semi-automatic from my days on the S-boat in Panama. I needed it to wear ashore when I was a disbursing officer. We had to pay the crew in cash back then…." His voice trailed off. He slowly walked back to his table and sat down.

Commander Lunsford glanced at the other members and then turned toward the new captain of the *Thornfish*, "LT Morrison you said you unloaded the pistol, is that correct?" Morrison replied, "Yes."

"Remember you are under oath, one final question, *was there **a round** in the chamber*?" Morrison knew the importance of this question. He said firmly, "Yes."

There was complete silence in the room for a long time. The board members sat motionlessly. Custer's counsel stared out the window. The sound of the ceiling fans whirling above reverberated throughout the warm conference room. In the distance a scout plane engine roared as it took off from Ford Island seaplane base. Custer wiped his face with his handkerchief and took a drink of water. Finally, Captain Jim Harris broke the eerie silence by saying "This board will be in recess for 15 minutes. When we resume, we will read the summary report of the medical departments and have closing statements from both parties. This will conclude the testimony phase of the BOI." Commander Lunsford was glued to his chair. He thought *this is truly Custer's last stand.*

When the board returned the Recorder provided the board and parties each a copy of the summary report of the findings of the medical examination conducted at Midway upon the return of *Thornfish's* patrol and copies of the evaluation done later at the submarine base.

Captain Harris said, "Gentlemen please read these summaries. If there are any objections, please advise the board. Complete copies are a part of Commander Custer's health record."

In summary the findings of my examination done October 31, of Lieutenant Commander John Jacob Custer USN, was that he was suffering from extreme fatigue and stress due to having just completed a 60-day patrol with contact of enemy forces, and being depth charged numerous times. He had high blood pressure, and rapid pulse, and anemia. He suffered from indigestion and should be further checked for an ulcer. During the time from his last physical, his weight had dropped 27 pounds. Conversations indicated a high degree of anger and frustration. Further psychological evaluation is recommended before his reassignment to active duty. Very Respectfully,

Commander Charles Phelps USNR, Medical Corps, US Naval Station Midway

The Recorder then handed out copies of the report from the medical department at Pearl Harbor. It confirmed the entire report from his examination at Midway with one additional comment: It said:

Commander Custer agreed to several sessions evaluating his psychological condition. This officer has an obsessive-compulsive disorder, striving for perfection in whatever he does. Failures, even ever so slight, lead to excess frustration and resulting depression. Carried to the extreme this could lead to a desire to take one's life. Further counseling is highly recommended. It is my professional opinion that this officer, when reassigned, should be precluded from any further combat billets.

Very Respectfully, Captain Patrick Ireland, MC USN, US Naval Submarine Base Pearl Harbor HI."

Captain Harris gave the parties and the board time to read the summary reports and then said, "Are there any questions or objections?" All eyes were on Commander Custer. He sat staring out the window to his right. He seemed incoherent. He knew his career was over in submarines, and maybe in any other capacity in the Navy. His counsel broke the silence by saying, "No sir. Not at this time. We reserve the right to appeal the conclusion of the medical department's assessment of reassignment though." The senior member of the BOI said, "Then we'll move on, with closing statements by first Commander Custer, and then the Respondent to the inquiry, LT Morrison."

John Jacob Custer rose and shuffled to the podium. "Gentlemen, I have served this nation honorably for twelve years, actually 16 if you count Academy time too, and I have been honored to command one of the finest submarines in the Pacific Fleet. Each member of this board has commanded submarines, and you know what a tremendous responsibility it is. I valued each member of my crew. Sure, some would challenge my decisions regarding some action that we took, but my intentions were always of the highest regard for my crew. I did not lose one man in some very dangerous situations. Read the patrol report and you'll see the damage we did to the enemy. Unfortunately, I had an overly zealous executive officer who made what I thought were bad decisions, and I had to countermand them. Of this I make no apologies. Let me be clear. This officer, LT Morrison, is a loose cannon and should not have command. He is reckless and overly ambitious. He should be court-martialed for his insubordination to my orders and my command. After weighing the testimony today, I trust that you will concur and so recommend to the convening authority. Thank you." The board members made some notes and then the senior member said, "We'll now hear from LT Morrison."

Dick Morrison had made up his mind not to be offensive. Custer's testimony was enough to acquit him of any nefarious endeavors to usurp his former commanding officer's responsibilities. Even if he had not taken command of *Thornfish*, Custer would have been relieved of command simply because of his lack of aggressiveness, as many other CO's had happened to them.

As he rose from his table and walked to the podium, he had an air of command authority about him. "Gentleman, I will be brief. We have heard words tossed around 'mutiny, insubordination,' and so on. I was never insubordinate, and never planned or even thought of mutiny. My concern was always to sink as many enemy ships as possible. I confess I did assume some risks, but not reckless risks. Taking a United States warship alongside an enemy is what courageous men have done since the Navy was born in 1775. Commander Custer was a good commanding officer. He was intense, a hard taskmaster, one who would not put up with poor performance by officers or crew. We were well trained, and we did sink ships, but we failed to attack far more that we should have. He has some serious problems both mentally and physically that I believe in time can be overcome, and he can contribute to the war effort. Looking forward, I want to take *Thornfish* back into Japanese waters and help shut that evil empire down. I am putting my trust in your good judgment to allow me to make that happen. Thank you."

Dick sat down and waited for the board's senior member to decide the next step. The board members were consulting among themselves. Then Captain Harris called the Recorder to come forward and they held a short conference in whispered tones. Captain Harris finally addressed the entire assembly. "I want to thank all participants for their input in this investigation. We have heard a lot of testimony, and the board will need time to assemble a comprehensive report for the convening authority. In the meantime, these proceedings are now closed."

CHAPTER 21

Covenant with Destiny

A Navy Jeep and driver were awaiting Captain Morrison and his junior officer outside the COMSUBPAC headquarters. The chief of the boat and the other two enlisted men had already found transportation on a Navy bus going to town and then to the Pink Palace. Commander Ben Miller got a ride with Rob and his boss to the nearby submarine squadron's office. After a few words of encouragement from Ben, they departed for their quarters in the Royal Hawaiian. As the little Jeep climbed the hill to the sub base gate, they could see a rain shower in the distant pineapple fields. Suddenly a bright rainbow appeared in the shimmering mist with its brilliant yellow, green, violet arc covering the entire horizon. Rob said, "Sir, look ahead, see the rainbow? Maybe that's a sign for the *Thornfish*." His captain said, "I'll buy that Rob. But maybe it's more than that. It could be a divine covenant for our boat." Rob remembered the last time he saw a rainbow. Lily had said the same thing as they sat in her steamy convertible overlooking the Halona blowhole. Rob mused, this can't be a coincidence, two rainbows in two different places, but both were giving credit to the Lord.... *What does this mean*?

As the Jeep bounced along Highway 92 heading back to the hotel, there was too much wind and traffic noise for them to carry on a conversation. Rob's thoughts turned once again to Lily, the rainbow, and her love affair with him. He knew he was getting too involved but how could he extract himself without hurting her? Molly's letters were so full of love for him. She was waiting for him, and he knew that the silent service was too dangerous for her to depend on him. He could be gone in an instant on his next patrol. Already five of Pacific Fleet's submarines had never returned from patrol, and 350 officers and men had vanished. Submarines have the highest casualty rate of all the naval service. Perhaps he should tell Molly not to wait for him. *It's unfair to her to keep her on a string,* he reasoned.

When they got out of the Jeep at the Royal Hawaiian, Captain Morrison told Rob, "I want to tell you that you did a good job today; your testimony was forthright and well received I believe. Commander Miller thinks the inquiry cleared the air and resolved a lot of issues. By the way Rob, he thinks a lot of you."

"Thank you, sir, I appreciate it very much."

"Now let's have a drink. I need one."

It was happy hour in the hotel's Tiki Bar when the new CO of the *Thornfish* and Rob entered the room. Christmas lights had been strung rather haphazardly over the rectangular bar, and the bartender sported a well-worn red and white Santa's hat. In the corner, the jukebox was playing *White Christmas* by Irving Berlin, the top song on the hit parade for the past three weeks. Rob saw Lily waiting tables on the veranda overlooking the water, so they quickly found a table nearby where the ocean view was terrific but especially the view of Lily dressed in a very brief cocktail dress. When Lily saw them, she glided over and said, "Merry Christmas gentlemen. Captain Morrison what would you like to drink this evening, I know what Rob wants." The captain said, "Merry Christmas to you too, and I'll have what Mr. Walker is drinking." The table they had selected offered some privacy, and they sat down as Lily leaned over and lit the candle at the center. Rob whispered, "You smell so good Lily… what perfume are you wearing tonight?" She smiled, "Chanel Number 5, of course." Rob wondered if he could buy some at the exchange for her Christmas present and Molly too. Before their drinks arrived, Lieutenant Abrams and Ensign Young came over to the table and asked permission to join them. "Permission granted," the *Thornfish's* captain said, pleasantly surprised. "How'd it go today sir?" Jerry Abrams asked. The captain said, "Well pretty well I think, time will tell. Please join us for a drink." Lily returned to the table and brought two gimlets and took orders for two more for the new arrivals. Jerry asked Lily how she survived the incident last Saturday night. Captain Morrison wasn't surprised. Rob had told him earlier of the incident. Lily still felt the embarrassment and disgust of that night. She simply said, "I'm OK."

John asked, "Captain, when are we going to sea again?" Dick Morrison was glad to have the subject changed to something he had in mind discussing. "We're going to have some sea trials next week, and we'll be going through an intensive training period; we have 17 new sailors coming on board to replace those leaving for new construction in the states so that we will be doing a lot of basic stuff. We plan to have Ensign Walker do one of our underway torpedo exercises to get him qualified. To answer your question, we have a busy schedule ahead of us. Of course, a lot depends on the progress that the relief crew is doing on our repairs. Mr. Abrams and I are going to check on them tomorrow." Jerry asked a question that had been on his mind for some time. "Sir, when will our new exec be on board?" Lily returned with the adult beverages and some macadamia nuts. Captain Morrison said, "Gentlemen these nuts are the best nuts you'll ever eat. I guarantee you cannot eat just one." He ate two to emphasize his endorsement. He continued, "I have a couple of announcements that I want to share with you in confidence for now. First, to answer Jerry's question, we are getting one of the top XO prospects. His name is Albert Buckhorn Rogers. They call him Buck for short. Buck Rogers! He's a character and a practical joker. He is a little ticked off by this assignment I'm told. LT Rogers was in line for new construction in the states, and he was planning to get married. Personnel pulled him off to be number 2 on *Thornfish*. He's a real go getter...aggressive and sharp. He'll be a real asset to our boat. He'll report sometime next week. Bucky is on his way from San Francisco now. The second thing I want to tell you is we are going to have a new Mark 1 mod 0 slot machine installed in the galley." The others around the table couldn't believe it. "Yes, it's true, the local Honolulu police department has donated one. They confiscated it from an illegal operation. I've cleared it with the staff and the chief of the boat agrees. The only criteria are that all proceeds go to the MWR fund for ship's parties. The chief of the boat will supervise it, and if anyone gets carried away in any debt, they will pay dearly to the chief. For your information, all the new boats coming off the shipyard at Manitowoc, Wisconsin, are equipped with slots donated by their police department. Our *George* will be responsible for working with the COB in keeping track of the monies." John Young knew what that meant; he had been the newest ensign and they were always called *George* because they were given the less demanding but important jobs, disbursing, commissary, and the like. Tony was now the new *George* which suited John just fine.

Jerry proposed a toast: "To the new *Thornfish*, the best damn sub for Uncle Sam!" Cheers went up from the table as Lily stood silently by wondering what all this would mean for her.

· · · · ·

Tuesday morning of Rob's last week of R&R began early for him. Rob convinced John to go with him to the base exchange to do some Christmas shopping. At 0900 they caught the Navy bus and were dropped off at the Navy Exchange forty minutes later. Rob quickly found what he was looking for, Chanel No. 5, and bought two bottles, one for Molly and the other for Lily. As he passed by the jewelry counter, he saw a beautiful Mikimoto Pearl necklace that he instantly knew would please Molly. It was expensive... twenty dollars. He had his purchases gift wrapped and tucked in a small Christmas card for Molly.

> *"My darling Molly, my heart's desire is that I would be able to give these two little gifts to you in person. Perhaps next year I'll be able to, but in the meantime, please remember me in your prayers. I love you. Your sailor sweetheart, Rob. Merry Christmas 1942.*
>
> *p.s. I'm dreaming of a white Christmas with you in '43.... XXXXOOOO. R"*

He handed the card and gifts to the clerk, and she promised to airmail them that morning. Both ensigns walked from the exchange to the pier where the *Thornfish* was berthed. The hull of the *Thornfish* looked good. It had a new coat of light gray paint to make it blend in with the tropical seas better than the previous dark gray. As they crossed the gangway, they saluted the flag at its stern and asked permission of the relief crew OOD to come aboard. Before going below Rob paused, looking across the harbor still coated in places with oil seeping from the wreckage of sunken ships, and it recalled what his Japanese friend had said years ago: "Imperial Japan is completely dependent on imports of all its raw materials, without them we cannot survive." Rob turned to John and said, "Our subs will be the weapon that will destroy Japan in this war."

They found the Officer-in-Charge in the wardroom having a cup of coffee and learned that the relief crew's work should be completed by the weekend. An award ceremony was scheduled for next Monday morning, and they wanted everything ready for the admiral's presentations. The OIC showed them the new surface radar PPI scope in the conning tower and the air search radar scope installed nearby. The range for both new radars was improved, meaning they could pick up aircraft and surface contacts sooner than before. Radar technicians were busy tuning the frequency of the surface radar; the PPI scope showed the entire harbor with some ships moving and the still sunken battleships masts and superstructures remaining as silent memorials to the infamous attack a year ago.

Inside, the *Thornfish* was impressive. Moving through the vessel, it was clean and neat. The new slot machine was bolted to the deck in the crew's mess, with a Navy gray canvass cover over it. A new phonograph, donated by the local American Legion Post, was installed on the galley's bulkhead near the ship's bulletin board. A smaller one was placed securely in the wardroom on a new stainless-steel shelf above the galley serving window. Lily was to donate records from the Royal Hawaiian spare jukebox supply. The sound system had been modified to allow the music to be played over the IMC announcing system at the discretion of the XO. When surfaced, the radio broadcast of Tokyo Rose's propaganda could be broadcast too, since she played the latest American songs on the Hit Parade.

LT Abrams was very pleased with the overhaul of #4 main engine. The main induction valve had been removed and a new one installed. *Thornfish* was nearly ready for sea. Several hours later Rob and John boarded a crowded bus for the hotel. Downtown Honolulu still showed remnants of the air raid on Pearl Harbor. The City Hall had bullet holes in one of the sides facing the ocean. A late model Oldsmobile taxi riddled with bullet holes and broken glass was left on display in the small park adjacent to the town center as a reminder of what had happened.

When they arrived at the Pink Palace, they checked for any messages and picked up their room keys at the front desk. There was a note from Lily asking if he was still planning to have dinner with his mother. Instead of dining out, her mom wanted to cook a real Japanese meal for him at her home. The only problem was that she had to work for the next few days and could they do it on the weekend? Rob knew that their R&R was to expire then but felt sure that he could get a one-day extension. He was looking forward to seeing Lily's mother again and for some real Japanese cooking. It was nearly five, Lily would be coming on duty in the lounge soon. Rob started looking for her and some of the *Thornfish's* officers sitting at the bar saw him and motioned for him to join them. Rob took a stool at the end of the bar. He sat next to the *Thornfish's* engineer, Jerry Abrams and his assistant engineer, Ensign Shane Montgomery, a reserve officer from Texas. His father's ranch sprawled over 2500 acres in the central part of Texas, considered a small ranch in Texas. Shane graduated from Texas A & M and took a Navy commission, rather than the Army, and served one year on a destroyer out of San Diego before going to sub school in New London. An outgoing and gregarious officer, he was a welcome addition to the wardroom immediately after he reported on board in early December. Shane had just been promoted to Lieutenant Junior Grade and was planning his "wetting down party." A tradition in the Navy, wetting down meant the newly promoted officer would buy drinks for the wardroom.

"Hey Rocky, welcome aboard. You're just in time. I'm planning on having my wetting down this Friday during happy hour, of course. Can you be here?"

Rob replied, "Sure Shane, I wouldn't miss it." Rob joined them as Jerry Abrams was telling one of his Jewish jokes for Shane about Texans: "Three guys are sitting at a bar in Dallas, Texas. Two had cowboy hats and the third a cap. The two big Texans were bragging about their ranches. "My ranch is 3,000 acres and we have 5,000 cattle. We call it the Rancho Gold." The second Texan, not to be outdone, said loudly, "Well I have a ranch of 5,000 acres and I run 10,000 cattle, I call it the Lucky Ranch," They turned to the little Jewish guy with the cap, next to them, looking for a response, and he finally said, "Vell, I have 30 acres, and no cattle." The two 'cowboys' smirked, "What do you call it?" He laughed, "Downtown Dallas!"

CHAPTER 22

The Train Ride

Despite a nagging cough, Mary Catherine Walker was determined to spend Christmas with her husband in Washington. Using her family's connections in Cincinnati, she was able to pull some strings and book a ticket for a Pullman coach on the C&O. She had stayed the previous night at the home of her uncle, Robert A. Taft, in Indian Hill. The ten-bedroom English Tudor home, set on a wooded 12-acre plot, had been her favorite place to visit during her childhood. It brought back fond memories of playing hide and seek, croquet, and later tennis with the other nieces and nephews. Christmas was a special time for her. After Christmas Eve services at the Episcopal Church, the entire family gathered in the living room to open one present before bedtime. They had the largest tree she had ever seen set in the huge living room.

This morning, after breakfast, the maid prepared a small lunch for her and called a cab to take her to the station. The 1939 Plymouth taxi took her to the front of Cincinnati's immense Union Terminal. She thought it looked like the half dome in Yosemite; a flat frontal escarpment, with sculptures, made this the most beautiful railroad station in the U.S. Completed in 1933, it merged four different railroad terminals into one striking edifice handling up to 216 trains per day. The *Cincinnati Enquirer* called it a 'Temple to Transportation.' Its beautiful steel arches stretched over the 100-foot rotunda. It was a city within a city; as she made her way through the throngs of passengers, she passed the bookstore, a toy store, food service, newsstands and an air-conditioned movie theater on her way to the ticket counter. She carried a heavy suitcase in one hand and a shopping bag with Christmas presents in her left. When she finally reached the ticket window, behind the bars stood an austere looking man with a green eyeshade on his forehead, his sleeves rolled up held by elastic bands. She showed him her reservation. He produced a ticket about an arm's length and stamped each section with an official looking imprint. As she was about to leave for her gate, a colored porter, feeling sorry for her, offered to carry her things aboard the C&O passenger train bound for Washington, D.C. Mary Catherine felt very lucky. Uncle Bob's office in Cincinnati got her a first-class ticket to Washington on the Chesapeake and Ohio Railroad's only air-conditioned passenger train, the George Washington. In fact, there were only two air-conditioned trains in America, the other one being Baltimore and Ohio's. Besides the engine, it had three baggage cars, a dining car, four coaches, three Pullman cars, and one lounge car. The cars were all named for people, places or events connected with our first president, George Washington. It had a crew of twenty-four. The dining car was renowned for its beautiful ambiance and its fine china.

The train sat at gate 11 and was already packed with passengers. Soldiers, sailors, and some civilians occupied every seat. Latecomers sat on their suitcases. Smoke filled the air in the high ceilings of the coach. This will be a train ride from hell she thought. She made her way through the coaches to the Pullman car named Martha and found the seating conditions much better. She located her reserved seat; after placing her things near her, she opened her purse and carefully unwrapped the lunch that had been prepared for her. She devoured her ham sandwich and carrot sticks, cauliflower stems, and celery pieces, and a small chocolate chips cookie before the train left the station. The train was already an hour late in leaving the terminal.

She needed to go to the bathroom and was about to abandon her seat when she looked up at a beautiful girl coming down the aisle. She was looking for her seat. She stopped and checked the number on the seat and smiled. Mary Catherine breathed a sigh of relief, she thought she would be a good traveling companion for the long trip to Washington.

"Hi, I'm Marianne Baker, I think my seat is here too. "

"Please sit down, I'm glad you're here."

"Lots of guys on this train. I had to almost fight my way through the soldiers in the other car."

"I can understand why," Mary Catherine said. She was beautiful she thought, sparkling blue eyes, smooth complexion and ruby red lips and a wonderful build. She took her seat and said, "I'm on my way to Washington." Mrs. Walker scooted over to give her more room, "May I ask what you're going to do, are you joining up?"

She smiled and said, "Well kind of, I've been asked to join a band tour for the USO. I'm a singer."

"I saw the USO room in the terminal. They're serving coffee and donuts to thousands it seems."

"Yes, they're doing great work for the troops. I hope to contribute some way too."

"What band are you joining?"

" Well I'm not sure yet. I hope it's Glen Miller. I'm from Bedford, home of the Bedford High School Stone Cutters basketball team. State Champs last year!"

"Why the name Stone Cutters?"

"Well that's where we mine Bedford limestone, architectural limestone used all over the world."

"Yes, I know, in fact its Oolite Limestone, minute fossils that got packed together millions of years ago. My husband is a geologist, so I am by default one too. Bedford limestone was used in building this terminal we are in right now." Mary Catherine went on to tell her about the architectural work done by four well-known artists that made the famous Cincinnati railroad station known for its Art Décor, a 'Temple to Transportation.'

She asked, "Tell me, how did you get in the band business?" She laughed. "Well I was Miss Indiana two years ago. My talent competition was singing pop songs, and the agent for the band heard me and gave me an audition. It worked out ok, I guess. But I'll sure miss being home for Christmas."

"So, will I." Mary Catherine shared sadly. "My son's in the Navy somewhere in the Pacific."

Just then the coach jerked. They were underway finally. One hour and twenty minutes late. Mrs. Walker finally made it to the toilet. It had been closed and locked while in the station because the waste emptied directly onto the track below.

◦ ◦ ◦ ◦ ◦

Even in the dead of winter the scenery was stunning. The train sped along the double tracks parallel to the Ohio River. Reminders of the tragic flood of 1937 remained. High water marks could still be seen on the farm buildings, damaged trees and debris on the low-lying hills. Crossing the Ohio River, the tracks led through the steelmaking town of Ashland, Kentucky, where Armco, The American Rolling Mill Company of Middletown, Ohio, manufactured the first rolled steel. Crossing the Big Sandy River, marking the border of the Kentucky, West Virginia state line, the first stop was at Huntington, West Virginia, named for the founder of the Chesapeake and Ohio Railroad, Charles P. Huntington. While people debarked and more came aboard, Catherine and her new young friend made their way through the crowd to the dining car. It was elegant; white table clothes, china and silverware. She was very impressed. The colored porter seated them at a table for two and took their orders for appetizers. Mary Catherine ordered a bottle of California Chardonnay. More than a few male patrons noticed the two very attractive unescorted women. They ignored their looks by carrying on a conversation about the war, family, and prospects after the war. Marianne was very interested in pursuing her career in music and was hoping to land a job with a popular dance band. "Well in your travels Marianne, if you ever get to the Pacific, try to look up my son Rob, he is a submariner on the USS *Thornfish*. He loves it, but I am trying to get him transferred to naval intelligence." Marianne seemed interested in knowing more about Rob. Mary Catherine reached into her purse and pulled out a photo of Rob in his Navy ensign uniform. "My gosh, he is handsome. I bet he has a steady girlfriend." Rob's mother looked out the window and finally said, "Yes he does, but I'm not sure she's the right one for him."

They both sat in silence as occasional West Virginia small mining towns flashed by, run down homes, built on hillsides with washing machines on the front porch, and broken-down cars in the front yard. Interspersed in the fading light of early December were beautiful views of the New River with cascading waters rushing down the rapids. Light snow was falling in the mountains covering some of the scars of open pit coal mining.

Mary Catherine recalled her husband talking about a little town in the hills that he had visited on a geology field trip a few years ago. Up one of the creeks flowing into the New River was a little town, Arthurdale. During the Depression in the thirties, poverty was rampant especially in West Virginia where some of the coal mines had been forced to shut down. Eleanor Roosevelt, President Roosevelt's wife, was a progressive and with her prodding, Washington initiated a trial of federal financial assistance to eradicate *one town's* poverty. Arthurdale became a laboratory for social scientists, an experiment in social engineering. The Feds provided a school, roads, a community building, and some fifty farmhouses, and invited fifty families to farm the land. They were obligated to repay the government within thirty years. It turned out to be a giant WPA program that created jobs mainly in construction. But as time passed, things began to depreciate and break down. When the town's school bus broke down, they sent for the White House garage to repair it. In time, Eleanor Roosevelt became despondent over the people's lack of initiative. Self-reliance and independence gradually gave way to dependence. She confided to one of her associates that the experiment failed because they felt that the solution to all their problems was to turn to the government. For the folks in Arthurdale, the dream became a nightmare when the program ceased.

Marianne broke her pensive mood by saying, "Mrs. Walker, after dinner let's go to the lounge car for a look." Mary Catherine thought, well I guess it won't hurt, we're together, as mother and daughter. "OK. Just for a few minutes."

The lounge car was named Mount Vernon, for Washington's home on the Potomac River in Virginia. It was furnished with comfortable chairs and end tables. Along one side was a bar made of Virginia Walnut. The ladies found a couple of high chairs at its end. Marianne was not 21, so she ordered a ginger ale. Mary Catherine had a scotch and soda. Soldiers and a few sailors filled the comfortable chairs; smoking was permitted, and the lights were low. It almost seemed like a charming pub in Watch Hill, Rhode Island, where Mary Catherine spent many summers as a girl. "Look there's a small piano!" Marianne exclaimed. "It looks like the one in the movie *Casablanca!*" The movie starring Humphrey Bogart and Ingrid Bergman, had just been out a few months and it was a hit. The piano Sam played in the film was a small upright, painted green and yellow. Marianne jumped up impulsively and sat at the small upright. She started playing the theme from the movie, *As Time Goes By*...and softly sang the words, her voice was so beautiful. Everyone in the lounge stopped and listened to her and applauded loudly when she finished. She smiled and then sang, *I'm Dreaming of a White Christmas*, from the movie *Holiday Inn* with Bing Crosby and Rosemary Clooney. Rosemary was from Cincinnati and got her start singing at WLW the 50,000-watt nation's station. As Marianne sang the last line, *I'll be home for Christmas if only in my dreams,* tears filled Mary Catherine's eyes.

When they returned to their sleeping car, the Porter had made up their beds, curtained off with heavy green drapes. They took turns using the toilet; Marianne still couldn't get over the fact that when they flushed the toilet the contents fell directly onto the track below. Changing into bed clothes was not easy in the cramped quarters, but they managed. Marianne took the upper bunk and they said goodnight. Mary Catherine turned off the light and said her prayers for her loved ones, especially for Rob who might be in harm's way at that very moment. And then she said a little prayer for Marianne, her new traveling companion. *Wouldn't it be nice if she would meet Rob someday?*

CHAPTER 23

The Last Night Ashore

As Mary Catherine was falling asleep to the cadence of the tracks beneath her Pullman berth, it was Saturday afternoon six-time zones west in Hawaii. Her son Rob was busy in his room at the Royal Hawaiian packing his things for his return to the *Thornfish* the next day. The officers had to check out of the Royal Hawaiian in the morning, and Rob was looking forward to Saturday night; it was going to be special, a real Japanese dinner prepared by Lily's Japanese mother at her home in the hills overlooking Pearl Harbor. Lily had to work till six, and her mom was going to pick them both up in front of the hotel after she got off work.

Rob had met Valerie Edmonds only one time while having his second breakfast in her home a week ago. He took a liking to her immediately. He could see where Lily had gotten her good looks. Tall for a Japanese, she had a slender athletic body complimented by a beautiful face; her firm countenance radiated calm serenity; her jet-black hair swept into a bun at the back had a tinge of gray giving her an air of wisdom, Rob thought. Mrs. Edmonds arrived promptly at six and parked her convertible with the top down in front of the hotel. The Marine guard posted outside of the entrance was about to tell her to move when Rob appeared and intervened. "Thanks Ensign Walker, the Marines don't seem to like people of Japanese ancestry you know... I guess it's understandable." While they were waiting for Lily, he hopped in the front passenger side. Mrs. Edmond said may I call you Rob? Yes, if I may call you Valerie. She liked that. "Are you famished, I hope?" and she added, "I've been slaving all day over a hot hibachi pot." She laughed. Rob said, "Well I hope not, but I must tell you how much I have been looking forward to being with you and having some genuine Japanese food. You know that I spent a couple of years in Japan as a teenager and loved the Japanese food." She looked directly into his eyes and said, "I'm glad you had that experience, it's very difficult here for Japanese-Americans now. Some of my friend's families are now in internment camps in the States. I can't believe what is happening; President Roosevelt ordered some twenty thousand families moved out of their homes on the west coast. The government has taken over the Santa Anita racetrack, and it's being used as a reception area before they are sent to internment camps."

Just then Lily appeared and jumped in the tiny rear seat. She was radiant, even after working a full shift waiting tables in the bar area. "Tips were very good today, mom." Her mother laughed, "They're spending their money like drunken sailors!" The officers were very generous with their tips. They consumed lots of beer and booze, especially since, for some, it was their last night in their luxurious quarters. Tomorrow they'd be crowded in their fleet boat, three hundred fifty feet long with seventy men, food for sixty days stashed in storage lockers, and in the compartments throughout the boat. Twenty-four torpedoes would be loaded in the next few days.

The little Chevy climbed the hills to her home in Aiea Heights in second gear. With the top down and the darkened streetlights along the way, the stars stood out almost as bright as those at sea. The view was spectacular from the top of the hill where her mother's home stood. They could see the lights of Honolulu in the distance, and the shipyard at the naval base, and to the west, Pearl City and Waipahu. Her husband Frank built the home five years before he died, the first home constructed on Waipao Place. The aroma of food in the kitchen met them when they opened the front door. "We are going to dine on the lanai tonight Rob," Lily said as she tossed her lei on the hall table. The hotel had provided her a beautiful lei of purple and white tiny orchids for waiting tables so well for the submariners. "I'm going to change; mom will tell you about her menu for tonight's dinner." Rob watched her walking down the hall toward her bedroom. Her silky black hair, tied in a bun, her hips moving in sexy motion, made him think of the memorable night spent in her bedroom only a few days ago.

Valerie interrupted his reverie, "She likes you a lot Robert; I must be honest with you, and I hesitate to say this, but I hope you both go slow because you are in a risky business. I know from personal experience how hard it is when your loved one is lost." Rob replied, "I understand Mrs. Edmonds, but we're all volunteers, and we have a super bunch of men and officers, especially the new CO. I believe he will take risks, but not senseless risks." She replied, "I hope so, why don't you pour yourself a drink? You'll find some really good sake on the buffet." Rob studied the bottle. The label was in Japanese script. "It's a very special brew, Rob, it's called *Darjinjoshu*. If you want it cold, I can put some ice in it." Rob poured it into a tumbler and tasted it, "No, room temperature is fine. Thanks." Valerie excused herself to attend to some things in the kitchen and Lily came into the living room dressed in a lovely pink and white loose-fitting Hawaiian dress. She chose a glass, and Rob poured it half full. He looked at her standing there with her lovely graceful hands extended toward him, raised his glass and said "Merry Christmas Lily. And Happy New Year." Lily clutched her glass, "Where will you be this Christmas Rob?" Rob told her, "Somewhere at sea." Lily glanced at him, "I just wish you could be here with us."

Valerie prepared the meal in traditional Japanese style right in the hibachi on the lanai. They sat in low chairs around a small round table containing the hibachi pot. They began with a Miso soup that Rob found delicious, followed by Saba Shioyaski, grilled Mackerel, cooked over the hibachi along with brown rice and cucumber salad. Each dish was served separately. For a beverage Mrs. Edmonds served cold Japanese rice beer made in Hawaii. Rob savored every morsel of what Mrs. Edmonds called a typical Japanese meal. For dessert she served peppermint ice cream made especially for Christmas that Lily had purloined from the Royal Hawaiian kitchen. Rob negotiated the chopsticks as if he were one of her former countrymen. Valerie watched him munch every bite. "Rob you're using those sticks like you've done it all your life. Where did you learn?" Rob repeated some of the story of his father's teaching in Japan and his friendship with Jimmysan. He said he hoped that they both would survive the war and be reunited someday. Mrs. Edmonds looked away sadly and said, "I too want Japan and the United States to one day be friends again. But it's hard to believe that will ever happen now."

A small Christmas tree filled the corner of the lanai decorated with colored lights and ornaments from all over the world that Frank Edmonds had collected during his years of Navy service. After they finished the excellent meal, they sat on the couch by the hibachi and watched the coals slowly disappear. Valerie spoke about the attack only a year ago on that fateful Sunday morning. Her husband, Frank, had left very early to be on board the battleship *Arizona* for the admiral's inspection later that day. Lily was asleep in her room. She drove her husband to *Arizona*'s boat landing in the Chevy convertible with the top down and returned home in time to get ready for church. She was in the bedroom when she heard some explosions. She rushed to the lanai and saw flames over Ford Island air base. She glanced at her watch, it read 8 o'clock. The roar of aircraft filled the air as dive bombers dropped their loads on the battleships tied up near Ford Island. Lily came to the lanai and stood by her side as they watched the carnage unfold. Suddenly there was a huge explosion, on one of the battleships. They learned later that it was Frank's ship, *Arizona*. A Japanese dive bomber placed a 500-pound armor piercing bomb on the forward deck that penetrated the ammunition magazine demolishing the ship. Her husband, the father of Lily, died instantly along with over 1200 sailors, including the admiral. She turned to Rob and said, "No one knew of the attack beforehand, it was a sneak attack. We did not have a chance." Lily said, "Some of the planes pulled out of their dives right over our house. We could see the pilots' faces in some of them. We didn't know what to do, we retreated inside the house and prayed." She described how huge fires erupted in the distance at Hickam Army Airfield where their aircraft had been placed wingtip to wingtip offering choice targets for Japanese fighter planes. Only a few Army fighter planes were able to take off in a vain effort to stop the onslaught. They turned their radio on and the local station told all civilians to remain inside, not to use the roads or highways. After the first wave departed, Lily went to the lanai and trained her father's new telescope on battleship row. In the smoke and fire, she saw the wreckage of her father's ship, the USS *Arizona*. She knew he was gone.

It was getting late. They had been talking for several hours, speaking in English and interspersed with some Japanese, Rob said, to improve his language skills. They talked about how long the war might last, rationing, Japan's need for raw materials. Valerie was interested in knowing more about Doolittle's raid on Tokyo in April. Rob said someone had sent him a clipping from *The Oxford Press* telling of one of Miami University's graduates, Robert John Meder, who was one of the pilots of the B-25's that bombed Tokyo. The Japanese said he had been captured. The article went on to say that Meder was the pilot of one of seven planes on their way to Dayton's Wright Field that flew over Oxford two months before they targeted Japan.

Lily's mother changed the subject, "Rob, did you get a chance to climb Mt. Fujiyama while you were in Japan?" Rob told her of his adventure with his buddy Jimmysan, leaving out the details. Valerie said, "Well I climbed it while I was in the Catholic school at the orphanage, I must have been about 15 years old." Valerie glanced at Lily and said, "My parents died in the worldwide flu epidemic in 1919. Some dear Catholic friends took pity on me and led me to the Catholic orphanage in Nagoya. The nuns raised me and schooled me. I learned to speak English there and it helped me get a good job here with Noritake China Company. But the best thing that happened to me is they led me to become a Christian." She added, "Rob, are you a Christian?" Rob looked at Lily and seemed at a loss for words. He finally said, "Well, yes, but I'm afraid not a very good one."

Valerie replied, "I guess I am too, we are all sinners, Rob, but the good news is that Jesus settled our debts on the Cross, and faith in him saves us. Before you leave, I'm going to give you a Bible, and I'd like for you to take it along with you, perhaps you can find some time to read a few verses each day. It will give you some strength when things get very trying."

"Thank you, Mrs. Edmonds, I will." Valerie said, "Now I'm going to bed, I'm tired. Robert, why don't you stay over tonight? This couch makes up into a bed and Lily will get some sheets and a blanket for you." Rob said he had to be back at the Royal Hawaiian by ten in the morning. "No problem," Lily said as she tried to hide her excitement, "I'll get you there."

After her mother retreated to her room, they sat on the couch listening to music on a local radio station. Rob told her they get Tokyo Rose on the radio in the sub while surfaced. She spreads the enemy's rumors of the war, propaganda of Jap victories, but she does play the latest hit tunes from the states. It's piped through the boat when possible. Lily said she was going to give them some of the latest records before they left. The folks that supply records for the jukebox in the bar where she worked gave her some extras for her personal use occasionally. She promised to get them to the boat. Rob squeezed her hand, "Better do it soon Lily, we're going to sea next week for some arduous training."

Lily drew close to him "I know, Rob will I ever see you again?" Her words were so lovingly direct that Rob didn't know how to respond to her candor. "Sure Lily, you know the Navy, we are in and out of Pearl just like the other boats homeported here. We'll be back after our next patrol I'm certain." She started to cry, "Hug me, Rob, and let's dance." The radio was playing *Moonlight Becomes You.* They took their shoes off, and as they danced, she sang softly the words that Bing Crosby made famous in the movie *Road to Morocco,* "*Moonlight becomes you …*" she drew him close and kissed him. They continued dancing as a full moon rose over Diamond Head.

After midnight, Lily put sheets on the couch and handed Rob a blanket and kissed him goodnight. Rob lay on the couch staring at the ceiling, thinking about all that had transpired since arriving in Hawaii; the meeting with the enchanting and voluptuous Lily, their attraction for each other, and especially the wonderful sex. He thought of Molly and his love for her. She was faithful in their relationship, while he was far too willing to be seduced by Lily. If he would only listen to his conscience, he would say no to her. But the thought that often overcame his willpower returned…this could be his last sexual experience. But deep inside, he wondered if he were falling in love with Lily. She was so beautiful, vivacious, spontaneous and very, very loving. He was confused. After tossing and turning a long time he finally fell asleep. In the middle of the night he was awakened by someone in the room. Lily was standing by the little Christmas tree with its colored lights still aglow. Rob whispered, "Lily you scared me." She was gorgeous standing by the rainbow-tinted Christmas tree lights. "Rob, I want to give you a Christmas present…me." She had a short terry cloth robe on her slim body. She dropped it on the floor and crawled in beside him on the little couch. The Christmas tree lights seemed to blend into one as they embraced. Rob didn't know she had been crying for hours.

CHAPTER 24

Union Station Washington D.C.
November 30, 1942

The George Washington, C&O's flagship train, arrived nearly two hours late at Union Station. The terminal serving Washington was built in 1934; it was a magnificent facility. Mary Catherine Walker and her new friend Marianne, dragging their bags, fought their way through the crowded station serving many thousands of passengers each day. Finding a porter was hopeless. When they finally arrived at the taxi stand outside the terminal, they were able to flag a Yellow Cab, and Mrs. Walker ordered the driver to take her to her uncle's residence in Georgetown. On the way they would drop off Marianne at the downtown YWCA headquarters on F Street. The USO was founded on the Y's seventh floor earlier in the year. Traffic was heavy. Gas rationing hadn't phased Washington's residents. It was Marianne's first visit to the nation's Capitol, and Mrs. Walker ordered the cab driver to drive down Delaware Avenue to Constitution Avenue so that Marianne could see the U.S. Capitol Building. She was impressed with the beauty of the building housing the U.S. House of Representatives and the Senate, set on the hill overlooking the National Mall. "I'll have my uncle Bob get you a special tour of the Capitol, Marianne, if you have time. Marianne said, "I'd love it Mrs. Walker, if it's not too much trouble." Mrs. Walker pointed out the Washington Monument, at its other end, standing some 555 feet high. "I once climbed all 898 steps years ago as a teenager during my first visit to Washington. My geologist husband says that if the Washington Monument represents the age of the earth, a sheet of paper on its top will represent the time humanity has been on this planet." Marianne was too busy to take her words in as she gawked at the many buildings and pedestrians going home from work in the rush hour traffic. The cab sped up Pennsylvania Avenue turned north on Ninth Street, passed the FBI building and the cabbie said, "Here's the first stop, the YWCA, The Young Womens' Christian Association, we sometimes forget what those letters mean, Ma'am." Mary Catherine wasn't too pleased with that, but she turned to her young friend, "When do you have to report to the USO, Marianne?" Marianne replied, "Well, my letter says two days from now." Her new mentor said, "You may not be able to get a room at the Y anyway; why don't you come with me and stay at my uncle's home for a couple of days? He has plenty of room." She was very persuasive, and

Marianne decided to accept her offer. It would give her a few days to get acquainted with the city and allow her some time to find a room and maybe sightsee a bit before going off to join her big band.

The driver got the new destination in Georgetown and pulled out in traffic and drove by 1600 Pennsylvania Avenue, the famous White House where Franklin Roosevelt had resided since 1933. Guards posted in sentry boxes were trying to stay warm in the December chill over Washington. The cab continued along the famous street until it became M Street in Georgetown. They passed beautiful old brick homes, many of them built in rows in the antebellum years. The senator's Victorian home was enclosed with a black iron fence. Two pillars, each with lion's heads perched above, marked the driveway. The cab slowly drove up the private gravel road to the front door. "Wait here," Mrs. Walker commanded the driver, as she exited the taxi. She climbed the few steps and rang the bell. A middle-aged maid, dressed in black with a white apron, answered the door and welcomed Mary Catherine. "Please come in ma'am, we've been expecting you," she said, "but Senator Taft is in a debate right now on the floor of the Senate chamber."

Robert Alphonse Taft, the eldest son of William Howard Taft, twenty-seventh President of the United States, grew up in Cincinnati and practiced law there until he was elected to the Ohio House and Senate before coming to the United States Senate in 1941. The senator, a strong conservative and one of the real intellectuals in the Senate, led a liberal newspaper reporter to write, "He has the brightest mind in the U.S. Senate until he makes up his mind." A graduate of Yale with a history major, and later Harvard Law School, editor of the Harvard Law Review, he was first in his class from grade school through college.

Mary Catherine dismissed the driver paying the fare plus giving him a generous three-dollar tip for helping her with the luggage. The maid showed her to her husband's bedroom on the second floor, and Marianne to a small bedroom at the end of the hall with a twin bed already comfortably made up. The young singer was thrilled and as she unpacked her small suitcase, she sang the words to the ballad everyone was listening to, *I'm Dreaming of a White Christmas*. Hearing her cheerful voice again, Mary Catherine softly strolled down the carpeted floor and stood by the open door of her room listening to the last verse, *If only in my dreams*. Startled, Marianne said "I hope it sounds better than when we were on the train, going clickety, clack down the track!" Mary Catherine replied, "I love your voice, it's beautiful. I can see you singing with Glen Miller someday, Miss Indiana!" Both women went to their rooms and enjoyed their first shower in over a day. Before dinner they met in the drawing room for cocktails.

A roaring fire was blazing in the huge fireplace. Above the mantle was a picture of William Howard Taft, twenty-seventh President of the United States and his wife and children. Her uncle was seated on the president's lap. A highly varnished fid, used by boatswain mates on the famous sailing vessel the USS *Constitution,* lay on the mantle along with a box containing some blue and gold buttons from a Revolutionary War soldier's uniform. Mary Catherine had a scotch and soda in her hand, when Marianne entered the room. "What can I fix you dear? Would you like a glass of wine?" Marianne was a teetotaler and not yet 21, but the fire looked so warm and inviting and she said, "Ok I'll let you decide for me." She found a bottle of French burgundy and offered her a glass. Both sat in large wing back chairs facing each other talking about family and friends. "Marianne in your travels with the USO, you may be in the Pacific someday, and if by chance you see a submariner, ask him about the *Thornfish,* my son's ship. I know it's a long shot but if you ever do please meet him and tell him about our adventure together." Marianne looked at her pleading glance and said "Yes, I will. I'd love to." Mrs. Walker reached into her small purse and took out a picture of Rob. The same one she had shown Marianne on the train. Marianne looked at it for a long time not letting on that she had seen it before. "He is very handsome in his uniform. What rank is he?" The proud mother replied, "Well he's an ensign now; he was commissioned after OCS last spring. I believe Rob's submarine is stationed at Pearl Harbor." Marianne took a sip of wine and sighed, "I'm sure you and your husband are very proud of him." Before she could answer, she said "I must confess, dear, he is in a very dangerous line of work. Frankly, one of the reasons I'm here is to try to influence my husband and the senator to get Rob transferred into the intelligence service. That's where he belongs." Marianne replied, "Are you certain, Mrs. Walker? He must have made his own decision about serving in submarines. Or did the Navy order him?" Mrs. Walker seemed a little taken back by Marianne's blunt comment. "No, they have to be volunteers in submarines. But it is a little strange that he didn't go to submarine school in New London."

The doorbell rang, and Doctor Robert Walker entered the hallway. The tall, lanky professor took off his heavy overcoat, and quickly strode into the drawing room greeting his wife with a hug and a kiss. He took both of her hands into his and said, "Hi Honey, it's been too long. Your look great! How are you feeling? Let me see you." He spun her around and hugged her once more. Mary Catherine, a little embarrassed, turned and introduced her husband to her new friend from Indiana. Dr. Walker greeted Marianne warmly and before sitting down made himself a scotch and soda. It had been a long day for him. His secret work at the intelligence agency included researching prospective sites for amphibious landings on some of the Pacific Islands, mostly created by volcanic eruptions ages ago. He had visited some of the islands held by the Japanese years ago during his two-year assignment as an adjunct professor of volcanology at Tokyo University. They chatted before the fireplace, and then he excused himself to get ready for dinner.

Dinner at the senator's home was usually semiformal. He always dined late usually dressed in his suit and tie. The grandfather clock in the hall struck seven when they gathered in the dining room. The maid said they shouldn't wait for the senator. He was running late as usual. They were eating their dessert of Key Lime pie when the senator returned home. Of medium build, with a slender face set with small horn-rimmed glasses, he resembled a college professor with his Phi Beta Kappa key dangling from the keychain on his vest. He greeted everyone and gave a special welcome to Marianne. The soft-spoken senator, looking very tired, apologized for being so late. He explained that he was in a labor relations committee meeting trying to figure out how to deal with Harry Bridges, the controversial head of the longshoremen on the West Coast. During the American landings on Guadalcanal in August, some of his civilian labor union men on merchant ships carrying vital cargo, refused to work on Sundays. That changed immediately when U. S. Marines came aboard and began to throw some of the union men overboard.

As he ate his dinner, he inquired about Catherine's health, and how she was holding up under her treatments. Marianne was surprised by the senator's inquiry and asked, "Mrs. Walker, I feel as though I have imposed on you too much. I was unaware of you having a problem with your health." Mary Catherine replied, "No, I have enjoyed your company so much. You have been such a help to me already."

The senator added some sugar and sipped his coffee saying, "How is Rob doing? I bet he's about ready to qualify in submarines." She looked at her uncle and said, "His last letter was from Hawaii; the navy yard was doing some work on his submarine, the *Thornfish*. Uncle Bob, you know full well how I feel about him being in submarines. With his background and language skills, he would be perfect for a job in intelligence. He could be stationed right in Hawaii where his ship is homeported. Is there anything you can do? I know you have more important things on your agenda, but just this once, could you intercede with the Secretary of the Navy about Rob?" Looking at Dr. Walker, the senator looked very uncomfortable, he said, "Mary Catherine dear, I already have, that's why he was ordered to submarines right after graduation from OCS!" Mary Catherine looked like someone had just struck her in her stomach, she gasped, "What? Who asked you to do this?" The senator turned to her husband who started to say something, but his words failed.

Embarrassed with the scene unfolding, Marianne got up from the table and started to excuse herself. She wanted no part of the family feud that was occurring. Looking directly at her husband, Mary Catherine said, "Robert, why did you do this to me?" She dropped her dessert spoon, stood, reeled around and left the dining room.

It was going to be a long night.

CHAPTER 25

Awards
Pearl Harbor Naval Base

Monday morning Rob was aboard the *Thornfish,* in the small stateroom that he shared with John Young, changing into his white dress uniform. The admiral was to be on board at 1000 for an awards ceremony. The Bible that Valerie Edmonds had given him was open on his small desk. Rob had promised Mrs. Edmonds that he would read some of the verses each day. This morning the Bible was open to a passage from one of Paul's letters. Valerie had placed a bookmark and underlined 2 Corinthians 5: 17, "Therefore whoever is in Christ, is a new creation, the old has passed and the new has come." As Rob dressed, he mulled those words over when John pulled the curtain aside and sat down in the chair by the desk. Glancing at the open Bible he said, "Hey Rocky, are you getting religion?" Rob ignored him. "You better get dressed John; we've got inspection in a few minutes." Not to be sidetracked, John said, "Well let's talk about that book later; you know it's still the best seller on *The New York Times* reading list."

Rob finished closing the neck clasp on his dress-whites and admonished John, "Ok, but let's get going, we can't keep the admiral waiting." A few minutes later the word was passed on the 1 MC announcing system, ordering all hands-on deck for inspection. Rob led the way through the newly refurbished forward torpedo room to the access hatch leading to the main deck. They emerged from the hatch in blinding sunlight. The new exec, LT Rogers, was busy getting the crew lined up on the crowded deck forward of the bridge. Those officers and men designated to receive awards were in the front row. Captain Morrison was standing by the gangway, alongside the OOD and six enlisted crewmen, who were side boys, a traditional naval honor for flag officers. At exactly ten o'clock, a Navy gray sedan drove up to the gangway, and Vice Admiral Lockwood, Commander of Submarines Pacific Fleet, got out and promptly climbed the small gangway to the *Thornfish's* deck. There he was saluted smartly and greeted by the officer of the deck and the commanding officer of the *Thornfish*, newly promoted Lieutenant Commander Dick Morrison.

"Welcome aboard admiral, we are grateful for your coming to the *Thornfish* this morning. We have a great crew, and we are anxious for action." The admiral replied, "Good morning captain. We know you're going to hit the enemy hard." The crew looked sharp. They were lined three deep on the forward half of the sub. A small microphone stand was set up in front of the crew. After the customary inspection, the admiral addressed the crew. He concluded his remarks by saying "The *Thornfish* has battled the enemy and won, it has battled the storms and won, and it has battled internally and won. I am pleased to award the Navy Cross to your Captain Richard Morrison, for exemplary courage in the face of enemy forces, sinking a destroyer, a 10,000-ton troop ship carrying reinforcements, sinking of a Jap cruiser, and even an enemy floatplane." The admiral pinned the medal on Lieutenant Commander Morrison's right breast, shook his hand and returned Dick's salute. Jerry Abrams received the Silver Star for his exemplary work as diving officer and overseeing repairs under extremely adverse conditions of depth charging. Ensign Robert Walker, USNR, received the Bronze Star for heroism during the boarding of an enemy floatplane and subsequent capture of a valuable prisoner of war and the Navy Commendation Medal for his heroic work in saving the sub after the forward torpedo room flooded. Rob was the last officer to receive an award. After the admiral pinned Rob's medals on his chest, he shook his hand and said, "How long have you been in the Navy ensign?" Rob replied, "Just a little over ten months including midshipmen's training sir." The admiral turned and spoke to Rob and his new commanding officer, "Well you've rung up an impressive start to your naval service Ensign Walker, keep it up son. Next time I'm here I want to see Dolphins on your uniform." Rob saluted and said, "Thank you admiral, you will." The admiral walked to the end of the line and presented the Chief of the Boat Larry O'Neil with a Bronze Star for his heroic leadership in the face of severe enemy depth charging. While pinning the medal on his chest, he said, "Chief, I remember you from my tour at the sub school, New London, after the *Squalus* went down. You did heroic work in helping to save that boat. Thanks to you most of the crew were saved. Did the Navy give you a medal for heroism?" The chief replied, "No sir. I was just doing my job." The admiral looked directly at the chief's weather-beaten face and said, "Well you deserved a medal and perhaps this one will make up for it. You are a real hero in my book. Congratulations chief. Thanks for your outstanding service." Then the admiral disregarded Navy tradition and rendered a salute to the old chief.

After the awards ceremony concluded, the admiral asked to say a few words to the entire crew. He strode over to the microphone and said, "I congratulate you on a fine inspection this morning. It was a genuine pleasure to present these awards; they are well deserved. But I want you to be the first to know that as convening officer for the Board of Inquiry, I have concurred with the findings of the board in that newly promoted Lieutenant Commander Morrison, your commanding officer, acted properly in accordance with Navy Regulations and the Articles of the Governing of the Navy, in relieving your former commanding officer. Lieutenant Commander Custer is a good man but was under great stress and not well enough to command. Commander Morrison has my complete confidence that *Thornfish* will succeed in the best traditions of the United States Navy. Thanks, and Godspeed." With that said, he turned and walked with the CO to the gangway. As he was about to leave, he said quietly, "Dick you did the right thing. Good hunting. By the way, I hear good things about that young Ensign, Walker. Keep your eye on him." He turned, saluted the officer of the deck, and then the colors and walked briskly down the gangway to his waiting sedan.

The new exec then ordered the crew to assume parade rest and Dick Morrison, commanding officer of the USS *Thornfish*, walked smartly to the microphone and addressed his crew.

"Men stand at ease." He paused as he gathered his thoughts. "I want to talk about the work that is cut out for us. We will be leaving at 0730 tomorrow morning December 7, for three days of intensive training. One year ago, this quiet harbor was suddenly filled with hundreds of enemy planes. You can still see the damage they wrought on our ships and sailors, some 1600 are still entombed in the hulks of the battleships on the other side of the harbor. Their blood was spilled here. *Thornfish* will help to avenge their deaths. But to do it, we will need to be prepared, one mistake on the part of any one of you can destroy us. We will train and then train some more. We have 17 new sailors aboard now for our next patrol. We will become one hell of a fighting machine before we even see the enemy. I expect nothing less than a total exceptional performance from each one of you. This crew will become what Shakespeare once called a 'Band of Brothers.' The admiral said, just as he left, that we are an outstanding crew. He expects great things from us. We're not going to let him down.

"Now I want to challenge each one of you. *Thornfish* will be going into harm's way. We will be a thorn in the side of the enemy. We are all volunteers. We are going to take risks. But I will not be reckless. But if any member of this crew wants to be transferred before we leave in the morning, you are at liberty to do so. Just tell your division officer after we leave quarters this morning. That's all."

The exec called out attention on deck as the captain departed for an early lunch with the squadron commander. After dismissal, one man asked to be transferred. He was the young seaman, who had debilitating seasickness during the last patrol. The exec interviewed him along with his junior division officer. Bucky wanted to make sure that he was leaving for the right reason. Satisfied that he was truly having a hard time from throwing up with the smell of sweat, diesel fumes, stale air and constant motion up and down while on the surface and sometimes even while submerged during storms, he signed off on his request. The afternoon was an all hands evolution to load stores, fuel, torpedoes, five-inch ammunition, 40-mm and 20-mm ammo. During the afternoon the exec took Rob aside and said, "Rob, I don't want you to be too disappointed, but I think we're going to postpone your oral exam for qualification until after the next patrol. You have a good chance of getting a shot at making your torpedo attack qualification this week while we are underway. But it doesn't leave much time to assemble a board of three commanding officers to interview you on everything you'll need to qualify. Sixty more days or so won't make that much difference anyway and you'll be better prepared I'm sure." Rob was a little taken back. He was hoping to get the earliest qualification of any junior officer in the fleet. He took it in good stride and said, "I understand sir. I'll be ready."

Albert Buckhorn (Bucky) Rogers, LT USN, was the *Thornfish's* new exec. Ben Miller had selected him for his charismatic personality that was needed to mend some of the fractures that might be lingering from the episode on 24 October and the departure of Captain Custer. Of medium build, the sandy haired officer with a pencil thin mustache and big ears reminded some of the crew of the movie star Clark Gable. The new exec had already gained the respect of the crew in the short time he had been aboard *Thornfish*. His broad grin and enthusiastic manners were infections. Bucky was just what was needed to heal any division that might remain with the crew. Bucky was a Naval Academy graduate ranking near the bottom of his class. But his yearbook picture carried the notation, *Bound to Succeed*. He often told his close friends that he had close company in class standing with that of Admiral Bull Halsey, who ranked near the bottom of his class at Annapolis.

Bucky was fighting mad when he received orders assigning him to the *Thornfish*. He was awaiting a new billet as the new XO of a new boat about to be launched at Mare Island Naval Shipyard near San Francisco. He had plans to be married in a few months and he would have time to spend with his new bride. Dick was very pleased to have him as his number two on the *Thornfish*. He assured Bucky that his new assignment would only last for one patrol and would help him toward qualification for his own command.

· · · · ·

That evening, Rob had a few minutes to dash off four Christmas cards he purchased at the Navy Exchange Sunday afternoon. One went to his parents in Washington, DC, one to his sweetheart Molly back home, and one to his new friend in Honolulu, Lily. The fourth was a thank you to Mrs. Edmonds for her hospitality and the wonderful dinner she served in her beautiful home overlooking the harbor.

To each he assured them he was fine and had a great time in the rest and recreation period. He didn't mention anything about the Board of Inquiry as that was still under wraps for the public as far as he knew. The letters to his parents and Mrs. Edmonds were easy. The ones to Molly and Lily were difficult. The letter he had just received from Molly before they were to get underway worried him. She enclosed a clipping from *The Oxford Press* about the enlisted school at Miami University. The Navy was asking for female volunteers to teach some of the men ballroom dancing.

Her final paragraph read,

"Darling, I know you wouldn't mind, so I volunteered. It's a Saturday night event in the town hall and the Campus Owls play swing music. I dance with a lot of cute men, but my heart belongs to you completely as you know. Please don't worry. I love you, Your sweetheart, Molly.

P.S. I pray for you and your shipmates every day. Be careful! Remember, <u>Our Love is Here to Stay</u>"

Rob tore up his reply twice before writing, "Dearest Molly, thanks for the mail and the article from the press, sure I don't mind, you should teach these sailors. They need some etiquette and dancing lessons, so it will be good for them. Just think of me when you dance with each one. I miss you so much. We leave soon for training. You'll not hear from me for a while. I wish I could stand you under the mistletoe and kiss you and hold you tight. I love you. Rob xo xo xo."

Ben Miller drove his Jeep to the head of the pier where *Thornfish* berthed. He got out and returned the salute of the sentry and walked quickly to the gangway of the *Thornfish*. Dick Morrison greeted him and the two returned to the Jeep for a short ride to the officers' club. Earlier that day the staff briefed the new captain of the *Thornfish* about his next patrol. The area chosen was a hot one. Reports from other submarines had indicated heavy traffic between the oil-rich island of Borneo and the Japanese mainland. Priority was to be given to sink tankers to shut off much needed oil to the Japanese mainland. Dick had spent the afternoon pouring over patrol reports from other subs reporting on their experiences on patrol in the same general area.

The two sat at the rectangular bar under the veranda on the south porch. The fragrance of Bougainvillea flowers invaded the place where they were sitting as they admired the setting sun over Ewa Beach and Barbers Point. A PBY amphibious patrol plane was laboring for a takeoff from the seaplane base on Ford Island, reminding them that an enemy submarine might be lurking under the Pacific off the entrance buoys to Pearl. Ben was a little low this evening. He confessed he missed his wife and two children. They had been evacuated a few months after the sneak attack December 7, a year ago. They had found a home near the base at Mare Island. It was going to be a blue Christmas for him and Julie, his wife of fourteen years. Dick Morrison had never married. He had been engaged once but his fiancé was not cut out for Navy life, and he had spent most of the years since commissioning at the Naval Academy in submarines. First in the old S-boats, cramped, with no air conditioning, foul smells, and danger lurking in so many ways. When he was assigned to his first fleet boat, it was like being in heaven. It even had showers, two aft for the crew, and a small one just forward of the officers' quarters.

Ben said, "Dick, our Navy has taken a real beating this year. In August we lost the heavy cruisers *Quincy, Vincennes, Astoria,* and the Aussies lost *Canberra* in a night action off Savo Island near Guadalcanal. They are calling it Iron Bottom Sound. The Japs are good at night fighting. They are trained for night action, gunnery and torpedoes. The only good thing for our side was the battle of Coral Sea last May; the entire battle was fought by air. The ships never saw each other. We lost the *Lexington* there. But the Japs took a beating too. The other was off Midway in June. Japs lost four carriers to our Navy air, including the *Kaga* that attacked Pearl Harbor." Then Ben added, "You know the enemy names their ships for weird things. For example, Kaga in Japanese means Increasing Joy! Well they had decreasing joy when our dive bombers sank her." Dick replied, "But what did our subs do in the battle?" Ben paused, "Not much. We did some scouting, but our silent service was petty silent in the very important battle I'm sorry to say; the Navy fliers, especially those in torpedo squadrons, took some terrific losses. One of them lost all their aircraft. Only one pilot survived, an Ensign Gay who floated around in a life jacket after being shot down. Those guys had a lot of courage, flying at 200 feet over water at 180 knots into all that flack. Takes guts for sure."

Dick changed the subject. "Ben, what about Custer? How is he taking all this?" Ben took a long sip from his beer and said, "Well I was given the job of telling him the results of the admiral's decision. He expected that the board would decide in your favor. So, he wasn't too surprised. He asked me what his next assignment would be. He knows his career is now on the rocks. I asked him what he would like to do, and he replied he'd like to get another command. Dick, he's not ever going to command a ship again, but he has some good attributes that the Navy can use. I think he'll be assigned to sub school in New London. He's on administrative leave right now and is staying close to his home on the beach at Ewa officers' housing." Ben took out a pack of Pall Mall's and lit one up. His Ronson lighter was a gift from his wife for Christmas. He showed it to Dick. It was silver and very slim so that it would fit in his pocket. Julie had it engraved with his initials. He smoked too much Dick thought.

Ben stood and walked over to the porch railing and motioned for Dick to follow him. Away from the crowd at the bar, he talked of his next patrol. "Dick, I've helped plan your next patrol. As you know the admiral is sending you into a real hot spot. Your area will be to patrol between Formosa and the Chinese coast. There's a lot of traffic there now. We especially want you to sink tankers. Warships can't run without fuel, and we can hasten the war effort by sinking those Jap tankers." Dick replied, "Understood."

Ben took a drag on his Pall Mall, the longest cigarette made, and said, "The Japs are now wising up and are convoying their tankers. So, you'll have some escorts to contend with for sure. I'm trying to persuade the admiral to let us form a wolf pack, as the Germans do. Three boats coordinated by a wolf pack commander. That's what I am pulling for. I'd like to be back in command of one and get back to sea again." Dick studied his chief of staff's face; his square jaw, peppered gray hair, strong physique made the former halfback at the academy still look good. Dick thought Ben would be a terrific commander of our first wolf pack in the Pacific. Dick replied, "Do you think the admiral will let you go, Ben?" He took a long drag on his cigarette and lamented, "I sure hope so, I'm anxious to get in the fray out there after being on this desk for a year now."

"Well maybe when we return, you'll know. I sure would like to be in your wolf pack."

"I'd be honored to have *Thornfish*, Dick. Now let's get dinner. You have a full day tomorrow and the next few days. What time do we get underway in the morning? "

"Our schedule calls for us to leave the pier at 0730, another boat is going to take our place as soon as we leave. Since its December 7, I want all men not actually on watch to be topside when we pass the *Arizona*. Ensign Walker's schoolmate was one of the aviators newly assigned to *Arizona* when she sank. He died with the other 1238 officers and men. Our next patrol will be dedicated to these men." Ben replied, "A good tribute Dick."

Promptly at 0730 Monday December 7, 1942, *Thornfish's* diesel engines were idling in preparation for getting underway. On the bridge, Captain Morrison, and Bucky, the new exec, dressed in working khakis were discussing some messages that they had just received regarding the day's exercises. Ben Miller was aboard from the staff over-seeing the three-day training exercises. The officer of the deck, Ensign Rob Walker, ordered all mooring lines to be singled up. Sailors on the pier were standing by the bollards awaiting the command to cast off the lines. It was Rob's first time getting the sub underway. As part of his qualifications, he was required to prepare for getting underway, maneuvering the vessel away from the pier and through the harbor into the channel leading to the sea.

Standing on the cigarette deck behind the bridge, he ordered the stern line taken in and then the breast line. Returning to the bridge, he glanced at the channel to make sure there were no other vessels in the way. The bowline was held with a strain as he ordered the port engine ahead for just a few seconds and springing the stern clear of the pier. "Take in number one, "he yelled. "All engines back slow," Rob felt a rush of excitement as the sub responded to his commands. What a thrill for a guy out of college for less than a year! Dad would be proud he thought. Then he ordered port engine ahead third, starboard back one-third. *Thornfish* slowly started twisting. Once clear of the pier, he ordered five degrees left rudder to start a turn to line up in the channel. He ordered all engines ahead one third. *Thornfish* glided down the channel. Ahead they saw the wreckage of the USS *Arizona*. *Thornfish's* new executive officer stood on the bridge with the captain and had ordered all hands to stand at attention to starboard as they approached the remains of the *Arizona*. "Attention to starboard he commanded. Hand salute." He held the salute for a long time as the submarine churned by the once proud flagship of the Pacific Fleet. Oil from *Arizona's* tanks still seeped fuel. Workers were cutting the superstructure down to the waterline, a sad reminder of the day of infamy only a year ago.

Ben Miller stood alone on the cigarette deck aft of the bridge in a pensive mood. His thoughts were on that beautiful Sunday morning, only a year ago, as he was preparing to surprise his wife and two children by cooking breakfast for them. He called them his crew. He heard a plane zooming over his quarters at Ewa Beach, so close he ran outside to try to get some identification to file a complaint with his superiors. He was stunned. It was Japanese! Not only one plane but scores of them were launching a raid on the base at Pearl Harbor. Bombs were falling on the seaplane base on Ford Island. He rounded up his family and took them to the nearby school that offered a little more protection and then he drove to the boat landing and commandeered a 36-foot motor launch. He wanted to get to his duty station at the sub base, but he never made it. On the way to base headquarters, he found so many men in the water that had been aboard battleships, badly burned and wounded, that he rescued as many as the launch would hold and took them to Hospital Point for aid.

As *Thornfish* sped down the channel, men topside were closing hatches, stowing gear in preparation for the first dive after upkeep. Ben's solitude was broken by Captain Morrison, who stood by him. Sensing he was reliving some moments, both men remained silent as the submarine passed Ewa Beach officers' quarters where Ben had a residence on that fateful day. Dick finally broke the silence by asking him what he thought about how long it would take to destroy the enemy. Ben guessed three more years at least, and that didn't count invading the Jap homeland. "When we invade the Japanese homeland, we're in for one hell of a fight. Lots and lots of casualties on both sides." Dick agreed and abruptly changed the subject, "Ben I'd like for you to take my bunk for the three days of exercises. I won't be using it much anyway." Ben hastily added, "No that's your stateroom and I'm not going to take your place. I'll sleep in the wardroom folding bunk. I would like to beat you at cribbage though." Dick chuckled, "We'll see about that." And he added, "Watch out for Ensign Walker, he'll clean your clock. He did mine."

Rob gave orders to the helm guiding the sleek sub along the right side of the channel, past the antisubmarine nets at the entrance, and into the beautiful Pacific Ocean.

He thought how good it was to be back to sea. Perhaps he could get some time to rethink his relationship with Lily. He was confused. He liked her and her warm affection for him. She was so beautiful and vivacious! Any officer would trade him places in an instant. In many ways she reminded him of Molly. He just needed time to think things through.

CHAPTER 26

December 8, 1942
Oxford

Molly Gaynor was busy studying for her final exams; the first semester of her senior year was almost over, and she was looking forward to her last semester at Miami and beyond; she was giving more thought about her life after college. Following her father's edict, she majored in education. During her last semester at Miami, she had to do her student teaching at McGuffey Elementary School in Oxford, but her minor in English was more to her liking. She thoroughly enjoyed writing and she intended to pursue a career in journalism. Several of her articles appearing in *The Student* newspaper were reprinted in *The Oxford Press*. One was an article about the recent graduation of sailors from the Navy's radioman school. She was thrilled and clipped the article and enclosed it in her latest letter to Rob. Another of her articles was not sent to Rob. It was about the twenty-five Miami men that had lost their lives in the war in 1942.

Molly met many fine young enlisted men that were being trained at Miami as radioman while she was teaching some of them to dance on weekends. She made a special effort to attend the graduation of the first 100 sailors held in Benton Auditorium. About 85 of those that completed the school were promoted to third class petty officers. Dr. Upham, president of Miami, addressed the men and commented on their fine performance in school and the challenges facing the new men in the fleet. Molly's articles impressed the editor of *The Oxford Press*.

But she was also considering joining the WAVES. With Rob in the Navy and her brother in the Marines, she felt she could contribute if she joined the war effort too. A few Oxford women had volunteered after seeing the young women in their smart uniforms being trained as radio operators at Miami's campus.

During Christmas break Molly took the train from Oxford to Lima, the closest town to Marion on the B&O Route. It was filled with students going home for the holidays. She had the good fortune to be one of the first on board and quickly got a window seat. A sailor, in his dress blue uniform, placed her suitcase on the luggage rack overhead. She grabbed her book bag and started to read her mail that arrived just as she was leaving her dorm. A Christmas card from Mrs. Walker was among her letters. But tucked in among other correspondence was a thin airmail letter from Rob. She tore it open quickly and read every word as the B &O train pulled out of the Oxford depot belching black smoke. Packed with kids, some sitting on their suitcases, the six-car passenger train wound through the dreary cold countryside with stops in Lima, Findlay, and Cleveland. Rob's letter was filled with his adventures while on R&R in Hawaii. He assured her that she should go out dancing with some of the Navy trainees, if her heart remained with him. His assurance worried Molly; he seemed too anxious and she began to imagine something might be wrong with their relationship. Could Rob have found someone else? Woman's intuition she thought, but she was usually right. She would love to be able to talk with Rob directly on the phone but that seemed impossible to her.

She disembarked in Lima amid falling snow. Her father greeted her and led her to his new Buick Special, parked just outside of the crowded station built by the City of Lima in 1920. He was so proud of the black automobile. Frank had purchased it brand spanking new for $980 just after war broke out December 7, a year ago. Her mother hugged her and helped her stow her bag in the trunk. Soon they were on Highway 30 East, heading for home in Marion for Christmas. Her father was driving 50 miles per hour despite the nationwide speed limit imposed by the government of 35 miles per hour. Gas rationing had been implemented in July, and all vehicles had to display a sticker, A for personal driving, B for business, and C for physicians, nurses and officials in government. Frank's car had a B sticker that enabled him to make trips such as this. Frank had moved up in the community and was now a new member of the city council of Marion. "Frank, you're speeding, you're going 50," her mother said, looking over his shoulder from the backseat. She knew full well that he would not pay any attention to her. He never did.

Eventually the conversation turned to an important item for her father. Molly's dad asked her about her studies, and her future after graduation. She hesitated to share her thoughts about her future, especially now. She needed the right time to inform her father of her change in direction. Teaching was an admirable career, but she had only studied education at the insistence of her father. Her heart was not in it. So, she spun his inquiry by asking about her brother. Frank said, "No we haven't heard from him in a long while. All we know is that he is in an infantry division in the South Pacific." Then Frank brought up the subject again as he finally slowed down due to the buildup of snow on the highway, saying "Molly, I have already talked with the Superintendent of Schools about you. He said he would be glad to have you come and discuss job opportunities with him over the Christmas break. You'll have a good job waiting for you right after graduation." Her mother broke in just in time, "Frank will you please turn the heater up? I'm freezing!" The 1941 Buick Special's heater located under the front seat did not suit her. She was still cold. Molly wanted to avoid an argument now.

"Dad let's talk about it later. I'm tired now." And she laid back in the seat and closed her eyes. She thought this might be a difficult Christmas break.

A few days after Molly arrived, her dad came home with a nine-foot Christmas tree, cut from a nearby farm, perched on top of his 1930 black Model A Ford four-door sedan. Frank discovered the antique Ford in an old widow lady's barn while helping her with some tile work. The little four-cylinder stick shift antique would go for miles on a thimbleful of gas. The car had been up on blocks for years. The interior was almost like new. The rear seat had a 'mother-in-law's' arms rest in the center, and because of gas rationing, Frank used it more than the big straight-eight Buick. The kids, however, were embarrassed when their dad dropped them off in front of their school in the morning in that old Ford.

The family had moved since Molly started college. They were able to purchase a four-bedroom home with a large front porch on Lafayette Street, an upscale neighborhood on the south side of Marion. Frank's business had expanded to include the sale of coal. Every home had a furnace and a coal bin in the basement. The Gaynor's new home had a stoker that fed coal automatically into the furnace. One of Gaynor's boys would fill the hopper once a day and bank the fire at night. Ashes were shaken down through a grate in the brick lined furnace and every few days they shoveled them into a bucket and took them outside. During icy days the boys would scatter the ashes on the sidewalk to give some traction when walking down to the mailbox at the curb. The upstairs bedrooms were heated in the winter by open grates in the floor, so that the heat from the first floor would rise to the bedrooms. Molly found the bedrooms cold at night, but her mother had plenty of quilts and blankets piled on the beds.

Gaynor tradition included having the entire family decorate the Christmas tree on Christmas Eve. The boys set it up in the living room, and they eagerly began adding ornaments, lights, and tinsel. The final decoration was to place the paper angel on the very tip-top of the beautiful Norwegian pine. That was Molly's job as the oldest girl in the Gaynor clan. Her little brother placed the step ladder and held it while Molly climbed to put the little angel at the very tip of the tree. It looked perfect. They all stood and admired the beautiful decorations, and then carefully gathered up all the discarded packing paper. Father plugged the string of lights into the wall socket and the tree came to life. Afterward, the family had a marvelous dinner of turkey and all the trimmings. After dinner Molly found a small package in the mailbox. It was postmarked Cleveland, Ohio. What could that be she thought? Could it be a present from Rob? But how could it be from Cleveland? She sat in a living room chair, hurriedly tore open the wrapping paper and opened the box. Inside was a beautiful silver filigree angel broach and a note: "To Molly from Woody, Merry Christmas." She was stunned. The note continued, "Molly, I saw this at Snyder's in Oxford and thought you'd enjoy wearing it.

I'll be driving back to Oxford on the 27th, would you like a ride back to school? I can stop by and pick you up. Please phone me as soon as possible at Clearwater 5683. Your friend Woody."

Molly's little brother Eddie was looking over her shoulder and read every word. "Molly, who is Woody?" Molly blushed. "None of your business young man. But just to be clear, he's a student at Miami and just a friend of mine who is on the staff of *The Miami Student* newspaper with me. And he's going to give me a ride back to school. That's all!"

Not to be deterred her little brother loudly announced to the family in a sassy sing song tone, "Molly's got another boyfriend! Molly's got another boyfriend!"

CHAPTER 27

Drills

The next three days for *Thornfish* were filled with drills. The captain and his new exec, Buck Rogers, and the squadron chief of staff, made plans for three days of exercises. First individual training; each man's job was important. The second was departmental training. And the third, entire crew training for battle, submerged or surface gun action. As part of his qualification in submarines, Rob would be the diving officer, making calculations for the first dive of the day. The submarine's fuel, stores, crew, and armament weight all had to be accounted for to properly trim the boat once it dived into the depths of the Pacific off the southern coast of Oahu. Each tank has weights assigned depending on the type of liquid, and capacity. Once the calculations are complete, the diving officer compensates the boat by trimming tanks, pumping from one tank to the other to satisfy neutral buoyancy. During every dive, whether in training or combat, the senior man in each compartment must personally go over the list posted in the compartment to ensure that all precautions had been taken before diving. One mistake could cost them their lives.

Thornfish's new executive officer stood in the control room and watched as the reports were received from each compartment. The chief of the boat, one of the survivors of the ill-fated *Squalus*, stood nervously beside the exec, receiving the reports, sweating profusely as images of his shipmates on the *Squalus* flashed in his mind. Men were crying for help as their compartments flooded after the main induction valve failed to close on that fateful cold winter day when the *Squalus* made its first dive after being in the shipyard for weeks. Only thirty-three men survived the sinking, rescued by a new rescue apparatus, a diving bell that fits over the submarine's forward deck hatch. The chief was one of the last to ascend in the diving bell, but his ordeal was not over as the cable nearly parted as they were hauled to the surface. His shipmates considered him to have nerves of steel, but internally he still fought off the horrific images of the sinking. The submarine was raised after many tries and later completely overhauled and renamed the *Sailfish*. After the accident, all subs had spring loaded hydraulic safety valves installed in the air induction lines going to the engine rooms that could be shut in seconds rather than by cranking by hand as on the ill-fated *Squalus*.

Under the supervision of the chief engineer, Rob completed his calculations and reported to the exec, "Sir, the boat is compensated and ready for dive." The exec glanced at Jerry to see if he approved, and when the engineer nodded, Bucky said, "Very Well," and turned to the general announcing system and reported, "Captain, control reports the boat is ready for dive, Sir." Two blasts of the klaxon sent *Thornfish* under for the first time in weeks.

"Green board, sir" Rob yelled as the "Christmas tree" in the control room showed all hatches, main induction, engine exhaust valves had changed from red indicating open to green showing shut. Immediately air was bled into the boat from the air manifold, and the second-class petty officer reported, "Pressure in the boat, Sir." The captain had the conn in the conning tower and ordered, "Make your depth 60 feet." Rob stood behind the bow and stern planes men, supervising their every move as they maneuvered their planes to achieve the ordered down bubble. Once at depth, Rob pumped some water from forward trim to after trim tanks to complete the trim of the boat. "Nice job, Rob," the exec exclaimed. *Thornfish* made twenty practice dives the first day, giving all officers at least two dives. Their guardian Destroyer Escort, the USS *Litchfield*, stood by to ensure that a friendly patrol plane didn't bomb them. The next day Rob would get his chance at qualification by being the approach officer in an exercise that would fire a dummy torpedo at the destroyer.

The evening meal was served at 1800. Seated at the tiny wardroom table were the exec, Buck Rogers, Jerry Abrams the chief engineer, Rob Walker, and John Young. On watch on the bridge were, Pete Robinson, gunnery officer, and a new JOOD, a brand-new *George* right out of sub school, Shane Montgomery, a reserve officer and a mechanical engineer graduate of Texas A&M, would serve as an assistant engineering officer and supply officer. In fact, all the officers were reservists except the exec and the captain, both of whom graduated from the Naval Academy.

They were awaiting the arrival of the captain and the Chief of Staff, Ben Miller, both in the captain's stateroom. The cooks made a special dinner for the captain, celebrating his promotion to Lieutenant Commander. Tonight's meal featured clam chowder, followed by a fresh green salad, baked potatoes and steaks topped off with a dessert of ice cream and a chocolate cake decorated with Lieutenant Commander's stripes.

Captain Morrison came in apologizing for his being late and motioned for Ben to seat himself to his left. Every officer watched in fascination as the captain sat down in his chair. Suddenly, a huge fart erupted. Dick's face flushed and gradually he began to roar with laughter. Bucky had placed a Bronx Cheer flatulence balloon under the cushion of the captain's chair. He reached under the cushion and threw it at Bucky, knowing full well his reputation for practical jokes. When the laughter subsided, Bucky started to apologize, but Dick wouldn't let him. He said, "This joke's on me. But I'll get even with you mister, so be on guard!" Rob thought how much the atmosphere in the wardroom had changed since Captain Custer left.

The *Thornfish's* new executive officer was like his captain in many respects. Both were energetic, aggressive, but sensible and very personable. They saw themselves as a team, leading men who were eager to excel. Bucky was selected to bring cohesion to the boat after the Custer fiasco. But his life had been interrupted by this assignment. He and his fiancé were in San Francisco, awaiting assignment to new construction and were planning to be married. All that changed when he received urgent orders to *Thornfish*. He didn't let on to anyone, but he still harbored some resentment for the sudden change of duty.

After dinner, Bucky had Rob stay for a few minutes. "Are you ready for the torpedo exercise tomorrow" he asked. "Yes, Sir," Rob replied.

"Good, this will complete your underway qualification, so don't screw up. Remember, each periscope observation should be very brief, just enough get a range and bearing, and angle on the bow. No more than ten seconds. Ride the scope up, so when it breaks the surface, you'll be ready to get the bearings. The tin can will be zigzagging. At the start of the exercise he'll be about five thousand yards away. Our usual tracking team will be assisting you."

"Yes, sir."

"The dummy torpedoes are scarce and expensive, so we 'll only get a few shots off tomorrow. I imagine you'll be up later in the morning."

"Thanks sir, I appreciate your confidence in me."

"Ok, but now I understand you're pretty good at cribbage. I'll challenge you to a couple of tracks."

Rob beat him two out of three.

· · · · ·

Rob had a fitful night. He was scheduled for the 4 to 8 watch in the morning and needed rest but was excited about the shot in the morning. He'd have only one chance. He tossed and turned. And then there was Lily. He was looking forward to seeing her one more time. But should he? He felt bad. He was leading her on, and guilt was beginning to gnaw at him. *I'm a real hypocrite*, he thought as he lay on his bed that was too short for his frame. He stared at the bottom of the bunk over his head for a long time thinking about his situation. Rob finally turned on his side and in the dim light he saw the picture of Molly taped on the bulkhead. She was looking directly at him.

At 0315 the quartermaster of the watch gently shook Rob's shoulder, "Sir, the OOD asked me to wake you. The weather topside is clear but cool, sea state 2." Rob shook the sleep out of his eyes, and said "OK, thanks." He slid out of the bunk, pulled on his khaki pants, washed his face and donned his wool watch sweater. On his way out, he grabbed his fanny life vest. At night watch standers topside in submarines were required to wear an inflatable life ring abound their waist, equipped with a small flashlight and whistle. An undetected rogue wave could float them right out of the bridge. Rob put on his red goggles and stopped in the wardroom for a cup of coffee. At 3:30 in the morning it looked like black molasses, so he went to the crews' galley and got a fresh cup. He entered the control room, looked at the chart and their position on the DR track, and read the notebook of the captain's night orders. He ascended the ladder to the conning tower and checked the radar scope. The PPI showed the destroyer escort ahead of *Thornfish* some two thousand yards. He climbed the ladder to the bridge asking permission from the OOD to come on the bridge. Pete said, "Permission granted Rocky, glad to see you." Once on the bridge he saw Pete standing by the windscreen. They huddled out of the wind as Pete brought Rob up to date on the course and speed, conditions of all hatches and openings, engines in use, conditions of the batteries, number of personnel topside, and radio call signs, weather conditions taking time to ensure that his relief was fully apprised of all the information needed to ensure the safety of the boat. Pete checked Rob's night vision by holding up two fingers, five feet from Rob on the darkened bridge. Rob identified them satisfying Pete that his night vision was ok. No lights were visible as both ships were darkened. Rob took a flashlight with red lens cover and checked the condition of the hatch leading to the conning tower to make sure no loose gear was present that would block shutting the hatch in an emergency. Once satisfied he said to Pete, "I relieve you sir."

It was a beautiful night the stars were particularly brilliant; Rob thought…*what a marvelous universe.* He recalled his freshman geology professor talking about the creation theories of the universe. *Did it all just happen or is there a creator that made the universe?* His classes in chemistry, and physics made him appreciate the precision of even the smallest atoms, protons, neutrons, and electrons. He recalled his Methodist confirmation class and the opening verses of Genesis, "In the beginning God created the heavens and the earth." His freshman geology instructor said he believed in the Big Bang Theory. Rob asked himself, *who created the bang?*

Dawn was just a few minutes away; Bucky would have a lot of good stars to shoot for his position this morning. The XO and quartermaster would be up soon to await the first glimpse of the horizon during twilight, that would enable them to determine the angle between the horizon and the star with the sextant. That would give them its altitude and coupled with the time provide a line of position for the navigator. Ancient navigators could determine latitude by observing the altitude of the north star, Polaris, but until accurate clocks were made, longitude remained just a guess.

A half an hour before sunrise, Bucky and the quartermaster asked permission to come up. "Come up," Rob shouted over the noise of the two diesel engines propelling them along on the calm waters at ten knots. This time of day is the most dangerous time for surfaced vessels; a submerged enemy sub can see the silhouette of surfaced ships and not expose themselves. The exec and his quartermaster went aft to the cigarette deck and started taking their star sights. That done they returned to the bridge and Bucky asked how the watch was going. The quartermaster had descended the ladder to the control room to start his calculations. "Well, sir, ok… we have a couple of new lookouts that are being trained, and I have been rotating them every hour." Bucky said, "Good Rob, we have new men plus one new petty officer from the repair crew to break in." Just as the XO was ready to go below, the forward port lookout yelled, "Periscope on the port bow!" Rob put his binoculars in the direction and confirmed the report. The early morning dim light disclosed a periscope two feet out of the water. Without hesitating he ordered left full rudder all engines ahead emergency and sounded the collision alarm. The patrol orders called for turning towards a periscope ahead of the beam, and away from one aft. He hit the speaker button commanding the control room to inform the destroyer escort of a sub sighted off our port bow. Down below the crew jumped out of their bunks, started shutting the watertight doors leading from each compartment. Rob barked orders "Helm, shift your rudder…steady on course 230. Control, tell the DD we are coming left toward the contact and stay away from us!" The captain rushed to the bridge and as the *Thornfish* accelerated, the periscope was more visible in the dawn's early light. The exec was on the port side of the bridge looking for the object and shouted Rob, "It's a mop handle! Some swabby probably dropped a mop while trying to clean it and it's floating towards Hawaii!" In the swells of the sea, the bobbing mop handle looked every bit like a submarine's periscope. Completely embarrassed, Rob recovered enough to order all engines ahead standard, and resumed the base course. Bucky pressed the microphone lever and announced, "Control, this is the exec, secure from the collision, and notify the destroyer that we have identified an enemy mop."

At breakfast Rob was the butt of a lot of good-natured jokes, "Rob did you see the mop bucket too?" Finally, the captain interjected, "Knock it off, I want everyone to know that the OOD did everything right. If that had been a Jap sub lying off Pearl this morning and we failed to do what Rob did, we'd all be dead. Better to react like Rob did than hesitate and be torpedoed. In fact, we were going to have a collision drill later today, I'm canceling it now because of the good work Rob and the crew did this morning." Ben Miller, sitting alongside the captain, said "Amen."

Rob felt a lot better, but he was a little nervous…in a few hours he would have his big test.

One of the requirements for qualification as a submariner, is to fire a torpedo and make a hit on a moving target. Not only did he have to position the submarine to fire the dummy torpedo, but he also had to prepare it personally and load it in the firing tube. After breakfast, the chief of the boat met Rob in the forward torpedo room to preview the proper procedures for firing with him. The fish gang, as they called themselves, said, "Sir we're pulling for you!" Everyone on the boat liked Rob. His gregarious manner, broad smile, courage under fire, and concern for his men made him a favorite among the crew. The torpedo men had painted "Rob's Rocket" on the head of the fish. And alongside, a crude figure of a mop. Rob said, "Thanks guys for the confidence and the mop!" The chief was satisfied that he had everything down pat, and they returned to the wardroom where the exec had laid out his plan of the day for the exercises. Exercises were scheduled throughout the entire day. Rob's turn was scheduled for 1300. The stewards laid out a buffet in the wardroom of fresh condiments, sandwiches, apples, and chocolate chip cookies to be eaten whenever the officers had time. Piping hot coffee was always available. The food for the submarine service was the best even during drills.

At 1230 Rob was in the conning tower. A half hour before, under the observation of the executive officer, Rob loaded the Mark-14 practice torpedo in the number one torpedo tube making it fully ready to fire. Now he was assuming the role of the approach officer making the periscope observations. The captain on the bridge told the OOD to dive the boat. Two blasts of the klaxon sent *Thornfish* at full speed into the Pacific off Pearl Harbor. Rob assumed the conn and ordered the diving officer in the control room to make his depth 60 feet. He heard the familiar "Green board, pressure in the boat sir." Rob acknowledged saying, "Very well, sonar report!"

"Sir I have sound bearing 185 degrees, sounds like twin screws of a destroyer. Estimated speed 15 knots."

"Very well. Keep giving me reports every two minutes."

"Aye sir."

"Up periscope!'" Rob squatted on his knees and as the scope rose, he opened the handles and stood up as it rose out of the well below.

Rob said, "I have the target's range 2500 yards, the angle on the bow, Starboard 20. Down scope." The quartermaster recorded the bearing from the bearing circle on the periscope. All this took less than 10 seconds. The information was put in the target data computer on the port side of the conning tower. It was quiet enough in the conning tower for Rob to hear the motors grinding out the initial information. "Come left to new course two zero zero." The helm acknowledged his order and then Rob reduced speed to minimize the wake of the periscope. *Thornfish* slowly turned toward the new target. Rob's calm, calculating manner radiated confidence. Sonar reported new target bearing and range. Rob ordered the scope up once again for another look. This time he was able to focus the range better and said, "Mark…bearing, range 1500 yards, target turning, angle on the bow port 15. Down scope, open outer door tube on number one, prepare to fire. Set depth 25 feet." Three minutes later the destroyer suddenly turned left on a new course that would bring it right in front of the *Thornfish*. Rob couldn't believe it. This would be a dead-on target. He yelled, "This is a final bearing and range, up scope." He took one more look and said, "Set gyro angle 10 degrees. Standby …mark bearing, range 900 yards…. Fire one!" The fire controlman pushed the firing lever, the dummy fish sped out of the torpedo tube at 45 knots, and ninety seconds later those on the bridge of the destroyer saw the wake of the fish as it went right under them on the port beam. As soon as the torpedo made its run, the captain took the conn, and after observing the sea around and once satisfied it was safe, he ordered, "Surface the boat." Three blasts of the klaxon and *Thornfish* broke the surface. Dick, looking through the scope said, "Bow out," whirled around and said, "Stern out. Start the low-pressure blow. Quartermaster open the hatch." The lookouts prepared to come up as soon as the captain standing on the bridge ordered them up.

The submarine division observer on board the DD radioed, "*Thornfish*, the last one was excellent. If it were a live shot, we'd be dead or swimming." Captain Morrison sent an acknowledgment, "Roger, our ensign did that one." Later in the wardroom over a cup of coffee, the chief of staff, said to the exec, "Rob, did great today, Bucky, he's going to be a winner for you." Bucky said, "Yes, sir. I concur."

CHAPTER 28

Farewell Dinner

Captain Morrison requested an additional day of exercises. He wanted more practice with his attack team and battle surface. Both evolutions required the best of teamwork. Ben concurred and in the four days they were underway, they made over fifty dives, and numerous approaches. While on the surface, four lookouts, two officers including the captain would be on deck. When the klaxon sounded, all of them would be down the hatch and underwater in fifty seconds. That took a lot of practice and teamwork. After their exercises, the destroyer dropped two depth charges set at 100 feet to acquaint the new members of the crew with actual depth charges. It shook the boat and the new men but did no damage. At 1600 Thursday afternoon the submarine docked alongside pier five at the sub base. Rob made the landing and fulfilled his last underway requirement for qualification SS submarines. The only remaining thing was the oral exam which had been postponed until after the next patrol.

Lily couldn't contain herself. She learned from one of the junior officers on the sub base that the *Thornfish* was due in late Thursday afternoon. She got off work early and drove her mother's convertible to the main gate, hoping to see Rob. She parked in the lot outside the gate and wrote a note on a slip of paper, folded it and put it in an envelope, marked with attention Ensign Robert A. Walker, USNR, USS *Thornfish*. She approached the Marine guard at the gate and handed him the note. "Sir, could you possibly have someone deliver this to the *Thornfish* for me?" The burly Marine didn't say anything. He looked at her beautiful body and then at his clipboard and said, "That boat is not here," and then corrected himself. Someone had penciled in the *Thornfish* on the list of subs in port. "Well it's unusual but I'll try." He called for the messenger of the watch posted nearby and said, "Sailor, deliver this to the OOD on the *Thornfish* right away."

Ben Miller was about to depart from the *Thornfish*. Before leaving he gave a brief evaluation of the exercises he had observed to the officers and leading petty officers in the wardroom. He was extremely pleased with the performance of the crew and commended them for their hard work in preparation for deployment on their second patrol. He complimented Rob for his quick response to the periscope episode, and his excellent qualification torpedo approach. The exec gave the crew liberty to expire at 0700 the next morning.

Dick escorted the chief of staff to the brow. Ben paused to shake his hand and said "Dick, we're confident *Thornfish* will do well. Bag one for me." Captain Morrison saluted smartly and just as the Chief of Staff Miller was leaving the Marine messenger asked permission to come aboard to deliver a message to Ensign Walker. He saluted the colors and then the two officers and the captain took the envelope and said he would deliver it. "The messenger, rather apologetically said, "Sir, the young lady is ... ah, sir, she is waiting at the gate for him." Both officers looked at each other and smiled, Ben said, "I'll wait and give him a ride up to the gate."

Captain Morrison found Rob at his desk finishing a letter to Molly. He had just sealed it and was about to place it in the outgoing mail in the wardroom when the captain stuck his head in the curtain and gave Rob the message from Lily. "Rob, a young lady is waiting for you at the main gate. Chief of Staff Miller will give you a ride if you hurry. Just remember to be back on board before 0700."

On the way to the gate, Ben Miller said, "Rob you've made quite an impression on your crew and officers. I want to give you something to think about during the next patrol. I'd very much like to see you stay in the Navy after this war is over. I think you'd have a great career as a regular officer. If you apply to transfer to the regular Navy, I'll be happy to give your letter my personal endorsement. Submarines are probably the fastest way to command in this man's Navy. Command at sea is what it's all about. There is nothing like it in any profession. Give it some serious thought. There's no hurry but if you have any questions please don't hesitate to contact me. All the best to you."

"Aye sir, I certainly will consider it. I like the Navy. Thanks for your confidence.... I'll do my best not to let you down. And thanks for the ride. ... Look, here's my friend."

Lily saw Rob getting out of the Jeep and ran to meet him. Lily was wearing the very short cocktail dress that she wore in the Tiki Bar. The tight-fitting Hawaiian dress accentuated her bosom and beautiful thighs causing her submariner customers to order more than one drink and tipping her very well. She hugged Rob tightly and kissed him. He was so glad to see her; they had only been separated a week, but it seemed longer. Rob introduced her to Captain Miller. He greeted her warmly and said, "Lily, Ensign Walker tells me you lost your father on the *Arizona*. I'm truly sorry for you, we lost a lot of fine men that day." Lily said, "Thank you sir. My father was doing what he signed up for, he even extended his enlistment when he saw the signs of war coming." Ben looked at her, "Bless you and your mother." He turned and got back in the Jeep; Lily watched him leave and holding Rob's hand said, "Let's go home. Mom has dinner waiting for us." Rob asked, "How did you know we were back?"

Lily said with a coy smile, "Ensign, I have my sources."

· · · · ·

The aroma of the freshly baked dinner rolls greeted Lily and Rob as they entered the foyer of the Edmonds' beautiful home overlooking the harbor. Mrs. Edmonds made a sumptuous dinner for Rob of Mahi cooked over the hibachi with rice, and steamed vegetables. During dinner the conversation turned to news of the war. They talked about the fierce fighting still ongoing on Guadalcanal and the bad news of the loss of cruisers in the Solomon Islands. Rob didn't mention the loss of six submarines in the first seven months of the war in the Pacific. Finally, Lily changed the subject to Christmas. She and her mom had a present for Rob. "This is special, Rob, mom found this in the surplus store downtown." Rob carefully unwrapped the package revealing a small New Testament Bible. Valerie Edmonds said, "It will fit in your shirt pocket Rob, but look inside. It's a Heart Shield Bible, to be worn in the shirt pocket over your heart." The front and back covers were made of stainless steel. If a bullet hits the cover, it would protect the person wearing it.

Inscribed were the words: *Rob, May the Lord bless you and keep you. Love Valerie &* *Lily.*

They sat on the lanai talking for hours, Rob and Lily sipping sake and Valerie green tea. Finally, Mrs. Edmonds said good night. Rob rose and hugged her and said, "Thank you Mrs. Edmonds for everything… the dinner, the Bible, everything you've done for me. I wish I could return some of the favors you have given me. I really appreciate the Bible. I 'll read it, I promise. We have a great ship. A terrific captain and a great crew. We'll be alright." She kissed him on the cheek and said she would be praying for him and his ship every day. Her eyes glistened in the rainbow of lights in the room as she retired for the night.

After Valerie left, Lily and Rob sat on the couch staring at the dimmed city lights below. Neither of them wanted to break the silence of the moment. The Christmas tree on the lanai filled the room with colored lights. Lily finally broke the silence saying, "Rob I have a request." Rob was surprised, "What is it Lily?" He looked at her as a sly smile graced her lips, "It's your turn to give me a present." She pulled him toward her and suddenly she was on him… it was déjà vu again. It was a night to remember.

Dawn was breaking over Diamond Head when Lily drove her mom's Red Chevy up to the front gate of the submarine base. In the trunk were two small stacks of records she rescued from the Royal Hawaiian bar jukebox spares. "For the ship Rob, handle them with care. They'll break you know." Rob started to acknowledge her admonition and Lily added, "But Rob my heart is breaking now." Rob held her close. They embraced once again, and Lily whispered, "I love you Rob," and quickly turned and ran to her car. Rob watched her leave until her taillights disappeared in the early light of dawn. He ordered the messenger at the gate to put the records in a Jeep and they drove to the gangway. The records would be a cherished treasure for the crew in the next months at sea.

Rob was exhausted. He got one hour of sleep before the general announcing system called reveille. He grabbed a quick shower, dressed and joined the other officers in the wardroom for a breakfast of scrambled eggs, baked beans and hash brown potatoes. The morning would be filled with taking on more stores, torpedoes and communication codes, documents, charts and weather forecasts. Most important for Rob, as communicator, were the recognition codes they would need to try to prevent friendly aircraft and ships from firing on them. Any surfaced submarine was a juicy target for Army air force pilots based on the island. At 1100 all departments reported to the exec that they were manned and ready for sea. Bucky acknowledged the reports and informed the captain that they were prepared for patrol. The Division CO, Captain Maurice "Mo" Brown, arrived at the gangway along with Ben Miller. They came aboard briefly for a cup of coffee in the wardroom and said goodbye to the captain. After they departed, John Young had the conn for the underway as *Thornfish* smoothly backed out of the pier and into the channel. As the submarine rounded the point across from Ewa Beach offices' quarters, the signalman on the bridge noted an officer standing on the boat landing signaling by semaphore with his hands. Dick asked the signalman, "What did he say?" He replied, "Well sir, all he said was "Good Luck and Good Hunting. C." Dick looked through his binoculars and saw his former commanding officer, J.J. Custer. Dick ordered the signalman to reply, "Roger, thanks." *Thornfish's* new captain and executive officer both saluted and turned to view the channel markers before them. Later, the *Thornfish* was met outside the harbor antisubmarine nets by their destroyer escort. Ahead some 1300 miles west was their first destination, Midway Island. *Thornfish* was on patrol to avenge the day of infamy exactly one year ago.

* * * * *

The bar at the Royal Hawaiian closed at ten p.m. The bartender, an old Navy retired petty officer, dressed in a wild aloha shirt, took Lily home. Her mother met her at the door. "Hi honey. I bet you're tired. Want some iced tea?" Lily said, "No mom, just bed." Not to be persuaded, her mother led her out to the lanai, and they sat down overlooking their favorite view, Honolulu and the base at night. A year ago, their lives were shattered when the Japanese attacked killing her father. The wrecked hulk of the USS *Arizona*, her father's tomb and 1237 other sailors, still protruded out of the oil slick waters around its former berth off Ford Island. Shipyard workers' cars, with their dimmed headlights, slowly made their way down Highway 1 at the top seed limit of 35 miles per hour.

They both sat there lost in their thoughts. Lily broke the silence on the darkened lanai, "Rob's boat is at sea now mom, off to only God knows where."

Lily's mom reached over and took her hand. "Lily, I know you care for Rob, maybe you're in love with him, but honey don't get too involved. He's in the riskiest branch of the Navy, and he may not ever come back. I don't want you to get hurt; you've had enough already with dad gone. Just be careful with your heart." In the dark, her mother didn't see the tears running down her only daughter's cheeks.

Part Two

The Road to Tokyo

CHAPTER 29

Midway

It's twelve hundred miles from Hawaii to Midway Island, west and a little north of Pearl Harbor. Ben Miller decided to ride the boat to Midway. A problem had developed with some logistics with the squadron's boats temporarily being outfitted at Midway. His boss wanted him to get them fixed pronto. *Thornfish* was escorted by a destroyer for the first fifty miles of the journey to prevent an attack by a friendly aircraft while *Thornfish* was on the surface. Submarines all look the same to pilots. Even though there was a safe passage zone ten miles wide for their journey, the *Thornfish* had to dive suddenly the next day after their escort departed, when an Army Liberator Bomber flew toward them and dropped two bombs; fortunately, the bomber was a lousy shot and the boat escaped any damage. *Thornfish* tried in vain to signal the plane with the assigned recognition codes. The captain was furious, and had the exec log the incident and report it when they reached Midway. It would take about four days to reach the Navy base on Midway going at standard speed 15 knots. There they would refuel and take on mail and additional provisions and depart as soon as possible for their destination in the South China Sea.

The Supply Officer, the new *George*, had managed to get a small artificial Christmas tree and decorations before leaving Pearl. It was set up in the crew's mess on a shelf above the slot machine. Chief O'Neil would preside at its lighting on Christmas Eve. New to *Thornfish*, besides the slot machine, was a small ice cream maker courtesy of the American Legion Post in Pearl Harbor. The fresh milk they took on board in Pearl would probably last until they reached Midway and from then on condensed milk would have to suffice. The exec scheduled multiple drills every day in route. With 17 new men and one inexperienced junior officer, training was a never-ending evolution on *Thornfish*. Captain Morrison was a stickler for doing every drill right. When the boat submerged, he required the men topside on the bridge to be down in the control room and the boat submerged in less than 60 seconds. Climbing down the ladders from the bridge hatch to the control room meant that the men had to slide down the ladders. Anyone lagging would find a body landing on his shoulders.

Before breakfast the third morning, the captain was shaving in his stateroom when he heard the exec on the bridge announcing system, exclaiming loudly, "Captain to the bridge!" Dick, with shaving cream still on his face, bounded out of his room up the ladders to the bridge, finding Bucky standing by the hatch with a stopwatch timing him, and yelled, "Good time captain, but I think you can do better!" Dick was expecting a serious problem awaiting him on the bridge; his demeanor changed from serious to relief and then to roaring laughter, "Ok Bucky. That's the second time you pulled one on me. You can expect some retaliation soon!" They both appreciated harmless practical jokes, and Buck had a reputation for some good ones.

Thornfish arrived off the entrance to Midway an hour after dawn lit up the eastern sky on the fifth day out from Pearl. The narrow entrance to the inner harbor required good seamanship to avoid hitting the reefs on either side. Captain Morrison skillfully conned the boat through the swift current in the constricted channel. They tied up next to the submarine tender, the USS *Fulton*, and were met by its executive officer and its repair and supply officers. The *Fulton,* during the battle for Midway in early June, got underway and rescued over two thousand of the crew of the sinking carrier, the USS *Yorktown*. Ben Miller knew the *Fulton*'s CO, a submariner from the Academy, and Dick felt that *Thornfish* would be given the best service possible. They sat in the wardroom with Jerry and went over the list of items. Their priority, besides refueling and taking on additional supplies, was a troublesome item needing immediate attention. The air-conditioning system was not performing well on the trip to Midway. AC is essential not only for the personal comfort of the crew but to maintain humidity within the sub to protect from electrical shorts. Jerry Abrams was not satisfied with its performance since leaving Pearl, and the tender was asked to try to fix it. After the conference, Ben and Dick reviewed the patrol plan along with Bucky. They were to patrol between Formosa and the Chinese mainland. Ben was an advocate of forming wolf packs as the Germans successfully did in 1942. COMSUBPAC, however, needed convincing. In the meantime, each sub would have its own territory communicating, as needed, with the other subs in adjacent patrol areas. Before departing the *Thornfish*, Ben Miller bade farewell to the officers and leading chiefs and announced to the crew over the I MC, "Good Luck and Good Hunting. And thanks for the ride."

Dick and Jerry continued monitoring the work in progress while the exec went ashore and got updated charts and intelligence information for the area they would be patrolling. A plane from Hawaii had landed in the afternoon bringing mail and packages for the boat. Rob received a packet of letters from Molly, a letter and a Christmas package from his folks, marked DO NOT OPEN TILL Christmas. Tucked in between was a small envelope, with the fragrance of Channel Number 5, from Lily.

Dick was anxious to get underway as soon as possible. The crew worked through the night and after topping off the fuel tanks and fresh water, they cast off all lines for their first war patrol under Captain Dick Morrison at dawn the next morning. Dick told his crew "*Thornfish* will live up to its name: a thorn in the side of the enemy. We intend to go in harm's way!"

A friendly aircraft patrolled overhead providing the additional security while heading west surfaced en route the Formosa Straits. At noon, the pilot flew low and wagged his wings in a salute as the plane returned to base. *Thornfish* was on its own.

Bucky had the officers' watch quarter and station bill updated to include the newest officer on board, a tall, slender athletic reservist just out of sub school named Anthony Kennedy. Tony was a graduate of Notre Dame and a star basketball player in his high school and college. His duties included Commissary Officer and *George,* the go for. He would stand his watches with Rob. John Young, the first lieutenant, would stand top watch as OOD as well, along with Jerry, and Pete, the gunnery department officer. They now had the luxury of four officers capable of standing OOD and diving officers' watches allowing them to stand one in four, while underway, at least for now. When in the patrol area, they would have two officers on the bridge most of the time, so they would stand one in three. If needed, Bucky could stand watch on the four to eight in the morning, giving him time to do the star sights for his navigation responsibilities. Both the captain and his exec believed they had the makings of a great wardroom.

Between drills and standing watches, Rob had little time to himself. Lying in his bunk, one evening after dinner, he began rereading his mail before going on the mid-watch. The ship's announcing system was playing some of the records that Lily had provided the crew. *White Christmas* with Bing Crosby was their favorite, and John Scott Trotter's Decca record of *I'll be home for Christmas* was another of the top ten records the crew enjoyed. He read Molly's first. She had finished her exams and was writing from the train carrying students' home for the Christmas break. Molly's letter included a picture of herself in a two-piece bathing suit taken last summer that he thought was every bit as good as Betty Grable's famous bathing suit picture displayed in every ship in the Navy. It was signed, *Rob, with all my love, Molly.*

As the *Thornfish* plowed through the seas toward Formosa, back in Hawaii the admiral's staff sent an urgent message to *Thornfish* altering its destination from the Formosa Strait to the Empire of Japan. Rob's duties as the communications officer included decoding incoming messages. This one was marked ULTRA, the top-secret code that only the captain was authorized to decipher. "Something's up Bucky," confided Captain Morrison to his exec. Bucky looked at the text of the secret message and exclaimed, "Sir, I have a hunch there must be a major deployment of a task force out of the Tokyo area." Dick replied, "We'll see soon enough, but we could be replacing one of our boats that is missing in the patrol area off Tokyo. Bucky get me a course and speed of advance to our new area. It looks like we'll spend Christmas with a view of snow on Mount Fujiyama!"

CHAPTER 30

Christmas Break

Molly's father was insistent. While she was home on Christmas break, her father planned for her to meet with the Superintendent of Marion Schools about a possible job. She had a good chance since several male teachers had been drafted or volunteered for the war effort, and her father had become good friends with the Super. Her father drove his big black Buick Special 8 to the school's office in the Marion's Harding High School. It had snowed the night before and there was ice on the sidewalk where the snow had been scraped; the janitor had sown ashes from the huge furnace in the basement to give pedestrians some traction on the slippery walks.

Molly and her father were greeted by the Superintendent, Mr. Nicholson, a rather short, balding man in his fifties, dressed in a brown three-piece suit that was a little tight on him. Frank Gaynor led the way into the office and after shaking Frank's hand the superintendent asked him to sit in a chair in the outer office. Frank was disappointed but didn't argue. The superintendent offered Molly a seat in front of the old walnut desk that had served his predecessors for many years. "Molly, you don't remember me, but I was a teacher in your elementary school when you were in the fifth grade." Molly remembered him well, as he once put her in the dunce corner for talking too much in class. Molly was usually bored in class. She was always ahead of everyone in her studies and tended to daydream. That deportment characteristic had been noted on her report card, causing her a lot of difficulties with her father. Molly said, "I remember it well, Mr. Nicholson, it scared me for life!" They both had a good laugh about it. "You know Molly, I always wondered why your father didn't send you to the Catholic School." Molly blinked several times, "Well, for one thing, it cost a lot of money for all of us kids, and he just didn't have the money, but more importantly for him, I believe, is that he had some bad experiences when he was a boy in Ireland with the nuns when he was in a Catholic school. I think he was always in trouble from the stories he told. Mr. Nicholson said, "I can believe it."

The superintendent's office was austere. Molly sat on a very uncomfortable wooden chair directly in front of Mr. Nicholson's large wooden well-worn desk. The window behind him was frosted with humidity, blurring the view of the open schoolyard where the kids played during recess when school was in session. Steam heat in the radiator was supplemented by a small electric heater that was on full blast but doing little good. Looking a little more professional, he began by saying, "Molly, I hear good things about your work at Miami. Why did you choose an education major?" Molly thought, *well I better tell him the truth*. "Well sir, I…that is my father, wanted me to major in education and become a teacher because that's what women do." She noticed the frown on his face. He paused, a little exasperated, and said, "You mean it was your father's choice not yours?" Molly replied, "Yes. I really like English studies though, particularly writing. I'm one of the student editors of *The Miami Student* newspaper. And I'm pretty good at it too." They talked at length for about half an hour. Finally, the super said, "Molly, why don't we do this: we need teachers, and I believe you'd be a good one. But let's not decide right now. Why don't we wait till spring after you have finished your student teaching at McGuffey? It won't be too late, as we can hire you this summer. That will eliminate some pressure on you at this time, and we can talk later. How does that sound?" Molly was thrilled with his decision, but she knew that her father would not be. On the way out, Mr. Nicholson remarked, "I'm impressed that you're doing your student teaching at McGuffey. William Homes McGuffey was a professor at Miami in 1826 and later wrote his famous series of books for early education. His books have sold over one hundred million copies. He was the single most important man in early education in this country. The *McGuffey Readers* shaped the lives of thousands of kids' early learning and helped mold good character too!"

On the way home, Molly's father couldn't wait to ask how her interview had gone. "Well, Mr. Nicholson is a very nice man, we talked a lot about a teaching career." Frank interrupted her, "But did he give you a job?" Molly took a deep breath, "No, father, we decided to wait until I complete my student teaching this semester and I graduate. He thinks that it would be best for both of us to wait." That didn't make any sense to Frank Gaynor. He thought she would need a job and should stay in Marion where she grew up. It would be a permanent job, something he yearned for during the Great Depression. "Besides Father, I might join the Navy or Marines after I graduate this spring. They are taking women volunteers and training them at Miami." Frank jammed the brakes of the Buick and glared at her… "No, Molly Lenore Gaynor, No! Your brother is in the South Pacific now in combat, and your two younger brothers are trying to get me to permit them to join the Marine Corps. I won't hear of it. And that's final. I'm unanimous in that!" Molly shrugged and remained silent.

Molly spent the afternoon of Christmas Eve shopping for last minute gifts at Frank Brother's department store in downtown Marion. She found a nice silk tie with regimental stripes for her friend Woody that cost a dollar. She had it gift wrapped for an additional 25 cents. Woody would be at her home on the morning of the 27th to drive her back to school, so she wanted to have a nice gift for him. Just the train ride to Oxford would have cost her over five dollars plus the time it would take her folks to drive her to Lima to catch the train.

Christmas Eve mass was celebrated at midnight in St. Mary's Catholic Church where she was confirmed as a little girl. The topic of the old priest was the Second Advent, the coming of our Jesus to complete the work of redemption of the whole world. His theme for his brief homily was Jesus would make everything new, so take courage even during a war-torn world our hope is in him. Comforting words, she thought.

The next morning the family had their traditional gift exchange after a sumptuous breakfast. Molly received a scarf and sock cap in red and white, the colors of Miami University, knitted by her mother. She gave her mom a new electric toaster that cost $1.29 and her father a beautiful cashmere sweater from Roy Young's college shop that cost her $5.00. Father read aloud a Christmas note they had just received from Bobby written from an island in the South Pacific. It said, "Dear family, I hope this reaches you all by Christmas. I would love to be with you this Christmas. I remember all the good times we have had in the past. But the Marines need me here now. So, I wish you all the best and trust that the Lord is taking good care of you. Please remember my buddies and me in your prayers as I do you. Merry Christmas with Much love, Bobby. 11/1/42."

Father's eyes misted, and tears flowed from her mother's cheeks. Frank Gaynor left the room and went out on the porch standing alone in the cold and lit a cigarette. Molly followed him out the door and put her arm around him. "Dad, I love you." Not given to show much affection Frank turned and hugged Molly, "Yes, I know."

Before dinner, Frank drove the black 1930 Model A Ford to the City Mission, near the railroad tracks and pulled up in front. The mission was in a storefront in the old part of town. Its minister met him at the door. "Frank, Merry Christmas! I have a couple of gentlemen I'd like for you to meet." Frank Gaynor had never forgotten the Christian hospitality he had received when he was a hobo and got out of the boxcar years ago and was befriended by the Marion City Mission. He became a regular supporter of the ministry, and each Christmas took one or two of the homeless men to enjoy dinner with the family. The minister introduced him to a couple of men in their mid-fifties he judged, wearing shirts and ties, probably for the first time in years. "I'll have them back this evening Reverend. Let's go men." They piled in the car shivering from the cold; Frank knew he would part with some of his sweatshirts and coats before they returned to the mission.

· · · · ·

Rob's mother and father attended Christmas Eve services at the Washington National Cathedral Episcopal Church in downtown Washington, D.C. She shivered through the entire service, trying to subdue a nagging cough that had been with her even before she arrived in Washington some weeks ago. She was anxious to return to their home in Oxford. Dr. Walker still shared a small apartment in the enormous home of her relative, the junior senator from Ohio. But she was longing for her own bed in the home she had lived in for over twenty years. With some assistance from the senator's staff in the Capitol, she was able to book a flight, December 27, on a Piedmont Airlines DC-3 from Washington to Cincinnati via Charleston, West Virginia. Her new friend, Marianne, had left before Christmas for her first USO tour with an Army Air Corps band. She was unable to tell Mary Catherine her destination for security reasons but hinted that they would be in England. Marianne was a delight to Mrs. Walker; vivacious, with a beautiful smile, outgoing personality and a marvelous voice, she thought Marianne would be the ideal girl for Rob to marry. And she came from a fine family and was a Protestant! She caught herself occasionally dreaming of Marianne meeting her son Rob in some far-off corner of the world as she traveled with the USO entertaining the troops. She and Marianne promised to correspond often.

CHAPTER 31

The Telegram

Sunday, December 27, was another snow-day in Cleveland. The lake effect weather pattern had caused some twenty-two inches of snow to dump on the city in the last weeks of December. Woody said goodbye to his folks outside their home on the lake shore in Rocky River and set out for Oxford in his Chrysler Airflow sedan. The light blue car slowly made the trip down Route 4 towards Marion at the new national speed limit of 35 miles per hour. Ohio was the first state to post the new speed limit. Woody was glad to have his car on campus since Miami students were prohibited from having cars on campus. Being sports editor of *The Miami Student* newspaper allowed him to have a car permit from the university to attend away games.

As he drove along the flat countryside, cattle were huddled by heaps of straw in barnyards, smoke coming out of the chimneys of coal-fired furnaces in farmhouses. *Man, it's cold*, Woody thought. As he made his way down the two-lane highway his feelings constantly returned to Molly and how much he missed her. Woody was looking forward to seeing her again. She had gladly accepted his offer to give her a ride to school. She was the most beautiful girl he had ever met. They had become good friends as they worked together on campus news and sports activities. Standing six feet-two inches tall in his socks, and weighing 200 pounds, Woody was both good looking and a very good athlete. However, he was unable to participate in varsity sports due to his hernia, so he did the next best thing, he became a sports writer. His infirmity kept him out of the service; he was classified 4F by his draft board in Cleveland, which pleased his mother immensely. Nevertheless, he was determined to be a Marine and had an appointment with a surgeon in Cincinnati in a few weeks to determine if his hernia could be corrected. Woody knew Molly was in love with a Navy man. The adage, "Out of sight, out of mind," occurred to him more than once. But she at least enjoyed his company and accepted his invitation to several campus dances featuring the Campus Owls band. He hoped that their relationship would eventually turn from platonic to personal.

Snow continued all the way to Marion. It was getting deep when the car pulled up in front of the Gaynor's new home on Lafayette Avenue. He climbed out of the car and pulled on his heavy jacket. He was glad he had kept on his galoshes as he walked up the snow-filled walk. He noticed footprints of someone on the walk. He rang the doorbell several times and waited a long time before the door slowly opened. Standing before him was a man he presumed was Molly's father. His face was ashen. He stood motionless. It was evident that he had been crying. "Sir, I must have the wrong address. I'm looking for the Gaynor residence. Could you direct me to their home?" Frank Gaynor tried to compose himself. "No son, you're at the right place. You must be her friend. As you can see, we are distraught. Come in please." Woody quickly unbuckled the clasps on his galoshes and pulled them off. He entered the warm living room, the Christmas tree, with some unwrapped presents still under its branches, stood in the corner next to the fireplace. Molly was sitting in the dining room with her mother, both crying uncontrollably. An hour before Woody arrived, a young Western Union Telegraph messenger came to the door with a telegram from the Navy Department. Frank, overcome with grief, couldn't speak and simply handed the message to Woody. It read:

> The Navy Department deeply regrets to inform you that your son Robert Patrick Gaynor Private First Class USMCR was killed in action in the performance of his duty and in the service of the country. The department extends to you its sincerest sympathy in your great loss. Due to existing conditions the body if recovered cannot be returned at present. If further details are received, you will be informed. To prevent possible aid to the enemy please do not divulge the name of his ship or station. Rear Admiral Jacobs, Chief of Naval Personnel.

Woody was shaken. He handed the telegram back to Mr. Gaynor. He wanted to leave and retreat to his car. Nevertheless, he said, "I'm so sorry sir, is there anything I can do? Please forgive me for intruding on you in this terrible moment for you all." Just then the doorbell rang, and Frank opened the door and greeted the Reverend Michael Mackenzie, the pastor of St. Mary's Catholic Church. "Thanks for coming Father." Frank took his coat and hat. The old priest put his gloves and scarf in the coat pocket and put his arm around the grieving father's shoulders. As they slowly walked over to the fireplace he said, "You know Bobby is with the Lord; his battles are over now." Molly and her mother joined them. Father Mackenzie laid his hands on them and prayed. "Father in heaven, we grieve now for the loss of Bobby, but we know that he is at peace with you and enjoying the praises of the saints that have gone on before. Bless now this family… send your Holy Spirit to comfort them and strengthen them now and in the days to come. In Jesus precious name, AMEN." Woody stood near the door struggling to hold his emotions in check as the family's grief began to envelop him.

· · · · ·

The Catholic Church in Marion was packed out for the memorial service of its fallen soldier, Bobbie Gaynor, on Wednesday, December 30. *The Marion Star* carried the story of his being killed in action in the southwest Pacific. The entire family and friends and classmates of both Bobby and Molly were in attendance. A picture of Bobbie in his Marine uniform was placed in front of the altar along with a triangular folded American flag. The mass was interrupted only for remembrances of some of his family and friends, of the young man from his days as an athlete and student at Marion's Harding High School. Father Mackenzie's eulogy was filled with scripture recalling the hope we have in Jesus. He concluded with the passage from John's Gospel, "Greater love has no man than to lay down his life for his friends." Afterward, the women of the church had a reception in the basement fellowship hall. Woody was with Molly most of the time. He had decided to remain in Marion to help the family if needed. He shared a bedroom with one of her brothers. He helped with the arrangements, and the family leaned on him a great deal in their time of sorrow. Molly saw a new side of him as a caring and compassionate man.

The next day, Woody and Molly said a sad goodbye to her parents and siblings and started their drive back to school on New Year's Eve morning. It was cold. The snow had been on the ground for the entire month of December. As they drove south down Route 4, the countryside looked like a fairyland. She told Woody stories of her childhood; times in the winter, when she and Bobbie would tie a rope on their sled to the bumper of the family car as her father pulled them down the flat snowy streets of Marion. Times were hard during the Depression; sometimes hobos would come to the door of their home on the south side of Marion and ask her mom if they could do some work for lunch. Her mother never refused any of them. Molly remembered seeing men employed by the government's Works Progress Administration, the WPA, replace the bricks on the sidewalks in front of their house and turn them over and put them back in place. Every family had a garden in the summer to put food on their tables. Mother canned fruit and vegetables and raised chickens. She was a great cook and made many delicious meals on her gas stove, a white porcelain stove with a built-in oven made by the Estate Stove Company in Hamilton, Ohio.

Molly was in a pensive mood, silent for a long time, her world was topsy-turvy. 1942 was drawing to a close, her mind was flooded with a swirl of events; Rob leaving for service in submarines, the loss of her brother in combat in the South Pacific, graduation in the spring, her need for a job and always the problem in the back of her mind of how an Irish girl from across the tracks could make it in an upscale university like Miami and especially with Rob's mother. Finally, Woody interrupted her reverie, saying, "Molly, you have a wonderful family. I especially like your dad, he is the real thing, and so are you."

· · · · ·

Mary Catherine Walker had a stack of mail awaiting her when she arrived in Oxford. The trip had been exhausting. She was so grateful that she was alive. The Piedmont aircraft nearly skidded off the slick runway when they landed in Charleston. The pilot brought the silver DC-3 to a halt just at the very end of the runway, carved out of the West Virginia hillside. A few more feet and they would have gone over the cliff. The pilot hated landing at Charleston. He felt it was like landing on an aircraft carrier but without the tail-hook wires.

She loved her old home on Spring Street in Oxford. The two-story white frame house with a broad sweeping front porch was built in 1829 and properly identified as a historic home in the village. The newspaper boy had stacked the papers in the alcove of the front door. The postman had left a box of mail there too. At the bottom was a small package from Rob. After hanging up her fur coat in the hall, she carefully opened the wrapped present and found a bottle of Channel No.5, her favorite perfume. The note read, "Mother, Merry Christmas. I know you like French perfume. Enjoy, with love, your son Rob. P.S. We're on our way again." She sighed, *O God, help him*. Her cough persisted. The house was cold even though her thoughtful neighbor had made a fire for her in the basement furnace; she trembled in the kitchen as she poured herself a hot cup of tea. She glanced at the December 31 edition of *The Oxford Press*. On the front cover was an article on the highlights of the year in Oxford. It read:

Outstanding Events in 1942

Highlights in the events of 1942 in Oxford include: Over 800 delegates attend National Assembly of Student Christian Association on local campuses.

State officials appropriate $30,000 for the purchase of land to be used by Miami University as an airfield. Site west of village was chosen, cleared and graded.

Classes in civilian defense are organized and activities, including two dim-outs continue through the year.

Stuart Holcomb is named Miami Football coach, succeeding Frank Wilton.

600 Bluejackets come here for radio training. Fisher Hall and Pines are turned over to them. New mess hall built.

St. Mary's church opens new parish house adjoining church on East High Street.

Teachers register citizens for sugar rationing.

Dale Shantz, radioman on U.S.S. *Houston*, reported missing. Philip C. Shera, a third engineer on an oil tanker, gives his life to save fellow crewmen; Cadet James W. Baer dies in a plane crash in Texas; Sgt. William A. Magaw drowns in Panama Canal Zone. Three McCoy sisters and Ruth Evelyn Clevenger are drowned at the gravel pit.

Village raises U.S.O. quota and county club room is opened in Halter building.

Volunteers assist with the registration of motorists for gas rationing book.

Litigation concerning the estates of Elizabeth McCullough and Daisy McCullough settled in favor of the village and way is cleared for the establishment of McCullough memorial hospital.

Over 65 tons of scrap collected in village and township.

One sailor killed, ten injured as a motorist drives into marching column of trainees.

Twenty-five Miami servicemen were killed in 1942.

As she turned the page, the headline on page 2 jumped out at her: 11 Sailors Injured by Car Tuesday. It went on, "Christmas pleasure in Oxford was marred by the tragic death Tuesday night of one of the trainees and the injury of 10 others. John Thomas Malk, age 22, seaman second class from Minneapolis, Minn. suffered a fractured skull and never regained consciousness after being hit by a machine driven by Edward Sladek, 34, of Hamilton. 300 sailors were marching back to Fisher Hall, after viewing a Navy film uptown. It was dark and Sladek said he never saw them in their dark blue uniforms until it was too late. He was being charged with manslaughter.

Mary Catherine put the paper down and sat motionless for a long time contemplating how much sorrow the young man's parents must feel at their son's loss, especially at Christmas. A thought immediately struck her that she might suffer the same pain someday for her only son in dangerous duty in the Pacific. But she decided this would be a good article to keep for Rob, so she cut it out and filed it away in a small notebook that would become her scrapbook of the war efforts in Oxford.

Christmas tree lights were bright in homes along Oxford's streets when Molly and Woody drove up in front of her dorm. She pulled the warm wool scarf her mother had knitted for her around her neck and drew the sock cap down over her ears, then plunged into the cold December air. Molly took the key and opened the door into the tiled entrance. Woody took her suitcase to her bedroom while Molly carried a cloth bag with her Christmas presents into her small living room. As head of the residence, Molly had a suite adjacent to the front foyer. No one was around. The students would not be arriving for another week, but the dorm had enough heat to be somewhat comfortable. Woody insisted they go uptown for something to eat. But Molly said she was exhausted from the entire week. She finally agreed to have him go uptown and bring back some sandwiches and Cokes. She gave him the key to the entrance to the dorm, and he left to try to find some burgers and 3.2 beers for himself and a Coke for Molly. He was famished. Mac and Joes, in the alley off High Street, was still open and he ordered four burgers, fries, Cokes and a six pack of beer to go. When he returned, Molly was in the shower. He put the food on a small table by the kitchenette and turned on the radio to WLW. They were playing the top twenty-five hit songs, some featuring Bing Crosby, Rosemary Clooney, and the big bands, Tommy Dorsey, Glen Miller, and Freddy Martin. Molly came in clad in a big terrycloth bathrobe with a towel wrapped around her beautiful blond hair. Woody thought she was the loveliest girl he had ever seen. "You know, I'd be fired Woody, if the university head of residences saw me entertaining a man in my room." Woody laughed and went to the windows and pulled down the shades. "Now you won't be fired!"

They sat listening to the music, munching the sandwiches and she said, "Woody could I have a beer? It's New Year's Eve and I've never had one." Woody was surprised. Twenty years old and never had a beer! "Sure honey." The word honey just slipped out of him. She didn't seem to mind. He handed her a Miller High Life, the champagne of bottled beer. She held it up admiring the amber color in the bottle's clear glass. It was nearing midnight, and she found the beer relaxing and enjoyable. "Molly let's dance." WLW was playing *Moonlight Sonata,* Woody slipped off his shoes, and the two of them danced across the living room rug. Woody's a good dancer she thought. She lay her head on his shoulder and dreamed of being with Rob once again. They paused dancing long enough for her to drink another beer. And then she wanted another one! WLW was playing *It had to be you*, and she pulled Woody off the chair and they danced to *It had to be you, wonderful you, I wandered around and finally found someone who…* and the words faded as Woody hands found the warmth of her body under her robe. Molly didn't hear the next words … *finally found that somebody who could make be true.* She felt as though lightning had gone off inside her as his hands ran over her. She reached up and kissed him hard, as the radio played *Auld Lang Syne.* It was midnight and she passed out… as she slumped to the floor her robe fell off.

Woody was stunned. He didn't know what to do. His mind was spinning. He felt her pulse, and it was strong enough. He had some training in emergencies for sports medicine, but he was unprepared as to what to do now. He covered her with her robe and carried her to her bed. She was pale and sweating. He recalled that medics call it syncope, passing out with a short loss of consciousness and muscle strength. He hoped that was all it was. Molly had been through a lot in the last week, her job interview, the loss of her brother, the memorial service, leaving home. All that had finally caught up with her. He thought, but what do I do now? If I call the university clinic no one would be there at this time of night with school out. Even if I found someone, how can I explain my being in her room? She could lose her job. Then he remembered her friend, Mrs. Walker. He found the telephone book on her small desk by the window, and hurriedly looked for her phone number. No luck. He returned to the bedroom and found Molly stirring. He grabbed a glass of water in the bathroom and brought it to her. Her eyelids fluttered, and she looked at Woody. "What happened?" Woody pulled a chair up by her bedside. "Well, you passed out as we were dancing. I didn't realize I was that bad a dancer!" She smiled, "I'm sorry to have been such bad company." Then she realized the robe lying on her to cover her nakedness. "My Gosh, Woody, you saw me naked!" Woody blushed, "Just briefly Molly, you've had too much stress lately and you're tired. It's best for you to rest tonight and sleep late in the morning. May I stay here with you?"

"No, there will be talk if you're seen leaving here in the morning. I'll be alright."

"Sure?"

"I'm sure, thanks for taking good care of me."

"I love to Molly."

After her friend left, Molly lay in her bed awake for a long time; feelings of guilt consumed her. I almost lost my virginity tonight. He felt so good to me. As she drifted off to sleep, she thought, I must be more careful. I want to save myself for Rob.

CHAPTER 32

The Operation

Bucky was awakened at three a.m. by the pharmacist mate second class, "Sir, we have a problem." Bucky rolled out of his bed and put his feet on the deck, rubbing the sleep out of his eyes. The deck was tossing in rough seas as they approached the coast of Japan. The exec sat on the edge of his bed. He grabbed a pack of Camel cigarettes and lit one. He liked Camels, they were strong cigarettes, and they only cost five cents a pack in the ship's store. "What's the problem doc?" He had only two hours of sleep and needed a lot more. "Well sir, it's the new man, Seaman Hawkins. He is very sick. He has a fever and is vomiting. I first thought he was seasick. However, it's been twenty-four hours since I had him stay in his bunk. I've been using ice packs on his stomach but, Sir, I'm sure it's appendicitis." Bucky recalled reading a recent patrol report from the *Seadragon's* fourth patrol out of Freemantle, Australia. They had a two and a half-hour operation for a sailor with acute appendicitis by the pharmacist mate that turned out successfully. Nevertheless, the staff medical officer in Freemantle was not at all pleased. Standard procedure was to pack the person in ice, feed only liquids and wait until the boat returned from patrol. Bucky frowned, "Well, can't it wait until morning?"

"I don't know sir, if it bursts, it'll be curtains for him."

"Ok, doc, go ahead and prepare. I'll talk to the captain. We will dive anyway at dawn. If he agrees, it can be done after we submerge and get a stable platform for you. Are you sure you can handle this?"

"I think so sir, I'll do my best. I've been reading up on the operation in my medical books. We'll need some retractors; the machinist mates can make them from spoons. I have catgut to sew up with and we'll need torpedo alcohol for sterilization. I have ether of course, and we'll use a tea strainer to administer it with gauze. We also have a new drug called sulfanilamide; we call it a sulfa drug. It is saving lives now for men that have been wounded. Every soldier is issued a packet to hang on his belt. It's sprinkled in the wound to resist infection. It's a miracle drug. The exec said, "We'll need a miracle doc."

The doc replied, "But I will need an assistant. Would you be able to do it sir?"

Bucky looked up at him for a long time taking a drag on his cigarette, "Well, I guess so, you're the doc. Get going!"

"Aye, Sir,"

The tiny wardroom table was stripped of ashtrays, table clothes, napkins, and sanitized as much as possible with alcohol. There would be no breakfast for the officers, just rolls and egg sandwiches served in the crew's mess. Captain Morrison agreed with his exec that Hawkins had to have the operation. He sent Bucky back to Hawkins' bunk in the crew's quarters just aft of the galley.

Buck Rogers was becoming a legend with the crew already. His gregarious positive attitude was contagious. Besides, he liked shenanigans and enjoyed playing the slot machine when the chief had it open. This time, however, he was serious. He stopped at the seaman's bunk and saw the gaunt, pale young man packed in ice bags, looking at him. Hawkins said, "Sorry to be so much trouble for you sir, I sure didn't want this to happen."

"Hawkins, it's not your fault, you're in need of an operation. The closest hospital is two thousand miles away. So, we are going to operate here in our little operating room. Are you up to it?"

"Yes, sir" he replied, "I want to get this darn thing out. It's killing me now." Captain Morrison didn't allow swear words in his command. There were too many young men on board; they didn't need to be corrupted.

"You're going to be fine Hawkins." Bucky returned to the control room and found his quartermaster ready to do star sights before dawn. Bucky enjoyed navigating, but he wasn't cut out to be a nurse. Fortunately, the navigator and his quartermaster assistant had a beautiful twilight with a good horizon and took their sights quickly. While his quartermaster was working out the lines of position on the chart table, the captain said, "Bucky are we ready to dive?" He replied. "Yes sir." Captain Morrison checked the radar screen in the conning tower to make sure it was clear of enemy vessels and aircraft, then ordered the OOD to take her down to 150 feet.

Bucky and the pharmacist stripped down to their underwear and scrubbed as much as they could. For gowns, they used clean bed sheets cut with holes in them for their heads and arms. As Hawkins was brought in the exec called the officers to come to the passageway outside the brightly lit wardroom, now the ship's operating room. "Ok men, we're going to need some help. I want a volunteer to pray for Hawkins. He added, and for me and especially the doc. Ok?" No one answered him. Finally, John spoke up, "I will sir." The ensign was interested in starting church services on Sunday mornings as circumstances permitted. He intended to speak with the exec about it soon. Bucky said, "Ok, Mr. Young, but I don't want any wishy-washy prayers, like, *if it be thy will.* I want a strong prayer with no room for God to misunderstand us, Ok?"

"Yes, Sir."

Bucky picked up the microphone for the general announcing system and said

"Shipmates, give me your attention. We are going to have to operate on our shipmate Jimmy Hawkins. Ensign Young will now lead us in prayer, please join in and agree with him. OK, Mr. Young, pray."

John stood erect and took the microphone. It was the first time he had ever used it. In a calm, strong voice he intoned, "Please bow your heads. Father in heaven, we bring to your attention our shipmate and friend, Jimmy Hawkins who is sick. We implore you to heal him of this appendicitis. Guide our doc and the others assisting him and give them supernatural ability as they perform this operation. We remind you the Bible says that Jesus was wounded for our transgressions and bruised for our iniquity and by his stripes we are healed. So, make it so now Lord for it is in the strong name of Jesus that we pray. AMEN."

"Good prayer, Mr. Young. Ok Doc let's go!"

The two-hour operation was a success. The pharmacist mate did a terrific job and the captain made the announcement as soon as the pharmacist mate agreed that Hawkins would live. Cheers rang out through the boat. He put the appendix in a jar and filled it with torpedo alcohol, for a souvenir. "Don't drink it," he cautioned his patient after he came out of the ether.

John Young was on watch on the bridge after *Thornfish* surfaced 100 miles off the Japanese mainland. When the word was passed about the successful operation, John said a silent prayer of thanks to the almighty for his help, "Jesus, our wounded healer, you're still in the healing business. Thank you." Later during the watch, the exec came up and got some fresh air. John said, "Sir, I thought you'd be getting some shut-eye. You've had a hard day."

"I just wanted to thank you for your prayer. Where did you learn to pray like that?"

"Well sir, I'm a Navigator."

"You are?"

"Yes, not in the sense of doing star sights, but I belong to a group by that name started by a Navy sailor on board the USS *West Virginia*, Dawson Trotman, who founded a small organization that encourages men to share their faith with one other person. They in turn do the same, and its spread all over the services now." The exec didn't say a word. John sensed he was pondering something.

"If I may, sir, if conditions allow, could we have a brief Christmas Eve service tonight in the crew's mess? The chief of the boat is going to light the tree and we can sing some carols and I'll share a few Bible verses."

"Sure, make it so ensign, thanks." He disappeared down the hatch just as the radar operator reported a plane coming toward them, range 15,000 yards.

John yelled, "Clear the bridge!" *Thornfish* slid under the water in 60 seconds, they were going to war again. The captain zoomed the periscope lens on the patrol plane. He identified it as a Mitsubishi and guessed it was patrolling ahead of a convoy. It didn't see *Thornfish*. As it disappeared over the horizon, he surfaced the boat and turned on some additional rpms to get to their intended position by dawn the next morning. Radar swept the horizon looking for the convoy that the Ultra message promised would be coming out of Tokyo Bay. *Thornfish* dived several times during the day to avoid being seen by patrol aircraft.

That evening the off-duty sailors gathered in the crew's mess for the Christmas tree lighting and some festivities. Chief O'Neil donned a red jacket and fake white beard with a red hat. He almost looked like the jolly old Saint Nick, in some Norman Rockwell painting. He passed out packages of candy, cigarettes and a surprise gift of a small decal of the *Thornfish* with a torpedo in its mouth and the words, *we sail in harm's way*.

Willie put records on the turntable of Christmas Carols by Fred Waring. The crew started singing along with the familiar hymns. John then led them in prayer and read the birth of Jesus account from Luke's Gospel. Then without notes, he began: "Yesterday before Hawkins was operated on, our exec said to the doc, we need a miracle. We got one, men. (AMENS were heard.) Hawkins came through fine. It was an answer to our prayers. Doc used a sulfa drug he calls a miracle drug before he sewed Hawkins up. It was invented six years ago and has saved many lives in the war. 2000 years ago, Jesus miraculously came into our world. When Jesus was born the world was in turmoil. Tyrants ruled. Later in his earthly ministry, he performed many miracles. Healing the lame, opening the eyes of the blind, and deaf ears to hear. He raised the dead. All to show the power of God. The greatest miracle of all was the fact that by his sacrifice on the Cross, he broke the power of sins over our lives, and for those who believe, he gives the power to become sons of God, and heirs with him in his eternal kingdom. The saying is true that there are no atheists in foxholes, and I think there are no atheists in submarines. As we head into enemy waters, the world is once again in turmoil. Tyrants rule where we are going. We do not know what trials are ahead of us. But we can have the assurance that we are on the right side. We will win. But most importantly, through Jesus, we can have life eternal no matter what happens." John closed in prayer. There was silence in the crew's mess. Heads were still bowed. Softly Willie began singing the verses of *Silent Night*. Everyone joined in. Someone in the galley tuned the overhead lights off. The little tree with its colored lights lit the little compartment. No one stirred. Finally, John said "Merry Christmas, men of *Thornfish*. God Bless our loved ones and God Bless us all, everyone."

Rob had the mid-watch but decided to give up some sleep to attend the program. He stood in the back of the compartment and joined in the singing of *Silent Night*. His thoughts turned to home, of Molly and his folks. But he also contemplated what

John had said about being a Christian …if we believe in Him, we can have eternal life no matter what happens.

Rob returned to his room and before going to sleep he opened his Christmas present from Molly. It was a beautiful stainless-steel identification bracelet engraved with his name and rank. On the back were the words, *to Rob with all my love forever, Molly*.

Rob's mid-watch was a long one. It was very cold and wet. The December wind had picked up and sleet was hitting him in the face. He consumed a lot of hot coffee brought to him from below. The radar screen was clear although the screen was blurred in patches of snow showers. Rob rotated the lookouts every half hour. One of them said, when he reached the warmth of the control room, that he thought if he touched his nose it would fall off. At 0345 John came up through the conning tower hatch to relieve Rob as the officer of the deck. "I'm just about frozen through and through John, I hope you put on some long underwear." John replied, "I sure did. What's going on?"

"Well, we have no contacts yet. We may have some in a few hours according to the captain. His night orders call for him to be awakened at 0500, did you get that?"

"Yes, and the exec wanted to be awakened at the same time if the weather was clear enough for him to get some star sights. No luck now."

The two of them went through the various items that the oncoming OOD needed to know. The engines online and on a battery charge, the motors and generators in use, battery ventilation, hull openings, the condition of ballast tanks, flood valves vents, variable tanks, pumps condition of the sub as to it being ready for dive, the condition of the radar and radios. Torpedoes ready in the tubes, course and speed ordered by the captain per his night orders, and a zigzag pattern if in use. Lots of things to rehearse and most of all remember. Watch standers were told to make it a practice to think of what they would do in an emergency. A half an hour before sunrise, they were to slow to three knots, put the sound head down and listen for enemy screws. Satisfied, John saluted and said, "I relieve you sir." Just before going below, Rob said, 'I liked your talk tonight, it was good. I've been thinking, I was brought up in the church, so I guess I'm a Christian."

John turned close to Rob's ear, and spoke over the noise of the wind and engines, "My pappy used to say, being in church doesn't make you any more of a Christian, then my being in a garage makes me a car." Rob was amused…maybe he's right. He shouted, "Let's talk more about it later." With that he quickly descended the ladder into the warmth of the boat. Sleep eluded Rob after his mid-watch; he had pumped too much coffee into his system. After tossing and turning, he got up and sat in his chair by the small desk in the room he shared with John. He glanced at the unopened bottle of brandy given him after a depth charge attack and decided to open it. He poured all of it in a small glass by the stainless-steel wash bowl and lifted it in a toast,

Merry Christmas everyone and to everyone a good night. The brandy tasted good and warmed his body. He found his Christmas presents from his folks unopened on the shelf above the desk. It was Christmas morning, and he unwrapped the package marked DO NOT OPEN TILL CHRISTMAS. He smiled, that's my mother for you. Inside was a small ditty bag with toiletries loaded with P&G products, an electric razor and a package of homemade Springerle cookies, German anise cookies that his grandma used to bake at Christmas time. Tucked at the bottom of the box was a slender package marked to Rob, Merry Christmas, Dad. It was a fountain pen. But one unlike any he had ever seen. His father had written a note: Rob this is a new pen. The RAF in Britain is using these. It writes well even at high altitudes. It's called a ballpoint pen. It was invented decades ago and patented by a gentleman named John J. Loud in October 1888. Some brothers named Brio started manufacturing them in Germany and later fled to Argentina in 1941. Their pen was marketed as Biros. I bet you'll be the first one aboard your sub to have one. It was inscribed, ENS R. A. Walker USNR.

Rob took the new present out and started to scribble some words on a piece of paper. Nothing happened. He picked it up, shook it a few times, and tried again. This time it wrote, gliding over the paper on a ball at the end of the pen. What will they think of next, thought Rob? He picked up the small Bible that Mrs. Edmonds had given him, and underlined the verse she had marked for him, *If anyone is in Christ, he is a new creation, the old has passed and the new has come.* Rob sat in the quiet of the moment, in the dimly lit room. A small fan, whirring overhead, was trying to stir the air. He pondered the verse he had read several times, deep down he knew that the scripture verse referred to a new person, like Molly, or Mrs. Edmonds, and John, ones who had turned their lives over to Jesus. John's strong words uttered just a few hours earlier, resonated in the echoes of his mind. "My pappy used to say that just by going to church now and then, doesn't make you a Christian any more than being in the garage makes you a car." Suddenly his quiet reverie was interrupted by a commotion outside the captain's stateroom. The quartermaster was waking the captain. "Sir, the OOD wants you on the bridge. We have lots of surface contacts!" As Rob pulled his pants on, he thought *to be continued.*

Captain Morrison rushed to the bridge. He stopped to check the radar screen in the conning tower. The PPI scope showed the outline of a convoy coming out of Yokohama. Seven ships, four large ones, covered by three escorts. John had the conn and had immediately changed course to directly head for the convoy. Down below, the tracking team assembled in the control room and began to plot the enemy's course and speed. The captain joined John on the bridge and yelled over the roar of the four diesels, "John, make turns for flank speed, we've got to get ahead of the convoy before daylight, submerge at dawn, and make our attack."

CHAPTER 33

Man Overboard!

A few minutes later the word was passed, battle stations torpedo and the crew raced to their battle stations. The XO told the men, "We have a seven-ship convoy coming out of the entrance to Tokyo Bay. Let's give them a Christmas present of some American fish!" Cheers rang out through the boat.

The convoy was on a zigzag pattern off a base course of south. Rob, manning the TDC in the conning tower, mentally calculated the course and speed necessary to get in front of the enemy ships before dawn. He reported to the captain, "Sir, I believe a course of 230 at flank speed will give us plenty of time to be ahead and wait for the convoy." The quartermaster figured the time of twilight to be 0545. At dawn they could dive and make the attack. Dick acknowledged the recommendation by ordering the helmsman to steer the new course of 230. The SJ surface radar was giving the range and bearing of the enemy's formation. Rob cranked in the true bearings and ranges fed by the radar operator across from him in the crowded conning tower. Captain Morrison and the OOD, John Young, remained on the frigid bridge. *Thornfish's* bow cut through the rough sea, causing salt spray to freeze on the bridge windscreen. Willie, one of the four lookouts, was high up on the periscope shears peering through the darkness. He was the submarine's best lookout. He exceeded the night vision tests at lookout school. The instructor told him he needn't stay for the entire course; he was that good. During the previous patrol, Captain Custer would not let him stand lookout watches because of his color.

The bridge target bearing binocular was useless as the lenses became covered with ice as soon as they were wiped clean. Bucky supervised the plot in the conning tower. The PPI scope showed a constant bearing and decreasing range to the closest escort in the convoy. Captain Morrison announced to the entire crew his plan of attack. "We're going into the center of the formation, we'll fire forward tubes on the two largest targets in the middle of the formation. Then we'll fire the stern tubes at the ship on the other side of the formation and go deep and hide under the thermal layer if a cold layer is present. Every man do your best!"

The captain ordered all the lookouts below except Willie. A few minutes later Willie, with his teeth chattering, yelled, "Sir, I can make out one of the escorts, it looks like a Chidori class patrol boat. I don't think he sees us.

"Good work Willie, keep your eyes on it like a hawk!"

In wartime, battle plans seldom go as planned. *Thornfish's* had to be altered due to the enemy ships zigging away from the convoy's base course. The intercom blared, "Captain, this is plot, the targets have zigged away from us. Recommend changing course to two zero zero to regain position."

Willie had spotted the escorts changing course too, and the captain altered course to the south to regain position. All four engines were online, and the sub speed was nearly 20 knots in the rough December waters off Japan. Dick's only hope was that the convoy would zigzag back to the original base course. If it did, they would be in a great position to attack. But the change of course allowed the wind and waves to come from behind the vessel. John, the officer of the deck, ordered the hatch closed to the conning tower in case a wave would wash over the bridge and down the hatch, endangering the electronics in the conning tower. A few minutes later without warning a huge wave rolled over the stern filling the bridge. Submariners call it a pooping sea, it floods the superstructure from aft causing the bridge to become a bathtub, floating men overboard. The captain and the OOD suddenly found themselves afloat as the following sea engulfed the entire bridge. Willie, high up in the periscope shears, held on and watched in horror as his captain and OOD struggled to hang on to anything. John was standing by the TBT when the wave hit. He grabbed it holding on with one arm and with his other arm tried to seize his captain by his foul weather jacket only to lose him in the swirling darkness. No one down below knew what had happened. When the wave drained out, John realized that the captain was overboard, he grasped the IMC and announced, "Man overboard! Port side! Left full rudder! All engines ahead full!" With full rudder on *Thornfish* completed an emergency procedure called a Williamson Turn that would bring the boat back to near where the man fell overboard. The submarine shuddered as it struggled to turn in the face of the wind and waves. The plotting team in the control room immediately marked the spot on the DRT, the dead reckoning tracer, where the submarine was when the word man overboard was passed.

The executive officer jumped up the ladder and cracked the hatch to the bridge. Water cascaded over him as he climbed to the bridge, his eyes were not completely adjusted to the blackness of the night. "John where is the captain?"

John yelled, "The captain was washed over the port side when the wave hit!"

"Oh shit!"

The exec yelled over the general announcing, "Quartermaster bring a searchlight to the bridge on the double!"

Captain Morrison thought his lungs would burst; when he surfaced, he knew he was in deep trouble. *Thornfish* was nowhere to be seen. His head submerged in wave after wave. Dick was a good swimmer at the Academy, but the weight of his clothes and foul weather gear kept pulling him down. He tore at his jacket trying to inflate his lifebelt; watch standers are required to wear them when topside in bad weather. He finally was able to pull the pin on the CO_2 capsule inflating the thin yellow life ring. He knew he could not last long in the frigid water. Not much of a religious person, he remembered the prayer his mother taught him as a little boy, "Jesus save my soul, amen!" Then he found the little emergency flashlight on the lifebelt. He grabbed it with his frozen fingers and held it high as he could, waving it back and forth.

It was decision time on the bridge. Bucky thought *if I light up the waters to search for the captain, an alert lookout on the Jap escorts might see it and we'd be in for a heap of trouble. If we stay surfaced looking for the captain, the convoy will get away.* He began to feel that the situation was getting hopeless. In what seemed like an eternity, suddenly Willie saw a faint light flickering in the waves; he yelled, "I see the light off our port bow!"

John screamed, "Willie keep giving me bearings on the light." *Thornfish* was still struggling to come about in the strong wind and wave action.

The exec hit the lever on the mike, "Chief O'Neil get me two swimmers on the bridge on the double."

John kept announcing the relative bearing of the man overboard as they tried to close the distance to him. *Thornfish* gradually returned to the place where the DRT plotters in the control room indicated the submarine was when the word was passed that a man was overboard.

John still had the conn and ordered, "all engines all ahead slow." With the exec's permission, the quartermaster on the bridge moved the searchlight's beam back and forth over the rough waves.

Suddenly Willie yelled, "I see him! he's dead ahead." The searchlight beam found the captain.

The XO said, "Good work Willie, keep him in sight. How far away?"

"Couple of hundred yards, sir."

John conned the sub so close that the swimmers could toss a line to Captain Morrison. But he was too weak to grab it. Boatswain mate Landfair jumped in the cold water and tied a rope around the limp captain. As the other swimmer on deck was desperately trying to haul him aboard, a wave came over the bow and gently floated the exhausted captain and Landfair up on the deck. John thought there must be an angel out there. "Thank you, Jesus," he shouted loud enough to be heard over the howling wind. The swimmers brought the captain to the hatch leading to the conning tower and gently lowered him below to the control room. The pharmacist mate immediately examined the captain and treated him for hypothermia. John, along with Willie and the swimmers, were given hot showers, and a shot of medicinal bourbon whiskey.

The exec assumed the conn and ordered the boat back on the course to intercept the convoy. It would be tough to overtake it now; nevertheless, Bucky was determined to try. *Thornfish* continued to plow through the grueling sea looking for the distant convoy. At first light the SJ radar picked up a contact of a patrol plane guarding the convoy, forcing the boat to submerge. Then a strange thing happened. One of the large ships in the formation had slowed to five knots and dropped out of formation. One of the escorts dropped back to protect it. Bucky thought it was probably due to some malfunction as both ships were only making five knots. He ordered the diving officer to make his depth 55 feet to keep the radar mast above the waves to track the contacts. Rob cranked in the course and speed and recommended they change course to intercept. Once they had a good target course and speed, Bucky lowered the radar mast and followed the two vessels with short visuals from the periscope.

Bucky announced that their new target was a large tanker, escorted by one of the Chidori patrol boats. Captain Morrison was still suffering from hypothermia, shivering and showing signs of confusion, he finally submitted to lying in his bunk. Normally the pharmacist would give him a sedative, but the exec would not permit it. Just a shot of whiskey.

The target was not zigzagging. A patrol plane was overhead of the two vessels giving some assurance of protection from submarines. Assisted by Jerry, Bucky made the approach perfectly. "Open the outer doors on tubes one, two and three," he commanded. "Stand by for a final range and bearing." Bucky squatted down and rode the periscope up. The scope broke the water for just an instant as he uttered, "Range 900 yards." The quartermaster noted the bearing ring and shouted out the bearing for Rob to check on his computer. It agreed. Bucky calmly said, Fire one… fire two… fire three. The three Mark-14 torpedoes shot out with a blast of air speeding to the target one aimed at the bow, one amidships, and one at the stern. Forty seconds later, WHAM, the torpedo aimed at the stern exploded and the tanker vaporized. But the other two fish were duds. Sonar man Harrington reported the sound of the patrol craft heading directly for *Thornfish*. "Take her deep," Bucky commanded. Make your depth 350 feet. It sounded like a freight train running over the submarine. There was a click, and then WHAM…. WHAM, two depth charges exploded close by. Bucky held on to the periscope now completely lowered into the well in the conning tower. He nearly was thrown off his feet by the burst of TNT. A moment later Dick Morrison climbed the ladder to the conning tower. Bucky looked at him, "Sir, are you ok now?" Captain said firmly, "Affirm Bucky, let's get the hell out of here, now." He knew that the sound of the exploding depth charges would block the enemy's listening gear, for a few minutes, so it was time to move out. He smiled, "I can't sleep anyhow, Bucky!" But his exec wasn't convinced his captain was ok.

The Jap had good sonar. For the next two hours he rained over thirty ash cans down near them. The Chidori was determined to get revenge for the sinking of the large tanker it was guarding, but fortunately for *Thornfish*, the damage was minor, but the little Christmas tree took a beating. All the ornaments were destroyed, as the tree hit the deck. The sub was blessed with a thermal layer that reflected the sonar's sound waves enough to enable the sub to steal away silently. During the Chidori's attack, Bucky walked back through the sub as they received the barrage of depth charges. He was grateful that *Thornfish* was constructed with the thick skin of the newer submarines coming off the ways in shipyards from Portsmouth, New Hampshire, to Mare Island, California. He was especially anxious to see how the new men were taking their first experience in combat. Most were doing ok, but one of the youngest recruits was sobbing and trembling so much that the pharmacist mate had to give an injection of a sedative to calm him down. Nothing to be ashamed of young man, the exec said, "We are all scared." The click of the detonator could be the last thing any of them would ever hear.

An hour later they surfaced to resume the hunt of the Christmas Convoy. *Thornfish's* 16-cylinder Fairbanks Morse engines were propelling them along making 18 knots. The members of the crew who were not on watch were ordered to turn in to get some shut-eye. More action awaited them in a few hours if they caught up with the convoy.

The enemy ships' speed of advance on its southerly course had accelerated after the straggler had departed the convoy. But they were now out of range of their land-based patrol planes, making the job of *Thornfish* easier by not having to dive when an enemy patrol plane appeared on their radar. While on the surface they were able to get a full charge on their batteries and let Willie and his cooks prepare Christmas dinner. Rob estimated that they could be in a position ahead of the convoy by midnight if everything went as planned. But it would be close. Pete had the watch on the bridge, and the captain and exec were below trying to warm up and plan for the next attack. Dick's hands were still shaking from the cold, so Bucky poured the coffee. Dick grabbed the cup with both hands and savored every drop of the strong black coffee. He said, "You know, Bucky, when I was in the water, I thought I was a goner. You should have left me and gone after those Japs. The convoy was more important than me. But I'm damned glad you did now. We may still have a chance of overtaking the rest of that convoy. You and John did a great job. Maneuvering in that sea state and wind was difficult enough, but I'm surprised you saw my little light." Bucky didn't hesitate, "Well sir, I'm glad we had Willie up there on the shears, he deserves a lot of the credit. He sure has good night vision. If he hadn't seen you, you would have frozen to death in a few minutes." Dick took a long sip of his drink, and said, "I know, Bucky when you put the bow near me, a wave just picked me up and put me on the deck. It was like a divine being had a hold of me!" Bucky smiled and said, "Just ask Ensign Young sir. He is certain that an angel had you in the palm of his hand. And by the way sir, he asked me about a week ago if it would be ok to have divine services when operations allow. He wanted permission to announce it and have brief services in the forward torpedo room. What do you think? You know article 3 of The Government of The Navy is about worshiping the Almighty."

Dick said, "Sure Bucky, I'll go myself. After what I just went through, I need to get right with God!"

"Sir, I think we all do in our line of work!"

The captain changed the subject to torpedo performance. "Bucky, are you sure you had a good set-up when you fired the torpedoes?" Bucky said," Yes sir, all of the three shots we fired didn't miss, two just didn't explode. I'm sure that those three fish went right where we aimed. Those magnetic exploders still are not reliable." Dick agreed, he remembered that the submarines based in Manila at the outbreak of the war, had lots of trouble with torpedoes that failed to explode. "You're right sir, I recall reading the patrol report of the *Sargo*, John Jacobs commanding, right after Pearl Harbor; he fired thirteen Mark-14's with the magnetic exploders during the patrol and all failed to blow up. Captain Jacobs deactivated them finally." It was the same throughout the fleet, Dick lamented. "The Bureau of Ordnance will not concede that they have a problem. They blame the skippers. Captain Al Taylor of the *Haddock* got in a lot of trouble for writing a nasty poem about the bureau. It got circulated among submariners based out of Pearl, and later Admiral English, the Commander of Pacific Fleet Submarines, somehow got a copy of it and started a full-scale investigation trying to find out who wrote it. Bucky, I had the same problem during our last patrol off Guam. We fired point blank at a tanker, and we could hear the Mark-14's with magnetics hit and bounce off the bastard. It got away. So, go ahead and deactivate the magnetic exploders. I'll take full responsibility. We'll use contacts instead. And let's do one other thing. Adjust the fins to make the torpedoes run shallower. Ok?" Bucky started to reply but the captain's eyes began to close, and he fell asleep with his empty cup still in his hand.

CHAPTER 34

The Necklace

The townies in Oxford liked the village most when the students were absent. Except for the merchants. The economy of Oxford, population 2845, not counting the students, hinged on the university. With its student enrollment declining as male students went off to war, the Navy, training some 600 sailors at Miami, added a lot of income to the village. An article appearing in *The Oxford Press* reported that the Naval School was bringing in extra business for local merchants. Capitol Dry Cleaning Company was handling the dry cleaning for the Navy. Petri's Men's shop was handling orders for uniforms. Folker's was providing candy vending machines; the Argonne Barbershop was doing the haircuts for the sailors and the Oxford Laundry was doing the laundry. Sloan's Shoe Store had a contract for the shoe repairing.

Students would return in a week, giving Molly some time to work on some articles for *The Miami Student.* She loved writing. The more she thought about her interview in Marion with the Superintendent of Schools, the more she thought she would decline any offer. Even though her starting salary would be seventy-five dollars a month, while very tempting, her heart was not in it. She would give student teaching a try to satisfy her academic requirements, and her father, but teaching was not going to be her life's vocation.

When she opened her mailbox in the alcove of the dormitory, she found a letter from the School of Education with a copy of her grades from last semester. The original grades always were sent directly to the parents. She had four A's and one B! She thought her folks would be proud of her, but she doubted that her dad would say anything to her. He never complimented her for fear that she would get a "big head."

Her heart skipped a beat when she found a note in the little mailbox saying she had a package to pick up at the Post Office uptown. She was sure that it was from Rob. Molly went to her room and quickly donned her coat, boots and her red and white sock cap with the Miami Redskin logo on the front. The snow was melting as she strode through the slush past the Miami-Western Theater where *Casablanca*, starring Humphrey Bogart and Ingrid Bergman, was playing. She wanted to see it and noted that the price had gone up to 55 cents, but matinees were still 45. Under the water tower in the town square were a dozen or so dried up Christmas trees that the Lions Club had not sold. She stopped in the grocery store to get some food for the next few days. She thought to ask Woody to give her a ride to buy groceries, but then thought better of it as she remembered their embarrassing New Year's Eve episode. No, she'd carry a few things back to the dorm herself. She loved coffee, but the government started rationing it in November. She didn't even have a rationing card. Miami students were required to get theirs from home if they needed them. She thought she might have to switch to tea.

Back in her room, she tore open the package from Rob. She read the note: "Wouldn't it be wonderful if we could be together next year?" Molly held it to her bosom, if only that could be true. Inside she found the bottle of Channel No.5, how can he afford it? she asked herself. Then she discovered a small box and found a beautiful chain and gold cross with a small diamond set in the center. In pencil another small note: "Dearest Molly, the necklace's diamond is a reminder of our love, and the Cross for Jesus love."

"Oh my God!" She sighed, "What's happening to Rob?"

The next day Molly awoke early and prayed for Rob and his shipmates. Afterward she decided to try to see Mrs. Walker. She found her outside her big white home on Spring Street trying to clean the slush from the sidewalk leading up to the porch. She was bundled up like an Eskimo.

"Mrs. Walker, you shouldn't be doing that! Let me help you."

"Molly! How are you? Come here." And she gave her a hug for the first time.

Molly said emphatically, "Let me finish this." She could tell Mrs. Walker was a bit relieved.

"Ok, but I'll go in and fix a pot of tea. I want to hear all about what's been going on in your life."

After Molly finished cleaning the walk, the two of them sat at a white table in the white kitchen drinking Lapsang Souchong tea from Fujian province of China. Molly thought it tasted like it was made from old railroad ties, but it was Mrs. Walker's favorite. The tea had aromas including dried longyan, pine smoke, and whiskey. She was down to her last large tin; this is it for the duration she told Molly. "What's been going on in your life? Start from the last time I saw you." Molly noticed that Rob's mom looked tired. She had aged since she last saw her. But Mary Catherine was dressed immaculately even when shoveling snow. She wore a white cashmere sweater over her dark brown slacks. Molly related the story of her interview for the teaching job in her hometown. She then told Mrs. Walker about the death of her brother in the South Pacific. She had to stop there as the stoic Mary Catherine started crying. Molly did too. Mrs. Walker did something completely unexpected. She rose and came over to Molly and put her arms around her, hugging her tightly. "Molly I'm so very sorry; I want you to know I am so very fond of you and I hate to see you hurt. Is there anything I can do for you now?" Molly tried to dry her eyes with her napkin. "No, not now, I am still having problems as you can see. I'll be alright in time. I know that Bobby is with the Lord. He's at peace. His war is over now."

Mrs. Walker said, "I agree, but I must be honest with you Molly, I hate the Japs. Nearly every time I read *The Oxford Press*, there is something about one of our boys injured or dying. Just the other day the paper said that Cadet James Baer died in a plane crash in Texas, Wm Magaw drowned in the Panama Canal Zone. Dale Schantz, radioman on the cruiser Houston, was reported missing. Billy Lawrence died on the *Arizona* in the Pearl Harbor attack. I know his mother. I'm really worried about Rob, and I know you are too. Submarines are so dangerous; I've tried several times to get Rob's duty changed to intelligence. He would be very qualified, but I can't influence the Navy brass." Molly straightened up, "I feel the same way, but I know that Rob is doing what he needs to do, so I am at peace with that." She didn't tell her of her feelings that something strange was happening to Rob. Just woman's intuition, she guessed.

Molly asked, "How was your trip to Washington? Did you see President Roosevelt?" She laughed, "No, but I did get to go to the Senate one day and sat in the gallery. It was very impressive, my uncle, the senator, was speaking about the war and the unions. Did you know that one of the union crew on a merchant marine supply ship off Guadalcanal refused to work on Sundays? That is until the Marines came aboard and started throwing them overboard. They got to work."

Molly shook her head, "My brother Bobby was killed on Guadalcanal. He was a private in the Second Marine Division." Mrs. Walker realized she had misspoken, "Oh, I shouldn't have mentioned it, I'm sorry Molly. Forgive me."

"That's ok Mrs. Walker, you didn't know."

The doorbell rang. Mrs. Walker slowly rose and walked down the hall and opened it to see a stranger standing on the porch shaking the wet snow off his rubbers. "Mrs. Walker?" He asked politely.

"Yes?" She had a puzzled look on her face,

"I'm Woody, a friend of Molly's on *The Student* newspaper. Is she here?" Mary Catherine started to say no; she was a very private person, and in her home, Molly came under her protection.

"Why, what do you want?"

"Well ma'am, the paper's manager wants to see her. There is a special edition being composed presently and she is needed."

"Please come in." She noted he was very handsome. About six feet two with strong facial features, a burr haircut and sporting a pencil-thin mustache. She thought *he should be in the movies. But why wasn't he in the service?* "Come this way." Molly, hearing Woody's voice, came out of the kitchen and greeted him warmly. *Too warmly*, Mrs.

Walker thought. Woody told her that she was wanted at the paper and that he would give her a lift.

"You have a car on campus young man? Her stern tone reminded Woody of his female geometry teacher in the tenth grade, a real witch. Somewhat sheepishly Woody replied, "Yes, ma'am, I'm the sports reporter and have to cover sporting events for the Redskins so I have a car permit and a B gas rationing card."

Mrs. Walker countered, "Well that beats me, I just have an A. But since you're here, could you give me a ride uptown to the Marathon gas station on the square? My car is having the oil changed and it should be done now."

"I'd be happy to. My car is still warm inside."

The three of them piled in his Chrysler Airflow sedan, one of the first real stream-lined cars. The curved front grill wrapped around the engine cowl sending the air around the car as it traveled its top speed of 60 miles per hour. It was painted a very light blue gray with large whitewall tires and lots of road salt splattered along the sides acquired during his trip from Cleveland. Mary Catherine sat in the rear seat. In front, Molly and Woody were carrying on a very lively conversation that she had difficulty hearing but sensed he had an unusual interest in Molly.

Mrs. Walker liked the service she got at the Marathon station. When she gassed up the Ford, they always checked the oil and washed her car's windshield. Woody parked in front of the gas station's two gas tanks. Each pump had a clear glass that filled when the attendant pumped the gas by hand. One was marked Hi-Test, the other, Regular. The OPA, the Office of Price Administration, had the price set at fifteen cents per gallon for leaded gas. The lead helped reduce the engine knocking when the car accelerated. Woody got out and opened the door for Mrs. Walker; she thanked him and watched as the two of them drove off. She thought he is smooth… just too smooth; he may be real competition for Rob. But then there is Marianne. Maybe they will meet someday. Wouldn't that be something, she mused.

As Woody drove down High Street with Molly, the car's radio was playing, *When the lights go on again all over the world,* another of Molly's favorites. When the car pulled in beside Irvin Hall, home of *The Student*, Molly asked Woody if he could find time to teach her how to drive. She had never been behind the wheel. Woody said he would love to as his hand slipped off the gearshift and casually caressed Molly's knee. She pushed it off, but there was a sly Mona Lisa smile on her face. She believed he's too fresh, but he is so cute!

CHAPTER 35

Christmas Dinner

Across the far Pacific, more than a dozen time zones from Oxford, Rob caught a couple of hours sleep. He was exhausted. The crew slept whenever they could on patrol. There was little time for him to relax anymore and play cribbage, the game he was learning to love. He seldom lost. He had heard that Dick O'Kane, exec of the *Wahoo*, had drawn a hand of four fives and a Jack, a perfect 29 cribbage hand. A mathematician had computed the odds at one in 216,580. But Rob made time to keep his promise to Valerie Edmonds to read his heart shield Bible that she gave him. The small Bible, with the Psalms and the complete New Testament, had such small print that he had trouble reading it as the boat rolled and rocked in the high seas. He had started reading the Gospel of Mark. He was impressed with the immediacy of everything Jesus did. It seemed to him that Mark was telling his readers that Jesus had dominion over sickness, demon possession, and even the weather. He remembered what John Young had told him of the miracle that he witnessed on the bridge when the captain was swept back on board after falling into the raging sea in the dark of night. John was sure Jesus helped bring him back on board. Rob wasn't too sure of that but, on the other hand, could it be just a stroke of luck? The odds of finding him in the dark of night in stormy seas off the coast of Japan were higher than the perfect cribbage hand.

There was a stack of Molly's letters jammed in the cubbyhole of the small desk he shared with John. He liked to reread them. She was a gifted writer, he thought, and he truly missed her. Her last letter was full of news of the campus, gossip and stories of the football team that beat Ohio U. at the homecoming game. It would be the last homecoming game for the duration. Stuart Holcomb was named as Miami's new football coach succeeding Frank Wilton. He wondered why they didn't pick Weeb Eubank, the coach at McGuffey High School. He applied and was turned down apparently. Rob loved Weeb, his coach in high school, a tremendous man and a great coach. She told him about some 800 delegates who attended the National Assembly of Student Christians on Miami's campus. Her priest, Father Tom, held an open house for the new addition to the parish house adjacent to St. Mary's Church on East High Street. One article that shocked Rob was a report of a shooting at the Purity restaurant uptown

March 14. Bill Davis of Okeana, a Miami sophomore, was fined $50 and costs for shooting four holes in the window of the pub. Davis will be required to pay for the new plate glass window that will cost from $80 to $100. I hope he isn't a Beta, Rob chuckled.

One clipping that bothered him was an editorial from *The Press* in a June 1942 edition, commenting on a proposal that would completely close Miami University and turn it over to the Navy for the duration to train enlisted men. The article said, "To disperse a teaching staff built up through the years, to break down the traditions of attendance at Miami, which have been established over a century, would be a step entirely unwarranted." In the same paper there was another editorial commending the university for purchasing 300 acres west of town for a flying field. "It is a step forward for this progressive school," the editor concluded.

Molly's letters always ended with sweet words of how much she missed him. In the last one she concluded with the words to the hit song, *Saturday night is the loneliest night of the week.*

> *Robbie, I miss our dances, but most of all I miss you every hour of the day, I love you forever. Xxxooo Molly.*
>
> *P.s. remember <u>our love is here to stay…</u>*

The letter fell from his hand as his head nodded, and he fell asleep sitting in his chair. Lying on the desk was a letter from Lily with red lipstick on the back of the envelope.

His nap ended when the word was passed for the attack team to report to the control room. As he passed the wardroom, he smelled the aroma of a fresh pot of coffee. Submarines have lots of odors. They usually stink. But the new fleet boats were not anything like the old S-boats that were not air-conditioned. Fumes from the stale humid air, diesel fuel, cooking odors, sweat, toilets, often were overwhelming. Bucky said he once spent a week, before the war, as an exchange officer on a Greek sub in the Mediterranean. It was awful. They used garlic and cooking oils that reeked throughout the entire boat. He said his clothes smelled for weeks afterward.

Rob paused and poured himself a cup of black coffee from a fresh pot that Marco, the Filipino steward's mate, had just made. The captain and exec were looking at a chart spread out on the table. He heard Bucky say, "Captain I don't think we're going to be able to get ahead of the convoy in time, they are just making a too good advance. They've stopped the wide zigzag swings and are making eighteen knots along their base course. I'm going to have the tracking team check my calculations, but I think I'm right." Seeing Rob at the Silex coffee pot, he said, "Rob, get to the control room and do some quick calculations for me. See if you think we can get ahead of the convoy at flank speed." Rob said, "Aye sir."

Captain Morrison looked at his exec, "Bucky I'm sorry. If I hadn't fallen over the side, we would be making an end run and would be attacking them in a few hours. You should have let me go."

"Captain you've got to stop thinking like that! We did the right thing. You would have done the same thing if Ensign Young had washed over the side. We'll have more targets on this patrol. Sir, with all due respect, get over it."

Dick's grip on his cup tightened. He rose and said, "OK, Bucky, if the attack team agrees with your calculations, then let's reverse course and head back toward Tokyo. I have a hunch we'll find some more activity up around the Tokyo area. We'll secure the attack team and slow to standard speed. We need to conserve fuel. We'll give our boys some rest and have a good Christmas dinner. But first radio Pearl that the rest of the convoy got away from us so that the *Pompano*, south of us, might get a crack at them."

"Yes, Sir." Bucky replied.

Rob and the attack team agreed with Bucky's assessment. Captain Morrison gave the word to dive the boat to provide a smooth ride for the Christmas dinner. The crew ate in shifts due to the limited number of places at the crew's mess. Christmas dinner was the best Willie and his cooks had ever made. The menu included roast turkey, sausage dressing, mashed potatoes and gravy, green beans, cranberries and peppermint ice cream and cake for dessert. Rob always marveled at how he could cook so many delicious meals in that tiny galley. The skinny little Christmas tree was back on the shelf minus most of the ornaments that had been destroyed during the last depth charge attack. The aluminum tinsel strips survived and helped hide the otherwise forlorn tree that served as a reminder of home and Christmases past.

Just before the meal, Captain Morrison left the wardroom along with John and went to the crew's mess. When he entered the compartment, they were about to rise but he said, "Keep your seats men. I just wanted to take a few minutes to say Merry Christmas to you and many thanks for saving my life. I had a close call, but you guys came to the rescue. I want to especially thank Willie McKinney, the best cook in the submarine service, and the best lookout in the Navy. If he hadn't seen my flashlight, I'd not be here enjoying his excellent cooking! To the swimmers who risked their lives on the bow, my heartfelt thanks, and to our exec and Ensign Young, for their superior seamanship. It is not easy maneuvering a surfaced submarine making a man overboard rescue in the rough seas. And finally, I want to give thanks to Almighty God for his protection. I've asked Ensign Young to pray a blessing on the food we are about to enjoy and for his divine protection for all of us." He turned to John and, over the general announcing system, the young ensign prayed: "Lord, we give you thanks for saving our captain. We pray for a safe and productive patrol; we are thankful for this meal and those who prepared it, and most of all for Jesus, who came into this world for our salvation. Be with our loved ones at home this Christmas and it's in His name we pray. AMEN." And throughout the boat, the crew joined in with the last AMEN.

After dinner, the crew relaxed listening to the records Lily had given them, playing cards, backgammon, reading, and writing letters that wouldn't be mailed until weeks later. Chief O'Neil walked by the slot machine as the phonograph played *White Christmas* for the umpteenth time. The chief put two nickels in the slot. When he pulled the lever with the second nickel, he hit the jackpot! Nickels started pouring out onto the deck. He put his hat under the machine to catch them as they gushed out. Cries erupted from the guys, "Chief you've got it rigged. We knew it!" The chief laughed and shouted, "No boys, it's the luck of the Irish! It's all going for a good cause!" From then on, he became known as Chief of the Boat, Nickels.

• • • • •

The following week was spent searching closer to the mainland. *Thornfish's* patrol area was known as the Rainbow area sprawling from Tokyo Bay along the coast of Honshu to below the tip of Kyushu including Kii Strait, Bungo Strait and the Osumi Strait. There should be many bountiful targets.

Thornfish had to dive many times each day to avoid patrol aircraft. The only targets were numerous sampans fishing and not worth a battle surface gun action and taking the chance of being exposed. Some of them clearly had radio antennas and could call in their position. Within minutes, a Mitsubishi would be overhead ready to drop bombs on them. Dick and Bucky believed a waiting game might bring a big one coming out of the naval base at Yokosuka. Sure enough, at dawn on New Year's Eve, the radar showed a large vessel and escorts coming out of Tokyo Bay. There were two problems: one was enemy patrol planes, the other weather. The barometer had been dropping for twenty-four hours. *Thornfish* remained on the surface making flank speed toward the oncoming enemy vessels. The air search radar swept the skies above for aircraft. The SJ surface radar swept the surface for enemy ships. Rob was standing watch as officer of the deck. Eight feet above him, in the periscope shears, were the four lookouts. Captain Morrison stood near the windscreen with the collar of his foul weather jacket pulled up around his neck. Rob noticed his face, especially his eyes, were showing the strain of command at sea. Bucky asked permission to come up. "Come up, sir" Rob replied. The executive officer emerged from the hatch zipping up his jacket and spoke to the captain over the noise of four 1600 hp diesel engines, "Captain, radar shows the convoy zigging away from us. We'll need to come to a new course; I recommend 240 for now and let's see what happens. If they zig our way, we'll be in a great spot to shoot. If the convoy holds their present base course, we should be ahead of them in about an hour." The captain didn't hesitate. "OK, make it so." Rob ordered the helmsman to come left to new course 240. Down below the quartermaster recorded the course change in the ship's logbook. Every change of course, speed, contacts all had to be faithfully recorded in the log that would become a permanent record of the ship's every movement.

The *Thornfish* plowed through the rough waters. Waves were crashing over the bow with increasing ferocity. Rob felt the excitement building up inside... maybe this would be the big one. Alone now on the bridge, as his eyes searched beyond the white caps for the enemy, he remembered it was New Year's Eve. Only a year ago he and Molly celebrated bringing in the New Year. They danced the night away, holding each other close dreaming of a new life together after the war. What a year it has been. As he tried to keep warm, drinking too many cups of coffee, thoughts flashed through his mind: graduation; midshipmen's school at Northwestern University's Chicago campus; commissioning; the flight to join the crew of the *Thornfish*; his first combat patrol; Captain Custer; the Board of Inquiry; and now under a new captain, the chance of a lifetime for a twenty-two year old to help sink a Japanese warship. He began to think of his relationship with Lily and of Molly; wondering what they were doing New Year's Eve? One thing for sure, Molly was not dancing with a new boyfriend. But ten thousand miles to the east, and across the International Date Line, Molly had celebrated New Year's Eve in her dorm at Miami University with her friend Woody. She had her first beers and passed out, naked.

CHAPTER 36

Dive! Dive!

The Bells of St. Mary's battle cry rang once again through the boat. Rob shouted, "Clear the bridge, clear the bridge!" The lookouts tucked their binoculars into their jackets and leaped down the ladders to the control room taking their new positions on the bow and stern planes. On the bridge, Rob reached under the windscreen sounded the klaxon diving alarm twice and announced on the IMC, "DIVE, DIVE!" The klaxon blasted. Aoogah! Aoogah! Rob heard the ballast tanks vents open and air escaped allowing seawater to enter the tanks from the bottom. Rob jumped down the hatch to the conning tower. Quartermaster pulled the lanyard and shouted, "Hatch secured sir!"

Commands rang out:

"Shut the main induction!"

"Green board, pressure in the boat."

"Flood Negative!"

"Flood Safety!"

Jerry Abrams, the diving officer, stood behind the men on the diving planes as they extended the bow planes, and ordered ten degrees down bubble.

Captain ordered, "All ahead one third. Jerry, make your depth 55 feet."

"55 feet, aye, sir."

Rob assumed his position in the conning tower as Target Data Computer Operator. The captain stood with his hands on the arms of the periscope making a last look around before the ice-cold waves closed over the optics. Before submerging, radar had the last bearing and range at 330 true and range 12,000 yards. The conning tower was quiet; no one spoke. Captain Morrison stood by Rob at the TDC and asked, "What course does the computer say we should take to get the best target range, Rob?" He had his course in mind but wanted confirmation from the TDC. Rob studied the dials for a moment and replied, "Well, sir, if they come back on base course, we should be able to get within 1000 yards of the center of the formation by taking course 289." Bucky came up the ladder from the control room just as the sound man reported, "Screws closing on bearing 300 true, sir." Dick responded with "Very well, give me a report every two minutes."

He turned to Bucky, "We'll stay on this course for a few more minutes and see what happens. Bucky, I want you to get us in 1000 yards from the big boy." Slowly the bearing and range closed on the enemy. The captain had decided to give the magnetic exploders one more chance. Dick made another periscope observation. "I see the escort now. The angle on the bow port thirty. He must be about two thousand yards ahead of the big boy. It's a Chiordi. "Mark my bearing! Range estimated 1300 yards. Come right to 290. Get me down Bucky now. We'll slip under the escort."

"Aye sir," Bucky ordered Jerry to go deep. The sound of the escort's screws reverberated throughout the boat as it passed overhead. *Thornfish* silently crept toward the target.

"Make your depth 55 feet Jerry. Let's see what we've got." Jerry trimmed the sub well, he had to be careful not to broach in the rough seas.

"Five, Five, feet sir." Jerry reported.

"Up scope." Dick squatted on the neck of the conning tower as the periscope rose. He pushed the handles down as soon as it cleared the well and rode the scope up. Waves broke over the lens but when the optics cleared, he saw the big one. An aircraft carrier loaded with planes!

Dick took another quick look. He described the carrier's silhouette to his executive officer. Bucky scanned the identification book and said, "Sir, it appears to be a Shinano class carrier." Dick acknowledged Bucky with a brief ok. His mind was racing processing angle on the bow, range, bearing drift, and a host of tactical items he needed to make an attack.

Dick said, "What do you think about firing all six bow tubes and then run under the target and fire stern tubes at the escort?" Bucky was surprised, "Sir, I don't think that is a good idea. The explosions of gasoline and ordnance could take us with it. I'd recommend full rudder after firing and use the stern tubes, if need be, on the carrier or on the escort that is sure to come after us."

"Good thinking Bucky. That is a good plan. Let the crew know."

Rob reported the range to the captain, "TDC range three oh, oh,oh sir. "

Captain replied "Very well. Open the outer doors." The hydraulic doors on the forward torpedo tubes opened with enough noise to be heard in the conning tower."

"All set forward sir."

"Very Well. This next observation is final and shoot. Up scope."

The slender attack scope broke in the waves enough for Dick to put the carrier in the vertical crosshairs of the periscope. The rangefinder set for the masthead height of the target showed thirteen hundred yards with the range closing. "Mark bearing." The crosshairs were right down the midship below the bridge of the carrier. "Set gyro angle ten. Standby to shoot. Fire one!" The XO reached up and pushed the firing button on number one. Rob noted the time in seconds on the TDC.

He ordered, "Fire two, fire three, fire four, fire five, and fire six." The sound reported all torpedoes running hot straight and normal. The three-thousand-pound fish were doing their thing. With the Mark-14 steam torpedoes leaving a wake, the escort on the side of the formation knew where to look for the enemy.

It was time to evade. "Flood negative take me deep Jerry, now!" Captain Morrison ordered in a calm but firm voice. Using full rudder would slow their decent, so Dick ordered left standard rudder as they plunged into the deep waters off Japan. Everyone could hear the high-pitched screws of the escort coming toward them. Captain ordered sternly, "Jerry, 25 degrees down bubble, 350 feet! All ahead emergency, rig ship for depth charge!"

Wham, Wham, Wham! Sounds of the torpedoes exploding rang inside the boat. As the crew held on, Rob yelled "premature, premature! The torpedoes exploded before hitting the target!" Then seconds later, one of the fish hit the fast-moving target. Dick was stunned. Why? It was a sure shot. Those damn magnetic exploders! Jerry blew negative to the mark and leveled off ordered depth. *Thornfish* went quiet. Slowly moving away from the datum point where they fired their torpedoes. Then came a rain of enemy well-placed depth charges. As *Thornfish* fought for its life, the crippled carrier made its way south under reduced speed.

Thornfish counted 39 ash cans dropped on them by two patrol boats during a three-hour attempt to escape. Captain Morrison ordered Jerry to take the boat to 400 feet. However, the enemy's depth charges were set deeper than any the crew had experienced previously. Dick conferred with his executive officer after he returned from an inspection of the boat.

"How bad is it Bucky?

'Well sir, it's bad," Bucky replied. "We're taking water in the engine room. We are going to have to pump soon. We've stopped the main leaks but the engine exhaust valve in the forward engine room is leaking petty badly now. I think it can be repaired when we surface."

Captain looked at Bucky, "We have to get out of here. Let's series the batteries and get the hell out of this mess."

"I agree, Bucky replied." He ordered Jerry to alert the maneuvering room to standby to series the batteries and prepare for flank speed. As soon as the chief in the maneuvering room acknowledged the order, Dick ordered "All ahead flank, right ten degrees rudder."

Bucky remained in the control room receiving damage reports when another explosion shook the boat on the starboard side. Then WHAM! Another depth charge exploded on the port side. It was too close. Lights went out. Pipes broke in the control room spraying seawater on electronic equipment. Diving planes were put in manual as their hydraulic lines leaked.

Then to make matters worse suddenly the word "Fire in the after-battery," came over the general alarm. The damage control party equipped with OBA's, filed through the control room to the after-battery well. No one spoke. The smell of burning electrical equipment filled the ventilation system. The damage party wearing their breathing equipment pulled the battery disconnect and dropped CO_2 fire extinguishers down the hatch to the lower battery. Fire on any vessel is a critical casualty, but even more so on a submarine at 400 feet. Captain Morrison remained in the conning tower maneuvering the boat trying to escape the reign of terror from above. Bucky went to the after-battery along with the chief of the boat. Chief O'Neil was trembling. It was déjà vu for him, as the scene of the fire in the battery of his former sub, the sunken *Squalus*, flashed in his mind. Bucky knew the problem. It was what they had feared. The copper buss bars in the battery well, carrying the electric load to the motors, were not large enough to handle the surge of electricity when the batteries were linked in series to enable flank speed. Dick had asked for larger ones during the two weeks of upkeep at Pearl, but the Navy yard did not yet have them.

It took hours to escape from their tormentors. The destroyers finally left to continue their guarding of the crippled carrier. *Thornfish* surfaced as the sun descended in the west. The boat was ventilated by taking air from within the boat by opening the forward torpedo room hatch and the after- torpedo room hatch to draw clean fresh air throughout the boat. The machinist mates fixed the damaged exhaust valves and repairs were made in every compartment. The radar and the radio worked! Chief O'Neil said it was the luck of the Irish! A message was sent to COMSUBPAC telling them of the course and speed of the damaged carrier; hopefully another sub would be able to follow the track and finish the job. Captain Morrison told them in the same message that the magnetic exploders failed again.

Dick said, "XO, break out the grog for the crew! They deserve their depth charge ration after all the shit the enemy gave us. We'll drink a toast to Josephus Daniels!" The former Secretary of the Navy issued orders in 1921 to remove all liquor from U. S. Naval vessels. The United States Navy is one of the few navies in the world that prohibit alcohol aboard ships. Bucky laughed, "You probably don't know this but after the attack on Pearl Harbor, the repair crew working on the heavily damaged USS *Maryland* found a bunch of bent copper tubing in the boatswain's locker in the very bow of the ship. They couldn't figure out what all that tubing was doing in the locker. It turns out the boatswain mates had made a still and were cooking alcoholic white lightning." The captain laughed, "Ingenious sailors!"

CHAPTER 37

The Job

Molly hadn't heard from Rob in a very long time. She was worried. News had filtered out about some of the submarine losses in the Pacific. It was disheartening. At times she felt despondent. She prayed for him and had her prayer group at church interceding for Rob during their regular small group meeting at Saint Mary's Church. She eased her anxiety somewhat by devoting herself to her studies, teaching third grade under instruction at McGuffey School, and writing articles for *The Student* newspaper. One story aroused some personal interest. Professor Read Bain of the Sociology Department was going to present some lectures about Marriage and Modern Life. The only fee was 25 cents for the book. His first lecture, "Selecting a Mate," really intrigued her. She knew that Professor Bain loved to shock students. He once asked a freshman class what a concubine was. A young female raised her hand and said, "Isn't that a machine you harvest wheat with?" He recently addressed the Phi Eta Sigma freshmen's honorary with an address on Postwar Men and Women. His topics included: greater equality between sexes, growing tensions between men and women because of competing interests, a stronger tendency toward birth control and more marriages in college life.

She dreamed that if Rob survived the war, they would be married. Sometimes though, as she read his letters, there was no mention of marriage and their life together after the war. *She wondered if he was really committed to her.* Perhaps it was a fear that he might not make it. She wanted an ending of the war to be a happy one... a life together forever and ever. But what if something should happen? She did not want to think about it. *Then there's Woody. She knew he was pursuing her. She liked him, and he's so good looking, and so charismatic.* He was such a great help during the week she learned of her brother's death in the South Pacific. During that time, she saw in Woody a depth of character that she had not sensed before. He always lit up the room when he entered *The Student* offices. They got along famously, sharing a lot of similar interests, writing, adventure and occasionally he asked her to go to a movie uptown and she usually accepted. After all, it's not a date she reasoned. Theirs was strictly a platonic relationship, as far as she was concerned, and his sense of humor helped her by cheering her up when she was down. One movie she refused to see was Tyrone Power in *Crash*

Dive. A movie about submarine attacks would only contribute to her fears for Rob. She loved *Casablanca,* one of her favorite movies. It became a classic almost as soon as it was released, and she saw it three times.

Woody finally had his hernia corrected. The surgery, performed at Christ Hospital in Cincinnati, caused him to miss the first two weeks of school in his final semester at Miami. His recuperation went smoothly and soon he was his old self at the newspaper office. Woody decided to reapply for Marine flight training before graduation in the spring. The Navy V 12 program, now in full swing, provided basic flight instruction for those in their program, at the new Miami airfield west of town. Woody convinced one of the flight instructors to give him flying lessons. He began his lessons flying in an Aeronca aircraft made in Middletown, Ohio. He loved it.

Molly faithfully wrote Rob a letter each week, often enclosing an article from *The Student* or *The Oxford Press.* She continued to keep him up-to-date with goings on in the town and school. She clipped an article from *The Student* regarding some 400 WAVES coming to Miami who would be housed in East and West Dorms. Their studies included radio theory, typing and radio signaling during four months of training. WAVES were filling shore billets in the Navy, allowing men to go to sea in combat roles. There were 1200 men on campus studying the same courses, including forty Coast Guard enlisted men. The article went on to say, President Upham stated the Navy does not want to crowd out regular civilian students. He wanted to quell rumors that persisted that the Navy wanted to take over the entire university.

Molly wanted to talk to her father about her vocation after graduation. But she was afraid. Her dad, being very stubborn, would be hard to deal with, but she was determined to get a job as a reporter, hopefully at *The Oxford Press.* She'd write to her father if she got the position, knowing that her dad would be more open to her having a real job so soon before graduation. He would be very disappointed though since the only college educated women he knew were teachers.

She loved Oxford and *The Press* being published weekly would give her time to gain experience in other areas of reader interest. After a year or so, she might move up to a larger paper like *The Cincinnati Enquirer.*

Redbud trees along High Street were starting to bloom as she walked with her resume in hand. Included in her envelope were several of her best articles from *The Miami Student.* She entered the small office of *The Oxford Press* and was greeted by a dour secretary who gave the impression that she was overworked and indispensable to the operation of the town's only paper. Molly politely introduced herself, "Hello, I'm Molly Gaynor, one of the editors of *The Miami Student,*" and asked her to give the envelope to Mrs. Avis W. Cullen, publisher and editor of *The Oxford Press.* The prim secretary wasn't a bit impressed with her. "Put it in the IN basket please," she said not trying to mask the disdain in her voice. Molly, a little taken back by her hostility, laid the large envelope on her desk and started to leave, when the door of the inner office opened, and a very elegant elderly lady said, "Miss, may I help you?" Molly picked up her resume and quickly scooted past the secretary's desk and entered the office of the owner and publisher of *The Oxford Press.* After an hour interview, she got the job!

Molly hurried back to *The Student* office. Woody rose from his desk and greeted her as she entered the building. "Hi Miss Molly! You look like you just won the Irish Sweepstakes!" Woody thought she looked radiant. "What's up, sweetie?" Molly ignored the term of endearment from her platonic friend. "Well, Woody, you won't believe it, but I just got hired by *The Oxford Press*! I begin work right after graduation." She described the interview she had with Mrs. Cullen and how she was very impressed with her work on *The Student.*

"You know she had already read some of my stories and knew me from my by-line. I'm going to be paid seventy-five cents an hour and if I do well, I could be getting a dollar in six months. I'm so happy Woody!"

He sat down beside her desk and said, "What will they have you do?"

"Well, we talked about me covering stories about the war effort from the home front perspective. It would include doing stories about the Navy on campus too. I would really like that; I'm sending clippings of stories about the home front to Rob now."

Woody knew that, but was sorry she had to mention Rob, his competition for the heart of the sweet Irish girl he was hoping to win.

"Let's celebrate! The Airflow is gassed up and we can drive to Cincinnati for dinner. How does that sound?"

"Great, but I have to get someone to cover for me at the dorm."

Woody picked Molly up in front of the dorm and drove east on High Street past Cook Field where hundreds of sailors were practicing close order drill. "I'll be doing that soon, Molly," Woody said. "If I can qualify, I'll be doing the drills at Pensacola after graduation."

"How long does it take to become a naval aviator?"

"I think it's now about a year. Basic flight and ground school and carrier qualifications. Then I'll be a full-fledged Marine pilot. Maybe you can come down and pin my gold wings on Molly."

"Thanks for asking but I'll probably be quite busy as a real journalist."

As the Chrysler Airflow sped down US 27 at 45 miles per hour, Woody acted as though he paid no attention to her remark but inside, he had a sinking feeling.

"Where do you want to eat?" Molly said to change the subject.

"Arnold's downtown Cincinnati. You will like it. It's the oldest restaurant in

Cincinnati. It was opened in 1861 by Simon Arnold and has been in continuous operation ever since. Great food. "

Molly said, "Sounds good to me."

Woody drove the big sedan past Crosley Field built in 1912 for the Cincinnati Red Stockings baseball team. The Reds were the oldest professional team playing their first game in 1869 in a field at the intersection of Findlay and Western Avenues. As they drove past the ball field, the dome of the Union Station a few blocks away glowed in the setting sun.

They rounded the corner on East Eight Street and found a parking place right in front of Arnold's Bar and Grill. Molly was not impressed by its appearance. It had an ugly brown brick front with two large plate glass windows with a red and blue neon sign in one of them advertising Burger Beer, Cincinnati 's finest. It had little atmosphere she thought. It looked more like a shoe store rather than a nice restaurant. They were shown to a table with a bold red and white checked tablecloth near the small bandstand. Woody held the chair for Molly and the waiter asked for their drink order. Woody looked at the wine list and ordered a bottle of French champagne. "May I see your ID please?" Woody glared at him, but handed him his driver's license and said, "We are celebrating tonight." The waiter smiled and said," I bet you're engaged." Molly coughed and said, "No I just landed my dream job." She watched as the waiter opened the sparkling white wine, thinking about the times she watched the same thing in the movies. Woody poured the wine into the slender wine glasses and raised his glass saying, "To my favorite Molly and her new job, may it be the beginning of a great career!" Their glasses clinked, and she sipped her very first champagne. She savored the wonderful bubbles. It was delicious. She wanted more. It was meatless Friday and Woody ordered Lake Erie whitefish for them. While waiting for the food to arrive they decided to dance. It was too early for the band, so Woody put coins in the jukebox, and they danced to *I've Heard That Song Before* with Harry James and his orchestra. It was on the Hit Parade for five weeks. The tempo picked up when more records dropped in the jukebox and they jitterbugged to *The GI Jive* and *Boogie Woogie Bugler* with the Andrew Sisters. Next, they slow danced Woody holding her tightly to Tommy Dorsey's orchestra playing *There Are Such Things*. They were the only ones dancing as they dipped and swayed across the small dance floor, Molly dreaming of Rob and Woody dreaming of Molly dancing like Ginger Rogers. No more records dropped. The silence was broken by approving dinner guests' applause watching them gracefully dancing.

They returned to the table. She smoothed her blouse, a little embarrassed, but Woody was more infatuated with her. The dinner was delicious as Woody had promised. She told him more of her interview with the owner of the paper and the sullen old maid secretary guarding the office inner sanctum. "You'll win her over Molly, so don't worry about her. Let's go," he said. "I want to show you Cincinnati by night."

He paid the bill and drove to the overlook on Mount Adams. He parked the car and they walked down the path hand in hand, to the overlook. Cincinnati, founded on seven hills with Mount Adams the highest, offered a spectacular view of the city. Even with the dim out, it was gorgeous. No wonder they called it the Queen City. They sat on a bench saying nothing for a long time. Tugboats pushing a stream of barges filled with coal from Eastern Kentucky plowed the calm Ohio River heading down river to provide power plants the fuel for wartime industries. Streetcars moved along Fountain Square downtown. Autos were moving slowly making their way down Highway 50 along the river. The Carew Tower was unlighted for the duration, but lights in the windows of workers laboring late in the night checkered the tall skyscraper.

Woody was the first to speak. "Breathtaking isn't it? Molly, here we are in this peaceful place, all is calm all is bright, as the Christmas Carol says, and thousands of miles away fierce fighting for the survival of our nation is going on." She didn't reply. Woody knew she was crying in the dark. He put his arms around her and drew her tight. Then turned her face toward him and kissed her wet cheeks. She kissed him back strongly and then suddenly drew away. No Woody, it's not right I'm …. I've promised myself to wait for Rob."

CHAPTER 38

Questions

Rob had the mid-watch and John the 4 to 8, so both turned in early after the evening meal. Mealtimes had changed while on patrol. The crew rested during daylight hours when they were submerged. Breakfast was generally served in the evening when they surfaced and hunted for prey. Rob and John, his roommate, played a couple of rounds of cribbage before turning in. Rob won as usual. The curtain on the doorway was closed. The room was dark except for tiny lights over each bunk. Rob, laying in his bunk was reading his daily dose of a page from the New Testament, before dozing off. He was struggling with a passage from John's Gospel, chapter 14: *No one comes to the father except by the son.* "I don't get it, this verse seems to say that there is only one way to salvation, and that is to believe in him and the one who sent him. Isn't that narrow of God? I mean what about others that believe in Buddha or the Japs that believe in Shintoism. It just doesn't seem fair to me. I mean if they live a good life and don't intentionally hurt others wouldn't they be welcomed in heaven too?"

His roommate turned over to his side to be heard better over the noise of the fans circulating air throughout the boat. John replied, "Well that's a problem we often hear when we Navigators present the word to a shipmate."

Rob interrupted him, "What're the Navigators, John?"

"It's an organization started a few years ago by a sailor named Dawson Trotman, on one of the battleships in the Pacific Fleet. His idea was to win one person to Christ, and disciple him, and then he in turn would win one and disciple him. It caught on and multiplied. We now have many sailors sharing their stories and leading men to Jesus. It is exciting, Rob. I joined right after I was commissioned. We even have a couple of members now onboard *Thornfish*."

"Very interesting. Let me ask you this… Hey, maybe I am keeping you up."

"No," John quickly replied, "I 'll get more shut-eye than you will tonight. Keep talking."

"Ok, what I was going to say is how about those human beings that have never heard about Jesus. Won't they make it too?"

"That's an excellent question Rob. One that I have thought about a great deal.

Here's my answer after a lot of pondering; first we who have heard the gospel message are to choose to believe it or not believe it. For those like the folks in the jungles of the Philippines, who may have never heard, we must leave that up to God's mercy. Someone has said that, when we get to heaven and ask that question, God's answer will satisfy everyone!"

"Thanks, John. I'll think about it." He turned the light off and blew a kiss to Molly.

A few minutes after Rob fell asleep, *Thornfish* surfaced in the dimming twilight. Only an hour had passed when the radioman striker came quietly in his stateroom and tried to awaken Ensign Walker, the boat's communications officer. He had to shake his shoulder to wake him. "Sir, I hate to bother you, but we have a Top-Secret message coming in that we need you to decode." Rob arose, splashed some water on his face and looked at his watch. Only an hour's sleep. He followed the radioman to the radio shack aft of the control room. He stopped in the wardroom briefly and poured himself a cup of coffee that poured like molasses and tasted like it too. It took him fifteen minutes to decode the message and he hand carried it to the captain's cabin. Dick turned the light on and sat on the edge of his bed. It was a message from Commander of Submarines, Pacific Fleet. The CO said, "Thanks, Rob, please have the XO meet me in the wardroom and get me the charts for the Sasebo-Nagasaki area." The message contained a report of a large convoy sighted by the submarine *Pickerel* that had not been able to make contact and notified headquarters of the course and speed of the enemy ships. Dick and his exec poured over the charts in the wardroom. Dick estimated they could intercept it if the boat could stay surfaced long enough and avoid patrolling aircraft.

Rob didn't try to get more sleep. He donned his foul weather gear and prepared to take the mid-watch. After the usual exchange of information from Pete, the OOD, he said the traditional words, "I relieve you sir." Rob was the one officer now solely responsible for the entire vessel, reporting only to the commanding officer. Rob felt a surge of adrenalin as he assumed the watch knowing the confidence his commanding officer had in him. Rob, alone on the bridge, zipped up the hood on his parka, trying to block out the cold and had a cup of fresh hot coffee sent up from the crew's galley.

The radar man in the conning tower interrupted his thoughts. "Bridge, we have a large contact on the PPI scope bearing north 30,000 yards." Rob passed the word to the captain, who came up to the conning tower immediately. He ordered a course change to the bearing of the contact. The Bells of St. Mary's chimed throughout the boat as the Thornies prepared for battle. Dick thought this one must have escaped our code-breakers. He was unaware that the Japanese had changed their codes in early January and our intelligence group in Pearl had not yet broken their new codes. Dick slowed to standard speed waiting to see the course and speed of the enemy track. Suddenly at 15,000 yards, it completely disappeared. A half an hour later, another large contact, the size of a battleship, appeared some 20,000 yards and then disappeared at 15,000 yards. A few minutes later another contact with similar results. The SJ surface radar operator insisted everything was operating normally. Cold dense air made for good radar reception. The lookouts and the quartermaster on the periscope observed nothing.

Bucky and the captain conferred in the conning tower. Bucky said, "Captain we're seeing ghosts, phony reflections from the mountaintops of the island 40 miles away." Dick looked confused, "Ghosts? Really?" The XO said, "Yes sir, we had them now and then when I was on the S-boat in the Aleutians, early in the war." Dick laughed, "My God, the admiral is going to have a fit when he reads our patrol report, chasing ghosts. All right, secure from battle stations Bucky."

"Aye, Sir."

Rob continued his OOD watch. One of the stewards brought him a hot cup of coffee and a ham sandwich. He devoured it. Less than an hour to go and he would be back in his bunk for a couple of hours sleep. It didn't happen. "Bridge, radar, I have a new contact five thousand yards ahead. Just popped up, Sir." In the pitch-black night, the lookouts couldn't see anything. Rob looked through the lens of the bridge TBT high-powered binoculars. Lookout school teaches to see better look off from the direct line of sight. As his eyes moved away, Rob saw a glimmer in the darkness; the outline of a submarine.

CHAPTER 39

Submarine!

"All stop," ordered Rob. "Sound get me a bearing on the contact off our port bow! Captain to the bridge! Captain to the bridge!"

Down below in the conning tower, Edwards the sonar operator said, "Sir, I have noise... it sounds like a sub is blowing ballast tanks. Bearing 350 relative."

Rob said, "Very well." Captain Morrison dashed to the bridge. Taking off his red night vision goggles, he said, "What's going on Rob, do we have another ghost? "

"No Sir. I sighted it on the TBT, it's a sub that just surfaced. Sound says they are starting a low-pressure blow. Radar picked it up at 5000 yards." Then he added, "Sir, do we have any of our subs in the vicinity?"

The captain said, "No, there shouldn't be, but we have to make sure. It could be the *Pickerel* off station. Shut down the engines and shift to the battery. Sound battle stations torpedo!" *Thornfish* began creeping forward toward the mysterious submarine. Rob remained on the bridge as OOD. Normally when at battle stations he would be operating the Target Data Computer, but because Rob's night vision was so good, the captain wanted him on the bridge to try to identify the unknown submarine. As *Thornfish* began to overtake the contact, Rob said, "Captain, I think it's an I boat. It's got the hangar forward of the bridge." Dick said, "We don't have any subs with a silhouette like that. Open the outer doors on tubes one and two." The range closed to 1000 yards, Bucky in the conning tower reported, "Already sir, anytime." Captain ordered, "Bucky you may fire when ready," echoing Dewey's famous words at the battle of Manila Bay in 1898. Two Mark-14 torpedoes launched from their tubes sped toward the unsuspecting target at 45 knots. Set for ten feet, and zero target angle, the fish would hit the sub in less than 60 seconds. Two lookouts on the enemy submarine saw the luminous wakes of the two torpedoes but it was too late. The explosion rocked the target and the *Thornfish*. Sounds of the sub breaking up as it sank in the depths rang throughout the boat. There was no joy in the sinking; everyone knew that it could have been them sinking had the enemy seen them first. They could feel the pain of the enemy sailors as they descended to their watery tomb. Captain Morrison conned the *Thornfish* over the spot where their target went down. Radar indicated no contacts;

he had a searchlight brought to the bridge. He needed to see if there was anything of value to secure for intelligence purposes. All bridge standers put on red goggles to maintain their night vision as much as possible. As the signalman aimed the searchlight in among the diesel oil, he spotted a survivor floating among some junk. The captain ordered, "All engines stop. Rig out the bow planes. Standby to rescue a prisoner."

Rob was standing by the bridge TBT observing the rescue attempt. Captain said, "I have the conn, Rob go down and talk to the Jap and see if you can coax him aboard, he may have some Intel for us."

Rob said, "Aye, sir."

The boatswain mate threw a line with a large loop tied with a bowline and fed it into the water for the enemy sailor. Then he saw not one but two enemy crew members trying to keep afloat. Rob called out in Japanese, "Don't be afraid. You will not be harmed. Come aboard." It worked; slowly they made their way up to the bow and took the line. It took a few minutes, but both were recovered, freezing in the cold and covered with oil.

Captain Morrison ordered the prisoners to be taken below in the forward torpedo room hatch. The alert boatswain mate found some papers floating near the bow. With the adroit use of the boat hook he was able to bring them aboard. Captain Morrison was anxious to move on toward Nagasaki. As soon as all men were below, he ordered Rob to take the conn and proceed at full speed toward the enemy convoy. The diesel engines came to life, and soon *Thornfish* started plowing through the dark waters at full speed toward Osumi Strait on the tip of southern Kyushu.

John relieved Rob as OOD after they secured from torpedo action stations. Rob exhausted, fell into his bunk with his clothes on. Two hours later, the aroma of steaks and fries being served in the wardroom revived him. He took a warm Navy shower conserving precious fresh water by wetting down, soap down and final rinse. Altogether, it took only three minutes. After putting fresh clothes on, he joined the officers in the wardroom. Bucky, seated at the head of the table, welcomed Rob and said, "The captain is grabbing a few hours sleep in his stateroom. He wants us to interrogate our new visitors after you have your meal." Rob said, "Yes, Sir." The steward poured him a cup of coffee, and he ordered steak, fries and eggs. While he was waiting, the XO said, "Rob, our prisoners are in the torpedo room and have been cleaned up and fed. One of them is a junior officer and the other may be a young quartermaster. Both must have been on the bridge after they surfaced. They may give us some important information about minefields, so we hope we can get them to tell us when you question them. We'll interview each one separately."

After the officers finished eating, the mess attendants cleared off the table, and the exec and Rob examined the Japanese charts that were recovered a few hours earlier.

They were of the area where *Thornfish* was heading showing the planted minefields in red ink. Finding them was a bonanza; however, were the charts up to date? There was no date on the charts as to when the minefields were planted. A few minutes later Chief O'Neil brought the young quartermaster into the wardroom still bound in handcuffs. He was wearing new clothes, Navy dungarees and a blue chambray shirt. All too large for him. He was scared. The exec sat at the head of the green-clad table, with Rob, his interpreter next to him. Rob asked the XO if the handcuffs could be removed, and he agreed. The prisoner must have been about 19 years old. He bowed and after the cuffs were removed, he said, "Dom ah Rigato." Thank you very much. Rob poured him a cup of coffee and began by asking him his name, rank, and if he had an identification number. What was his job on board? The name, hull number of his sub. It was, as they had assumed, an I Boat displacing approximately 2500 tons. He learned that they had been on patrol looking for enemy submarines and had just surfaced to charge batteries. He had just come to the bridge when the *Thornfish* torpedo exploded, killing the lookouts. Bucky offered him a cigarette, which he refused. It was evident he wanted to talk. He told them he was a quartermaster striker and the charts that they recovered were up to date. Their captain, he explained, was on the bridge and survived but chose to remain and went down with his crew. Only he, and his officer of the deck, survived. The OOD was the third officer, the engineer.

The interview lasted about half an hour. At the conclusion, he looked at his translator and then the exec, and said, "Please do not tell my officer of my talking so much to you. He might harm me." Chief O'Neil had him cuffed and moved to the after-torpedo room. Rob thought they had gained his confidence enough to get more information regarding coastal navigation and perhaps more about the operation of the I boat. They would like to find out more about sonar ranges, and radar equipment. It would be very important to keep the two prisoners separated at least for a time. Bucky had the Japanese charts removed and ordered the Jap officer to be brought in for questioning.

Rob refilled his coffee cup and said to the exec, "Sir, I think it would be wise not to disclose any information we just got from the sailor. We need to compare the officer's story with that of the enlisted man if he talks."

"Agreed, Rob. Let's see what the officer has to say."

Chief O'Neil returned later with the handcuffed Japanese lieutenant in tow. The chief had blindfolded the prisoner. The tall Japanese officer had striking features. Jet black hair, head erect, strong jaw, giving him the air of one used to command. The chief had him seated. Rob decided to have the blindfold remain on as it might give him a bit more insecurity. Rob began in Japanese; you are a prisoner of the United States Navy Submarine *Thornfish*. While you are in our custody, you will be well treated. Upon our return to our home base, you will be turned over to our Marines for forwarding you to a POW camp. The Red Cross will be notified in due time of your capture. In the meantime, we must have your complete cooperation. You will first give us your full name, rank and serial number and unit assigned.

Speaking in Japanese he said, "I am a Kaigun Chui, lieutenant junior grade, number 257689, assigned to I-13 based in Yokosuka, Japan. I am an assistant engineer and navigator."

"What is your name?"

He hesitated. "My name is Jimmu Kamatsu."

Rob was stunned. It could not be. He nearly spilled his coffee. "Chief take off his blindfold!" Chief O'Neil hesitated, and then reluctantly removed the blindfold.

Rob and his teenage friend from the American School in Tokyo sat looking at each other. Finally, Rob stammered, "Jimmu, do you remember me? I am Rob! Your friend at the American School in Tokyo!'"

He spoke in English, "You were my American friend!" Bucky was astonished at the exchange. It's impossible that this could happen. The two junior officers, now enemies, rehearsed some of the good times they had together as teenage friends. Bucky had the handcuffs removed. He wanted to get on with interrogating. Rob poured Jimmu a cup of coffee and Bucky offered a cigarette. Their prisoner gladly accepted both. "Camels! My favorite brand before the war." He took a deep drag and exhaled, "Wonderful cigarette, made in Winston Salem, North Carolina. My father enjoyed them when he was our naval attaché in Washington, years ago."

Rob interjected, "Where is he now? I imagine he is flag rank now."

Jimmysan said, "Yes, he's my boss. He oversees submarines based in Yokosuka."

"How does he see the war going now?" The young officer paused and said, "Now…. good. In the future, no. We are an island nation. My father says that someday we will be able to walk on the American submarines from Singapore to Tokyo. We can only hope for a negotiated settlement to this war." He halted briefly, pondering his next words, "We started it. I am sorry."

CHAPTER 40

The Blowhard
Submarine Base, Pearl Harbor

The phone rang and rang. Ben Miller, the admiral's chief of staff, rolled over in bed and reached for his bedside phone in his suite in the BOQ of the submarine base. He glanced at the luminous dial of his alarm clock. It was 4 a.m.

He answered it, growling, "Miller. What the hell is going on?"

"Captain Miller, it's LT Begovich, the duty officer, we have a problem sir. Can you come in sir?"

"Why can't you tell me now? It four o'clock!"

"Well I'd rather not discuss it over the phone, sir."

"OK, I'll be in. Send me a Jeep."

"It already outside, waiting for you captain."

Ben did not like what he was hearing. He put on his working uniform and grabbed a stale piece of toast stuck in the toaster from yesterday's spartan breakfast. The driver gave him a salute, and he hopped in the passenger's seat. He glanced at his watch, 0415. "Let's go!" He ordered.

The five-minute drive down the hill to the submarine squadron headquarters gave Ben a little time to think. *We must have lost another boat. Probably due to the magnetic exploders.* Lieutenant Begovich met him at the front door. He saluted and ushered his boss into the conference room. Two officers were seated at the conference room oval able. The Deputy Chief of Staff, Commander Lou Hansberger, and the Staff Assistant Communications Officer, Bill Nelson.

"OK, gents. What's the problem?"

"Well sir," Lieutenant Commander Nelson, a veteran of four combat patrols, began, "Captain, the mainland wire services are carrying a story about Congressman Andrew Jackson May from Kentucky. You met him recently when he was here on an inspection tour of the war zone."

"Yes, I certainly remember him. He was probably trying to get out of the winter weather in Washington. I call it a junket tour. But don't quote me, of course. He has a big job in Congress though. He's the Chairman of the House Military Affairs Committee."

The sixty-eight-year-old Democrat senior member of Congress was known for his outspoken remarks. He never worried about adverse publicity. The folks he represented in Kentucky's Seventh Congressional District loved him. In fact, all the Kentuckians admired him almost as much as they admired the legendary Daniel Boone. His seat in the Congress was as secure as anyone. He was born in eastern Kentucky, the heart of the coal mining industry. He worked his way out of the Kentucky hills after he graduated from Tennessee's Union Law School, first becoming a county clerk, then a lawyer for the coal companies and later a judge on the county bench in Lawrence County. "Well, sir, on his return from his junket he called a press conference late yesterday in his House Office. During the session with the reporters, he remarked, "Boys, you know how much I admire the men of the silent service. Well you don't have to worry about our submarines; those damn Japs are setting their depth charges too shallow!"

Ben put his head in his hands, and murmured, "Oh, No!"

"But you won't believe this sir; the reporters carried this story over all the wire services."

Ben's jaw dropped, he shouted uncharacteristically, "Oh, Shit! Shit! Shit! This is crazy! Can this be true? Lou are you sure they carried the story?"

Lou, Ben's deputy replied, "Sir, I have double checked it. The wire services have carried the story and I just found out that the *Honolulu Star-Bulletin* is going to publish it in their early morning edition. The admiral will be told this morning at his morning intelligence briefing. We need to be ready; he's going to blow a gasket!"

"I already have blown a gasket. Lou, get on the phone right now with the Star. I want to talk to the editor. Maybe we can head this report off here in the Pacific. I can't believe May and the wire reporters would be so careless with top-secret information. They ought to be put in prison for the rest of the war."

Hours earlier, Professor Dr. Albert Walker Sr. was busy working late at the newly constructed temporary office buildings housing the OSS, near the State Department's headquarters at Foggy Bottom, Washington, D.C. The renowned geologist having experience with Pacific islands, was pouring over photographs of Tarawa, an atoll in the Gilberts chain in the central Pacific, looking for the best place to land Marines. The fifty-year-old professor of volcanology was tired. He had been working all day on this top-secret project. The door to his office opened and his colleague rushed in waving a copy of the *Washington Post*. "Al, you won't believe this. That old fart Congressman May just gave away some of our secrets to the Japs!"

"What? Let me see it?" He handed the newspaper to the professor. The second page headlined a wire service article regarding Japanese antisubmarine warfare. He quickly read the story. The Japs were setting their depth charges too shallow. Our subs can escape by going deep. Al could not believe it. He said, "My son Rob is in a sub in the Pacific now. He might be killed by this SOB's doing." He reached for the phone and gave the operator the senator's private number. He was the ranking member of the Senate Armed Forces Committee. The old man answered, "Al, I know what you're calling about. I saw the Post's article. I've already called the Navy Secretary. His line is constantly busy. I'm sure Frank Knox is really upset. That Democrat congressional representative has some explaining to do. But he is a very powerful member of Congress. They will never censure him."

The Honolulu Star refused to pull the article. They said the presses had already run the story. Admiral Lockwood, Commander of Submarines, Pacific Fleet, was furious. He ordered no more press briefings and no publication of our submarines' successes or losses. He estimated many of our submarines would be lost due to this leak in security. He was correct. Some ten submarines and 800 men would lose their lives because of this blunder.

CHAPTER 41

Lily Worries

Lily was worried. Driving home in her mother's car late at night after work at the Royal Hawaiian, she stopped at the overlook on Ka'amilo Street on Aiea Heights. Down below, welders' torches flashed in the shipyard, in the naval base. Occasional red or green sidelights of vessels underway in the harbor made a beautiful scene. The evening was beautiful. The stars shone brightly over the dimmed lights of the city. Her thoughts drifted back to her childhood when she and her father laid on a blanket one night in their backyard, and he pointed out the stars and constellations and even named them. Now she loved another Navy man. But did he love her?

It was near midnight when she finally pulled into the driveway of the home that her father had built on Cocci drive. She thought of her dad. She loved him but did not get the time to spend with him as she would have liked. Being a career Navy man meant lots of moves and separations. In his later years, he was lucky. He was stationed at Ford Island seaplane base. He thought about getting out of the Navy after his twentieth year, but the oncoming threat of war made him change his mind. He loved the Navy and the country he served. Two weeks before the attack on Pearl Harbor, he reenlisted in a ceremony aboard the USS *Arizona*, his new duty station. Lily loved her father. He was her best friend.

Lily had missed her period. In fact, she had missed two. She had to tell her mom. She needed help. Lily remembered the time with her father, after he returned from a long deployment, when he told her about the birds and the bees. "Lily if you ever get in trouble you call me. I know a doctor that can help you if need be." Her mother had always had apprehensions about Lily getting involved with someone in the service. She understood the problems military families often had, frequent separations, missed birthday parties, school plays, and the loneliness of Christmases apart. Valerie Edmonds was concerned about Rob. Serving in submarines is probably the most dangerous branch of the service. She did not want Lily to lose Rob as she had with her husband Frank. Mrs. Edmonds liked Rob. He's not only good looking, but she thought he has a kind heart; he is truly an officer and a gentleman. No wonder Lily had fallen head over heels for him.

The light in the foyer was still burning bright when Lily pulled in the driveway. She entered the door quietly and tiptoed down the dark hallway toward her room. "Lily come in and see me," her mother called. Lily was tired. It had been a long day serving drinks to rowdy submariners. The Navy had a lease on the entire hotel facility for the duration. She had a good job and made terrific tips. The sailors spent money without thinking about tomorrow. She dreaded having to tell her mother of her condition. She decided to see what her mom wanted. She opened the door and Valerie turned on the light and instantly sensed something was wrong. "Honey what's wrong, you've been crying. Come here and sit beside me." Lily's mother was an angel. A Catholic with deep faith, she had raised her only daughter to be a strong Christian. Her husband never converted to the Catholic faith but, in his own way, he knew and respected the Almighty. "What's wrong honey?" she said. "Mom, I'm afraid I'm pregnant." Valerie sighed, and hugged her. They both cried. She always wanted the best for her only daughter, marriage and family. This war had destroyed so many lives. Now this. Lily got up and paced the floor. "Mom I need to see a doctor to be sure." Valerie replied, "Ok honey, I'll take care of it. Let's not panic. It's in the Lord's hands."

The next morning at breakfast, Lily told her mom she wanted an abortion. Her mother stiffened, and her hand was shaking as she poured Lily's coffee into a beautiful Noritake cup. "No, let's not talk about it. You need to find out if you're pregnant first. What happened to you, Lily?" Lily reached for a Kleenex on her mother's night table, "I don't know mom, I just … I am so in love with Rob, it just seemed so good. I want you to know I was the aggressor, not Rob." Her mother said, "I can understand how you could fall for him. He is such a wonderful man; he will make a great husband someday if he makes it through the war ok." Lily rose and went out on the lanai and sat on the couch sobbing. She couldn't stop.

CHAPTER 42

Nagasaki

Lieutenant Kamatsu was not as forthcoming about his service in submarines as the young quartermaster shipmate. Despite their reunion, as fate would have it, questioning by the executive officer and Rob, only yielded his name, rank, and serial number in accordance with the Geneva Convention, which Japan never signed. But Rob decided to make his boyhood friend as comfortable as possible and try to get him to be more talkative as time went on. Being an officer, he was provided with a cot to sleep on in the forward torpedo room. His enlisted shipmate, however, slept on the deck in the after-torpedo room. The crew did not like either of them. The chief of the boat kept each prisoner's wrist handcuffed to a stanchion, except to eat and do their toilet.

Thornfish raced along the 100-fathom curve off the eastern portion of Kyushu, diving only to avoid aircraft during the day. Bucky got a good star sight at twilight and confirmed his position by sighting the lighthouse off Oji point, still lighted by the Japs for navigation at night. They rounded the southern tip of Kyushu and by dawn were in the sea-lanes off the seaport of Nagasaki. At 0900 the next morning, they sighted a convoy showing six ships on the PPI radarscope. They were out of range for *Thornfish* to catch up with them, so Captain Morrison decided to submerge and draw closer to the shipping channels. He would wait for the next one.

About four in the afternoon, the soundman reported distant screws. Dick ordered periscope depth, sixty feet. The sea was smooth as glass. "Up Scope." Dick searched the surface seeing nothing but distant haze on the horizon. "Down scope. Make your depth 90 feet." The diving officer below him in the control room replied, "Nine zero feet, aye sir." Suddenly two bombs went off directly under *Thornfish* blowing the sub up at a steep angle. It was a horrific explosion. They were about to broach. Jerry Abrams was the diving officer and immediately ordered the manifold operator to flood all tanks. "Get me down!" the captain yelled. The explosion knocked out the electric system in the control room. The bow and stern planes were jammed and whirled uncontrollably. Rob was in the head going to the toilet when the bomb hit. The force of the shock wave jammed the head's door and he had to smash it open. He ran to the control room and saw the spinning bow plane's wheel and rushed to grab it only to have all 200 pounds of him thrown into the bulkhead knocking him unconscious. They had to get down. That plane circling above them would have more depth charges but none came. Captain Morrison ordered all hands forward to the torpedo room to increase the boat's descent. *Thornfish's* bow started down at a steep angle, sinking like a rock as fifty men jammed into the forward torpedo room. The depth gage read 350 feet, near test depth! The fleet submarine was unmanageable. Jimmu was in shock. Handcuffed to the lower torpedo rack, he was helpless and was nearly trampled by the rush of sailors. He was certain that this would be the end. His wrist was broken. Fortunately, the weight of about 8000 pounds of men got them deep. Now, however, they were too deep! The captain backed the sub emergency full astern and ordered the fifty men aft to the after-torpedo room. They scrambled past the control room as the depth gage passed 500 feet far below the boat's test depth. During this calamity, Chief of the Boat O'Neil had an idea. He took a plastic toothbrush and placed it between the two jammed breakers on the electric panel and immediately power returned to the diving planes. Finally, the diving officer was able to control the submarine.

Later, when Rob came to, he was in his bunk with a terrific headache. The pharmacist gave him some aspirin and applied a bandage to his forehead. All compartments reported damage to the captain as the boat returned to 90 feet. The damage was severe, but the *Thornfish's* thicker skin saved their lives. Jimmu thought his handcuffed wrist was broken during the melee, and he later asked for a change of clothes as he had lost control of his bowels in the crisis. The pharmacist mate confirmed that his wrist was broken and had to be immobilized. He administered morphine to ease the pain while he carefully applied a splint and bandaged the prisoner's right wrist. Captain Morrison, his executive officer and LT Abrams, diving officer, performed their duties in a cool, professional manner during this terrifying descent into the depths of the Sea of Japan. They surfaced at nightfall to repair the damage.

At dawn the second day off Nagasaki, a convoy emerged out of the fog with two escorts. Three large freighters, one of them a passenger ship loaded with troops, moved single file preparing to form up with the escorts in the lead. Bucky made the periscope observations and Dick maneuvered the boat into a firing position only 1800 yards from the largest target. The captain fired all six torpedoes from the forward tubes, three at the freighter in the front and three at the passenger ship. The magnetic exploders had been deactivated. In two minutes, the lead ship exploded, and the troop ship burst and broke in two. "A double whammy!" Dick shouted. He maneuvered the *Thornfish* to avoid the shellacking of the escorts by going under the sinking freighter and staying at 100 feet. A few hours later, after the escort had left to rejoin the decimated convoy, *Thornfish* surfaced; its radar picked up a pip of a very large ship. Dick raised the periscope and to his amazement, he cried out, "Bingo! A carrier is coming our way!"

Thornfish submerged, and the battle stations alarm once again sounded throughout the boat. Dick maneuvered the sub toward the fast-moving carrier and its escorts. He fired three torpedoes that had been reloaded in the forward torpedo tubes. One exploded prematurely after running only 24 seconds, but the other two found their mark, and the sound of the explosions rocked the *Thornfish*. Dick could not risk another periscope observation as the destroyers were on him in minutes dropping 35 depth charges on the sub over two hours as it twisted and turned, going deep to avoid destruction.

Thornfish had endured a terrible beating from the Japanese escorts, but the damage was not only physical damage to the boat itself, but damage to the men enduring the tremendous strain of the sound of enemy screws coming in at them, and the click of depth charges about to explode. Stress can make the strongest weak. One of the new members of the crew, a seaman recruit, had to be sedated during the depth charging. He had just turned 18. When rigged for silent running, air-conditioning and pumps are secured, temperatures reach over 100 degrees and in some compartments over 120 due to the electrical equipment and batteries surrounding them. Leaks abound, decks are slimy, and men vomit. The men in the maneuvering room get dehydrated sooner due to the heat from the motors. Those able to withstand the punishment the best are doing something, officers and men in the control room and conning tower working on ways to evade the rain of death. After the shellacking, Captain Morrison decided to remain submerged for the remainder of the day giving the crew some rest, and they got their ration of medicinal whiskey having survived two severe depth charge attacks. *Thornfish* spent the next week off the southern coast of Kyushu sighting only sampans fishing. Submerged off the naval base at Sasebo one night, the submarine ran into fishnets strung out for miles. Every five hundred feet a marker buoy floated along suspending the net, and marking with a bold v, the submarine moving it from below. Dick Morrison tried everything to shake it loose. He backed, and changed depth, to no avail. Finally, just before dawn Dick decided to surface. The sun rays in the east were breaking the darkness as the gun crew armed with knives started cutting the nets from the bow to the periscope shears. Once free, he stayed on the surface charging batteries. The Japanese fishing industry was the lifeblood of their population. At night off Sasebo, the lights of a myriad of fishing sampans looked like a floating city. Dick Morrison considered using his forty millimeter and 20 mm guns on some of them, but he was reluctant to do so, it would be like shooting ducks at a carnival. His exec was visibly upset. Bucky reminded his captain of the *Thornfish's* operation orders, "You shall attack all enemy ships encountered with gunfire or torpedoes." Dick took his young executive officer aside and told him he would not attack any defenseless sampans unless they intended to harm his vessel. Dick could tell that Bucky was not at all pleased. Captain Morrison told him he recalled meeting Slade Cutter at Midway, commander of the

Seahorse, who told him after seeing the slaughter of families and kids in their fishing boats, he ordered no more attacks on innocent fishermen. He said *his crew had gotten to like the surface action too much.*

Toward the end of the month, messages arrived that indicated that the code breakers in Pearl Harbor had once more broken the Japanese naval codes. Dick Morrison deciphered a top-secret Ultra Code: two convoys were heading north from Formosa to Nagasaki and *Thornfish* was assigned to attack the lead convoy of tankers coming from oil-rich Borneo. Ten torpedoes remained. Six in the forward tubes, and four aft. Dick had a feeling that he would need every one of them. Seventeen ships were in the convoy including five escort destroyers.

The officers and leading petty officers gathered in the wardroom for a plan of attack. Tankers are the primary targets of U.S. submarines after heavy warships. Dick spoke first, "Gentlemen, this will be our most important attack." He rolled out the chart of the area and laid it on the wardroom table. Pointing to the island on the chart, he said, "My guess is they will slow after sighting the lighthouse off the island and will want to enter the port of Nagasaki after sunrise. If we lay low with a full battery charge, we can surface and intercept them in the dark. We will make a high-speed surface attack firing our torpedoes in the middle of the pack. Any questions?" No one spoke. The captain looked at the expression on each face. They had been through a lot of combat and fatigue had set in. They all knew not only the danger from the antisubmarine destroyers, but also the danger of collision during the high-speed action among seventeen darkened enemy ships. Finally, Rob spoke, "Sir are there any minefields to be aware of?"

"Good question. I've marked in pencil the minefields from the chart we rescued from the I sub we sank. We will stay just outside them, and we know they won't zigzag toward the minefield."

"What about the enemy radar, sir?" John asked.

"We have some information that their radar is not very good. However, we must be careful about the Chidori patrol boats. They are good; they have very good sonar. They are tenacious but not as fast as a destroyer. Chidories carry a lot of depth charges."

Pete, the gun boss, asked, "what about our torpedoes, do we deactivate the magnetic exploders?"

Without hesitating the captain replied, "Affirmative. I think the increased magnetism of the larger displacement ships, causes them to detonate before they hit the target. So, I'm taking the responsibility of deactivating them for the rest of the patrol." He heard some Amen to his statement. Then he gave instructions to the attack team. He said, "It will be a surface torpedo attack. *Thornfish* will be low in the water, so we may not be seen. The exec will oversee the approach in the conning tower and observe the radar PPI scope. Rob will be on the TDC. Pete will be the fire control officer. Jerry will be in the control room with Chief O'Neil preparing for diving. John will be on the bridge TBT, and we will have only one lookout, Willie. They both have excellent night vision. I'll be on the bridge directing traffic. We will shoot three on each tanker. Spread will be amidships, bow, and stern on each. Torpedo depth ten feet. The after-torpedo room will be ready to fire their stingers at the destroyers that will come bounding over to us. The tankers will light up the sky like daylight when they are hit. We will clear the bridge and make a crash dive as soon as they explode."

Bucky, the navigator said that there might be some glow on the horizon from the lighthouse to the east and the quarter moonrise to occur at 0247. The captain asked if there were any more questions. There were none.

As he rose to leave, he told his executive officer to go through the boat and tell the crew of the plan. Bucky had made a hit with the crew from the beginning. They recognized him as a smart, personable, caring superior who leveled with them. As he made his way through the boat, he told them of the battle plan and how proud he was of the job they were doing. In the short time he had been aboard, he knew every member of the crew's name. A lean lanky man who wore cowboy boots most of the time and spoke with a slow Texas drawl. He was a Texan through and through. As he passed the slot machine in the crew's mess, he put in a nickel and hit the jackpot. Coins fell out of the machine onto the deck. The crew loved it, and they called him Lucky Bucky, but not to his face. It seemed a good omen of things to come.

At 0210, *Thornfish's* radar picked up the convoy proceeding north and east toward Nagasaki. The speed of advance 13 knots, zigging 10 degrees off base course. Heavies in the center, with three escorts in front and one on each side of the convoy and three in the rear. The Bells of St. Mary's rang battle stations torpedo throughout the boat. Most of the crew had already been at their battle stations, waiting ready and anxious for the battle to begin. To avoid detection, *Thornfish* ballasted down so that the deck was awash. With captain and John on the bridge with Willie as the lookout, they lurked, like a lion in the bushes, waiting for its prey to appear. They did not have to wait long as the convoy moved closer and the radar operator repeated the distance to the track. It was very cold on the bridge. The sea state five made it advantageous for them to avoid detection. In the conning tower, bathed in red lights, Bucky watched the enemy ships on the radar PPI scope and noted the ships had zigged away from their baseline. He planned to penetrate the formation from the side passing behind the patrol boat and entering the formation from behind. Captain concurred and ordered full speed ahead and changed course to fall in behind the convoy. The *Thornfish* went in still undetected. Morrison sought after the first target, a freighter but before the set up could be made, the freighter suddenly changed course and almost collided with the *Thornfish*, coming within 200 yards of the submarine. The captain swung *Thornfish* around and fired two stingers from the stern torpedo tubes and missed. The freighters change of course blocked the escort from attacking and revealed two huge tankers in the middle of the formation. Pouring on the coal, the sub gained on the tankers ahead. After six minutes they gained a position to strike, firing three torpedoes at the first target and after swinging hard right, sent off three Mark-14's at the second tanker. Both hits erupted and lit up the sky for miles around. Dick figured they must have been carrying gasoline. The ships disintegrated leaving an oil slick behind. The formation turned chaotic. Ships were milling around, guns sent salvos over the *Thornfish's* bridge. Dick ordered Willie and John below and conned the submarine from the bridge by himself. Using the available light from the sinking tankers, he aimed torpedoes in the after room at a large freighter. The enemy Maru was hit in the bow and stern and began to sink. Another Maru took up the chase and tried to ram the *Thornfish*. Dick ordered right full rudder and the ramming ship missed by 50 feet. Machine guns blasted away from the ship now gliding by forcing the *Thornfish* captain to take refuge on the other side of the bridge. But dead ahead was a passenger freighter. Two fish had been reloaded in the bow tubes. Dick fired a down the throat shot at the oncoming ship. The oncoming Maru exploded and came to a full stop only 500 yards ahead. Morrison had enough. He hit the diving alarm sounding two blasts and jumped down the conning tower hatch just in time as water flooded over the hatch. He ordered the diving officer "make your depth 400 feet, rig for dive and silent running." Then the escorts started to lay down their depth charges. Two escorts worked effectively moving back and forth over the sub as it moved quietly in the cold depths below, snaking away from the menace overhead. In two hours, the Chidoris dropped 31 ash cans, causing only minor damage to the exhausted submarine. When the escorts finally rejoined the remnants of the convoy, Captain Morrison congratulated the crew and broke out the medicinal grog. In just a little over an hour, the *Thornfish* had decimated the Jap group. They had only one torpedo left. The Commander of Submarines Pacific Fleet sent a highly complementary message to the Commanding Officer for one of the most successful patrols thus far in the war. *Thornfish* was ordered to return to Midway for repairs and R and R.

CHAPTER 43

Gun Action

Homeward bound to Midway the crew relaxed. Many of the new men were reviewing their qualification manuals learning every aspect of submarine systems. Rob and John resumed their cribbage game contest and caught up on their long-neglected correspondence to family and girlfriends. Rob continued his interrogation separately of the two prisoners. They were no longer handcuffed. LT Kamatsu's broken wrist was beginning to heal. He began to be more cooperative, especially after the care he received for his broken wrist. The captain allowed Rob to speak with him in the wardroom when it was not occupied. Over a cup of hot coffee, Rob learned that Jimmu's father had been assigned to the Japanese embassy in Washington before the war, and he gained an appreciation of American culture and way of life. It was so different from his country. While there, Jimmu visited the U.S. Naval Academy at Annapolis. An avid sailor, he persuaded his midshipman guide to arrange for a sail in one of the academy's new Luder Yawls. The forty-four-foot sailboat was beautifully trimmed with a blue hull and teak decks. One weekend in the spring, Jimmu participated in a Sailing Squadron race down the Chesapeake to St. Michaels on the Eastern Shore of Maryland. He told Rob of the thrill of racing, rounding the buoy and setting the spinnaker on the last leg of the race course. He loved the Naval Academy and wished he could go to school there. However, his father insisted that he gain an appointment to the Japanese Naval Academy at Etajima, Japan.

Rob offered him a cigarette. He eagerly accepted it and took a deep drag. 'I'd walk a mile for a Camel' he joked, saying the words of the commercial he had often heard on the radio in the States. Although Rob did not smoke, he had purchased a whole carton of Camels from the store in the crew's mess. He thought, as he questioned Jimmu, he would offer him an occasional cigarette hoping that, as he relaxed, he might provide some details of the boat he was on and the strength of the submarine fleet.

Rob brought the subject up of the depth charge attacks he had experienced while on board *Thornfish*. Jimmu said he was scared to death, especially when the captain ordered the men to run to the forward torpedo room to get the boat down faster. He was surprised to learn that the attack had come from a plane. He said the Japanese airplanes were terrible marksmen; however, he went on to compliment the Chidori patrol boats that worked them over. He told Rob of the new sonars they carried, and some of the tactics they used on enemy submarines to get cross bearings and drop their ash cans. Their radars had limitations, having poor range and resolution. Rob was aware of the improvements made to American radars, thanks in part to the ultrathin electric steels produced at Armco Steel in Middletown, Ohio, twenty miles east of Oxford.

During one session Jimmu said, "Do you remember our trip to Mt. Fujiyama?" Rob replied, "How could I ever forget?" What an adventure. It was the time of our lives! And your father paid for it!" Rob took the opportunity to query his captive once again about his father. "Your father took us aboard an I boat in Yokosuka, do you remember?"

"Sure, it was the first time I had been aboard a sub also. Japanese are very cautious about security; I'm surprised they let us aboard."

"Your father was commodore then, right?" Rob asked casually, "Where is he now?" It was the same question he had asked before. He wanted more details.

"In a tunnel in the naval base at Yokosuka. He is a vice admiral, commander of our submarines now!"

"Big job," Rob said. "I hope when this damned war is over, if we survive, I would like to meet him again." Jimmu stared off in space without saying anything for a long while.

"I am not sure I want to meet him. My father will not want me to be a prisoner. The Japanese Bushido says it is a dishonor to surrender." The young Japanese lieutenant was familiar with General Hideki Tojo's Field Service Code Order of January 1942, telling Japanese military and civilians how to view prisoners of war. "To live as a prisoner of war is to live without honor." Jimmu said, "to Japanese living a life without honor is worthless. I should have gone down with my ship." He crushed out his cigarette in the ashtray and sat lost in thought.

Rob sensed his prisoner's distress, and after waiting a long time said, "You will be well treated Jimmu, your father will be notified by the Red Cross."

"I know. The Japanese Army is not so kind. They are cruel. Japan does not recognize the Red Cross; it is too American. We heard about the terrible treatment of the thousands of American soldiers that surrendered last May in the Philippines. It is called the Bataan Death March. They were forced to march over sixty miles in the terrible heat without food or water. Many were bayoneted if they stumbled. There is a secret POW camp near Tokyo called Ofuna. I hope submariners never go there. Run by the Navy. They are bad. Very bad." Their conversation was interrupted, "Captain, to the bridge!" The OOD announced. "Smoke on the horizon." *Thornfish* was returning to combat.

It was a large trawler. Most likely a fishing vessel. It was not worthy of the last torpedo, so the captain ordered gun action. Dick Morrison decided to send a boarding party aboard her to see if they could recover any codebooks, charts and other information that might be valuable to Navy intelligence people. Rob would lead the boarding party assisted by the new ensign and two gunner's mates.

With guns manned, *Thornfish* closed on the Japanese trawler. The exec had the conn as they slowly approached the trawler. But unfortunately, the Japanese captain of the boat made a foolish decision. He decided to ram the submarine. He turned his trawler and aimed at the bow of the submarine. Captain Morrison ordered all guns to open fire. In a matter of minutes, the trawler was dead in the water.

"Cease Fire! Cease Fire!" Captain Morrison ordered. "Boarding party away!"

The rubber dingy with Rob and his companions, armed with 45 pistols, and the gunner's mates with Thompson Submachine Guns, were on board the enemy vessel in a matter of minutes. In the eerie quiet, Rob made his way along the deck of the sinking vessel. Rob sent Ensign Kennedy forward with one of the gunner's mates, and he went aft looking for the shattered chart house. Suddenly shots rang out. From behind the remains of the bridge, a wounded Japanese officer opened fire on the *Thornfish* with a machine gun hitting one of the gun crew on deck and the executive officer on the bridge. He then turned and fired at Rob and his companion; Rob felt a burning sensation on his left shoulder as he rolled on the deck emptying his semi-automatic 45 pistol, killing the assailant. Crawling along the deck, he reached the bridge and entered the chart room. His band of brothers then gathered up charts, logbooks, maritime publications and a large Japanese flag. The deck of the trawler was awash when they returned in the dingy to their boat. Rob was hurting, but he soon learned the sad news. His executive officer was dead, and the gunner's mate was wounded. Once again, the wardroom table became an operating room table. It would be a long night as the *Thornfish* resumed its way toward Midway.

Dick Morrison was depressed. He berated himself for not being more cautious. There was a solemn atmosphere throughout the boat. Few slept that night. His executive officer did not want to come on this patrol; he was conscripted. Bucky had a better term for it, he once said, "I was shanghaied." His orders to the construction of a new boat in Mare Island had been canceled. He was disappointed because he would not have time to be married. Ben Miller hand picked him for this billet because of his personal attributes needed due to problems with the former commanding officer, LCDR Custer.

The gunner had been lowered down the hatch and gently laid on the wardroom operating table. His wound did not seem too serious at first to the pharmacist mate. He had taken a bullet in his shoulder. But he soon started coughing up blood uncontrollably. The bullet had penetrated his lung. There was nothing that could be done for him. LT Robinson, his division officer, stood by him. As he was administered morphine, he whispered to him, "Sir please kill that son of a bitch Jap prisoner for me." An hour later, the young third-class gunner's mate coughed and died.

Rob's wound was attended to last. He sat in the wardroom stripped to the waist. The bullet from the lone gunman had left a deep flesh wound, but there were no broken bones. The pharmacist numbed the wound enough to allow him to probe the wound, remove the bullet, and clean everything with ample amounts of iodine, followed by a liberal sprinkling of a sulfa drug. Rob sat still through the treatment, still stunned at the events that had turned out so badly. Dick Morrison sat at his desk in his stateroom, his head in his hands. There was a knock on the door. Jerry Abrams, the third officer on *Thornfish*, entered pushing the curtain aside. "Sir, could I have a few minutes please?" Captain replied, "Sure come in." He motioned to him to sit in the chair by his bunk. Jerry Abrams had blossomed under the tutelage of Captain Morrison. He had become the best diving officer Dick Morrison had ever had. Calm and cool in even extremely dangerous situations, he had the respect of the entire crew. Rather reserved by nature, he had a marvelous way of telling Jewish jokes about himself. His men loved them.

Now he was as somber as anyone on the *Thornfish*. "Sir with your permission, I'd like to conserve fuel by going to two engines on propulsion and one charging the batteries. We should have a full pack by 0200."

"Very well Jerry, thanks," The captain looked tired. After weeks on patrol, exhausted commanding officers sometimes had to ask for relief upon completion. "Jerry we'll need to do some rescheduling of the watches. I want you to take over Bucky's duties as exec and navigator. You may have to take over some of the OOD watches, such as the 4 to 8 so you can do your stars then."

"Yes sir. I would like to suggest that Pete take over the diving officer and engineering duties, and we can fleet Rob up to the gunnery officer's job. He will stay on the TDC of course. Ensign Young will take over as communicator."

"Sounds good. Make it so."

The captain asked, "How's Rob doing? Will he be able to stand watches on the bridge?"

"I don't think so sir. His wound is not too serious according to the pharmacist, but he would have difficulty going down a ladder if we had to dive."

He stood up and said, "Jerry, get John to bring me a Bible. We will have a burial at sea in the morning. I want John to help me with this. Tell him to meet me in the wardroom as soon as it is cleaned up and put back together again."

"Aye Sir."

During the night the gunner's mates in the forward torpedo room sewed both men into clean canvas bags and weighed them down with rocks normally used for weighting trash. At dawn the next morning with the seas very calm with little wind, the *Thornfish* came to a complete stop. All hands not on watch assembled on the deck. Captain Morrison dressed in a clean starched khaki uniform addressed the crew.

The two fallen shipmates were placed on the leeward side draped in American flags. Captain Morrison spoke words that Ensign John Young had suggested. His voice was loud and clear. "Shipmates, we sailed in harm's way yesterday and lost two fine young men." The captain's voice broke, then he said, "LT Rogers and Gunner's mate Meijer gave their lives in service to their country and in serving each one of us. They will be missed." He paused trying to hold his emotions in check. "Jesus once said that greater love has no man than to lay down his life for his friends. We are not only shipmates, but we are also friends. These fine young men gave their lives for us. We will be eternally grateful for their sacrifice." Then he read Psalm 23: *The Lord is my shepherd, I shall not want...* John, standing on the bridge, said the first verse of the Navy Hymn, *Eternal Father Strong to save, whose arm has bound the restless wave, who bade the mighty ocean deep Its own appointed limits keep: Oh, hear us when we cry to thee for those in peril on the sea. Amen.*"

The captain then bowed his head and began the Lord's Prayer, "Our Father who art in heaven...." As he led the prayer, all hands joined in.

Then he said, "And now we commit our brother to the deep." Jerry ordered, "Hand salute!" Two men lifted each canvass bag and their bodies slid silently off the edge of the deck. The flags covering their fallen brothers would be given to their next of kin. The hand salute ended. Immediately the diesel engines came to life and *Thornfish* was on its way to Midway.

Down below, Jimmu was apprehensive. He got some bad looks from the men in the forward torpedo room. He did not sleep that night afraid that someone would put a pillow over his head and smother him to death. He shared his feelings with his former friend the next morning. Rob assured him that he would not be attacked and later told all the torpedo men, now in his division, to be sure that no harm fell to the prisoners, they were providing some valuable information that could help our war effort. En route, the prisoners were more open about the tactics and hardware used by the latest submarines Japan was producing.

The night before landfall, Rob and his former high school friend had a long talk about life after the war. Jimmu said he would like to meet one day when the world was finally at peace. Rob gave him two packs of Camels, candy bars, and chewing gum along with a note from him asking for good treatment by the Marines in charge of POWs. Being a submariner, he would be given further interrogation upon his arrival In Pearl Harbor.

Thornfish entered the narrow channel at Midway in the early morning and tied up alongside the USS *Fulton*, a submarine tender. The two Japanese prisoners were blindfolded and escorted off the sub by Marine guards. Rob bade them farewell in Japanese and went ashore with them.

Thornfish's second patrol of 55 days was outstanding. They steamed 12,769 miles, used 136,000 gallons of fuel, making torpedo attacks and one gun action, sinking a total of five ships and damaging two large carriers. The admiral's endorsement of the patrol reports commended the captain and crew for an aggressive and highly successful patrol in the face of hard-hitting enemy opposition. He added some somber words of condolence for the entire crew on the loss of a great officer and gunner's mate. *Thornfish's* crew was authorized to wear the coveted submarine combat award. The admiral's representative would present awards in a few days.

Sacks of mail arrived when the crew checked in the 'Goony Bird' Hotel for two weeks of rest and recreation. Rob, John, and Tony, the new ensign, shared a room on the second floor. The first thing they did was to get some beers. They found a cooler downstairs in the bar filled with ice; Rob reached in with his good hand and pulled out two ice-cold Pabst Blue Ribbon Beers. Rob drank them almost without stopping and nearly passed out. When he returned to his room, there was a stack of mail on the desk, most of them from Molly. What a sweetheart he thought. She had written at least one letter every week. He arranged them by date and started reading from the earliest one. It was a small envelope with an engraved invitation to the 100th commencement of Miami University. She wrote on the back,

> *"I wish you were here darling. I'm so excited! I have a job. I start next week as a reporter for The Oxford Press!! I am going to make a scrapbook for you of any significant articles, so when you return you can be caught up with all the events of the year. My father is so disappointed that I'm not going to teach school in Marion, but he seems reconciled to it now. The family is coming to the graduation ceremonies. I'm the first one in our family to go to college! I will send you a picture of me in my cap and gown. My only wish for a graduation present is to have you with me. Love forever, Molly."* And she added: *"Our love is here to stay…"*

Rob looked out the window. The white sand beach was glistening in the hot sun. The blue-green water sparkled. Gooney birds and seagulls milled around the water's edge. The tranquil scene was not so peaceful nine months ago when one of the great battles of the war was fought in the ocean just miles north of Midway. The Japanese lost the four carriers that had launched their planes during the sneak attack at Pearl Harbor some seven months earlier. America lost one, the *Yorktown*.

Rob put the invitation back in the envelope thinking how much he missed Molly. He would love to be the first to congratulate her on her graduation with honors from Miami. He was very pleased that Molly would be remaining in Oxford, for his mother was learning to appreciate her more and more. It would give Molly time to develop her writing skills and keep him up to date on things happening in town and the university.

There were seven more letters from Molly, and three from his folks. There was one from Lily. He opened hers next. Lily's was puzzling. It was written sometime after the New Year. She wrote how much she missed him and the wonderful times they had at the Royal Hawaiian and the officers' club. She was making good money from tips for the submariners coming in after patrol. But she seemed worried. Perhaps it was because of her mother. Mrs. Edmonds was still having trouble finding a good job. There was a great deal of resentment in the Island of anyone with Japanese ancestry. The last line of her letter said that she was not feeling well, and she was going to see a doctor. She signed it: *I love you Rob* and put her lipstick below her name.

There was a knock on the door, and the captain came into the room. Rob and John both jumped to attention and Dick said "Relax; I've got some news for you both." John sat on the edge of his bunk and Rob stood by his bed as Dick took the seat at the small desk. "Arrangements have been made to have both of you gentlemen have your oral exams by three submarine commanders next week. We're putting the horse before the wagon for you John, as we'll do your torpedo shoot during makeup training after we complete our repair period. I'm going to ask Jerry to mentor you both for this exam. He knows what it's like and how best to prepare." Then he turned his attention to Rob. "How is your arm coming along? I want you to check in with the medical department tomorrow morning. We want you aboard when we leave in a few weeks. You're my new gun boss and official TDC operator. John, you will be the new communicator."

Shortly after colors sounded at 0800, Rob reported to sickbay for a checkup of his wound. The medical department was housed in a large Quonset Hut painted white, with a large red cross on each side. A young doctor, a Navy lieutenant who Rob figured was a recent graduate of medical school, examined his wound. Just to be sure there were no broken bones, he ordered an X-ray. After a long wait, the doctor came back in the examining room and announced, "Ensign you are lucky. Had that bullet been an inch to the right you would have had a broken shoulder. You will be fine, and you should be able to resume your duties after some physical rehab I'm going to prescribe."

At quarters several days later, with the crew in whites, Vice Admiral Lockwood presented the Navy Cross to the commanding officer, and the Navy Cross posthumously to LT Albert Buckhorn Rogers, USN, and the Purple Heart. LT Gerald Abrams received the Silver Star for his heroic work as diving officer. The Chief of the Boat, Chief Electrician Lawrence O'Neil, received the Silver Star for the heroic efforts in saving the vessel during the fire in the after battery. Rob received the Navy's Bronze Star, his second, for the action while boarding the Japanese trawler along with the Purple Heart for his wound during the gun battle. Gunner's mate Jonathan Meijer received the Bronze Star and Purple Heart, posthumously, for his action on *Thornfish* during the gun action with the Japanese trawler. Ensign John Wesley Young received the Navy

Commendation Medal for action in the recovery of Captain Morrison when he was washed overboard. In presenting Rob's awards, the admiral noted that he did not yet have his Dolphins. Dick Morrison said he would have them before they departed in a few weeks. At the conclusion, the admiral addressed the crew. "Men of the *Thornfish*, I want to congratulate you on a tremendous patrol. Your efforts have done a great deal of damage to the Japanese war effort. Yours was one of the best patrols in the war so far. Your courage under extreme battle stress was magnificent. I join you in sorrow for the loss of two extraordinary men. Their sacrifice will not be in vain. You are a team and I know you will perform once again to the highest standards set by your captain. It is an honor to be here this morning, honoring the men of *Thornfish*, a submarine of honor for our nation. Smooth sailing and fair winds for your next assignment. Well done!"

As he departed, the admiral took Dick aside and said, "Dick, I will tell you in advance, *Thornfish* will be transferred to the Southwest Operating Area. You will be based at Freemantle Australia for a while. They need some fleet boats in their area of operations to replace losses they have suffered recently. You will be under the direction of Rear Admiral Christie. I know you will do well for him. I hate to see you go but there's nothing I can do about it." Dick frowned, "Honestly, I'm concerned sir. Admiral Christie believes that the magnetic exploders are working ok. I know they are not. It is going to be tougher making hits with them. I deactivated the magnetic exploders at the beginning of our patrol."

"I know. Admiral Christie has a lot invested in them, he helped develop the mags when he was at the Bureau of Ordnance. However, many folks are working on this problem. It will be solved soon. In the meantime, do as he *says*, and we will trust that you will find a way to do what is needed." Dick thought this was a veiled signal not to use them anyway.

"One other thing admiral, I would like to have my third officer, Jerry Abrams, become my new exec. He is a fine officer and well qualified. He is a reserve officer, however, a graduate of Purdue in electrical engineering. I don't think we should exclude highly motivated and qualified reservists from being XO, and in my opinion, some to command." His old boss looked directly at him. "Dick, I agree. Make it so. Before you leave, I will get you another officer to fill your complement."

· · · · ·

The following days were filled with study for both Rob and John. Chief O'Neil and LT Abrams coached them in what to expect from the qualification board. They studied the rules of the nautical road, communications, engineering, gunnery and all the systems of a submarine, air, hydraulic, electrical, casualties, and on and on.

The next Monday at 0900 they reported to the OOD on the quarterdeck of the *Fulton* and were escorted to the Commodore's conference room. Three commanding officers from subs tied up alongside the *Fulton* introduced themselves and began their questioning, first of Rob and then later of John. Each took about an hour. The exam was tough, but they were well prepared. When they returned to the 'Gooney Bird' Hotel, they were met by Captain Morrison. He had just been notified that they passed with excellence. "Congratulations Rob and John! You both did very well. I am proud of you. We will pin your Dolphins on when we return to the boat and in the meantime, I think tonight you will want to have a wetting down party at the club."

CHAPTER 44

Good News and Bad News

Lily drove her mother's Chevy convertible along the highway to Waipai. She had written the name and street address of the doctor her mother had recommended on a notepad and searched for his office high up on the hills overlooking Pearl City. It was a gorgeous day, not a cloud in the sky, but that could all change in just a few hours in the warm Hawaiian climate. She could be in a deluge before she left the office. She parked the bright red convertible behind the office and put the top up. Her mother had made an appointment at 11 o'clock with Dr. Sakamaki, a Japanese American gynecologist, who received his medical degree from Stanford. The receptionist had her fill out several forms describing her medical history, and, in a few minutes, she was ushered into an examining room. The nurse had her disrobe and put on a gown and left. Lily waited and waited. There was nothing to read but she noticed some charts on the wall depicting the development of the baby starting at conception. She was amazed at how quickly in the early stages of pregnancy the little appendages such as feet developed in as soon as ten weeks. The heart begins to beat during the fifth week.

The doctor came in and introduced himself. A man about fifty she thought. He had a slender build with strong Asian facial features and a pencil thin mustache. He apologized for the delay in seeing her and asked about Lily's mother saying he knew her from the church.

"What can I do for you Lily?"

"Well, I'm here to get a checkup to determine if I am pregnant."

He said, "I see." He then asked questions about any medicines she was taking, history of illness and any female problems. She told him of her recent morning sickness. "Well there are two tests. One a blood test to measure something we call hch and the other a urine test. "We will do both to be sure. We can do the urine test in the office. The blood test has to be sent to a laboratory and will take a few days." After the exam, she dressed and waited for the doctor to return. A few minutes later, he came in smiling, "Lily you are pregnant!" She began to weep. The doctor said, "I thought you'd be happy." Lily reached for a Kleenex and wiped away tears streaming down her cheeks. "No, you don't understand. I am single. I am not married. I must work and help support my mother. It can't be. Can you… She didn't get to finish the sentence. "Lily if you are asking me if I can perform an abortion for you the answer is no. For two reasons, one, it is unlawful and two it is morally wrong. I'm a Catholic and our church forbids it."

"But can't you make an exception for me?"

Doctor Sakamaki, shook his head. She could see she wasn't making any headway with him.

"Do you know of anyone who could help me out?"

"Lily I wish there was a way but look at the posters on the wall. Do you see what the baby looks like at ten weeks? Look at the tiny feet. The fingers, the little heart beating trying to survive inside you. Do you want someone to destroy it?"

Lily left the doctor's office and got in the car. She was crushed. She needed to think. She drove up the mountain toward the Army base at Schofield Barracks. A few miles before the guard posts she pulled the car off the narrow highway and came to a halt near the cliff overlooking the plains around Pearl Harbor. A thousand feet below stretched fields of lush pineapple growing in the rich red soil, the city of Honolulu and Diamond Head in the distance. The bright sands of Waikiki shone in the afternoon sun in front of the beautiful 'Pink Palace,' the Royal Hawaiian Hotel. The Japanese planes on December 7 flew close overhead where she was parked, after strafing the Army barracks, on their way to attack the sleeping sailors in their ships below. Amid the beauty of the island she dearly loved, thoughts of ending her life invaded her mind. She could easily let the car out of gear, and it would carry her over the cliff and down one thousand feet. Her problems would be over.

Lily sat in the car for a long time thinking of her choices. She was so in love with Rob that she had done something very foolish. It was her fault entirely. Rob was in a different world now, with no time for her. Her father's words flashed in her mind: *Lily if you ever make a mistake, I know of someone who can help you.* She put her car in gear, backed out of the overlook and drove slowly down the hill to home. As she approached the driveway to her mother's house, a black official looking sedan backed out and drove down the street. She wondered what had happened. She jumped out of the convertible and rushed through the front door. "Mom are you alright?" Her mother met her in the hallway and said, "Lily you won't believe this: I may be getting a job, a real job!" She grabbed Lily's hand and led her into the kitchen. "You will never guess who was just here…the FBI!" Lily was dumbfounded, "Mom, what have you done?" Valerie Edmonds laughed, "It's not what you think. Months ago, I applied for a job as a Japanese American translator. They came here to check me out for a job requiring top-secret clearance."

Valerie started dancing around the small kitchen. "Mom I hope it happens, but don't get too excited yet. Remember you are Issie." Valerie said, "You're right. Let's go out on the lanai."

Lily poured both a glass of sake. "Mom, you have good news. I have bad news." Her mother sat on the wicker couch. "What is it Lily?" Lily sat on the chair opposite her mother, "Mom, I am pregnant. Dr. Sakamaski confirmed it today. What am I going to do?" Her mother was silent.

"Mom, I want an abortion. What will people say at work? How can I handle taking care of a baby? What about *my life*?"

"I know honey. But think about the life of the tiny baby. It has rights too. It will work out ok, I trust the Lord. I know I'm going to get a good job with the Navy. We will make it. Abortion is wrong, legally and more importantly it is not moral." Lily sat on the couch thinking about Rob. They had made love there the night before he left on patrol. *Would he marry me? No. He was so in love with his Molly.*

. . . . .

Molly Gaynor graduated Monday, May 31, 1943. Before Miami's graduation, the Navy held a commissioning service on Tuesday, May 4, in Cook field, home of the Miami Redskins for decades. Many top coaches played their varsity games there for Miami University; Paul Brown, presently coaching at the Naval Academy prep school, Red Blake, Army's head coach at West Point, and LT Weeb Eubank, USNR, Oxford's McGuffey High School coach, got their start playing for the Redskins. The stadium playing field, filled with 1000 sailors, WAVES, and SPARS passed in review for the Commanding Officer and other dignitaries. Special guest for the occasion was Miss Mary Snyder, Miami Coed, voted by the sailors as the prettiest Recensio Year Book beauty, and named Commissioning Day Queen. Woody, the sports reporter for *The Miami Student*, had press box privileges and invited Molly to attend. They had great seats, but Molly was uneasy. Women were not allowed in the press box, but no one challenged her for being there. They stood proudly at attention as the colors passed by and the band played the National Anthem. Woody was excited about joining the Marine Corps. His hernia surgery was very successful, and he passed his physical. He would report to the Pensacola Naval Air Station in June after graduation. Upon successful completion of flight training, he would receive his commission as a second lieutenant USMCR. He hoped Molly would come to his graduation and pin his wings on his uniform.

Although it was a beautiful bright summer day, Miami's graduation ceremonies May 31 were held indoors in Withrow Court, home of the Miami Redskins basketball team. There were more women graduates than men as many males were either drafted or volunteered for duty in the military. The academic procession began at 10 o'clock. The commencement speaker was Dr. Raymond Molyneaux Hughes, class of

1893 and president of Miami University from 1911 to 1927 and presently emeritus president of Iowa State College. The Baccalaureate speaker, Rev. Hardig Sexton, class of 1918, a graduate of Princeton Theological Seminary, had held pastorates at Cincinnati, Philadelphia and Baltimore, spoke at the service on Sunday at 10 a.m. preceded by an academic procession.

Molly's first assignment for her new employer, *The Oxford Press*, was to write a story about the commencement. Her work would be in the paper the following week. She wrote that Dr. Hughes made three strong points in his commencement address: First, young people should not look for the easiest job or the one that pays the most, but for the one which will enable them to use their talents to the best advantage and provide an enjoyable worthwhile life work. Second, keep the colleges clear of students who are not truly students. Third, for those people who are more interested in serving people than in mechanical or scientific achievement, the liberal arts curriculum has much to offer, "*Science had not made man better, it has only made him better off.*" Dr. Hughes added that the liberal arts college should give students a broad view of literature, history and philosophy so that they could develop standards by which to distinguish the good, beautiful and true friends of graduates.

Molly's parents and siblings drove down from Marion early Monday morning and got good seats on the main floor. They were very proud of their daughter, the first in her Irish family to graduate from college. Molly graduated with honors. Her dad shared the family's pride, but he would not tell Molly that he was pleased with her accomplishments for fear she would get a big head. Her father was very disappointed that she turned down an opportunity to teach second grade in Marion, but he finally became reconciled to her having a newspaper career. As Frank Gaynor watched his only daughter receive her diploma from Dr. Upham, he thought she was headstrong, like most Irish. Nevertheless, she now has a teaching degree, and it is something she could fall back on if newspaper work did not pan out.

Woody had three weeks after graduation before reporting for duty, so he had time to spend with Molly and to continue his flight training at Miami's airport. Woody loved flying. He began his flight instruction in the winter. The cold dense air made for great flying conditions. The new hangar at the Miami Airport was now in use and was to be dedicated by Ohio's Governor, John Bricker, in honor of Ensign Lawrence Williams, the first Miami student killed in the war.

Weeks before graduation, Molly made luncheon reservations at the Huddle Restaurant uptown by the water tower in the center of Oxford. After the ceremony, Dad Gaynor loaded the family in his 1941 black Buick Special and drove them to the restaurant. The new automobile was his prize possession. It had a straight eight-cylinder engine, with big whitewall tires and chrome from bumper to bumper. He paid $989 for it at McDaniel's Buick agency in Marion. He really wanted a Road Master, but it would have cost another two hundred dollars. Frank Gaynor was happy that he bought the automobile in early November 1941, as the dealers' new car inventories were exhausted soon after Pearl Harbor. Rationing of fuel and food began in 1942. Each family had ration books with stamps that were surrendered when purchasing meat and other rationed items. The Huddle was the finest dining room in Oxford. The restaurant was filled with parents. The Gaynor family was seated at a large round table, with a white tablecloth and elegant Noritake China. Before the food arrived, father had the family hold hands, and he offered a prayer of thanks for Molly's graduation, a blessing for the food and for the safety of Molly's boyfriend Rob. Molly was grateful but could not help from shedding a few tears. As she wiped the tears from her face with her napkin, her dad said, "Where is Rob now?" Molly looked away, "I don't know. His last letter said he was very busy preparing for qualifying in submarines. I am so worried. His letters don't say much about the war."

"Well he *is in the silent service*," her young brother said in a vain attempt to make her feel better.

Woody graduated from Miami's College of Arts and Science. His father, a prominent lawyer in Cleveland, and his mother lived in the wealthy village of Rocky River, a suburb of Cleveland. They had driven down Saturday and had a reservation at the Elms Hotel on Main Street. Woody told them at dinner Saturday night that he had joined the Marines. They had hoped he would not pass the physical, but seeing his enthusiasm, they were resigned to his decision.

Woody had made reservations at the Huddle for his parents. When the Collingsworths entered, Woody saw Molly and her family and went right over to her table to greet his beautiful friend. Molly looked positively gorgeous. Her blue blouse and not so modest length white skirt set off her beautiful legs. Her long blonde hair fell gently on her shoulders. Woody was ecstatic. The Gaynor family appreciated him so much for his help when Molly's family received word that her brother had died in action in the South Pacific. He drew up a chair and chatted with the family. Frank liked him even though he was a Protestant. He could tell that Woody liked Molly.

To his embarrassment, Woody realized he had left his parents at their table. Woody apologized and brought his parents over to Molly's table and introduced them to Molly and her family. Molly stood feeling some uneasiness, which was quickly dispelled by Woody. "I want you to meet my friend and colleague from *The Student* newspaper, Molly Gaynor. She's from Marion, and you know about her losing her brother last winter." Molly interrupted him, "Yes, Woody was very helpful in our time of despair when the Western Union message came from the Navy about my brother's death." Mrs. Collingsworth said, "We are so sorry for your loss, we owe your brother a debt of gratitude for his sacrifice. I just wish this damn war would end. It's so tragic for everyone. You probably are aware that Woody passed his physical and has been accepted to begin flight training at Pensacola in a few weeks." Molly was fully aware of his plans, "I'm very proud of him, as I know you both are. He will be a good officer and an aviator. He promised to take me for a flight around Oxford next week." Woody's mother was shocked. She looked at her son, "Have you been taking flight lessons? You didn't tell us!" Woody stammered, "Well mom, I just didn't want you to worry. I took lessons last winter from an instructor at the new Miami Airfield west of town. I've soloed already!"

Molly glanced at her parents; her father was getting impatient. Molly said, "I'm sure your all are famished. Please sit and enjoy your meal. It was good to meet you both. I have heard so much about you." Woody's father finally spoke up, "Molly, perhaps you can visit us someday if Woody ever gets leave. We have a nice place right on the lake, and we have a sailboat. We'll take you for a sail on Lake Erie." Molly looked at him and felt the invitation was genuine. She said, "I'd like that very much."

As they left the table, Mrs. Collingsworth whispered to her husband, "She is a very beautiful girl, but she is Irish and Catholic.

CHAPTER 45

Decisions

Ensigns Young and Walker and five enlisted men of the crew dressed in crisp white uniforms, stood at attention on the cigarette deck aft of the *Thornfish* bridge. The entire crew stood at attention on the main deck below them as Captain Morrison, assisted by the chief of the boat, pinned the newly awarded Dolphins on their breasts. The captain remarked that Ensign Walker had become qualified in submarines without the benefit of having been through submarine school. He said, "Both of these officers have proved worthy of these Dolphins through hard work and in the heat of combat. Quite an accomplishment ensign, and well done." He then addressed the crew. "Men we've been given a great patrol area to sink Japs. We will be departing about 1400 this afternoon at slack water; so once again, you all know the deal. We will be going in harm's way. You're all volunteers, but if anyone feels that he will not be willing to share in some risky situations, you are free to leave the crew. Just tell the exec and he will be able to counsel you. I expect only the best from each man on this boat." There were no requests for transfer.

The *Thornfish* began backing away from alongside the submarine tender stationed at Midway at 1350. Jerry Abrams, the new exec had the conn. Tony Kennedy, his junior officer of the deck, stood by his side assisting. The deck hands were preparing for sea, stowing gear, mooring lines and ensuring that the lifelines were taunt. Captain Morrison watched the other boats slack their lines enough to allow the *Thornfish* to ease away from the tender. Below, Chief O'Neil walked the deck from bow to stern inspecting for any omissions. *Thornfish* followed the destroyer escort out through the slot in the narrow channel entrance of Midway's Atoll. It was slack water, when the current was almost at a standstill, making it easier for the vessel to navigate the treacherous entrance through the coral reefs surrounding the tiny island. A month earlier another submarine trying to navigate the restricted channel went aground on the reef and had to be pulled off with the assistance of a tug. Once in the open sea the exec ordered all hands below in preparation for the trim dive after having been in repair period for the last three weeks. The boat had a full load of torpedoes; both Mark-14 steam and new Mark-18 electrics and enough food to last over 60 days, stored in the storerooms, freezers, lockers, and any available space. All fuel and fresh water tanks were topped off. Jerry Abrams was very excited to be the new executive officer. He hated that it had to be because of the loss of LT Rogers, but he was very confident he could do the job. Jerry would be the youngest in the squadron and its first reserve executive officer. Early in the morning Pete, the diving officer, worked up the computations of weights and measures of tanks, supplies, weapons and crew, which permitted the boat to submerge with just enough negative buoyancy to permit trimming as they descended into deep waters surrounding Midway. Once satisfied, he reported to Captain Morrison in the conning tower, "Trim satisfactory sir." Dick responded, "Very well." After taking a good look around through the periscope and the soundman reported all clear, he ordered, "Surface the boat."

The previous week both Dick and Jerry met with the staff. The chief of staff asked Dick where he would like to go on his next patrol. Captain Vogel in Pearl Harbor sometimes rewarded captains having completed a very successful patrol, with lucrative hunting grounds for their next assignment. Dick had asked for the East China Sea area around Formosa, but it was suddenly changed by higher authorities in Washington. The *Thornfish* was needed to replace one of the boats lost during the last six months in the southwest area based out of Freemantle, Australia. By the end of 1942, three fleet boats and two S-boats had been lost operating out of Freemantle. As their submarine set course to the west guarded by the vigilant destroyer, Dick and Jerry went over the operation plan in the wardroom with the officers and the chief of the boat. Their new mission: to patrol near Palau, one of the main convoy routes from oil rich Borneo to the Marianas, and sink enemy ships, especially tankers. From there they would proceed south to Darwin, Australia, and then to Freemantle, *Thornfish's* new operating base. Submariners had grown to love Freemantle and Perth. The Australians welcomed them with open arms, especially the young women.

John Young knocked on the exec's door and hearing "come in" drew the curtain aside. Jerry had had a long day and was at his desk in his skivvies, preparing exercises for the next day. *Thornfish* would dive many times after the escort departed, practicing crash dives, man overboard drills, battle stations surface, battle stations torpedo; teamwork was stressed, as every man had a vital part to play in the survival of their boat. "Sir, if I could have a few minutes I'd like to talk with you about resuming our weekly church services." Jerry Abrams was a Jew and had been raised in a reformed Jewish family. After graduation from high school in Indiana, he drifted away from his Jewish roots. In college, however, he joined a Jewish fraternity at Purdue and enjoyed the fellowship, but his studies in electrical engineering took priority. He found little time for social life. John described what he had in mind and Jerry nodded approval. He added, "John, the Articles for the Government of the Navy strongly support religious services. In fact, a person disrupting a service can be court-martialed. If it does not interfere with our training too much, I think it would be well received by the captain. In fact, he may even join in. I might come too if you have an Old Testament reading sometime." John was elated. "Thanks sir, I'll keep you posted of our progress." As he was about to leave Jerry said, "Mr. Young, your timing is just right. The crew… we're very despondent over the loss of our two shipmates. Perhaps there may be some healing for us. You know, after the shellacking we took off Nagasaki, I don't believe there is an atheist on board." Jerry received prompt approval from Captain Morrison.

When John returned to his room, Rob was seated at the desk reading a letter. John said, "I didn't know we stopped at a mail buoy Rob." In the peacetime Navy, recruits were often told by old-timers to look for a mail buoy when they were at sea, where letters would be left for the ship to pick up. Rob laughed, "No, John boy, I'm rereading some letters I received before we left Midway." John said, "You sure have a lot of girlfriends Rob, and good-looking ones too. Which one do you like the best? The Ohioan or Hawaiian?"

Rob was taken back by John's forthrightness once again. He replied, "Thanks buddy, I'm pinned to Molly." John asked. "What's pinned? Remember, I'm from VMI, we are all male there."

"Well it means we are going steady."

"You sure can't go steady out here."

"Well it's kind of like engagement, but she is more faithful than me."

"I know …you have a thing for Lily too. Are you serious?"

Rob did not like the way the conversation was going. He turned the desk light off without replying to John. As he turned in the bunk in the dim light, he saw Molly's beautiful picture taped to the bulkhead…she was gazing at him. John's words *what does it mean to be pinned* echoed through his mind before he tried to sleep. His thoughts turned to Molly and how unfaithful he had been to her. And then gorgeous Lily. In the back of his mind, however, was the present worry that the chances of his surviving the war were slim. It eased his troubled conscience. Perhaps the Lord would forgive him. He started to say a little prayer he learned as a child, "*Now I lay me down to sleep, I pray the Lord my soul to keep, if I should die before I wake…*" Rob thought about some of his brother submariners who may have said that simple prayer, *if I should die before I wake*, and never woke up when their submarine struck a drifting mine during the night. He drifted off in uneasy slumber.

· · · · ·

Lily liked working at the Tiki Bar in the Pink Palace. She met some terrific sailors, got great tips, and enjoyed the lively conversation. She had to fend off many young men high on booze and testosterone trying to bed her down. As she smoothed her white apron on her short Hawaiian skirt, she saw her friend Kimo, the bartender.

Kimo Kaumana, a retired Navy petty officer, stood wiping the bar with a rag preparing for happy hour that always began at the Royal promptly at five. Everyone loved Kimo, the Hawaiian name for Jim. Especially the waitresses, he was a combination of a father figure, and bouncer for them. A native Hawaiian with a perpetual tan and black hair turning grey at the edges, his massive build and loud gangway voice made the crowd know who the boss was. When things would tend to get out of hand, he would come out from behind the bar and make peace in no uncertain ways. Lily was his special friend. Lately he sensed something was wrong. She seemed as if she was in another world at times. So, this evening before the sailors arrived, he had a chance to say something to her.

"Lily is there anything wrong? You don't seem to be yourself lately." Lily sat down on a barstool at the end of the bar. The old bartender handed her a cola and they talked. She finally confided in her friend, "I'm pregnant Kimo." He picked up his rag and scrubbed the bar even though he had cleaned it beforehand. "Well honey, it's not the end of the world. You're young, and the guy that got you this way will have to own up and marry you."

"Well it's not that simple. He is a submariner somewhere in the Pacific. I am so in love with him, but he loves someone else. I'm heartbroken."

"Oh, that changes things a lot. I'm sorry." He thought about what he could say to help her. "What are you going to do?"

"I don't know. I went to the doctor and asked for an abortion, but he won't do it. I am scared to death of what will happen. I'll lose my job for sure."

Kimo looked at the setting sun glimmering through the straw hut over the bar, thinking about her dilemma. After a while he said, "Well honey, I may know of someone who may be able to help you." He took a notepad and wrote a name and address on it. See Dr. Noe on Alakawa Street in Honolulu. He may help you. Lily took the note and put it in her bra. She was determined to see the doctor in the morning.

She went to work on the lunch shift the following morning. Her mother dropped her off in front of the Royal Hawaiian. Valerie was so excited that the Navy had told her to come to the base for another interview. Lily wished her mom well and watched her drive west toward the Navy shipyard. Lily was confident that her mother's language skills, in both written and verbal Japanese, would enable her to get a good job finally.... perhaps in intelligence.

But instead of reporting for work, Lily waited a long time for the next bus that would take her to downtown Honolulu. As the bus wound through the busy streets, she saw a reminder of the Jap attack, a late model black Plymouth sedan riddled with bullet holes from a Jap Zero that had been parked near the front gate of Fort DeRussy guarding Waikiki. She got off the bus a block from Alakawa Street and walked the remaining distance looking for the doctor's office. She checked the slip of paper with the address and found a door in a rundown frame building marked Dr. Inouye Noe, DDS. Lily could not believe it. He was a dentist! She double-checked the name and address that Kimo had given her. It was correct.

The waiting room had a couple of chrome plated chairs covered with dirty plastic, a table with a lampshade cocked askew and some well used National Geographic magazines. The ashtray had not been emptied for a long time. The receptionist office was empty. A small sign by the receptionist window said, "For service please ring the bell." Lily stood looking at the sign for a long time. Should she ring it and inquire about the abortion side of his practice? She held the tiny bell in her hand. The picture posted in the gynecologist's office of a ten-week old fetus flashed before her eyes. Little hands, little feet, swimming inside her. No, she could not ring the bell. She turned and walked outside into the warmth of a beautiful Hawaiian day. She took a deep breath and made her decision.

CHAPTER 46

Kauai

The island of Kauai lies some 70 miles west of Oahu. The most beautiful of all the Hawaiian Islands, it is called the garden island of the Hawaiian chain. Like most of the islands in the Pacific it was formed from volcanoes deep below the ocean's surface eons ago. The lush vegetation, beautiful canyons, and pristine beaches became a hidden resort for many who looked for an out of the way vacation. The Navy developed a testing station at Barking Sands along the isolated western coast of the island. The Navy occupied the only hotel on the island, leasing it for contractors and naval personnel manning the radar and testing facilities. Besides the hotel, the town of Lihue had an airport with one runway, a general store, post office, and a gas station that sold gas only three days a week. The only restaurant was open air with a tin roof. Small tables were crowded in the room. A parrot greeted the customers as they entered the tiny dining room. Dogs, looking for a treat, frequented the sidewalk waiting outside the open windows for a handout from one of the tables. Steaks and seafood were the only menu, complemented with three sides, baked beans, baked potatoes and salad. Patrons cooked their steaks or fish over a huge open pit charcoal fire in the center of the dining area. Sammy Orita was the owner, an old Japanese American, and a cousin of Valerie Edmonds. Her daughter, Lily, seven months pregnant, had become the only waitress and sometimes bartender. Lily lived with the Oritas in their home outside of town. He and his wife welcomed her into their home with open arms. They knew Lily from the time she was a little girl and wanted to help her through this stressful time in her life. They had a beautiful home on Nawiliwili Bay set high on a cliff overlooking the ocean.

The restaurant was only open in the evenings but was generally bustling with military customers from the hotel on the weekends. The circular bar, covered with bamboo, was the real money maker for the old couple. That is if they could get liquor. The Barking Sands' supply officer seemed to have an in with the suppliers on Oahu, and with his help, managed to keep the bar going. Lily loved the new job, but she hated to leave her mother and the Royal Hawaiian Tiki Bar staff. They were disappointed that she decided to leave but understood her predicament. Having a child out of wedlock was frowned upon by many. Valerie Edmonds shared her daughter's fears of shame and exclusion that would arise once her secret was disclosed. Among her friends and relatives, Lily's baby would be called a bastard. The family's unwritten code called *for honor at all cost*. Her mother would take care of everything. She would arrange for adoption with the Catholic Family Organization of Oahu. Plans would be made before the birth of the child. Then life would go on as before. She blamed the war more than anyone.

Lily was concerned that there was only one doctor on the island, and he was drunk a lot of the time. Nevertheless, the old doctor had delivered hundreds of babies over a lifetime of family medicine. Lily generally wore a large Hawaiian shirt from Hilo Hattie's in Honolulu to work. It covered her swollen belly nicely. Navy officers attached to the testing station came in regularly on the weekends to enjoy a good meal away from the base. Lily thought of Rob constantly. She wanted him to know of her pregnancy but believed it would upset him if he knew and only add to his stress. There was nothing he could do anyhow. She was lonely and despondent. She needed him, but she never knew where he was or if he would ever return. She was fearful that when he returned to Pearl, he would tell her that he wanted to stop seeing her. It would break her heart. She was so confused. Thoughts raced through her head: *if I tell him we are having a baby, he will marry me as soon as he returned from patrol. But she wanted him to marry her for love, not honor.*

After an exhausting evening at work, Lily couldn't sleep. She was so depressed. She repeatedly debated about writing Rob and telling him everything. She glanced at the alarm clock by her bed. It was 2 a.m. The cool ocean breeze lifted the curtains on the windows of her cozy room overlooking the ocean. On the cliffs below, breakers were rolling over ancient volcanic rocks that had resisted erosion for eons. The moon was rising in the east. The beauty of the night reminded her of the night months ago when she and Rob were together on the lanai high above Pearl Harbor and made love. She arose and sat at her wicker desk taking a pen and began to write…

Dearest Rob, I know you haven't heard from me for a long time, and I want you to know why. You see I've moved to Kauai at least for a time, and I am living with my mother's relative and working in his Island Bar and Grill. It's a good job but doesn't pay as much as I was making at the Pink Palace Tiki Bar, but I am surviving. Their four-bedroom home was built in the early part of this century and has a wide veranda and bedrooms facing the ocean on the cliffs below. I have a nice room overlooking the water. As I write this, the moon is coming up over the Pacific and everything is so peaceful. But the world is such a mess and so am I. Before going on I want to tell you my mother received her security clearance and is now working for the Navy at Pearl Harbor. She can't tell me what she does, but we are so happy that she has steady work. Her check for dad's loss on the Arizona December 7 finally arrived, and with the ten thousand dollars, she was able to pay off the car and the house mortgage. The Navy presented her with my father's Purple Heart in a ceremony at the naval base last week. I couldn't be there, but she wrote to me that it was a very solemn and moving experience. The battleship's superstructure is being cut up with welder's torches and oil is still seeping out from under the hull. Kauai is very beautiful and peaceful. I think Hollywood should make a film about the Pacific here someday. The reason I am here though is that I am pregnant. Yes, I'm going to be a mother in less than two months. Being unmarried and bringing a baby into the world is not acceptable in our community, so mother suggested going to stay with my relatives in Kauai. I contemplated having an abortion, but I just could not bring myself to kill an innocent baby. So here I am stuck in a difficult situation in wartime and with no husband. Now you may ask who the father is. You have been my only lover. But I am not asking you to marry me. I know you're tenderhearted and would marry me if you were here. But I want a marriage of lasting love and devotion, not one of obligation and duty. Love more than honor is my heart's desire.

I love you. Lily

Lily folded the letter and slipped it into an envelope and laid it on the desk. She worried, *If I send it, he couldn't do anything about it, and he has enough to stress. Maybe I should wait a while.* Sleep eluded her. Finally, she quietly stole out of the house and walked down the slope to the edge of the cliff. The roar of the breakers seemed to grow louder the longer she stood there. The wind caught her hair and nightgown in a whirl around her. It would be so easy she thought. Just step off into the churning sea below her, and everything would be solved. Lily stood on the brink of destruction for a long time. She recalled first meeting Rob on the beachfront of the Royal Hawaiian and the love affair that unfolded around them. As she stepped closer to the edge, she suddenly felt the baby in her womb move and kick her. Her hands clasped over her belly; it was like the little one was telling her not to do it. She turned and walked back to the house. As she lay on her bed the Bible verse that her mother recited many times after her father was killed came to mind. *Sorrow lasts for a night, but joy comes in the morning.*

Before falling asleep, she put the letter under her pillow; she would think about sending it *in the morning.*

CHAPTER 47

The Palaus

The Palaus Islands became Japanese mandates after the First World War. They are a group of some two hundred small islands, part of the Carolines, situated in the central Pacific. Located some five hundred miles east of Mindanao in the Philippines and north of New Guinea, they were heavily fortified and served as a staging area for Japanese expansion to Java and northern Australia. Thornfish plowed through the seas from Truk to their patrol area surfaced most of the time. Dick Morrison was very happy to be assigned to Palau. It would provide many targets especially tankers taking oil from Borneo to Japan and was a port for the assembly of convoys going southwest to the Solomon Islands and New Guinea.

Rob spent his spare time reading the many pages of his ship's instructions for his new department. As head of the gunnery department and as its division officer, he was now responsible for the efficiency of the ship's armaments. Rob learned the lesson that all junior officers eventually recognize, that chief petty officers and leading men run the Navy. Torpedoman First Class Grabowski, his senior petty officer, became his best source for learning the technical side of the gunnery department and he knew his men. He was very fortunate to continue to have him as his leading P.O. Grabowski helped save the boat on Rob's first patrol when the fathometer shaft broke and nearly flooded the forward torpedo room compartment.

Gunnery practice was held several times during their run to Palau. Four days later, *Thornfish* arrived off the entrance to Malakal Harbor in the Palaus. The following day, two patrol boats proceeding out of the narrow channel announced the coming of several larger freighters. Dick submerged the boat and deftly maneuvered in front of them. He let the two escorts pass and the periscope observation disclosed that the freighters were troop ships loaded with soldiers. Dick closed within 1000 yards and fired Mark-14's at each vessel. Sound reported all hot straight and normal. Less than a minute later, two explosions jarred everyone in the boat. The wakes of the four steam torpedoes, however, alerted the escorts to the firing position. There was no time to get another periscope observation. Dick ordered 400 feet as depth charges thundered from above. The chief of the watch in the control room, observing the outside water temperature, reported a layer of cold water and the captain maneuvered under it and escaped. *Thornfish* had received a new and improved instrument during upkeep at Midway. The submarine *Scorpion* was one of the first submarines to be equipped with the instrument that became very useful during the war for evading enemy sub chasers. It simply measures the temperature of the water outside of a boat, thereby enabling submarine commanders to evade sound detection by going below heavy cold water that deflected sound waves from the enemy escorts. The instrument was in the control room near the diving officer's station. A drum chart had a stylus that recorded the temperature at every depth.

Dick Morrison took advantage of a cold dense layer of water off the harbor entrance while submerged during the daylight hours. Pete, the diving officer, trimmed the boat to perfect neutral buoyancy. The crew not on watch rested in their bunks as walking around from stern to the bow would disturb the trim. The soundman listened for enemy screws coming out of the harbor. The captain lay in his bunk with his clothes on including his foul weather jacket catching some sleep. John Young was in his bunk contemplating the talk he would give during the first church service. He was thinking about a passage in Mathew's Gospel, chapter 25, 'Go into the world making disciples of all nations…' Jerry and Rob were playing cribbage in the wardroom. Rob was winning as usual. Pete interrupted the game. "XO, sound reports high-speed screws coming from the entrance to Malakal." Jerry rose from the table and said, "Ok Pete, wake the captain and make turns for three knots. Make your depth 60 feet. We'll go up and look." Jerry ordered the stationing of the tracking party and climbed the ladder to the conning tower. He met the captain as he was rubbing the sleep out of his eyes. "Sir, we have some high-speed screws coming at us, I've ordered periscope depth."

"Ok Jerry, we need to be really careful there may be aircraft above them. We'll try out our feminine periscope." Some "expert" in the bureau in Washington did some research and found that pink periscopes are less visible in tropic waters than the Navy gray or black. While at Midway, the squadron ordered their boats to have their periscopes painted pink. Pete reported, "60 feet, sir." Dick said, "Very well, up 'pinky'!" Dick rode the scope up as it broke water in a flat calm sea, even at three knots the periscope would show a wake. A scan of the surface disclosed masts on the horizon; he estimated three or four ships in column. Fortunately, no aircraft was in sight. From the position of the masts, he made a rough estimate of the course; another observation would be needed to get course and speed. He ordered down scope and a course change to intercept the enemy ships. With no aircraft in sight, he took a risk by coming to 55 feet and powered up the radar. The PPI scope showed four ships. Three small patrol boats, and a little larger ship in the center of the formation. As the convoy approached closer, Dick submerged to 100 feet and increased speed. He was soon in a great firing position ahead of the enemy ships.

After a few more observations with 'pinky,' the tracking party made a recommendation. The exec said, "Captain, we think this may be a trap. The guy in the center may be a Q ship." They were warships disguised as merchant ships that had very shallow drafts so that torpedoes would pass harmlessly underneath them. Then the escorts, seeing the torpedo wakes, would charge in blasting the submarine with depth charges. The escorts were pinging sound waves but had not detected *Thornfish*. "All right," Dick said, "We'll find out if it's a Q ship. Stand by to fire at that SOB Q ship with Mark-18 electrics from the after-torpedo room. Set torpedo depth for four feet, with one degree spread." Submariners loved the electrics. Though they were slower than the Mark-14 steam torpedoes, they left no wakes, a real advantage in daylight attacks. Each torpedo had been painted with names of the *Thornfish's* fallen executive officer and gunner's mate.

Within minutes, the range to the target had decreased to 1000 yards, a perfect set up for a stern shot. One final observation and Dick commanded shoot! Two electrics sped out of the after-torpedo tubes. A minute and fourteen seconds later, the target exploded, and the escorts came looking for the *Thornfish*. Dick ordered deep, and as they descended, pinging became louder. Several escorts had locked on to their nemesis. Then came the rain of thunder from above. Men were knocked off their feet by the explosions. More explosions came each one closer and closer. Lights blew out; cork insulation flew around the control room, and the pressure hull started groaning from the punishment and seawater began flooding into the engine room. Dick found a cold dense layer of water to hide beneath. However, for some strange reason the Japanese commander broke off the attack. Had he continued, the Japs would have inflicted mortal damage to the *Thornfish*. Dick remained submerged until it was safe to surface to repair damage and recharge the batteries. Damage to the main induction valve required several hours to repair two gaskets. Then the lookouts saw that they were leaving a trail of oil on the water. An oil leak had occurred caused by damage to the fuel oil refueling valve. All repairs were completed by sunset. It was time to return to the fight.

· · · · ·

Rob had the 4 to 8 watch on the bridge and was looking forward to some fresh breakfast rolls and then sack time after he was relieved. The eastern sky was aglow with the sun's red rays bouncing off the low clouds. He remembered the sailors' limerick, *"Red sky in the morning, sailors take warning; Red sky at night, sailors delight."* *Thornfish* had just completed its battery charge, and Pete had finished his compensations. He alerted the exec that he was ready for the trim dive, the boat's first of the day. The captain came up to the bridge from the conning tower and greeted his officer of the deck. "Morning Rob, are we ready to dive?" Rob replied, "Yes sir, we are ready now." Dick Morrison trained his crew well. He had complete confidence in his officers and men.

The average age of the *Thornfish* crew was 21 years. Dick took a long look around the horizon, "Great day Rob, I have a feeling we are going to find some contacts today. When you're ready, pull the plug and we'll trim out the boat for the day." As the captain descended the ladder, Rob had the word passed, to standby to dive. He ordered the lookouts below and then reached under the windscreen and pulled the lever on the klaxon twice, and on the announcing system said "Dive, Dive!" The hydraulic vents on the tops of the main ballast tanks opened, air gushed out and sea water filled the tanks. The boat started to disappear below the waves. Once satisfied that the trim was satisfactory, Pete reported "Trim Satisfactory Sir." The captain acknowledged his report with the familiar words, "Very Well" then he added, "Good job Pete." He turned to his exec and said, "Jerry, we will surface later this morning. We'll have 'Rope Yarn Sunday' to rest the crew and have divine services in the mess deck for anyone wishing to attend. John is going to conduct it. Grabowski is going to play his harmonica, and the chief will lead the singing." Jerry said, "Heck, if they'll let a Jew in, I'll come too!"

John Young slept in after having the mid-watch, but the sound of the diving alarm awakened him. He washed his face, shaved and put on a clean uniform and sat down at the desk he shared with Rob. His well-worn Bible was open to the book of Genesis. He went over once again the outline of what he intended to speak about. He decided to begin with a reading from Genesis chapter one. In the beginning, God. He wanted to share some thoughts about God's creative power. He uttered a silent prayer, "Lord, please let me have an anointing this morning as I try to tell the good news to my shipmates."

An hour later, the executive officer announced "Now give me your attention: Divine Services are now being held in the crew's mess. All not on watch are invited. The smoking lamp is out throughout the boat." John stood by the slot machine covered with canvass, as the crew filed in. In all eighteen crowded in the small compartment. Later the captain came in unannounced and stood near the compartment's door. Willie had prepared some delicious donuts along with piping hot Navy coffee and while the men were helping themselves, he handed out words to the hymns on mimeographed paper. John welcomed everyone and opened with a short prayer. He beckoned to Chief O'Neil to come and lead the first hymn. Grabowski pulled the harmonica out of his dungaree pocket and played the melody to the familiar hymn, *Holy, Holy, Holy, Lord God Almighty, early in the morning our praise shall rise to thee.* The men began to sing the words printed on the handout and after a few feeble attempts and prodding by the chief, they finally chimed in.

John gave a brief homily about God's creation, which was well received. He noticed a hand go up in the back of the compartment. It was the young gunner's mate who had been on the deck loading the five-inch gun when LT Rogers and the gunner were killed. He said, "Sir, I just wanted to tell the guys that I have been giving a lot of thought about my life recently. Why wasn't I killed instead of gunner? I was right beside him when he got hit. He was married with kids, and I'm single. I kind of feel guilty." John looked down searching for words; the captain interjected, "This is a question a lot of men ask themselves in war. We said we were going in harm's way. And we did. The hardest thing I have had to do, as commanding officer, was to write letters to the next of kin for LT Rogers and the gunner. There is no satisfactory answer to your question. Only the Lord knows why you were spared and only time will tell. I think the most important thing for you to do is make the rest of your life a testament to duty, honor and loyalty to your band of brothers to help make this world a better place than when you came in. I'm proud of what these two men did for their country …they gave their all. I am very proud of all of you. Let's dedicate our time together to be the best we can be and make them proud of us." There were many Amens. Without being asked, Grabowski began playing his harmonica, *Amazing Grace, how sweet the sound…* As the senior chief sang the words, he went over to the young man who asked the question and put his hand on his shoulder. He began to sob unashamedly. When he finally stopped, no one spoke. No one moved. It was a somber time of reflection.

The services concluded with a closing prayer by Ensign Young. Then the word was passed that the smoking lamp was lighted. John was disappointed that Rob had not attended. Captain Morrison went over to John and thanked him for doing the service. He joined the men in a donut and coffee.

Fifteen minutes later *Thornfish* surfaced on a beautiful cloudless day, making standard speed for Freemantle. The cover was removed from the slot machine and Chief O'Neil was the first in line to feed it nickels. The men still called him Chief Nickels for his luck. Some played cards; a few men started writing letters that would not be mailed for weeks to come. The boat's radioman began playing some hit tunes from Tokyo Rose over the general announcing system. *In the Mood* by Glen Miller's orchestra was playing in the crew's mess. It came from Tokyo on a program called the Zero Hour. It featured the latest hit tunes from the States and interspersed with propaganda broadcast to all U.S. forces in the South Pacific. The disc jockey was an American woman born in Los Angles, her real name, Iva Ikuko Toguri, was born of Japanese- American parents in Los Angles July 4, 1916. The name she chose, Tokyo Rose, was also known to her audience as Orphan Annie. Her soft lilting voice introduced each song designed to make troops homesick and was accompanied by propaganda telling the American military how the Japanese were winning the war. After Glenn Millers' piece ended, she announced, "Our fleet has again shown its superiority over the American submarines! In a recent landing in the South Pacific, our forces ran into a nest of them. Not one enemy submarine was able to accomplish a successful attack. It will not be long before we have eliminated the last submarine from Pacific waters." The *Thornfish* sailors had a good laugh listening to this bullshit, but the crew loved the songs she played of Jimmy Dorsey, the Mills Brothers, and the Glenn Miller orchestra.

· · · · ·

'Rope Yarn Sunday', a tradition in the Navy since sailing days, when captains gave time off to the crew, ended when Captain Morrison was told radar had a contact. The SJ radar had a convoy on the PPI scope, range 30,000 yards and closing. The music suddenly stopped as the sound of the Bells of St. Mary's rang throughout the boat. Rob awoke and dressed quickly stopping in the wardroom to grab a cup of stale coffee.

The captain and exec were huddled around the DRT. The plotter, showing true bearings and ranges to the convoy, indicated a base course of 220 and a speed of 12 knots. "Looks like we may have a couple of good size ships in the center sir," said the exec. "I agree, Jerry. Let's track and give me a recommended course to intercept while we are on the surface." Rob had passed them climbing the ladder to the conning tower. His arm still pained him from the gun wound while climbing the ladder, but he never let on to anyone. He lit off the power to the TDC and fed the initial range and bearing into the computer. The words "Surface, Surface, Surface," rang out throughout the boat and *Thornfish* smartly surfaced; diesels cut in and as the quartermaster opened the hatch, water poured down the ladder soaking the captain as he climbed out on the bridge. Dick ordered flank speed taking a southwesterly course to intercept the enemy ships. The exec in the conning tower took the handles of the pink periscope; the extended scope would provide the first visual observation of the convoy. In high power, he could see the tips of the largest vessel's masts on the distant horizon. Jerry climbed to the bridge and conferred with the captain. He said, "Captain, I'm surprised they don't have any air cover sir. They know we must be out here. The radar is showing the convoy zigzagging about twenty degrees off their base course. But the radar is showing some weather turning ugly with intermittent rain squalls." The captain said, "this may help us a bit Jerry; I think we can stay on the surface a little longer. This may account for no air cover. Let's get a mile ahead of them, and we'll pull the plug. Jerry I'm going to let you do the periscope work and I'll make the approach on this one. OK?" Jerry appreciated his captain's confidence in him. The captain continued, "If we are lucky, we will duck under the escorts and hit the biggies in the center. Then shoot an escort with our stern fish." Jerry replied, "Sounds like a good plan sir."

Thornfish's four diesels churned up the wake as the submarine gained position at flank speed. As the weather worsened, the OOD had foul weather jackets brought up for the topside watch. The tracking plot still showed a twenty-degree zig on either side of the base course. Torpedomen in the forward and after-rooms checked and rechecked their fish. As the range closed to 5,000 yards, Dick ordered John to dive the boat. Once at periscope depth, the captain ordered speed reduced to three knots to minimize wake. Jerry made the first observation. "We have two freighters in a column in the center; one of them is a troop transport. The angle on the bow port 10, give me a radar range." The radar man said, "Aye sir, Range four-five, oh, oh." Jerry commanded, "Down scope!" Rob fed the information in the TDC including base course, speed and range from the last radar observation. Jerry told Dick, "The escorts look like Mikura class frigates." Two minutes later he ordered, "Up scope!" He took a quick look around the horizon and then announced, "Angle on the bow port 40, down scope!" The captain shouted, "Target zigging," and Rob cranked in the new estimate in the TDC. Sonar reported sounds of pinging coming from two of the escorts. Standard practice for antisubmarine warfare, with three escorts, two would use active sonar and the third listen. "High-speed screws coming toward us sir!" shouted the sonar man in the conning tower. Dick ordered full dive on the planes, as the frigate passed overhead. The crew braced themselves for the expected blasts of explosives, but none came. They were still not detected. *Thornfish* returned to periscope depth, and Jerry took his second observation, "Angle on the bow port 50, bearing mark, range mark." Rob fed the new information as Dick ordered a course change to close the targets. He increased speed; it would be close if the Japs continued the present course. Range closed to 1000 yards and Jerry took his final look. "This is a final and shoot."

When he shouted mark, the quartermaster took the bearing off the periscope bearing circle and shouted it to Rob. Rob acknowledged it and said, "TDC checks. Range, 1000 yards sir." The correct solution light came to life, and Captain Morrison said, "Fire one…Fire two… Fire three." Three electric torpedoes swam out on their way to the troop laden ship.

Jerry swung 'pinky' to the other ship in the center of the formation and focused long enough for the firing team to lock on the target with the correct target angle and spread. Fire four, Fire five, and finally, Fire six. The sub shuddered as three steam torpedoes were expelled aimed at the second ship in the van. WHAM! WHAM! The men in the conning tower were shaken as two of the three fish hit the first troop ship in amidships and its stern. Dick ordered, "take her down. Fast!" Screws of two frigates were bearing down on them. "Flood negative. Rig for depth charge." The diving planes man's bubble passed twenty degrees as the sub twisted and turned trying to evade a rain of depth charges. The enemy frigates had them boxed in. As they descended, the captain yelled out to the chief of the boat in the control room, "Chief, watch the thermal chart do you see any cold water yet?" The old chief calmly replied, "No sir, the water temperature is about the same." The depth gage passed 350 feet. Pete the diving officer called out the depth to the captain and as they passed 400 feet the chief shouted, "We have a cold layer sir." Dick responded "Hallelujah! Make your depth 450 feet."

They found refuge from the enemy and went quiet. No movement of men or machines was allowed. The rain of enemy explosives continued for over an hour. Over fifty depth charges were recorded by the quartermaster. During the time Jerry walked through the boat trying to encourage the crew. He ordered them to get in their bunks, knowing full well that no one could sleep through the terror of the thunder from above. There was one exception. Chief O'Neil was somehow able to sleep either from exhaustion, or from an abiding faith in the Lord. Finally, the enemy frigates' barrage ceased, most likely for trying to rescue survivors of the ships they were guarding.

Just before darkness fell, *Thornfish* surfaced to repair damage and charge the batteries. Dick ordered the search periscope up and to his surprise, could not see anything. Upon surfacing the captain emerged on the bridge to find a Jap soldier's coat from one of the ships they had torpedoed covering the number one periscope.

They had had a hard day's work over. But the stout hull of the *Thornfish* stood the test once again. American steel forming the hull made from ore of the Mesabi Range in Minnesota, coal and coke from West Virginia, and limestone from Ohio melted in blast furnaces in steel mills from Indiana, Ohio, and Pennsylvania, were producing steel for submarines made in Wisconsin, New Hampshire, Connecticut, and California, at a rate of four per week. Japan's shipbuilding capacity began to dwindle as supplies of raw materials were reduced as freighters were being sent to the bottom of the Pacific by American submarines.

Dawn broke just as repairs were completed. They had one more day on patrol, and then *Thornfish* would be released to begin the long haul to Australia. During the night they had received a radio message from Pearl Harbor Headquarters congratulating them on a very productive patrol. Peter was getting concerned about the fuel situation. He recommended cruising with two engines for conservation whenever possible as there would be no refueling until they reached Darwin Australia, over two thousand miles.

In midmorning a patrol plane caused them to dive. Several more were sighted as the day wore on. Dick told Jerry there must be something up and sure enough, he had no more said this, and the radar operator reported ships coming out of the harbor. Jerry standing in the conning tower looking at the PPI scope said, "Sir, it looks like a big one!" Dick climbed down the ladder from the bridge and conferred with his exec. "I'm surprised Jerry, they know we are out here," Jerry said. "This guy is making smoke... he is tracking at 19 knots. It may be a heavy, perhaps battleship." The target began to zigzag, and plot said they would have a hard time catching up. Dick ordered all four engines to come online and they tore after their newfound target. Jerry went back into the engineering spaces and told them to override the governors and give them all the speed they could crank out of the four Fairbank Morse diesels.

Submarines' advantage in warfare is invisibility, stealth and surprise. But luck is also involved. And this time lady luck was on the *Thornfish* side. A zig toward them sent them diving below the rough seas. The Bells of St Mary's rang out and within two minutes all compartments reported manned and ready. If the enemy ships remained on this zig toward them, they would be in excellent firing position. And they did.

Dick raised 'pinky' and set the scope on the bearing Rob provided from the computer. Dick was astonished. "It's an aircraft carrier!" he exclaimed. Jerry passed the word on the general announcing system. He could feel the tension rising in the boat. The range was closing fast. Everyone had to do their job and do it right. No mistakes. Dick called out commands: "open outer doors. Set torpedo depth 15 feet. High speed. Spread degrees. Stand by for a final observation and shoot." Rob quickly fed the information into the computer. Rob called out "Range 1800 yards to the carrier." Dick called out target angle starboard 20, standby, "Fire one, fire two, fire three, fire four." The familiar lurch occurred as the four forward steam torpedoes were launched with high-pressure air. But after twenty-four seconds the first fish exploded prematurely. "Damn torpedoes!" Dick yelled. "Right full rudder, standby aft, we'll shoot one remaining from the stern." As the sub swung around two explosions were heard. "We got him!" Cheers erupted through the boat. One more to go. Upon the command, "Standby aft," Rob lined up on the final shot. "Fire when ready Rob," Dick ordered. Rob pushed the firing button and the remaining Mark-14 sped out. Sonar started to say it was hot, straight, and normal but then checked. "Captain, it's coming back at us!" The steam torpedo ran out, circled and was coming back at *Thornfish* at 45 knots!

"Full Dive! Flood Negative!" the captain barked. He did not order full rudder as it would slow their decent. Moments later the erratic torpedo whizzed overhead. White knuckles relaxed as the danger passed. The destroyers, however, came in furious pursuit of the *Thornfish*. The ocean thundered below as the enemy launched tons of explosives trying to destroy the sub that damaged the carrier. By going deep and silent Dick was able to guide them to safety. Surfacing after midnight, Dick got a message off to headquarters about the damaged carrier and its longitude and latitude so that another submarine could sink it. The code breakers in the basement of the Navy yard at Pearl Harbor learned about the carrier being damaged and that it had to return to port. The admiral said to chalk up another victory to the Thorny!

But *Thornfish's* danger was not over. The captain, first on the bridge upon surfacing was heard to exclaim, "OH SHIT!!" Upon hearing the captain's unusual cuss words, the exec rushed up the conning tower ladder to the bridge.

"What's wrong, skipper?"

"We've got company. Look over the deck below."

On the deck, wedged in between the bridge and the five-inch gun, was an unexploded Japanese depth charge. Both men were astonished. If that ash can had exploded, all of them would be at the bottom of the Pacific. The Captain and his exec conferred about how to dispose of the dud. Or perhaps it wasn't a dud but failed to explode because the depth setting was incorrect. If they tossed it overboard it could detonate and blow them sky high. Dick passed the word for Rob, the gun boss, and the first lieutenant, Tony Kennedy, to come to the bridge. As they explained the alternatives, Rob interjected. "Sir, I have an idea. I'll get some of the strongest hands we've got, and we'll put that sucker in one of our rubber rafts and flood down a bit, float the raft off and then we'll shoot it with one of our twenty millimeters.

"Great idea Rob!" The captain, however, was concerned, one mistake could be costly. "We will do it now." Tony got his men on deck and inflated one of the ship's rubber life rafts while Rob and his men wrestled with the ashcan. First, they tied straps around it and then rotated the five-inch gun back toward the bridge and using it as a crane, lifted the explosive high enough to place it in the black inflatable boat. Rob copied all the printed information on the side of the depth charge, and then signaled that they were ready to launch their new weapon. The exec made a change in plans. Instead of shooting the contraption, he decided to hole the raft with a knife so that it would slowly sink as they left their patrol hunting grounds and headed to Darwin. With the crew below, Rob and the captain watched as the submarine slowly flooded down enough for the raft to float away from the *Thornfish*. The captain said, "Maybe it will drift back to the harbor and give the Japs a memento from us!"

The patrol off Palau was about completed. A message from headquarters in Pearl Harbor confirmed their orders to report, upon completion of the patrol, to Commander Submarines Southwest based in Freemantle, Australia. It would be a long voyage to Darwin on the northwest coast for refueling so conservation of the remaining fuel was of primary importance now.

Willie prepared a huge chocolate cake for the captain's 33rd birthday. The crew loved their commanding officer. They would do anything for him. He ran a taut ship, demanding the best of each man but treated them all fairly. He knew each man's name and some personal information. Some came from farms in the heartland of America, a few from the big cities. Their Navy experience was limited as most were reservists. Since most were young, Dick didn't permit swearing and foul language to be used aboard the boat. His can-do attitude flowed through the ranks. The crew admired their commanding officer's calm cool response in crisis situations. Jerry, the new executive officer, was an inspiration for the crew; they regarded him as very smart, aggressive and enthusiastic. He handled stress fearlessly, and the crew loved his jokes and Jewish humor. He shared the same ideas of leadership and aggressiveness as his commanding officer that was sometimes lacking in other boats, particularly when the commanding officer was older and aligned with prewar concepts of submarine warfare. The younger officers tended to be more aggressive in their approach to tactics. As the command age decreased, tonnage sunk increased. However, two years into the war the silent service remained plagued by poor torpedo performance. Particularly controversial was the Mark-6 magnetic exploder. Dick and Jerry began the outline of their patrol report and decided to state the reasons for most of their misses were due to defective torpedoes. The Bureau of Ordnance, responsible for the weapons, continued to disbelieve submarine commanding officers' reports of premature explosions, poor depth control and erratic runs after torpedoes were fired, blaming the problem with the poor performance of commanding officers. Admiral Christie, their new boss in Freemantle, agreed with the bureau. Dick and Jerry agreed that it would be a problem for the *Thornfish*.

Captain Morrison had just finished cutting the cake in the crew's mess when John Young came in and handed him a message. He glanced at it and told him to have the exec meet him in the wardroom right away. Dick grabbed a piece of cake and thanked the crew and especially Willie for the very nice birthday surprise. A few minutes later, the captain and exec sat in the wardroom over cups of coffee, discussing the new message ordering them to proceed immediately to the south part of the island of Mindanao in the Philippines.

It read:

COMSUBPAC To Thornfish 499 x Upon Completion of Thornfish Patrol, Proceed to Pagadian Bay Mindanao PI to Evacuate Major Sean Smith Royal Australian Army Reserve Coast Watcher x Rendezvous TBD at Later Date Depending on The ETA of Thornfish x Confirm Receipt

Dick asked, "Jerry before we reply, I want an accurate plot of where we will go, the fuel needed to get to the rendezvous, evacuate and make it to Darwin. Do we have charts of the waters off the southern Philippines?"

"Yes Sir, we got a full packet from Midway before we left since we were going to report to Freemantle." Jerry had his quartermaster bring the latest chart to the wardroom. Jerry had him remain and the three of them carefully examined the new chart. "Sir, I heard Chief O'Neil once talk about Mindanao; he had been on an S-boat in the Philippines, and he might know a lot about the waters there."

"Good suggestion. Please have the chief join us. Also ask LT Robinson to come to the wardroom too."

"Aye, sir."

A few minutes later five of them were reviewing the chart. The captain said, "Chief, the quartermaster says you were on an S-boat, based out of Cavite, near Manila."

"Yes Sir, it was a good tour but those S-boats without air-conditioning were horrible to be on. Equipment was continually breaking down due to the humidity."

"Were you ever at Pagadian Bay on southern Mindanao?"

"Just once sir. I remember we were concerned about going aground as the bay is very shallow. Jungle surrounds the bay. I remember there is a Catholic Church in town and a Muslim Mosque. I went to mass there one Sunday, I mean at the Catholic Church not the mosque." Laughter broke out as the chief blushed.

The captain said, "Thanks chief, we may need your help later. It looks like we're going there to pick up an Aussie."

CHAPTER 48

Empty

Several weeks after graduation, Molly found a room to rent in a home on High Street, across from Oxford College, and just three blocks from the office of *The Oxford Press*. Mrs. Walker had offered to let her stay with her. She had a very nice room with a private bath upstairs. Molly turned her down because she wanted to have a place near her office. But the main reason was that she did not want to feel indebted to her. She liked the house on High Street when she first looked at it. With all brick construction and a large front porch with a swing, it looked comfortable and safe. She had a bedroom on the second floor with a desk and a private bathroom across the hall. The owner, LeRoy Douglas, was a retired farmer from College Corner. His wife, Myrtle, let Molly know she would not put up with any shenanigans. Molly knew what she meant but was not opposed to her restrictions. The rent would be five dollars per month with the first month paid in advance. Woody helped her move in and Mrs. Douglas kept a sharp eye on him. After moving her things in, he asked Molly to come with him for a ride. He drove out Contreras Road, past the Oxford Country Club west of Oxford and parked his Chrysler. "Now you drive," he commanded.

Molly said, "What! I don't know how." Woody said, "You will soon. Just get behind the wheel and I'll give you instructions." It was a flat road with no traffic. She reluctantly got behind the steering wheel and said, "Now what?" Woody told her how to use the clutch and shift gears. He turned the engine off and let her get used to shifting the gears one by one. Then he let her turn the engine on and to his complete amazement, after a few jerky starts, she smoothly engaged the gears and got the sedan back on the road toward the university airport. Woody enjoyed watching her pretty legs as she learned to use the manual clutch. Molly was thrilled. She drove to the Miami Field and, with some help from Woody, parked the big sedan. "Congratulations Molly, you are going to be a good driver." He leaned over and kissed her. "Now let's go flying!" Woody led her to a small yellow and black Piper Cub J3 airplane parked on the grass by the new hangar. "I rented it," he said. I'm going to take you for a joy ride over Oxford." While Molly climbed in the back seat and fastened her safety belt, Woody performed the visual checks over the plane. Once satisfied, he jumped in the front seat and set the throttle, and the engine came to life. "Here we go Molly," as the tiny airplane taxied down the grass strip to the end of the grass runway. The Piper turned facing into the west wind. Woody revved up the engine, released the brake and they sped down the field rising above the distant line of trees and were airborne on the way to Oxford.

Molly was thrilled. It was her first ride in an airplane. Woody steered the little plane right over High Street. She saw her apartment at 210 High Street and then the post office in the next block. Woody made a slow turn over the town square. She could see graffiti painted on the water tower by some freshmen's last homecoming. He banked the J3 to the right and flew over Harrison Hall, known as old Maine. Down below she saw Elliott dormitory where Rob lived during his senior year. As they flew east, Woody dipped the plane's wings as they passed over Fisher hall, the sailors' barracks now guarded by sentries 24 hours a day. Woody climbed higher and signaled for Molly to take the stick and fly the plane. She could not believe he would do that. Here she was learning to drive a car and fly a plane for the first time all in one day! He leveled off at 1500 feet and let Molly try to control the plane. He was amazed at how easily she controlled the Piper Cub. Woody had her turn and bank without losing altitude. She would be a natural he thought. He took control as they approached Middletown, and he did a long circle around Armco Steel's Middletown Works. The mill was turning out rolls of steel for the war effort for Jeeps, ships, and tanks. Armco was the inventor of rolled steel. Their fabricating division was producing thousands of tons of 12 gauge hot rolled steel interlocking strips that formed instant runways for new airfields in the South Pacific Islands. Galvanized steel, produced on their continuous hot-dipped lines, another first by Armco, was being used in the manufacture of Quonset Huts for use in every war zone throughout the world. In a small lab in the Research Center on Curtis Street, Armco Steel was producing ultrathin electrical steels used in the manufacture of radar equipment. It enabled the allies to have superior radar detection giving our military great advantage revealing enemy ships and planes.

Woody eased the rudder and lined up on State Route 725 west from Germantown toward Camden. A troop train loaded with soldiers and tanks had stopped in Camden blocking the highway while the train crew took on water for the steam engine. Soldiers milled about, and a few ran to the grocery store looking for snacks and beer. Flying southwest Woody pointed out the Hamilton Boy Scout camp, Myron Kahn below. He had been at its dedication in June, with John Dolobois, and had written a story a year ago about it. He wagged his wings at some boys below paddling a canoe on the large pond. As he pulled up to gain altitude, the engine started to sputter. He yelled, "Oh my god, Molly we're nearly out of gas. We're going to have to set this crate down." The J3's gas tank is gravity fed and located just in front of the instrument panel. As he started to descend, the engine caught on with some gas in the bottom of the tank.

But it wasn't enough. "Molly fasten your seatbelt tight, I'm going to land in that hay field off to the right." The plane banked, descending slowly its engine sputtering, and Woody carefully glided over a fence at the far end of a farmer's newly mowed pasture. The Piper Cub landed with several bounces on the field and coasted to a stop near the far fence. "Thank you, Jesus!" Molly shouted!

Woody was embarrassed. He said, "Molly I'm sorry, in my haste I checked everything but the most obvious thing, the gas gauge. It must have been almost empty. I won't do that again! I promise."

Molly responded, "Woody you did a wonderful job in that emergency. Thanks for saving our lives." Woody grinned, "Well now I've got to get some gas so that we can get back before sunset."

Molly looked up, "Woody, we have company." In the distance, a pickup truck made its way down the road and turned into the hay field. A kindly looking old timer got out of the rusty Studebaker pickup truck. "Welcome to my farm young man! You out for a joy ride today?" Woody grinned and replied, "Well sir, I'm giving my girlfriend a tour of the countryside before I leave for naval aviation training in Pensacola. I sure am embarrassed about running out of gas. A poor way to impress my girl!" The old man's wrinkled face broke into a wide smile as he looked at Molly. He thought about how this young man must hate leaving such a beautiful blonde girl. "Let me take you to the airport and we'll get some fresh gas."

The three of them piled in the truck and sped down Oxford Germantown road past the entrance to the proposed Heuston Woods State Park and soon were at the airfield. Woody was able to get two five-gallon cans of aviation grade gasoline and placed them in the rusty truck bed. They drove to Molly's rooming house on High Street and let her off over her strenuous objections. She wanted to return to the hay field and take off with Woody. "No way Molly. It will be easier for me to take off anyway with only me in the plane. I'll visit with you when I return, it won't take too long. I have to get the plane back before dark." Fortunately, the State of Ohio was on wartime and in June the daylight is very long. Woody hopped in and the old farmer drove the old truck at top speed, 35 miles per hour. "I see you have a C stamp sir." The red stamp stuck on the right side of the windshield permitted the owner to have more gas than the public, most of whom had A stamps. The A stamp allows four gallons per week. The B is issued to businesses and permits them to buy 8 gallons a week. The price fifteen cents a gallon for regular. The C is issued to farmers, contractors, maintenance workers, priests, ministers, military and physicians, who needed more gasoline in their work. "Yes, sonny, I need the C. Got it through the Office of Price Administration last December just as the government made the maximum speed 35." He went on, "The real reason they tell me for the speed limit is to conserve tires. The Japs have cut off our rubber supplies from Southeast Asia." He changed the subject, "Sonny, you sure have a pretty young lady for your girlfriend." Woody put his arm out the window and glanced at the corn in the fields now almost knee-high, "Yes she sure is a wonderful gal, but I'm afraid she's taken though by a Navy guy overseas now." He nudged Woody, "Well as they say out of sight out of mind." That thought had crossed Woody's mind many times. "Well you don't know Molly. I think she may have written the song don't sit under the apple tree with anyone else but me till I come marching home." He added, "She's really in love with him I'm afraid."

The truck slowed as he drove in the gate to the farmer's field. "What kind of plane is that?" he asked. Woody replied, "It is a Piper Cub J3, the plane used for training pilots to learn to fly. It has a four-cylinder opposed air-cooled engine and can cruise at 75 miles an hour. It is fun to fly. I would take you for a spin, but I'm going to need every foot of grass to take off in."

"I don't mind; you've got to get back to the airport and that pretty girl." Woody filled the tank with ten gallons of aviation gas and checked over the landing gear. He said, "All's well" to the old man. They shook hands and Woody got in, put up the door and fastened his seat belt. He yelled, "Thanks again for all your help …I'll be careful and not tear down your fence." He laughed. Woody pressed the switch and the engine came to life. He revved it up, released the foot brake and taxied down to the end of the hay field. Then with the throttle wide open the plane raced along the field skimming over the fence at the far end. He waved goodbye to the old man and headed west to Oxford.

Molly sat at her desk in her new room and inserted a paper in the new Royal Portable Typewriter her parents had given her for graduation. Molly thought of what a blessing learning typing had become. She learned to type as a junior in high school. Her classmates were all girls, aiming at secretarial work after graduation. They learned to touch-type by using typewriters with all blank keys. She began typing a letter to Rob telling him of the wonderful time she had with Woody trying to learn how to drive and even taking the controls of the little Piper airplane over to Middletown. She mentioned that her friend, a colleague from *The Miami Student*, had given her the ride. She didn't tell him he ran out of gas while they were flying. "He likes me a lot, but don't worry darling, I'm still in love with you and besides Woody is leaving in a few days for flight training at Pensacola Florida." She continued, "I like my new job as a reporter for *The Oxford Press* very much. They are keeping me very busy writing stories about the military in our area. I'm enclosing a copy of an article I wrote about 650 V12 sailors and Marines about to arrive on campus for 18 months of training, 400 to be commissioned upon completion in the Navy and 250 in the Marines." Alongside the article was another she wrote about the Black Condor's visit to Oxford.

Colonel John C. Robinson, Negro aviator, flew the Emperor of Ethiopia out of the country during the Italian invasion of his country in the thirties. Colonel Robinson worked in Chicago for the Curtis –Wright Aeronautical Company and went to Ethiopia to introduce them to American made aircraft. While in that country, he received a commission as a Colonel in the Ethiopian Air Force. He flew missions in Ethiopia carrying medicine and information to the troops and was shot down three times. Coming home, New York and Chicago honored him as a hero. He now works for the U.S. Army Air Force. And Rob you won't believe this, the house down the Street from your mother is being rented for $40 per month. Of course, it's a very nice large place but think of it, $40 a month!

"Rob, there's an article in this week's paper about Dr. Wolford leaving. I am not sure how the Geology Department is going to survive. Your dad is in Washington; Dr. Wade is in the service, now Dr. Wolford is leaving to become a first lieutenant in the Army air corps. Rob, WLW Radio just made an announcement on their news broadcast that Congress has just passed a mandatory withholding tax by employers, so they will have to withhold 20 percent over what is exempt from all wages and salaries. My paycheck will be reduced before I get my first one! I'm wondering now if I can pay the rent here but don't worry about me, as the song says, 'I'll get by as long as I have you!' Love and kisses always. Your sweetheart, still waiting for you, Molly. Our Love is Here to Stay!

P.s. I can still buy a Coke for a nickel! But it's still six ounces.... Pepsi is twelve full ounces for a nickel.

I like their jingle I hear on the radio:

Pepsi Cola hits the spot, twelve full ounces, that's a lot. Twice as much for your nickel too, Pepsi is the drink for you!"

CHAPTER 49

The Visit

Across town, Mary Catherine Walker sat on the front porch of her home on Spring Street. It was a hot summer day; she had her handyman put a black oscillating fan on the large front porch by the swing to try to keep cool. She had a portable radio that her husband had given her for Christmas beside her. Powered by a large dry cell battery, it seemed to her that it weighed a ton. She generally kept it tuned to WLW, 700 on the radio dial, so that she could hear the latest news and the broadcasts of the Cincinnati Reds games. Mary Catherine loved baseball. As a young girl, she often joined her father at the Reds' games at Crosley field near Union Terminal. They had front row seats over the third base side of the infield. Once a hard line-drive foul ball came right at her; fortunately, her dad caught it. The souvenir still shared a prominent place in her kitchen. Her favorite Reds announcer was Wait Hoyt, a former big-league pitcher, who began his career at the age of 15 with a contract from the New York Giants. He later became a New York Yankee, and in his first season with them won 19 games and pitched three complete games in the World Series without giving up an earned run. Wait broadcast the Reds home games as well as the ones on the road. He even did the away games in the WLW studios by receiving the play by play from Western Union Teletype. Between pitches he would make up the action on the field. During rain delays, he would tell stories of his baseball career with Babe Ruth and other major leaguers. Mary Catherine often wanted to correct his grammar. He would say, "There was the pitch." He used the past tense so often that the radio audience did not mind it at all.

The paperboy, delivering *The Oxford Press,* came down the street riding his Huffy bicycle. He stopped in front of the Walker's home and instead of throwing the paper on the walk, as was his custom, seeing Mrs. Walker sitting on the porch, he got off and brought the paper to Mrs. Walker. "Here's your paper Mrs. Walker, hot off the press, who's winning the game?" Mrs. Walker replied, "Listen to this sonny. Hamilton High School's baseball star is playing his first game for the Reds. He's not doing too well." They both sat listening to the historic game.

A young lad from Hamilton by the name of Joe Nuxhall, only 15 years old, was pitching for the Cincinnati Reds in his first major league game. Due to a shortage of players in wartime, the young lefthander pitched one inning, becoming the youngest pitcher in the major leagues. Joe had a rough day. The Reds were playing the first place St. Louis Cardinals. He retired the first batter but then he walked five, had one wild pitch, gave up two hits, and five runs scored.

Mrs. Walker said, "Well he at least gave it a good try sonny." The young boy nodded in agreement but seemed more interested in the new portable radio than in the game itself. With his canvas newspaper bag slung over his shoulder, baseball cap tilted up, and his freckled face staring intently at the radio dial, he looked like a living Norman Rockwell painting.

When young Nuxhall was relieved, Mrs. Walker thought that at least the Reds were staying with males. She disliked Philip Wrigley of the Chicago Cubs, who was starting an all-female professional league due to the lack of male athletes. Somehow, the Rockford Peaches playing the Racine Belles did not fit in her world of baseball. Mercifully, the Reds' game ended.

She turned off the radio just as a light blue Chrysler sedan pulled up in front of her home. A man got out and bounded up the wide worn steps of the porch, "Mrs. Walker, do you remember me? I'm Woody, the reporter for *The Miami Student*, Molly's friend." Woody was dressed in khaki pants and a red Miami athletics tee shirt. His white tennis shoes were well worn. Mary Catherine stared at him for a moment and said, "Of course I do. You gave me a lift to the gas station recently."

"I'm leaving in a few days for Pensacola to enter flight training for the Marines."

"Well, I hope you become a better pilot than a few days ago. I hear you ran out of gas while on a joy ride the other day, using up valuable resources for the war effort!" Woody blushed and said, "Boy word gets around fast; yes ma'am, and I learned a valuable lesson that is for sure. Anyway, Molly asked me to drop off a book you wanted, and I wanted to say goodbye. I hope you and your family are going to be ok and this war will be over soon." Mrs. Walker sensed a real sincere attitude behind his words. "Thanks, we are going to be alright." She offered him a seat in the white wicker chair by the swing. Two huge potted geranium plants along the porch railing were wilting under the hot sun. She fanned herself and said, "It's too damned hot; the porch is the coolest place in the house. Can I offer you some iced tea?" Woody gladly accepted and waited on the porch while she brought out a pitcher from the kitchen. He was eyeing the beautiful portable radio. He turned it on hearing Wait Hoyt winding up the broadcast of the game that the Reds lost to the Cardinals. Mary Catherine poured two glasses of sweet tea and they sat listening to Wait. "He's a great announcer Mrs. Walker, and I think the young pitcher from Hamilton will become a major league star someday."

"I hope so they need him, and a lot more like him. I'm disgusted with the Cubs trying to have females play professional ball."

"Me too. I'm the sports editor or was I should say, of *The Miami Student*, and I see no future for women in athletics especially baseball."

"I agree. Now tell me about yourself. May I call you Woody?"

"Sure." "Well there isn't much to tell. I'm from Cleveland. My dad is an attorney and my mother is a volunteer for charities and the war effort. I like sports, flying, and the Marines. I am going to be a good pilot."

"I hope you will Woody, but I think there is something else you like. Tell me about your friendship with Molly." He was surprised by her directness. Woody took a long sip of tea and nearly choked. "Well, we are just friends." She paused and gave him a penetrating look, "Woody, my woman's intuition tells me you regard her as more than just a friend. Am I wrong?" Woody felt like this attractive but stern lady was seeing inside of him. He looked away for a moment, then took another sip of tea, "No, ma'am your right. I must confess I am in love with her, but I'm afraid she doesn't love me. She is head over heels in love with your son Rob. I wish she weren't, but I respect her for that."

"I understand. She is a beautiful and talented girl. Rob loves her deeply and is waiting for her."

"She tells me a lot about Rob. She constantly worries about him. I know he's in a very dangerous branch of the service."

"Woody, I tried and tried to convince him to go into naval intelligence, but he wanted combat."

"Well I am certain he is getting it." He realized he should not have said that. Mrs. Walker did not say anything for a long time. She took a Kleenex and wiped her forehead.

"I hope I didn't upset you ma'am."

"No, it's OK."

Woody put his glass on the tray and thanked her for the tea. "I will be leaving for Pensacola in a few days. I'm going home to see my folks first and then on to the Marines." Mrs. Walker said, "I'll be praying for you Woody. You're going into a dangerous branch of the service too."

"Thanks Mrs. Walker, I appreciate that. I'll try to keep in touch with you if possible. Goodbye."

"Goodbye Woody and God bless you."

Woody started down the steps and paused, "Oh, I almost forgot the book!"

He ran to the car and brought her the book Molly asked him to give Mrs. Walker; she thanked him and as he drove off, she opened the new book she was anxious to read, Ayn Rand's *The Fountain Head*, just published in April 1943.

CHAPTER 50

The Rescue

Captain Morrison, Jerry, the exec and navigator, and Peter the engineer, conferred and decided they would have enough fuel to last to Darwin. It would be close and might limit chasing enemy ships that might be encountered on the way. Upon arrival at the rendezvous, Rob would lead the shore party assisted by his leading petty officer, Grabowski. Both had training in boarding parties at Pearl Harbor.

En route, Rob had a chance to write some letters, first to Molly, then Lilly and his folks. Rob told them how much he liked his officers and men. What a great 'band of brothers' they had become; however, he did not mention the loss of the exec and gunner's mate on the last patrol. He was still the cribbage champion of the wardroom, was reading his Bible almost every day, and enjoyed the companionship of his room-mate, John, 'the Baptist' as he affectionately called him. He told Molly, *"You know he makes me think. I stand watch at night on the bridge and look up at thousands of stars and can't believe that this was the result of just a chance explosion of matter. Somebody up there is a very good architect."* He went on to tell them of achieving his coveted Dolphins signifying he was qualified in submarines, and that he would be promoted soon to lieutenant junior grade.

Mindanao lay some one thousand nautical miles west of Palau. The rendezvous would be in four days if everything went as planned. Rob and his Buccaneers, as they were called, began planning the evacuation. Some valuable information was provided by several patrol reports of the submarine *Trout* commanded by a classmate of Captain Morrison. Earlier in the year, *Trout* landed Lieutenant Commander Charles Parsons, USNR, in southern Mindanao. He had lived in the Philippines before the war and was very familiar with Mindanao. He served as a coordinator with the remnants of the US Army and the Filipino guerillas. Commander Parsons' reports identified enemy garrisons, strengths and ways to avoid contact with their patrols. Rob and Jerry sat in the wardroom looking at the chart of the southwest coast of Mindanao and planning the arrangements for the pickup. A message had been received hours earlier giving instructions about the rendezvous point, signals to be used and the timing of the contacts. But added the ominous words that the Aussie coast watcher, a major in the

Royal Australian Army Reserve, had contracted malaria. The pharmacist was notified to review the medical books on the treatment of this tropical disease. Jerry was concerned about the shallow water at the pickup point, and word had been received that a Japanese submarine had been sighted recently off the southern coast. Rob suggested a simple plan: there would only be two in the landing party, himself and Grabowski. They would get ashore, find their man while *Thornfish* would stay offshore submerged and surface before daybreak to retrieve the men. They would arm themselves with 45 pistols, and two Browning Submachine Guns and hand grenades. Each man would have a Bowie style long knife strapped to their legs. Emergency flares would be enclosed in waterproof containers in the rubber boat along with a first aid kit. A new device was added: an SCR 300 Walkie-Talkie. It could transmit and receive voice communications within a one-mile range. If the radio failed to operate, they would use their signal light. If the Aussie could not be located, they would return to the boat and try the following night again.

After the four-day transit to the rendezvous area off the south coast of Mindanao, the captain conned the submarine into the lagoon as far as possible using the propulsion by the battery to avoid making any sound. He ordered a complete blow of water from all ballast tanks to decrease their draft in the shallow waters. It was midnight and a new moon, which added to their invisibility. Rob and his companion dressed in black, made last minute checks of their equipment while the men on the bridge looked for the anticipated signal from the shore. After a half hour Captain Morrison called Rob to the bridge. There were no recognition signals from the beach. Jerry and the captain were concerned that it might be a trap. Rob said, "Captain, we've come a long way to rescue the sick Aussie, I'd like to go ashore and look for him. He might be unable to come down to the beach." The Captain said, "Jerry, what do you think?" The XO said, "We've got five hours before daybreak. Let's give Rob three hours to scout around for him. He can let us know by the walkie-talkie." The captain voiced his concern once again, "The range of the radio is only about a mile, we have to get further out, and may not be able to communicate with them." Captain paused thinking it through and made the decision. "OK it's a go. We will back out and stay offshore and come back in at 0400. Synchronize your watches. Shove off when you are ready. Good hunting."

Rob and Grabowski climbed in the rubber boat and Rob made a final radio check with the bridge, "I hear you loud and clear, Roger out." They started paddling in toward the beach, carefully gliding through the breakers that almost overturned them. The narrow beach was nearly covered over by the jungle. Rob wished that they had brought a machete, but it was too late. They tied the little black inflatable boat to a mangrove tree and started down the beach toward a ridge of ancient rocks or coral. Rob figured that the Aussie would have gone to the highest point to be seen. When the two men reached the pinnacle, they stopped suddenly. They heard voices in the distance. Rob whispered, "We've got company." Japanese were yelling "Talk, Talk!" Rob and his big petty officer started through the thick jungle towards the sounds echoing through the brush. They threaded their way into the dark maze climbing over vines that seemed like snakes hanging from trees and swamps that held unknown squirrely things, and startled birds that flew in their faces. It took a half hour to reach where the screaming was coming from. The Japs had discovered the coast watcher's secluded camp. There, in the dim light of a campfire, was the emaciated coast watcher bound to a tree with two enemy soldiers taking turns beating the helpless Aussie. Two other soldiers were sitting on a log, casually smoking cigarettes guarding three other prisoners huddled together bound in a sitting position watching the torture. Their weapons were beside them near the small campfire.

Rob peering through the long grass at the edge of the clearing whispered to his companion, "Grab, we've got to rescue this guy. I don't want to start a firefight here unless we must, there may be other patrols in the area. I've got an idea. You circle behind the guys on the log, when you're in position, I'll jump out and order them to surrender. If they make any effort to resist, use your knife. They each pulled the slide back on their 45's and chambered a round just in case. When Grabowski was ready, he emerged from the trees and Rob jumped out in the clearing shining a flashlight in his face and screaming in Japanese, "Stop, surrender, you are surrounded!" The eerie light on his face and loud commanding words completely shook the shit out of the confused enemy. One of the soldiers sitting on the log jumped up and went for his gun only to be dispatched with one blow of Grabowski's knife. Rob ordered the remaining nips to sit and using the rope from the Aussie started to tie them up. Suddenly one of the Japs pulled a pistol and fired at Rob. It missed him by inches, and Rob returned his fire and killed him. Grabowski used his gun and killed the remaining two men who had tortured the Australian. In less than a minute it was all over. The coast watcher said, "Thanks, Mate, I wouldn't have lasted much longer. Have you met the Bishop?" With those words, he collapsed.

Rob was stunned. The three other prisoners were a Catholic Bishop and two nuns. In broken English, the man explained that he was the island's Bishop and had been imprisoned for months by the Japanese. He and two of his nuns were set free by Filipino guerrillas two days ago. They were brought to the coast watcher's camp by the guerrillas only to be left there. The coast watcher said they might get a ride with the Americans. Unfortunately, a Japanese patrol found them hiding in the jungle.

Rob asked them, "Can you all walk now? We've got to get to the beach right away!" He was worried that enemy soldiers would hear the gunfire. The small elderly cleric said, "Yes, we able to walk. I show you path to the water, faster, better than jungle."

Rob was anxious to get to the inflatable boat and radio the sub when it surfaced before 0400. Timing would be close he thought. The Bishop showed the way down the hills to the water. Rob was in the lead, followed by the Bishop and his two frightened nuns. Grabowski carrying the coast watcher on his back, brought up the rear. Traversing the steep slope with his strange entourage seemed like an eternity to Rob. The nuns fell several times slowing the group to a halt. The flashlight was used sparingly to avoid detection. Before reaching the beach, they had to cross a marshy area wading through water up to their knees. Grabowski had to stop several times to rest. But the group finally made it to the water's edge. They put the Aussie down, and Grabowski administered first aid, while Rob untied the boat and dragged it to where the brave man lay. "He's beaten up pretty bad sir," Grabowski said in a low voice. "Don't know if he is going to make it." Rob and his leading petty officer gently laid him in the boat.

Rob got on the walkie-talkie. "Lollypop, this is Buccaneer over."

"This is Lollypop, come in Buccaneer." They used L's as they are difficult for Japs to pronounce.

We've had a little skirmish with a Jap patrol; we have our man, but he is in bad shape. Please have the pharmacist mate standing by to receive him in the wardroom first aid station."

"Roger, WILCO."

Rob added, "And one other thing; we have some company, a Bishop and two nuns. Over"

There was silence on the other end.

"Repeat, say again Buccaneer!"

"Yes sir, three others: an elderly Catholic Bishop and two nuns who have been imprisoned by the Japs and were just freed by friendly guerrillas."

"Ah…. OK, how do you propose to get them aboard?"

Rob replied, "We'll have to make two trips. Grabowski is taking the first load with the Aussie and the Bishop and I'll remain on the beach with the two ladies, until he returns for us."

"Roger, understood." The exec got on the SC300. "Rob this is Jerry, we don't have much time before dawn. Can you possibly fit everyone in the boat and get out here?" Rob thought about it. The girls were small, the problem was the unconscious Australian. It could be done but it was risky. "OK sir, I'll try, the problem is getting through the surf without capsizing." Jerry said, I know you two can do it. And have the Bishop say a prayer, a strong one. We'll have some grog waiting for you." Then he added, "I'm signaling with my light. Do you see it?" "Affirmative, sir. Thanks for the aid to navigation." Rob had the two nuns sit in the bottom with the Aussie on their laps. The old priest was in the stern with Rob and big Grabowski manned the bow.

The two sailors stood in the water and launched their tiny craft into the increasing surf. They jumped in and began to pump their paddle strokes deep and hard. As they left the lagoon, a giant dark wave rolled over them, nearly overturning their rubber dingy. It was only by the extraordinary strength of the two men that enabled them to stay upright. Guided by the signal lamp flashing for two seconds every minute from the *Thornfish*, the Buccaneers reached the welcoming sailors. Strong arms helped the Aussie first and then the guests and finally the two heroes of the night's action down the hatch to the air-conditioned interior of the American submarine. Before their equipment had been stowed, Rob felt the diesel engines roar to life underway for Darwin. On the bridge, Jerry took the conn and backed out of the shallow lagoon into the blackness of the channel leading to the open Philippine Sea.

The pharmacist mate began working on the Aussie coast watcher. The captain stood in the doorway and said, "This is a brave man. "The doc said, "Yes sir, the Japs worked him over a lot. May have some broken ribs, dislocated shoulder, some broken teeth and a smashed nose. But Ensign Walker said he didn't give away our rendezvous." He administered some morphine. "I'll need some help getting the clothes off him. Which reminds me sir, please have the guests stripped and clothes shit canned. They may have lice and I don't know what all. I'll look at them after I get the Aussie fixed up a bit." Captain Morrison thought this might be a little tricky with the nuns.

John came in to help the doc. He gently removed the Aussie's filthy clothes, took a bowl and washed the blood off, cleansed his wounds and saw the patient's chest moving. He prayed out loud for healing, "Lord, I am reminding you that your word says *By Your Stripes, Jesus, we are healed*." Doc took his blood pressure again and said it was coming up. "Hang in there Mate," the doc whispered to the prone man on the wardroom table, now a first aid station.

The trip from Mindanao to Darwin took a week. The two nuns did not speak English but enjoyed the food and even their new Navy clothes. The old priest led daily prayers on the intercom and had a Sunday mass and sermon about forgiving and loving our enemies. After all he had been through himself, his message had authenticity and was well received by those who heard it. John really liked it; he wondered what Rob thought of it. One evening before going on watch they were both in their small stateroom and Rob was at the desk trying to write a letter that could be mailed in Darwin. John climbed in his upper bunk and leaned over and said, "Rob what did you think of the padre's message about forgiveness?" The tall lanky ensign got up and stretched, "I don't know John, and I don't know how he could do it. The pharmacist mate told me about the terrible marks on his body from flogging by the Japs. He has several teeth missing too. You have to hand it to him though, he's a real tough man." John remarked "Yes, he is. I liken him to the Apostle Paul. He was flogged many times, beaten, imprisoned, stoned, shipwrecked, hurt by his enemies and his brother Jews. Yet he could write: "Don't avenge yourself for vengeance is the Lord's. Be not overcome with evil but overcome evil with good." Rob sighed, "I admire those that can do this John, but I'm human, hell, John, I just killed a man and Grabowski killed three in our firefight with the Japs that were torturing our Aussie soldier. I killed that guy on the trawler who killed our men. Was I just to stand there and let them kill us?"

John thought before answering his friend, "Rob, we're all in the same boat, no pun intended, because we are in a war of survival of our country, and for people of honor and goodwill. Think about all the ships we have sunk and the men that have gone down with them. I know that God will understand on the final day when we stand before him, that we were defending ourselves and our loved ones."

Rob said, "I sure hope so."

There were no enemy contacts during the trip to Darwin. Rob was the officer of the deck as *Thornfish* neared the secure harbor of Darwin. On the bridge, standing alongside the captain and the exec, Bishop Masagi stood proudly as the crew exchanged customary honors with the senior ship, the USS *Holland*. The submarine tender had been stationed at Darwin since early in the war. They had received permission to come alongside the tender to receive the wounded major and his companions, assist in some minor repairs, and provide some provisions and mail from home. Movies would be exchanged with them as well. The Bishop, dressed in his new dungarees and Navy baseball cap, bade farewell to the crew. He and the nuns dressed in their newly acquired habits of dungarees and chambray shirts climbed the ladder to the ship and were directed to the quarterdeck where they would be assigned further transportation to their new parish in Perth, Australia. The Navy doctor from the *Holland* came aboard the submarine to examine the wounded Aussie. He was afraid that the coast watcher might have TB in addition to malaria. They both emerged later and the captain, exec along with Rob and Grabowski, shook his hand and all men topside rendered a salute to the courageous man as he hobbled up the ladder to the waiting medical team. Pete was busy overseeing the refueling operation from the barge alongside. They had consumed nearly all available diesel fuel. If they had had to be at sea one more day, they would have run out completely and would have had to come in on battery power alone.

Darwin was a crummy port for submariners just coming off patrol. There was absolutely nothing to do. The temperature was 110 degrees F. when they arrived. The town looked like something out of the Wild West. Stores were boarded up. Townspeople had evacuated in fear of a Japanese invasion. The port was in the range of Japanese bombers flying out of Java, or Timor. The old non-airconditioned S-boats operating out of Darwin found the heat extremely difficult to tolerate. Freemantle over nineteen hundred miles south, however, was considered a submariner's paradise. Fortunately for the men of the *Thornfish*, their stay in Darwin would be brief.

Later the captain and exec went aboard the *Holland* and were directed to the captain's quarters for Captain Morrison to pay his respects to the captain of the *Holland* and review some of *Thornfish's* patrol just completed.

Later in the evening, dinner was served in the hut loaned to the Navy by the local Salvation Army. The wags called it the Salvation Hut. Overhead circulating fans and open louvered shutters allowed what cool breeze there was to make the evening more pleasant. It was John's wetting down party. Drinks were on him for all the wardroom officers in celebration of his being promoted to Lieutenant Junior Grade. Jerry proposed a toast to the newest LTJG. "Gentlemen, to John Young, Lieutenant Junior Grade, United States Navy Reserve, for his outstanding service to our ship, the United States Navy, our great nation, and our Lord." Brown bottles of Pabst Blue Ribbon Beer clinked, and the men shouted to John, "Cheers!"

The wetting down party ended early. Everyone was exhausted. Rob and John were the last to leave. John paid the bill. They said little as they made their way to the quarterdeck of the *Holland*. As they came aboard on the officers' gangway, they, saluted the officer of the deck, saying "Request permission to cross over to the *Thornfish* sir." The OOD replied, "Permission granted." They went through the passageway to the ladder going down to their air-conditioned submarine and a welcomed relief from the heat and humidity.

A stack of mail awaited them both. There were three from his mother and one from his father, but none from Lily. He was beginning to worry about her. There were lots of letters from Molly though. Rob eagerly sorted the mail by postmark starting with the latest one. He opened the letter from Molly first and found two new photos of her. One was her graduation picture from college and the other a new picture of her in a bathing suit taken at the Oxford swimming pool. She was in a not so modest two-piece white bathing suit that showed every curve. She was more beautiful than ever. She had signed it *with all my Love, Molly*. Rob wondered who took the picture. Maybe it was that guy Woody. She said it was beastly hot. She saw his mother often and his father once in a great while. He was still working in Washington and came home when he could get transportation. Her letters were full of news from Oxford. She had written an article for *The Press* about Mrs. Ruth Lawrence finally receiving her son William Lawrence's Purple Heart a year and a half after he was killed when the USS *Arizona* was blown up during the attack on Pearl Harbor. A branch of the National Association for the Advancement of Colored People had been organized in Oxford. The first meeting was held May 20, 1943, at the Bethel AME church with colored and whites invited. The article said that, "A few people have referred to its promoters as agitators, and troublemakers." It was noted that a colored recreation center was being considered by the city council. Governor John W. Bricker came to Miami in July 1943, to lay the cornerstone for the Miami Airfield Hanger named in memory of Ensign William Lawrence. Mrs. Ruth Lawrence, Ensign Lawrence's mother, helped lay the cornerstone. The governor gave the commencement address at the mid-summer graduating class and later the governor reviewed the Navy radio trainees at Cook Field.

"You'll be interested in this Rob," she wrote. "Two Japanese boys are to study here this fall. They will be enrolled at McGuffey School this year having been sent from Topaz, Utah, where they with other Japanese were interned following the Declaration of War with Japan. The two brothers are from a family whose father had been in America for 35 years and their mother 25 years. Under the War Relocation Authority, the Japanese who are interned are being classified. Those found loyal to the United States will be sent to relocation centers from which they may be released to work or may be granted indefinite leave.

Another letter told Rob of the village's participation in an all-Ohio blackout to be observed from 8:30 to 9 pm on Thursday evening April 8. And in April the subscription rates for the weekly *Oxford Press* will be advanced from $1.50 a year to $2.00. Molly wrote,

> *"Maybe Rob, they will now be able to hire me full time. Ha! By the way I hope you don't mind, but I went to see a movie last weekend at the Miami Western with Woody. They had a showing of Casablanca starring Humphrey Bogart and Ingrid Bergman. I saw it before and loved it just as much the second time. Woody leaves soon to join the Marines. He's going to be a pilot. So, don't you worry, like the song says, 'I'm saving my love for you.' And I'm still wearing your fraternity pin even though graduation is just around the corner. With adoring love, Molly.... xoxoxo. p.s. The Marines have landed. Yes, 35 women enlisted Marines arrived last Thursday for training in code and typing in a new contingent of 100 females including 35 WAVES and 30 SPARS. They'll be here for four months and reside in East Hall."*

WAVES in radio training. Photo by Gilson Wright

Oxford's Honor Board circa 1944. Photo by Gilson Wright

WAVES marching. Photo by Gilson Wright

Sailors marching past the Beta Bells to reviewing field.
Photo by Gilson Wright

CHAPTER 51

The Way to Freemantle

The *Thornfish* was ready to depart Darwin en route to Freemantle. The exec reported to the captain that all hands were aboard, and they were ready for sea. Lines tying them to the *Holland* were taken in and the exec maneuvered the boat smartly away from its host. Jerry became an excellent ship handler and Captain Morrison believed he would one day command his own submarine becoming one of the few reservists awarded command.

The crew, not on watch, assembled on the deck as they made their way through the beautiful natural harbor. It was a gorgeous day. Not a cloud in the sky. As they made their way out of the channel, Ensign Wright, the first lieutenant, accompanied by the chief of the boat, walked from stem to stern checking all equipment to ensure that nothing was left topside that shouldn't be there. At the harbor entrance all hands, except the bridge watch, went below. Once out of the channel Jerry turned the conn over to the OOD. Hatches were secured and ready to dive. Air search and surface radars were working perfectly sending out the pulses of energy that would give warnings of any enemy, surface or air. The major threat would be enemy submarines lurking in the depths watching for departing ships. Rob was in the forward torpedo room with his division checking the storage of some new Mark-18 electric torpedoes. Torpedoes were still in short supply. Over two hundred Mark-14 torpedoes were left in storage racks at the naval base at Cavite in the Philippines after the Americans surrendered in early 1942. In the control room, Pete, the engineering officer, went over his compensation forms once again, rechecking his figures for weights of fuel, water, personnel, ammo, torpedoes and condition of all tanks, to ensure an accurate trim dive, the first dive of the day.

Prior to getting underway the exec and his quartermaster had spread the charts of the southwestern coasts of Australia out on the wardroom table. They laid out the track for the next leg of their trip to Freemantle. The navigator estimated that the total distance from Darwin to their destination was 1900 nautical miles. They carefully plotted the submarine safe passage corridor from Darwin to Freemantle. A ten-mile wide swath of ocean off the Australian coast was set aside as a zone in which no allied planes were to attack submarines. The captain reviewed the track and approved it, saying "we still have to be very careful. When those plane jockeys see a sub, they attack. Jerry, I want you to put the largest American flag we have on board on the staff at the cigarette deck while we are surfaced. And make sure that we have green flares on the bridge to signal any numb nuts flying those planes. We need to maximize surface time to get to Freemantle as soon as possible. Have you sent out a message with our estimated time of arrival yet?" Jerry replied, "No sir, I wanted to wait till you approved our plan. If we can remain on the surface most of the time my estimated time of arrival is about 1700 off the entrance buoy, in six days using standard speed on three engines." The captain was satisfied. "Make it so Jerry." As he started to leave, he said, "Do we have a movie tonight? "Jerry answered, "We do sir, and it's a good one, Ronald Reagan in *Desperate Journey*, a spy film behind enemy lines in Germany! Tomorrow night we have a Disney movie, *Bambi.*"

Rob had the afternoon watch underway and at 1600 turned the duties of officer of the deck to John. Ensign Kennedy stood his watch with John as his junior officer of the deck. Rob went below and washed his face in the stainless-steel wash basin in the stateroom he shared with John. He had just sat down at his desk when the captain knocked at the entrance guarded by a curtain. "You up to a game Rob?" Dick loved cribbage as much as Rob. He replied, "Sure Sir, I feel lucky today!" It was an invitation he couldn't refuse and a challenge he enjoyed. He dealt and as they spread their cards, the captain said, "Rob you did a great job back there rescuing the Aussie and his companions. I'm recommending you and Grabowski for the Silver Star." Rob studied his cards, "Thank you sir. We were just doing our job. We couldn't have done it without the help of our shipmates." As he folded his cards the captain said, "Well you did a marvelous job. Keep up the good work." Over the next hour, Rob won two out of three boards. The steward came in and asked permission to set the table for dinner. The captain looked up to give him permission when the sub was rocked by two explosions. The word Dive, Dive was shouted over the I MC announcing system. The captain jumped up from the table spilling cards and ran to the control room. John and his JO were coming down the ladder to the control room with the lookouts who immediately manned the diving planes. "What the hell is going on John? Get us down deep now!" John was breathless, pale as a ghost. "B-24 sir came in out of the sun at 200 feet and crossed our bow from starboard to port. We saw him too late. I fired two green flares, but he dropped two bombs. Fortunately, he missed by a mile." Captain Morrison ordered the firing of a red flare as the boat descended to the ordered depth of 200 feet. The emergency red flares work only above depths of 250 feet. They are fired from a tube in the after-torpedo room and emerge at the surface indicating a submarine in distress. As the pilot of the Liberator bomber was turning to make another run, he saw the flares and turned back to his base. Rob never saw the captain so angry. After a half an hour the *Thornfish* returned to the surface as the sun was setting in the Indian Ocean. He sent off a blistering message to headquarters in Freemantle reporting the incident in no uncertain words. *Thornfish* was in the center of the sub safe passage zone. After things calmed down the captain returned to the bridge and spoke with the watch. Now composed, he asked the OOD, "John, can you explain how the Liberator could drop two bombs before the diving alarm was sounded. Were you all asleep up there?" John said, "I'm sorry sir, it's my fault. He, the bomber, came in out of the sun close to the surface. The radar didn't pick him up and the lookouts simply didn't see it in time."

The entire watch knew the consequences of their inaction. Survival in peacetime and more so in wartime on a submarine depends on every man doing his job one hundred percent of the time. Captain Morrison told John "I am going to assign two additional lookouts whenever we are surfaced until we reach Freemantle." John replied. "Yes, sir." John felt terrible. He had screwed up, but he determined that it would never happen again.

Down below in the control room, Rob felt for John. He was going through the same thing he had experienced on his first watch with Captain Custer. It was déjà vu again. But with Captain Morrison, a mistake like this would be a learning experience not punishment.

· · · · ·

Thornfish missed its ETA in Freemantle. The episode with the American Army Airforce Liberator bomber and two more later had slowed their speed of advance. They arrived outside of the entrance to Freemantle's harbor as the sun was setting behind low slung clouds over the Indian Ocean. Submarine nets were strung over the mouth of the harbor each night at sunset to prevent enemy submarines from entering the busy port. The harbormaster would not open the nets under any circumstances despite urgent pleas from Captain Morrison. They had to wait all night. Dick was worried. Waiting for the nets to be removed at dawn, while silhouetted by the city's lights, would make them a perfect target for a Jap sub. Fortunately, two Navy destroyers returning from antisubmarine patrol were caught in the same predicament and anchored between the *Thornfish* and the channel to the open sea giving them some protection.

The *Thornfish*'s crew was disappointed. Freemantle was becoming famous for liberty, but liberty would have to wait another night. Many on board were suffering from what the old-timers called 'channel fever,' that is longing for female companionship after being on patrol for nearly 60 days. The exec had Rob and the other junior officers seated at the wardroom table reading the crew's letters before they were mailed to ensure that no classified information was sent home.

Jerry received a message from the headquarters staff on base that the admiral would be on hand when they tied up on the pier in the morning. He had the crew 'turn to.' Compartments were cleaned once again; laundry done; showers taken. Men shaved off beards and trimmed mustaches. By 2200 the exec and the chief of the boat made a quick tour through the boat and found things shipshape. The next morning the boat moved down the channel past the submarine nets. The base was huge. Cranes capable of moving heavy equipment moved slowly back and forth loading supplies from merchant ships; dry docks held damaged ships in need of repair. The harbor was a beehive of activity at eight o'clock in the morning. Dick and his exec dressed in fresh khakis were on the bridge as Ensign Kennedy conned the boat alongside pier 2A at the sub base. The signalmen had made small pennants marking the number of Jap ships sunk on this patrol and strung them from the periscope shears to the railing on the cigarette deck. The Commander of Submarines Southwest Pacific was already on the pier as the gangway was placed from the pier to the sub's superstructure. The admiral was the first on board. Ralph Waldo Christie, Naval Academy class of 1915, had his first submarine command in World War One. He knew submarines and torpedoes. A graduate of the Massachusetts Institute of Technology, he was assigned to the top-secret development of the Mark 6 magnetic imploder and as recently as 1938 had been assigned as Officer-in-Charge, Torpedo Section, in the Bureau of Ordnance. Christie had convinced Admiral King, the Commander in Chief of the Navy, to increase the number of submarines based in Freemantle from twelve, to twenty-two. *Thornfish* was one of them.

The crusty two-star saluted the colors and then the officer of the deck and greeted the captain. Dick saluted smartly and said, "Welcome aboard, admiral." The admiral returned his salute and said, "Thanks Dick, and congratulations on a fine patrol." Looking up at the pennants celebrating the sinking of Jap ships, he started counting them and gave the crew thumbs up. Turning to the captain, he said, "How about a cup of Navy coffee?" Dick said, "Yes Sir, it's fresh and hot." He led him below. The wardroom table, covered with the traditional green cloth, had a tray of fresh rolls and cookies from Willie's ovens in the galley. The admiral took one of the cookies and dunked it in the hot cup saying, "the sub service still has the best food and coffee in the Navy." After the pleasantries, Admiral Christie wanted to talk about their patrol, tactics used, enemy capabilities, and the successful rescue of the coast watcher and the bishop and nuns. "Where did you put them up, Dick?" Dick smiled, "Well the two nuns were given one of the officer's rooms and the bishop had a bunk with the exec. The coast watcher was on a bunk in the forward torpedo room where the pharmacist's mate could better take care of him. We had room for him and a couple of our officers to bunk there because we unloaded all of our torpedoes at the Japs." The admiral stirred his coffee before saying, "Which brings me to ask you a question and I want a straight answer." Dick took a long sip of coffee. "I know what you're going to say, sir. It's about the performance of our fish, right?" The admiral looked Dick straight in the eyes, "Yes, on a score of 0 to 10 with ten the best, how would you rate them?" Dick handed him his patrol report, "Well sir, it is in here. But to answer your question, the Mark-18 electrics I'd give a ten, I wish we could get more of them. But the Mark-14's I'd rate a five. For both when armed with magnetic exploders I'd give them a zero. They simply don't work. If it's a large ship, the magnetic mass of the enemy ship is so strong it detonates the torpedo before it reaches the side of the target. Our torpedoes sometimes run deeper than set." The admiral didn't say anything. He drank the last drop of his coffee. Pointing at his coffee cup, "Like the commercial on the radio says, 'good to the last drop.' But I don't like what you're telling me, Dick. I still think a lot of the torpedo problem is poor performance by the captains and execs. And you have proved me right. You did a super job with your ordnance." Dick blushed. "Well, sir I have a confession. We finally disarmed the magnetic features and went with simple contacts, even then, if we hit dead on, they were duds. Only striking at an angle did they perform as they should. We had several that prematured 30 seconds after firing. One ran a circular run and came back on us and only by the grace of God we escaped. It's all in the report." The admiral was visibly upset. His fingers tightened on the handle of his empty cup. His order to the subs under his command was not to disarm the magnetics. He would forgive Dick, coming from another command at Pearl Harbor, but he was still not convinced. He agreed with the assessment of his former department that nothing was wrong with their torpedoes. "Well Dick, we'll see. There's a move on now to do some static tests in Oahu that may help solve the mystery." With that, he rose taking the patrol report under his arm and followed Dick topside.

Freemantle had become one of the favorite ports for U.S submarines, even surpassing Pearl Harbor for many underwater sailors. Midway was spartan; just beer, sand volleyball courts, baseball fields, snack bars, canteens, and an old white frame hotel previously owned by the Pan American Airlines that stopped at Midway for refueling before the war. There were no girls or entertainment. Freemantle, however, had bars, Australian beer, parks, movies, welcoming town folks, and best of all lots of women. One of Australia's largest towns, Perth was only a dozen miles or so away by car or bus. Months earlier there was a real scare for folks living in Southwestern Australia that the Japanese would bomb or try invading the coast. Even the road signs were removed to avoid giving the enemy directions if they invaded.

The populace was relieved when the Yanks came. They welcomed Americans and were especially fond of submariners. Stories were being circulated about how American subs had made risky special missions at Java and other islands rescuing Australian troops who were trapped behind enemy lines. Recently, the USS *Searaven* had rescued thirty-one Australian troops and returned them safely to Freemantle. The crew became the toast of the town.

The weather in this southern hemisphere country was mild, and many thought it reminded them of southern California. Admiral Christie had leased two hotels in the nearby city of Perth for housing returning submariners. Within a day after arriving, subs coming off patrol would turn the repairs over to a relief crew. Credit was given to Admiral Lockwood who, as one of the early commanders of submarines, initiated the relief crew concept so successful for returning submariners in Hawaii. Before his policy, returning submariners sometimes had to sleep in their crowded bunks on their submarines even while round the clock noisy repairs were being made. Commanding officers, in deference to their rank and responsibilities, were provided cottages in the exclusive area of Dalkeith. Another perk for skippers was access to an automobile and driver.

Submarine officers were housed in the hotel, two to a room. Room service included house boys serving breakfast in their rooms, horseback riding, beach parties, swimming and tennis, all supervised by an attractive lady who served as sort of a house mother type and maintained a taut ship. Both hotels had excellent facilities including dining rooms, community rooms, bar and recreational areas. Perth was a great town; some thought it was like a Midwestern city in the US. After the American military began arriving, several nightclubs sprang up offering booze and local entertainment. The new Coconut Grove was one of their favorites. The United Services Organization opened on the east side of town, and the YMCA began having dances on Tuesday, Wednesday, Fridays, and Saturdays providing dance partners and supper. But on Sundays, everything shut down.

Two large rented buses pulled up alongside the pier, and the crew of *Thornfish* embarked on their trip to Perth for R & R. It was Saturday, and everyone was looking forward to a great night of partying. John and Rob sat on the front seat of the bus. "John, what do you want to do while we're here?" Rob asked. John looked at the beautiful scenery passing by them as the bus rolled on, farms, cattle ranches, and said "You know, I'd like to go horseback riding. And I'd like to have a huge steak for dinner." Rob added, "With Foster Beer too?" John, a teetotaler, said, "Yes, even a beer!" When they pulled up in front of the hotel, John the senior officer present, stood on the steps of the wide veranda of the hotel and addressed the men. "OK everyone, give me your attention. We want you to have a good time. A safe time. And one that will reflect well on the United States of America and your ship. So be careful, behave reasonably well, and if you go to the beach tomorrow use plenty of suntan lotion. Or better still stay covered up. After 60 days of no sunshine, you will burn easily in the Aussie sun. One other thing: there's a dance down at the USO here in town tonight. One of America's top bands will be playing, and there is a dance contest. You may want to enter. If you do, win it! Dismissed."

Rob and John checked into their room; a large room with private bath, desk, chairs and a balcony overlooking the beautiful wide Swan River leading to the ocean. As he unpacked, Rob placed a large stack of letters from home. Molly had written ten letters, his mother three, and his father one. Missing was any from Lily. What's wrong Rob thought? He'd write her soon and try to find out if she was all right.

John stretched out on his bed. "Gosh, this is swell Rob, wish we could stay here a month." Rob replied, "Don't get too comfortable, John boy, we going to the USO dance tonight. There's a contest remember? We're going to have fun tonight."

The USO van pulled up in front of the hotel at 7 p.m. Rob and John both were wearing loud Hawaiian shirts not tucked in and their khaki uniform pants. They sat in the front seats as the van pulled away from the hotel. Some of the submariners had already had a little too much to drink. Fortunately, it was a short ride across town to the USO dance pavilion. It had a large dance floor with high ceilings with fans blowing cool air. Tables and chairs surrounded the dance floor and in the small food court off to the side. The USO was famous for its donuts, and there were ample ones of assorted flavors. The USO didn't serve liquor, for which John was particularly grateful. They went over to the canteen to get a sandwich and coffee. There were lots of young women there without partners. They found a table as the band began playing Glen Miller's famous song, *Moonlight Serenade*. The girls from Western Australia were very pretty and athletic, and it didn't take long for both handsome young men to meet some very attractive local girls. As they were about to sit down, a striking beauty came up and asked John to dance. She was nearly as tall as he and had a gorgeous figure. Her beautiful shoulder length blonde hair and fresh sunny smile exuded loveliness without a hint of makeup. John looked at Rob as she grabbed his hand and led him to the dance floor. Rob thought it was a terrific welcome to the land they called 'down under.'

"Do you jitterbug, mate?" an Aussie lass asked Rob as she sat down in John's chair, "If you do, let's dance!" Americans had brought the new dance, many conservatives called crazy dance, to Great Britain as millions of American troops were stationed there, and it became the competition dance in Australia. She was another gorgeous girl, one of many adoring young females that welcomed the U.S. servicemen, especially submariners. She didn't wait for an answer. "I can see from your pale skin that you're a submariner. You'll do then. Come on let's dance." She grabbed Rob's hand and pulled him to his feet. The band was playing *Jukebox Saturday Night*, with a vocal group that sounded just like the Crew Chiefs on the Glenn Miller Album that Lily had given the *Thornfish*. The dance floor was swinging as they moved in the crowd. Rob hadn't jitterbugged since college, but it came naturally to him, and this girl was a terrific dancer.

When the number was over, he was able to catch his breath as the crowd applauded loudly. She said, "I'm Matilda, and you're a bit out of shape my man; we need to get you some exercise. What's your name sailor?" Rob studied her; a brunette with an impetuous face, sparkling blue eyes, high cheekbones and lovely lips. "Well ma'am, my name is Rob...Rob Walker, and I am very pleased to meet you." She frowned, "Please don't call me ma'am, I just turned twenty." Fortunately, the next number, *Deep Purple*, was a slow one and as they danced, she snuggled up to him. "Are you sad Rob?" Rob was a little taken back by her inquiry. "Well, I admit I am a bit. I was thinking of home when you came up and asked me to dance. It was nice of you. You cheered me up." She lifted her face to him, "Well, we Aussie's have to be a little more direct these days. Most of our boys are off fighting in Africa, Europe or captured by the Japs. I hate them. My brother is a prisoner of the dirtbags in Burma. She stopped dancing and looked directly into his eyes. "Rob, why don't we enter the contest tonight? I think we'd have a good chance of winning." Rob taken back again said, "Matilda, we haven't had any time to practice." She replied, "Well nobody else has either!" She led him to the USO table and signed them up. The band struck up another jitterbug tune, *Jeep Jockey Jump*. It was a hit with the crowd too. Rob was getting worn out, but Matilda was just getting warmed up. After serval more numbers, the USO hostess announced the contest and the names of the contestants. When Rob and Matilda's names were read, the band's beautiful singer gasped. She was sure that it was Mary Catherine Walker's son, Rob Walker, the one she said to look up if she ever got to the Pacific. She was a little rattled when it came time for her to sing the lead in the band's rendition of *Speak Low,* a song made famous on the hit parade by Johnny Desmond. Marianne, Miss Indiana, sang the heartfelt rendition to Rob as he danced with his partner for the evening. Before the contest, during intermission, Marianne made her way through the crowd and found Rob just as he was leaving the dance floor. "Rob Walker," she called out shouting at the top of her voice. Rob turned to see the beautiful singer in a blue evening gown coming full speed toward him. "Hi, you don't know me, but I know you. I'm Marianne Baker, a friend of your mother. Could we sit down and talk a bit?" Rob stammered, "You're the singer in the band. How do you know me again?"

"Well, from your mother. You see, she and I once shared a train ride from Cincinnati to Washington, DC, and I couldn't find a room, and she offered me a place to stay for a few days at your uncle's home in Georgetown. I even have your picture! A class photo of you from Miami University."

"My gosh, it's a small, small world!" Matilda was getting visibly uncomfortable with this new intrusion. She excused herself and went to the ladies' room. Rob and Marianne shared bits of their life stories as the intermission was about to end.

Marianne said, "Could we get together tomorrow sometime? It's Sunday, and I have the day off." Rob replied, "Sure, when and where?" She said, "Let's meet at noon at my hotel, and we'll go over to the park a few blocks away and have a picnic. OK?" Rob was thrilled. "Sounds wonderful. I'll be there." She gave him a slip of paper with her hotel's name and address. They shook hands, and she went back to the bandstand for the introductions of the contestants.

Rob and his new dance partner Matilda, had to jitterbug, foxtrot and two-step. And some of the crew of the *Thornfish* that were present, whistled, clapped, and shouted for them during each event. Rob and Matilda won the contest easily. They embraced as the exhausted winners sat down on the stage. They were presented with the prize: two bottles of Australian champagne and a dinner for two at the Coconut Grove. Rob thought *this is getting interesting.*

CHAPTER 52

News from Home

Rob returned to his hotel by himself with the two bottles of very fine champagne each wrapped in a fine woven basket. Matilda said she would not be allowed in her parents' home with alcohol and in no way would she be permitted to dine at a nightclub. So, Rob decided he'd take one of the bottles to the picnic with Marianne tomorrow. He could not find John after the dance was over. He figured that he had made a friend with one of the girls, so after waiting as long as he could, he caught the USO bus to his hotel. He was tired, but before turning out the lights, he decided to read some more of his letters from Molly and his folks.

Molly's letter enclosed an article she had written for *The Oxford Press*, about the war bond sales. The area had not met their area goals for the War Loan Drive. "Some people do not seem to realize that our government is making a supreme effort at this time to strike the decisive blows of a winning war. These people do not realize how much money it takes to buy guns, tanks, ships, planes and equipment for our armed forces. Others are making real sacrifices to buy bonds. The editor was told today of several persons who had borrowed money to buy bonds. One farmer received a check for $2500 for hogs and when he cashed it, purchased $1500 worth of bonds. Small purchases also help, and many school children have bought $25 and $50 bonds. And Rob, Kyger Motors has an ad in the same paper for seven used 1941 automobiles and two 1940's. Oh, how I wish I could buy one! But I sure get a lot of exercise walking to work and making the rounds for news." The same clipping had a note about real estate for sale. "For sale: extra nice 8 room modern house, with two complete baths three squares from campus. Also 2 1/2 acres with a 3-bedroom house, $3200."

She wrote,

"Rob I wanted to go to the Presbyterian Church last Sunday, they were ordaining a man for Christian Ministry by the name of Merlin Ditmer Jr. Do you know him? Anyway, I wanted to hear the preacher Rev. G. Jarrett Rich's sermon on the subject 'Why does God not speak?' I hesitated to go without permission from Father Tom.

Rob, do you ever hear God speaking? Sometimes I do. And He's encouraging to me. Hope you are too. All my love, Molly.

Remember, Our love is here to stay…

p.s. Ms. Cullen, our editor, and I went to a lecture at the Methodist Church the other afternoon to hear Woodyerick Libby, Executive Secretary of the Council for the Prevention of War. His three points are: curb the growth of hate and intolerance; plan for lasting peace after the war; and be open to negotiating the end of the war. My comments: Fat chance bargaining with Hitler and Tojo!"

Rob lay on his bed, thinking about how lucky he was having such a wonderful girl waiting for him. He thought about their first kiss, and the last dance they had in Oxford on December 6, 1941. The world wasn't the same after December 7. *If I make it through this war, I'm going to marry her if she will still have me.*

He put the letter down and the door flew open, and John came rushing into the room, turned on the lights and exclaimed, "Rob, I'm in love! I met the most awesome girl you could imagine. Did you see me dancing with her?" Rob had to confess he did not; he was too busy dancing with the pretty imp he had for a partner.

"Well tell me about her."

"Well she is an Aussie, of course, her name is Isabelle, and she is a knockout and what a wonderful dancer. She is very sharp and witty. We hit it off right away. What brown eyes and boobs to go with them. She invited me over to her parents' home for dinner tomorrow night. I even got to kiss her good night!"

"Well I'm glad for you John; I hope you have a good time with her folks too."

"What about you and Molly? Have you heard much from her? "

Rob pointed to the letter he was reading, "A brief mention that her *Student* friend, Woody, has finally joined the Marines. He is entering aviation training at Pensacola. She had a few driving lessons, and she's talking like she would like to buy a car, but she would have to work for years to pay for one."

The two talked for a long time. John finally went to bed after he realized he was talking to himself; his roommate had fallen asleep.

CHAPTER 53

Oxford Night Out

Molly was walking along High Street toward the Post Office to deposit another letter to Rob, when a Chrysler Air Flow sedan pulled up to a screeching stop. "Hey babe, want a lift?" yelled Woody. Molly pretended to be very aloof and said, "I'm not a babe and I don't ride with strangers, sonny," and she continued walking down the street. Woody pulled ahead and parked. He jumped out and ran to Molly, "Sorry, I was just kidding. I would like to apologize by inviting you to have dinner with me tonight." Molly said, "Oh, Woody you know I'm not dating for the duration." They sat down on a park bench beside front steps leading up to the door of the post office. "I know, Molly, it's really not a date. I thought we could go to a movie and then have a nice dinner at the Huddle. It's strictly platonic between old *Student* newspaper colleagues. Molly thought *he's leaving in a few days, perhaps forever. We are just friends. Couldn't hurt. I deserve some companionship anyway and even though I've seen Casablanca before I would love to see it again.* She relented saying, "Ok but we'll skip the dinner. Let's go to the movie. Woody didn't need any further persuasion.

They sat in the last row of the nearly empty auditorium of the Miami Western Theater as the Pathe newsreel told the story of American tanks led by General George S. Patton defeating the Germans in Tunisia. Next was the somber story of ten American prisoners of war in Mindanao, Philippines, who escaped the Jap Davao Penal Colony, and for the first time told of the terrible atrocities committed by the Japanese during the infamous Bataan Death March. Teardrops started down Molly's cheeks as the newsreel ended.

The main feature was one that she had seen before, *Casablanca* starring Ingrid Bergman. Tears flowed again at the end of the movie when she watched her favorite actress say goodbye to her former lover Rick, played by Humphrey Bogart. Rick says the lines that captured movie goers forever, "Here's looking at you kid." Molly's hand grasped Woody's as the movie neared its end, and Ingrid's plane took off into the early morning fog, leaving her lover, Rick standing in the mist with the French captain Louie Renault, played by Claude Raines. As they watched the plane disappear in the foggy night, Rick utters the famous line, "Louie, this is going to be the start of a great relationship."

Woody sat still in his seat until the words came on the screen, The End. Molly mumbled, "I'm sorry, I just get caught up in the tender moments of this love story." They sat for a long time in the now empty theater. Woody put his arm around her as she took her handkerchief and blotted the tears. He leaned over, and their lips met, and they kissed, and kissed again. And Molly wanted more and more. It was getting heavy when the lights came on and the attendant came in to sweep up the popcorn. It was time to leave.

As they came out of the theater Molly straightened her hair and took a deep breath of the fresh summer night air. It revived her and relieved her as well. "I'm sorry Woody. I don't know what came over me. I'm embarrassed." Woody said, "Molly no apology is needed. We both are human with human needs. It's ok." They started walking down High Street toward Woody's fraternity house where he had parked his car. "Why don't you go into the house and use the restroom on the first floor. Besides me, there is no one living there until summer school starts. I'll wait in the living room." Molly went in and found the small powder room off the hallway while Woody stayed in the empty living room. He went to the Victrola and found a record and placed it in the machine. When Molly entered the large living room, she heard music playing. It was a record of the familiar hit song, *Till Then* by the Mills Brothers. "This song is one of my favorites Woody." He took her hand and they started to dance. Woody said, "Molly I'm really going to miss you. I'm leaving in the morning. Will you write to me now and then?" Molly didn't reply… she was lost in reverie. She knew the words of *Till Then* by heart. She started to say yes to his question and suddenly they were on the couch and embracing once again. "I love you Molly Gaynor. Could you ever love me too?" His hands were all over her and she felt electricity flowing through her heaving body. "Woody, please. I can't. Please don't." I want you too, but I promised…." Woody rose and sat in a chair opposite her. "Molly, I know you have Rob in your heart now. But I'm leaving for flight school, could you …would you…." He paused, if something would ever happen, could you love me? I love you so much." She sat on the couch with her head in her hands, then looked at him through tear-filled eyes, and softly said, "Yes."

CHAPTER 54

The Picnics

Dawn broke over the Australian plains. Kangaroos were up early searching for breakfast. Australian sheep dogs were busy rounding up their charges on sprawling sheep farms, and the city of Perth was stirring and coming to life. Rob was sound asleep and was awakened by the sound of a brass band playing in the streets below. John was up and in the shower. He glanced at his watch; he couldn't believe it. It was ten o'clock. The band was playing an old hymn, *Rock of Ages, Cleft for Me, let me hide myself in thee."* He scrambled out of bed and looked out the window. It was the Salvation Army Band serenading the troops. He pounded on the bathroom door. "John come out and see the band!" Sailors were standing by their windows. No one took offense at them as they played more familiar hymns, including *When the Saints Come Marching In.* "This will be our Sunday Service Rob," John said. He dressed quickly and went downstairs and gave them a five-dollar bill.

Rob arrived at Marianne's hotel a few minutes before noon carrying the bottle of champagne. He found her in the dining room where she had the chef prepare a picnic lunch for two. "Thanks for doing this Marianne, "Rob said. Dressed in a blue blouse, with white shorts, she looked lovely. "Let's go, Rob; I have two wine glasses too. They walked to the park a few blocks away. It was a beautiful park, with shade trees and a large white gazebo in the center. They opted for a small picnic table nearby. They sat down opposite each other. Marianne took a checkered tablecloth out of the basket and carefully spread it. Rob helped to place the paper plates and wine glasses. He opened the champagne and poured two glasses. "Let's toast to life!" Their glasses clinked. Rob gazed at his beautiful new friend admiring her graceful beauty. "Tell me about yourself," he said. She quickly described her upbringing in Richmond, Indiana, her schooling at Indiana University and her winning the Miss Indiana contest and finally the audition for the USO gig. "It's been such an exciting time Rob; I am so happy to be doing something that brings home to our troops overseas." Rob said, "Marianne, you have a marvelous voice. Have you any thoughts about what you'd like to do after the war?" She said, "It's funny, your mother asked me the same question the last time we were together. To answer your question, I haven't given it a lot of thought, with the war on. Maybe I could have a singing career with a big band. Right now, I want to get through this one ok. You know we face danger too. Do you recall what happened to a wonderful bandleader, Glenn Miller? He was lost on a flight over the English Channel. I am trying to live one day at a time. How about you? What are you thinking about doing?" Rob paused, "Well, I'm kind of like you. I have been just living one day at a time. I love the Navy, and I might stay in after the war. My folks will be after me to go back to school and get my master's. I like mineralogy. I might go into mining someday if I decide to get out of the Navy." He looked at Marianne's lovely face and said, "But we face danger every day. I have a friend on the sub who has me thinking more about life and the hereafter. We lost some good men on one of our patrols. We had to bury them at sea. It made me think more about the meaning of life and our role in making things better for others." Marianne reached out and took his hand. She squeezed it and said, "I understand." They ate mostly in silence. The picnic lunch was delicious: flank steak sandwiches, home fries, and coleslaw. The Australian wine was perfect. Rob noticed a pigeon looking for a handout and tossed him a crust of bread. After lunch, they packed the remains in the basket and went for a walk. Marianne took his hand in hers as they strolled down the path through the trees to the Swan River. The wide blue river flowed lazily down to Freemantle and then to the Indian Ocean. They found a small pier with a bench and sat down. They sat watching the boats go by, "Rob, it's like there is no war going on at all. It is so peaceful here, it's like we don't have a care in the world. She began humming a song she loved for years, *Down by the Riverside.* The lyrics were so appropriate she thought.

> *Gonna lay down my sword and shield*
> *Down by the riverside, Down by the riverside,*
> *Down by the riverside,*
> *Gonna lay down my burden*
> *Down by the riverside.*
> *I ain't gonna study war no more*
> *Study war no more*
> *Ain't gonna study war no more*

Rob was moved not only by the sweet lyrics, but the lilting way she sang them to him. *Gonna study war no more…* He put his arm around her, and they simply sat watching the clear blue water for a long time. She turned her face to his and kissed him. Rob responded, and kissed her. He thought: *Can this be happening? Here we meet during a war, down-under, halfway around the world from our roots. How marvelous to have met her at the dance. If I hadn't entered the contest, we would probably have never met. But was it chance…just coincidence? Luck? John says life's crossroads are not chances. Chance is a gamble. Life's crossroads are not.*

Marianne looked at him wondering: *What is he thinking? Am I too forward with him? Maybe not enough! I don't know, he is so nice, a real gentleman. So handsome. I want to know him better and I know his mother will be so happy to know that we met. But we haven't enough time.*

She pushed his hair back. His forehead was getting red. "Rob, you're getting sunburned. Your pale skin can't take much sun now. Let's go back." As they walked hand in hand, Rob thought what a wonderful girl Marianne is, no wonder mother likes her so much. On the way to her hotel, she said, "Rob, the band is moving this week to Freemantle for some USO shows for the Navy next weekend. I can get some time off. Why don't we do something? The USO director told me that she'd lend me her car if I needed it. Let's do some exploration. What do you think?"

"It sounds great to me. Let's plan on it."

"I'll pick you up at noon. Bring your swimsuit and suntan lotion. We'll find a place to swim I'm sure."

· · · · ·

Rob found the recreation room at the hotel. He asked for a beach umbrella. They didn't have one, but the attendant gave him a small umbrella tent with bamboo mats to use. He bought a boxer swimsuit and suntan lotion. He purchased a pair of goggles thinking that they might go swimming looking for tropical fish among the corals. Armed with his supplies, he went to the parking lot to meet Marianne promptly at noon. It was Monday and a gorgeous day, not a cloud in the sky. Marianne pulled up in a green and black two-door Ford coupe, vintage about 1935, with a rumble seat in the back. "Where did you find this beauty, Marianne?" She explained, "My new friend, the USO Director in Perth, loaned it to me for as long as I need it while we are here. Isn't it nice? These Australians are wonderful people." Rob agreed. He put his swim gear in the rumble seat and hopped in the passenger seat. She engaged the clutch smoothly and drove along the highway toward the ocean. They were off on their great adventure.

Rob liked the way she drove the car, "You're a pretty good driver." She smiled, "I've been driving since I was fourteen. I learned to drive an International Harvester tractor on my dad's farm in Indiana." As they drove through the countryside, there were no road signs. So, they stopped at a small grocery and gas station on the outskirts of town and got directions. The clerk told them that the commissioners had all road signs taken down in case the Japs invaded their district. No need to give them any help in directing traffic. He suggested they look for Sand Trax Beach up the coast, a great place to see reef fish. Rob purchased some things for lunch: peanut butter, bread, sausage and a bottle of white wine. They soon found the road north from Freemantle along the ocean. The gravel road wound along the shoreline beaches and limestone ledges. The rock formations interested Rob, a geology major in college, and the view of the Indian Ocean was awesome. Rob pointed out the small island called Rottenest, with its lighthouse that welcomed sailors to Freemantle for decades. Rob said, "When our sailors see the channel buoys or other navigational aids like the lighthouse at Rottenest, leading into home port, they get what is called channel fever. The engineers call it the "finishing rate." Marianne asked, "what does that mean, channel fever and the finishing rate." Rob blushed, "Well the finishing rate is a term used by the engineers to indicate that the batteries on the subs that propel the submarine underwater are just about charged. The channel fever and finishing rate are kind of nasty terms that the crew sometimes use indicating the need for feminine companionship, i.e., the need for intercourse!" Marianne laughed. "I understand now. You know we women sometimes have the same feelings." Rob didn't know what to say, so he just let it pass. She drove on looking for a good place to swim.

They found the isolated beach called Sand Trax Beach north of Freemantle. It was named for its empty sparkling white dunes. It was a small and out of the way bay, sheltered from southwesterly winds and waves by the northernmost breakwater of Freemantle port, so waves were smaller and sea breezeless. It was perfect for swimming and picnicking. And there wasn't a soul around as far as they could see. Rob quickly set up the little green umbrella tent that the R&R department had loaned him. Marianne changed into her swimsuit in the tiny tent while Rob got the food out of the car and arranged the lunch just as she emerged from the tent. She was gorgeous. She wore a one-piece white bathing suit that made him think of the famous pinup picture of Betty Grable prominently displayed in the crew's mess. It was his turn to change. He left his white tee shirt on and put on the black swimsuit. Its baggy shorts weren't pretty but covered some of his body from the sun.

They talked about home as they ate their lunch. She was so happy that she had met his dad and mom. She said that they were so gracious to her; even his uncle, the senator, was so hospitable letting her stay in his home in Washington. "Your mother is very proud of you Rob. She told me all about your honors in school, and in athletics too. She sure didn't want you to go into the submarine service though."

"I know that Marianne, it's funny you say she was full of complimentary remarks about me. It's ironic in a way because she never tells me that. I think it's in her upbringing. She doesn't want me to get a 'big head.' My father helped me to get right into subs out of Midshipmen's school at Northwestern. He pulled some strings with some contacts he has. But, Marianne, never let my mother know that." Marianne grimaced as she recalled the scene last Christmas in the senator's dining room. She did not tell Rob of the incident during dinner when the senator told his mother that he had prevailed on the Secretary of the Navy to get Rob assigned directly to a submarine at the request of her husband. It was a difficult night for all of them.

After they finished, Rob applied suntan cream on his legs and neck. Marianne asked him to do her back. It felt so good to her, and she allowed him to do the back of her legs. Careful now, Rob cautioned himself. Before getting carried away, Rob took her hand and led Marianne to the water. It was cold, but they got used to it once they were immersed. Rob pulled the goggles over his eyes and saw a myriad of fish; Blue Tangs, yellow, orange and green Parrot Fish, Butterfly Fish, Black Sturgeons and even silver Trumpet Fish. He had lost time, and when he came up out of the water, Marianne was nowhere to be seen. Rob was worried. He had stayed in the water too long. He searched the cold water and didn't see her. He rushed to the tent and found her inside laying on the mat with a towel pulled completely over her. She was shivering. "I was so cold; I had to get out Rob." Her wet bathing suit was hanging on a tent peg. He pulled his mat inside, and they talked for a longtime about home, the orchestra, her singing career, the audition for Fred Waring's chorus; and then she noticed Rob was sound asleep. His slumber was interrupted by a hand pulling on his swim trunks. "Marianne, what are you doing?" She stammered, "I want to come out of the virgin forest Rob, I'm 21 and still a virgin. I want you to bring me to womanhood."

"No, this isn't right. You need to save yourself for your husband."

"I don't know if I'll ever have a husband, Rob."

"Well don't think that way. Stop it!"

"No, I want you, right now," and she rolled on top of him. It was déjà vu all over again.

* * * * *

When Rob returned to his hotel, there were three letters in his key box. One from Molly, one from his mother and another from Valerie Edmonds. He opened Lily's mother's first. It was a very brief note saying that Lily had moved to the island of Kauai for a time and was living with her relatives on the island and working at their restaurant. Her health was good, and she might remain on the island for the duration. Mrs. Edmonds finished by saying she enjoyed her new work, "*it is demanding but I feel I'm contributing to the war effort, and I think that Frank would be proud of me. Blessings to you from all of us. Stay safe. Fondly, Valerie.*"

Rob wondered why she would leave her mother for an island 100 miles away. It didn't make sense. He wanted to get her new address, but Valerie didn't include it. Strange. He opened Molly's letter just as John burst into the room. "Rob, I am, I am… still in love. Even more. We hit it off so much. I want her to be my mate for life. "

"Whoa, John, better slow down, you just met. Is this your first love?"

"Well yes, but Rob this is for real. I've met her folks; we had dinner. They treated me like a king!"

"How old is she?"

"Well she's just 18, but very mature for her age."

"Ok, just play it slow. We have a war to fight. Remember."

"You're right Rob. It just seems as if time is so short for us. I remember a phrase from Ben Franklin's *Poor Richard's Almanac, "Lost time is never found again."* Then he changed the subject: "How is Marianne? She sure is beautiful. She is the hit of the USO show."

"I know. We are having a fabulous time; we went swimming along the coast today. We enjoy being together. She's a wonderful person, John. The band is going to have a USO show this weekend at the Navy base in Freemantle. So, we plan to see each other until then."

"Strictly platonic right?" Rob didn't answer right away.

"Well, John, I could say it's none of your business, but you are my best friend. He paused trying to muster up some courage. "We have been intimate. It wasn't my doing but it just happened, and I am at fault too. It takes two to tango. We both rationalize it as a wartime interlude. Is that wrong John? It's like eat drink and be merry, for tomorrow we die. You know that the Freemantle based subs the *Grenadier* and the *Grayling* were lost a few months ago. They just disappeared. I mean we could be next."

"I'm sorry Rob. I didn't mean to put you under the law. Jesus ushered in the era of grace. He came across a bunch of guys one day who were going to stone a woman caught in adultery. He asked them "which one of you are without sin?" They put down their rocks and went away. Jesus saved the lady. Saved by amazing grace. But Jesus cautioned her to go but sin no more."

"Where is that story?" He went over to the bedside table and found a Gideon's New Testament placed there by the Gideon Bible Society of Australia. He started thumbing through the pages of the New Testament. "I think it may be in John's Gospel. Try chapter eight."

Rob finally found verse 11 and read and reread it. He put it down. And looked at his friend, "Well John, maybe there's hope for me."

"There is Rob. You'll see."

．　．　．　．　．　．

Rob invited Marianne to share his dance contest winnings of a complete dinner for two at the Coconut Grove on the waterfront off Hay Street in downtown Perth. The new club was named after the famous one in Boston. On November 28, 1942, the worst fire in Boston's history swept through the crowded popular nightclub killing over 490 patrons. 160 were injured. Before the war, there were few nightclubs in Perth. The beach town of Cottesloe had one of the first clubs to open, called the Lido on the waterfront. Coconut Grove opened soon after.

Marianne had some music matters to attend to. She told Rob to go on ahead and get a table, and she would join him after she finished work. He had selected a secluded table for two overlooking the water. A full moon reflected in widening ripples over the water. The small dance band was playing some American pop tunes from the hit parade as Marianne came in looking for Rob. Rob rose and went to meet her. She said, "Rob, let's dance." The number one on the hit parade for weeks, *Paper Doll* was being sung by a vocalist who Marianne thought was a little flat. As they glided across the small dance floor, she whispered, "Rob will you forgive me?" Rob was startled. He held her tight, "No need to, Marianne. It takes two to tango as they say. We both were caught up in the moment thinking that our lives may never meet again and might end sooner than we would like to think. So maybe we both need forgiveness. I'd like to tell you a little story about forgiveness." She said, "let's sit down I want to hear every word." After they were seated the waiter came over with the menus. They were large with orange covers decorated with palm trees just like the famous ones used in the club in Boston. They ordered wine and an appetizer. "Tell me your story, Rob."

"Well, please don't share this with anyone. On our last patrol, we picked up a passenger. I can't tell you any of the details for security reasons. But I'll call him a preacher. He had been horribly mistreated by the Japs, tortured for his faith. His body showed the marks of it. While on board he gave a sermon on Sunday to the crew. We held the service in our torpedo room; he spoke about forgiveness amid the instruments of war. His words were based on what Jesus said, *that we are to forgive when others sin against us, and if we don't forgive others, the Lord won't forgive our sins.* He said we must forgive others. He talked a bit about his being held in prison and how he was able to forgive the guards even when they beat him unconscious for no reason. I've always thought of forgiveness as a two-way street. I won't forgive unless he apologizes and forgives me first. It got me to thinking. I have a friend who lives in Hawaii. Her husband was killed on the USS *Arizona* when it exploded December 7. She's a Japanese and has learned the lesson of forgiveness the hard way. After the attack that Sunday, she couldn't get a job for a long while because she looks Japanese. But after she forgave those who oppressed her, a job opened, and she now is doing something important for the war effort. My roommate, John, is so innocent. He has a simple altruistic view of life and lives it. He's our lay minister on board. His talk one day at our services was about forgiveness. They paused while the waiter poured the wine, Lindeman's Pinot Grigio, Southeast Australia's finest. Marianne said, "Rob, I was selfish. I must confess I'm self-centered. You didn't have a chance." Rob replied, "Marianne, I had channel fever too!" Rob raised his glass, let's toast. "To life and its serendipities." Marianne raised her glass, as the sparkle in her eyes gave way to tears streaming down her checks. "The USO tour leaves Thursday for Freemantle. I must go too. I'm so thankful that we met…I hope we can see more of each other this week but for now, let's enjoy tonight, and dance the night away." Their glasses and glances met.

CHAPTER 55

Goodbye

Marianne and the band started rehearsals for the Navy and Marine Corps Show next weekend at the pavilion on the Navy piers. They added two new numbers, all on this year's hit parade: *When the lights go on again all over the world,* made popular by Vaughn Monroe, and *Praise the Lord and Pass the Ammunition*, by Kay Kyser's band. He was a former professor of music before forming his own orchestra. Marianne requested a third number, *People will Say we're in Love*, a ballad originally sung by Bing Crosby. Marianne was so excited. She loved the lyrics to that song, it seemed to reflect her feelings for Rob. Rob would be attending, and she managed to have a seat saved for him in the third row. The first two rows were reserved for senior officers.

Marianne and Rob saw each other as much as possible during the time she entertained the troops in the Perth area. They drove her borrowed car down the coast to the Cottesloe beaches, swam, dined and danced often. Rob loved being with her. Maybe it was making up for lost time. Lost time is never found, he remembered. But deep down he did not want to become more involved with women. His life seemed complicated enough with his true love in Ohio, passionate Lily in Hawaii, and now lovely Marianne; but what a wonderful problem to be enmeshed with three beautiful and completely different women.

The USO Freemantle concert had about a thousand attending. Saturday evening's weather was perfect. Marianne was the hit of the show again. Her vocal style and phrasing of the lyrics of familiar songs reminded the boys of home. She wore a low-cut black dress hemmed above the knees, and high heels. She looked like a million dollars. Her troop included a new act, a comedian and a male singer who played the guitar.

After the show, Rob went backstage and met Marianne as she emerged from her tent dressing room. "Wonderful performance Marianne!" Rob exclaimed. "Thank you, Rob, it was fun to do. Where do you want to go?" Rob said "I bet you're tired. Why don't we just go for a drive?" She frowned; he could tell she was not keen on that idea. "Rob, I don't like driving at night on the left side of the road especially. Could we just have a nightcap at my hotel? I need to return the car to the owner tomorrow morning. We leave for Brisbane in the afternoon." When they arrived at her hotel downtown, the bar was just closing. Rob ordered two Blue Swan beers and found Marianne sitting in the lobby with her shoes off. "My shoes are killing me," she laughed. "Let's drink these Aussie beers in my room. It is just up the stairs on the right. Being the only female in the band, I have my own private room." It turned out to be a long night for both. She felt that she was falling in love for the first time. But she knew about Molly. During the night she whispered to him "Rob, if anything ever happened to the wonderful relationship you have with her, I would dearly love to take her place in your heart." Then she added, "We could be a great couple!"

* * * * *

The two-week rest and recreation period for the *Thornfish* crew ended too soon for them. Besides nightclubbing, they enjoyed swimming along the pristine beaches near Perth, hiking, horseback riding, and even trips to the outback where some hunted kangaroo. John continued advancing his new romance. He had pictures of his new girlfriend, Isabelle, to show Rob. "Isn't she gorgeous Rob?" Rob replied, "She sure is. You're a lucky guy to find such a swell girl, John. How do her parents treat you?" He didn't hesitate, "Like I'm part of the family!"

While they recuperated from the stress of patrol, the relief crews from the sub tender *Pelias* worked night and day repairing battle damage, loading torpedoes, supplies, food for over 60 days, and charts of patrol areas. Near the end of the upkeep period, Captain Morrison and his exec met with the staff of the squadron to review patrol assignments. Unfortunately, the torpedoes were still equipped with faulty exploders. There was nothing that Dick could do as Admiral Christie was adamant that they were good weapons. One of the submarine commanders, A.H. Taylor, former CO of the *Haddock*, wrote an 'anonymous poem' about the lousy magnetic exploders. It caused a firestorm when Admiral English, Commander of Submarines Pacific Fleet, learned that it had been widely circulated among submarine squadrons in the Pacific theater of operations. He wanted whoever wrote that 'damn thing thrown out of submarine service.' After two years of constant complaints, by submarine commanding officers, including A.H. Taylor, the 'anonymous author', live tests were run firing a torpedo at a cliff off Oahu. Repeated tests showed that the firing pin had been changed from copper to aluminum to save money. And when struck head-on, the aluminum pin did not fire. The Navy lost two productive years as the Bureau of Ordnance refused to admit they had a problem. Admiral Lockwood, Commander of Submarines based in Hawaii, ordered deactivation of the Mark 6 magnetic exploders months before the first patrol of *Thornfish* out of Freemantle. The improved exploders were the first step in the advancement of submarine performance. However, it would take Admiral Christie almost seven months to finally order the deactivation of the controversial exploders for Southwest Command boats. He had a lot of investment in them from the beginning.

During the repair period, a new S J surface radar had been installed on the *Thornfish* and with the introduction of reliable surface radar, U.S. submarine tactics changed. Night surface attacks on enemy convoys and warships became common.

The increase in the use of Ultra Code messages improved Navy submarine tactics. It was the most highly classified code and only seen by submarine commanding officers. The breaking of the Japanese Navy's code was the most significant advance in destroying the enemy's capabilities in the war. Further aiding the submarine war in the Pacific was the breaking of the "Maru Code." Japanese merchant ships, Marus, transmitted position reports twice a day to Tokyo. By finally breaking the Maru Code, operation staffs were able to direct boats to intercept merchant convoys, a huge tactical advantage. It also enabled boats to sometimes pair up with other submarines in the area for wolf pack attacks.

· · · · ·

Rob and John returned to the boat before Saturday's inspection. Rob found a small package on his stateroom desk. He opened it and found two silver Lieutenant Junior Grade collar insignias, with a note on the captain's calling card: Rob well deserved. Keep up the good work. R/ RM. Your promotion by the way is retroactive two months!

Saturday morning, the crew was at quarters on deck dressed in their white uniforms for Admiral's Inspection. *Thornfish* had been moved from being alongside the tender *Pelias,* to the pier. Promptly at 1000 the admiral came aboard in white dress uniform. Captain Morrison was awarded the Navy Cross, and the Silver Star was awarded to the executive officer, Jerry Abrams, for his performance during their outstanding recent patrol. The Silver Star Award was pinned on the uniform of Torpedo- man First Class Grabowski and newly promoted LTJG Robert A. Walker, USNR, for action against the enemy in the rescue of allied personnel. Rob was surprised to also receive a Commendation Medal with Combat V for his superior work in disposing of the dud enemy depth charge that was found on the deck after a shellacking of depth charges by an enemy destroyer. After the awards were given, Admiral Christie said that the combat patrol badge was authorized for all hands on their patrol. He then gave a stirring speech to the men telling them how much they had done on the last patrol to destroy the enemy and how grateful the Australians were for rescuing the Australian coast watcher. Word got out as soon as the survivors were released. Nothing was published, however, in the local *Freemantle Gazette* or the *Freemantle's District Sentinel* newspaper. Perth's seven newspapers and magazines failed to mention the rescue. Deliberate censorship was imposed on any reports of ill-treatment of Allied prisoners by the Japanese for many months into the war.

. . . . .

Sunday noon the USO tour group loaded their instruments and luggage aboard an olive drab Army DC 3 aircraft, destination Brisbane, Australia. They were scheduled for a weeklong performance at the military facilities where American submarines were based. Rob had hitched a ride with Marianne on the USO bus to the airport. They sat in silence for most of the trip. It was a sad time for them both. They were the last to leave the dusty bus. She started to cry. "I'm going to miss you, Rob. I enjoyed being with you so much. I hope we will meet again someday, 'When the lights go on all over the world.' Sounds corny doesn't it, but it is the way I feel." They kissed deeply, and it was time to board the aircraft. Rob stood on the tarmac until the plane roared down the runway. He waved a final goodbye.

During the long flight across the continent to Brisbane, Marianne had time to write a long letter to Mary Catherine Walker in Oxford, telling her of the serendipitous meeting with her son in Perth and what a wonderful time they had. She knew that she would be thrilled.

Brisbane was the home of the Army and Navy headquarters for the Southwest Pacific. General Douglas MacArthur, Commander of all allied forces in the Southwest Pacific, was pleased with the submarine service. He directed many missions for supplying guerillas in the islands held by the enemy, landing commandos that took time away from the Navy's primary purpose of destroying enemy shipping. The Navy wasn't pleased with the General especially when he decided to present the Army Distinguished Service Medal to one of the submarine commanders.

When he returned to his hotel, Rob opened a letter from his mother. One line read,

"I just read an article in The Oxford Press about Miami University's Naval Radio Training School wanting old radios from its readers. Any condition will be accepted. Navy enlisted trainees will take them apart and put them together again as part of their training while they are here."

His mom added,

"I'd like to give them all your father's radios in our attic, but I know he would have a fit. So, I'll leave them alone for the duration. Our mailman just delivered new application forms for new ration books for sugar, coffee, and shoes. Miami students will have to get their ration book applications from their parents at home. Also, I must get a new application for a gas ration sticker for Dad's car. I sure don't need much. A tank of gas will usually last me weeks. And you should know that Dr. F. Alton Wade, your father's colleague in Geology, has been ordered to report to Greenland for duty. The Army must know of his experiences with Admiral Byrd's expedition to

Antarctica. He'll add to his resume after being there. And by the way, I know you enjoyed your surveying class in Miami. Well, the State is doing some surveying at Hueston Woods in preparation for a future state park in the postwar years."

She closed by saying,

"Merry Christmas 1943 and Happy New Year 1944. Your packages are on the way. Stay safe. Love, Mother."

Her letter, postmarked weeks ago, reminded him that Christmas was coming soon, and he needed to buy some presents for Molly and his folks. The next morning, he went shopping in downtown Perth. The stores were much like those at home with large full-length windows, and small tiled alcoves, made to invite customers to come in. In a few hours he had completed his Christmas shopping. He got his father a silver cigarette box with his initials engraved on the front. And for his mother, a pearl necklace. The proprietor agreed to wrap and mail the packages to Oxford, Ohio, USA.

In a clothing store, he saw a white cashmere sweater perfect for Lily. He had it gift wrapped and mailed to her mother's home on Oahu. He enclosed a small note:

Dear Lily, I hope you are ok. I haven't heard from you. The sweater will really look good on you. Please write when you can. Love Rob. P.s. off on patrol soon

He found a gift for Molly, a beautiful red-brown kangaroo leather handbag with a strap long enough for her to carry books or folders over her shoulder as she walked to work. He enclosed a picture of himself taken by a Navy photographer, being awarded the medals by the admiral. He wrote on the back, 'me getting a medal from the admiral.' After having everything mailed, he went back to the hotel and got a Foster Beer and sat in an Adirondack Chair overlooking the water. He had an ominous feeling about the next patrol. He hadn't shared his gloomy feelings with anyone. But it caused him to do some serious thinking about his life. Over the last few years he had become involved with three women, Lily, the vivacious and passionate one; Marianne, the impish, innocent girl who wanted to be his lover, and Molly, his first love. What a dilemma. Molly had remained faithful to him; but he had not been faithful to her. Thoughts about his involvement with other girls bothered him a lot but he did his best to put them on the back burner.

Rob's Christmas packages from home did not arrive before departing on patrol. He would never receive them.

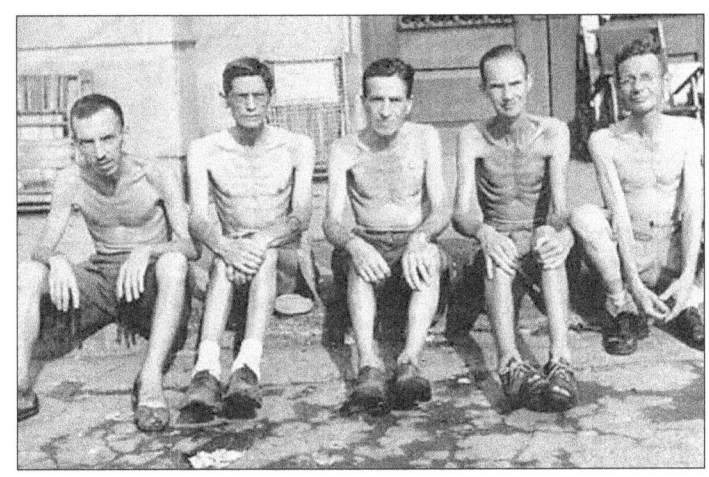

PART THREE

Prisoners of War

CHAPTER 56

The Last Patrol

Thornfish sounded one prolonged blast of the whistle signaling my engines are going astern. Ensign Wright had the conn, his first attempt at getting the submarine underway. As the Fairbanks Morse diesel engines throbbed, he conned the sub away from the pier at the Freemantle shipyard, where they had been moored. Captain Morrison stood by him coaching as needed, making sure that he was not making any mistakes. It was Christmas Day. Church bells in the city were chiming and a carillon was playing Christmas Carols. *Oh, Come all ye Faithful* echoed over the town of Freemantle. The crew, dressed in whites, stood at attention as the boat exited the slip into the channel and on to the sea. Their destination was only known to the captain and his executive officer. Days preceding, they were given their patrol area by the admiral's chief of staff. The tall lean commander stood by a large map of Western Australia, Java, Borneo, Sumatra and Malaysia. Tex McLean was apologetic when he told them they would be going into the Straits of Malacca. *Thornfish* would be the first U.S. submarine to penetrate the shallow and confined waters. This was an area that was controlled by British submarines. However, the British requested that reconnaissance be made of shipping in the area between Singapore and Rangoon by an American fleet submarine. Also, photographs were to be made of harbors and routes used by convoys. A new camera was provided to be used with the periscope observations. It would be a tough assignment he said. And he was right.

Thornfish proceeded north to Exmouth Gulf to an advanced base some seven hundred miles north of Freemantle, stopping to top off fuel and water. From there, they set their course through the Indian Ocean to the Great Channel at six degrees north latitude, into the Sea of Andaman and then north toward Rangoon. A month after leaving Freemantle, they were disappointed. Little traffic of any size worthy of a torpedo was to be had. Dick turned south and decided to take a look at the port of Penang down the Malaysia coast toward Singapore. Their SJ radar picked up a two-ship convoy and Dick gave chase. In the distance they could see the Malay coastline a few miles away. It was early morning, and Dick decided to remain on the surface. Suddenly a low flying aircraft appeared off the port quarter. Dick ordered, "Clear the bridge!

Dive! Dive!" As they passed 130 feet, they breathed a sigh of relief but then an aerial torpedo exploded directly over the after part of the sub. The shockwave drove them to the bottom at 250 feet. The damage was horrible. Lights went out and power was lost in the conning tower. The maneuvering room and the after-torpedo room took the worst blow. Compartments in the after part reported that the hull had been dished in four to six inches. The engine room reported damage to the diesels. The torpedo tubes were bent causing the propeller shafts to bend. The main induction and after hatches had sprung large leaks. Captain Morrison went aft to assess the damage. The damage was more than Dick could imagine. The electric and hydraulic lines were destroyed. The compartment doors were warped and would not close. An electrical fire broke out in the maneuvering room housing the electric motors that drove power to the propellers. A firefighting party equipped with OBA's went through the crew's berthing, engine rooms, to the maneuvering room to fight the fire. The captain got on the announcing system telling the crew to stay calm they would be ok. The men in every compartment were valiantly trying to stop the leaks. A bucket brigade had to be established during the day to transfer water from the motor room to keep them from being flooded to the forward torpedo room. Finally, after jury-rigging electric lines, one of the bilge pumps was started removing most of the water. More electric fires were continuing to occur. The worst news was that the damaged propeller shafts would not turn. The situation was in extremis. The only solution was to surface and try to get a radio message sent telling their operational staff of their condition and position. Any allied assistance could not arrive in time to help. The crew was near exhaustion. The foul air with low oxygen made minds confused, and fatigue set in. Pete, the engineer, tried to get the shafts to turn without success. Dick finally ordered surface. High-pressure air blasted the water out of the ballast tanks and *Thornfish* wallowed out of the mud and surfaced. It was night.

Upon surfacing, radiomen got the radio working and the captain sent off a message telling of their plight and position. But no acknowledgment was ever received. Jerry had the captain's approval to make a sail and try to get in close to shore. If they could get closer to shore, they would blow the boat up and swim in and perhaps they could find some guerillas or friendly natives in the jungle. While the destruction of codes, confidential papers, charts, radar equipment, sonar gear, the TDC and even Australian money continued below deck, the boatswain mates supervised the making of sails from mattress covers. At dawn the sails were raised from the periscopes. But there was no wind. Then to make matters worse, a Japanese plane homed in on the helpless submarine. The gunners fired twenty millimeters at the oncoming fighter. As it pulled up the bullets hit the plane but didn't prevent it from dropping a bomb that landed harmlessly away from *Thornfish*. The pilot would have undoubtedly alerted surface forces in the area.

Finally, Dick ordered the men to prepare to abandon ship. The crew lined up on deck in life jackets. Each division officer accounted for his men. Rob stood with his men in his division. Sick men and those that could not swim were placed in rubber boats. Below deck, Chief O'Neil prepared to open the vents on the ballast tanks to scuttle their boat.

Over the horizon a Japanese merchant ship accompanied by a small escort came towards them as the order to abandon ship was given by the captain. His order was shouted down the hatch to scuttle the ship! The men went into the water and when safely clear, the ballast valves were opened. Chief O'Neil came up from the control room and went over the side and the captain was the last one overboard. They watched in sadness as their magnificent boat, their home for many months, disappeared in the Malacca Straits, sinking stern first. Some of the men were crying. It was just the beginning of their troubles.

CHAPTER 57

The Capture

The Japanese merchant ship and its escort circled taking pictures of the 70 American sailors in the water. Finally, the ship stopped and picked up all the Americans. They were herded into one of the ship's holds. En route to Penang, the captain of the Maru had Chief O'Neil brought to his cabin. He thought that, being the oldest looking man, he was the captain of the submarine. None of the chiefs and officers had insignia on their shirts. When asked, Larry O'Neil simply gave him his name, rank and serial number. "Who is your captain, chief?" he said in very good English. Chief O'Neil was surprised at his speaking English. He explained that he had made numerous trips before the war as a merchant marine captain to America bringing tons of scrap metal from the West Coast to steel mills in Japan. He asked to see the submarine captain. Chief O'Neil made no reply. The Japanese captain had the *Thornfish* captain identified, by the second oldest looking man in the crew. He had him brought to his cabin. The small Japanese Maru captain said, "Your name please." Dick replied, "Richard M. Morrison Lieutenant Commander USN, service number 376890." "Welcome aboard Captain Morrison." Dick was surprised that he spoke English. "Well it's not my choice to have your hospitality. I want you to know captain, that it is the responsibility of the Japanese to treat our men in accordance with the rules of war and the international treaties regarding prisoners of war. The Maru captain said, "I regret sir to inform you that I am not a part of the Japanese Navy. They conscripted me, but the government of Japan has never recognized the Geneva Treaty. I am sorry, but I am afraid you are not going to like the Japanese treatment of prisoners. The Army is especially bad. The Navy is not much better from what I have heard." Dick knew what he was talking about. The harsh treatment of POWs was kept secret for months by the allies. After General Wainwright surrendered the US forces in the Philippines in April 1942, the word of the atrocities of the Bataan Death March leaked out infuriating the world. Unbeknownst to Captain Morrison, on January 8, 1942, the most important man in Japan, General Hideki Togo, minister of war issued a Field Service Code for the treatment of prisoners of war. "To live as a prisoner of war is to live without honor." For the Japanese, living without honor is worthless living. Therefore, treat prisoners, especially white prisoners, as worthless. To their captors, they are merely a number pinned on their dirty clothes. They are people without honor. But to the Japanese corporations, these prisoners were very important to maintain production of the Japanese war machine.

During the short voyage to Penang, the captain of the Maru gave all the prisoners a meal of rice and beans. When they arrived, they were blindfolded and led off the ship to waiting trucks on the pier. The first leg of a long journey of sorrow was just beginning.

As the blindfolded prisoners were driven to their destination, the captain told the men in his truck, "Remember, name, rank and serial number; that's all we're to give these bastards. Hang tough." Jerry, the senior officer in the other truck, told his men the same. After about a half an hour the trucks pulled up in the courtyard of an old convent. The crew, still blindfolded, was ordered out of the truck holding each other by their shoulders, some fell and were hit by guards. The walled compound had a courtyard at the center. The blindfolds were removed, and the men were lined up in rows and the prison commander addressed the men in broken English. "Anyone speak Japanese?" he asked. Rob gulped. But no one answered. "Your subs sink merchant ships. You criminals." Segregated by rank, interrogations began soon after they arrived. Each one of the *Thornfish* officers was put in former convent nuns' rooms now made into prison cells. The cell had a bed with no mattress, a small barred window and a pot to pee in. The temperature must have been over 100 degrees.

The Japs were interested in technical information about American submarines. They started with the *Thornfish's* captain. A soldier led Captain Morrison into a large room that formerly was a chapel. He was introduced to a Japanese naval officer who spoke very good English. "I studied at UCLA before the war, he announced. I'm here to help you avoid any strict interrogation captain. So, if you can answer some simple questions, I think your stay here will be more pleasant." Dick answered him, I appreciate that, but I can only give you my name rank and serial number according to the rules of war and international treaties. The interrogator replied, "We don't recognize them. We Japanese do not have any of our military held as prisoners by Americans. To be a Japanese prisoner is to be without honor." The following day he was bound hand and foot to a narrow bench. With his head hanging over the end of the bench, and his feet elevated, his torturers asked him questions about his vessel, its home port, refueling bases, codes used, radar ranges, sonar capabilities, and his mission in the Malacca Straits. He refused to tell them anything. They then poured water into his nostrils while holding his mouth shut. After he swallowed enough water, they beat him on his stomach with a bamboo stick until he passed out. The questioning was repeated over and over again. He refused to give in. Later, when he came to, he found himself bound to a chair with his hands tied tightly to the arms. Bamboo splinters were inserted under each fingernail and then set on fire. His screams could be heard throughout the convent prison. He still refused to divulge any information. He went without food for an entire week. As he dragged himself into the toilet after a beating one day, he found a pieced of charcoal and wrote on the wall for his fellow shipmates: "Stay tough, don't talk, and don't give up!"

Throughout their ordeal, the *Thornfish* crew's respect and admiration of their captain grew and gave them confidence.

· · · · ·

The stay at the convent prison lasted for 100 days. The Japs were frustrated. After abuse and torture for that many days, they had learned little information of any value from the Americans. Rob and the other officers received daily beatings. Rob understood the guards' language. They were very fond of beating what they called the 'dirty white men.' One favorite implement used by the guards was a piece of bamboo about three inches in diameter and about four feet long with holes every few inches. A prisoner would be ordered to stand at attention. Then the guard would take the stick and, when hit on the back, the holes in the stick created holes in the prisoner's skin that made running sores for days.

Finally, the *Thornfish* crew was again blindfolded and herded into trucks and driven through the hot, teeming Penang streets. The crowd jeered when it was discovered that the cargo was American prisoners. But some had enough courage to throw fruit into the trucks as they passed open-air markets. The crew eagerly shared what had been given to them.

Once on the pier downtown, they were forced up the gangway of a small rusty merchant ship. Guards made them climb down into a hold where the temperature was well over 100 degrees. There was little room for them to sit down. Captain Morrison demanded to see the captain. After much argument with the guards, he was permitted to take Rob with him to translate and was ushered to the bridge as the ship steamed down the Malacca Straits to Singapore. His tattered uniform hung on him after being nearly starved for over three months. He told the ship's captain that he had some very sick men, and they needed water and medicine. Rob translated his requests. The old Maru's captain was not going to provide anything to the Americans. But he was impressed with Rob and his ability to speak his language. "Where did you learn Japanese?" he asked. Rob told him and that he had met his old Japanese classmate from the American School in Tokyo recently and was able to rescue him from a sinking submarine. This really impressed the Japanese captain. He finally agreed to provide some medicine for dysentery and malaria and an ample supply of water for the *Thornfish* crew. "Thanks, Rob," Captain Morrison said as they were escorted back to their cramped hold. "Looks like we are on our way to Singapore."

Singapore, the gateway to the rich oil fields of Southeast Asia, controlled for decades by the British, fell to the onslaught of Japanese soldiers in less than three months after the start of the war in December 1941. The evening of February 10, 1942, The British Prime Minister, Winston Churchill, cabled the commanding general saying: There must be at this stage no thought of saving the troops or sparing the population. The battle must at this stage be fought to the bitter end at all costs. The 18th Division has a chance to make its name in history. Commanders and senior officers should die with their troops. *The honor of the British Empire and the British Army is at stake.*

The British surrendered on February 15, 1942.

The Japanese invaded from the thick Malaysian jungles rather than from the anticipated route by the sea. The battle lasted just over a week. The Japanese with 36,000 troops, 440 military pieces, and 3000 trucks defeated the combined British, Australian, and Indian forces of over 85,000 men, 300 military pieces, and 54 fortress guns. Prime Minister Winston Churchill called it the worst disaster in British military history. 80,000 troops were captured. The Japanese forces under the command of General Tomoyuki Yamashita were ruthless in the victory. On February 14 the Japanese forced their way into the western part of the city. As they advanced towards the Alexandra Barracks Hospital, a young British Lieutenant walked toward the Japanese lines with a white flag and was bayoneted. The Japanese entered the hospital killing 50 soldiers, including some undergoing surgery. Doctors and nurses were murdered. The remaining male staff and patients were ordered to march some two miles, and any that stumbled were bayoneted. Those that survived were herded into small rooms without ventilation and were bayoneted the next day. Only a few that played dead survived the massacre.

Ironically, the Japanese invaders were almost out of ammunition before the British surrendered. General Yamashita would say later that his attack on Singapore was a bluff. A bluff that worked. If the British could have held out one or two days more, the Japanese conquest might have failed.

The *Thornfish* crew was about to land in that hell hole.

Once disembarked in Singapore, the Japanese segregated the crew; they did not want anyone to know that they had captured an entire American submarine crew. Further information was needed from these highly valued prisoners, especially regarding American codes. Junior officers usually had communication billets on board U.S. submarines. Japanese interrogators would take their time to extract more information from them during the next stop on their journey. The crew of the *Thornfish* was held in Changi Prison for a week. They soon learned about the terrible conditions that thousands of Australian, British, Indian, and Dutch forces had been experiencing for nearly two years as prisoners of war. Emaciated British, Australian, and American soldiers, and even Navy survivors of the sinking of the American cruiser *Houston* early in the war, were being loaded into merchant ships en route to slave labor details in Japan. Japanese heavy industries were pleading for POWs to fill their needs for laborers due to military conscription of their male employees. Many of these white prisoners had been forced into building a railroad from Rangoon to Thailand and thousands of slave laborers perished under the harsh conditions in the Malay jungles from disease, malnutrition and torture. A booklet by the Japanese issued in 1943 provided instructions to commanders about the interrogation of *white* prisoners. "That he will not receive the same treatment as other prisoners of war; in the event of an exchange of prisoners, he will be kept till last. He will be forbidden to send letters, will be forbidden to inform his home that he is a POW."

CHAPTER 58

Missing in Action

It was springtime in Washington, the Cherry Blossom Trees were in bloom. In 1912 three thousand cherry trees were given in friendship by the Mayor of Tokyo to the United States. On March 27, 1912, the wife of President Wm. Howard Taft, Helen Herron Taft, and the wife of the Japanese Ambassador to the United States, planted the first two trees along the north shore of the Tidal Basin.

An Army Twin Beechcraft airplane from Andrews Airfield outside of Washington flew over the U.S. Capitol, along the Reflecting Pool lined with cherry blossoms, past the White House and the Washington Monument carrying Professor Dr. Robert A. Walker and four Army Air Corps officers on a flight from Andrews Army Air Base to Dayton's Wright Field.

Dr. Walker had finally gotten time off to come home for a couple of weeks. His expertise about South Pacific islands was proving very valuable in preparations for amphibious forces making landings on volcanic islands. He seldom had any time off from his secret work in the Navy Department. As the plane came in for a landing in Dayton, it flew low over Huffman Field where the Wright Brothers had test flown one of their early aircraft at the beginning of the Twentieth Century.

The Army provided him with a car and driver from the air base to take him to his home in Oxford forty miles away. The dull brown Army sedan pulled up in front of his home on Spring Street. He took his B-4 bag out of the back seat and thanked the driver, a young female Army corporal, a member of the Women's Army Corps, commonly called WACs. The Dogwood and Redbud trees lined the street outside his comfortable historic home. It was a welcome sight for his homecoming. Spring was his favorite time of the year.

Doctor Walker walked up the sidewalk and climbed the familiar four well-worn wooden steps to the front porch and opened the door to his home. "Honey, I'm home," he exclaimed. There was no answer. The family's car was parked in the driveway alongside the house. He went into the kitchen. It was spotless as usual. He climbed the back stairs and entered the master bedroom. There he found his wife of thirty-two years laying on the bed sobbing. He rushed to her side. "Honey, what's wrong?"

She held a crumpled piece of paper in her hand. "It's Rob!" she cried. "It's Rob!" He took the paper from her shaking fingers and read:

THE SECRETARY OF THE NAVY REGRETS TO INFORM YOU THAT YOUR SON LIEUTENTANT JUNIOR GRADE ROBERT A. WALKER JR USNR IS MISSIING IN ACTION

The rest of the telegram became a blur. He fell beside his wife and held her. Memories flooded his mind of his trip to Hamilton with his only son to enlist in the Navy, his eagerness to be in submarines that led his father to intercede with the highest echelons of the Navy to get his son directly assigned to a submarine. He was stunned. It must be a mistake. He reached for the phone to call his contacts in Washington, and then paused and put it down. She needed him as never before. He lay on the bed they shared for so many years and held his trembling wife.

Molly Gaynor closed and locked the door on *The Oxford Press* office on High Street. She had just finished her weekly column, *News of Men Serving in the Military*, including a short story about the USO in Oxford offering a party and smoker for men to celebrate the third anniversary of the founding of the National USO. She was pleased with her articles. Her writing career was becoming very rewarding. She was convinced more than ever that she had made the right decision. Teaching school is a noble profession, but it was simply not what interested her.

Molly put some papers in her new kangaroo leather handbag that she received from Rob for Christmas. She loved it. It was beautiful…. soft, dark red brown with pockets for the notebooks and camera used in her work for *The Oxford Press*. She thought how caring Rob had been to buy this expensive bag, but she really had wanted him to give her an engagement ring. As she walked along the brick sidewalk, she breathed the scent of the trees and flowers along the way to her small rooming house. She enjoyed the beauty of Oxford in the spring with white blossoms coming out on the Bradford Pear trees. Spring was in the air. Students walked past her on their way to their Oxford College dorm. She stopped at the post office, climbing eight steps to the front door and once inside the lobby she opened the little door to her post office box, hoping that there might be a letter from Rob. It was empty once again. She hadn't heard from Rob in months. She felt certain that something terrible had happened. His last letter included a loving Christmas card and her present, the kangaroo handbag.

As Molly approached her rooming house, she noticed a black late model Ford coup that looked familiar parked in front of her house. As she started to pass by, the driver side door opened, and a man got out and said, "Molly?" She recognized him; it was Rob's father. "Hello, Doctor Walker, I'm surprised to see you! You're still in Washington, right?" He came over and shook her hand, "Yes, I have a couple of weeks off, my first in a long time. How are you?" She looked intently at his face. He was pale and looked very tired. "Well I have a great job here in town working for the newspaper. I'm writing stories about the news of men and women in the armed forces. I send some of the more interesting articles to Rob. But Dr. Walker, I'm worried, I haven't heard from him in months. Have you?" He did not reply but asked her if she had time to come to their house. Molly was happy to join him. It had been a long time since she had seen Mrs. Walker. She hopped in the passenger side, and he drove his Ford coup down College Street, the cobblestones singing against the tires. There was no small talk. Turning left onto Spring Street they were soon at the front of Walker's home. He led her up the steps. The front door stood open and a breeze was flowing through the hallway. When she entered the living room, she found Mrs. Walker sitting in her chair, a photo of Rob in her hand. When she saw Molly, she burst out crying. "Mrs. Walker, what's wrong?" Mary Catherine turned to her husband. "Tell her Robert!"

"Molly, I'm afraid I have some bad news. A few hours ago, we received a telegram from the Navy Department. Rob is missing in action."

"Oh no, it can't be!" She stumbled and started to faint, Dr. Walker held her from falling and gently helped her to sit down in a living room chair. He went to the medicine cabinet and found some smelling salts. Molly revived in a few minutes. She looked at Rob's father, "Are you sure? What did the Navy say? How was the sub lost?" Dr. Walker handed her the telegram, wet with tears.

THE NAVY DEPARTMENT DEEPLY REGRETS TO INFORM YOU THAT YOUR SON LTJG ROBERT A. WALKER JR. USNR IS MISSING FOLLOWING ACTION WHILE IN THE SERVICE OF HIS COUNTRY. THE DEPARTMENT APPRECIATES YOUR GREAT ANXIETY BUT DETAILS ARE NOT AVAILABLE NOW AND DELAY IN RECEIPT THEREOF MUST NECESSARILY BE EXPECTED. TO PREVENT POSSIBLE AID TO OUR ENEMIES AND TO SAFEGUARD THE LIVES OF OTHER PERSONNEL, PLEASE DO NOT DIVULGE THE NAME OF HIS SHIP OR STATION OR DISCUSS PUBLICLY THE FACT THAT HE IS MISSING,

REAR ADMIRAL JON WALDRON FOR THE SECRETARY OF THE NAVY

Mary Catherine Walker said, with anger shaking her voice, "Molly, Doctor Walker is trying to get more information. We are hoping that he may be a prisoner of war." Molly sobbed, "Oh, God, help us."

• • • • • •

Weeks earlier Ben Miller received a call from the Commander Submarines Southwest's office in Freemantle, about three in the afternoon Hawaiian time. It was Tex McLean, Chief of Operations, on the admiral's staff. "Ben, we've got bad news. *Thornfish* is overdue and presumed lost." Ben was dumbstruck. He took a deep breath, "Tex can you tell me any more details." "Not over the phone," He replied. "I'll send you a message as soon as I'm authorized. I just wanted to let you know first in case you got the info from someone else." Ben said, "Thanks, I'm really sorry to hear this. I have a lot of friends on that boat."

Tex said, "I know. The staff at Freemantle is shaken, they have already lost three submarines in just a few months. The *Flier, Robalo,* and *Harder* were lost; the speculation is that mines sank them. *Thornfish* was in a treacherous patrol area. We assigned *Thornfish* to it only because the British had urgently requested the mission. News of these losses will have to be released soon. It's going to be a public relations nightmare. Undoubtedly the Navy will convene a Board of Inquiry. I think Admiral Christie is coming under some serious criticism from those up the chain of command." Ben interjected, "News is already out about the *Flier. The New York Times* reported that all the *Flier's* crew survived but then had to print a correction later. There were only eight survivors, including the captain. They were able to swim miles of open sea to land and got help from Filipino guerillas."

"Have the Japs said anything publicly about sinking a U.S. Submarine lately?"

"Nothing that we can identify for sure except there was an interesting item on Tokyo Rose's program some weeks ago. She said that an American submarine had been sunk and some captives were taken. No word as to which submarine. She makes up most of her stuff anyway. If you believe her, the Japs have sunk all our submarines."

"OK, please keep me informed of any word about the *Thornfish.*"

"Roger."

Ben thought maybe there was hope for the *Thornfish.*

· · · · ·

Valerie Edmonds arrived on Kauai just in time for the birth of Lily's baby. She had a difficult time getting time off from work. Her job as a translator with cryptology in the Navy at Pearl Harbor was demanding and much needed in winning the war. She was worried about Lily and the baby. The medical facilities on Kauai were not good. But Lily stubbornly refused to come back to the home island. Fortunately, the island's only doctor was sober, and Valerie helped with the delivery of an 8-pound baby boy. Lily had a long delivery and was exhausted when Lily's mom came in holding the new baby wrapped in a white towel. "Here's your new baby honey she exclaimed. A beautiful little boy!" Lily was so happy. She held him close. Her life would never be the same, but she was convinced that she had made the right decision. She would keep the little one and raise him without a father, at least for now.

Lily was devastated when she heard the news of the loss of Rob's submarine. She cried for days on end. She longed to see Rob once more, but it would never happen.

She grieved for the other members of the crew that she had gotten to know at the Royal Pink Palace. She remembered John and his innocence, Jerry with his latest Jewish jokes, and Captain Morrison, the seasoned veteran, who showed real leadership and was so admired by his men. All gone. The war had been devastating for so many, and Lily descended into the depths of despair after losing her father and now her lover. She determined to name the baby Robert and Franklin after Rob and her father Frank, but she wasn't certain which name would be the first or the middle name.

CHAPTER 59

The Voyage from Hell

The entire *Thornfish* crew was loaded on a Japanese merchant ship made by Mitsubishi along with some 1100 other white prisoners having been held in Singapore's infamous POW camp for over a year. Some were very sick with dysentery, malaria, and malnutrition. A second Maru, made by Kawasaki, was carrying over 1200 prisoners. Both ships became part of a convoy headed for Japan.

The conditions were terrible. They were forced down ladders into cargo holds that had been used for hauling coal and animals. As early as 1942, the Japanese Minister of Transportation ordered every returning merchant vessel to carry, in addition to their normal cargo of rice, munitions or troops, as many white prisoners of war as possible. Regulations promulgated in English for treatment of prisoners while underway were posted and given to each prisoner before embarkation:

"Punishment by immediate death include, those disobeying orders and instruction. Those showing antagonism and opposition. Those disordering the regulations by individualism, egoism, thinking only about yourself, talking without permission and raising loud voices. Those walking and moving without order."

The men were packed in like sardines. There was no room to sit or lie down. They had to take turns trying to find enough room to rest. Hatches were kept covered except for the time once a day required to empty four buckets used for toilets. Breathing became difficult and the temperatures in the tropical climate made the cargo hold unbearable. Many men died en route from dehydration, and lack of food, and their bodies were tossed overboard from the stern of the ship. Rob and most of the *Thornfish* crew were separated in the chaos. All the POWs were very frightened. It became almost impossible to breath. Men screamed. Panic set in. A bucket of water would be lowered and if some men were not near it, they would not get any. When the Maru encountered rough seas vomit from the seasick prisoners flowed all over the deck making it so slippery it was hard to stand. Beatings of the men were common, mostly for sport for the Jap guards. Rob being one of the tallest received many beatings. The guard would use bamboo shafts or sometimes baseball bats. His back would be raw. A young Catholic Priest suffering from malaria and dysentery tried to lift the spirits of the men after some sailors besides Rob were beaten. The Priest began by reciting the Lord's Prayer. As he spoke the words, *give us this day our daily bread and forgive us our trespasses as we forgive others….* his words trailed off and he died. Rob was almost ready to give up until the priest began to say the prayer. He became very angry. When the hatch cover was removed to haul the slop buckets up, he shouted in Japanese to the guard above. "You bastards killed a holy man of God! Let us bury him." The guard was infuriated. He ordered Rob to come up on deck. Rob slowly climbed the ladder; he was totally exhausted. When he finally reached the top of the ladder onto the main deck, he saw his punishment. The guard held a sword in his right hand. He was going to be beheaded.

Rob shouted to the guard, "I am an officer. Only an officer can do this to me." He was bound hand and foot and laid prone on the hatch cover. The guards began to talk among themselves; their conversation grew louder as they argued about what to do. Finally, after a few minutes a Japanese naval officer appeared on deck. Each ship carrying POWs had an officer assigned. He came over to Rob and had him turned over. "Remove his ropes," he ordered. He looked up at Rob "Stand up! You speak Japanese?" Rob struggled to pull himself up; every bone in his body ached. "Yes, I speak a little. I lived in Japan years ago." Rob could see that this lieutenant was curious to learn more.

"Why," he asked.

"I was going to school in Tokyo."

"Do you realize you have violated the rules for prisoners?"

"Yes, I am responsible for asking for a decent burial for a holy man of God, a Catholic priest who just died."

The Japanese junior officer said, "I am Shinto. We have holy men too."

"Can we give him a burial at sea?"

"No, you are in trouble. You have violated our rules. You deserve death. I should behead you now. You should be buried along with the priest. What is your number?"

Rob showed him the patch pinned to his ragged shirt, "Number 135." Rob said "Our men are dying every day. You must allow us more water and medicine."

"Don't tempt me anymore, you are getting the same treatment as all other white prisoners of His Majesty's Imperial Government. Now go below before I change my mind and you lose your head. You may be called upon to assist me with translations later."

Rob turned and took a deep breath of fresh air, and as he descended into the filth below, he said a silent prayer of thanks. He was still alive.

· · · · ·

On the other side of the earth Molly Gaynor woke in the middle of the night. Her heart was beating rapidly.

She had just had a nightmare. It was Rob. Something was wrong. She got up from her bed and walked to the window overlooking High Street. The street was empty. The luminous dial on the clock by her bed read three a.m. She knew that something terrible had happened to Rob. She sat in the rocker by her bed and started praying for Rob and his shipmates. On her nightstand was a small Bible, with the Psalms and the New Testament. She opened the book to Psalm 42, Verse 7, and the words leaped off the page: *Deep calls to deep, in the roar of your waterfalls; all your waves and breakers have swept over me. By day the Lord directs his love, at night his song is with me—a prayer to the God of my life.* Molly remained in prayer for the rest of the night.

· · · · ·

A few days later, Rob heard an explosion. A ship was hit by a torpedo. The Kawasaki built merchant ship in their convoy ahead of their vessel, was hit by an American submarine. Aboard were 1200 American and British prisoners. As the ship began to sink, the Japanese crew took to lifeboats. Those prisoners that were able to reach the main deck jumped in the water, trying to find anything to cling to as the Japanese beat them off when they tried to be picked up by the lifeboats. All the prisoners drowned.

After the attack, the guards on Rob's ship beat their prisoners in retribution. Any that fainted were thrown overboard. Eighteen days after leaving Singapore, the ship docked at Yokohama.

When they left the ship, the men were dizzy from dehydration, suffering from disease, malnutrition, and beatings by their sadistic guards. Some had difficulty seeing, due to lack of vitamin C. Rob's butt was badly bruised, so that he could barely sit. He looked in vain for John and any of his shipmates. The men were put into groups of 70 each. The Japanese Prisoner of War Ministry representative recorded the name, rank, date of birth, serial number, branch of service, and the job of each prisoner. Then they were given a small ball of rice, and a drink of water and marched to the rail yards. Along the way, Japanese civilians lining the sidewalks and alleys, spit on the prisoners, occasionally throwing stones at them. At the rail yard the prisoners were segregated according to their destination of assigned camps. All submariners were being sent directly to Ofuna, a secret prisoner camp operated by the Japanese Navy. The men in his group were jammed into canvas covered trucks for the short trip from Yokohama. Captain Morrison, Chief O'Neil, John and some of his shipmates from the *Thornfish* were in the truck with him. These highly valued officers and senior enlisted men were sent there for intense interrogation purposes. The internment camp was located at Kamakura, close to Yokohama. Rob had visited Kamakura as a teenager when he traveled there with his Japanese friends to see the famous metal statue of Buddha.

Camp Ofuna was opened in April 1942. It was operated by a unit of the Yokosuka Naval District. Most of the Prisoners of War camps were run by the Army. Ofuna was never listed as a POW camp and many of the residents of the city did not know of its existence. The Red Cross was never allowed in the camp. There were two sections of the camp. One with three main buildings in the former elementary school surrounded by a large field. The perimeter had an eight-foot-high wooden fence. The interior was divided into small individual cells, about six feet by ten feet. Each room had a bunk or just a bamboo mat, a blanket, an electric light with bulb and one window with bars. Guards were housed in each main building. Prisoners were not allowed to speak to each other, and silence was always maintained. Although it was cold, the prisoners were not permitted any clothing except what they had on when captured. Initially POWs were allowed out once a day and would have to stand at attention in the hallways.

The second section was partitioned off with a wooden fence and gate. The buildings there were newer but not as good as the old buildings. The roof and sides were covered with tar paper, and windows had no glass.

Interrogations began immediately trying to pry out information regarding submarines. Individual interrogations were repeated to compare notes with previous sessions. Answers that did not suit the guards were punished with beatings with a 2" by 4" stick about six feet long. Ofuna soon became known as the torture farm.

Rob held out during the worst of times until one day while in the dungeon in the basement of the old school, he saw his shipmate John being beaten mercilessly. He shouted out in Japanese, "Stop, you assholes! You're killing my friend." They left John on the floor and immediately turned on Rob. He was bound by his hands and a rope tied over a beam in the ceiling. They then took turns beating him front and back turning him from side to side. Hours later he was brought to his room and dumped on the floor. When he awoke, he was lying in a pool of blood. He had lost all sense of time. He had no idea how long he had been unconscious. It was dark outside. He started to get up but couldn't. He lay on the floor until early the next morning when the door opened, and two guards picked him up and took him to the little dispensary down the hall. An orderly treated his wounds and gave him some food. The following day, he was taken to the shower. "Take off those filthy rags white man!" the guard shouted. A small bar of Red Cross soap was handed him, and he could bathe in warm water and shave. Rob took a towel and carefully dried himself. Every bone in his body hurt. He was certain he had a broken rib or two. Breathing hurt. He was given underwear, new pants and a shirt. Afterward he was handed two Hershey's chocolate candy bars with Red Cross emblems stamped on the wrappers. Rob was bewildered. He wondered, what is going on? What's next? He was escorted back to his small cell. He sat on his bunk and tried to tear the wrapper off, but his hands were so swollen and bruised he started eating the candy, wrapper and all.

Earlier in Rob's second week at the Torture Farm, Rear Admiral Kamatsu, soon to become a Vice Admiral, left his home situated near the top of one of the many hills overlooking the Yokosuka Naval Base and walked down the 103 steps to the street level below striding briskly to his office near the waterfront. His headquarters, in one of the myriad tunnels carved in the hills of the Yokosuka Naval Base, housed the command center for all Japanese submarines. In his fight with the enemy he also had to continually battle the Japanese Army bureaucracy that wanted to relegate Japanese submarines to be clandestine supply ships for their embattled troops on Pacific Islands. And he had to battle the Navy bureaucracy pleading with them to build more subs to fill the void created by so many losses to American antisubmarine warfare. He had lost his only son when his I class submarine was sunk off the Honshu coast months ago. It was Monday morning. His chief of staff was already there reviewing the latest patrol reports of submarines in his command. It was not going to be a good morning.

The admiral's face was showing the strain of the war. Wrinkles spread across his broad face. His gray hair had thinned. Standing six feet tall in his early years, time and stress had slumped his body; however, his mind was as sharp as ever, and his eyes never missed a thing. The old man was worried. He had served in submarines since he was commissioned at the Japanese Naval Academy over thirty years ago. His shore duty included a wonderful tour as Naval Attaché in the Japanese embassy in Washington. While in Washington he toured the steel mills of Bethlehem Steel in Baltimore and its shipbuilding yards. He visited Norfolk, Virginia, and toured the U.S. Navy Base on a Sunday afternoon. The public had full access to the base; there was no security. The Japanese naval officer drove his car right on the pier next to where the aircraft carrier *Wasp* was berthed. He took many pictures with his little Nikon camera. He marveled at the Americans' openness. The public would never be allowed to tour any of His Majesty's bases. During his tour he learned to appreciate the enormous resources and the industrial might of America. He knew that Japan would never win a war with the Americans. Their only recourse would be to sue for an early peace.

As he entered his office his chief of staff rose, bowed and said, "Good morning sir, I trust you had a good night." The admiral growled, "No, I was informed before bedtime that we lost another I boat yesterday off Luzon. The Americans are sinking them faster than we can build them." The chief of staff said, "Which boat sir?" The admiral turned and looked at the chart of the Western Pacific on the wall. "The I-29 off the Luzon Straits. We believe an American sub sank it. The damned Army is being allowed to use our boats to move supplies and troops into some of these battles in the islands. We can't go on like this much longer. I am responsible but have little control anymore." The chief sat down in front of the angry admiral's desk. "Sir the Americans have improved their sonar. We are trying to find out more by interrogating submariners held at Ofuna. Here is a list of current captives." Admiral Kamatsu took a handkerchief and started to clean his glasses. "Just read me the names of the senior enlisted men and the officers there." The senior officer is a man named Lieutenant Commander Morrison, captain of the *Thornfish*. He is a very tough man. Won't give us any information. The next in command is an LT Jerry Abrams, a Jew I believe. The third is LT Peter Robinson, engineer, and the next is LTJG John Young, communicator, and the next in rank is LTJG Robert A. Walker Jr, gunnery officer." The admiral looked up, "Read that last name again." His chief of staff was puzzled, "Yes sir, LTJG Robert A. Walker Jr. USNR." The Admiral leaned forward, "I think I may know that officer. If it's the same Robert Walker, he and my son were students at the American School in Tokyo before the war. I want you to have him brought here as soon as possible."

"Aye sir, there is a note here that he speaks some Japanese."

The Admiral's eyes narrowed, he said, "He is the one I'm sure!"

"I will take care of it immediately."

CHAPTER 60

The Interview

Rob was ordered into the corridor outside his cell. Two guards came to him, "You go for ride." He was bound and blindfolded and led to a vehicle in the courtyard, but he was able to look down and peek at the ground before him. Then he saw a hubcap of a car with a Chevrolet emblem stamped on it. The two guards accompanied him in the back seat as it traveled along the streets of Kamakura, past the iron statue of the great Buddha and onto the highway leading to Yokosuka Naval Base. Rob was terrified. He was certain that he was being led to a public beheading. But why would they clean him up and give him clothes? It didn't make sense unless it would be for a propaganda film. Maybe he would be the subject of Tokyo Rose. He had really violated the harsh rules by interfering with John's beating. As the sedan bounced down the narrow road, he remembered the scripture passage in the little Bible that Lily's mother had given him... *God is our refuge and strength, A very present help in trouble. Therefore, we will not fear.* Rob prayed silently, "Lord please help me."

The sedan came to an abrupt stop, and the driver started arguing with men guarding the entrance. Finally, he heard the driver saying *arigatou,* thank you, and the Chevy drove slowly through the streets of the largest naval base in Japan. Still blindfolded, he could hear the familiar sounds of a Navy shipyard, cranes moving, riveting, motors of trucks moving cargo. When the vehicle stopped, other guards met them and led him into the tunnel marked His Imperial Majesty's Submarines Pacific Fleet.

Rob shuffled into the long tunnel. Noise from the large circulating fans greeted him drowning out any other sound. His blindfold had slipped enough for him to see the ground beneath his feet. There were patches of light and dark. "Halt!" His escort yelled as they entered the admiral's offices. "Stand at attention." Rob dutifully obeyed. He stood motionless for a long time. His body was still radiating the pain from his barbaric beatings. Finally, he was led into a large room and told to sit. A guard came over to him and spoke in Japanese. "You are to bow to the person you will meet. Now stand up and put your hand on my shoulder and follow me." Rob struggled as he got to his feet and placed his right arm on the guard's left shoulder. They moved into the admiral's office. A curtain covered the tactical map of the Pacific on the wall behind where the admiral sat at his teak desk. Rob stood at attention and bowed slightly.

"Your name." The admiral in Command of Japanese Submarines demanded.

"Robert A. Walker junior."

"Your rank and serial number."

"I am a lieutenant junior grade, USNR, serial number 517510.

"What is your specialty in the Navy?"

"I am a submariner."

"Name of your vessel."

"*Thornfish*."

"What is your billet?"

"Gunnery Officer."

"Who is your father?"

Rob was startled. He stammered, "Doctor Robert A. Walker Sr."

The admiral said, "I have met your father, and I met you once when you were a student with my son at the American School in Tokyo years ago. Guard remove his blindfold!"

Rob's heart leaped. His eyes were trying to adjust to the bright light. He was surprised to see the distinguished Japanese Admiral sitting behind a large ornate teak desk. His jet-black hair had streaks of gray, his eyes deep-set, and his strong square jaw gave him an intimidating look. He ordered his aide to dismiss the guards. He said, "Sit down." Rob slowly sat in a straight back chair. Standing or sitting caused intense pain. "I am Admiral Kamatsu, you may remember me. I am the father of your former schoolmate Jimmu Kanatsu. Rob was stunned.

"How are you being treated?" he asked. The admiral need not have asked. He could see the pain in Rob's face. His clothing hung on him. His tall frame was bent. His eyes were gaunt. His jaw, scarred.

Rob said, "Ofuna is a torture farm. We are beaten with baseball bats for no reason at all. We are not allowed to talk except when told to. Food is terrible, rice with bird feed filler added and that only once a day. My shipmate was nearly beaten to death by two guard's days ago, I don't know if he survived. We are told that the Red Cross will not be informed that we are prisoners. The Japanese government and your Navy are violating all the rules of war for the treatment of prisoners." The admiral interrupted. He called his orderly into the room. "Get me a meal…soup, and boiled fish, rice cakes, coffee and a bottle of sake." He turned to Rob, "I'm sorry lieutenant, the confinement of guests of our Emperor is beyond my control. As you may know, we signed the Geneva Convention of 1929 for the treatment of prisoners of war, but it was never ratified. The Geneva convention allows for enlisted POWs to be used for labor if they are physically fit. Officers are exempt. They are to maintain control over their men. I understand, however, that they can volunteer to work and will be paid. But we Japanese do not recognize any of our military taken as prisoners. It is not honorable for the Japanese military to be taken as prisoners. Japanese tradition for centuries impressed on military and civilians, that to be taken prisoner is shameful. The Military Code of 1941 says plainly we are to have regard for our family first. Rather than live and bear the shame of imprisonment, the soldier must die and avoid leaving a dishonorable name. Honor is an important matter for the Japanese."

Rob summoned up as much courage as possible, "But you, Sir, do have one of your own as a prisoner of war held by the Americans, your son Jimmu!" The bright light prevented Rob from seeing the anguish on the old man's face. He jumped up and ran from behind his desk and shouted, "How did you know about his capture?" Rob was shaken. Beads of sweat ran down his forehead. The admiral paced back and forth, "I received notice from the Red Cross months after his I boat was lost that he had survived and was taken prisoner. I am relieved but at the same time our family is dishonored by his surrender. Japanese sailors should go down with their ship. It is the honorable thing to do.

Rob could no longer stand it. "Is it honorable for a professional Japanese naval officer to beat prisoners and throw them overboard, deny medicine, deny food and water and sanitary conditions that we have experienced as so-called guests of your Emperor? Is it honorable to behead helpless prisoners if they talk too loudly or when they cry out in pain? Is it honorable to not tell their loved ones that they are being held captive? Is it honorable for mothers and fathers to worry themselves sick for months and even years not knowing if their son is alive or dead?" The admiral was outraged. He was about to respond but hearing the commotion, a guard ran in the room and started to hit Rob with a pistol. The admiral told him to stop and leave the room. He looked at Rob, "You could be killed for talking to me like that." Rob said, "I know, I have been beaten for far less."

Just then the meal arrived. He commanded Rob to sit in a chair at his long conference table. Rob bowed his head and offered a silent prayer for saving him and the food. Admiral Kamatsu sat opposite him at the long table and watched him bow his head and eat his first real meal in months. "Eat slowly lieutenant or you'll vomit." Rob heeded his warning.

As he slowly spooned his soup, with real meat, the admiral said, "Now lieutenant, tell me how you came to know about my son becoming a prisoner of war." Rob replied, "Because I helped capture him."

The admiral was speechless. He stood, paced back and forth and suddenly turned, "Impossible! He was on patrol off our coast, and his boat was not heard from again. Don't fool with me. I have ways to make you tell the truth young man." Rob said,

"I know, I have been tortured sir. I am telling you the truth. We captured your son who was the navigator, as well as his quartermaster on his I boat. I'm sure that they were on the bridge getting ready to take evening star sights, when we torpedoed their submarine." The Japanese officer said angrily, "Who else was taken prisoner?" Rob answered truthfully, "No one sir, those two were the only survivors. The captain went down with his command."

"Good, my son should have also. It's a *matter of honor*."

Rob replied, "I believe he would have had we not fished him out of the water. He must have been blown overboard when the torpedo hit. Before we surfaced, we heard a submarine blowing ballast. We thought it might be an American boat, so we carefully identified it as the enemy. If the timing had been different, we might have been torpedoed instead."

"Your entire crew survived. Even your captain. He survived. Tell me about him. He is at Ofuna. He is very uncooperative. He should have gone down with his boat."

"He is a great commanding officer. Our crew loves him. He is courageous and looks after his men."

"What was the condition of my son?"

Rob replied, "He was shaken up but not wounded. We took him below and our doctor examined him and his enlisted man and gave them food and clothing. Our captain insisted that both prisoners be treated in accordance with international treaties." Admiral Kamatsu glanced at his watch, he seemed unimpressed. "This war will come to an end eventually. Your forces will have to invade our homeland and the casualties on both sides will be enormous. I must go, but first is there anything I can do for you? You speak enough Japanese that could be useful to us. Perhaps I can get you assigned to one of our industries. I'm well acquainted at Mitsubishi and Kawasaki, and I might be able to get you assigned to one of their plants." He took a small bottle of sake and poured two small glasses, one for Rob and one for himself. The old man offered a toast: "To Peace!" Rob didn't respond but took his and drank it. It was a good sake. It would be his last drink for a long time.

Rob sensed that the interview was over. He said, "I do not want any favors, Sir. I have one request. I would like to have the Red Cross notified of our POW status, so that our loved ones will be informed of our capture." The old man stared at him and said simply, "I doubt that will be possible, but I will see what I can do." He called out, "Guard!" The guards came in and bound and blindfolded Rob. The interview had ended. As he was leaving, the old officer said in English, "I hope we meet after the war. Good luck."

CHAPTER 61

Oxford, July 1944

A silver Navy standard trainer, the SNJ Texan made by North American Aviation, swooped down on Oxford in the afternoon sun. It glided down to less than 500 feet and zoomed over the water tower in Oxford's town center. The pilot applied full power and the engine roared over the university town. The low-winged Navy trainer headed west over High Street and circled the tiny airport at the west end of the village. The pilot checked the wind direction from the windsock at the end of the grass strip. The plane landed near the end of the grass runway and taxied up to the hangar. The pilot cut the engine, slid the canopy back, pulled up his goggles, unstrapped his parachute and hopped down from the left wing and onto the grass. Woody Collingsworth was completing his final solo cross-country flight before being awarded his wings and commissioned as a Second Lieutenant in the United States Marine Corps Reserve. He was excited to be back in Oxford and a chance to see his girlfriend Molly. He was going to surprise her.

Molly sat at her desk in the tiny offices of *The Oxford Press* on High Street completing the editing of a story by her colleague, Fern Patten, about the price of cocoa. During the cocoa scarcity the price jumped from twelve cents a pound to sixty cents for the popular Our Mothers brand. Complaints to the Office of Price Administration had forced the distributors to lower their prices. The article said, "The outlook for the remainder of 1944 looks good for not only cocoa, but coffee and tea. You may be limited to one can, but it will be at a price set by the OPA."

When the plane flew over the town, Molly heard the roar of the engine and rushed out to see what was happening. The engine sounded like thunder and frightened her. It was so loud that she thought the plane might crash. Seeing nothing, she returned to her desk and finished her work on the page for the Thursday edition. She was writing a one-paragraph story about the movies being shown uptown at the Miami Western Theater. The price for a ticket had gone up to forty cents. The movie to be shown on the weekend was *Going My Way*, starring Bing Crosby and Barry Fitzgerald, about a talented young man who leaves a life of singing and dancing to become a Catholic priest at a rundown church in New York. Molly immediately decided that she really wanted to see this one.

Everyone had gone home for the day when she finished her story. Her thoughts drifted as they often did, to Rob and his loss. It had been over a month since she was informed by the Walkers that the Navy had reported the loss of the *Thornfish*. She wept every night. Sometimes she got out of bed and sat in the rocker praying for Rob. In her heart she believed he was alive. Her daydream was interrupted by a knock on the office front door. Molly went to the outer office and opened it. Standing there was a very handsome Navy man in khakis. "Hi Molly, remember me?" Molly was shocked! "Woody what are you doing here? Was that you buzzing the town? I bet you nearly clipped the water tower!" He hugged her tightly for a long time. "Molly I have just a few hours, I have to leave in the morning to return to Pensacola, could we go to dinner tonight? I don't have my Chrysler, but I have a borrowed U.S. Navy Jeep waiting outside. Let's go someplace where we can talk!"

Molly locked the front door to the office, and they headed for Mac and Joe's in the alley next to John Minnis' drug store. Woody wanted to take Molly to Cincinnati to the Maisonette, but it would be too long a drive, cost too much precious time, and be a little dangerous for them to be on the highway after dark in the little gray Navy Jeep. They found a small booth at the very end of the pine-paneled room and Woody ordered two Miller High Life beers. Molly said she wanted tomato juice, but Woody overruled her. "This calls for a celebration Molly. We don't have champagne, but we have the *champagne of bottled beer*." Molly looked at him, he was more handsome than ever. Gone was his pencil thin mustache. His face was tanned, and black hair shortened to comply she thought with rules for Marine trainees. "How is flight training going Woody?" she asked. "Ok I think, but first I want to tell you how sorry I am to have learned about Rob's loss. He was a fine man and a good submariner I'm sure. When did you learn that his boat was missing?" Molly started to shed a tear, took a napkin and wiped her tears. "Two months and five days ago. I still can't believe it. Somehow, Woody, I feel he is not dead. I recently read of eight survivors of a damaged U.S. sub that made it to some islands in the South Pacific and they were able to get help and eventually made their way to Australia." Woody took a long swig of beer, "I hadn't heard of that, they were really lucky. Maybe Rob will too." She changed the subject. "Tell me how do you like flying? Have you run out of gas again?" Woody laughed, "You really know how to hurt a guy Molly. No, I haven't, in fact I am more careful than others in doing my preflight checklist. I learned my lesson with you. Right now, I'm doing my solo cross-country and next week I will be doing six carrier landings in my SNJ. I love that plane and I really love flying. I am applying for advanced fighter aircraft training at Corpus Christie Texas. Would you like to come and see me there? Or better still you could come to my class graduation at Pensacola and pin my wings on me." Molly blushed, and smiled, "Oh that would be fun, but I don't think I could get time off." Woody said, "Well maybe you could convince your boss that you should cover a story of a Miami graduate who is finishing flight training. It might make an interesting story of what we do to learn to fly and fight our common enemy." Molly smiled, "That would take a lot of doing with Mrs. Cullen, believe me."

Woody went to the bar and ordered two hamburgers with the works, and two Millers. When he returned Molly excused herself and went to the ladies' room. Woody was troubled. Molly still loved a man who most likely was not alive. She was in love with a wish dream. He was aware that his chances of her loving him were slim, at least until she came to the realization that Rob was gone forever. She returned and sat down in the tiny booth, he said, "You smell good. What are you wearing?"

"Chanel No. 5."

"Wow, that's expensive."

She smiled, "it was a Christmas present." Woody could guess who it was from.

The conversation turned to parents, Mrs. Walker, *The Oxford Press* job, her future goals for writing. She told him of the scrapbook she was doing for Rob and that his mother had caught the same idea and had been clipping articles from the magazines and newspapers and putting them in a large scrapbook for Rob, but she had stopped when the telegram arrived. She said that his mother was taking it very hard. His missing in action and presumed death was a terrible loss for her. Dr. Walker had returned to Washington determined to help as much as he could in his work for the Navy. Mary Catherine had told her of a letter she had received from a friend of hers, by the name of Marianne, who had a chance meeting with Rob in Australia. Marianne was a singer with a USO troop touring the far-flung bases entertaining the soldiers and sailors in foreign bases. She had learned of the loss of the *Thornfish* from newspaper reports and was quite devastated apparently.

Molly and Woody finished their meals and went outside, and walked down the sidewalk past Snyder's variety store, and on past St Mary's Catholic Church. "This is where I go to church Woody. My Pastor, Father Tom, is a source of comfort for me in the last few months." Woody reached out and took her hand. They walked hand in hand, on past the entrance to Slant Walk. They stopped and took a drink from Tobe's fountain, made of odd size uncut stones, still spouting delicious water from wells deep under Oxford's Ordovician surface. Woody reached over and drew Molly's face to his and kissed her. She seemed to melt in his arms. Molly recovered and said, "Tobe is still having dreams on Friday nights during football season of Miami Redskins' football victories. He even predicts the scores. At the pep rallies he wears his red and white striped suit, with a matching umbrella, and dances in front of the crowd to loud cheers." Woody recalled seeing him perform at football games while he was busy covering the games from the press box high above the stands. Woody said, "And I am having dreams too. Not of football but of you." She smiled, and said, "Woody you are so sweet." They turned around and started back to the Navy Jeep parked in front of the Purity Bar. When they arrived at the Jeep, they found some sailors sitting in the front seats enjoying watching the girls go by. When they saw Woody coming, they jumped out thinking that Woody was an officer. "They saluted, "Sir, sorry to have taken liberty with your vehicle." They had not seen a Marine Cadet before; Woody returned their salute, and ushered Molly in the front passenger seat and took off. "Golly, that was my first salute! And I'm not even an officer." They laughed. It was liberty night for many of the Navy students. Two shore patrol enlisted men walked past them casting an eye on Molly. 'Eyes in the boat sailors,' thought Woody. A sign outside the city hall advertised the USO dance for the evening being held in Withrow Court. "Why don't we join them for a few minutes Molly? It'll be like old times again." She quickly agreed.

As they drove down High Street, Molly asked, "Where are you planning to sleep tonight?" Woody immediately thought *with you honey*, but he restrained himself. "I don't know, probably at the frat house." Molly laughed, "No you won't. It's been taken over by females for the duration. Why don't we go over to see Mrs. Walker, maybe she'd put you up for one night?" Woody was not keen on that, but he conceded and reluctantly turned down Campus Avenue and stopped in the driveway by the Walker's home on Spring Street. They got out and walked to the front door and rang the doorbell. No answer. There was a light in the hallway, but no one seemed to be at home. "Well it's early," Woody said, "We can come back later."

When they arrived at Withrow Court, The Campus Owls, student swing dance band, was playing a Glen Miller hit tune, *Jeep Jockey Jump* and the dance floor was crowded with sailors jitterbugging with young coeds from campus. Molly and Woody joined right in. It had been so long she had almost forgotten how much she enjoyed dancing and being with Woody. It was like old times again, she mused, and he is such a good dancer, almost as good as Rob. He is good looking in his uniform, but not as much as Rob was or...is.

The dance numbers changed, and the lights dimmed as the band played, Glen Miller's *Moonlight Serenade*. Woody held her close as they slow danced, and she didn't resist. He whispered, "Molly, I love you and have since the first time I met you." Molly said, "I love you too Woody." She looked away, "but somehow deep in my heart, I feel Rob is still alive."

Woody said, "I know you do but if he isn't, do I have a chance? Even if it's one in a million!" She kissed him and said, "Sure." It was intermission, and the lights came on very bright. Woody said, "let's go." They exited the building and walked along Talawanda Street. Tuffy's was still open, "Let's have a toasted roll!" They went in and found a booth and ordered two rolls topped with vanilla ice cream. "It's like old times.

I've missed these." He put his spoon down and held her hand, "Molly if things work out for us, we could be married right after I am commissioned. I'll be making $275 per month. We could live well while I'm in advance flight school. We'll have a ball." Molly looked at him. *He's so wonderful to be with. But I am so confused now.* She said, "I need time to think and pray a lot about everything." Tuff's soda jerk was preparing to close. "Woody, we need to find a place for you to stay. Let's go back to Mrs. Walker's house and see if she's returned."

When they got to the borrowed Jeep they drove right over to Walker's home. They went to the door and rang the bell. No answer. Molly said, "She must be gone for the weekend. What will we do now? You're not going to sleep on the street. I have an idea. We will go to my room. There's a couch long enough for you. But we will have to be very quiet and absolutely no hanky-panky. Is that clear?" Woody nodded. "If they find me with a man I'll be thrown out on the street!" Woody couldn't believe it. It was too good to be true. *Me and Molly* sleeping in the same room!

They parked the Jeep in the alley behind her rooming house and quietly walked around the side of the house to the front door. Molly put her key in the door, turned the knob and was quickly inside with Woody right behind her. The old folks lived in the downstairs, and their bedroom was in the back of the house. So far so good. She closed the big glass front door and turned the deadbolt. She took off her shoes and tiptoed up the stairs. Just as she got halfway up the stairs, Mrs. Douglas yelled from the back bedroom, "Molly did you lock the front door?" Molly's heart skipped a beat, "Yes Ma'am." The elderly lady was always careful about locking up all the doors and windows at night. "Just can't be too careful you know. Good night." Molly said, "Good night Mrs. Douglas." She and her guest continued up the carpeted stairs to her room. They went into her room, Molly whispered, "Woody, I'm going to use the bathroom down the hall. Take off your shoes and be very quiet. When I return you go to the bathroom and I will be in bed. You use the couch. There are blankets in the closet if you need them. But remember, no hanky-panky." Woody nodded his head and watched her beautiful back as she went out the door.

Earlier that afternoon, Mary Catherine Walker, became very daring. She drove her husband's black Ford coup over route 73 to Middletown and then onto highway 4 leading to Dayton's Wright Field Army Air Base. She had received a phone call a few days prior from her dear young friend, Marianne, inviting her to attend the USO show at the base. She was the lead singer for the USO's Big Band Sound, playing hit tunes from the list of Hit Parade songs. Doctor Walker had arranged through a friend in the Pentagon, to get her a VIP pass and overnight accommodations through the base Protocol Office. Mrs. Walker was excited to see Marianne after all these months, and especially so since she had seen Rob just before his submarine had been lost on patrol.

She had great seats in the officers' section of the hangar at the base. A stage had been erected in a hangar and about a thousand soldiers crowded in to see the performance of Bob Hope, Jerry Colona, and the band with the featured singer, Marianne.

Mary Catherine could not get over how beautiful Marianne looked. She was positively gorgeous. Dressed in a tightfitting short skirt and white lowcut blouse that accentuated her beautiful curves, she was an instant hit with the troops. The band opened with an up-tempo version of *There'll be a Hot Time* followed by the *Little Brown Jug*. Then Marianne came on singing, *Saturday Night is the Loneliest Night of the Week*. The troops clapped and cheered wildly and wanted more. A vocal followed, *Jukebox Saturday Night*. Bob Hope, the Ohio born comedian, cracked jokes and barbs with Jerry Colona whose big eyes were only exceeded by his big black handlebar mustache. It was a fun evening. After the show, Mary Catherine made her way backstage, finding Marianne signing autographs. When she saw Rob's mother, she ran to her and hugged her and kissed her on the cheek. "I am so glad to see you Mrs. Walker, let me change and we can go someplace and talk." It didn't take long for her to join Mrs. Walker, and the two slipped out of the back of the hangar and she drove the Ford to the BOQ where Mrs. Walker had a suite. When Marianne entered the room she said, "WOW what a room! You have a bedroom, a sitting area, a kitchenette, and look, a wet bar stocked with adult beverages!" Mary Catherine laughed, "Help yourself honey. It's on the house." Marianne chose Johnny Walker Red Label Scotch and poured a drink for each of them.

"Now tell me about your life on the road, do you like it?" Marianne said, "Yes. It's fun, exhausting, and sometimes dangerous entertaining the troops, but I feel we are really doing something to contribute to the war effort by bringing a little bit of home to the guys overseas. Mrs. Walker, I want to tell you how shocked I was to learn about the loss of Rob and his shipmates. I cried for days. I feel so sad, more than you realize. I know you are suffering from your loss. I am still depressed. She started to cry. Mary Catherine crossed the room and hugged her and held her for a long time. "Tell me about the last time you saw Rob. How did he look? Was he OK?"

"He looked great. A little pale from being in a submarine for months, but he was in good spirits, full of fun and looking forward to his next patrol. He liked Australia, as did all the sailors I met. The folks there treated American sailors like their saviors, as I guess they were."

Marianne went on to tell Rob's mother of their meeting by chance at the USO dance in Perth and the fun they had for a few days touring the countryside. She took a drink of scotch and stared at the glass, "You know, I think if time had stood still a bit for us, we both might have fallen in love."

"I wish it had, Marianne."

. . . . .

Molly lay in her double bed; Woody on the couch. They talked very quietly for a long time after turning out the lights. He told her what flight training was like and asked her to come to his graduation and commissioning. "With flight pay I'll be making about $300 a month, and we could be married Molly, if you'll have me!" Molly didn't say anything for a long time; she stared at the spokes of light from the street lights outside her room that danced across the ceiling as she lay there thinking about his words. After a while she whispered, "I don't know Woody, I may have to wait a while longer." Finally, Woody got up and went over and sat on the foot of Molly's bed. He said, "Honey, I'll wait." He made no advances, which surprised Molly.

Woody found the knobby couch in Molly's bedroom uncomfortable, but it didn't bother him a bit. The exhaustion of the long flight, the excitement of being with his girlfriend and the evening of dancing, caused him to fall asleep within minutes after they said a final goodnight. But Molly couldn't sleep. She disliked the bed…it sagged in the middle. Molly glanced at the luminous dial on her alarm clock. It was two a.m. She thought of how her life might be like if she married Woody. *He is a wonderful man, spontaneous and risky at times, but has his serious side too. He is fun to be around, and he really loves me.* She remembered how kind he was when she learned of her brother having been killed in action. He stayed with the family in Marion and helped with some of the arrangements. She had worked with him when he was the sports editor of *The Miami Student.* She thought that *after the war he'll probably go into sports broadcasting. And he didn't take advantage of me when I fainted after having just two beers New Year's Eve. He carried me naked into my bedroom. He was a gentleman then and now here he is sleeping in the same room with me. Any girl would jump at the chance to marry Woody, and even sleep with him before going off to war. But I still feel that Rob's alive, somewhere as a prisoner or in a jungle with guerrillas. I want time to see if it is real or a wish dream.* She finally dozed off with the words of the last song at the dance, reverberating in her dreams, *'It had to be You, it had to be You. I wandered around and finally found someone who could make me be true….'*

The alarm went off at five a.m. She shut it off immediately. Molly put on her robe and gently shook Woody. "It's time to go, Woody." He went down the hall without his shoes and used the bathroom. When he came back in the bedroom, he said, "I used your toothbrush, hope you don't mind." She laughed, "No, it's for the war effort." He pulled her tight and put his arms around her. "Molly I love you even in the morning. Please marry me!" Molly said, "I love you too, we'll see." He held her closer and whispered, "Please don't wait too long, we may not have a lot of time." He kissed her again and finally eased out of the room with his shoes in hand, descended the stairs, unbolted the door and was quickly out in the dark alley where his Jeep was waiting.

Farmers, even retired farmers, are used to getting up early. Today was no exception. Mr. LeRoy Douglas sat in the kitchen drinking his first cup of coffee for the day when he heard the front door being unlocked. He glanced down the dark hallway and saw the back of a young man leaving the house. He didn't say anything but moved down the hall to the front door and locked the deadbolt. Something will have to be done. He liked Molly. She was a good tenant, but Mrs. Douglas doesn't want any hanky-panky here even in wartime.

· · · · ·

Molly was sitting on the porch swing of Mrs. Walker's home on Spring Street when she drove up in her 1941 Ford coup. She parked and grabbed the small overnight bag and climbed the stairs to the front porch when she saw Molly. Molly was crying. "Molly, what's wrong?" She hurried over to her and sat beside her in the white swing. "I was thrown out of my room. I don't know where to go." Mary Catherine Walker put her arm around her and tried to comfort her. "What Happened? I thought you liked the place you were staying." Between sobs, Molly told her the story of Woody and that there was no hanky-panky at all. "Mrs. Douglas wouldn't accept the reason for Woody staying overnight, and she was the one who threw me out." Mrs. Walker hugged her and said, "Well don't you worry honey, you can stay with me as long as you like. I will enjoy the company, and we have plenty of room. Now let's go inside, and I'm going to fix you some of my favorite tea, and we'll talk." They both sat at the kitchen table and talked for hours. Molly told her about Woody flying in and buzzing the town and that they couldn't find a place for him to sleep. She even tried to see if the Walkers could put him up overnight. "Well tell me about Woody. Do you like him?" Molly said "Yes I do. I've known him for several years. He's a wonderful person. Kind, gentle with a great sense of humor, and he's very handsome." Then she added, "He's asked me to marry him." Mrs. Walker looked directly into Molly's eyes. "Do you love him, Molly?" She asked. "I'm not sure; I think I could… but I still love Rob, and I believe he is alive."

Mrs. Walker got up and went to the stove and fiddled with the tea kettle. She turned and said, "What leads you to think he is?" Molly looked up at her. Her stern countenance seemed to demand evidence. The tall slim elegantly dressed woman standing at the white stove was so much like Rob, confident, smart and very practical. Molly took a deep breath and said, "Mrs. Walker, *have you ever thought you could talk with God? I mean that you could hear a word from him specifically directed for you?* I want to tell you I had such an experience one night. It was a short time after you received the telegram from the Navy. I awoke in the middle of the night. I was sitting in the rocker in the bedroom praying for Rob. It was just as if I had heard an audible voice in my room. It was just two words, "He's alive!" Mrs. Walker sat down and held her hand, "Molly, I hope you are right. Help me to believe too, will you?" Then she looked directly into Molly's eyes, "You build up my faith so much. I want you to remain here for the duration with me. Let's continue to do the scrapbook I've started for Rob. Someday he will enjoy reading about all that was happening on the home front here in Oxford while he was away!"

CHAPTER 62

Ofuna

Rob was led back to his cell in Ofuna's torture farm. His blindfold was removed, and he was shoved into the tiny room. The only light came from a small barred window high above the room. He still had not had any contact with any of his shipmates since arriving at the secret Japanese Navy POW camp. Prisoners were not allowed to talk to each other. In camp his captors never addressed him by his name or rank, just the number he was assigned, number 135 pinned on his breast pocket. The only real meal he had eaten since his capture was the one he was served in the admiral's office. While eating the dinner, the old man, speaking English to avoid being overheard by others, told Rob that he appreciated the care that he gave his son during the time he was on the *Thornfish*. Rob was praying that the admiral would reciprocate by somehow notifying the Red Cross of his capture and his shipmates. His prayer was interrupted by a commotion outside in the hallway. He thought he heard John's voice saying something. He ran to the door and put his head against it hoping to hear some words of the yelling going on. The Japs were beating a prisoner for refusing to talk. He was pretty sure it was John. Perhaps he was right next door. After the turmoil stopped, he looked for a way to communicate with the prisoner next door. He found a broken piece of wire hanging underneath his rusty short bunk made for a Japanese. Along the ceiling, a conduit used for the wire of a single overhead light bulb ran to the next room. He stood on the bunk bed and fished the wire in the crack where the electric wire conduit ran into the next cell. He wriggled it. No response. He tried again, with the same result. Rob thought he might be unconscious. He'd try later.

Ofuna was never intended to be a prisoner of war camp. The Imperial Japanese Navy operated it. After the interrogations of captives were over, they were generally transferred to work in Japan's heavy industries such as shipyards, mines, factories and steel mills. But some prisoners were held at Ofuna for years. One of the Marine pilots held there was Major Gregory 'Pappy' Boyington, who had chalked up twenty-two kills before being shot down over Rabaul in early January 1944. Rob learned later that an Army pilot by the name of Louis Zamperini, an Olympic gold medalist runner, was being held there and was tortured unbearably because he was such a well-known athlete. Dick O'Kane, commanding officer of the submarine *Tang,* was a prisoner at Ofuna and suffered terrible punishment from the interrogators. The *Tang* was sunk by one of its torpedoes that malfunctioned during a fast attack on a convoy in 1943. Only nine crew members survived.

To the Japanese, prisoners had no rights. They were considered war criminals. Taking more than a normal share of atrocities at the torture camp were American submariners who targeted "innocent merchant ships." Captain Morrison was singled out especially. Upon arrival at Ofuna, the captain was led out in the courtyard in front of all newcomers and beaten with a baseball bat to impress on the new arrivals what awaited them if they didn't cooperate. They hauled him off to his cell unconscious. It was just the beginning. He would be subjected to countless episodes of water torture, beatings, his fingernails pulled out, but he never gave in.

The guards were not the sharpest knives in the drawer. Most had failed to meet the conscription standards for the Army. Their superiors abused them; beaten for the slightest infraction of discipline, they frequently took their rage out on their helpless prisoners. The rules for Ofuna prohibited prisoners from speaking to anyone other than guards. No eye contact was allowed. Heads always had to be bowed. The day began with the ringing of a bell, assembly in the yard, roll call by counting off by each prisoner, bowing to the emperor, and calisthenics to the point of collapse. They were required to stand at attention outside in all kinds of weather without any warm clothes. Breakfast was a bowl of sloppy rice that was consumed in each prisoner's cell. Rob soon learned that the old-timers had a way of communicating while standing in line at roll call. They used Morse Code with hand signals while they had their hands behind them. A clenched fist was a dot; a flat hand was a dash. So, the letter R, for Roger, was a fist, hand flat, and a fist. Dot dash dot.

Prisoners were hauled out at random to be interrogated and were asked the same questions that they had been asked before to see if they gave the same answers, and they would compare answers given by others from the same unit or ship. The interrogators spoke good English. Some had gone to school in America. One had been assigned to the Japanese embassy in Washington. A few days after returning from the interview with the admiral, Rob had a chance to see John. He was in bad shape. It was a cold morning after calisthenics, Rob saw him in line about to fall, but he managed to remain standing. He's a real tough guy, Rob thought. The guards were laughing making fun of their prisoners. When they weren't looking, Rob found a broken pencil dropped by one of the guards. He quickly put it in his pocket. He had to be very careful about putting his hands in his pocket. It was an offense punishable by a severe beating. Later that morning when he was eating his meager breakfast in his cell, he managed to write a note on a piece of toilet paper. *John hang tough. I'm praying for you. Rob.* He stood on his bed and using the wire poked the note through the crack in the walk where the conduit ran between rooms. The next morning Rob found a returned note. Thanks Rob J. It was written in blood.

· · · · ·

"You're lucky 135," said the young Jap interpreter to Rob. "You are going to be transferred to a comfortable assignment. You are going to go to work for the Mitsubishi Company. You and several of your crew are leaving tomorrow." Rob was not happy; here at Ofuna at least, they were not helping the Jap war effort. Working for one of the largest suppliers of war equipment was not only contrary to international treaties for POWs but completely reprehensible. He wondered if the old Jap Admiral arranged his assignment. Rob asked about his executive officer, LT Abrams. The well-dressed interpreter he called 'Pretty Boy' said, "He is a Jew and is being sent to Mitsui's plant, the Deakin Kogo Co, an electrical chemical subsidiary, at Aomi, near Tokyo, known as POW Branch Camp No. 13. This is where undesirables, Jews, and the very sick are sent." He added a somber note, "You're lucky that you are not beings sent to Camp 13, life is hard there, they work in open iron pits, and furnaces with hot molten metal. Very, very dangerous work. You mess up and get beat very much." He refused to tell him any more names except to say that his commanding officer, Morrison, was being held at Ofuna.

It was getting very cold. December in the Kamakura area was much like that of Cape Cod, raw, blustery wind, and some snow. Men wore their blankets when outside as much as they were permitted by the guards. The men of the *Thornfish* were concerned about their fate, and what might be happening at home. By this time the Navy would have sent telegrams to the next of kin. Wives, sweethearts and mothers and fathers would think that their loved ones had perished, like so many others in the submarine service had, when they received news of 'overdue and presumed lost.'

But about the time Rob and his shipmates arrived in Japan, Admiral Lockwood received some good news. The code-breakers in Pearl Harbor had intercepted and decoded a short transmission from a Japanese merchant ship *Teiwa Maru* that had departed Singapore and was approaching Yokohama with 1123 prisoners of war including the crew of the American submarine *Thornfish*. The ship was requesting that transportation arrangements be made for the prisoners when it docked.

Only the admiral responsible for the entire submarine force in the Pacific, and a few of his staff were made aware of the news. Admiral Lockwood wanted to tell the families about the *Thornfish* crew, but he and his staff were pledged to silence to prevent disclosure. If the Japs knew that their code had been broken, it would set back the war effort for months.

* * * * *

The torture farm of Ofuna was losing some of its guests. There were seventy-two of them. On a cold December morning, they were loaded in two Jap trucks that chugged and backfired on low octane fuel. Three shipmates from the *Thornfish*, Rob Walker, John Young, and Larry O'Neill shared one of the tarp-covered trucks with other high-value prisoners from other boats and aircraft. Although John was the senior man in rank, it meant little to the men with the common goal of survival. The cold wind blowing through the truck penetrated the men's thin clothing. They had to leave their issued blankets behind. As the truck wound through the crowded streets near the waterfront of Yokohama, the men were speculating where their destination might be. The guards had told them sordid stories of the coal and copper mines run by Mitsubishi. 'You dead if you go there' one remarked. Rob ran his fingers over the ID bracelet that Molly had given him last Christmas. It was the only personal item that he was able to keep as the *Thornfish* sank. The words inscribed inside were written in his heart as well. The Lord Bless You and Keep You and Give You Peace. And the words "all my love forever. Molly." He said a prayer, "Jesus, help us. Amen."

When they got out of the truck, they heard airplanes. Lots of them. They looked up and saw formations of beautiful silver American B-29s flying high above Yokohama leaving contrails in the blue sky. The men were overjoyed. "They're on their way to Tokyo," Rob remarked. "Hallelujah!"

CHAPTER 63

The Mitsubishi Copper Mine

Of the many Japanese corporations during the war that needed large numbers of American prisoners, five were the major consumers of slave labor. They were Mitsui, Mitsubishi, Nippon Steel along with Showa Denko and Kawasaki Heavy Industries. The need was so great the companies paid the Japanese Army a daily fee for each POW assigned to their company. Mitsubishi Industries' complex extended from the Japanese homeland to the jungles of Thailand, and to the cold northern plains of Manchuria. They manufactured the Zero fighter plane and other aircraft at Nagoya, ships at Nagasaki, mined copper and coal in northern Honshu, steel mills at Zosenjo. The company was one of the largest consumers of slave labor during the war, and they made a handsome profit. One very lucrative venture was supplying railroad ties for the famous Burma-Siam Railway, cut through hundreds of miles of impenetrable jungle, using some 61,000 Allied POWs. Some 13,708 would die in the building of the railroad. In 1936 British engineers investigated the possibility of building the railroad but rejected the idea due to the dense jungle, and the high probability of malaria and disease that would be encountered in building it.

In early 1942 the Japanese government instituted a Prisoner of War Bureau to oversee the distribution of forced labor. Mitsui was the largest 'employer' of slave labor. The Mitsui family was one of the most powerful magnates in Japan. POWs were transported in merchant ships built by Kawasaki, Mitsubishi, and others. Many upon arrival were too sick to be used. One shipment had over 100 men that were so sick they were left on the pier at Yokohama upon arrival and were never seen again. The supply was endless, however, and sick men were seldom given medical treatment.

Half of the seventy-two 'graduates' of Ofuna were assigned to the Kawasaki shipyard at Nagasaki, and the others to the Mitsubishi copper mine at Hanawa in northern Honshu. Rob and John Young along with some of the crew of the *Thornfish* including Rob's mentor, Chief O'Neil, were loaded into railroad cars and transported to the northern mountains of Honshu; their destination, the Osarizawa Copper Mine at Hanawa. The camp was designated as Sendai POW Camp no. 5.

In September 1944, hundreds of white prisoners arrived at the camp. Rob and his buddies arrived in December. The cold was unbelievable. The barracks had no insulation. The wind howled through the wood slab boards. The steep roofs, to deflect snow, were covered with tar paper. Buildings were connected by covered walkways. A small guard shack sat at the camp entrance housing a half-frozen sentry. The fence around the camp was only eight feet high, and with snow of two to three feet, a prisoner could easily vault over the fence and escape, but where could he go? A white man didn't have a chance to find a way out to the ocean. That was one of the reasons that the Japanese POW Bureau requested only white prisoners for assignment to Japan. Their skin color would make it difficult for them to escape very far.

The new arrivals were issued blankets but no toilet paper, sanitary supplies, toothbrushes or soap. One small stove was the only source of heat and that for only two hours in the night. The guards confiscated even scraps of wood that the prisoners collected to feed the tiny stove. Each prisoner was issued a new number. Rob was assigned 244. *I'm moving up* he thought. John Young's new number was 232.

The ancient Osarizawa mine has been in operation for over 1000 years, and Chief Electrician Lawrence O'Neil, assigned to the repair shop, thought that the equipment was almost as old. The shop had many old GE electric motors badly in need of repair. The chief needed repair himself. Age and cold were wearing down the old man. John and Rob had to sign a document in Japanese that said that as an officer, he was volunteering to work for Mitsubishi and that he would be compensated at the rate for labor in the area, paying overtime as appropriate. The rate would be about three cents a day in U.S. dollars. None of the prisoners ever received any compensation. Meals of rice and something like seaweed were made available only twice a day. Fish meal was occasionally provided. Tea was the only beverage and that at night. Old-timers told them that during the summer they would catch grasshoppers to supplement their meager meals with some protein.

The snow was two feet thick when they arrived. The men had to climb nearly two miles up a narrow mountain road to get to the mine hanging on to a rope along parts of the road to avoid getting lost while climbing through the blinding snow. Some men succumbed to pneumonia and died; their bodies were laid out frozen until they could be buried when the ground thawed out.

The damp mine had icicles hanging from the roof of the tunnels. But hundreds of feet below the cold surface, the temperature in the mine became more tolerable. Each day POWs would be lowered down the elevator to various levels of the mine. The copper was in veins threaded through the tunnels in igneous rock. Dynamite had to be used periodically to blast the rock. An electric drill machine, made in the USA, was used to drill out holes for the dynamite. The POW's task was to gather up the pieces after the blast and load them into buggies to be pushed to the elevator shaft for transport up to the surface. Occasionally silver deposits would be discovered. Dim electric bulbs lighted the tunnels. Some workers had to wear carbide lamps fastened to their foreheads with a tight band, to see within some of the dark tunnels under Honshu. Each laborer had a pick with an ax on one end and a hammer on the other to bust the rock into smaller pieces. They were so emaciated that it was difficult for them to raise the pick after three or four hours in the tunnel on what they estimated was about 500 calories per day.

Rob thought it ironic that he would be in a Mitsubishi copper mine during the war. He had spent a summer during college working at a copper mine in the Upper Peninsula of Michigan. The copper country in the Keweenaw Peninsula jutted out into Lake Superior and was a major source of the nation's copper for decades. The first mining of copper was done by the Native American Indians. They melted copper from veins that extended to the surface along the shores of Lake Superior. Rob loved hard rock mineralogy, and his summer work allowed him to get a good income and earn college credit as well. His work took him thousands of feet below the beautiful forests of Michigan. The Finnish people came to America and settled in the Keweenaw because it reminded them so much of their native country. Steam hoists lowered the men into the mines in the early morning. They brought with them pasties made of potatoes, meat, and vegetables all enclosed in a hot bun. Rob loved them and dreamed of eating them often at night in the frigid mountains of Honshu.

The Japanese Mitsubishi employees treated the white prisoners as brutally as the halfwit Japanese soldiers guarding them. One of the company's honcho foreman hated white people. He regularly beat John because he was tall and made a good target for his bamboo rod and because he was the senior officer in the camp. The prisoners called him the Mitsubishi gorilla because he looked like one. His long black hair covered his head and shoulders. Massive arms and belly were as large as a sumo wrestler. Discharged from the Army for insubordination and theft, he was drunk more than sober.

Just before Christmas a truckload of Red Cross packages arrived for the prisoners. Each man was given a small package but told not to open them until all POWs had received theirs. Then they were ordered outside to stand at attention in the cold night. While they were standing at attention for hours, the gorilla had the Red Cross packages removed and put in a storeroom for his personal use and to be sold on the black market. When the men returned to the bunks, they found all their packages had been stolen. John was furious. Rob had never seen his calm, cool friend so angry. He ran to the Japanese commander, an old Army Lieutenant who had been passed over for promotion and demanded that they be returned. After much argument, the old officer agreed to have them given back. However, he required that all prisoners be photographed with the Red Cross packages by a Mitsubishi photographer at a Christmas 'celebration' in the dingy mess area. John knew that they would use the pictures as propaganda.

The Mitsubishi gorilla was not in a good mood. He would get his revenge soon.

CHAPTER 64

More News!

Molly had a new home in Oxford. The Walker's home on Spring Street was perfect for her. She could walk to work and church. She had a large bedroom at the front of the house overlooking Campus Avenue. There was plenty of room for her desk and a small sitting area, and an adjacent private bath. Mrs. Walker bought her a full-size Philco radio set in a beautiful walnut cabinet and put it by the couch. Molly had the dial set most of the time to 700, WLW, but one feature that she really appreciated was it had a shortwave band. Occasionally she and Mrs. Walker would sit on the small settee and listen to the radio reports from the BBC station in London. One evening they heard a live broadcast of Prime Minister Winston Churchill announcing the first V-2 rockets that the Germans began firing indiscriminately into London in September 1944.

Mrs. Walker wouldn't charge her rent. She insisted that she appreciated the company of Molly and she could learn to cook and help with doing some light housework. An additional benefit was that she was continuing to learn how to drive. Mrs. Walker gave her instruction sitting at the dinner table one evening, "Here's how to shift gears Molly." She took a knife and showed her how to go through the four forward gears and how to engage reverse. "Now tomorrow we'll make sure you can do it. We'll drive over to College Corner if the weather cooperates."

Despite her poor health, Mary Catherine Walker remained a big wheel in the Oxford community serving as a volunteer for the war effort in Oxford. She sat on the rationing board, the local USO board and was being considered for an appointment to the Trustees of Miami University. She worked with the newly established chapter of the NAACP to establish a colored recreation area in town. She read the *Cincinnati Enquirer* every day and loved the crossword puzzles. She read as much as possible of the *Wall Street Journal* and the weekly *Oxford Press*. Her favorite place in Oxford was the newly formed Lane Library, and she was soon enlisted to be on the library board.

She liked the articles that Molly was writing for *The Press*. She was very impressed with the editorial Molly helped write in September 1944, about Miami discriminating against women. Women were not permitted in the Press Box at Cook Field, Miami's football stadium. Molly wrote, "We understand the ban is not so much against bona fide women reporters as against women visitors desiring an extra good seat in the press box, but it's the principle of the thing. Miami University, long a coeducational school, should open its press box to accredited women of the press."

Mrs. Walker led her into her study on the first floor. "I want to show you something I have been doing. For months I've been clipping articles from the newspapers and magazines about the war effort." She opened a huge scrapbook. The dark blue hardcover had an emblem of the United States Navy emblazoned in gold. After she had received the news of the loss of Rob, she stopped working on the scrapbook. "Now Molly I think you can help me. It will be a treasure for my husband and Rob to see after the war." Molly said, "I'm doing the same thing. I have clipped a lot of articles from *The Miami Student* and *The Oxford Press*. We'll have fun doing this together!"

On the first page was a picture of Rob and his father taken at Rob's commissioning at Northwestern University in downtown Chicago. Molly gazed at the photo for a long time. Mrs. Walker interrupted her reverie by gently turning the pages. "Look dear, I've been capturing some of the major events in the war each year since 1942. I'm currently working on 1944." Molly turned the pages, lots of articles had been clipped and not mounted. She'd help do it in her spare time. Some of Mrs. Walker's scrapbook that needed to be mounted were:

Oxford Press September 28, 1944

The price of flour in 25 lb. Bags $1.14; Tomato soup two cans for 15 cents; coffee Kroger 59 cents for 3 lb.

The film showing at the Miami Western Movie Theater, *Going My Way* with Bing Crosby and Barry Fitzgerald. Matinees cost 40 cents.

Major Gravitt, who was from Oxford and attended Miami University, was killed on his 30th combat flight over Germany, and leaves a wife and baby he had never seen.

In August 1944, attendance at the Oxford USO was 3,042.

The price of gasoline at the Marathon station at Main and Park Street is now 20 cents per gallon. Phone # 121

Sept 1944, A Colored Youth, Number 1 Man on Miami's cross-country team, Sylvester Stewart 18, set a new state record for the half-mile run.

An article that captured Mrs. Walker's attention was one that mentioned that the Miami University student body was composed of mostly women and that the staff of *The Miami Student* newspaper had a female business manager. Mary Catherine sparked, "Molly you're right. Women are doing jobs that men have traditionally done. Why women are even working in the steel mill at Armco in Middletown doing tough jobs that only men have done for decades. And they damned well should be able to be in the press box at Miami University!"

Mrs. Walker continued, "And here's another one I just read in the Christian Science Monitor: The War Department, believe it or not, has just issued a booklet of instructions for G.I. Joe on the mysteries of women! And a booklet, *Do you want your wife to work after the War?* has just been published. One section of the pamphlet dealt with men assisting their wives with washing and drying dishes!"

An article from the pages of the *Cincinnati Inquirer* fell to the floor, that carried the story of the Battle of the Philippine Sea, nicknamed the Great Marianas Turkey Shoot by Americans, that had taken place. The U.S. Fifth Fleet won a decisive battle near the Marianas Islands. Over 200 Japanese planes were shot down while the Americans only lost 29 to enemy action. In the first five months, the Japs had been defeated in the Marshall Islands; Kwajalein, the world's largest atoll and a major Japanese naval base was secured in February. And the Navy bombarded the Kuril Islands, northernmost of the Japanese homelands.

June 6, 1944, the long-awaited invasion of Europe began with 155,000 troops landed on the coast of Normandy, France.

July 10, Tokyo was bombed for the first time since Jimmy Doolittle's raid in April 1942.

July 18, General Hideki Tojo resigned as Chief Minister of the Japanese Government due to increasing military losses and the Emperor, Hirohito, asked General Kumiaki Koiso to form a new government. In the same month Marines landed on the island of Guam in the Marianas on the march to Tokyo. On the 10th of August, Guam was reported liberated after fierce fighting. A few days later the Marines landed on Tinian Island the last of the Marianas, and it will become a base for B-29s to bomb the Japanese homeland. Soon all the Marianas islands will be under the control of the Americans.

Mrs. Walker sparkled, "Molly this war is turning. We are winning! Pray that Rob will be coming home soon!"

CHAPTER 65

Sandia Camp no. 5

Rob and John were struggling to stay alive at Sandia POW Camp no. 5. Rations had been cut. Some new arrivals joined them; some were airmen recently shot down over Japan. One pilot, badly burned, had been treated by the Japanese doctor in the mining town. He was never hospitalized and left by the medic on a cot in the prisoners' barracks. Prisoners took turns trying to clean his bandages and give him nourishment from what they could from their rations, but several evenings later the doctor came in the barracks and gave the young lieutenant an injection. He said it was for infections. A few minutes later he was dead. His companions believed it was an injection to put him out of his misery.

The new POW arrivals brought some good news about the advancing allied forces in the Pacific. Saipan had fallen with thousands of Jap casualties including many civilians who committed suicide rather than face capture. They learned that MacArthur had returned to the Philippines, as the United States Army landed on Leyte October 20. And on November 6, Franklin Delano Roosevelt won his fourth term as president. And a few weeks later, the U.S. Navy started bombarding Iwo Jima preparing the beaches for the Marines to invade the small but important volcanic island some five hundred miles from Japan. It would provide the closest base for B-29s to make emergency landings on the way back from the aerial bombing of Japan.

A senior British enlisted radioman was among longtime POWs in camp no.5. He had been badly wounded in the battle for Singapore and was assigned to the kitchen. Rob was amazed that he had been able to construct a small radio. By bartering with some townspeople that came to the camp daily bringing meager supplies, he was able to get enough radio tubes and parts to make a small receiver. For power he jury-rigged a lamp cord and tied into the electric wire for light bulbs. Tokyo Rose came in strong. In the cold December night Tokyo Rose played some Christmas Carols, and a song was sung by Bing Crosby, "*I'll be home for Christmas*" specially designed to depress rather than cheer allied troops. The men crowded together to hear the latest music from home and laughed at her trying to persuade the Americans to give up the war. "Don't stick your neck out sailors…you'll lose it!" she said softly. Rob thought of Christmases past;

last year, the celebration was in the warm confines of the *Thornfish* with Christmas carols, cake and ice cream; now their only tree was drawn in charcoal on the floor by one of his compatriots.

There was no celebration in camp on New Year's Eve 1944. As the bombing of Japanese bases in the homeland increased, the beatings by the Mitsubishi's honchos increased. Japan's war production bureau demanded more production. Prisoners were working 14 and 16 hours a day doing hard labor. The gorilla selected the men he wanted to work each day. Sick or infirmed men were not exempt. His disdain for officers was apparent. He particularly had it in for John since the Red Cross package episode. John was showing the damage to his body from the beatings. He looked terrible. His handsome face had scars, his front teeth were loose, and he would probably lose some of them at least. Rob thought he must weigh about 90 pounds. He encouraged him, "John hang in there. We're going to make it. Remember the girl you left behind in Australia. She is waiting for you. We've got to believe we will win soon."

The New Year 1945 began with a problem. It happened on a bitterly cold winter day at Osarizawa copper mine. There was fire in the gorilla's eyes as he ordered the work crews to assemble outside the steam hoist as dawn broke over the bleak countryside. He had been drinking and was obviously hung over from a night of hard binging. He was more sadistic during his drinking bouts, and today was no exception. As the workday began, he ordered men from the selected work detail to get in the elevator, deliberately overloading it. The cab groaned under the load of men and materials. They stopped at different levels as the men fanned out to work. Of interest to Rob, as a geologist, was a large vein of mass copper in the level that he and John had discovered the previous day. John, Rob and one other prisoner had spent all morning chipping at the surrounding rock to free it, and it finally broke loose. It took all three of them to load it in the wheelbarrow and they started back to the main shaft toward the elevator. They came to the large corridor, awaiting the elevator, and decided to eat their meager ration of a rice ball loaded with chicken feed. They heard the elevator creaking down the shaft and looked up as the elevator arrived and saw the gorilla. The five-foot-five hulk had a kamikaze bandanna on his forehead. Hung by his right side was a machete. "We're in trouble," John said. And he was right.

The honcho yelled, "Why are you sitting down? You are loafing. Get back to work you white bastard mercenaries." As he walked toward them, the elevator started back up to the surface leaving the rickety gate hanging half open. Without warning he drew the machete and struck John in the side of his head with the flat blade. The sudden blow knocked him down on the floor of the tunnel. The gorilla then turned the machete and stood over John's prone body with the raised blade. He was about to behead him. In an instant Rob summoned all the strength he could muster and tackled the monster from a football crouch and shoved him over to the edge of the elevator shaft. The hulk lost his balance and started to fall into the mineshaft but managed to hold onto the rickety gate by his fingers. He looked at Rob with fear in his eyes pleading for help. But Rob, knowing he would kill them, kicked him. The gorilla disappeared screaming down the dark shaft and seconds later the splash of ice-cold water at the bottom sealed his doom. John stirred. Rob tried to explain to him what had happened. They sat on the floor of the tunnel trying to decide what to do. "Do we report it, or just not say anything?" asked John. The sound of the elevator coming back down filled the chamber. They needed a plan right now.

John prayed out loud, "Jesus help us!"

The third man on their work detail spoke up. He saw everything. He was an Aussie, an engineer by profession, who had been captured at Singapore in early 1942 and later taken to Burma to work on the infamous railroad with some 61,000 other captives. After the bridge over the River Kwai was nearly completed, he was transferred to Japan in a Mitsubishi merchant ship to what he thought would be a decent camp. Engineers, especially white engineers, were in high demand in the homeland. He was offloaded at Moji and transferred to Mitsubishi's aircraft manufacturing plant at Nagoya, where they manufactured the famous Zero fighter. He was caught later sabotaging the Zeros by putting sand in the gas tanks. He told John and Rob about his punishment. He was beaten unconscious and starved for a week without food or water. As further punishment, he was transferred to Mitsubishi's copper mine. He became a friend of John and Rob. His positive attitude lifted their spirits on more than one occasion.

"Mates" he said, "I've got an idea. We had a similar thing happen on the Burma railroad. One of the sad sack guards, came up missing one day. He was killed by an Aussie buddy of mine. He was tripped on the edge of the bridge when my friend stuck his foot out and the bloke fell a hundred feet to his death in the river. It was deemed an accident. Let's tell the camp commander that the gorilla was drunk and fell after he got out of the elevator. Case closed!" Rob looked at John. "What do you think?" John replied, "Well the camp commander may buy it. It's worth a try."

LT Toshinori Asaka, the camp military commander, listened passively to John as he explained the demise of the Mitsubishi honcho dramatically. The old lieutenant knew full well of the gorilla's drinking habits. He had reprimanded him more than once and threatened to send him to Mitsubishi's Mukden Manchuria plant, the hell hole of POW camps, if he didn't stop drinking. Competition for slave labor by POWs among the forty or more Japanese companies wanting them was intense. But Mitsubishi got 2000 allied prisoners early in the war, the majority American, to work in their manufacturing plants at Mukden. The temperature dipped to 40 degrees below zero in the severe winters. They were housed in earthen huts, with sod roofs, and prisoners were always cold. Nearby was the site of the notorious Unit 731, falsely named *The Anti-Epidemic Water Supply and Purification Department*. Many believed that POWs were subjected to medical experiments and died. Jap medics would sometimes come in the barracks at night and inject prisoners while they were asleep. The next morning, they would be dead. Beatings were common, and prisoners were often made to stand outside naked in subzero temperatures. Three hundred died the first winter at Mukden.

The threat to send the gorilla to Mukden, however, didn't work. He liked his sake too much, so LT Asaka seemed satisfied with John's explanation. But to be sure, he interviewed Rob and the Australian soldier separately and they both told the same story of how the honcho died. They hoped the case was closed.

· · · · ·

The camp commander was depressed. He sat in his office outside of the compound staring at the snow coming down. When he was younger, he loved the snow. He took to skiing and spent time when he could in the north country of Hokkaido. He thought it would be a great place for holding the winter Olympics if peace ever came to the world again. He was worried; reports of American bombers flying over Honshu without any Japanese aircraft opposition, meant that the invasion would come soon. Certainly, this year. Guam and Saipan had already fallen, as had Iwo Jima. General Tojo had resigned as Prime Minister. Next would be Okinawa and then the invasion of the mainland. There would be a bloodbath when that occurred.

He unlocked his file cabinet and found the file he was looking for. It was a copy of an instruction from the top echelons in the military government regarding the treatment of prisoners of war. The policy, going back as far as 1942, stated that they were to be publicly mistreated, humiliated, used as slave labor and then killed. If a POW camp commander believed that the enemy would overrun his camp, they should use all means to kill all prisoners by whatever methods necessary, and any documents regarding their captivity should be immediately destroyed.

He had received word of the Palawan massacre in the Philippines December 14, 1944, in which Japanese soldiers burned 150 Marines alive thinking that their camp was to be invaded by the Americans. Only a few remained alive to tell about the massacre. Aska was familiar with killing, having served in the Japanese infantry brigade that raped Nanking, China, in 1937. He had participated in the rape and massacre of innocent Chinese civilians. Thousands were bayonetted or beheaded by gleeful Japanese soldiers. But he could not understand why he was passed over for a promotion and given this godforsaken duty with Mitsubishi. Someone had it in for him he was sure.

As the snow piled up outside his window, he pondered the best way to annihilate all the prisoners under his responsibility. He concluded that all POWs would be ordered into the mine for daily work, and then he would dynamite the steam hoist collapsing it over the mine entrance and sealing off all below. Any prisoners topside working in the repair shop or kitchen or warehouses would be shot by the guards. Their bodies and all documents would be incinerated by gasoline. He would work with the Mitsubishi personnel office to destroy their records. It would not be easy, but it could be done. He placed the only copy of the order he had back in the file cabinet and locked it. He would personally take it with him when and if he had to escape from the mine headquarters. It would be his cover should he ever be arrested. It would show that he was just obeying orders.

After he returned to his desk the phone rang. It was the Army headquarters in Tokyo. He thought, what have I done wrong now?" He picked up the telephone.

"Lieutenant Asaka speaking." It was his superior officer. "Good Morning, Sir." The general was abrupt as was his custom. "Lieutenant, you are ordered to transfer a prisoner to Ofuna camp in two days. He is needed for further interrogation. His name is Robert A. Walker Jr. and his service is Navy and his serial number is 517510. Do you understand?"

"Yes sir, but I must tell you we need every prisoner to make our production quotas."

"I know that you numbskull!! You may get additional workers later. Make sure he is presentable. He will be seeing a Navy Admiral." And he hung up.

CHAPTER 66

Oxford, Christmas 1944

There were two letters on the hall table in Mary Catherine Walker's home. One for Molly, postmarked U.S. Naval Air Station Pensacola, and the other postmarked U.S. Armed Forces United Services Organization, for Mrs. Walker. She had built a fire in the living room fireplace and was sitting in one of the two large wingback chairs. Green garland and small lights trimmed the fireplace mantle. The only other decoration she put up this year was a small Christmas tree set on a Queen Ann table near the front window.

Molly took the two letters into the large living room and handed the one from Marianne to Mrs. Walker. "Thank you dear," she said. "I'm hoping Marianne has some good news for me." She tore the envelope open and began to read. "I am so saddened by the loss of Glen Miller," she wrote. "They say he is missing but rumors are that his plane mysteriously disappeared on a flight over the English Channel. He could have stayed as a civilian but elected to join the Army. He was on his way to join his band in France on December 15, 1944. He will be missed by all of us on tour but also by the entire nation. His musical arrangements became a standard for the big bands in America. He combined the clarinet and the saxophone to make a new sound resonating through the music world." Mrs. Walker took off her glasses and gave her letter to Molly to read. When she finished the two-page letter she said, "Marianne has become your friend hasn't she?"

"Yes, and you missed seeing her just by a few hours when she was here. You would really like Marianne. You know she was the last one we know to see Rob alive." Molly was hurt but tried not to show it. "I know, I'm sure that she was fond of Rob even though she only must have known him for a short time."

"I am sure of it too." She sighed saying, "Marianne sent me a letter expressing her feelings when she learned of Rob being missing in action."

While Mrs. Walker went to the kitchen to make some tea, Molly eagerly opened her letter from Woody. He had received his commission and was selected for advanced fighter training. He said it would be an accelerated course, since they need pilots in the Pacific. He wrote, "I am hoping to be assigned a combat squadron in the Pacific where the final action will soon take place. The war in Europe is winding down. The American Army under General Patton has taken one of the large cities in Germany, and on the way to Berlin he stopped long enough to piss in the Rhine River! The Russians are in Poland. Germany will be crushed from both sides." Woody's letter ended, "Molly I dream of you every moment, day and night. I love you so much, <u>will you marry me</u>? Please tell me soon, <u>we don't have much time</u>…all my love, W."

Her gracious landlady returned with a pot of tea, cups and some Christmas cookies that she had baked that afternoon. Molly said, "Woody is predicting the war in Europe will be over soon. General Patton is on his way to Berlin."

"I know," Mrs. Walker said, "I heard about it on the BBC shortwave broadcast from London earlier today." Then she added, "But Molly I know these damned Japs, they won't give up easily, and it will be a lot longer war than people think. I lived in Japan for two years and met some of those SOB leaders. They have this damned honor code that goes back centuries. It's called Bushido. The word loosely translated means *the way of the warrior*. It is a code of principles that the soldier must master. It includes honor, obedience, duty and self-sacrifice. They believe surrender is a dishonor for the soldier and his family. And the summation can be hara-kiri. My husband told me that they have already had what they call Kamikaze pilots that fly their aircraft right into our ships."

Molly changed the subject. "But Mrs. Walker, I need some advice, this letter… Woody is getting deployed soon and has proposed in the letter. He wants us to get married as soon as possible. I don't know what to do, I'm so confused." Mary Catherine was moved. She sat on the settee next to Molly. She loosened the knot holding her hair in back, letting her graying locks fall around her shoulders. She looked less severe, even gentler. "Molly, I'm not the one to talk with you about such a momentous decision. I'm prejudiced of course. The question I would ask is, are you in love with Woody? Do you want to spend the rest of your life with him?"

She waited for Molly to respond. When she hesitated, she said, "I know you believe Rob is still alive. I want to believe that too. But realistically speaking, his chances are very slim. Let me tell you about a conversation I had recently with one of the crew's wives. I had a phone call from Mrs. O'Neil, the chief of the boat's wife. She called to see how I was getting along now. She mentioned that some of the younger wives had begun dating, and one had remarried already. I'm telling you this in confidence since you have a big decision to make. What I'm trying to say is that some of the survivors' dependents are making efforts to get on with their lives. It has been over seven months since we got the telegram. Molly, perhaps you should consider it too." Molly sighed, "I know, Mrs. Walker, I understand. I need to pray about this."

CHAPTER 67

The Vow

Rob was freezing. It was the coldest night of the year. The men in his barracks huddled together to get a little warmth. The fire in the little stove had gone out, and the guard had confiscated the remaining firewood that they had managed to steal. As punishment, the bastard had opened the windows to make their lives even more miserable. The Brit radioman had his makeshift radio on to Tokyo Rose's broadcast. She was describing the atrocity of the B-29-night raid on Tokyo. Snow had fallen on the entire city. Hundreds of bombers unloaded gasoline jellied incendiary bombs on the city of wooden and paper homes and light industry. Over 50% of Tokyo's industry was among residential and commercial neighborhoods. She said it was estimated that over 100,000 people were killed in one night that they now call the night of black snow.

Earlier in that day, Rob had been ordered to come to the camp commander's office. LT Asaka waited for Rob to bow and then said. "You are being transferred back to Ofuna tomorrow. Someone there wants to talk with you. A big shot I am told. So, mind your manners. You can tell them you learned a lot from your experience volunteering at Sendai POW Camp no. 5. You are very fortunate not to have been sent to Mitsui Corporation POW Camp, where the copper we mine is used. You get burned with nitric acid, and the chemicals you breathe will kill you. Men die every day. Count your blessings and tell the others what a good learning experience this has been in the Mitsubishi copper mine."

Rob was shocked. *Why am I going back to the torture farm?*

That night, despite the cold, Rob, John and Chief O'Neil huddled together for the last farewell. The chief shared a Hershey bar he was given by one of the guards, undoubtedly stolen from a Red Cross package, for repairing a small electric heater he used in his room. "This is a little treat for you Rob. I don't know if you'll ever be back in this hell hole. I hope not." John interrupted. "Fellows, whatever happens, let's make a vow that if any of us makes it to the end of this bloody war, that he will tell our loved ones that we love them and are honored to have done our part in this war." Chief O'Neil asked that his wife in California be told. John gave his folks' name and his girlfriend Isabelle in Australia. Rob said he wanted his folks in Oxford to be told and the love of his life, the girl he wanted to marry, Molly Gaynor of Oxford and Marion, Ohio. The chief added, "I'm very proud to have served with you men. You both have become great officers, and I'm glad to have been your shipmate." John said, "Could we pray for Rob before he leaves us?" They gathered together holding hands, as John led them: "Father, I commit to your loving care my friend and brother in Christ. I ask that you protect him and guide him. Lord we've all been through a lot of bad things. I ask you to help us to someday forgive our tormentors. We remember the prayer that Jesus taught us, saying, *Our Father, who art in heaven, thy kingdom come, thy will be done on earth as it is in heaven. Give us this day our daily bread and forgive us our sins as we forgive those that have sinned against us. Lead us not into temptation but deliver us from evil, for thine is the kingdom and the power and the glory forever. AMEN.*

The next morning Rob and a guard boarded a train headed south to Yokohama. The blinds were drawn. The main train tracks followed the coastline, passed Taria, Hatchi and Mito where it turned southwest to Tokyo. The guard raised the blind to see the devastation he had heard about for himself as the train passed slowly through the charred east side of the capital city. Burned out cars, and bodies littered the streets. The odor filled the train with the stench of the effects of the incendiary bombs. Nothing was left.

The military knew this was just the beginning. More would come.

．　．　．　．　．

Rob found himself once again in the compound of Ofuna. Night had fallen along with more snow. Nothing had changed. There were still lines of sullen prisoners standing outside for hours. Smirking guards were beating their POWs even more since the bombings began. Rob was placed in the newcomer's section of the camp. The next morning, he was led into the office of the commander who was surprisingly pleasant. His orderly gave him a new number to pin to his shirt. The commander was a naval officer. As required, Rob bowed to him and the officer said, "You stink." He told his orderly to get Rob a shower and shave. "Tomorrow you will be going to see a superior officer. You need to look better for him." Rob knew he would be seeing his friend Jimmysan's father once again.

The routine was the same. He was ushered into the Yokosuka Naval Base blindfolded and cuffed. While waiting for permission to enter the naval base, sirens sounded announcing another wave of B-29s. There must be a hundred of them Rob thought. The sound of the four-motored airplanes drowned out the noise around him. He overheard the guards talking, 'Americans won't bomb this base because they will want to use it after the war if they win.'

A few minutes later the Chevrolet sedan stopped in front of the tunnel entrance to the Commander of Submarines Japanese Imperial Navy. Still shackled and blindfolded,

Rob was led through the maze of corridors to the admiral's office. He was ordered to sit on a chair in the cold and damp passageway outside of the admiral's office. It was a long wait. Hours passed when suddenly a command, "Stand up" was given. He was led into Admiral Kamatsu 's office once again.

Rob gave the perfunctory bow and looked straight ahead. The old man broke the silence, "I understand you are at the Mitsubishi's copper mine up north, is that right?" Rob answered, "yes sir." The admiral laughed, "I think they knew you were a geologist. After you left the last time we met, I tried to get you sent to the Mitsubishi Zero aircraft manufacturing plant at Nagoya. Someone of their management must have had other needs." He motioned the guards to remove Rob's shackles and blindfold and leave the room. He pointed to Rob to sit in the chair by his desk.

The admiral seemed to be in a talkative mood. He spoke in fluent English, "Anyway, I had you sent here for a reason. When you were here before, you dared to lecture me on the meaning of honor. I have been giving that some thought lately. I sometimes wonder who is more honorable, America or Japan. We have an honor code called Bushido; you have a code of laws including international treaties that call for decent treatment of prisons of war. I have learned firsthand about your treatment of your prisoners. I have had several cards from my son who is a POW of yours in America. He is being treated very well and is learning English in classes. He gets the news in a prison newspaper. He is doing farm work if he likes. His health is good, he has medical care if needed. He is gaining weight. Sometimes I think you have more honor than we Japanese. But while we have killed many prisoners, I learned about the deaths of civilians in Tokyo from the firebombing by your B-29 bombers. The report is that over 100,000 died in one night."

Rob turned and looked the admiral in the eye, "Yes sir, I saw some of the results the other day while coming through on the train. It's terrible."

"One of your submarines killed hundreds of our soldiers that survived the sinking of our troop ship. They were machine-gunned in the water." Rob had heard about it. The Wahoo, under Mush Morton's command, did that. Unrestricted submarine warfare was ordered on December 8, 1941, and Mush believed it and carried it out.

There was silence in the room for a long time. Finally, Rob's captor went behind his desk and opened the top drawer and took out a small postcard. The front had a Red Cross, and postage free marked on the outside. "Lieutenant, you asked me last time to see if I could inform your crew's families of their being captured. Unfortunately, I was not able to do that. But I want you to sit here and write on this card and address it to your next of kin. You are only allowed a few words; you can tell them that you are a POW…but do not give your location. I will have it delivered by one of my contacts in the Swedish embassy in Tokyo. It may take several months for it to reach the States, but hopefully they will be informed." Rob could hardly believe it. He sat with a pen given him and quickly wrote: *Mom, Dad and Molly, we are POWs and I am working. I miss you and want this war to end soon. All my love ROB.*

On the front he addressed it to: Dr. and Mrs. Robert A. Walker and Molly, Spring and Campus Street Oxford, Ohio, USA.

As he signed the postcard, Rob said a prayer, "Lord please give this card wings and send it safely home."

Rob handed the postcard to the admiral and said, "I'm grateful." The old man said, "We both are submariners. We train to kill the enemy. But I do have admiration for those enemies who are valiantly serving their country. You have helped my son, now it is my turn to help you. I am going to try to have you assigned to Kawasaki's Drydock Company at Kobe. They need workers, and if you choose to volunteer, I can help to keep a close eye on you. I must tell you that I have heard rumors to the effect that if the Americans invade Japan, all prisoners of war will be eliminated." Rob nodded, "Yes, I have heard that as well. The commander of Sendai Camp no.5, where I was attached, hinted that same thing before he sent me to Ofuna. If this should happen, Japanese leaders will be guilty of the greatest atrocity of the Pacific War." The admiral concluded their conversation by saying, "If that happens, I will try to send someone for you to come to my home for protection. You will be safe there." Rob was amazed.

Just then the orderly arrived with Rob's meal. Included were some candy bars and Juicy Fruit chewing gum. He devoured the meal, and then the admiral said goodbye. Rob stood looking at him for a solemn moment thinking this would be the last time they would meet. He then saluted him, and the Japanese Admiral returned the salute. He was shackled once again for the return to the torture farm.

A few hours later Rob was back in Ofuna. To his great surprise he saw his commanding officer, Dick Morrison. He hardly recognized him. He was emaciated. He must have weighed no more than 80 pounds. The first thing that his CO asked was how he and the others were doing. Rob brought him up to date about the *Thornfish* men at the copper mine. He recounted his talk with the Japanese Admiral and the postcard. He mentioned that he would probably be sent to Kawasaki's shipbuilding at Kobe. "That's bad news, Rob. I 've heard that prisoners are treated very badly there. They have several hundred civilian contractors captured when the Japs took Wake Island. They are working them twelve to fourteen hour shifts without any safety equipment. It takes six men to lift five by ten steel sheets." Rob passed on to him what he had learned about the elimination of POWs when the invasion begins. Commander Morrison said, "I have heard the same report. We are beginning to see what we can do to resist if that happens. We must have a plan." A guard approached. They had to stop talking.

CHAPTER 68

The Confirmation

Molly sat at her desk in her bedroom in the Walker's home. Woodie's letter lay open, and she read the line again, 'I love you so much. Will you marry me? Please answer soon, we don't have much time.' She looked out the window. Sounds of children playing in the alley across the street drifted into her reverie. She thought of her childhood in Marion, playing games, kick the can, marbles, hopscotch, until time for her radio programs. The kids would go home to listen to the radio before dinner. Captain Midnight, Jack Armstrong, the all-American boy, and the Lone Ranger, were her favorites. She still remembered the stirring words said at the beginning of every program of the Lone Ranger originating from station WXYZ in Detroit: 'Out of the past come the thundering hoof beats of the great horse Silver, the Lone Ranger rides again. Heigh-ho Silver.'

She needed fresh air. She pulled on her coat, and tiptoed downstairs and started walking toward town. She stopped in the center of the town square where the Honor Board listed the names of over 600 local men and women serving in the war. She found Rob's name and put her fingers on it and said a prayer. A gray bus loaded with sailors went by and the guys whistled at her. A few minutes later she arrived at the front of the door of St. Mary's Church. A sign on the front door said, 'welcome, come in and pray.' She opened the door and walked down the narrow aisle to the front row of pews. She sat before the simple but beautiful altar. She was alone and welcomed the serenity. Molly poured her heart out in prayer. She lost all sense of time. She repeated: *Lord, I need to know your will about Woody and Rob. My heart tells me Rob is alive and to wait for him, but I need some confirmation.* Then she heard a rustling around the altar. "Who's there?" she said. No answer. She repeated louder this time, "Is anybody there?" Then she saw it. It was a bird. A little sparrow had somehow entered the church and couldn't get out. It landed on the altar right in front of her. It seemed exhausted from trying to find its way out. The little bird just looked at her. She rose and went over to the little fellow and it jumped in her open hand. She took it to the side door of the nave and released it outside. The little brown bird flew up and circled back toward her as if to say thank you. She had her answer. She felt in her spirit that Rob was a prisoner, and one day he would be released as had the sparrow. She had her confirmation. Her burden lifted.

That night, as she said her prayers during her devotions, she recalled Jesus telling the story not to worry, that none of the sparrows are forgotten by God. She took her fountain pen and filled it with Parker Ink and wrote Woody:

Dear Woody, I am so honored by your letter. You are so sweet. I love you more than you can imagine… But honestly, I am still in love with Rob and I know in my heart that he is alive and will come back when this awful war is over. I have prayed much about our lives together and the answer is to wait. I hope you'll understand. I know you will be a good pilot. I pray for you each day. Stay safe.
Blessings with love, Molly

* * * * *

At Admiral Kamatsu's order, Rob was sent to Kawasaki's shipyard at Kobe the following day. The Kawasaki Dockyard Company was one of the first companies to request POW laborers after the war began in 1941. Wake Island fell December 23, 1941, and the island had over one thousand civilian contractors working on the facilities there. The admiral commanding the invasion forces debated with his superiors for two days whether to kill all prisoners or transfer them to Japan. International law required that belligerent nations transfer civilian contractors to their homeland. The Imperial Japanese Navy had no such intention. While the decision was being made, all POWs and civilian contractors were held on Wake Island's pockmarked hot runway without food or water for two days. These men were skilled tradesmen in construction. Japanese industries were clamoring for slave laborers, so the decision was made to ship the prisoners to Japan. Kawasaki wanted at least 250 of them. On January 12, 1942, 1235 men were crammed in the hold of the Mitsubishi built ship *Nitta Maru* bound for Yokohama and Woosung China.

Later, 98 Marine defenders of Wake who were left behind, were blindfolded and executed by machine-gun fire by order of Admiral Shigemitsu Sakaibara, the commander of Japanese forces on Wake.

Rob was sent to Osaka POW Camp no. 2 near Kawasaki's shipbuilding facilities. Allied bombing increased and the prisoners asked for air raid shelters. None were made available. The old-timers told Rob not to worry. The drydocks, some of which were the largest in the world, were not being bombed.

The sound of riveting penetrated the ears of the POWs, no ear protection was provided, not even wads of cotton. The honcho had been informed that Rob understood Japanese and gave him the job of marking plates that would be fabricated into steel hulls. Rob deliberately mismarked several each day which resulted in confusion when the assembly was attempted. The second day Rob had a wonderful surprise, he met his former shipmate Petty Officer Grabowski. The huge man looked like a scarecrow.

Gone were the bulging biceps that could easily move a heavy piece of ordnance, and the clear eyes that served well as a scout in the jungles of Mindanao during the rescue of the Aussie Coast Watcher. When he saw his former division officer, he ran up to him and gave him a big hug. "Sir, how are you? I 'm glad you're here but it's the asshole of the earth. Look at my head." Rob saw a terrible gash in his scalp. "What happened Grabby?"

"Well sir, a couple of days ago I was hit with a rivet while working below a scaffolding on new construction. The honcho deliberately hit me. If I weren't Polish, it would most likely have killed me. The bastard laughed and told others about his fun with a white rat. Well, the next day I was high up above him working, and he came right underneath my workstation. Somehow a bucket of rivets 'accidentally' fell off the scaffolding and killed the son of a bitch!"

"Well, they will be after you."

"I hope not. There is one honcho here that has been a help to us. You'll see him soon, he is the tallest Jap here. And he has been trying his best to keep the guards from hurting us. He sneaks food in too. He speaks some English and he is a Christian." Rob listened intently, "How do you know?"

"Well sir, right out of the blue one day he was in our barracks and came up to me and asked me, "Are you a Christian?" I was dumbfounded. First, because he spoke pretty good English, and then I didn't know how to respond. I thought, if I say yes and he's a Shinto he might want to cut my head off for being a Christian. But I didn't care, I'm Polish and a Catholic, so I told him, I am a Christian." Then he added, "You know what he said?"

"Me too." And that was all we said. Grabowski turned to Rob, "Could I ask you a question? You are a Christian aren't you sir?"

Rob said, "I am. More than ever now."

"Well you remember the Filipino Priest we liberated on Mindanao. Do you recall his sermon while he was on our boat? The one about forgiveness?" "Well a little bit."

"He made me think. That priest was horribly abused by the Japs and yet he forgave them. He said he had no choice and that we're commanded to forgive seven times seven for every wrong we have received. I don't know. I'm all mixed up. I hate these guards. I've seen them kill a man for no reason at all. Some just for sport. So here I am supposed to be a Christian, and I just killed a man the other day. Even though he could have killed me with that rivet, I dumped a bunch of them on him and intentionally killed him."

Rob said, "Well I did the same thing just a while ago. I killed a guard in the mine who was a monster…we called him the gorilla. I pushed him down the elevator shaft in the mine after he nearly killed Lieutenant John Young."

Grabowski said, "You mean our Mister Young?"

"Yes. He was beaten unconscious, and I thought the guy would cut his head off with a machete. He was evil. And there is a lot of evil in this war. I remember John talking about something the Bible says about evil. It says: the two things God hates, devising wicked schemes and feet that run swiftly to evil."

Rob said, "The Japs think there is no honor in being a prisoner. And they especially hate white prisoners. John is a better Christian than I am. He says the Bible says we are to hate evil and love our enemies. And forgive our enemies, even seven times seven. Grabby you and I have killed a lot of people in this war with torpedoes, guns, knives and even rivets. I don't know about you, but before I check out of this earth, I hope I can forgive and be forgiven." Grabby looked up and said, "AMEN."

The air raid sirens sounded. In the distant horizon, wave after wave of B-29s covered the sky. That night, as the men tried to sleep on their wooden bunks after working 18 hours, the guards came in banging trash can lids exclaiming 'Roosevelt is dead! Roosevelt is dead!'

CHAPTER 69

The Postcard

It was raining in Oxford, Thursday, April 12, 1945. Skies had been gray for several days, but the crocuses were sprouting yellow blossoms and the robins had returned to Oxford. Molly was in her office, working late, finishing some articles for next week's *Press*. She was alone and was listening to the radio while finishing her work. The station was playing a record of Bing Crosby singing, *Red Sails in the sunset, way out on the sea*. Molly was singing along with Bing, when the announcer interrupted the music saying, "We interrupt this program to bring a bulletin. President Franklin Delano Roosevelt has died. The President succumbed about one o'clock this afternoon at the Winter White House in Warm Springs, Georgia, where he was enjoying a two-week rest. As more details become available, we will bring them to you, in the meantime please stay tuned to this station."

Molly cried, "Oh my God, what are we going to do?" That plea was echoing throughout the nation.

At five-thirty that afternoon Vice-President Harry Truman was summoned to the White House, unaware that the President had died. Eleanor Roosevelt broke the news to him. He was stunned. Trying to recover he said to Mrs. Roosevelt, "Is there anything I can do for you?" She replied, "Is there anything we can do for you? For you are the one in trouble now." About seven p.m. Chief Justice Harlan Stone administered the oath of office to Harry Truman, senator from Missouri, as the cabinet looked on. The nation was in shock. Some Americans had never known another President. That same day the U.S. Ninth Army crossed the Elbe River fifty miles from Berlin.

· · · · ·

Six days earlier, the Japanese battleship Yamato got underway from Kure along with the light cruiser *Yahagi* and eight destroyers. The force had been spotted by the U.S. Submarines *Threadfin* and *Hackleback*, April 6. Their mission was twofold: First, attack the U.S. Navy forces off Okinawa in coordination with a massive kamikaze air attack. Second, preserve the nation's honor. The Yamato had only enough fuel for a one-way trip. It would be a suicide mission by the largest battleship in the world. It was 863 feet long and displaced over 73,000 tons. Its main battery of nine 18-inch guns could hurl a projectile weighing 3200 pounds some 22 miles. A veteran of the battles of Midway, Leyte and the Philippine Sea it was equipped with radar and had a complement of 2500 officers and men. Its sleek design coupled with four turbine engines propelled her at a speed of over 27 knots. Its antiaircraft defense was formidable …150 guns.

Marine second lieutenant Woodrow Wilson Collingsworth, USMCR, was the newest pilot on the aircraft carrier *Essex,* VT Avenger Torpedo Squadron. In a short time, he had become a favorite in his group. His friendly affable manner, cocky at times, and storytelling about sports made him fit in right away. His cool head in difficult landing approaches gave him high marks. He was a natural pilot. He loved to fly, and he loved the Marines, and his squadron welcomed him as one of them.

The weather was misty with a low overcast when he took off from his carrier in the early morning and joined up with his squadron. Aided by two slow-moving Navy PBM patrol planes shadowing the enemy fleet, Woody and his wingman were vectored into the enemy task force. At noon dive-bombers from the carrier were the first to attack diving through the clouds and dropping bombs on the huge ship. Two bombs and one torpedo hit the battleship in the first ten minutes of the action.

Woody and his wingman followed the Douglas Dauntless dive bombers attack. Bursting through the clouds, they approached the Yamato two hundred feet over the water at 180 knots. Antiaircraft guns blasted away, but he was surprised that they were not very effective. Woody barreled in aiming for the after part of the ship hoping to disable its propulsion while his wingman concentrated on amidships. At 1000 yards from the target his bomb bay opened, and he launched his 2000-pound torpedo that hit the water and ran true into the stern of the Yamato. Woody pulled up right and his wingman left. Woody radioed, "We got 'em." But as his plane climbed for altitude, a stray burst of machine gun fire from the after guns of the Yamato hit his TBM. Woody valiantly tried to keep flying but his oil pressure dropped, and it was only then that he felt the wound to his left leg. He radioed "Mayday, we're hit! Avenger 15 going down."

Altogether over 300 American aircraft pummeled the ships. The Yamato took a 35-degree list and at 1423, a little over two hours after the attack began, the largest battleship in the world and the last, sank in 1200 feet of water. Only a few of its 2488 officers and men survived. Over 1100 perished when the cruiser *Yahagi* and four destroyers were sunk. The U.S. Navy lost four planes and eight crew members that day.

Woody was one of them.

· · · · · ·

Molly and Mrs. Walker sat at the kitchen table pasting clippings in their scrapbooks. Molly had designed her book by categories: People in Oxford and Miami University; the Navy at Miami; prices and rationing; men in the armed forces. Her landlady Mary Catherine Walker arranged hers chronologically. "Molly here's one that I found in an envelope from Robert in Washington. I misplaced his letter. I remember he was furious when he read this in the newspaper." Molly started reading the clipping. Congressman Elmer J. Holland of Pennsylvania made a speech in the House of Representatives, attacking *The Chicago Tribune* for "unthinking and wicked misuse of freedom of the press.... American boys will die because of the help to our enemies. Somehow our Navy had secured and broken the secret code of the Japanese Navy." Mary Catherine sat straight up and shook the article. "Molly, that bastard should have been shot! Giving away our top secrets just for his own ego. Robert said his comments were printed in several newspapers." The congressman was referring to an investigation by a special prosecutor, William L. Mitchell, ordered by President Roosevelt himself, because of an article printed in *The Chicago Tribune* by one of their reporters. The culprit was an Australian war correspondent by the name of Stanley Johnson who had become friends with the captain of the USS *Lexington* during the battle of the Coral Sea in May 1942. He had personally observed some ULTRA Secret documents outlining the Japanese battle plans before the battle of Midway in June 1942. The author's story was devastating to the intelligence community and the highest echelons of the Navy. He found out that our intelligence service at Pearl Harbor had broken the Japanese Navy code. It became the greatest secret of the Pacific war. Dr. Walker believed that only by the grace of God did the Japs not read the article and the congressman's comments. Molly gasped, "This could have killed American sailors including Rob. Why these people can't think of our country before their own interests is beyond me."

Finally, Molly turned to her book, "here's one that was in *The Oxford Press* article about a local man who saved his friends on Saipan." Mary Catherine took the clipping and read:

> "**Local Boy Loses leg as he Saves Companions.** Marine Pfc. Charles Arnold, the 18-year-old son of Mrs. Lois Alexander of Oxford and a former Stewart School student, is listed as one of the Saipan heroes. He deliberately chose to cover a Jap hand grenade to save his companions, and as a result lost his right leg. He had been on Saipan just seven hours. He wrote his mother, "A Jap threw a hand grenade at a group of us. It landed by me and I saw that unless something blew it down instead of spreading all over there would be many of us killed and injured so I laid down on it with my right leg." The Navy doctors tried to save his leg, but gangrene set in and it had to be amputated above the knee. He saved his buddies. There was no mention of a medal for his sacrifice.

The doorbell began ringing incessantly, Mrs. Walker jumped up saying, "Who the Hell is that?"

She walked briskly down the hall to see who was so much in a hurry. She opened the door. It was Hank, their postman of many years. Mrs. Walker seemed a bit irritated, "Hank, what's wrong? You're out of breath."

"Mrs. Walker, you won't believe this! I just happened to read this postcard addressed to you and Molly. Look!" He handed it to her, and Mrs. Walker shouted, "My God it's from Rob! Molly come here quickly…look at this!" Molly ran down the hall and realized that her friend was about to faint. Molly ordered her, "Sit down Mary!" It was the first time she had ever called Mrs. Walker by her first name; with the help of Hank they eased her into a chair. The lady looked up at Molly and through tears, "Molly, Rob is a prisoner and he is alive! Your prayers worked!" Her hands were shaking so much that she nearly dropped the faded card. She handed it to Molly. She saw the Red Cross emblem on the front, and then turned it over and read the words Rob had written in his handwriting. Molly was stunned. She looked at the card and read and reread the words, ending with, All my love, ROB. She started to cry and holding the little card, raised her hands toward heaven and shouted, "Thank you Jesus!"

The postman and Mrs. Walker said in unison, "AMEN. AMEN!!"

Part Four

To Total Victory

CHAPTER 70

Victory in Europe,
Good News and Bad News

The war in Europe had ended. It was a time of rejoicing. VE Day was sunny, cool and quiet in Oxford. *The Oxford Press*, Thursday, May 10, 1945, edition said, "VE Day was observed with thanksgiving, but no fanfare. At the union services held Tuesday night in the Memorial Presbyterian Church, Dr. S.R. Jamieson spoke on 'Things to Remember' and Dr. Burton L. French talked on 'We Dedicate Ourselves to the Task Ahead.' The McGuffey school chorus sang under the direction of Miss Catherine Adams and Mrs. H. A. Moore presided at the piano. Councilman J.W. Heckert, cooperating with the ministerial association, planned the program.

Special assembly programs were held at Miami and Western College. Phillip Henderson, vice-president of Western College, spoke and the students listened to President Truman's address by radio. LCDR. Robert W. Stokes of the V 12 unit said the struggle with Japan would be difficult and urged sticking to the job. Ted Martin, returned veteran, also spoke."

There was good news in Oxford that day, but bad news in Cleveland, home of Woody Collingsworth. It was a chilly day in Cleveland. A cold front had moved down from Canada and the wind off Lake Erie was fierce when the Collingsworths came home earlier in the afternoon. The newspaper was on the front porch and Mr. Collingsworth began reading it after they shed their coats. "Look here Martha, there's a story in the *Plain Dealer* about the Navy off Okinawa. Lots of ships are being hit by suicide bombers called kamikazes. They're aiming for our carriers. I hope that Woody is not there." They had finished late lunch when the doorbell rang. The Western Union Telegraph boy had ridden his bike up the long driveway to the beautiful home on the shore of Lake Erie. Mr. Collingsworth went to the door and saw the Western Union boy. He froze, knowing that telegrams were not good news. He accepted the message and gave the lad a tip and then went to the library off the man floor sat in the chair by the fireplace, and opened the message:

The Secretary of the Navy regrets to inform you that your son, Lieutenant Woodrow Wilson Collingsworth, USMCR, has been killed in action in the Pacific. We share your grief and want

```
you to know that his sacrifice will not be in vain. You will
be informed of more details as they become available. For
security reasons do not share any details of his loss with
others.
Sincerely, James Forrestal, Secretary of the Navy. Washington,
D.C.
```

Woody's father was crushed. Woody was their only child. It wasn't possible, he had only been in the service eighteen months. This must be a mistake. When his wife came into the room, she knew something terrible had happened. She saw the look on her husband's face, his hand holding the telegram and the envelope on the floor, and she knew it was Woody. She burst out crying, her heart pounding in her breast. She grew angry, damning everything, Roosevelt, Hirohito, the Navy and Marines and everyone. It would be a long night for those in the beautiful lakeside home in Cleveland.

Molly received the bad news from Woody's father in a telephone call the next day while at work. She was so distraught, she had to leave the office. She walked down High Street, past the water tower, the movie theater, to Slant Walk. Ahead was Tobe's water fountain where Woody had kissed her before he left. The words in his letter, 'Will you marry me, we don't have much time,' reverberated in her heart. Oh God, where are you? Why do you allow this evil to exist? A platoon of sailors marching to class passed by her as she sat on the bench in front of Harrison Hall. She wondered how many of them will die before this war ends. She gave thanks that Rob was alive and a prisoner, but how long could he survive? She had read of the terrible atrocities committed by the Japanese military…stories of the awful Bataan Death March, the murder of civilians and soldiers in Hong Kong and Singapore, all exploded in her thoughts. It was hours before she could return to work. The office was closed. She entered and sat at her desk for a long while. Then she uncovered her Underwood standard typewriter and began to write:

Sorrowful yet proud were the thoughts of citizens of the community on VE Day.

Sorrowful because so many lives have been lost, so many families have been broken. Proud because our American men and boys had the courage and faith to fight for all they hold dear. The day passed as it should have been all over the nation in quiet and sobriety. Schools and business places continued as usual. Many took time to listen to the President's message, and many attended the union prayer service held in the evening.

The hope of all is that the heroism of our armed forces and our allies shall inspire us to carry on to total victory and that the Greater Guidance, which has led us to VE Day, shall lead us to peace which will end wars.

Molly took her pen and started to write a note to Woody's parents: *Dear Mr. and Mrs. Collingsworth, I am so grieved by the loss of your son and my dear friend Woody....*

* * * * *

Rob lay on his wooden bunk. It was hot. It was August. The latitude was thirty-five degrees north, but the prevailing winds blowing off the sea that made it so cold in the winter had now become calm. He had worked 18 hours straight and was exhausted. But he felt good about marking the steel plates going into ship construction incorrectly. Grabowski was sabotaging the heating of the rivets making them seem smooth on top but fully capable of popping out prematurely. Kawasaki was running low on steel and other critical supplies. The prisoners were worried that they might be killed once the shipyard work ceased. The war of attrition by the submarines was making a dramatic effect on the Japs. He finally dozed off, and sometime during the night he had a dream. There were three women looking for him in a forest. They were beautiful, but each one had been hurt. One girl was blond, the other brunette and the third had red hair. As he walked through the forest, huge trees that appeared like monsters were trying to grab him. When he awakened, he was trembling and soaked in sweat. The dream or nightmare was about his three sweethearts. Molly the angel, Lily, the temptress, and Marianne, the innocent. He had been involved with each, but he knew in his heart that his true love was Molly. But his conscience was bothering him. If he survived the war could he be forgiven for his indiscretions? And could he forgive himself?

The next day as he worked in the shipyard, the inventory of steel was almost gone. The constant bombing of factories by the U.S. Army pilots and the Navy shore bombardment of Kawasaki and Nippon steel mills, had caused steel to be rationed and some Jap ships could not go to sea for lack of repairs.

The tall muscular Kawasaki honcho walked over to Rob in the afternoon and said, "You Christian? He searched Rob's eyes waiting for his reply.

Rob said "Yes."

"Me too." The honcho was the tallest Japanese Rob had ever seen. His very athletic appearance and the words he had just uttered awed Rob. He looked around to see if anyone was looking and handed Rob a small package of candy. Then to his surprise he gave Rob a small English edition of the Gideon Bible, with the book of Psalms and the New Testament.

He cautioned Rob, "Keep quiet."

Rob said, "Arigatou, thank you." Then the man whispered, "Hiroshima bombed. Destroyed by one bomb!"

"What, how could this be?"

"New bomb. Atomic. The city is gone. Thousands dead." Rob's first thought was maybe we wouldn't have to invade Japan.

The honcho paused before turning to go back to work. "Time to stop the war. Time to forgive."

Later, when he got a chance, Rob opened the little Bible. There was a ribbon marking Matthew's Gospel chapter 6, and verse 12 had been underlined: "Forgive us our debts, as we also have forgiven our debtors."

· · · · ·

Mrs. Walker sat in the kitchen working on her scrapbook. August 6 was another hot afternoon in Oxford. She wished she had air-conditioning. The only cool place in town was the air-conditioned Miami Western movie theater. She was listening to the small tear-shaped walnut Zenith cabinet radio. Her team, the Cincinnati Reds, was playing the Brooklyn Dodgers in Brooklyn. The announcer interrupted the game by saying, "We bring you a special bulletin from the War Department. A United States Army Air Force B-29 bombed Hiroshima, Japan, just hours ago with a single atomic bomb. The force of the new weapon was equal to thousands of tons of TNT. The entire city, home of Japan's Second Army, was destroyed. Stay tuned to WLW for more details." Mrs. Walker, muttered to herself, *what's an atomic bomb anyway? I've got to call Robert in Washington. He will know.*

On July 26 the heavy cruiser USS *Indianapolis* unloaded some special cargo on the newly captured island of Tinian in the Marianas. The first atomic bomb to be used in war was loaded into a B-29 bomber named the Enola Gay after the mother of the command pilot, Colonel Paul W. Tibbets, Jr. On the morning of August 6, 1945, at 2:45 a.m. the plane roared down the long runway at Tinian in the Northern Marianas and was airborne. Its destination Hiroshima, Japan. About 8:15 a.m. it dropped an atomic bomb over Hiroshima, and it exploded 2000 feet above the city. The force of the bomb, as reported to the American people hours later by President Truman, was over 20,000 tons of TNT. It killed an estimated 72,000 and another 68,000 were wounded. The United States Truman said, is developing more powerful bombs that would eliminate the capacity of Japan to conduct war. He called on the Japanese to surrender or face prompt and utter destruction.

The Japanese government had rejected the Allies' proposal to surrender made two weeks earlier. As a result, on August 1 the Army Air Force launched the largest flight of B-29 bombers in history: over 800 bombers dropped more bombs on Kyushu and Honshu than at any time in history. Their continued refusal to surrender made the atomic bomb necessary. Another new weapon would be dropped on Nagasaki three days later. Killed in the second attack were over 100 allied POWs in camps around the city.

For the next week, after the Nagasaki blast, the Emperor, his military and ministers of state argued. Hirohito wanted to accept the Allied terms, but the military wanted to fight to the bitter end defending its nation's honor. However, at 1449 Tokyo time on August 14, 1945 the Emperor's decision was broadcast over radio Tokyo. President Truman announced it to the nation at 7 p.m. Washington time. The most destructive war in the history of mankind had ended, and the atomic age had begun.

CHAPTER 71

Japan Surrenders

John learned about the surrender from the British radioman. He had heard the Emperor's broadcast on his crude radio he had assembled from spare parts and picked up enough of the Japanese language broadcast to confirm that the Japs had indeed surrendered. Shouts of joy rang throughout the camp. The first thing that John and his band of brothers did was to arrest the camp commander, Lieutenant Asaka. But before they could get to him, he had burned most of his records. He was not sure if the Mitsubishi office had destroyed theirs. The liberated prisoners held him for three weeks while awaiting American units to arrive. They took him with them when they left for Yokohama and turned him over to the U.S. Navy shore patrol. The next thing they did was to paint the letters POW on the roof of the buildings. A little later a B-29 bomber came over the camp and dropped food, medicine and clothing in 55-gallon drums. Three weak prisoners were killed when they could not get out of the way of the falling drums.

Rob and his compatriots at the Kawasaki shipyard were told of the Japanese surrender by the honcho they now called 'hero.' Rob and his buddies were so worn out they could not celebrate except to raid the warehouse, finding Red Cross packages that had never been given to the prisoners. Rob lay on his wooden bunk covered with flies. The next day most of the guards had disappeared. POWs wanted those guards held for war crimes trials. One of them, a Wake Island civilian prisoner valued for his construction skills, told Rob and Grabowski of how he was frequently beaten while held at the Kawasaki shipyard. He wanted to kill his former captors.

"For punishment the Japanese would take a piece of bamboo about three inches wide and four feet long with quarter-inch holes drilled in it, made me stand at attention and then beat me over the back with the bamboo stick. When it hit my back, it would pop holes in the skin, so I had running sores most of the time. They would never get a chance to heal before I would get another beating. Since the only clothing I wore was a breech cloth, these beatings were extraordinarily cruel."

He would have a hard time forgetting and forgiving.

Dick O'Kane, former commanding officer of the *Tang*, sunk by its own torpedo, heard the announcement of the surrender while a captive at the Omori POW camp in Tokyo Bay. The camp's loud speaker played the recording of the Emperor's surrender message. Although spoken in an arcane Japanese language that was difficult for ordinary Japanese to understand, it was authoritative in tone. But in Hirohito's words, "We have resolved to pave the way for a grand peace for all the generations to come by enduring the unendurable and suffering the insufferable," helped soften the hard realization reflected in the countenances of the Japanese guards and civilians around the camp.

They knew they had lost the war.

Immediately after the Emperor's message, Japanese POW camp commanders and industries that used prisoner slave labor began the systematic destruction of records.

In Honolulu Admiral Lockwood began receiving lists of liberated submariners that had been under his command and began notifying their next of kin. Nine officers and men from the *Tang* and its commanding officer Dick O'Kane were reported in bad condition. Especially O'Kane, he was given up for near dead during the triage by medics. And so was Lieutenant Junior Grade Robert A. Walker Jr. at the Osaka POW camp.

Rob was completely dehydrated from a massive attack of dysentery. In the days leading up to the surrender, he had become delirious and eventually was unconscious when the Army medics reached the camp. The medics were about to give up on Rob and had turned to others when Grabowski grabbed a medic by his jacket and threatened him if he didn't give him medicine and fluids intravenously. They complied with the gaunt man's demands and saved Rob's life.

· · · · ·

Rob lay in the ward of the hospital ship USS *Rescue* anchored in Tokyo Bay. The USS *Rescue* and sister ship *Benevolence* and the Army's *Marigold* were caring for the hundreds of emaciated and terribly sick former POWs.

Rob awoke as the planes flew overhead, and he panicked, not realizing where he was. Rob was awake now, "Where am I? What day is it? What's happened to me?"

You've got a lot of questions young man." A nurse in a starched white uniform stood over him and assured him he was safe at last. She said, "Welcome back to America sailor!" She hovered over him taking his temperature and blood pressure. "You're looking a lot better. You were a 'sight for sore eyes' as my mom used to say, when you were brought aboard here. You are on the Navy Hospital Ship, USS *Rescue*. We are anchored in Tokyo Bay right now, but we soon will be moored at the Yokosuka naval base. We have a ship load of you poor guys that were prisoners of war. Some are in very bad shape. You will be OK soon. You need to gain some weight and muscle strength."

"Thanks ma'am." And he fell asleep.

There were only a few military men remaining in the tunnels of Yokosuka Naval

Base when U.S. Navy personnel arrived. One tunnel marked in Japanese, Commander IJN Submarines Pacific Fleet, interested the new occupiers. A young Navy lieutenant along with five Marines went into the tunnel looking for anything from boobytraps to gold taken from the Philippines. They found neither. But in the last tunnel they discovered the offices of the Commander of Submarines. When they entered, they found Vice Admiral Kamatsu sitting behind a large teak desk, surrounded by large wall maps of the Pacific. A bottle of sake and a glass sat before him on his large desk. A small samurai sword lying on the desk with the point facing him. It was obvious that he was planning to commit hara- kiri.

The lieutenant quickly knocked the sword off the top of the desk. He said, "Sir, I cannot allow you to do that. You must submit to our authority now! Please stand." The admiral obeyed the command and stood with his hands raised. "State your name, rank and serial number." The admiral replied and gave him his full name, rank and Navy registration number. One of the Marines searched the admiral and found no weapons. The admiral noticed his Dolphins. "I see you are a submariner." The young naval officer said, "Yes, I'm on the staff now but was the number three on the *Gato*."

"Oh yes, I am familiar with that class."

The lieutenant was impressed with his fluent English. He continued, "You are aware that Japan has surrendered. I will be escorting you to the offices of the staff of the submarine division on the USS *Proteus* for interrogation. You will be quartered there for the time being. Do you wish to have anyone notified of your whereabouts?"

The old man sighed, thinking of the dishonor he had done to his family by surrendering. He finally said, "No."

The lieutenant took the samurai dagger and put it in his belt. He posted two Marines to guard the tunnel, especially the records in his office, and left for the *Proteus* with the Vice Admiral of Japan's Imperial Navy Submarines as his prisoner.

Oxford's VJ day celebration of Japanese' surrender, August 15, 1945
photo by Gilson Wright

Navy trainees marching to VJ Day Celebration Oxford's town square
photo by Gilson Wright

CHAPTER 72

V J Day

Miami students listened to the radio for news and at 4 a.m. Tuesday, August 14, they heard the broadcast of surrender and began shouting, blowing horns and bugles. When word was officially proclaimed from the White House later that day, fire sirens were sounded, church bells rang, and students paraded uptown. VJ Day had finally arrived. It was glorious. The Thursday, August 16 edition of *The Oxford Press* headlined:

News of Jap Surrender Brings Rejoicing, Religious Services, Parade and Dance; Dr. French Chief Speaker at Ceremonies.

Protestants held Union Services at the Memorial Presbyterian Church and the Catholics at St. Mary's at eight o'clock Tuesday. Official ceremonies were held Wednesday afternoon on the Oxford Public Square. Navy officers and 250 trainees, including a Navy band and American Legion color guard, along with Boy and Girl Scouts, marched around the town square. Dr. French spoke and read the names of men from the Oxford community lost in the war. The same day *The Oxford Press* carried a story that manpower controls of the War Manpower Commission were abolished immediately. The United States employment office would begin to assist returning veterans and every displaced war worker, so every man would be able to be gainfully employed. And the nationwide brownout was canceled. Oxford's offices, streets, and businesses would turn the lights on again!

Ironically, the **Victory Edition** of the *Press* had an editorial about the local telephone service and the future of atomic energy:

"Seventh Day Adventist operators do not want to work on their Sabbath. The *Press* asked: should we give one faith privilege over another. Some work must be done seven days a week. Telephone service is now improved; however, it is decidedly on the slow side. A new line between Oxford and College Corner has not yet been completed. Come another 50 years and telephone operators who will work on Sunday may not be needed. *We're told there is a portable telephone which one day could be used in one's automobile, or airplane or vest pocket maybe.*

We wonder though if it won't be a mixed blessing. Dr. R.L Edwards, professor of physics at Miami, wrote a piece about the *future uses of atomic energy.* He said it might even be used to generate electric power, even for autos and railways!"

Molly clipped all these events for her scrapbook. Later she and Mrs. Walker walked up Campus Street to the town square as the VJ day ceremonies began. They worried, however, because they had not heard any news about Rob. Dr. Walker, still in Washington, appealed to his connections within the Navy Department to find out any information about his son. After several days he was informed that Rob was ill but was doing well while recuperating on a Navy hospital ship, the USS *Rescue*, in the Tokyo area. He would need time there to heal. Molly was thrilled when Dr. Walker called with the good news, finally knowing he was in good hands. She rushed from the Walker's home holding Mrs. Walker's hand and led her up Campus Avenue to the St. Mary's Church. It was the first time Mary Catherine had been in a Catholic Church. She followed Molly to the altar where others were praying. It was there, months ago, that Molly had received confirmation that Rob was alive. Without urging, Mary Catherine Walker fell to her knees weeping at the altar rail beside Molly as she raised her hands and prayed aloud, "Thank you Jesus, my savior, for saving Rob." Tears of joy flowed as they prayed together...*Our father, who art in heaven....*

· · · · ·

The second day of September was overcast. Tokyo Bay was crowded with 258 anchored warships. Every type was represented except aircraft carriers. They were at sea launching planes in the event that some Jap rogue would make a suicide sortie. The nation's newest battleship, the *Missouri* BB 63, was honored to host the surrender ceremonies. At its flagstaff flew the flag that had flown over the Capitol in Washington on December 7, 1941. At 8:05 in the morning Fleet Admiral Chester Nimitz came aboard 'Mighty Mo.' His five-star flag and General MacArthur's were broken out flying from the yard arm. A few minutes before nine the Japanese delegation arrived on a U. S. destroyer. They were given the traditional courtesy of side boys and piped on board the *Missouri*. Near the number 2 turret general and flag officers of allied services stood awaiting the longed-for surrender of the enemy. The crew jammed every place possible in the superstructure to see the surrender. A few minutes later General MacArthur accompanied by Admirals Nimitz and Halsey appeared on the main deck where a simple mess table covered with green felt served as the signing desk. The General called the ceremonies to order. Flanked by his side were Lieutenant General Wainwright USA, who surrendered the Philippines, and Lieutenant General Sir Arthur Percival, British Army, who had surrendered Singapore in early 1942. Both were emaciated and showed the strain of nearly three years of humiliating captivity in the infamous Seihan Manchurian Prisoner of War camp, where important prisoners were held.

MacArthur made a brief but poignant speech appealing for a "better world founded on faith and understanding, a world dedicated to the dignity of man and the fulfillment of his most cherished wish for freedom, tolerance and justice."

Foreign Minister Shigemitsu signed for Japan followed by MacArthur signing for the allied powers. Then representatives of all nations that had been at war with Japan signed the document. When all had signed, MacArthur closed with "Let us pray that peace be now restored to the world and that God will preserve it always." General MacArthur was named Supreme Allied Commander with complete authority over the former Japanese empire. The Emperor would be subject to him. After the surrender in late September, the deputy Prime Minister had ordered the recall of every former prostitute, taxi dancer, masseuse, and waitress to volunteer for sex amusement centers for the American occupation forces. The thinking was that there would be mass rapes of women once the surrender had taken place. They were shocked when the GI's wanted to take pictures, sightsee and have a couple of glasses of beer. Admiral Halsey had given strict orders to those occupying forces that there were to be no incidents.

One important item in the surrender document was a statement that no harm will come to any Allied prisoners of war.

The entire ceremony was over in less than half an hour. The sun came out as 450 carrier-based aircraft along with hundreds of Army Air Force planes flew over the *Missouri* and her sister ships.

The most destructive war in history had ended with an estimated 50 million killed.

· · · · ·

The POWs were coming to Pearl Harbor. Medical centers were clearing their decks for action. Most of them wanted to get out of Japan as soon as they could. C-54 planes were ferrying the emaciated men to Hawaii or directly to Naval hospitals in the continental U.S. The admiral called Ben Miller into his office. "Ben, I know you are busy with arranging for the care of our submariners' return. Dick O'Kane and Dick Morrison are going to stay here in Hawaii while they recuperate. The Navy has the Commander of Japanese Submarines held on the *Proteus* in Yokosuka. I want you to go to Japan right away and interview him. We need to learn more about their subs' ordnance, radar, sonar and anything else we can learn from them. In fact, I'd like for you to arrange to bring one of their latest boats back here, so we can evaluate it. The Japanese boats have snorkels and excellent torpedoes. You should get someone with Japanese language ability and a combat submariner to be Officer-in- Charge."

Ben said, "Yes sir, I agree it could provide some good intelligence for us. I think their torpedoes were one of their best weapons."

"I concur Ben. We'll have your orders cut immediately. Now go to it. But the first thing to do when you get there is to check on our submariners that were POWs; we owe them a lot. Our boys were brutalized. I just got word that all but four of the *Thornfish* crew had survived in various POW camps. The Chief of the Boat O'Neil was one of them that didn't make it. I learned that the Jap SOB's accused him of sabotaging conveyor motors, and he was made to stand outside in freezing temperature in a tub of ice water. When asked by a guard sarcastically, if he needed anything he replied, 'Yes, a cake of soap!' He later died of pneumonia."

"I'm sorry to hear that sir. I knew the chief… he was a real hero even before the war started. You may know that he helped save the men on the *Squalus*. The Navy never gave him a medal."

The admiral said, "He will get one now but regretfully too late."

As Ben started to leave, the admiral called after him. "Oh, one other thing Ben, the Jap Admiral Kamatsu's son is a submariner and a POW of ours. He's being held on the mainland in California. He has been treated very well as our prisoner.

The next morning, Ben was able to catch an Army C-54 bound for Tinian and then to Tokyo. In two days, Ben was aboard the USS *Proteus* now moored at the Yokosuka Naval Base. Ben Miller was anxious to meet the Japanese admiral. On the long flight to Japan he outlined some of the things he wanted to learn from the admiral in charge of all Japanese submarines during the war. 1. Strategy and tactics used to include the use of *kaitens*, suicide midget subs. The Navy wanted to know why the Japanese didn't use their I class aircraft carrier submarines to try to bomb the Panama Canal. If they had done that it would have severely slowed the progress of the war. 2. Technological advances in radar, sonar, and snorkel masts. 3. The info they received from the German U Boat exchange. 4. Loss of Face, i.e. effects on Japanese submarine forces at Pearl Harbor and after the attack. 5. Shipbuilding priorities. 6. Sub losses, 29 lost in first six months 1945. 7. The Navy wanted to bring an I boat to Pearl for inspection.

But the first thing Captain Miller wanted to do was to go to the hospital ship and see some of the submarine survivors on board for treatment. A list had been transmitted to him by the staff in Hawaii. He wanted specially to see LTJG Walker.

· · · · ·

The USS *Rescue* AH18 was tied up to pier 5. Rob was still recuperating from his injuries. He had gained some weight but was still skin and bones. X-Rays showed no broken bones, but his body was still bruised from the beatings he received by the Japs. As he walked about the deck on the ship, Rob noted that the base itself suffered little damage from American bombers or Navy ships. He saw some of the entrances to the caves and tunnels drilled into the hills about the base. Memories of his meeting with his Japanese friend's father flooded his mind. He wondered if the old admiral had survived the war.

On one occasion while walking through the ship's passageways, Rob came across a nurse posting a list of all patients on the ship. It's called the binnacle list. He quickly scanned it to see if any of his *Thornfish* shipmates had been admitted. They were listed alphabetically. Grabowski's name appeared and John Young's. Rob was elated! He found Grabowski in a ward on the third deck. He looked up in time to see his former boss. "Mr. Walker! How are you sir?" The two hugged each other. The big Pole was about to cry. He seemed embarrassed, "You know we Polish can't hide our feelings. Sir, you sure look a lot better than when I saw you in camp. You were about dead. I made the medics treat you… they were going to give up on you!"

Rob said, "Thanks! You saved my life. I owe you one!" Rob had been through some rough times with this terrific petty officer who had taught his junior officer a lot in the months they had been together. Grabowski was sitting on a cot beside a man who was in a lethargic condition. Grabowski said, "I want you to meet someone, your best friend, LTJG John Young." Rob knelt down by John and whispered to him, "You're going to be ok John. You need some rest and you'll be seeing that beauty from Australia before you know it. Hang in there." John smiled and fell asleep. Rob turned to Grabowski, "How are you doing now?" He answered, "Well they x-rayed me and found a spot on my lung, so they're evaluating me now. Could be nothing, but they want to find out for sure." He looked around and not seeing anyone looking, he reached in his bathrobe and handed Rob a small bottle of Bourbon whiskey. "Where in the world did you get that?" asked Rob. "Can't tell you sir, but I have my sources!" He poured some Jack Daniels, Kentucky's finest bourbon whiskey, into paper cups and they made a toast, "To Victory and Home!"

· · · · ·

The naval base at Yokosuka was a beehive of activity. U.S. Navy Attack Transports were unloading cargo alongside the piers with Japanese cranes overhead that only weeks ago were working feverously on hundreds of midget submarines that were to be used on suicide missions against the American armada. The Navy was setting up offices in the former tunnel complex on the base.

Ben Miller got out of his gray Navy Jeep and went up the gangway of the USS *Rescue,* saluted the colors and the OOD as the boatswain mate announced, "Captain, United States Navy, arriving." A messenger escorted him from the quarterdeck to the captain's office, where he met an old friend and classmate from the Naval Academy. Ben told him of his mission. "You're in for a shock Ben," the captain said, "These men have been through hell and back. Their captivity was the most inhumane thing I have ever known. I've heard stories that you would not believe that a civilized nation would do to another. While some of these men's appearances may seem well enough, they are all suffering internal injuries. Their mental issues will be with them for a long,

long time." Together they made their way into a ward where men were lying on cots. Hospital beds were reserved for the worst cases. Some men wore only boxer shorts, their ribs showing through their white skin. They looked like skeletons. Most had been brought here September 5, a few days after the formal surrender had taken place. Ben believed he was going to throw up. A medic led them to where some of the *Thornfish* men were being treated. Ben didn't recognize Rob at first. Rob looked up when he saw the two captains coming down the rows of sick men and recognized Ben Miller right away. He rose and greeted the captain. "Sir, I'm Rob Walker of the *Thornfish*, do you remember me? It's good to see you again." Ben was shocked. Rob's frame was still tall and straight, but his thin body showed the strain of torture and malnutrition. Ben greeted him warmly and tried not to show his dismay at his appearance. Rob quickly introduced Grabowski standing by John Young's cot. John, in his torpid condition, tried to stand but was unable. The ship's captain excused himself, and Rob and his former staff officer talked at length about home, the Navy and finally the purpose of his visit to Japan. "Well Rob, I'm here for two reasons. One to check up on our submariners' condition and need for recuperation and two, to meet with the Japanese Commander of Submarines, Admiral Kamatsu." Rob was stunned. "I know him sir! I knew his son when we were teenagers here in Japan years ago. His father was a squadron commander then and even got us a tour on one of his I-boats. I was called to his office twice after I was captured. He is now, a Vice Admiral." Rob went on and explained his capture of the admiral's son and how he had helped him try to get word of his capture to the folks back home. Ben said, "Rob, your folks and Molly did get your Red Cross postcard. It was a godsend for them." Then he changed the subject back to the interview. "Do you think you would be able to accompany me on my first visit with the Jap Admiral?" Rob nodded. Ben continued, "It would help break the ice and give me an entrée with him that might take a lot longer if I did it by myself." They agreed to try to meet the next morning after breakfast. Ben talked with John for a long time, and finally had to say goodbye, and went on looking for any more of his submariners on board.

The following morning Rob met Captain Miller on the quarterdeck of the submarine tender. The OOD was busy 'directing traffic' as several submarines were coming alongside for some needed upkeep. Ben brought a new submariner's Dolphin Pin and Combat Patrol Award and gave them to Rob to put on his breast pocket. Despite his gaunt appearance, he was alert and ready to meet the admiral who had helped him and was now a POW himself. They entered the large comfortable wardroom and had some coffee and hot donuts that had just come from the ship's bakery. Ben discussed the items he wanted to cover with the admiral. He had the tender provide him with one of their portable wire recorders. The interview would be transcribed later for distribution for naval intelligence services and submarine commands. Their first meeting, however, would be informal and a get acquainted session without a wire recorder present. Ben's plan was to have Rob wait in the wardroom until he had an appropriate time to bring him into the meeting.

A Marine guard stood outside the cabin of Japanese Admiral Kinaki Kamatsu. He snapped to attention when Captain Miller came up the ladder to the passageway on the 03 level. Captain Miller returned the salute, knocked on the door and entered. The Japanese Admiral stood and saluted the young American Navy captain. In fluent English he said, "Good morning sir. Pardon my appearance, I haven't dressed for the occasion." The admiral had Navy issued khakis with no insignia. Ben looked at him for a long time. He was in his fifties he thought. His black hair had too much gray for his age. His face was drawn, and wrinkles surrounded the corners of his eyes. His square jaw remained firm and radiated command. Ben knew some of his background. A graduate at the top of his class at the Japanese Naval Academy, and former attaché in the Japanese Embassy in Washington, he had studied at Harvard; altogether an impressive resume. He put out his hand and Ben took it. His handshake was strong and warm. He looked Ben directly in his eyes. Ben introduced himself and his job on the staff of the Commander of Submarines Pacific Fleet. He offered the admiral a Lucky Strike cigarette, and he eagerly accepted. The stateroom was a good size for a naval vessel; it had its own bath and toilet, a steel desk of Navy gray, a brown leather couch and chair and a small coffee table. The porthole with dark blue curtains overlooked the 03 level and the Navy yard beyond. Ben asked if his accommodations were ok and called the wardroom and had coffee and pastries delivered within minutes.

Ben said, "Admiral tell me a little about yourself." Admiral Kamatsu replied, "There is little to tell. I am a graduate of the Japanese Naval Academy, spent most of my career in submarines. The highlight being the command of two I-boats. I also had shore duty in the States at the Japanese embassy in Washington DC. as its naval attaché. I had the opportunity to spend some time at Harvard as well. I am married and have not heard about my wife yet. I am concerned about her welfare. She lives in our home on the base." Ben made a note on a small notebook he carried. "I'll see if I can arrange to check on her for you. Before I leave please give me the particulars of her whereabouts." The Admiral seemed very pleased. Ben said, "Tell me about your son. He is a prisoner of ours now held in California." The admiral crushed out his cigarette in the chrome plated ashtray the machinist mates had made from the casing of a five-inch shell. His lips tightened, and he folded his arms over his chest. "How do you know about my son?" Ben replied, "We know from an after-action patrol report from one of our submarines that sank his submarine, an I-boat I believe. One of my officers helped rescue him before his boat sank. You know him, LTJG Robert A. Walker Jr., a reservist. He became a prisoner of war after his boat, the *Thornfish*, was scuttled off the Malay Peninsula. I understand you have seen him and helped him." The admiral nodded, his frown betrayed his feelings, "Yes, I did what I could. He and my son were friends before the war when his father taught here at Tokyo University. And I believe the lieutenant personally treated my son very well. Perhaps they will still be friends someday." The admiral added something that Ben did not expect. "Captain, I must confess that our treatment of Prisoners of War was reprehensible. My country does not respect the military who surrender. We still do not accept the fact that we have soldiers and sailors who became prisoners of the Allies. It goes back to our centuries old tradition. The Bushido code of honor for the samurai." Ben interrupted, "Mr. Walker is in the wardroom below us right now and would like to see you for a few minutes." As Ben picked up the phone to call Rob, the admiral said, "OK, it's all right." He was resigned to the fact anyway that there would be no sense in refusing to see the young lieutenant. While they were waiting for him to come up Ben asked if he had heard anything from his son recently. "No, as you know we have had very little commerce or contact with the outside world for months. The American Navy has so many ships off our shores, we could almost walk on them from here to Okinawa." Ben smiled at his faint attempt at humor. There was a knock on the door, and Rob entered the stateroom.

CHAPTER 73

Another Interview

When Rob entered the stateroom, Admiral Kinaki Kamatsu rose and greeted him. "We meet again lieutenant, and under different circumstances. You look much better."

"I'm getting better food now, the daily rice ball laced with cat litter we POWs were being fed makes you lose weight rather quickly."

Admiral Kamatsu said, "I know, we treated our prisoners badly." Rob said, "That's an understatement Sir, in fact, your camp commanders were given orders to execute all POWs in the event of an invasion." The admiral did not reply. He knew of the order. Captain Miller, sensing the awkwardness of the situation, said, "Please be seated gentlemen. Now tell me how you know each other."

Rob began by telling about his time in school with the admiral's son, and later by some quirk of fate, Rob's vessel sank his submarine and the admiral's son was rescued. "Your son was treated well by our side, and we honored the international laws regarding prisoners of war."

The admiral sat in the leather chair and finally spoke. "You are correct. You did it the honorable way, we did not. I'm sorry. To make amends perhaps I can share with you both, now that the war is over, some of my assessments of the war from the Japanese perspective. I think that is what you are here for anyway."

Ben perked up. "Yes, admiral we do want to get you assessment of your submarines' operations. I intend to do some interviews with you over the next several days, and I will record them in order not to miss anything."

The admiral replied in Navy lingo, "Very well."

For the next several days, Admiral Kamatsu shared his recollections of the war beginning with the five submarines that were part of the Japanese task force attack on Pearl Harbor. They carried midget subs, which did not do any damage. In fact, none of the Imperial submarines did anything during the attack. It had profound implications during the war. To many of the military leaders such as Tojo, their poor performance caused loss of face and often submarines were diverted from sinking Allied ships, to ferrying supplies and troops to beleaguered island bases. On the last day of the interview, he disclosed that 29 of their submarines had been sunk during the last six months of the war. Mostly from depth charge attacks by American destroyers. Only one or two I boats were still afloat. Toward the end of the war, the loss of face overwhelmed Admiral Kamatsu, and he seriously considered committing hara-kiri, the Japanese samurai self-disembowelment by the sword for disgrace. The U.S. Marines interrupted his unsure attempt.

Ben said, "I have orders to take one of the latest I-boats to Pearl Harbor for our evaluation of your technology. We are particularly interested in your torpedoes, radar, and snorkel masts and how your submarines used them."

"Yes, we have one of our surviving I-boats, I-36, it was alongside pier 3 here in Yokosuka during the surrender; if you can arrange it, I will give you a tour of one of them tomorrow if you would like."

Ben said, "For the trip to Pearl Harbor we will need the captain of the I-36 and some of his key personnel to man the vessel underway along with reporting to our American Officer in Charge and crew. The trip will be on the surface only. We will need an American officer that can speak some Japanese.

The admiral said, "I know of one, and he pointed to Rob."

Ben smiled, "I've already thought of that. Rob would you be up to it? You would have to volunteer for this assignment. It will delay your homecoming."

Rob didn't hesitate. "Yes sir, I'd like to do it." But he added, "I'd like to have my leading petty officer Grabowski and LTJG Young to be a part of the crew." And if I may, sir, I suggest that LT Abrams, our exec on the *Thornfish,* be assigned as OIC. He is in line to command a fleet boat even though he is a reservist." Ben said, "I know of him. I've heard good things about his job on the *Thornfish.* In fact, he is being released from the hospital ship presently at Yokohama. I'll see if he is interested, and we'll have to get the doctors to agree to release you all to resume active duty."

Before he excused Rob, he added, "Rob I would like for you to try to locate the admiral's wife. She lives on the base up by the radio tower. Admiral Kamatsu is anxious to know about her welfare." "Aye sir, I'd be pleased to do it."

"I want you to join us for the tour of the I-36 tomorrow…you're going to become very familiar with the operation of a Japanese prize of war."

The next morning Rob had a Jeep and Marine driver take him to the top of the hills above the naval base to try to locate the admiral's home. The radio tower that sat on the very top of the hill had been destroyed. The admiral's home was below the road some 100 yards, down a steep embankment. There were steps down the hill leading to the alcove in front of a beautiful Japanese style home. He noticed a small pair of rails alongside the stairs for a cargo lift that had been used to carry food and household items up and down the steep incline. Rob had the Marine wait at the top of the hill, and he knocked on the door. In a few minutes a Japanese lady dressed in a violet kimono appeared at the door. Seeing an American naval officer, she said in English, "Yes, may I help you?" Rob saw an elegant lady, "Mrs. Kamatsu, I'm Lieutenant Robert Walker, and I have some news from your husband." Her face turned ashen. "Oh my god, what's happened?" Rob saw her concern. "I didn't mean to cause you concern. Your husband is fine. He asked me to find out if you were all right. He is worried about you since he had no word of your welfare since the surrender. He is on a U. S. Navy ship moored alongside a pier at the base. He is confined to his cabin for now."

"Won't you come in?" she asked. Rob took off his shoes and entered the foyer. A polished wood floor accented with bamboo and teak decorated the entrance to the small sunken living room. Several leather couches sat opposite the low table in the center of the room.

"May I offer you some tea?" Rob said, "Yes, please." She offered him a seat while she prepared some tea in an adjacent room. Rob stood admiring the beautiful wood block prints decorating her living room walls. When Mrs. Kamatsu returned, she said, "Are not these beautiful prints? They are by Sadanobu Hasegawa, a famous Japanese artist." Rob said, "Yes, they are, I especially like the Princess painting." She looked at Rob, whose demeanor pleased her. For a victor he was very humble she thought. "Yes, it is one of my favorites too." She placed a tray on a small table with a teapot and cups of Noritake China along with some rice cakes. After pouring tea she said, "Now please tell me about my husband. How is he now? Is he a prisoner of war? I was fearful that he had committed hara-kiri. I find the Bushido code of honor reprehensible. That arcane code is not honor in my opinion. It's a coward's way out."

Rob said, "Mrs. Kamatsu I have the same opinion. But I must tell you that your husband is well and being taken care of while confined aboard a ship moored at the base. He tried to help me while I was a prisoner of war here at Ofuna and later at Mitsubishi's copper mine." She sighed, "Yes, he told me about some of those horrible camps. I'm so sorry." Rob continued, "You see we met because he learned that I was a prisoner of war. I had news of your son's capture." She leaned forward, eager to hear more. Beginning with the action of the two submarines off the coast of Japan, Rob told her of Jimmu being rescued after his sub was sunk, and his being taken prisoner by the *Thornfish*. He assured her that Jimmu was well treated as a POW. When he finished, she started to cry. "Why do we have these damned wars? These old proud men get us into these wars, and the young men fight and die. Look at Hiroshima and Nagasaki. We'll never be the same again. A horrible weapon has been unleashed." She took a small lace handkerchief and covered her eyes. Rob waited and then said, "If we would have invaded Japan the loss of life would have been monumental on both sides. Perhaps the bomb saved many hundreds of thousands of lives. I know it saved many prisoners of war like myself. Time will tell."

Rob looked at his watch, it was time to go. He started to leave and gave her the name of the ship, its hull number and location on the base where her husband was being confined. She would be able to come and see her husband soon. Rob said that he would try to send a vehicle to pick her up. She said, "Thanks, so very kind of you. I want to thank you for what you did for our son. Perhaps someday we can repay you." As Rob was saying goodbye, she went to the wall and removed the Princess woodblock and gave it to Rob. He refused, but she insisted. "I want you to have it in appreciation for your kindness shown to my family. Please remember us when you see the Princess after you return home." Rob finally accepted her gift. She signed it on the back: To LT Robert Walker USN, gratefully, M. J. Kamatsu.

• • • • •

Mary Catherine Walker sat at the kitchen table drinking a fresh cup of Lapsang Souchong Chinese Black Tea, the one Molly thought tasted like old railroad ties. Mrs. Walker loved the heavy-bodied flavor accented with anise. *The Oxford Press* was spread out before her, and with scissors in hand, she was cutting out articles that she thought should be included in the history of Oxford during the war. As she started to cut an article about VJ Day, she noticed an editorial that made her angry.

One Sad Part of War

"One of the saddest things about war is the intolerance and hatred it breeds. The atrocity stories about the Japs have created a wave of comments about the 'dirty yellow beasts,' and unquestionably those who treated American prisoners as they are reported to have done, are beasts. The thought we should not overlook, however, is that there are some kindly Japanese people. Particularly do we feel sorry for people of Japanese heritage born and reared in this country and now under surveillance as an alien people.

"In the last war, we remember persons of German ancestry that were subjected to the same intolerant treatment. One of our favorite college professors, who had married a German woman while studying in that country, was placed in a most unpleasant position. He was shunned as 'pro-German.' Right here in Oxford, we are told that families now prominent were looked upon with suspicion 25 years ago. Because of their German forebears.

"Japanese who have lived in this country for years and have been good citizens are regarded with even greater distrust. The government has moved these people inland, often taking families from successful businesses and attractive homes, housing them in one-room tar paper shacks. If they are fortunate enough to get an offer of a job someplace, they are given $25 with which to start a new life in a hostile world. Tough prospect. Wouldn't the Christian thing be to give these people a chance and treat them as human beings?

"All Germans are not Hitlers and all Japs are not sadistic monsters. Generations ago some of them chose to come to America where we boast that there is equal opportunity, where a man has a chance to get ahead if he works and tries to do right."

Mary Catherine thought, *what's wrong with these people, anyway?* At the beginning of the war, the FBI had identified 700 Japanese spies embedded on our west coast. There was fear that Japan would try invading and a submarine had shelled Santa Barbara that same day. *Molly is so forgiving. I'm not built that way. An eye for Eye, Tooth for Tooth was the way I was brought up.*

She heard Molly coming in the front door. She must have gotten off work early. "Molly come in here, I want to show you something." Molly tossed her Miami Redskin jacket on the hall chair and joined her landlady for a few minutes.

"Would you like a cup of tea? It's hot on the stove."

"No thanks I'll only stay a few minutes, I have some letters to write. Have you heard when Professor Walker will be coming home permanently?"

"Yes. The Navy will be closing his unit In Washington soon, and he hopes to begin teaching again at Miami next semester. You know he made a huge contribution to the war in the Pacific. He knew so much about some of the islands that the Navy invaded on their way to Tokyo. He is getting the Navy E for Excellence award from the Secretary of the Navy."

"Wonderful!"

"By the way have you heard from Marianne lately?"

"I had a letter from her a few days ago. She is going to try out for the Fred Waring Chorale in New York this fall. She has another option, an opportunity to go to Hollywood for an audition for a new movie. But she wants to come here as soon as she can. She is so excited that Rob is alive and that he'll be here someday before too long. They had so much fun together in Australia."

Molly didn't say anything, but Mrs. Walker could tell that Molly wasn't too keen on her being here. She said, "Now Mrs. Walker, what was it that you wanted to show me?"

"I just read an editorial that I hope you didn't write about the Japanese here in America. Doesn't the paper know that the Japs had plans to invade the West Coast of the United States, and that the FBI had arrested over 700 Japanese spies on the west coast? One of their submarines shelled one of the California cities. And the U.S. Supreme Court upheld Roosevelt's decision to move the Japanese- Americans." Molly didn't want to argue with her. So, she opened the latest *Oxford Press*, "Look, let me read this. It's hot off the press!

"Forty Officers Coming to Teach Navy Men,
Seek Homes Here; Candidates Arrive November 3.

Homes, at least temporary, must be found immediately for 40 naval officers who will teach in the naval ROTC program which is to open at Miami November 3. These men plus three civilian teachers are being added to the Miami faculty and will be in Oxford by the first of November. This group of Navy men has been specially selected for the work of training future officers. Many of the men are married but will not bring their families to Oxford until they can find suitable housing. Any person with a spare room which can be used even temporarily will relieve the situation by that much. The ROTC unit will bring 550 officer candidates to the Miami University campus, 173 of them being trainees who have been here under the Navy's V12 program. Miami is one of 27 colleges that have been assigned permanent NROTC units."

Mrs. Walker was aware of President Upham's desire to have a unit of the Navy ROTC here on Miami's campus, and had written the Navy department in March and later submitted a formal application. It was granted in August and made effective 1 November 1945.

Molly exclaimed, "WOW, wouldn't it be wonderful if Rob could be assigned here?"

She folded her arms across her chest, "No, absolutely not. Rob is not going to stay in the Navy. I'm sure he will be discharged as soon as he recuperates. Submarines are too damned dangerous. Look what happened to him on the *Thornfish*! He will have a career in geology like his father … he likes mineralogy and will get his master's."

Molly wanted to say Rob should have something to say about his life career. But she didn't. She excused herself and went to her room. She fell into her armchair in the bedroom and thanked her guarding angel that she didn't explode at Mrs. Walker. She would be looking for a new place to live soon since Mr. Walker would be coming home to live.

Mary Catherine Walker sat at the table staring at her empty cup, thinking, *why did I say that? I'm too darned hard.*

CHAPTER 74

Hawaii

Valerie Edmonds sat on her lanai reading the Sunday edition of *The Honolulu Star*. She was starting on her third cup of Kona coffee. The VJ day had come and gone. The Island's celebration had been electric; people filled the streets and the Navy had a huge parade along Highway 92 to downtown Honolulu's Ala Moana Avenue and on to Diamond Head. The Royal Hawaiian had become civilian again and was being refurbished. The barbed wire had been removed from Waikiki beach. Fort DeRussy had an open house, and many residents of Honolulu were invited to see its fortifications for the first time since December 7, 1941. Ships in the harbor strung bunting and flags from the forecastle to the stern. The brownout had finally ended, and the bright lights came on again all over the island. But Mrs. Edmonds was in a pensive mood. The joy that came with the end of the war did not resonate long in her soul. She thought of the day of infamy as Roosevelt called it, when her husband Frank, chief petty officer air group on the USS *Arizona*, died along with over 1200 of his shipmates. The hulk of the old battleship containing their tomb was still lying at the bottom of the harbor rusting away and still oozing oil from its bunkers. The fourth anniversary of the attack that changed the nation was coming up in a few months. She hoped that there would be a solemn remembrance of that awful day. She intended to lay some flowers over the wreckage if she could get a Navy boat to take her there.

Her job with the Navy intelligence branch was going to be eliminated one of these days. What could she do? She did not want to go back to cleaning houses. Her work with the code breakers in the basement of the nondescript building at the base administration had been very rewarding. Valerie Edmonds felt good about what she had done for the war effort. There would probably be work for the after-action summaries that would come from the Navy and its review of the strategy and tactics used during the war. The Naval War College would be war-gaming some of the battles over again she thought. She was already hearing about the formation of teams called Joint Army-Navy Assessment Committees which would be sent to Japan to compile from Japanese sources losses of merchant and warships. She resolved to consider employment with them. She translated many documents for the Navy, every day. Top secret ship movements, logistic reports, and submarines' positioning all were a part of an average day.

There was one that was very personal. While on duty one evening in the spring of 1944, she translated a rather routine message from the Maru code of a Japanese merchant ship, carrying allied prisoners of war. The vessel, owned by Mitsubishi, said that among the prisoners were the crew of an American submarine, the *Thornfish*. Valerie could hardly contain herself. What a joy for Lily and the families of the survivors. But she realized that if she revealed the good news *to anyone* it could disclose the fact that the Americans had broken the Japanese code. She had to keep the top-secret information private even from her only daughter Lily.

Lily was crushed when she learned of the loss of the *Thornfish*. Although it was technically listed as missing in action, the submarine community knew what the word *overdue* meant. Lily grieved for months. But her mother's frequent letters were a source of inspiration for her. They gave her hope for a brighter future. Then, while on Kauai, Lily met a handsome Navy aviator who came often to eat at the Sunset Bar and Grille, where she worked. She first met Bill a few months after the report of the loss of the *Thornfish*. He was on temporary additional duty at Barking Sands and came to town as often as he could. He and Lily hit it off from the start. It was love at first sight for him. Of medium height with crew cut red hair, and a marvelous athletic build, what attracted her the most about Bill was his sense of humor, his infectious smile and cheerful attitude. During his last TAD, Temporary Additional Duty, to Kauai, he asked her to marry him. She was falling in love once again, but the winds of war interrupted their romance. Bill's squadron was deployed on the aircraft carrier, the USS *Hornet*, and he flew F6 fighter planes in the battles of Philippine Sea, Iwo Jima, and later Okinawa where its aircraft helped sink the Japanese battleship *Yamamoto*.

Before he left for combat, Lily said yes.

CHAPTER 75

The Inspiration

Molly had an idea. In Rob's last letter he told her he had recovered from dysentery. All things considered, he was making good progress according to the Navy doctor on the hospital ship. He told her of Chief O'Neil's death while a prisoner. He liked the man so much. He was more than his mentor in submarines. They had become good friends especially during the months they shared as 'guests of the Emperor.' He told her of how the old chief of the boat had died in the Japanese Mitsubishi's copper mine camp. John told him that he conducted a very brief funeral service in the cold at the copper mine camp. But he said he had some exciting news to tell her, but he could not say anything at this time. She wondered what that could be. A promotion perhaps.

She had an inspiration. What if she were to get permission from Mrs. Cullen, the publisher of *The Oxford Press*, to fly to San Francisco or wherever Rob would disembark and interview him about some of his wartime experiences. It might be a capstone to all their reporting during the war of their coverage of the news of the military, especially the Navy. She had read about some reporters from big newspapers trying to get interviews with ex-POWs upon their return to the states. Molly would give it some thought though; she did not like to make snap decisions.

Letters from Rob were more frequent now. He said he was still trying to find out about the status of his other shipmates from the *Thornfish*. He had seen Dick Morrison, his captain on the *Thornfish*, who was near death when the medics found him at Camp Omori in Tokyo Bay. He was going to be flown directly to Hawaii for treatment of his wounds. Jerry Abrams made it through one of the worst camps. He was sent there because he was a Jew.

Rob wrote Molly:

"I think Jerry will stay in the Navy. (And they want me too.) He was a terrific engineer for the Thornfish and would make a great commanding officer one of these days. He made a comment to me when we met on the hospital ship recently that atomic energy could possibly be used to propel submarines and ships someday. He said he would like to do some research on atomic energy for submarines. Can you

*imagine? And Molly, news from Japan: Tojo tried to commit suicide and bungled the
job when American Marines came to his home to arrest him for war crimes. And our
favorite Disc Jockey, Tokyo Rose, has been arrested in Yokohama. She is American.
She should be tried for treason.*

*"John Young is with me now on board the Rescue and is improving every day. He
is an inspiration to me. He saved my life more than once. He is like a brother to
me. John has given a lot of thought about forgiveness as he gets well. Not that I am
without fault myself, I know I'm a sinner... I have killed men in the war.*

*"Molly maybe you can help me. I have a lot of resentment and anger at my captors.
John says that as a believer in Jesus, we are called to ask God to forgive them. We
called the guards dumbbells, gorillas, numb nuts, and words I don't want you to
know, even to their face when they couldn't understand English. But they deserved
it. Let me have your thoughts next letter.*

*Love and Kisses, Rob. P.S. I miss you soooo much. Will you take a chance on me
and spend your life with me now that this war is over? I will be home soon. <u>Will
you marry me?"</u>*

Rob Walker had made his decision. Of the three lovely women in his life, Molly
was the first one he truly loved, and he was ready to make her the last one forever.

Several weeks later, she received the letter from Rob postmarked USS *Rescue* AH18
FPO. Molly read the letter in the privacy of her bedroom in the Walker's home. When
she read the last line, she screamed, and she clasped it to her breast. "Oh my God,
we're going to be married!!" But then she began to worry. She went over to the mirror
on her little vanity chest and looked at herself: it's been almost three years since we
saw each other. Will he still like me? She sat at her desk and dashed off a reply in the
best handwritten script.

Dearest Darling Rob:

*Yes!!!! I love you and always will, please come home soon. I will marry you the minute
I see you. Your sweetheart, Molly.*

News of the treatment of the Allied POWs was leaking out. But the military had put
a gag order on the Americans held by the Japs. It seemed to many Americans that the
U.S. government wanted to avoid "Japan bashing." Homecoming orders to ex-POWs
told them they were not to discuss their captivity unless cleared by cognizant bureaus
of Public Relations. Some were required to sign documents acknowledging the orders.

· · · · ·

Dr. Robert A. Walker checked in at the operations office at Andrews Army Air Base.
He was able to catch a flight out to Wright Army Air Base in Dayton. His B 4 bag

was loaded with his personal effects and some books he had acquired in Washington. His job in the Navy Department was over. His knowledge of the geography and geology of certain islands the Navy invaded in the Pacific benefited the Marines Corps immensely. He was anxious now to resume his teaching at Miami. His colleagues, Dr. Wolford, Wade, and others would be returning soon as well. He loved teaching. His specialty, Volcanology, was his favorite subject, and he was eager to begin mentoring others to enter the field. The Geology Department was considering offering a master's degree, and he hoped to oversee the program. He loved old Brice Hall with its creaky wood floors, high ceilings and large windows. The basement labs in paleontology and mineralogy would soon be filled with returning veterans studying under the new GI Bill that Congress had passed.

The C-47 Dakota twin-engine airplane took off on a clear day, and as a courtesy to the VIP passengers, circled the city. As he viewed the Capitol Building, the Reflecting Pool, and the Lincoln Memorial, he thought of all the men that fought and died for this beautiful country, the land of the free and the home of the brave. He thought of his son, and how he had helped him get into submarines against the objections of his strong-willed wife, Mary Catherine. She hated him when they learned of the loss of his submarine in early 1944. He knew she had not forgiven him, and he was so grateful to the Lord for protecting Rob. God had not only saved his only son but saved his marriage too.

After the airplane leveled off at 6000 feet for the flight home, he opened his briefcase and took out a couple of magazines he had brought along to read. As he thumbed through the first one, the October copy of *Wireless World* magazine, an article caught his attention. The author, Arthur C. Clarke, interested in science fiction, put forward an idea of a geosynchronous communications satellite. It was fascinating to this geologist. He mused, what if we could use the rocket technology of the German scientists, like Warner von Braun, and put an object in space over the earth, in sync with its rotation, that we could bounce radio waves off and have worldwide communications. What a feat that would be! Dr. Walker resolved to follow that guy's work in the future.

Later as the plane crossed the Alleghany River below him, the steel mills of Pittsburgh were making smoke and rolling steel for the new trucks and cars, refrigerators and wringer washing machines, things that Americans had gone without for years and were now eager to buy. Happy days are here again he thought. He turned to the second magazine, *Time,* and read about the formation of the new United Nations organization on October 24, 1945. Made up of 50 democratic nations, the big five, the United States, Great Britain, the Soviet Union, France and China, became what is called the permanent members of the Security Council, charged with overseeing the peace of the world. As the plane was about to land, he finished reading and put the magazines in his briefcase thinking that perhaps now, there would be an end to wars.

CHAPTER 76

'The Pig Boat'

The Japanese submarine I-36 was built for extended patrol and with the added capability of an aircraft carrier. It housed a small floatplane that could be launched on a tilted catapult. The plane had been removed for the voyage to Hawaii and loaded with equipment that the Navy wanted to inspect. Admiral Kamatsu had told Ben and Rob that the Japanese Navy had built 20 of the B 1 submarines, also known as the I-15 class. Displacing 2600 tons, 357 feet long, with a beam of 30 feet, it was a powerful but awkward boat to handle.

It needed work. Lots of it. The sub was given priority when it was drydocked at Yokosuka. The Japanese workers went over the entire submarine, running from one job to the next on the list. Rob was surprised at the performance of the Jap workers. The dockyard workers were fast and usually good at what they did. But after two weeks, the Navy inspected the work and still found lots of problems. The biggest one was the engines. The gaskets were worn causing lack of compression and wasting fuel. The entire sub was dirty by American standards. The boat reeked of soiled food, and poor sanitation. The head was a hole in the deck. The waste would fall into the open tank below and later blown to sea. The odor was awful. To make things worse, there were no showers, and roaches inhabited even the wardroom. The American crew soon named it the I-36 'Pig Boat.' The executive officer's stateroom was paneled in beautiful wood, but the bunk was for a midget, Rob thought. He had a cupboard at the foot of the bed removed so that he could stretch out somewhat when trying to sleep. Name tags on valves in Japanese had to be translated into English. Fortunately, most of the Japanese crew knew some English. Jerry Abrams came aboard the submarine tender and was given orders to command the I-36 as its officer-in-charge. John would be the communicator, Rob would act as exec, and navigator, but he needed more officers, an engineer and a first lieutenant. He located additional officers from a list of ex-POW submariners provided by Captain Miller. Petty Officer Grabowski volunteered to join the crew. He would be a help to watch the Jap crew, as there was some concern that one of them might attempt to sabotage the sub while en route. Finally, after a month of scrounging parts and a thorough cleaning, they went alongside a pier and had an air pressure check to make sure the boat was watertight. It passed.

A normal load of 17 Japanese torpedoes was put on aboard. Some thought the Jap torpedoes were better than the American torpedoes. Navy Ordnance people wanted to find out why. The empty hangar was loaded with radar and sonar gear as well as plans for the snorkel and aircraft launching procedures. The I boat floatplanes never really accomplished much during the war according to the Japanese submariners. With a surface range of 16,000 nautical miles, an I-boat aircraft carrier submarine could launch an aircraft and bomb the Panama Canal thereby slowing the war effort to reinforce the Pacific fleet after Pearl Harbor. For some strange reason it was never tried. But on February 24, 1942, the I-17 slid through the Santa Barbara Straits north of Los Angles and bombarded several targets on shore. It fired ten rounds and then skirted by an oncoming destroyer. In June the submarine I-26 shelled the Wireless Navigation Station at Vancouver Island firing seventeen rounds with little damage. Later that month a sister sub, the I-25, fired twenty rounds at the submarine base at Astoria on a clear moonlight night again with slight damage. Japan lost almost all the I-boats during the war, mainly to anti-submarine warfare by destroyers. Some twenty-nine of I class submarines were lost in the first seven months of 1945. The I-37 was sunk on 13 August, two days before the cessation of hostilities. The I-36 was one of the few patrol type submarines of the Imperial Japanese Navy that had not been sunk by the end of the war.

The interview with the admiral revealed that radar was one of the main reasons they lost so many of their submarines. For most of the war the Japanese military bureaucracy's hierarchy refused to believe radar had any value on submarines. They were invisible anyway, they reasoned. Some of the Japanese staff officers believed that the reason they lost the war was due to science. The technology of the atom bomb caused them to lose the war, not their military. Blaming science was a way to save face. *It was a matter of honor.*

· · · · ·

When he had a chance, Rob and John would go into town. The people were very nice to them. They were polite, and some would offer them gifts. Rob wondered, *how can these people who have half of their city destroyed, harbor so little hatred?*

On Monday morning in early November, the I-36 got underway from its pier at the naval base at Yokosuka. It was a test run into Tokyo Bay, with its two powerful diesel engines fed with U.S. Navy diesel oil and guarded by two LCVPs. Rob had the conn, Jerry stood by him on the bridge, Grabowski was in the control room watching every move of the Japanese sailors. The sub glided past the myriad of U.S. Navy ships. Yokosuka was becoming the U.S. Navy's principal base in Asia. After successfully holding several tests, including submergence to periscope depth to check periscopes, and the snorkel, the I-36 returned to the base, and took on provisions for the trip to

Hawaii. The Japanese submarines normally based at Yokosuka had been moved. Their commanding officers had orders to transfer them to the naval base at Sasebo near Nagasaki on the western coast of Honshu. The large subs and the midgets were all programmed for destruction by a U.S. Navy team headed by Commander Paul Schratz, a former executive officer on two fleet boats. Rob's mentor, Captain Ben Miller, had departed a few days earlier for Hawaii and promised Rob he would meet him on the pier at the sub base when he arrived.

Rob and John shared a stateroom on the sub tender now alongside a pier at the Yokosuka naval base. When they returned to the ship on the eve of their departure for Hawaii, there was a stack of mail for each of them on the gray steel desk. John's was postmarked from Perth, Australia, and Rob's from Oxford, Ohio. Rob tore the earliest letter finding her reply saying, YES! Rob was so excited, he jumped up and grabbed John and showed him the letter "Molly said she'd marry me! John, I'm getting married!"

Early the next morning, after 8 o'clock colors honoring the American flag throughout the naval base, the senior officer afloat came to the pier and bade the young officer-in-charge and his crew farewell. A Navy public affairs officer and his photographer took pictures. Jerry along with Rob was photographed on the bridge with the American flag proudly blowing above them in the superstructure.

With a prolonged blast of the whistle, Jerry Abrams, commanding, ordered both engines back one third and he conned the I-36 out of the harbor into Tokyo Bay. It was a thrill he had never expected to have, commanding his own submarine, even though made in Japan, on a long slow voyage to Hawaii. As they neared the entrance buoy to Tokyo Bay, Rob standing on the bridge took a long look back over the stern of the sub at Mount Fujiyama in the morning mist. The sunshine reflected off the low hanging clouds, and the cone of the 12,000-foot mountain he had climbed with Jimmysan years ago glowed with golden fire. He wished that he still had the little 35 mm camera he had purchased used from John Minnis' drug store years ago. It had gone down with the *Thornfish* in the Malacca Straits.

It had taken America 45 months to beat Japan. United States submarines had ground the Japanese Empire to a halt. Their vital imports of oil, rubber, and food-stuffs had been completely shut off. They couldn't make steel for ships, or aluminum for aircraft. By the summer of 1945 nearly all of Japan's fuel had been depleted. Their submarines were burning fuel for their diesels made from soybeans. Yet the Bushido military wanted to fight to the last man, military and civilian, **for the honor of the Emperor and Empire**. They had never lost a war until the two blasts of the atomic bombs altered the Emperor's thinking.

The most evil war in history had ended. Tens of millions had died in Europe, Africa and Asia.

It was estimated that American submarines had sunk 4000 Japanese vessels. But the silent service had the highest casualty rate, twenty-two percent, in any military branch. Fifty-two United States submarines were lost, and 375 officers and 3,131 enlisted men never came home.

CHAPTER 77

Homeward Bound

The I-36 was two days out of port. John had the deck while Rob made a quick below deck inspection. While in the control room, the Japanese radio man handed him a weather notice: a strong low-pressure area with strong winds was directly in their path. It could become a serious storm. Rob informed Jerry and then ordered the crew in Japanese to begin tying down any loose gear. He recalled the infamous Typhoon Cobra that hit Halsey's fleet in December 1944, when three destroyers capsized and over 700 sailors lost their lives while battling a huge typhoon 300 miles east of the Philippines. The USS *Pittsburg* CA72, a Navy heavy cruiser, lost its entire bow in a typhoon off Japan's southernmost Island, Kyushu in June 1945.

While they were in upkeep at the naval base at Yokosuka on October 9 and 10, a typhoon hit the western shores of Kyushu and Honshu causing ships to go aground and damaging buildings with 200 mph winds. Hundreds of lives were lost. However, Yokosuka was spared as the typhoon stayed on the west coast of Japan.

The one that I-36 was heading into could be a real doozy.

· · · · ·

Valerie Edmonds stooped to pick up her morning paper left on the driveway of her home. The paper boy had done it again. He threw the paper just under the rear bumper of her convertible. She would have to talk to him about it. She had a little time before leaving for work at the naval base. Glancing at the headlines of the *Honolulu Star-Bulletin*, she saw in the mast head on the front page a headline "**Jap sub comes to Pearl Harbor.**" She turned to the second page and saw a wire service photo of a large Japanese submarine leaving Japan en route to Hawaii, and on the bridge, a Navy lieutenant named Robert A. Walker. She could hardly believe it. She went back to the house and phoned Lily, "Rob is coming to Hawaii!"

· · · · ·

Molly had just finished an article for the Thursday edition about the change of status of the Navy ROTC program at Miami. In an interview with the commanding officer, Captain Granville A. Moore, USN, Molly learned that the students in the program will change from active to reserve, effective February 1, 1946. Molly finally got up enough courage to talk with her employer about doing the story of one of their home town heroes coming home from the war as a survivor of the Japanese prison camps. And, to top it off, coming home in a Japanese prize of war, one of their most sophisticated submarines. She pulled the typewriter paper from the Underwood typewriter and took it into Mrs. Cullen's office.

She knocked on her door. "Excuse me Mrs. Cullen, may I speak with you for a few minutes?" Mrs. Cullen was a person of few words. She was stingy with her time as her words. She believed that a reporter should be able to tell the story as succinctly as possible, and not with the goal of impressing the reader with her vast command of the English language.

"Come in Molly." She seemed in a good mood. Molly entered the spartan office and handed her the story she had just written. She put on her pinch-nose glasses and, as usual, took out her red pencil and started to read Molly's epistle. After one or two red notations, she returned it to Molly and said, "Good job!" Molly, thus encouraged, told her boss of her idea of going to the West Coast to interview Rob. "Molly, I think you have a personal goal in mind here too. Am I right?" Molly blushed, "Yes Ma'am." Mrs. Cullen put down her glasses and pencil, and said, "Well, I'll think about it. There may be a good storyline here. One that even *The Cincinnati Enquirer* might try to steal. I'll let you know tomorrow."

· · · · ·

The operation order for the I-36 trip required the sub to provide a noon position report each day to the squadron commander in Hawaii. By the second day they had made good distance, some 700 miles east of Tokyo. Rob, the ship's navigator, had the quartermaster report to him each hour on the hour, the barometer reading and record it in the ship's log. He made his way up to the bridge early at twilight the third morning and took a round of star sights with the quartermaster standing by his side recording the time of each observation. As the dawn broke across the eastern sea, clouds in the east glowed a beautiful red. He remembered the sailor's lore of ages ago, 'Red sky at night sailors delight, red sky in the morning, sailors take warning.' We need to get an updated weather report as soon as possible. After the disastrous typhoon that hit the Halsey fleet, the Navy established weather stations on Guam and other island locations in the western Pacific.

A few minutes before reveille sounded, there was a knock on Rob's stateroom door. Rob awoke immediately, "Yes, come in." Grabowski stuck his head in the stateroom, and said, "Sorry to bother you sir, but we have a problem." Rob rubbed the sleep from his eyes. He had only slept a few hours during the last day. "We have a stowaway, sir."

Rob responded, "What, are you sure?"

"I have her right here."

"What do you mean *her*?"

"Yes sir, it's a girl, I think she may be a Korean."

Rob was in his skivvies and quickly pulled his pants on. Come in here he ordered. The big man had a young girl in tow. "She speaks Korean and some Japanese, I think. I found her hiding in a storage room in the after-crews berthing." Rob looked at the pathetic girl. Speaking Japanese, Rob demanded, "What are you doing here?" Speaking softly in Japanese, she replied, "I want go America."

Rob learned that she was a sex slave kidnapped by the Japanese military from her home in Korea along with thousands of other girls to provide sexual services for the Japanese Army and Navy. Rob guessed she was probably about 16 years old. She had been a sex slave for the last two years servicing Japanese submariners in the area. She and her other girls would meet a sub when it came back from patrol and start in the bow and work their way to the stern for two hours. When she learned that the I-36 was going to Hawaii, she sneaked aboard at night while the hatch to the after-torpedo room was open during the time workers brought food and supplies on the submarine.

She smelled bad. So, Rob gave her soap and towels and a clean set of his underwear, and let her take a sponge bath in the officers' toilet, and use his room to clean up in. He closed the door for her privacy while he and Grabowski sat in the wardroom trying to figure out what to do next. A few minutes later Jerry came in the wardroom and Rob told him the story. Jerry said, "Well we need to inform the crew and the squadron of our guest." Rob agreed. "I will announce at breakfast both in English and Japanese that no one is to lay a hand on her, under penalty of me throwing any offender overboard."

When he returned to his stateroom, he found the girl in her clean clothes, sound asleep on his bunk. He had her filthy clothes thrown overboard.

*   *   *   *   *

Molly applied for and was granted a war correspondent identify card. It would give her some priority in transportation and entrance to military facilities. When she read the wire service report of the departure of the Japanese submarine, she rushed to get an airline ticket to San Francisco. From there she hoped to get a seat on a military plane to Hawaii. The day before her flight, she received the most wonderful letter from Rob that she had ever had. It was full of interesting things that he was doing in preparation for the long voyage to Hawaii. And it closed with the sweetest words she had ever heard from him. "I told the Lord when I believed I was going to be beheaded... I made a promise that if he'd get me out of this I would serve him. I am, and I love you with all my heart." Rob. Molly cried.

CHAPTER 78

Typhoon

It's 3859 miles from Japan to Hawaii. The operation order called for the former Japanese submarine to make a non-stop trip if fuel permitted. If in doubt they would have to stop at Midway to refuel. It would only add about 50 miles to their track if they had to refuel there. The voyage would last about 16 days at speed of advance of 10 knots. A storm had formed as a tropical depression four hundred miles northwest of Midway Island and was moving toward them at 20 miles per hour. A recent radio message received from the newly established meteorology center on Guam, reported gale force winds of 40 knots with waves of 5- 6 meters. The 64-dollar question was which way would it track? Most lows that form in the northern hemisphere are usually between 20 to 30 degrees latitude and travel counterclockwise. Jerry wanted to change course to the weak side of the storm as soon as they could determine its track. From midshipmen training in navigation, he recalled the 'Buys Ballot's Law.' Buys Ballot was a Dutch meteorologist in the 1850s whose observations helped ship captains determine the danger area of a potential storm. It says: *Stand with your back to the wind. Extend your left hand and the low pressure is to your left.* Jerry and Rob consulted and after receiving several messages from Guam, decided to alter course to the southeast, the weak side of the storm that Guam now called a typhoon.

Jerry didn't have a lot of confidence in the former enemy 's submarine. It looked strong enough, but the welds of the hull made him apprehensive about it holding together on the surface in a severe storm. Jerry discussed his concerns with Rob and John and with the former I boat commanding officer, a Japanese graduate of its naval academy, who spoke some English. They went over the charts of the vast Pacific reviewing the possible paths of the typhoon. Rob asked the former CO what he would do in a typhoon. He said, "Must dive in a bad storm." There was a problem, however. The operation order called for them to remain on the surface. To make matters worse the starboard engine started acting up. It had to be shut down temporarily while repairs were undertaken. Speed was reduced to 6 knots. Waves were now breaking over the airplane hangar just forward of the bridge. Rob had the lookouts and watch standers on the bridge tie themselves on with ropes. All hatches were checked and secured tightly.

At night the only men topside were the officer of the deck and junior officer of the deck, a Japanese ensign. The radar was almost useless. It was secured.

Down below the Korean lass was beginning to smile. Now dressed in Navy dungarees and shirt, she assisted the steward serving in the wardroom and helped herself to the pastries made in its tiny ovens. The tossing of the boat as it plowed through angry waves didn't seem to bother her. The foul odors from engines, body odors, and food, were very bad, but she seemed to be used to it. The Japanese did not do much to make their submarines habitable. Rob had the shipyard install commodes over the holes in the deck the Japs used for their toilets and curtains for a little privacy.

Seas were increasing each hour. The barometer was dropping at a rate of over .05 mm per hour, a sign of trouble ahead. The anemometer read 70 miles per hour winds. The howling sea made talking on the bridge nearly impossible. The navigator had not had a star sight in over two days. The gyro was working well, however, and the chart table had a dead reckoning track laid out with the sub's estimated position marked each hour. About midnight Rob decided to make a trip to the bridge. He put on a warm foul weather jacket and walked through the control room now bathed in red to assist watch-standers with their night vision. A qualified lieutenant junior grade was standing watch on the bridge, tied in with a hemp rope. He had ordered all the lookouts below and the hatch closed. Once on the bridge, the officer of the deck yelled at Rob, "Hang on sir there's a huge wave coming!" Rob just had time to crouch down and put his arms and legs around the binnacle as the wave broke over the bridge. The blackness of the water was highlighted by the white foam of the angry sea. Daybreak was two hours away. There was no need to man a bridge watch in these dangerous conditions. So, Rob ordered the OOD to go below and stand his watch in the conning tower. He descended after him closing the hatch securely behind him. He was soaked through and through. He climbed down the ladder to the control room and said a few words to Grabowski and went to his stateroom next to the control room. He shed his wet jacket in the passageway and stepped in his stateroom and began undressing. As he reached into the closet to get a towel and some dry skivvies, he heard a noise and turned the red night light on. Then he saw her. The Korean girl was laying naked on his bed, arms outstretched, begging him to come to her.

For an instant he was tempted. It had been over eighteen months since he had been with a woman. No one would know. But he couldn't betray himself and his shipmates. He reminded himself of the words of admonition he had given the crew. "No one lays a hand on her." It was a matter of honor. In Japanese he ordered, "No, now get dressed and go to your room!" For security the Korean had her own stateroom in officers' country. It was the smallest of all five of them, but it was private and easily seen just outside the wardroom. Rob dressed and started to lie down when the sub's bow shot up then dove and pitched and rolled some 35 degrees. When he reached the control room John and the Japanese former commander of the submarine, were hanging on to the chart table. John said, "We both recommend that we dive the boat." Rob paused for a moment; he had reached the same conclusion. He had to talk with Jerry who was in command. Just then Jerry came in the control room grabbing onto anything that he could find to keep from falling. It didn't take long to convince Jerry that they really needed to submerge. Jerry ordered the Japanese former CO to put air in the boat. Immediately the machinist mate opened the air manifold and pressure started to build inside the entire submarine. The pressure held.

Jerry ordered John to get a message out with the latest estimated position and the reason for diving. "We need to inform Pearl Harbor of our situation and our position. Try to get a message out now...." Jerry ordered, "Stand by to dive. All compartments report when ready to dive." He checked the barometer. It was below 29 mm of mercury. The wind speed was 80 knots! "Pressure in the boat, sir" yelled the diving officer. "Green board!" Normally they would be ready to dive in a minute or less, but the crew checked and doublechecked valves, fittings, and systems to ensure that nothing was overlooked on this old Japanese I boat. Finally, all compartments reported ready to dive. Jerry took the general announcing system microphone and announced, "Dive, Dive," and the same words in Japanese. The main induction, snorkel and overboard exhausts valves were shut. With five degrees down bubble, the I-36 descended into the depths of the Pacific Ocean, the bottom being 7000 feet below. Grabowski stood in the control room with his fingers crossed watching the crew as they completed their first dive.

Before submerging, the radioman sent a dispatch to Pearl Harbor giving them their position and need to submerge. But there was no reply. Fortunately, the sub had a full charge on its batteries. Jerry leveled off at 65 feet, periscope depth. It was still very rough, so he went to 100 feet. The ride was better but still not comfortable. When they reached 150 feet, the storm's fury abated. John and Grabowski made a tour of the submarine from bow to stern. A few minor leaks were found but nothing serious so far.

Jerry told his watch standers, "We'll continue on this course for a few hours and then see how the storm is behaving." He ordered all hands not on watch to get some sleep. Rob turned in with his clothes on and fell asleep immediately. The I-36, making 6 knots submerged speed, continued underneath the storm heading southeast, the weakest side of the typhoon. At 0700 Jerry awoke and went to the conning tower. He ordered the boat to come to periscope depth and after coming to a depth of 55 feet he could see the bright sky above. They were in the eye of the typhoon. There was blue sky above, and in the distance walls of water surrounding the center of the storm were stacked in an ever-widening circle slanted like bleachers in a football stadium. The men on the diving planes were having trouble controlling the depth, so he took the boat down again. This time to 200 feet. Breakfast was served in the crew's mess. Their main dish was rice. The former POWs would have no part of rice. Grabowski had commandeered a Navy coffee pot from the tender and the Americans enjoyed hot coffee and a typical Navy breakfast, powdered milk and scrambled eggs, biscuits, sausage and baked beans.

After the wardroom was cleared, John and Rob sat talking about their lives after they reached Pearl Harbor. They both had enough points to be discharged in a few months. The first thing John wanted was 30 days POW leave, so he could return to Freemantle to see if the Australian lass would still be there and hoping she would marry him. Rob said he wanted the same. He wanted to see his Molly again and be married as soon as possible. "But you know, John, I sometimes feel like a real heal. I mean, Molly has been faithful and probably had lots of opportunities what with all those Navy guys around her at Miami. Especially after the *Thornfish* was lost and none of us reported as surviving by the Japs. And here I've been doing extracurricular things." John listened intently as Rob continued, "I feel rotten. You know I think I could eventually forgive those Jap bastards that treated us so bad, but I don't know if I can forgive myself. Does any of this make sense?" John took a gulp of his coffee, "You know the Jap mess boy is learning to make some good coffee now. Isn't it weird, Rob, that here we are in a Jap sub with Jap sailors working side by side, and a few months ago we'd be trying to kill each other? Rob, here's the thing, our tendency when we are hurt is to want to get back at them. But as followers of Jesus we are called by God to forgive them. The best example is Jesus on the Cross, forgiving those who were killing him." Rob said, "But John weren't his words *Father forgive them*? Maybe we should pray that God will forgive them." John's eyes gleamed, "You are right. Maybe we can't forgive them now when our pain is still with us, but we can hope that someday we will be able to forgive them ourselves."

Rob looked away, "I think of my killing the guy on the trawler we boarded, and that Mitsubishi guard in the mine that day when he was about to kill you. And I think about our friend Chief O'Neil. They killed him at the copper mine. They put him outside in a barrel of ice water in the winter. And I can just hear him say to the Jap guard, 'give me a cake of soap'! He was more than a mentor to me. He was my friend. He took me under his wing when I came aboard, green as grass, and taught me the sub's systems, helped me in casualty drills, and most of all, how to treat my men." John sighed, "Yes he was a good man and a tough hombre. He loved the Navy. But now about forgiving yourself. I understand what you are saying. I guess there is some comfort that as Paul says we are all sinners. The psalmist wrote centuries ago telling God, '*Remember not the sins of my youth and my rebellious ways.*' Here's what I think, If God can forgive others, he can forgive you. And because you are forgiven, you can forgive yourself. Sometimes

I think our Catholic brothers have it right in confession. *"If we confess our sins, he is faithful and just and the blood of Jesus cleanses us and makes us whole."*

John got up and poured another cup of coffee. He thought of something else. "Rob, you know I am a Navigator. Dawson Trotman, our founder, always witnessed to a sailor each day. I haven't done that in a long time. But I want to witness to the Korean girl before we reach Pearl. You can interpret for me." John could see that Rob was hesitant. He finally said, "I don't know. Maybe I should…penance for me perhaps. Ok, if the opportunity comes about, I'll do it, provided you lead the discussion."

The next evening just about sunset the I-36 came to periscope depth. "Up Scope," Jerry commanded. When the periscope broke water, it was a glorious evening. "Stand by to surface." Then came the familiar words, Surface, Surface, Surface! Said in Japanese and English. High pressure air hit the ballast tanks and the submarine surfaced with a glorious red sunset over its stern, Red sky at night, sailors delight. The storm had passed. They were homeward bound, but they were still in rough waters.

There was a problem. The radio mast had broken and was lost in the storm. They could not transmit or receive. It would have to be fixed. The Japanese radioman came to the bridge and said he knew how to make a temporary antenna, but it was too dangerous to put men on deck at night. The seas were still rough, and repairs would have to wait for morning. Fresh air was finally being drawn into the boat. After being submerged for days, the foul odors were overwhelming. The smell of sulfuric acid, sweat, diesel fumes, urine and shit and the dangers of electrical shorts, made life miserable for everyone, especially the American sailors who were accustomed to air conditioning and good sanitary systems.

Rob had the mid-watch. They were on the surface with all running lights on. No more darkened ship. "All lights are bright lights, sir" the quartermaster reported. The red port light showing an arc from the bow to 120 degrees, the green starboard light covering the starboard side from the bow to 120 aft, and a white range light high above them. The stars were out with a quarter moon rising in the east. The I-36 was making a good fifteen knots even in the rough seas. The long voyage to Hawaii gave him time to contemplate about life. He was so grateful to be alive after all he had been through. He loved the sea, and it's ever changing moods. He loved the sounds of the diesel engines muffled by the turbulent waters and the ocean spray that reached for him as he stood watch on the bridge. He thought about staying in the Navy and making it a career. He had done a good job on the *Thornfish*, and he was sure that Captain Morrison, his former commanding officer, would give him a good recommendation for augmenting into the regular Navy. He liked the challenges of submarine service, its need for excellence from everyone in the crew. In a way it is remarkable he thought how a guy in his early twenties, could have so much responsibility. He had wanted combat, and he sure got a lot of it. They had sunk many enemy vessels, rescued sailors, fought the Japs almost hand to hand on the junk and rescued an Aussie coast watcher. It was a life of sometimes boredom interrupted by the sheer terror of combat. He had seen the other side of humanity in the brutal Japanese prison camps. Their imperialistic leaders, obsessed by Bushido and its honor code, had driven them to begin the war and almost destroyed their nation at the end.

He had experienced two different commanding officers. One who ruled by the book and clawed his way up in the Navy bureaucracy, the other a warrior who didn't give a damn about brown nosing his way up the chain of command. Rob felt that he would be able to make a real contribution to the country if he remained in the Navy. But he wondered about Molly… would she be willing to be a Navy wife? Separations are hard on families. If he got out of the Navy, he'd probably go back to Miami and get his master's in geology. He and Molly might have to live with his parents for a while until they could find a place to live. The thought of living with his mother bothered him a lot. After his master's degree, he would have to get a job, but he had had enough of mining. Maybe he'd go into oil. Dr. Shiedler was one of the most well know paleontologists in the country, and he could study under him. That might lead to a job in petroleum geology. He'd likely wind up someplace in the middle of Texas sitting on an oil well in the hot sun. He would like to talk about it with Molly. There was so much to get caught up with. He would call her when he reached Pearl Harbor.

The thing that bothered him the most was his indiscretions with Lily and Marianne. *Should he tell her? She might never know, but if he did tell her would she forgive him? What did the Psalmist say: Lord, remember not the sins of my youth? John said the most difficult part of forgiveness is to forgive yourself. Maybe it would be better not saying anything. He didn't want to hurt Molly. The thoughts about his life with Molly made the watch go quickly.*

CHAPTER 79

Molly Goes to Hawaii

Molly was excited as she neared the Dayton Airport. Dr. Walker drove her to the small terminal to catch her early morning flight to Chicago. Dressed in a blue two-piece suit, with a white blouse, pearl necklace and her hair done up in a bun in the back, she thought she looked very professional. Dr. Walker told her he was so pleased that she and Rob were going to be married, and he hoped that they would come to live in Oxford someday. He waited while she bought her ticket. She paid cash for her fare to San Francisco and checked her one piece of luggage all the way through. Dr. Walker went with her to the gate by the tarmac guarded only by a waist-high chain-link fence. The cold November air was raw and biting. As the attendant opened the little gate in the fence, Dr. Walker gave her a big hug and kissed her cheek. "Safe trip dear. Tell Rob we love him and are very proud of him. Here's a note for Rob; it's a present for both of you, and some money for you to take along for some travel expenses." He pressed the thick letter and four twenty-dollar bills in her hand. Molly thanked him and gave him a big hug. After she boarded the silver TWA plane, he waved goodbye as the two-engine Douglas DC-3 aircraft taxied to the runway.

As he climbed back in his black two-door Ford, Dr. Walker wished his wife shared his feelings about Rob marrying Molly. She had grown to like Molly very much especially for the contagious faith and confidence she radiated while there was no news about Rob. But she had harbored some hope for another girl for her son, a beautiful girl he had only met once in Washington when she stayed at Senator Taft's home overnight. He sat in the car with the engine running and the heater on full blast as he watched the Douglas Commercial, DC-3, climb in the November air and turn west. Thousands of the two-engines planes were built during the war, and it became the workhorse of the military. They flew tons of supplies to the Chinese Army over the Burmese mountains called the hump. Hundreds of the airplanes dropped the Army airborne troops over France on D-Day.

Molly's plane seated 21 comfortably. Mrs. Walker had prepared a nice box lunch for her, and Molly took it on board in her small bag that fit under her seat very nicely. Once airborne, a stewardess dressed in a modest brown uniform with cute fore and aft hat, came down the aisle passing out chewing gum to passengers to help their ears adjust to the change of air pressure when they reached their cruising altitude of 6000 feet. Molly thought what a wonderful and exciting job that would be, but airline stewardesses had to be registered nurses to qualify for the position. Passengers were well dressed, coats and ties for the men and dresses for the women. Molly ate her ham sandwich and carrot sticks before the plane swept over the south shore of Lake Michigan and landed at Chicago's Midway Airport. She had to change planes in Chicago and boarded a four motor DC-4. The DC-4 was three times larger than the DC-3, and with four 1400 hp. Pratt and Whitney engines it could cruise high over the Rocky Mountains. Molly, sat in a window seat, and watched the snowcapped Rocky Mountains below, as the plane ascended. Although the plane could fly nonstop from Chicago to San Francisco, it landed in Salt Lake City taking on more passengers and fuel before departing for the final domestic leg to the Golden Gate.

As they approached San Francisco, the pilot told them that they would be circling the field waiting for landing instructions as there were several flights ahead of them. The landing pattern took them over San Francisco Bay, Alcatraz prison, the Golden Gate Bridge, and the port terminals busy bringing troop ships disgorging soldiers and Marines from China, Japan, Okinawa, even Australia. Men and some women in uniform were rushing to get home for Thanksgiving, or to their mustering out base near their hometowns.

After landing and securing her bag from the baggage area, Molly went to the military police counter nearby and asked for directions to Alameda Naval Air Station. There was a bus outside marked NAS Alameda, and she boarded it with the help of an eager sailor. She was the last one on the busload of sailors, and the only woman. To many whistles and cheers, she was given a seat in the front by a chief petty officer. As the bus passed through the city she was fascinated with its hills, colorful crowded homes stacked side by side, cable cars and in the distance the famous Golden Gate Bridge lit up with hundreds of bright lights glowing in the fog settling in over the water. Molly thought this would be a wonderful place to explore for their honeymoon.

The guards at the main gate to Alameda NAS came on board the bus checking everyone's ID. They asked Molly for her driver's license and she blushed, "I don't have one." Molly showed her press credentials, Military Editor of *The Oxford Press* the title Mrs. Cullen insisted on her having, and the bus driver let her off at the BOQ. It was late when she checked in at the front desk. There were lots of admiring looks by officers in the lobby. She took a room on the second floor, locked the door and fell exhausted on the bed. It had been a long day. The room was very spartan, but it had a little radio and alarm clock. She set the clock to ring at 6 a.m. and the radio to the local San Francisco station. The disc jockey was playing. "I'll be seeing you in all the old familiar places that this heart of mine embraces...." And she fell asleep dreaming of Rob.

The next morning after showering and breakfast at the canteen, she called the base protocol office and, after identifying herself as a newspaper correspondent, she learned that there was a military hop going to Hickam in Honolulu that afternoon. She might get a seat if there was space available. Then she asked when the Japanese submarine was scheduled to arrive in Hawaii. They would check. An hour later she received a phone call saying that it appeared that the submarine would probably arrive in two days. She would see Rob for the first time in nearly three years! She said, "Hallelujah."

Molly went to the base operations office and enquired about the plane to Hawaii. She learned she had just missed a flight, but there was a plane of VIP's leaving in a few hours for Pearl. She was told she could stand by and if space were available, she'd get to board. She grabbed her bag and sat in the waiting room praying. She really needed a seat on that plane. Hours passed. Suddenly there was a commotion as a group of senior Navy and Army officers arrived in the room and went in the VIP lounge. Her heart sank. There were so many of them. She waited a few more minutes and then decided that she would check on her space available seat. A pert Navy lieutenant WAVE on duty behind the desk greeted Molly, "I understand you're a member of the press waiting for a flight to Hickam. Right? Well, this is your lucky day. We have just one seat left and it's yours, unless some officer is late and needs the space. If you get on board, you're safe." Her heart rate increased as she watched the entourage go through the gate one by one. As the last one boarded, a Navy petty officer motioned for her to come to the gate. "Go ahead miss, you're the last one. It'll be a long flight, 2400 miles."

The plane was a four motor Douglas DC-4 converted for use during the war and designated the C-54 Skymaster. The C-54 aircraft was used by President Roosevelt, and General MacArthur during the war, and took a delegation to the Casablanca, Morocco, Conference in January 1943. The four motors had more powerful engines, the R2000 11, and carried 44 passengers. Molly was number 44. She found her seat near the rear of the passenger compartment. A Navy captain was occupying the aisle seat and got up to allow her to take the window seat. She sat down and after putting her carry-on bag under her seat, opened a small turkey sandwich that she had purchased before leaving. She apologized to the captain by saying "I'm famished. Hope you don't mind me eating now." He laughed, "No, help yourself, I don't mind. It will be a while before the steward will come by with some C-Rations, or worse." He glanced at her for a longer time than he should. She was a very pretty young woman. He didn't mind a bit for her companionship on the long flight to Hawaii.

"Are you from the fourth estate?" He asked. She was uncertain what he meant, estate? She said, "I'm from Ohio." The captain smiled. Molly continued, "I am a reporter for *The Oxford Press*. You probably have never heard of it. We are a small-town newspaper with a lot to say." The engines roared, and the plane started down the runway; Molly tightened her seat belt and said a quick prayer. She thought of her first plane ride in the little yellow Piper Cub with Woody at the controls. He loved flying, and she suddenly felt the pain of his loss once again. The officer sensed her anxiety and said, "Are you OK?" She thought, *he must have noticed my fingers holding tight to the armrests.* "Yes, I was thinking about my first ride in a plane, a Piper Cub, and the pilot, my friend, ran out of gas. He became a naval aviator, a Marine. The captain said, "Oh, where is he stationed now?"

"In heaven now. He died in April, sinking a Jap battleship."

"I'm sorry. He may have been in on the attack of the huge battleship Yamato."

"Yes, that was the one. His was one of four planes that were lost that day." The captain said, "He must have been a very courageous young man." Molly said, "I'm sure he was, he loved flying and most of all being a Marine. We worked together in our college newspaper."

As the plane rose and turned west, she looked below and saw the Golden Gate Bridge, and a submarine was coming into the Bay. She said, "I see a submarine coming under the Golden Gate!" The captain said, "Yes, many are coming home, to be put in mothballs at Mare Island."

When the Skymaster leveled off, the plane's captain came on the intercom and welcomed the passengers and gave a little spiel about the comforts of the plane and that they would be flying at 10000 feet en route to Honolulu. It would be a long flight, 2400 miles at 200 mph and, would take 12 hours. Molly took a notepad out from her bag and started to write some thoughts of the sight she had just witnessed out the window. She wrote, "The famous Golden Gate Bridge's arches were welcoming the returning heroes, Marines, soldiers and sailors, coming home at last in ships of all types, streaming into San Francisco Bay."

The Navy captain took up the conversation again, "Where is Oxford, in Ohio?"

"Well, it's in Southwest Ohio, near Dayton, Ohio, the birthplace of aviation. Oxford is the home of Miami University, where I graduated."

"I know someone from Miami. Maybe you may have met him. He is a submariner, a reservist named Robert Walker."

"My god, she gasped, "Do you know Rob?"

"Sure do. I am on the staff of the commander of submarines. In fact, I was with Lieutenant Walker in Japan a few months ago. Right after the surrender. I am going to meet his submarine when it arrives at the Pearl Harbor submarine base. What's wrong?" He thought she might pass out. "Did I say something wrong?"

"No, sir, I am just speechless. Rob is my fiancé. We are going to be married soon. I haven't seen him for almost three years. I can't believe that of all the people in this world, in this Navy …that I would be sitting next to an officer who knows Rob."

"You must be Molly. I am Ben Miller." He extended his hand, and she clasped it tightly.

"I know you sir; Rob has written about you in his letters. He thinks so highly of you."

"I think highly of him also. Your Rob is a real hero. Let me tell you about him."

"Tell me first, how is he? How does he look? Is he sick? I'm worried about him. He had a horrible experience as a POW."

"Yes, he did. I think he came through it because of his strong will to live. And I believe his faith sustained him."

Molly listened intently as he told her about Rob's health, and how he had persuaded him to join the crew of a Japanese I class submarine and bring it to Pearl Harbor for Navy evaluation. She was fascinated with the story. Then the captain told her about the loss of the *Thornfish* and Rob's heroic work in captivity. After he finished, she told him: "Sir, what you have told me is something I believe the nation should know. These men were all heroes and deserved to be recognized. Wouldn't this make a good newspaper story or even a book?" Ben didn't answer her. He smiled, "Rob has been awarded the Silver Star for valor, and already has two Bronze Stars for combat and a Letter of Commendation, plus he will certainly get two Purple Heart awards."

Molly said, "WOW! I hope I can be there when he gets the awards. I want to write up these stories for our paper. I hope it will be permissible to write all these stories. But I need to know about the Purple Hearts. How is he, what happened?" Ben calmed her fears about Rob's wounds but then told her, "There is one thing the Navy is doing that disturbs me. They don't want any bad publicity about the Japanese treatment of our POWs. Some commands are requiring the returning POW veterans of Japan to sign a letter pledging not to reveal stories of their ill-treatment. I think most of them sign… they want to get back to life in the States and forget the bad stuff. So, anything that pertains to the treatment of Rob and his crew is strictly off the record for now. Understand?"

Molly said, "Yes, but honestly, I mean, I really don't understand; I think it is a terrible decision. These veterans deserve to have their stories told. The public has a right to know about these atrocities."

Ben added, "Perhaps MacArthur wants to get the Japanese industries up and running. Truman wants to conclude a peace treaty before too long. Maybe before he leaves office if he wins reelection."

"But sir, what about these perpetrators of the atrocities. Can't they be punished?"

"Well there will be war crime trials like the International Military Tribunals now beginning in Nuremberg, Germany."

Ben could tell that Molly was not satisfied. She was tired, however, and soon dozed off just before the Navy mess man came by with a delicious meal. Ben looked at the beautiful young woman now resting her head on his shoulder and wondered how Rob finally made a very tough decision on which one to marry…Lily or Molly; both were gorgeous, vivacious and intriguing. What a choice! As he ate his meal he thought, Rob made the right choice. He would not say anything about Lily to Molly.

· · · · ·

Rob and John were having breakfast in the wardroom. Ji Su, the Korean girl, was serving them coffee. Rob was about to leave when Jerry came in and sat down. Ji Su poured him a cup of hot coffee. "We've got the radio operating now. The base says that they are assigning us to starboard side pier one. We may expect some senior officers to meet us." Looking at the Korean girl, "we'll probably have some MPs come and get her. They have to figure out what to do with her." Jerry saw Rob's countenance was troubled.

"Anything wrong Rob?"

Rob said, "Well sir, yes, I hate to see her put in confinement. She's been through a lot of terrible stuff in her short life. She's a nice girl. I hope some accommodation can be made for her. Maybe we could find someone to take her in temporarily. I know a lady that could help. She is a Christian, and I could ask her."

"Who might that be?"

"Well it's the mother of Lily Edmonds…you remember Lily from the last time we were at Pearl on R and R."

"Yeah, who could ever forget her? She is one gorgeous gal. I remember that she was your date the night at the O club when she slapped Custer after he insulted her."

Rob blushed, "Yes, that was a bad one. Her mom has a place up in the hills, and she would have plenty of room for her, if she and the authorities would agree to it."

"Well it's worth a try. The problem will be with the base police. For some reason they don't like submarine sailors very much. Too rowdy, I guess. Navy headquarters won't like to have any publicity for obvious reasons, and they don't want others to get the idea of coming to the U.S. illegally."

Jerry went to the bridge, and John brought Ji Su in and had her sit at the wardroom table. She was very hesitant.

John said, "We are going to try to help you after we arrive in Hawaii." John paused while Rob translated.

"What is your full name?" She looked away and finally said, Ji Su Kim.

"Where are you from? What city in Korea?" Rob waited as she tried to answer the question. As best they could determine, she was from Pusan in the lower part of Korea. The two of them got as much information as possible, and John made notes for the record. He glanced at Rob and said to her, "Ji Su, have you ever heard of Jesus?"

Her eyes lit up when she heard the name of Jesus. "Hai, she said in Japanese, "Hai!" Rob translated, "Yes, Yes." She had come from a Christian home in Korea! Both parents had been murdered by Japanese soldiers when she was taken captive. John said, "We," and he pointed to Rob, "We are Christians."

"How I be one?"

Rob translated her words. John was as startled as Rob. "Well, I want you to know that we are all sinners, saved by the grace of God through Jesus." He waited for Rob to translate. "Ji Su, I am going to say a simple prayer, will you pray it with me?" She nodded. "Lord Jesus," and her eyes filled with tears. Rob was translating every word, "I know that I have sinned; please take away my sins and cleanse me and make me new. I ask this in your name. Amen." They stood in the wardroom, and John hugged her. She was crying. Rob was having a hard time not breaking down too.

Ji Su would need some help along her new way. Maybe Valerie Edmonds could help.

CHAPTER 80

The Arrival

Rob had a few minutes to pack his things in a B-4 bag before leaving the 'Pig Boat' next day. He was glad to leave it to Navy research teams to go over the entire submarine and evaluate the enemy vessel. It didn't take long, he had very little to pack. He would have a lot of back pay coming, if they could ever reconstruct his pay record. He learned the grim reality that the Navy would not give them submarine hazardous duty extra pay while as a POW, and even on this voyage which was hazardous; the Navy considered them not eligible for hazardous duty pay because they were not aboard an American submarine.

Rob knew that the Japanese companies that used slave labor, Mitsubishi, Kawasaki, and others should have paid all the POWs but that would never happen. The poor men who had slaved building the Jap Burma Railroad, got $2.50 a day from the American government for every day they were prisoners and nothing from the Japanese government after the war. Not even an apology. A real insult.

After dinner that evening, Jerry had a prearrival conference of the officers including the I-36 former commanding officer. Rob, the navigator, discussed the navigation details, reviewed charts of the harbor, tide and current at the time of entry, and honors to be given if they passed any warships on the way in. The fuel for the diesel engines was nearly gone. If they ran out and had to shut down the engines, they would shift to battery power for the remainder of the voyage. Jerry decided to give the honor of making the landing to Rob. He would take the conn at the entrance buoy and bring the sub alongside the pier. He wanted the first line over to the dock done at exactly 1000, their estimated time of arrival.

"What are we going to do with the Korean girl, sir?" John asked. Jerry said, "Good question. Rob has an idea that has merit." Rob spoke, "Well, we have to tell the Navy of her status, and I have a suggestion. I have a good friend, Lily's mother, who is fluent in Japanese and might be willing to take her into her home for a while. Let's send a message tonight to the squadron, attention Captain Miller, and ask him if he could arrange to have Mrs. Valerie Edmonds come to the arrival to act as a translator for our Japanese crewmen. She works in Navy Intelligence on the base. The prisoners will be handed over to the Marines upon arrival I suppose, and she might be persuaded to help with the transition as they depart the 'Pig Boat.' When we arrive, I'll talk with Ben Miller about the Korean situation and let him take it from there."

Jerry said, "Sounds like a plan. One thing though, I think it would be best for all of us not to say anything in public about our stowaway. No one would believe it anyway. So, mum's the word. The Navy will have to figure out a way to take care of her. If Mrs. Edmonds can be at the pier when we arrive, you can ask her if she'd be willing to take her in for a while." Rob looked around at the men at the table and said, "Aye, sir."

* * * * *

It was past midnight when the Skymaster pilot informed the passengers to fasten their seat belts in preparation for landing at Hickam Army Airfield. Molly looked out the window as the plane passed Diamond Head, and off to the right the lights of Honolulu were burning bright. It then flew past the base and made a turn to head into the wind, flying over Barbers Point, and Ewa Beach Navy housing, and with full flaps and wheels down made a gentle landing on the east-west runway. As they deplaned, a gray Navy bus pulled up at the side of the C-54 and the tired passengers were taken to the base BOQ. With Captain Miller's influence, she was given a separate VIP room at the Navy Bachelor Officers' Quarters on the submarine base. When she entered her VIP suite, she thought, this is grand, this is living. She opened the doors to the balcony and went outside looking at the view of the harbor, the lights of the city and the cars filling the highway even at this late hour. A gentle breeze filtered into the room and the fragrance of Bougainvillea gave her a warm welcome to beautiful Hawaii. *This sure beats Oxford, Ohio, in November,* she mused. And Rob is coming in the morning. She lay down to sleep thinking of what tomorrow held for them. They had not seen each other for over three years. *Will he still love me? Will he think I'm attractive? Will he still want to marry me?* These thoughts tumbled through her mind for hours, before she finally slept.

In her dreams Rob had found another love.

* * * * *

As Molly slept, the 'Pig Boat' fifty miles off the northwest tip of Oahu, was preparing to enter the Navy base at Pearl Harbor. Jerry had slowed the submarine's speed to about six knots to not get ahead of their scheduled ETA of 1000 on Thanksgiving eve. He wanted to make sure the boat was as clean as possible just in case the admiral might come aboard. He ordered a field day. Every inch of the former Japanese submarine was being scrubbed and any debris was thrown overboard. The small laundry worked feverishly cleaning uniforms, sheets and table clothes. Sanitary tanks were blown out to sea. The cleaning continued into the night. Ji Su helped clean the wardroom and the small officers' galley next to it. The next morning Jerry had a huge American flag 'borrowed' from the submarine tender displayed from the flag hoist aft of the bridge.

Dawn crept over the eastern horizon and the boat's lookouts shouted, 'Land Ho!' The steep mountains, covered in green foliage, came in view with the binoculars. In a few hours the I-36 rounded the west shore and hugged the coast rounding the Waianae area and then on to the entrance buoy to the famous harbor. Jerry called the crew, Americans and Japanese, to fall in ranks topside in dress white uniforms. The I-36 slowed to ahead one-third as they passed where the anti-submarine nets had once guarded the entrance against Japanese submarines. In a few minutes the rusting hulk of the USS *Arizona* came into view. The order was given for all hands, American and Japanese, to render a salute in respect for the 1238 men still entombed in the ship as it sank on December 7, 1941, nearly four years ago.

Jerry stood by Rob as he smartly conned the submarine around Merry Point, past the destroyer piers and toward the submarine piers that lay ahead. Jerry trained his binoculars on the people on the pier. There was no band, or hula girls or crowds as there had been just a few months ago on VJ Day celebrating the end of the war, for returning ships. But there was a group of high-ranking Navy officers awaiting its arrival and what appeared to be a band of photographers and reporters huddled at the end of the pier, held back by the guards. Molly was among them, frustrated that the Navy was holding the press back. *The Honolulu Star* reporter yelled, "We should be allowed on the pier right now!" A reporter from *Stars and Stripes* was there also. Molly knew about the killing of one of its reporters, the beloved, Ernie Pyle, who was killed during the invasion of Okinawa in April. Molly noticed a very well dressed Asian looking woman, standing behind the noisy reporters. She seemed nervous and a little anxious. Molly decided to talk to her. "Hi, I'm Molly Gaynor." Mrs. Edmonds was stunned. How can this happen? This is the girl Lily told me about. She is Rob's girlfriend and even prettier than I imagined. "Is something wrong? May I help you?" Valerie Edmonds recovered enough to say, "No I'm fine. I'm waiting to see one of the officers on the Japanese I boat." She asked, "So am I, who are you looking for?" Valerie said, "LTJG Walker. I am a translator for the Navy. Molly said excitedly "Oh, what a coincidence! He and I are engaged, and I am here to do a story for my paper, *The Oxford Ohio Press*, about LTJG Walker, our hometown hero. He has been a prisoner of the Japanese for over a year and a half. His entire crew was captured." Valerie said, "I know. They were given up for dead. The Japanese never revealed that they were prisoners of war." Molly's curiosity was aroused. *How would she know?* She started by asking her interest in the Japanese sub. Valerie said, "Well I was just asked by the Navy to come to help with the translation of the Japanese sailors on board. They are still technically our prisoners and will be confined for a while I suspect." The two of them chatted along while awaiting the submarine.

Jerry put his binoculars down after checking to make sure line handlers were awaiting them on the pier. "Rob we've got company, it looks like the admiral is waiting for us and some of his staff, and we may have some reporters on hand for our arrival. There are some Marines there too. I guess they are there to take care of our Jap crewmen." Rob replied, "Well that's ok I guess, we are just delivering this boat, that's all. And we did it well."

Rob ordered, "left standard rudder, steady as you go," as he aimed the bow for pier 2 to moor with the sub's starboard side alongside the pier. About fifty yards out, he ordered, "all stop." With the engines stopped, and with just enough headway, and help from the wind on his port side, Rob ordered the helm right ten degrees. As soon as the bow started swinging, he ordered, "Rudder amidships, all back one-third," and the bowline was thrown over to the dock. "All stop!" he shouted, as the wind took the huge submarine's stern in and the stern lines were cast over to the dock. Rob had made a perfect two bell landing. "Good job Rob," said Jerry. "I couldn't have done better." It was exactly 1000.

Rob was busy attending to the details of mooring and setting up a deck watch in anticipation of the arrival of the Commander of Submarines to come aboard for a look at the I boat. Jerry rushed down the ladder to the main deck to greet the admiral as soon as the gangway was put over to the sub.

The three-star Vice Admiral Lockwood was honored with side boys in dress whites: three Navy sailors, and three Japanese. Lieutenant Jerald Abrams, USNR, Officer in Charge of I-36, greeted him with a sharp salute and offered him a tour of one of Hirohito's few surviving submarines. Then the word was announced, "Captain, United States Navy arriving," and Captain Ben Miller came aboard with honors. Rob met him on the main deck and said, "Welcome aboard Sir, we made it." Ben smiled, "I knew you would Rob, if anyone could do it you men could. I have some good news for you lieutenant...but before he could finish his sentence, he was interrupted by a young Marine second lieutenant and his shore patrol asking permission to come aboard to take the Japanese crew ashore. Rob looked at Captain Miller, "Beg your pardon sir, we have a problem, excuse me for a minute." He went over to the Marine, and said, "You'll have to wait on the pier for a bit, we have a lot going on right now. Just be patient. You can come aboard in a few minutes. OK?" The Marine could only say, "yes." He then went back to Captain Miller, "You see, unbeknownst to us we had a stowaway on board. We discovered her several days after we left Tokyo and before the typhoon." Ben said, "Her, did you say her?" "Yes sir, she is a Korean girl who was abducted by the Japs and held for over two years as a sex slave for their submariners when they returned to port. She was terribly abused. She wants to go to America. I hope we could avoid getting her put in confinement. I know someone locally, Mrs. Valerie Edmonds, who speaks fluent Japanese, and may be able to help her while her case is being resolved. We sent a message last night to the squadron to ask her to come to act as a translator for the Japanese crew, do you recall?" Ben looked over to the pier and said, "Yes, I was told there was a Korean aboard, but I didn't catch that it was a girl. I just assumed it was routine. My aide sent for Mrs. Edmonds." Ben seemed perplexed. "Rob, I don't think we want this in the newspapers, at least not just yet. And I'd like to have her out of the admiral's way below decks. Can you get her up here pronto?" Rob replied, "Yes sir, right away." Rob turned and saw Grabowski. He ordered, "Grabowski, go get Ji Su and bring her to the gangway right away!"

Ben said, "Now, Rob go and find your sweetheart! "He pointed to the beautiful blond now standing in among a group of reporters and photographers from *The Honolulu Star.* "It can't be!" Rob exclaimed! "It's Molly!" Without waiting to salute the colors Rob rushed down the gangway and took Molly in his arms and kissed her. He kissed her again and again and held her in his arms for a long time and whispered, "Molly I love you, I can't believe you're here. How did you manage?" He held her arms looking at her face, "You're more beautiful than ever! WOW!" Flashbulbs went off as the *Star's* photographers were getting terrific pictures of the young Navy officer greeting his girlfriend. They would make the front page of the next morning edition of *The Honolulu Star-Bulletin.* As he held her close, over her shoulder, Rob saw Valerie Edmonds. He shouted, "Valerie… Mrs. Edmonds, wait!" He grabbed Molly's hand and ran toward her. "Mrs. Edmonds, please come here, it's good to see you, and I want you to meet Molly." As the three of them stood at the foot of the gangway, Rob started to introduce Mrs. Edmonds to Molly. Valerie couldn't resist giving Rob a hug; she said, "We've already met, while waiting for your submarine to come in. Welcome home Robert, you look good. You are blessed to have such a fine girl. She has waited a long time for you. I'm here to help with translation for the Japanese crew members. I have a note for you from a friend," and she handed him a small unmarked envelope which he stuffed in his pocket. Rob said, "Thank you…." and he was interrupted by Captain Miller who bounded down the gangway. He greeted Molly warmly. Turning to Rob he said, "She was my companion on the long flight to Hawaii." Then he spoke to Mrs. Edmonds, "You must be Mrs. Edmonds. Rob has told me about you. I'm Ben Miller, and I wonder if I could have a word with you for a few minutes privately?" Valerie was surprised having only just met him, but she said, "Why, yes, I suppose so." Ben took her aside and explained as much as he knew about the situation with the Korean girl. "Could we persuade you to take her in to your home for a little while as we try to figure out what we can do with the girl? She has been terribly abused …a throw away for the Japanese military, like thousands of Korean and Chinese girls we are learning about."

Ben led Mrs. Edmonds on board the sub and around the superstructure to gain some privacy, away from the Marine guards. Petty Officer Grabowski was there holding the frightened girl's hand. Valerie and Ben looked at her standing there as Ji Su was shaking about to cry. Grabowski came to attention and smiled sheepishly, "Sir, this is the Korean girl who hitched a ride with us from Japan." Ji Su was dressed in dungarees that were too large for her small frame, and a blue chambray shirt with sleeves that were too long. Her hair was bundled up under a Navy white hat. Valerie looked with compassion at her pretty face and spoke to her in Japanese for some time. A slight smile broke through Ji Su's tears and soon beamed across her face. Ben had a lump in his throat; whatever she said in Japanese sure spoke to the girl's heart. She has some hope.

Captain Miller told the Marine lieutenant that he would take temporary responsibility for one of the crew, a Korean, and together he and Rob escorted her off to Mrs. Edmonds car, the red Chevy convertible. She looked like a small sailor to the reporters and went unnoticed while the Marines came aboard to take charge of their prisoners.

Jerry was meeting with the admiral down below, and Ben joined them in the tiny wardroom. He handed Ben the patrol report including the mentioning of the stowaway. He read aloud the abstract of the many pages of the report that Jerry had prepared. The admiral listened intently to the summation of the observations of the American officers regarding the performance of the I boat. The boat was difficult to maneuver, controls were complicated, living conditions and sanitation were extremely poor. Its radar and electronics were terrible. And the I class did not have escape hatches. In summary, they were lousy submarines. The I-36 could not compare with U.S. Fleet submarines. It had a German Snorkel, but the men were afraid to use it in transit due to the possibility of flooding the submarine.

When told of the stowaway, the admiral was not overly concerned as he was aware of the imprisonment of Korean girls by the Japanese for use as sex slaves.

Ben Miller was very pleased with the summary Jerry had presented. He took it with him as he prepared to depart. The entire crew assembled on the main deck, and the admiral congratulated the crew for their work bringing it safely to Hawaii in extreme seas and difficult conditions. He apologized that, due to regulations, there would be no submarine extra hazardous duty pay allowed because they were not aboard an American submarine. Jerry looked at the others but didn't say anything. Ben determined that he would recommend the American officers and crew for the Navy Commendation Medal, and Jerry for the Bronze Star.

CHAPTER 81

The Lunch

Before departing the sub, Ben invited the officers, and Molly to a noon luncheon at the admiral's mess at the sub base. The elegant white frame building set on the hill overlooking the submarine piers looked like a southern plantation. Prior to the meal the group had drinks at the bar adjacent to the dining room. A Filipino steward took orders for beverages, and Molly chose iced tea with lemon, unsweetened. Rob ordered a gin gimlet with lime. Ben ordered last, a Johnny Walker Black Label Scotch on the rocks. Ben invited them to sit out on the veranda overlooking the entire base. Below them were so many submarines that they had to be nested and anchored in the harbor. Most were being readied to go to San Francisco or Bremerton Washington for mothballing. Ben waved his glass at them and spoke to Molly, "Our subs were the main reason for Japan's capitulation. I believe that in time they would have had to surrender as their supplies were cut off. We might not have had to use the atomic bombs." Rob interrupted, "But sir, with all due respect, if they had any reason to believe that we were going to invade the home islands, I and most of us gathered here would be dead. They had orders to kill all POWs if their homeland was invaded. No, I believe that the bomb was necessary and saved not only American lives but thousands of Japanese." And Jerry added, "I agree, the camp commander told us that we'd be executed if they were invaded. The casualties would have been enormous on both sides." Ben didn't say a word, except to say, "Let's eat."

As they sat down at the large round table Ben looked at John and said, "I'm going to ask LT Young to say the blessing." John was caught off guard, cleared his throat and said, "Lord, we are grateful to be alive and able to be together this beautiful day. Bless our great nation, and the loved ones of those who did not make it home. Thanks for the food we are about to enjoy. And it is in Jesus name we pray. Amen." Ben had Molly sit next to him, then Rob. To his left Jerry and John and the other officers.

The food was delicious. The California wine was excellent. Molly enjoyed her first Mahi Mahi served with wild rice, and steamed broccoli. Rob ordered a New York strip steak, and baked potato. The chatter at lunch was more relaxed, until Captain Miller got everyone's attention by saying, "let's raise our glasses to the officers and men of the

U.S. Navy Submarine Force, our nation's first in combat and the last to leave, and to the men who gave their lives in the boats that are still on station on some unknown location in the Western Pacific." Glasses clinked in unison. "Now I want to urge some caution. What we have said here before lunch and now is off the record as far as the press is concerned. Right Molly?" Molly smiled sheepishly, "Yes, sir."

Ben smiled and looked at Jerry, "First of all, I want to know from Jerry Abrams, how you got a stowaway on board your submarine." Molly was surprised. Jerry replied matter of factly, "Well sir, we didn't let her come aboard." Laughter echoed around the table. "The Korean girl was well acquainted with the I class submarines as she was required to service the crew on many of them. She sneaked aboard the I-36, during the evening hours before we departed while we were busy loading stores. She went immediately to a small storage locker she knew about in the crew's sleeping quarters. She had learned that we were going to Hawaii, and she wanted to escape the Japanese forever. When we discovered her, we were over two days out from Japan, and she was famished. We put out a stern order that no one was to touch her en route to Hawaii. And no one did. We made her a mess cook and she did a good job. That's about it sir." Ben said, "OK Jerry, you've dumped the disposition of her case on me, I guess. But that's OK. I'm glad Mrs. Edmonds is going to look after her for now." Molly was stunned. Rob noticed her expression of disbelief. She was unaware of what had happened that morning. Molly recovered by thinking it was because she was so caught up in seeing Rob. A good reporter would have noticed that something was up.

Ben called the Filipino steward to the table and ordered dessert, Baked Alaska, for everyone. Then he continued talking, "New subject. Before lunch I was given a message that a Japanese POW being held in California, Jimmu Kamatsu, son of Admiral Kamatsu, whom Rob and I interviewed a few months ago in Yokosuka, is now at a holding compound near Hickam waiting for transportation to Japan. I think Rob might want to see him." Rob was delighted. He replied, "Yes sir." Looking at Molly, he said, "We rescued him from a Japanese I boat that the *Thornfish* torpedoed off Honshu. When we were teenagers, we were schoolmates at the American School in Tokyo. His father, at that time, was commodore of a Japanese submarine squadron, and when I was in school, he once arranged for his son and me to tour an I boat. During the war he rose to be a vice admiral and became the commander of all Japanese submarines. I sure would like to see him, sir, if it can be arranged."

Ben replied, "OK, I'll take care of it." Molly piped up, "Sir, would it be permissible for me to accompany Rob? It would make a good story." Ben replied, "I'm not sure Molly. It would have to be cleared with our Public Affairs Office. I'll see."

He continued, "When we talked with Admiral Kamastsu, he was concerned about his son because in the Jap culture becoming a prisoner is a dishonor to the family and the nation. Admiral Kamatsu told us of a story of the surrender of a Japanese officer during the attack on Pearl Harbor, and I checked this out and it is true. America's first Japanese prisoner of war was a submariner by the name of Salamaki, the officer-in-charge of one of their five midget submarines, that were launched from I boats prior to the attack. Due to some mishap, his small sub got stuck on a reef off Bellows Air Base. He tried to scuttle it but failed, and he was captured. When he surrendered to the Marines, he asked them to kill him. He felt disgraced and did not want the Navy to inform the Red Cross that he was a prisoner of war. As an officer in the Imperial Japanese Navy, he was well treated by us as a POW. Somehow, a few months later, word of his capture reached the Navy in Japan. Kamatsu told us that Admiral Yamamoto was furious and called his staff submarine officer into his office and got red in the face and stomped his feet because of the information the Americans might gain, but also because the code of honor calls it a disgrace to be captured." Rob interjected, "Yes that was my experience with LT Kamatsu, when we rescued him. He wanted to die."

Ben said, "But in my talks with the old admiral, he seemed to be discouraged with their code of honor." Rob turned to Molly and added, "At one time he told me that we Americans treated our prisoners honoring the Geneva Convention, but Japan dishonored humanity in the way they mistreated all of their prisoners."

Then Ben made a profound comment: "We learned some significant things from our interviews with the Japanese admiral. The failure of Japanese submarines to do any damage at Pearl Harbor changed the view of many of their senior Navy staff about the use of their submarines during the war. Many felt they were only good for resupply and special operations during their campaigns. But most importantly, we learned from Admiral Kamatsu that the Japanese General Staff concluded a study of the war in September 1943, *before* we had the massive B-29 raids on Japan's mainland, that Japan could not win the war and they should seek a negotiated peace settlement. The reason was that the American submarine offensive was decimating their ability to import raw materials essential for the war. They could not keep up with America's industrial might."

Lunch was over and before leaving Ben said, "Remember our conversation was off the record, we'll see what changes are made in Japan by MacArthur. I think his address at the surrender on the USS *Missouri* was magnanimous, almost as much as President Lincoln's Gettysburg Address during the Civil War."

· · · · ·

Shortly after lunch, Rob was provided with a Jeep and a Marine driver from the squadron and he and Molly set off to the barracks where Jimmu was housed. The base Public Affairs Officer agreed it would be permissible for a reporter to go along as it might make a good story about how well we treated our prisoners. The only condition was that they are given an advance copy of any article she would write, but they did not threaten her with censorship.

A half an hour later, Molly and Rob arrived at the barracks housing the prisoners. The two-story frame building had been an Army barracks for those guarding the air base. Inside the high fence was a basketball court, and weight lifting equipment. Rob showed the Marine guard a letter on the vice admiral's stationery granting Rob and the reporter contact with one of the prisoners, a Japanese officer by the name of Jimmu Kamatsu. "Do you know where we might find him?" Rob asked. "Yes sir, I think he is playing basketball over there." The guard went over to the court and stopped the game calling out Kamatsu's name. He promptly came over to the guard and bowed. He then noticed two people waiting to see him and wondered what was going on. Rob recognized him instantly. "Jimmu, it's me, LT Walker!"

As the other players looked on in amazement, the two men faced each other, and shook hands. Rob said in Japanese, "It's over. Thank God it's over Jimmu! I want you to meet my fiancé, Molly." They went over to where Molly was standing and Jimmu bowed, and said "Pleased to meet you, Miss." The guard watching all this shook his head thinking how soon things can change. Rob said, "Let's find a place where we can talk." The guard led them to a recreation room in the barracks where they found some lounge chairs, and they sat down to reminisce. Rob told him of his encounters with his father while he was a prisoner, and the interview he had after the surrender. He recounted his meeting with his mother at their home overlooking the naval base and her concern for her son and how much she wanted him to come back home. Jimmu said he had dreaded the time he would have to face his father. He knew that his father strongly believed in the warrior's code that Japan should have no prisoners. But then several weeks ago, he had received a letter from him. He took a folded piece of paper out of his pocket and said, "Please read." Rob opened the envelope from his father written in beautiful Japanese penmanship, but Rob's ability with written Japanese hieroglyphics was limited. He apologized, "I'm sorry, you will have to read it aloud." Jimmu took the letter and translated the words:

"Jimmu, your mother and I are grateful that you have survived the war and will be on your way home soon. We are now living off the base in Yokosuka; the Navy will give you the details. This ugly war has revealed to me and your mother some very bad things about our culture in Japan. We have been guided by a decadent code of honor that has led to the destruction of our moral fiber as a people. The samurai that inspired us for centuries, has brought about the destruction of our homeland. We look forward to your homecoming. Do not be ashamed of being a prisoner. General MacArthur is showing us the way of compassion and tolerance that we really do not deserve… If there is any honor left in war, I believe the Americans have honor. K."

No one said a word. The letter said it all.

Jimmu's eyes moistened, Molly stifled some tears. Rob was choked with emotions of what had been read, but he remembered the terrible times he had had…the evil gorilla, the voyages in hell on ships Mitsubishi and Kawasaki used to transport thousands of white prisoners of war to be slaves, and the torture and starvation so many endured in over forty Japanese industries. It was hard to believe that the old admiral had changed, but he hoped it was genuine. Only time would tell. Rob broke the silence, "I know you're going to be well received at home. I am amazed at how well we were treated by the Japanese civilians while I was there a few months ago. Jimmu, we must go but perhaps, after we are married, Molly and I may be able to come to Japan, though I won't climb Fujiyama again!"

Jimmu laughed, "Me too."

Rob remarked, as they were about to leave, "Jimmu, you've gained weight since I saw you on the *Thornfish*." Jimmu blushed, "Yes too much good food; we got the same as your troops." As they climbed back in the Jeep, Rob said to Molly, "I'm glad I got to see him. He is a former enemy and now once again a friend."

Molly held Rob's hand tightly, "Rob this story could not be made up. It needs to be told someday, but not now."

CHAPTER 82

The Note

Rob returned to his room at the BOQ thinking what a great day this had been. He was preparing to take a shower and was emptying his B-4 bag containing all his worldly effects on the bed. As he started to put them in the bureau drawer, he found the note in his pants pocket that Mrs. Edmonds had given him when they arrived in the morning. In the excitement he had forgotten it. He opened the flap and the aroma of the perfume Lily always wore met him. It was a short note. A picture of a little boy, probably about two years old, fell out. The little boy with blond hair was dressed in a sailor suit. He was cute he thought. He read her note:

"Dear Rob: I want to share my heart with you in this note. I've hesitated even to write to you but after praying, I think what I am going to tell you is needed. You see after you left for patrol, I found that I was pregnant. The first thing I thought of was to abort the baby, but after much prayer I decided on my own to keep it; I could not bring myself to kill an innocent baby. So, to avoid some shame for not being married and dishonoring my mother, I decided to go to live with my mother's relatives on Kauai. I worked in my uncle's small restaurant and there met a young Navy pilot named Bill. And about that same time, we learned of the loss of the Thornfish. I was crushed and almost came to the point of doing away with myself. After the baby was born, Bill wanted to marry me. I was hesitant at first, but time passed, and it seemed that you were gone forever, it was the best thing to do. But our relationship was interrupted by the war, and Bill deployed on the Hornet for months. While he was at sea in combat in the Western Pacific, I learned that the Thornfish crew had survived. I was so excited! I knew in my heart that you made it. Bill returned from the war about the time you were liberated from Japan. He is a kind, gentle and a very handsome man. He will make a fine husband and father for Frankie. He has orders to be a flight instructor at Pensacola and wants me to marry him and move to Florida. We are going to be married and I am so happy! Rob, I was the aggressor in our relationship. Bill has forgiven me for my indiscretions, and I have asked for forgiveness from the Lord and have received complete absolution from my priest.

The Lord healed me and set me free of guilt and shame, but I must confess some of the pain remains. I can only hope you will forgive me too."

With Love, Lily

P.s. Enclosed is a picture of Frankie. **Isaiah 43:25**

Rob put the letter down. Sweat formed on his forehead, his hands were shaking. A sudden pain shot through his stomach. That's why he had not received a letter from Lily. He thought, *what should I do now*? He lay on his bed, his head spinning. He saw stars as he closed his eyes. He was in shock. Thoughts of his past with Lily swamped his mind. *What about the baby?" I'm responsible for him!* And his escapades with Marianne invaded his heart as he felt sudden pains of guilt in the loneliness of his room. Fear began to creep in his emotions making him feel more dread than the time off the Malay coast when he took to the water after the *Thornfish* was scuttled. *Should I confess all this to Molly or just not say anything? She might not ever know. Would I lose Molly if I told her? I can't lose Molly. Not now or ever.* For the first time in his life, he was not in control of his emotions.

His thoughts were swirling in his head. *What should I do?* He was rescued as the Thornfish sank; he needed to be rescued now. He needed some advice. Maybe John could help.

John was in his room at the BOQ writing a letter to his girlfriend in Australia. Rob knocked once on the door and entered and said, "John, I need your help. And I need it now!" John glanced up from his writing at the desk and saw Rob's ashen face. "What happened, Rob? You look like you've just seen a ghost! Sit down. Do you want a drink?" John didn't drink, except after being depth charged when he gladly accepted the ration of whiskey the pharmacist mate handed out. Rob said, "Sure. Whatever you've got." John opened a small bottle of Jack Daniels from the bar that each room had and poured it into two plain glasses from the bathroom.

He began, "John I need some advice, not only human but divine advice."

John said, "Well I may help with the human, but God will have to do the rest. Now tell me what's wrong." After swallowing the bourbon, Rob began by telling his confidant about his relationship with Lily, starting with the incident after the swim at Hanauma Bay, to the departure of the last patrol out of Pearl Harbor. Then he handed him Lily's note.

Rob waited while John read and reread it. John stood and started pacing the floor. He turned and looked directly at his friend sitting on a chair with his head down.

"Well, she's dropped quite a load on you. There is a principle of life that says, you will reap what you sow. You and Lily have made some bad decisions, and there are consequences. But there is hope Rob for both of you. She is telling you about it in her letter.

Let's look at the scripture passage she mentioned in her note. Rob, here's my Bible; read the passage from Isaiah. Rob took the little Bible and read out loud from the prophet Isaiah, chapter 43, verse 25. *"I, even I, am he who blots out your transgressions, for my own sake, and remembers your sins no more."* John said, "Rob, all the bad things you have done, God can erase them. He won't pack them in a sea bag and bring them out now and then… no, he completely erases them. He throws them overboard and it's gone forever. But that's not the end of the story." John took the Bible and turned to another passage. "The New Testament adds this admonition: I John 1:9, *If we confess our sins, he is faithful and just, and will forgive our sins and cleanse us from all unrighteousness.* Rob those words are for you right now."

John sat down at the desk, "You know Rob it seems to me that Lily has already done that. She has found forgiveness. Now it's your turn. You first asked for my advice, and then you asked for divine advice. First let's look for divine guidance. It's better than mine. Here's what I believe the divine guidance is: Go to your room and confess your sins and ask for His forgiveness. And then *my advice* is to take the letter to Molly and let her read it. She needs to know about the situation including the child. And I believe she will forgive you." But Rob said, "Will she ever trust me again?"

Rob couldn't wait to go to his room to confess. He knelt and made his confession right then and there. John was silently praying for him for what seemed to be an eternity.

Finally, when Rob arose, the heaviness had left him. It was a new day, and life was beginning with a closeness to the Lord that he had ever experienced. He remembered the words he uttered when he feared the Japanese were going to behead him: "Lord if you get me out of this, I'll serve you for the rest of my life."

Rob knew he was forgiven. He knew what he had to do.

CHAPTER 83

The Choice: For Honor or Love

The sun was setting over the red rich soil of the pineapple fields west of Honolulu, when Rob drove his borrowed Jeep up to the front of Valerie Edmonds' home in the hills of Aiea. Rob was more nervous than when he stood his first watch as an officer of the deck on the *Thornfish* in enemy waters off Japan. He rang the bell expecting to see Lily, but her mother appeared. "Rob, come in, I was hoping to see you. Come and see Ji Su. Lily is working, I expect that she'll be home shortly. She has a job as a head waitress at the O club at Barber's Point Naval Air Station."

Rob entered the familiar foyer and heard a girl singing on the lanai. It was the chorus sung by kids in every Vacation Bible School; she was mixing Korean, Japanese and newly acquired English to sing *"I've got the love of Jesus down in my heart, down in my heart, down in my heart, today!"* Valerie told Rob of the change in Ji Su since she came to live with her. "Rob, she has joy for the first time in her life. She is already learning some words of English!"

Rob saw a new person. Her face was radiant, her black hair pulled back into a ponytail, she was dressed in a Hilo Hattie Hawaiian dress, with new white shoes, she looked beautiful. When she saw Rob, she rushed to give him a big hug. "Thank you for my saving," she cried in broken English. Rob was having a hard time controlling his emotions. As he started to say something, Valerie came into the room with a large pitcher of iced tea. She poured as they sat on the lanai and spoke of her work for Naval Intelligence. "My job is about over. They are asking me if I would return to Japan and work with a group called JANAP, short for Joint Army Navy Assessment Program of the war. It would be a challenge, but also very worthwhile. I would be assisting with the investigation of Japanese naval war records." Rob said, "That would be a very challenging job, but necessary, and your language ability would be needed for sure."

Valerie poured another glass of iced tea, and Rob turned the conversation to the reason for his visit. "Mrs. Edmonds, I came to see Lily. I need to ask for her forgiveness." Valerie Edmonds sat down by Rob. She knew a lot about forgiveness. She had been on the receiving end of discrimination due to her race, and had learned the hard knocks of life, it's not always fair. She was thrilled to hear Rob's desire for forgiveness.

She said, "Rob I'm glad, forgiveness can't undo the past, but it will enlarge the future. The Lord is still in control, even when things seem so chaotic, that's where faith comes in. I believe all this is in His hands. Frankie is not an accident. He could have been aborted, but by the grace of God, he is a beautiful healthy boy that we all love dearly." Valerie paused, "This war has caused so many hurts; I believe, you are at a crossroads in your life. You don't have to tell me, I know you have chosen Molly, she's a lovely girl, and I believe you will be very happy. Do you plan to stay in the Navy? Are you going to remain in submarines? Is she open to your shipping over?"

Rob smiled, "I think so."

"Rob, if you're married here, I'd like to go to your wedding, may Ji Su go too?"

"You bet. Will Lily be here soon?"

"Yes, but first I want you to meet Frankie, he should be waking up from his nap in Lily's room, I baby sit a lot."

Rob wasn't prepared for this. Just meeting Lily again would be hard enough but meeting the little boy he fathered would make things a lot more difficult for him. Valerie excused herself and went into the bedroom to get Frankie. Ji Su sat on the floor of the lanai with a stack of cards with words in Japanese on one side and the English word on the back. She looked at Rob and tried to say, "Pleased to meet you." Rob smiled and took some of the cards and began to teach her the correct words.

Rob heard tiny footsteps in the hall, and around the corner came Frankie, a beautiful little blond blue-eyed boy dressed in shorts and a NAVY tee shirt. He ran over and put his hands out for Rob to hold him. Rob picked the boy up and put him on his lap and hugged him tightly. Rob, the coolly composed submariner was choked with emotion, he began to cry. The two-year-old was ready to jump down and pick up his toy firetruck on the lanai floor. Valerie returned and saw Rob's distress. She went over to him and put her hand on his shoulder and began to pray. She knew it was a tough situation for him. She heard the sound of Lily's car. "I think Lily has arrived Rob. Just stay here, I want to tell her you are here. I'm sure she will want to go to her room and freshen up."

Rob stood awaiting Lily, trying to compose himself. When Valerie told her daughter that Rob was here, she didn't wait, and came directly into the lanai. She cried, "Rob! Rob," and ran over to him and gave him a hug, she whispered, "Will you ever forgive me?" As they sat down on the couch where, in years past, they made love, Rob replied, "Lily, yes, but I'm the one who needs forgiveness for all the things I did that hurt you terribly." Lily said, "I already have forgiven you."

Valerie excused herself and took Frankie to his room. Rob and Lily sat on the lanai talking for a long time. Rob was in more pain than he had experienced at the hands of his Jap torturers. His heart beat faster, and adrenaline flowed. His thoughts were of little Frankie. *What's going to happen to the little boy? My boy. What is best for him?*

Finally, Rob subdued his emotions enough and, on an impulse, said, "Let's go for a short drive in my Jeep. We can talk some more." And he needed to clear his mind. Lily agreed and after checking with her mother, making sure that Frankie was attended to, they hopped in the Jeep and Rob took the narrow road up the mountain towards Scofield Barracks, the Army Base, one of the first targets of Japanese planes during the attack December 7 almost four years ago. As he drove neither of them spoke, but his foot on the gas pedal increased, finally Lily said, "Rob, slow down Frankie needs his mother!" Rob slowed, but he thought, *Frankie needs his father too*. Her comment only added to his misery. They parked at the overlook, and Rob helped Lily get out of the Jeep. He took her hand and walked over to the edge of the cliff. Stretching a thousand feet below them in the sunset, were fields of pineapples, and beyond, Barbers Point Naval Air Station, the Naval Base at Pearl Harbor, and Ford Island Airfield. The spires of Honolulu could be seen in the distance and Diamond Head, the hallmark for the island of Oahu. Rob said, "Sure is beautiful isn't it? I can see why your father wanted to stay here."

Lily's mind flashed back to the time, ages ago, when she parked almost in this very spot and thought about ending her life after learning she was pregnant. She said, "Rob, let's talk about the future not the past. What are you going to do now that you can be discharged? I hear you have done a tremendous job in the Navy, are you staying in?" Rob said, "Well that's secondary, the most important thing for me is our relationship and Frankie's. He paused, looking for words, "You know I am engaged to Molly, and we are planning to be married here in Hawaii. But Lily, I know that I am responsible for Frankie. If I had known earlier, I would have married you and taken care of Frankie." Lily broke in and put her fingers over his lips, "Rob, I know that, you are a kind and honorable man. I knew you would do the right thing, the honorable thing. After I learned I was pregnant, and you were my only lover, I moved to Kauai, and one night I wrote you a letter telling everything. But I never mailed it. I often thought about what our lives would be if I had mailed it that night on Kauai. You would have been devastated, and you didn't need me to worry about, you had to fight a war. That's why I didn't mail the letter."

Rob interrupted her, "Lily you should have, I want to take responsibility for my actions. *I chose intimacy over virtue*. We can blame it on the war, but at the end of the day, I am responsible." Lily started to cry. She sobbed, "Mom says all this is in the past, and God is still in this. I am so grateful for Frankie. I have been blessed with Bill a wonderful man, much like you. He came into my life after you and your crew went missing. We all knew the *Thornfish* was gone forever. And Rob, the good news is that I have found real true love with Bill, and he loves Frankie, and someday, when the time is right, Frankie will be told. We will be married soon. He is going to stay in the

Navy and is going to be transferred to Pensacola for duty as a flight instructor. I want you to be happy with Molly, she was always number one in your life, and I knew it. If you married me, I would *always feel* that it was because of your obsession with duty and honor. Cherish Molly, as I cherish Bill and Frankie; I am making them number one in my life for life."

Rob drew Lily to him on the windswept precipice and caressed her tears away. They got in the Jeep. He put it in gear and drove down the mountain road.

Both had chosen love over honor.

CHAPTER 84

The Confession

The officers' club at Hickam Air Base had changed little since Rob had been there years ago. The wide sweeping veranda filled with tables overlooking the Pacific Ocean looked the same, except that the barbed wire fences and gun mounts outside on the beach had disappeared. Gone too were the many customers that came each night to forget the war and have fun and a good meal. Eighty-five percent of the Navy during the war were reservists, and most had now left Hawaii for the mainland to be discharged, and their ships and planes put in mothballs. Rob had made reservations for a table but really didn't need to. The place was almost empty. Rob and Molly were seated by the waiter, at a table on the veranda with a white tablecloth decorated with a candle and a small fake turkey in a basket to remind their guests of Thanksgiving.

They were holding hands as the three-piece ensemble played, *I'll be seeing you*. Molly knew the words to the song by heart. Rob asked Molly to dance, and they were like one as they glided across the smooth tiled floor. Molly was in heaven. It was their first dance in three years. The dreams of many months had come true. She was in beautiful Hawaii with the one and only man she had ever loved completely. But as they swayed to the music, Rob remembered the last time he was there with Lily. They danced on the same veranda, and she asked him if he could ever have room in his heart for her. Molly's intuition was aroused. "Are you OK, darling? I feel you're a bit up tight. Am I right?" Rob avoided her glance, and replied faintly, "No, I'm OK." Molly was not so sure, as they danced Molly was troubled. *This shouldn't be. What's wrong with me?* After they sat down, the waiter took their dinner orders. Mahi and rice for her, broiled Mahi with a baked potato for Rob. He hated rice. She put aside her concern while they ate their delicious meal, served with a choice California Chardonnay wine.

During their meal the conversation turned to Molly's work with *The Miami Student* and *The Oxford Press*. She told Rob of the excitement she felt interviewing interesting people and writing stories about the war and how it impacted Oxford and the military from Miami University and the village of Oxford who were serving all over the world. Then she said something that made Rob nervous. She said, "Rob what would you think about helping me write your story? I mean the adventures you had in the

Navy. Each of those medals you were awarded has a story to tell. And America needs to be told about the atrocities done by the Japanese on our POWs in the name of their Bushido honor code. I would like to write a book about your experiences someday; *would you help me?* I have loads of material from the scrap books we saved for you and you can contribute your experiences in the silent service. We could write a story of the incidents, but more importantly, the stories of your shipmates, and the people you were involved with during the war."

Molly waited for a response for a long time. She searched his face. Rob looked away. He couldn't look at her. She felt his uneasiness and she became worried. *Did I say too much about his trauma, did I hurt him?* Finally, Rob said, "Molly I'm sorry, right now I want to forget everything."

Molly thought…*Something is wrong.*

After the waiter cleared the table, Rob took her hand in his, and they walked out on the stone patio overlooking the ocean. He was anxious. Summing up more courage than he needed in combat, he looked directly at her saying, "You know, honey I have loved you from the moment we met in the library at Miami. You always told me you were a virgin. I am not. Molly smiled, "I know. You needn't have told me, I sensed that from the first time we met." Rob was amazed at her perception. Molly held his hand as they walked along the long veranda. The music from the dance had stopped. The only sound was the ocean waves breaking on the reef off shore. Molly continued, "During the months after we learned of the loss of the *Thornfish,* I drew closer to the Lord. I prayed a lot. And the Lord gave me a confirmation that, against all odds, you were alive!"

Rob took a deep breath, "Well there's more to the story. You met Mrs. Edmonds on the pier. She is a friend of mine. She kind of took me in when I was back in Hawaii on R and R, that's Navy lingo for rest and recreation. I met her daughter on the beach at the Royal Hawaiian where she worked. We became friends too, *and I must confess* we were more than just friends. We had an affair." Molly was shaken. She hardly heard the next words that Rob uttered. Everything seemed to be in slow motion. Her heart ached. Rob continued, "I guess that the war made us both reckless. I thought I might not make it through the war. The submarine service had the highest losses of any branch of the military in the war. So, I wanted you to know about this and a brief encounter I had with a girl with the USO troop I met while in Perth, Australia. She is a friend of my mother… her name is Marianne."

Molly was crushed, not one but two affairs. Then Rob handed her the note from Lily. She tried to read it in the dim light on the veranda and cried, sobbing uncontrollably for a time. Rob started to hold her close and said, "You see what a rat I am. If you don't want to marry me, I'll understand. But Molly I have a friend… my shipmate John.

He and I went through hell together as POWs. He is a very strong Christian and has helped me though this. While we were prisoners, we talked a lot about forgiveness. I have confessed my failures and received Jesus forgiveness. I feel like a new man. I hope you will be able to forgive me too. I love you Molly more than you'll ever know."

She handed the picture of Frankie and Lily's note back to Rob and walked away, tears streaming down her cheeks. She staggered down to the sandy beach. The full moon gleamed over the placid water. She found a small stone bench and sat down alone. The evening, which had begun with so much joy and expectation, had turned to dismay and sorrow.

Molly sat there for a long time thinking of her own mistakes over the years that they had been apart. She was not so innocent either. Woody had been very persuasive, and she almost had succumbed to his charms several times. She wanted to be physical with Woody more that she wanted to admit. The fog of war, as military experts called mistakes, caused a lot of personal mistakes in their lives as well. Rob told her just a few minutes ago that he had asked the Lord for forgiveness for his mistakes; he felt clean and new. She thought, *and didn't he say that he had resisted the invitation by the Korean girl while on the Japanese submarine? Having been without a woman for over a year and a half, his temptation must have been very strong. Rob is such a good man at heart. I love him so much. Can I be strong and willing to forgive? The Lord has forgiven him, shouldn't I?*

She sensed his presence even before he got to the bench where she was seated. He sat down beside her. No words were spoken for a long time. The tide was coming in, the breakers closer than before. The turbulent waters that once had enemy subs lurking off shore, and men dying from torpedoes, had all ceased. The world had survived somehow, and a new beginning was emerging from the ashes of conflict. Molly took her shoes off and waded in the warm water, the foam glistened in the moonlight. She turned and Rob was by her side reaching for her hand, she took his hand and held him close. She kissed him and whispered, "I love you so much. I understand. I forgive you Rob. Let's erase all the past mistakes and forget them." She kissed him again and again. As the ocean water swirled around their feet, Rob reached in his pocket and produced a diamond ring that his father had sent him in the note he had given to Molly for them. It was his grandmother's diamond engagement ring, platinum and set with a one carat diamond. "Molly this is to seal our love," and he placed it on her finger. It fit perfectly.

CHAPTER 85

The Wedding
December 7, 1945

Molly hung up the telephone in her room at the Royal Hawaiian. It was Friday, December 7, 1945. Exactly four years ago, on this date, the Japanese made their attack on Pearl Harbor. She had just called her folks in Marion telling them that she was about to be married on Waikiki Beach in Honolulu, Hawaii. Her father, awakened from a nap by her call, said he worried that she couldn't afford the call, but was so glad to hear from her. He was so proud of Molly, even though she had not become a school teacher as he wanted her to be. He knew she was engaged but was surprised that she was being married in Hawaii and not Marion. He had always planned a large Catholic wedding for his oldest girl. Nevertheless, he blessed her wedding and was sorry that he and mother could not be there, but he understood. "Just make sure he becomes a Catholic, Molly. I love you. Goodbye."

At 0800 that morning, most of the wedding party attended memorial services on Ford Island near the site of the sunken battleship *Arizona* marking the fourth anniversary of the bombing of Pearl Harbor that brought America into World War Two. Valerie Edmonds was there and placed a small wreath of Hawaiian flowers close to the barbet of number one turret, now rusting a few feet below the water. Oil still seeped from the storage bunkers below. She thought of the oil as tears from the sailors and her husband Franklin, Chief Aviation Boatswain Mate, still entombed there. When Rob returned from the memorial ceremony, he received a telegram from his parents.

"Rob and Molly, God bless you both on your Hawaiian wedding. We wish we were there with you, but we will leave the porch light burning when you come home. With Love Mom and Dad. P.s. There is a teaching position in the Geology Department waiting for you if you want it. New instructors are starting at $1800 a year!"

The Royal Hawaiian's workers were finishing a small tent by the beach to shelter the wedding party from the sun, and any threatening showers like the one now in the distance over Diamond Head. Rob and John, his best man, came down the stairs from their rooms at the Royal Hawaiian wearing their crisp Navy Officer's dress white uniforms. "Where's the ring?" Rob asked once again. John replied, "Rob stop worrying, I have it right here in my pocket." They had two bars on their shoulder boards, both having just been promoted to full Lieutenant. On Rob's left breast were medals, the Silver Star, the Bronze Star with Clusters, the Purple Heart with Cluster, and the Navy Commendation Medal with Cluster, along with service awards for the war.

Rob and John took their positions beside the small makeshift altar the chaplain had installed. The table had a gold cross, with silver communion ware set on a white tablecloth.

Seated on folding chairs around the periphery of the tent were: Commander Dick Morrison, former CO of the *Thornfish*, still recovering from the abuse he suffered while a POW; Lieutenant Jerry Abrams, former executive officer of the *Thornfish*; Chief Petty Officer Marvin Grabowski, newly promoted former leading petty officer torpedoman of the *Thornfish*; Mrs. Valerie Edmonds; and Ji Su, the young Korean girl, dressed in a beautiful blue dress.

Mrs. Edmonds served as Molly's Matron of Honor, and Captain Ben Miller stood in for her father to give the bride away. As the captain and Molly waited by the main entrance to the beach, he said, "Molly I feel like I've known you for some time. You're getting a wonderful man as your husband; I am hoping that he will stay in the Navy. We need officers of the caliber of Rob. He is a man of character, courage, integrity, and honor. I've seen him in action and the Navy needs him." Molly replied, "I agree, if he wants to make the Navy a career, I will be happy too. I'm a bit like Ruth in the Old Testament, "Where you go, I will go." Captain Miller squeezed her hand. "Good."

Rob had orchid leis delivered for all the guests, including Ji Su who sat next to Mrs. Miller. Chief Petty Officer Marvin Grabowski played the harmonica, "Here comes the bride." At the first note, Molly took Captain Miller's arm and walked slowly down from the hotel to the wedding tent on the white sands of Waikiki. Molly looked lovely, dressed in a gorgeous white dress, knee length, and cut low in front. She wore the necklace with the gold cross that Rob had given her for Christmas the year before he was declared lost. Valerie, dressed in a gorgeous pink dress clinging to her slim body, preceded them walking in the sand, wearing her new sandals. Captain Miller led Molly to the front of the altar, and took his seat next to his wife, Joan. Molly and Rob looked at each other and held hands. John stood to the right of Rob nervously holding the ring. The Navy chaplain, Commander Morgan Burnett, a Lutheran, greeted them and the attendees.

He began, "This morning we are gathered here to witness the joining of this man and woman into Holy Matrimony. I say Holy because it has from the beginning been ordained by God. Speaking from experience, having been married for years, I have found that there are two ingredients to a happy and successful life together. They are

Love and Forgiveness. They go together like a lock and key. You can't have one without the other. Without love you cannot forgive and be forgiven, and forgiveness keeps love fresh and new every day."

As the minister spoke those words, Rob squeezed Molly's hand. Her smile said it all...*yes*!

"Molly and Robert are Christians. Both have endured trials during this war. They have been in love for years and are now ready to dedicate their lives to each other and have The Lord as the center of their lives together."

The bride and groom faced each other and held hands and repeated their vows. The minister concluded saying, "Robert and Molly by their promises before God, and in the presence of this congregation, have pledged themselves to one another as husband and wife." Then he said, "By the authority of the Department of the Navy and the Territory of Hawaii, I now pronounce you man and wife. Ladies and gentlemen, I present Lieutenant and Mrs. Robert A. Walker Jr." Then the decorated Navy chaplain quickly added with a broad smile, "You may kiss the bride!"

Everyone stood, clapped and cheered. Rob and Molly kissed. And as the chaplain's final words were pronounced, in the distance a rain shower had fallen over Diamond Head, and through the mist, a beautiful double rainbow appeared and then melded into one.

Rob drew her close and kissed her again, "Molly, look at the rainbow!" She whispered, "It's a promise for us, Rob!" As they walked hand in hand over the warm sands of Waikiki's oceanfront playground toward their reception at the Royal Hawaiian's Tiki Bar, Molly said, "Rob, they're playing our song! Listen, the jukebox is playing *Our Love is Here to Stay*!" Rob smiled, "I know honey, I had Kimmo, the bartender, play it for us."

The little Tiki Bar was crowded with well-wishers for the bride and groom. Red and white orchids adorned the small tables along the dance floor. Several well used Christmas trees decorated each end of the bar along with a large three-tiered wedding cake, courtesy of Kimmo, the retired Navy chief petty officer, bartender, bouncer and newly appointed wedding planner. The white cake was decorated with wavy ribbons of blue icing on its sides and a small submarine on the bottom layer cutting through the white vanilla ocean waves. The words *Our Love is Here to Stay* circled the second layer. On the very top was a small cross made of wood from the palm tree overlooking the Tiki Bar that Kimmo carved himself. Mai Tais and gimlets flowed from Kimmo's well.

Captain Morrison stood watching the festivities, his white uniform hanging loosely on his frame. When the music stopped, he nodded to Kimmo who said in the booming voice of a Navy boatswain mate, "Now Hear This!" Jerry Abrams, wearing his new Lieutenant Commander shoulder boards strode to the center of the dance floor. "I have an announcement." He smiled, "I'm not going to tell you any jokes, so relax.

Seriously, we had a very courageous leader for our captain, in the line of the heroes of the United States Navy from John Paul Jones to the Fleet Admirals of today. He took the Thornfish in harm's way and never flinched. In times of the worse crisis that you can imagine, he never failed us. He served bravely in the face of enemy torture and upheld the highest traditions of the Navy." His voice cracked, "Sir, the crew wants you to have this sword inscribed with the words, 'To Captain Richard Morrison, with love and honor from the crew of the USS Thornfish, December 1945.'" Dick Morrison was visibly moved. Tears started to flow from his tired eyes. He looked around searching the faces of those men he had served with, John Young, eager to learn, full of faith, who had saved his life; Jerry Abrams, the intellectual and personable executive officer; Marvin Grabowski, the fearless Polish chief torpedoman; and Rob Walker the bright, courageous leader whom he hopes will be a submarine commander one day.

He said, "You men served with honor and endured more than words can describe. It is with gratitude I receive this." Overcome with emotion, he paused to gain his composure. He continued, "We lost some good men. The world is a better place for their sacrifice. It has been my honor to serve the nation we love with you. God bless you all, God bless the bride and groom on this happy occasion, and *God Bless America*." Cheers erupted from the crowd. Holding the new sword, he said, "Now let's cut the cake!"

Later Rob and Molly danced cheek to cheek as the jukebox played, *Red Sails in the Sunset*. Rob hugged her tight and said, "Molly I'm glad you waited for me. Even when we were given up for lost, you waited.

Finally, the bridal couple slipped away from their friends and made their way up four flights to the suite formerly reserved only for senior officers. Rob picked her up and carried her over the threshold and led her to the balcony overlooking Waikiki. In the twilight the moon reflected off the gentle waves creeping ashore; in the distance a beacon was lighted on the top of Diamond Head. The white stone bench near the beach, where Rob made his confession, stood as a solitary reminder that their love was stronger than his mistakes.

Molly gazed at Rob and said, "Rob, it's hard for me to even imagine being here on this beautiful island with you. It's a dream come true. We have a lifetime ahead of us. Let's make the most of it. Someday I want to tell your story. Will you help me?" Rob looked away feeling as if he were again in combat; images of Sandia Camp no. 5, the gorilla, gun battles, and depth charge attacks flashed like lightning through his mind. He sighed, "No, not now... maybe never." Molly, sensing his pain, replied, "If you ever do, I want to write the book for you."

As twilight descended on Waikiki, lights were coming on in Honolulu. In the distance a silver Pan American four motor civilian airliner took off from Hickam Airfield homeward bound. The war weary world was returning to peace.

SURFACE, SURFACE!
A U.S. submarine surfacing in Tokyo Bay at war's end. Painting by the Author.

The Spires of Oxford

Winifred M. Letts
"The Spires of Oxford and other Poems"
E.P. Dutton and Company, 1918.
Courtesy of The Penguin Books

As I was passing by
The gray spires of Oxford
Against a pearl-gray sky.
My heart was with the Oxford men
Who went abroad to die.

The years go fast in Oxford,
The golden years and gay,
The old Colleges look down
On careless boys at play.

But when the bugles sounded war
They put their games away.
They left the peaceful river,
The football field, the quad,
The shaven lawns of Oxford
To seek a bloody sod.
They gave their merry youth away
For country and for God.

God rest you happy gentlemen,
Who laid your good lives down,
Who took the khaki and the gun
Instead of cap and gown.
God brings you to a fairer place
Than even Oxford town.

With thanks to Daniel Maynard for the drawing of the Beta Tower

The Oxford Press

Alvis Cullen, Bob White, Bob Ratterman
All Honor to Your Name

Every Thursday <u>The Oxford Press</u> appeared.
Prize winning journalism at its best.
Editors Cullen, White and Ratterman passed every test.
They gave us the news, they covered the games,
Graduations, promotions, awards - all the names.

They love the town and even students, no less,
They visit the schools and knew the kids,
Never resting 'til they went to press.
Always correcting syntax and spelling,
Proofreading the info about gardens, speeding tickets, pot-lucks and more.
Letting the townspeople editorialize - especially when sore.

The townspeople learned all the news from <u>The Oxford Press</u>.
Not to mention, kindness, patience and truth from the Editors.
Can you imagine Halloween uptown without Bob & Bob photographers?
What about Santa and Sleigh Bells in the Park?
What about town meetings with nobody on the beat?
What about "Under the Water Tower" with scoop Bob White?

It is not easy to survive with Sunday Ratterman Press,
He has limited space, but never complaining.
He continues the legend of good 'ol <u>Oxford Press</u>'
Let's give Editor Bob a big hand indeed,
"Just the facts" is still his eternal creed.

<u>The Oxford Press</u> was in the mail or at any store.
But times do change and radio and newspapers disappear.
Still, I'll take the old days any day of the year.
<u>The Oxford Press</u>, like flowers and sunshine brought us ever so near.

Courtesy Randy Listerman, *Poems of Oxford, Ohio*, and Braughler Books

Cast of Characters

Robert A. Walker Jr. Ensign USNR, bright, strong and athletic, courageous, weak at times with women, aggressive when needed, and eager to learn.

Robert A. Walker Sr. Professor of Geology, Miami U., Father of Robert Jr. congenial, a good husband, and Volcanologist. OSS in Washington D.C. during the war.

Mary Catherine Walker, Mother of Rob, strong willed, with a stern, and to some an intimidating personality, proud of her heritage, pillar of the community.

Molly Gaynor, Miami Coed and girlfriend of Rob, bright, ambitious, beautiful and full of the Holy Spirit.

J. J. Custer, LCDR USN commanding officer USS *Thornfish* strictly by the book. Obsessive compulsive personality, humorless, good trainer, relieved of command in combat.

Dick Morrison, Lieutenant USN. XO *Thornfish*, forced to relieve the Captain during combat. Intelligent, athletic, well liked, loves his men, never married, strong personality, withstands Jap torture.

John Young, Ensign USNR shipmate of Rob, innocent and strong Christian.

Lawrence O'Neil, Chief Electrician and Chief of the Boat *Thornfish*, tough as nails crew loves him, Irish Catholic, mentor to Rob, a hero on the *Squalus*.

Jerry Abrams, LT USNR Engineer *Thornfish*, Jewish and smart, loves jokes, and loved by the crew.

Albert Buckhorn Rogers, New XO of *Thornfish* after JJ Custer was relieved, loved by all, practical joker, knows his men and well liked.

Pete Robinson, LT USNR Gunnery Officer *Thornfish*.

Anthony Kennedy, First Lieutenant, and asst. gunnery officer. Notre Dame graduate.

Ben Miller, Commander USN, Chief of Staff Submarines. Great boss and a compassionate, good administrator.

Shane Montgomery, Assistant Engineer, Graduate of Texas A & M.

Lily Kaga Edmonds, Waitress Royal Hawaiian, enticingly beautiful, seductively passionate and deeply in love with Rob, but always knew Molly was his first love.

Valerie Edmonds, Mother of Lily, born in Japan (Issei). Strong Christian, loves life, well versed in language and culture, remarkable woman who finally is accepted in the Navy intelligence community.

Marianne Baker, Miss Indiana, Singer USO, gorgeous, vivacious, innocent and in love with Rob.

Marvin Grabowski, Petty Officer, torpedoman on *Thornfish*, big tough Polish. A hero.

Jimmu Kamatsu, LTJG Imperial Japanese Navy, a classmate of Rob's in Japan and later a POW of Rob.

Admiral Kamatsu, Imperial Japanese Navy, father of Jimmu, Commander of Japanese Submarines.

Woody Collingsworth, Miami Student Newspaper reporter and Navy pilot who falls in love with Molly Gaynor.

Glossary

Air Banks. Groups of air bottles used for storing high -pressure air used to blow tanks and charge torpedoes.

Angle on the bow. The angle formed by the longitudinal axis of a ship and the line of sight from a submarine intersecting the ship.

Ballast tanks. Tanks located between the outer hull and the inner pressure hull of a submarine when completely flooded give negative buoyancy for submergence. When blown dry enables the sub to surface.

Bathythermograph. An instrument to record sea temperature at a submarine's depth. The cold water helps to reflect an enemy ship's sonar echo.

Bow buoyancy tank. A ballast tank located in the bow to provide extra buoyancy when surfacing., especially in an emergency.

Bow planes. A pair of large horizontal rudders, that help give the initial down angle when submerging and later in conjunction with the stern planes, to control depth.

CinCPac. Commander-in-chief Pacific Fleet.

ComSubPac. Commander Submarine Forces Pacific Fleet

ComSubSoWestPac. Commander Submarine Forces, Southwest Pacific Fleet.

Conn. The officer having sole authority for directing the maneuvering of a ship.

Conning tower. A small cylindrical compartment between the bridge and the control room, housing the search and attack periscopes, the torpedo and ship handling controls, steering stand, sonar gear, target data computer and angel solver (TDC), radars, torpedo firing panel, bathythermograph and chart desk.

Control Room. The compartment directly below the conning tower containing the sub's controls, the bow and stern planes, the gyrocompass, auxiliary steering stand, the AC switchboard, and the radio room.

CPO. Chief Petty Officer.

DE. Destroyer Escort.

DD. Destroyer.

Div.Com. Division Commander.

Dogs. The pawls securing a watertight hatch or door.

DR. Dead-reckoning position obtained from a ship's course and speed over a period of time.

End-around. Maneuver to gain a position ahead of a target.

Engine-air-induction. A large valve and piping to provide air for the diesel engines when surfaced.

Fire control. The directing of gunfire or torpedoes.

Fix. A position obtained by visual bearings or star sights and plotted on a chart by the navigator.

Forward trim. A variable ballast tank to adjust the boat's weight and trim.

Fox. A radio broadcast usually daily of messages for submarines.

Gradient. A layer where the temperature of seawater and density changes quickly and may bend sound waves of an enemy sonar.

Gyro angle. The angle set into torpedo's gyro by the TDC, so the torpedo's steering mechanism keeps the course to hit the point of aim.

IC switchboard. An interior communication switchboard that handles AC electricity for gyrocompass, torpedo data computer, radios and sound.

Mark-14 torpedo. A steam torpedo fueled by alcohol and compressed air, with a range of 5000 yards at 47 knots and 9000 yards at 31 knots.

Mark-18. An electric powered torpedo leaving no wake when fired and having a speed of 27 knots and a range of about 4000 yards.

Maru. A name for Japanese merchant ships.

Navy Regs. U.S. Navy Regulations the official rules and regulations for the orderly conduct of the Navy and Marine Corps.

Negative tank. A tank holding 14,000 pounds of ballast when full that accelerates diving.

Normal approach course. An approach course perpendicular to the bearing of the enemy ship in order to reach the target.

OBA. Oxygen Breathing Apparatus. A mask with oxygen canisters providing oxygen for use in damage control, firefighting.

One-bell. A single order to engines for maneuvering.

1 MC. The submarine's general announcing system including the diving alarm, collision alarm, and general alarm for battle stations having a bell sound and commonly called the Bells of St. Mary's.

Pressure Hull. The inner hull of a submarine designed to withstand sea pressure at a particular depth.

Relative bearing. The direction or bearing in degrees measured clockwise from the bow of the ship.

Safety. A special ballast tank, with the same pressure hull strength that can be blown to compensate for flooding in the boat.

S boat. World War I class submarines with some still operating in World War II.

SPARS. US Coast Guard women's reserve in WWII.

Stern Planes. A pair of horizontal rudders that control the angle of the submarine when submerged and in conjunction with the bow planes the depth.

TBT. The target bearing transmitter, one forward on the bridge and one aft of the bridge, having special 7 x 50 binoculars with vertical crosshairs for sighting on target vessels.

TDC. Torpedo data computer. Maintains the target range and displays relative aspects of own ship and target continuously. The angle-solver section computes the gyro angle continuously and keeps it set on the gyros in the torpedoes prior to firing.

The Bells of St. Mary's. A melodic bell tone that summons the crew to battle stations.

Torpedo gyro. The internal gyro in a torpedo that is spun on firing and guides the torpedo on course set at the instant of firing.

True bearing. The bearing in degrees measured clockwise from the earth's true north.

Ultra. A high priority classified message containing information derived from broken Japanese codes. Normally decoded for the captain's eyes only.

Wag. Colloquial for a joker.

For Further Reading

Some of the books and materials that were used in the research of *For Honor and Love* that may be of interest to the reader for further information:

Batfish The champion 'Submarine Killer of World War II.' Hughston E. Lowder, New York: PrenticeHall. 1980.

Dec.7 1941 The Day the Japanese Attacked Pearl Harbor. Gordon W. Prange, New York: Wing Books. 1991.

Freemantle's Submarines, How allied submarines and Western Australians helped win the war in the Pacific. Annapolis, Maryland: Naval Institute Press. 2015.

Maru Killer The War Patrols of the USS Seahorse. Dave Bouslog, Sarasota, Florida: Seahorse Books. 1996.

Miami University 1809-2009 Bicentennial Perspective. Curtis A. Ellison, Editor, Athens, Ohio: Ohio University Press in association with Miami University. 2009.

No Ordinary Time Franklin and Eleanor Roosevelt The Home Front in World War II. Doris Kearns Goodwin, New York: Simon and Schuster. 1994.

Silent Victory The U.S Submarine War Against Japan. Clay Blair Jr., Annapolis Maryland: Naval Institute Press. 1975.

Slade Cutter Submarine Warrior. Carl LaVO, Annapolis, Maryland: Naval Institute Press. 2003.

Submarine! Commander Edward L Beach USN, New York: Henry Holt and Company. 1946,1952.

Submarine Commander A story of World War II and Korea. Captain Paul R. Schratz USN (Ret.), Lexington, Kentucky: The University Press of Kentucky. 1988.

Sunk The story of the Japanese Submarine Fleet 1941-1945. Mochitsura Hashimoto, Joshua Tree, California: Progressive Press. 1954, 2010.

The Two-Ocean Navy A short history of the U.S. Navy in World War Two. Samuel Eliot Morrison, Annapolis, Maryland: Naval Institute Press. 1963.

The Miami Years 1809-1969. Walter Havighurst, New York: G.P. Putman's Sons. 1969.

Thunder Below! The USS Barb revolutionizes submarine warfare in World War II. Admiral Eugene B. Fluckley, The Board of Trustees of the University of Illinois. 1992.

Truman. David McCullough, New York: Touchstone Simon and Schuster. 1992.

United States Submarine Operations in World War Two. Theodore Roscoe, Annapolis Maryland: Naval Institute Press. 1949.

Unjust Enrichment, How Japan's companies built postwar fortunes using American POWs.

Linda Goetz Holmes, Mechanicsburg, Pennsylvania: Stackpole Books. 2001.

Wahoo, The patrol of America's most famous World War II submarine. Rear Admiral Richard H. O'Kane Ret., Novato California: Presidio. 1987.

PERIODICALS

The Miami Student. Oxford, Ohio: Miami University Archives. 1939-1945.

The Miami University Bulletin, 1946.

The Oxford Press. Oxford, Ohio: Micro Film, Lane library, Smith Library of Regional History. 1939-1945.

The Spires of Oxford and Other Poems by Winifred M. Letts. E.P. Dutton and Co. 1918. With grateful appreciation to Penguin Random House Publishers, New York.

About the Author
James H. Maynard, jr. Captain USNR Ret.

Jim Maynard's interest in the Navy began in his childhood years when his family lived near Norfolk Virginia, the home of the largest United States Naval base. His father worked in construction helping build Navy facilities during World War II, receiving the Navy's Award for Excellence.

He took the military oath as an NROTC midshipman when he entered Miami University in Oxford as a freshman scholarship student. He had a double major in Naval Science and Geology. After graduation he was commissioned an Ensign USN, and served on the USS Quincy CA 71, a heavy cruiser, as a Combat Information Center watch officer and air controller during the Korean War, and later as an instructor at the Naval Academy teaching navigation, seamanship and sailing. He enjoyed sailing and made several ocean races representing the Naval Academy Sailing Squadron. Sailing gave him a great appreciation for the effects of wind, tide and current while sailing forty-four foot Luders yawls.

Following his release from active duty at the Naval Academy, he joined the Submarine Reserve unit at Baltimore and made his first active duty tour on the USS *Sarda*, the submarine school boat at New London, Connecticut. Subsequently he trained on the new *Sailfish*, the *Piper*, the *Dog Fish*, and the *Sea Robin*.

His reserve duty continued after being transferred by his employer to Dayton, Ohio, and he later commanded a Navy Reserve Surface Division and was subsequently selected to serve as Naval Reserve Group Commander for all Naval units in the greater Dayton area. Afterward, he was promoted to the rank of Captain. During his Naval career, he served on active duty and later as a reservist on over fifteen ships during a twenty-seven-year span including cruisers, destroyers, submarines, aircraft carriers, patrol craft and shore assignments including serval tours at the Naval War College. In 2005 Jim was honored by the Miami NROTC Alumni Organization, of which he is co-founder, with the Admiral Sidney W. Souers Award, given annually to one of their alumni for Distinguished Service.

Jim met his college sweetheart, Billie Ann Baldauf, at Miami, and they married after her graduation, and have three sons, all Miami graduates. Along the way, Jim and Billie developed an interest in their spiritual formation, eventually leading them to obtain their Master of Divinity Degrees from United Theological Seminary. They established a parachurch ministry, Pleasant Vineyard Ministries, offering Christian retreats and youth camps. In 2012 they received their Seminary's award given annually for Outstanding Effective Ministry.

After retiring, Jim continued his interest in naval history, and particularly submarines, and with encouragement from many others, he decided to write this narrative of the courageous men who left Miami and their loved ones at home during this epic war. It's to them that this book is dedicated.